P9-BJE-919

Praise for
THIS FAR FROM PARADISE

"Just what you need for a day in the hammock . . . Full of the rich and famous, their betrayals and revenge set in the fictitious Angeline Islands and starring a most formidable heroine."—*The Seattle Times*

"A lush backdrop and an excellent mixture of suspense and romance make this tale of a woman trying to regain her heritage and fortune perfect escapist fare."—*The Chattanooga Times*

"Shelby's tale is well-told, and his settings and characters are well-developed."—*The Orlando Sentinel*

"Fast-paced, intriguing, and absorbing . . . The heroine's . . . love affairs are cleverly weaved into the story, giving it added suspense and flavor."—*South Bend Tribune*

"Fast-paced, compellingly plotted."—*Publishers Weekly*

THIS
FAR FROM
PARADISE

PHILIP SHELBY

BANTAM BOOKS
NEW YORK · TORONTO · LONDON · SYDNEY · AUCKLAND

THIS FAR FROM PARADISE
A Bantam Book
Bantam hardcover edition / August 1988

Bantam paperback edition / July 1989

ISBN 0-553-27814-2

Published simultaneously in the United States and Canada

Bantam Books are published by Bantam Books, a division of Bantam
Doubleday Dell Publishing Group, Inc. Its trademark, consisting of the words
"Bantam Books" and the portrayal of a rooster, is Registered in U.S. Patent
and Trademark Office and in other countries. Marca Registrada. Bantam Books,
666 Fifth Avenue, New York, New York 10103.

PRINTED IN THE UNITED STATES OF AMERICA

O   0 9 8 7 6 5 4 3 2 1

Although the characters and events in this novel are fictional, readers familiar with the Caribbean and Central America will recognize certain islands in the composition of the Angelines.

My deep gratitude goes to the people in various Caribbean nations who, over the years, allowed me to enter their lives and share the "paradise" experience.

Others to whom I am indebted include:

Betty and Grant McLean of Dallas for their unswerving support and encouragement,

Beverly Lewis, my editor, whose skills and advice added greatly to the finished work,

And Joyce Davis who, over a period of two years, faithfully typed the novel in its various drafts.

To all, my sincere thanks.

Philip Shelby

"She that leaveth nothing to chance will do few things ill, but she will do very few things."

—after George Saville,
Marquis of Halifax

PROLOGUE

She was a legend almost as famous as her mistress, dominating the horizon between an indigo ocean and the dying persimmon sky that stretched beyond Windemere Key into the northern reaches of the Caribbean.

Rising from an aggressive stance, her beauty was molded by curves and contours that flowed one into the other. But beneath her polished trappings beat a heart impatient to be under way.

Mariners who sighted her from a distance, even if they knew her well, were seized by her beauty. These waters had been her domain for thirty years, and she had shared them generously. But in the gathering October dusk all gave her a wide berth.

Tonight was different. Tonight the legend was waiting, watching, hunting.

Rebecca McHenry stood on the bow of the *Windsong*. The dying sun caught and transformed her copper-colored skin to a deep bronze, profiling the slight curve of her nose and the full, parted lips. The wind swept up from the waves, misting her long sable hair with sea salt. Absently Rebecca brushed away the strands, her fingertips sensitive to the tiny furrows and creases the years had left behind, like swallows' tracks on glistening sand. Her eyes, the gray of heirloom pearls, continued to scan the horizon in anticipation.

Rebecca thought she saw something flash across the water. Her fingers slid down the gold chain around her throat until they curled around the sea-horse pendant. Rebecca squeezed the gold figurine, and the diamond-studded spine bit into her palm.

But there was nothing on the swells except dancing whitecaps and the wind, which suddenly turned very cold as it ran between her toes, set in soft-sole sandals, and up her bare legs. Rebecca shivered and drew the Sea Island cotton jacket tightly around her shoulders.

Be patient. You'll hear him long before you see him. He'll be coming out of the sun, on your blind side, the way he always has. But he's out there. He's coming this way.

If she had wanted, Rebecca could have had the location of the still-invisible vessel pinpointed instantly. The *Windsong* was far more than one hundred feet of teak, mahogany, and exotic alloys. Above her four double staterooms where Rebecca lived and the main salon that served as the nerve center for her business empire was a bridge crammed with state-of-the-art electronics: color radar, satnav, loran, and weatherfax. The *Windsong*'s captain, Ramon Fuentes, could locate anything that moved on or under these waters.

But Rebecca wanted to smell her quarry, hear him and finally see him coming toward her. She had waited too long for this confrontation to spoil it now. She continued to scan the sea around her.

To the north lay Windemere Key, the sliver of sand on which, an eternity ago, she had built her first resort, a ramshackle collection of *palapas* she had called The Tides. Over the last decade those huts had become a resort empire flung across the globe, from the Pacific coast of Mexico, across the Caribbean, to the Mediterranean and the shores of North Africa. An industry phenomenon, The Tides had exploded to rank in the Fortune 500 companies, its stock eagerly sought after—when it was available.

But for all its solidity as an investment, The Tides had something more—an aura of glamour, a patina of magic that made its attraction irresistible. Some traced this to the exotic fact that The Tides was the only blue-chip corporation to be headquartered on a luxurious yacht. Others believed its mystique was an extension of Rebecca McHenry herself.

Such speculations drew only a smile from Rebecca. That indefinable yet undeniable quality existed, but few recognized what it really was. The Tides was her weapon, forged over ten long years. Just as she had wielded it ruthlessly in the past, so today it lay unsheathed, ready to be used one last time.

Rebecca shifted her gaze to the southeast. Nothing natural or man-made broke the water, yet Rebecca knew as surely as her heart beat that that was the exact spot where she had consigned her father's body to the deep. The man Rebecca was waiting for would have to pass over the unmarked grave just as she wanted him to do. It seemed only fitting that her father's murderer unwittingly pay final homage to his victim.

Rebecca was sure she heard the sound then. It wasn't the flutter in the air caused by flying fish or the distant airburst of a surfacing whale or the scythelike hiss of a shark's dorsal fin. The sound, a powerful bow splintering the waves, curled within her ear and resonated.

On the bridge Captain Ramon Fuentes was looking for her signal.

You've waited ten years for this moment! Ten years of building and planning, suffering and hoping. This time he has to pay!

Rebecca raised her arm. Immediately the twin diesels rumbled to life and the *Windsong* rose in the water.

As her vessel turned due west, Rebecca shielded her eyes from the sun, bloodred against the horizon. It singed the feathery clouds, setting them on fire. She had seen the Caribbean sunset a thousand times, but in her mind's eye it became something else, a devastating inferno caused by the one man who, in the blink of an eye, had changed her life forever.

PART ONE

———————————

THE ANGELINES
1962–1963

· 1 ·

The man had almost reached the top of the last obstacle to his destination, a ridge lined with ceiba trees that drew themselves up like parade soldiers. He had been traveling since midnight, and although the sky was still ablaze with constellations, he sensed dawn in the warming air. Trekking through the jungles of the Maya Mountains alone and at night had been foolhardy. But he had crisscrossed the interior of the Angelines hundreds of times in the last quarter century. He knew where the dangers lay, how to avoid them, and, when necessary, how to deal with them. This particular trail, stretching into the rain forests like a meandering stream, was invisible except to those who knew it existed at all. To the man it was as familiar as the path to his own house.

Although only five foot five, Maxwell McHenry—or Midas Max as he was known throughout the Angelines—was a giant of a man. His barrel-chested torso was anchored by strong, sturdy legs, his arms were slablike, with thick, corded muscle. His hands were rough and callused, like the rocky earth from which he had wrested his fortune. His face, reflecting his tenacious New England heritage, resembled an ancient limestone tablet on which his tale could be read. The hawklike nose ruled over a stubborn jaw, but the eyes dominated: gray, flinty eyes whose depths revealed the determination of a man who had discovered the largest gold reserves on the Central American isthmus.

Grunting with effort, Max McHenry plunged through the last of the undergrowth and scrambled up to the pinnacle of the ridge. Suddenly his night vision was destroyed by the brilliance of high-intensity lights set in a ring on the plateau below. Within the circle was an entire city, rising from the cleared jungle floor like an otherworldly apparition.

"I have brought you home," Max whispered, gazing reverently upon the silent ruins and temples.

7

Shouldering his backpack and rifle, he set off down the trail, his right hand firmly gripping the leather pouch tied to his belt, his fingers kneading the smooth stones through the chamois.

A millennium ago Pusilha had been the royal seat of Mayan civilization in the Angelines. Nineteen years earlier, when Max McHenry had first stumbled across it, it had belonged to the jungle, its treasures and pyramids hidden from the world by an impenetrable canopy. Now, as he walked along the *sacbe,* a Mayan ceremonial road, Max believed he was seeing Pusilha as the high priests and noblemen must have seen it.

Almost two decades of painstaking excavation had unearthed architectural marvels. There was the Plaza of the Thousand Columns, dedicated to the warrior elite; the Caracol Observatory, whose hieroglyphics, inscribed by Mayan astronomers, recorded the movement of heavenly bodies; the Platform of the Eagles, with frescoes of plumed serpents and human figures referred to as "Atlanteans." Surrounding these centerpieces were smaller temples as well as mysterious ossuaries and ghostly ball courts.

As Max walked through this reincarnation, he gave silent thanks to the hundreds of men who, with patience and dedication, had resurrected Pusilha. The millions he had spent to finance their efforts meant nothing to him.

Max passed the observatory, quickening his pace. Beyond the Temple of the Jaguars, set in a rough semicircle, were the bunkhouses for the archaeologists and field workers, as well as the kitchen, baths, storage sheds, and a rudimentary field laboratory. In spite of his fatigue, Max was bursting with the news that his elusive goal, one he had been pursuing for twenty years, had finally been realized. He had solved the riddle of the whereabouts of the woman he had loved and lost, a woman he had spent years searching for, to bring her home, first to Pusilha, and then to the daughter she had never known.

Finally, Max thought to himself, feeling the smooth stones, I know the truth. And so can Rebecca.

Near the perimeter of the dig Max saw a new excavation under way. It was a *cenote,* a sacred sacrificial well, forty feet in diameter. Moving to the edge, Max noted that in his absence his teams were already twenty feet down. He was wondering what treasures the *cenote* had yielded so far, when he felt the earth give way beneath him.

The storm that had impeded Max's progress two days earlier had loosened the normally hard-packed soil around the well.

Max heard the telltale rain of dirt and pebbles and threw himself around, scrambling to anchor his fingers into the earth at the edge of the *cenote*. Weighed down by his backpack and rifle, he lost first his grip, then his balance, and catapulted into the pit. Even as he screamed, Max couldn't believe he was falling. The sky and stars were spinning crazily for no reason at all. Then he hit the rough ground twenty feet below. The backpack absorbed most of the impact, protecting his spine. But Max was unable to keep his head from snapping back. The skull fractured instantly as it struck a sharp outcrop of rock.

The last vision Max McHenry experienced was that of the heavens closing in on him and the smooth stones rising into the night, floating beyond his reach forever.

Two hundred miles to the south, in Angeline City, Andrew Stoughton threw his pencil on the paperwork littering his blotter and stretched back in the old-fashioned, leather-padded barrister's chair.

The managing director of McHenry Enterprises was a tall, slender man of thirty-three whose flaxen hair had been bleached white by the tropical sun. His dark skin contrasted sharply with sapphire eyes, and the white *guayabera* stuck to his chest.

Andrew Stoughton lit a cigar and surveyed his night's work. A reply to the telex from the Franklin Mint, which needed more gold for another series of coins, had been drafted. A letter had been prepared for the World Exhibition Committee in Montreal regarding the proofs of their commemorative medallions for the 1967 World's Fair. The order from a major medical equipment firm, whose new device for cancer research used three times the normal amount of bullion, had been processed. That left the monthly shipments to the big jewelry houses—Bulgari in Rome, Cartier of Paris, Tiffany in New York, and Asprey of London—to be looked after as well as McHenry Enterprises' bread and butter: the orders from major American defense contractors— General Dynamics, McDonnell-Douglas, and Hughes.

Although this was Andrew's fifth year with McHenry Enterprises, he was still fascinated by the company, the way in which it drew the world into itself because of one thing: gold. The gold Max had wrenched from the earth beneath the jungle. Gold that had enabled him to carve out a mighty empire that demanded homage. As he attacked the remaining correspondence, Andrew felt not only was he in control of some giant engine, but that in some strange way he had become a part of it. Working for a legend like Max wasn't a job, it was a vocation.

The shrill blast of the telephone startled Andrew. Glancing at his diary, he saw that no transatlantic calls were expected. Who the devil would be calling the office at four in the morning?

The connection was poor, riddled with static from atmospheric interference. Twice Andrew asked the caller to repeat his message. Even then he couldn't believe what he was hearing.

Three hours later the seaplane carrying Max McHenry touched down in Angeline Bay and throttled up to a private pier, where an ambulance waited. For Andrew Stoughton, time had crawled.

In spite of his gnawing concern, Andrew had fallen back on his iron discipline. He had instructed Pusilha not to mention anything more over the airwaves about Max's accident. Too many ears might inadvertently hear the open transmission. Although he made certain of the whereabouts of Max's personal physician, Dr. Bishop, Andrew didn't call him until he himself was ready to meet the plane. Likewise, the ambulance was summoned at the last minute.

Until he knew just how badly Max McHenry was hurt, Andrew was determined to keep the accident a secret. Once the news was out, the shock waves throughout the Angelines and the world financial community would be enormous. Andrew needed time to plot a strategy to protect McHenry Enterprises.

And there was something else that had to be done immediately.

As soon as the plane was made fast to the pier, the physician climbed on board to check his patient before moving him. When Max, still unconscious, had been transferred to the ambulance, Andrew drew Dr. Bishop aside.

"I need a minute with him alone."

"Impossible! I have to get him to the hospital at once."

Andrew's voice hardened. "Then let me ride with you."

The physician took one look at Andrew and shrugged. He was shocked by what happened next. As soon as the ambulance roared away, Andrew Stoughton began going through the pockets of Max's bush jacket and trousers.

"What are you doing?" Bishop demanded.

Andrew ignored him and continued his search. When the other man tried to pull him away, he turned on him.

"Max was on an expedition in the interior. Maybe he found a new strike. Maybe he wrote down its location, or even drew a map. Whatever he's carrying is confidential information that belongs to the company. I won't have nurses or orderlies going through his clothing finding something that's none of their business!"

The doctor watched helplessly as Andrew pocketed papers, a small notepad, and Max's wallet. Everything he had been told about this young man seemed to be true. Responsible for the day-to-day operation of McHenry Enterprises, Andrew Stoughton had, over the years, developed a reputation for loyalty to Max that bordered on obsession. Anything that could possibly affect the company was dealt with quickly and decisively— ruthlessly, when need be.

He might be a bastard, Bishop thought, *but he's McHenry's bastard.*

In spite of Andrew's best efforts, news of Max's accident traveled the length and breadth of the Angelines in less than a day. But for all the speculation that buzzed in the air, there were few details. Andrew Stoughton made certain no one except handpicked doctors and nurses attended to Max, and even these he swore to secrecy. He himself left the hospital only once, to meet a specialist he had had flown in from Miami.

"There's nothing I can do," the neurosurgeon told Andrew.

He had examined Max carefully, studied the X rays and reports of the attending physician.

"Ninety-nine percent of the time, two things will happen when a man falls twenty feet onto hard ground: He'll either snap his neck or else walk away with nothing worse than a concussion. If only Max hadn't hit his head on that outcrop. . . . That blow is probably what dislodged the aneurysm that is now sitting in his brain."

"No chance of operating on it?" Andrew asked.

The specialist shook his head.

"There's nothing to do except wait. If he comes out of the coma, it won't be because of anything modern medicine can do." The specialist hesitated, then added, "I think you had better send for his next of kin, just in case."

· 2 ·

Mid-September was the most beautiful time of year along the California coast. The ocean winds, rich with salt, dissipated the summer heat, making for languid days and cool evenings. Sitting on the window ledge in her dormitory room, Rebecca could see the icy blue Pacific breaking upon the jagged coastline. At that moment she didn't want to be anywhere else in the world.

Rebecca looked across the emerald-green quadrangle bounded by the neo-Gothic buildings of the most exclusive girls school in the United States. Modeled on the Swiss system, Briarcrest had the highest entrance requirements of any preparatory school in the country. Each year thousands of hopeful girls from around the world applied for admission. Only one hundred were accepted. Rebecca had often wondered what she would have done had she not been one of the lucky few.

Since this was the beginning of the fall semester, the grounds were teeming with students new and old. Rebecca watched the girls in their white blouses, dove-gray skirts, and green jackets with white piping hurry along the asphalt paths that connected the buildings. She noticed a group of new arrivals, twelve years old, timidly following one of the administrators, like goslings behind their mother goose.

I couldn't have looked like that, she thought to herself, then grinned. *No, I probably looked worse*.

"Miss the old place already, do you?"

Rebecca almost jumped off the windowsill.

"Bix!"

Rebecca rushed up and flung her arms around her best friend and roommate.

"When did you get in?"

"Just now. Help me with this stuff, will you?"

Rebecca grabbed Bix's enormous suitcase and dragged it over to the bed.

"What have you got in here, your latest boyfriend?"

"Don't I wish," Bix grunted as she pulled the steamer trunk in from the corridor and kicked the door shut. She plopped herself down on the trunk and leaned back against the bed.

"Oh, Bix, it's so good to see you!" Rebecca breathed.

The daughter of a U.S. Navy admiral, Beatrice Ryan was an incorrigible dynamo. An inch or two shorter than Rebecca and a month older, Bix had flaming red hair, the freckled face of a leprechaun, and a Junoesque figure. Rebecca had watched her drink dates under the table and use language that made even the admiral blush. Bix could surf all day without straining a muscle and dance until her last partner dropped. There wasn't another like her in the whole world.

"How was Newport?" Rebecca asked. "You must tell me everything."

Bix rummaged in her bag for a hairbrush and tried to restore some order to her outrageous titian hair.

"Nothing changes. Mother drank and played bridge. Dad spent most of his time in Washington and Norfolk. I did a lot of sailing and fell in love with an Italian count. He said he had a palazzo on the Grand Canal in Venice."

Beneath the nonchalant words Rebecca felt her friend's pain. Bix's mother was old Newport, her father a war hero. They lived separate lives that had never accommodated a daughter born late in the marriage. Bix's fiery independence stemmed from having had to fend for herself at an early age. It was a quality Rebecca admired enormously.

"Are we going to visit him in Venice?" Rebecca asked. "Has he proposed?"

Bix hooked her thumbs into the pockets of her jeans.

"Principe Massimo Sabatini was a perfect lover and a splendid divertissement. However, he was also a lowdown swine who tried to steal my jewelry. When I left him, he was enjoying the hospitality of the Newport News jail, where I hope he rots!"

Bix paused. "What about you, Becky? How was your summer?"

"The best!"

Breathlessly Rebecca ran down the list of everything she'd done, from diving with a Scripp Aquarium marine biology expedition in the Sea of Cortez to attending oceanside concerts given by a new group called the Beach Boys.

Bix regarded Rebecca suspiciously. "Come on, kiddo. What else went on? You look like the proverbial cat after the canary disappeared."

Rebecca sat up against the headboard of the bed, hugging her knees.

"Andrew came by in August while I was staying with the Forsythes," she said. "He had business in Los Angeles and San Francisco. We went out to dinner three times!"

"And?"

"And what?"

"Did you finally make love with him?"

"Bix!"

"Becky, Becky!" Bix groaned. "You're crazy for the guy. Do something about it! Christ on a sidecar! What's going to happen to my reputation if I let you leave Briarcrest with your virginity intact?"

The two girls chuckled over the threat to Bix's reputation for amorous escapades, then turned to more serious matters: the planning of a European trip over the Christmas holidays.

"Actually," Bix said, unfolding a pamphlet describing the skiers' paradise of St. Moritz, "I would rather go somewhere warm this year."

Bix regretted her words as soon as they left her lips. Rebecca seldom went home to the Angelines and she had never asked anyone to come along. Only Bix knew why.

"Becky, I'm sorry. I wasn't fishing . . ."

"Don't worry about it," Rebecca said with a faint smile. "I'm the one who's not being fair."

When Rebecca had arrived at Briarcrest that blustery February day five years before, the cachet of the McHenry name immediately made her the object of speculation and gossip. Some girls, whose fathers held high-level positions in government or industry, had heard the name mentioned at home. Others recalled stories in the society pages and gossip columns that detailed the extravagant parties Midas Max McHenry held for charity on his out-of-this-world estate. A senior from Palm Beach threw in a different nugget. She remembered an afternoon tea at the Breakers during which her mother had waxed eloquent about "Midas's" wife having died so young and how the poor man had never remarried. All that money and no one to enjoy it with . . .

Before Rebecca had even set foot at Briarcrest, everyone knew the most important things about her. Her father was fabulously rich. The fact that she was an only child made her an instant heiress. Not having a mother gave her a faintly tragic air. And, of course, she lived in a Caribbean paradise. It was also conceded that she had to be smart. Nobody, but nobody, had ever been permitted to start school in mid-term unless the teachers agreed she could hack the curriculum.

The claws sharpened a little when it turned out Rebecca McHenry was beautiful as well.

In spite of the obvious curiosity about her, Rebecca was quickly accepted. Even though she had never been to California, she had visited the southern and northeastern United States with her father. The girls who came from those regions discovered that Rebecca knew the right people and places. That she was willing to share everything from her designer toiletries to the most recent edition of *Mademoiselle* made her one of the girls. Within a month of her arrival Rebecca also became the school's champion swimmer. When she made the national swimming finals, the entire student body traveled to Los Angeles to watch her capture the gold medal in the regional finals. After her victory everyone agreed that no matter what had brought her here, Rebecca McHenry was a real Briarcrest girl. The exception was Beatrice Ryan.

Brash, outspoken, and impulsive, Bix was exactly the kind of roommate Rebecca had wanted: someone so caught up in herself and her intrigues that she had no time for anyone else. She soon discovered there was more to Bix than that.

During her first months at Briarcrest, Rebecca suffered from severe recurring headaches. Sometimes they left her in such agony that it was all she could do to get out of bed to make her class.

"At this rate you're going to dig yourself an early grave," Bix told her one morning. "Why don't you talk about what's bothering you?"

"I'm fine," Rebecca told her, reaching for the aspirin. The next day she fainted in the gym.

"You know, kiddo," Bix said, sitting by Rebecca's bed in the infirmary, "you might have convinced the nurse that it's all because of your period, but not me. You're just a little too damn perfect, Becky. The minute you waltz into Briarcrest you have everyone eating out of your hand. No one knows where you came from or why you're here."

"That's nonsense," Rebecca said weakly. "Everyone knows I live in the Angelines—"

"Sure they do," Bix said sarcastically. "And we all know who your father is, that you attended Miss Potter's, the fanciest school in creation, and blah, blah, blah. But what about *you*, Becky? Who are you? What are you really doing here? Maybe nobody else has noticed, but you're walking around with your lid screwed on so tight I shudder to think what's going on inside.''

The harder Rebecca ignored Bix's probing questions, the more of them she had to endure. And the headaches kept getting worse.

"Christ, Becky, don't you see?" Bix would say. "The whole school doesn't have to know what's eating you. Just me. Give yourself a break, talk to me.''

Despite her promise never to tell anyone about her humiliation at Miss Potter's, Rebecca reached the point where she could no longer cope with the painful memories by herself. She had gone over them again and again in her diary, yet they still had the power to hurt her. Even leaving the Angelines had brought her no peace. But more than the pain, it was her inability to understand why she should have been victimized that haunted her.

Had it not been for Bix's persistence, Rebecca might have found a way to continue the facade, by day being the model student, at night retreating to her own private hell. With a saint's patience and a bulldog's tenacity, Bix slowly coaxed the truth from Rebecca. When at last it was out, Rebecca felt terribly vulnerable. Bix had a remedy for that too.

"I know it's going to take a long time for you to understand what happened," Bix told her. "But remember one thing: those who hurt you are trash, Becky.''

A few days later Bix presented Rebecca with a T-shirt that read DON'T LET THE TURKEYS GET YOU DOWN! It was the sweetest tonic in the world.

After that Rebecca and Bix became inseparable. Amused by her roommate's blushing attitude toward sex, Bix led her through a crash course in the illicit works of Henry Miller and Frank Harris. On the winding coastal roads she taught a white-knuckled Rebecca to drive LeMans style. It was Bix who found a way to get in and out of Briarcrest undetected and introduced Rebecca to the smoky roadhouses along the Pacific highway, where black musicians jammed into the early hours of the morning. Together they got sick on beer, choked on cigarettes, and learned the steps to every new dance that came along.

Their adventures continued throughout the summers. Bix brought Rebecca home to Newport and taught her how to sail the rough Atlantic. They spent weeks visiting Bix's innumerable relatives scattered up and down the seaboard, exploring Boston museums and discovering roadside stands along the Massachusetts coast that served sensational deep-fried oysters and onion rings.

Somewhere along the way they also discovered a profound, lasting friendship.

Yet for all that she shared with Bix, Rebecca never invited her to the Angelines. As much as she wanted to see where Rebecca had grown up, Bix did not insist. Rebecca hadn't yet come to terms with what had happened to her there. Besides, they had their whole lives ahead of them.

"Becky, are you all right?" Bix asked.

"Fine." Rebecca smiled, stirring from her reverie. "I was just thinking about everything we've done over these last five years, how wonderful they've been." She paused. "How much you've done for me."

"Oh, pooh!" Bix sniffed, then added, "I guess we were an unbeatable combination. All that's left for me to do is to get you into the sack with Andrew."

"You have a one-track mind, girl! Here, start going through these brochures."

For the next half hour they lost themselves in the dazzling images of sun-washed Spanish beaches and idyllic Greek islands.

"What the hell is that racket?" Bix demanded, cocking her head.

Rebecca went to the window, and Bix squeezed in beside her. Both girls stared in amazement at the helicopter that was settling down on the quadrangle.

"That's someone who's either very, very important or really dumb!" Bix said. "Any second now you'll see Old Lady Wright hoofing out there to find out—"

"Oh, my God, Bix—look who it is!" Rebecca grabbed her friend's arm.

Bix saw a tall figure emerge through the rear door of the helicopter, the rotor wash sending his white-blond hair askew.

"Well, well, well." Bix chuckled as she watched Andrew Stoughton duck beneath the spinning blades. "If it isn't Prince Charming come to sweep his princess off her feet. Becky, you scheming bitch! Why didn't you tell me the love of your life was arriving?"

Rebecca blushed furiously, but her eyes were riveted on Andrew Stoughton.

"Why is he here?"

"Because of you!" Bix groaned. "Christ on a crutch, Becky! He's finally come to his senses. He's going to take you away from all this."

Rebecca watched as Andrew trotted past gaping girls and

disappeared into the administration building. A few minutes later he was walking swiftly toward the dorms, Miss Penelope Wright, the headmistress, matching him stride for stride.

"They're coming up here!"

Rebecca looked at Bix uneasily.

"Don't jump to conclusions," Bix warned her, taking Rebecca's hand. "He quite literally dropped in to see you, that's all."

The words sounded hollow even to Bix.

"Would you rather I go?"

"No, please."

It seemed like an eternity before they heard staccato footsteps on the ancient floorboards. There was a sharp knock on the door, and Miss Wright entered, her usually ruddy complexion pale.

"She's here, Mr. Stoughton," she started to say as he pushed by her.

Rebecca found herself staring into Andrew's pain-filled eyes.

"You've got to come home right away," he said, his voice hoarse. "There's been an accident. Rebecca, it's Max. . . ."

· 3 ·

What happened next was reduced to a blur in Rebecca's memory. One minute she was shaking her head violently, screaming "No! No! No!" The next Andrew was beside her, his arm around her shoulders, talking quickly, quietly.

"You have to calm down and listen to me, Rebecca. Max was at some ruins Dallas Gibson was working on. He was standing at the edge of a well and the earth gave way. Max injured his head in the fall."

"How badly was he hurt?"

"His condition is stable but he hasn't regained consciousness," Andrew said carefully. "I've got him at the hospital in Angeline City." Andrew paused. "He needs you, Rebecca. He needs you now."

Bix kneeled before Rebecca and grasped both her hands.

"Go, Becky! I'll pack the essentials. Don't worry about the rest. I'll look after everything for you. Just go!"

Rebecca rose and stood very straight, her eyes glittering like newly minted coins.

"He is not going to die," she said very clearly.

"No, he's not," Andrew replied, then realized that it had been a statement, not a question.

Of course he won't die, Rebecca thought to herself. Max is indestructible. Look at everything he's been through. He would never do anything to hurt me.

The memory of her father's strength sent a shock through Rebecca. She felt ashamed for having thought of her own pain.

How can you be so selfish? For the first time in your life the tables are turned. He needs you!

"Are you all right, Rebecca?" the headmistress asked anxiously.

Rebecca looked at her, then down at herself.

"Yes, I am, Miss Wright. But I can't very well meet my

father in my Briarcrest uniform, can I? Give me a minute to change, Andrew?''

"Don't worry, Rebecca. We have plenty of time.''

At first Andrew didn't think she had heard him. Absently Rebecca selected a beautiful red and white linen skirt with matching peasant blouse. Before she disappeared into the bathroom, she said to him, "What about my father? Does he have time too?''

Andrew slumped forward, burying his face in his hands.

"Oh, Jesus,'' he whispered.

McHenry Enterprises had been one of the first customers for Bill Lear's sleek new executive jet. As soon as the plane lifted off the runway at San Diego, Andrew Stoughton called the steward to bring him a glass of water.

"I want you to take one of these.'' Andrew handed Rebecca the water along with a tiny white pill.

She spoke into her reflection in the Plexiglas.

"What is it?''

"A tranquilizer. It'll help you sleep.''

Rebecca stared into his fathomless eyes, bloodshot with fatigue.

"I'm glad you came for me,'' she said.

"Everything will be all right,'' Andrew soothed her. "Go on, take the pill.''

"No, Andrew,'' Rebecca said. "I'm not going to hide from this. You're here with me. That's all I need.''

Andrew intertwined his fingers through hers and held them tightly. As the engines continued their hypnotic drone and twilight appeared on the horizon, he felt Rebecca's grip loosen. Her breathing became shallower and her head rolled lightly against his shoulder. Except for the two rivulets of tears that streaked her cheeks, he would have sworn she was asleep.

She had grown up a child of the sea and her crib had been the pond between the beach and the reef created by a half moon of rocks sunk in the shallows.

Rebecca could remember being in the water, lying on her stomach, supported by very strong hands, kicking her arms and legs as she learned to swim. The man who held her was her father, a laughing giant who rolled her in his arms and tumbled her into the water only to hoist her up and toss her in the air. Her father would catch her and whirl her around as she threw her head back and cried out in joy. In her father's arms she did not know the meaning of fear. That came only when he left her.

As a child, Rebecca had realized that her father's frequent absences were to be a constant part of her life. She learned to recognize the change in him when he was getting ready to leave, the quickening pace around the house, the excitement in his eyes and voice. And Rebecca always tried to stop him with tears and pleas. One evening she even waited until he had gone to bed, then unpacked half his gear before, exhausted, she finally fell asleep in the midst of the jumble of bags.

Even though her father solemnly promised to return, Rebecca always feared he wouldn't. She remembered that first time Max had told her about her mother, explaining as simply and kindly as he could how she had left one day and never come back. For a long time the image of this unknown woman walking away and not once turning back had haunted Rebecca, making the first night her father was gone a bitterly tearful one.

The only person Rebecca had to turn to was Jewel, a matronly black woman with a gleaming gold tooth, whose laughter sounded like wind chimes and whose body jiggled when she walked. Rebecca had never known life without Jewel and, although she knew Jewel wasn't her mother, she lavished a child's love upon her. It came back to her threefold. Jewel was always there to teach her the ways of the islands, explore the natural beauty of the Angelines, and help her understand the new wonders she discovered each day. Later, when Rebecca was old enough, Jewel took her to school and in the afternoons helped her to make small gifts to give to her father when he returned—an imprint of her hand, fingers spread apart, set in plaster and painted a vivid blue, or a wood carving that cost Rebecca countless scratches and cuts. Rebecca would hoard her treasures until she heard Max's telltale step in the house, then rush to his side and drag him off to her room. Her father would look carefully at each gift as if it were a precious stone, then kiss and hug her.

Over the years a comfortable pattern was established for the first night her father was home. After dinner, when he came out onto the terrace, his pipe lit, Rebecca scrambled onto his lap. Together they watched the sun set and he told her wonderful stories of where he had traveled and what he had seen. Placing a rough gold nugget in her hand, he described the shining mountains in the north and how it took days to reach them by boat and on foot. He told Rebecca all about the creatures he encountered in the jungle, the clever golden orb spider whose web was strong enough to catch young bats, the patient margay, predator cat of the treetops, the beautiful melanea butterfly that lost its innocence as soon as it ate from poisonous plants and became inedible itself.

These stories fascinated Rebecca as much as her father's descriptions of the mining camps and the tales of his early explorations. She shared his excitement when he spoke of the rough camaraderie among his men, the din of the heavy machinery, the cries of the miners as they labored beneath the blazing sun, and the glow of the gigantic smelters that lit up the sky at night. On his words Rebecca traveled to the frozen tundra of the Yukon and Alaska where, in the early twenties, Max had begun his search for gold. She felt the icy waters sluicing in the California gravel beds and the searing heat of the Australian outback, a territory Max had crisscrossed for ten years in a vain search for gold. She was beside him when he set foot in the Angelines, penniless and in despair, until he met Jewel, who gave him the money for one last expedition.

Yet for all the excitement and love Rebecca heard in her father's words, she also sensed a note of sadness vibrating within them. Several more years would pass before she understood the deepest reason for Max's continual expeditions into the Angelinian jungles.

Christmas was the season Rebecca loved most. Not only was her father always home, but the big house, empty for so much of the time, was filled with people, music, and laughter. The year Rebecca turned eight was particularly special since her father had promised she would be allowed to stay up with the adults.

The beginning of Christmas was marked by the arrival of the F.A.O. Schwarz catalogue from New York. Rebecca and Max would spend hours poring over it, with Rebecca carefully making a list of the toys she wanted. Although the final letter was always addressed to Santa Claus, Rebecca strongly suspected that it was Aunt Lauren and Uncle Ramsey who brought the gifts from the United States.

The guests began to arrive on the twenty-third, some coming in large vessels that rode anchor in the bay below the house, others by plane. Wearing a favorite cherry-red dress with white lace, white stockings, and black shoes, Rebecca stood beside her father at the door, greeting the arrivals and promptly offering to carry off the armloads of presents to the twenty-foot tree that dominated the living room.

Rebecca was very proud of the care her father took to introduce her to the hundreds of people who milled through the house. She was awed by how eager they were to talk to him and by the respect they showed. The best part came after Christmas Eve dinner, when the band on the terrace began to play and her father escorted her onto the floor for the first dance.

As exhausted as she was, Rebecca should have slept right into Christmas morning. But in the middle of the night she got up and tiptoed through the silent house toward the tree. Then she saw the partially open door and the shaft of light coming from her father's library.

Max was sitting at his desk, his back to the door. At first Rebecca thought he was staring through the windows at the panoramic view of the ocean. She noticed that the curtains across the wall were drawn back, revealing something she had never seen before.

On the wall was a life-size portrait of a regal Mayan woman standing before ruins partially obscured by jungle. She seemed to be looking directly at Rebecca, her gaze quiet, reassuring, a ghost of a smile on her lips. Rebecca drew in her breath and, as though hypnotized, moved closer to the portrait. The resemblance between the woman and herself was unmistakable. When she looked at her father she saw the overwhelming sadness of the woman's eyes reflected in his.

Her father glanced at her, and his surprise at seeing her faded. Shivering, Rebecca climbed onto his lap.

"Her name was Apho Hel," her father said, not taking his eyes off the portrait. "She was your mother and the only woman I ever loved. . . ."

His voice caught as he said the rest. "I know I told you she had gone away. And she did. But now I know, as surely as I know I love you, that she's dead."

Her father lapsed into a silence Rebecca dared not break even though her heart was bursting with questions. Staring into his pain-filled eyes, she suddenly had to know everything about this woman—who she had been, where Max had met her, what had happened between them. Rebecca looked at the portrait with loathing. How dare this woman hurt her father so deeply, first by leaving, then by dying?

Rebecca reached up and brought her arms around her father's neck, hugging him tightly. She had to make him understand that she would never leave him. She would never die or make him cry, because now they had only each other. The question she asked so much later—what had Max found that had convinced him her mother was dead?—never entered her mind that Christmas Eve.

And when I did ask him, he never told me. He kept going back into that damn jungle, searching for something he never shared with me. Is it too late now for him to tell me?

The whine of turbines and the pressure in her ears as the plane began its descent stirred Rebecca from her reverie. She looked across at Andrew, feeling a rush of gratitude for his presence.

"Are we there yet?"

He passed her a glass of cold orange juice and Rebecca drank gratefully.

"Look for yourself."

Even the distortion caused by the Plexiglas window couldn't detract from the beauty unfolding beneath the sky. Rebecca watched as the midnight blue of the Great Trench gave way to lighter shades until the green of the reefs was mixed in to render a gentle aquamarine. She recognized the frothy white line that marked the outer limit of the reef and the silver glitter of the beaches along the large keys: Chapel, Corker, and Paradise. Beyond them, across another expanse of water, was the Angelinian mainland, 110 miles long, 50 wide, divided into a northern swampy plain, a slight plateau in the east, and a mountainous mass—the Maya Ridge—in the south. As the jet arced, Rebecca saw the first cream and rust colors of the island dwellings.

"Are you sure you're all right?"

"I'm fine, Andrew, really."

At that moment Rebecca fooled even herself.

The Lear taxied to its assigned position and the engines were turned off. Rebecca stepped into the brilliance of an Angelinian afternoon, and the dry heat enveloped her like a cloud. She glanced at her watch.

Could it have taken only three hours? Three hours to bring me to another country, another time?

Then she saw Jewel. Jewel, with her head done up in the familiar yellow kerchief, gold hoop earrings flashing in the sun, gold tooth gleaming. Rebecca felt herself swallowed up by matronly arms. She looked down at the tearful face whose lines and ridges resembled those of a baked apple.

"Thank the Lord you're home," Jewel whispered.

And with that Rebecca's own tears finally came.

"There is nothing more we can do for him, Rebecca."

The diminutive physician who, after twenty years, knew every scar on Max McHenry's body, uttered the words with quiet finality. To Rebecca it sounded like a death sentence.

The hospital room gleamed from a freshly applied coat of white paint, the color almost painful to the eyes when the sun poured in. Outside the window, screened with hurricane louvers, Rebecca heard the call of the Angeline swallow.

Max McHenry lay in the bed with his arms stretched over the blankets. His eyes were closed and his expression was serene, as though he were sleeping peacefully. Even the bandage near the crown of the skull seemed meaningless.

A bubble of air. Something no bigger than the tip of a pin. After everything he's survived, he's being killed by something he can't even see.

"There's absolutely no way to tell when he'll regain consciousness?" Rebecca asked.

Dr. Bishop shook his head. "Mr. Stoughton and I have consulted with a leading specialist from the United States. His opinion is the same. The coma might last only several more hours or else it could go on for years."

Years! What would be left of him after "years" if in just two days his body, once seemingly indestructible, was already diminished?

"Mr. Stoughton is having the best medical equipment flown in. Your father will require round-the-clock nursing attention which, I'm told, has been looked after. Rebecca, we can and will keep him alive indefinitely."

Rebecca gripped the cold enamel of the bed frame, struggling to maintain control of herself.

"If there's nothing more you can do for him here, can I bring him home to Skyscape?"

To her surprise the physician did not object.

"There's no reason why not. But you must be sure you want to do this. Having an invalid at home can be very difficult."

"He's not an invalid! He's my father."

Bishop inclined his head. "I'll tell Mr. Stoughton. He and I will make the necessary arrangements for the transfer."

Rebecca was alone with her father. She placed his rough, callused hand between her palms.

There are so many things I want to tell you, so much we have to do together. I promised you I wouldn't die and leave you. Why are you doing this to me now?

The scraping of the door intruded on Rebecca's anguish. She looked up to see a young man in his late twenties standing on the threshold. He was an inch or two taller than she, about five ten, with weathered skin almost as dark as his chestnut hair. He wore jungle clothing—baggy green pants of thick cotton, a bush jacket made from the same material, and underneath his arm he carried a stained Australian slouch hat. His hazel eyes were filled with a pain far greater than his broken left arm might have caused.

"I'm sorry," he said, starting to leave. "I didn't know anyone would be here."

"Wait!"

Rebecca leapt to her feet and closed the door behind Dallas Gibson. She had seen him only a few times and at first hadn't recognized him. He was the archaeologist her father had hired just before she had left the Angelines.

"I'm Rebecca McHenry," she said. "You probably don't remember me."

"Oh, yes, I do," Dallas said softly, his gaze dropping before Rebecca's furious eyes. "I'm so sorry about what happened. . . ."

"What exactly did happen?" Rebecca demanded.

Dallas jammed his clenched fist into the pocket of his bush jacket. His voice was a monotone, that of a man who can't believe what he's saying.

"No one expected Max to come out of the jungle in the middle of the night. But then, he was always one for the unexpected. When I first saw him he was walking by the *cenote*. That's the—"

"I know what it is!"

Dallas recoiled at the anger in Rebecca's voice and his own tone became more subdued.

"I was taking a walk around the perimeter, having a cigarette. I was just about to go inside the bunkhouse, when I saw him, standing near the well. Before I could call out to him, he was gone . . . as if the earth had swallowed him up. I heard him cry out when he fell and ran to the well. As soon as I saw what happened I yelled for help, then scrambled after him and got this."

Dallas tapped his cast.

"How could you let him get so close to the edge of that damn well?" Rebecca whispered. "Why wasn't it roped off?"

"Miss McHenry, you don't understand," Dallas said desperately. "Max wasn't in any danger where he was standing. There was plenty of light around the *cenote*. The earth shouldn't have given way so far back from the edge."

"You should have realized it might, Mr. Gibson," Rebecca lashed out. "You were the expert on the site! You were responsible for the safety of everyone around you! You were responsible for my father!"

Every coil of fear and pain within Rebecca was unleashed. She was not even aware of her fists hammering Dallas Gibson's chest. Rebecca was still trying to kill the terror within her, when Andrew Stoughton rushed into the room, stepped between her and Dallas Gibson, and dragged her away.

Two days later Rebecca brought her father home. The vigil, whose end no one could foresee, had begun.

· 4 ·

The great house called Skyscape sprawled across the edge of the cliff that shot vertically from the beaches on the leeward side of the Angelines mainland. Only two stories high, the house followed the contours of the terrain, its sections laid out at seemingly incongruous angles to one another. From the air the structure resembled the disjointed spine of some prehistoric skeleton.

Yet when Max McHenry had built Skyscape he knew exactly what he had been doing. Even this protected side of the Angelines lay in the path of Caribbean hurricanes. Sometimes the worst ones appeared only once in a decade but when they arrived, the tall proud homes along the unprotected shorelines were battered mercilessly. Anchored into the stone and earth, Skyscape had survived them all.

From the second floor master bedroom window, nurse Violet Lhuiller looked across the rolling acres of cleared jungle that made up the grounds of Skyscape. Lamps dotted the crushed-shell drive and cinder paths that meandered through manicured lawns. The warm October night trembled faintly with the rhythms of *balché*, the annual festival being celebrated in Angeline City three miles away.

Violet, a short, lithe woman of forty-five, with caramel skin and dark Indian eyes, glanced at her watch. Her crisp white uniform crackled as she checked the medical equipment that surrounded the canopied four-poster. The oxygen tanks, respirator, electrocardiograph, and intravenous drip were all functioning properly. On her chart Violet noted the time, eleven o'clock in the evening, and wrote the same comment she had made for each of the past twenty-one nights: No change in the patient's condition. Nor was there likely to be.

Violet rolled a stool to the bedside and, dipping a cloth into warm water, began to swab Max's face around the oxygen mask; the skin looked almost translucent against the skull. As she

28

worked, her gaze wandered around the palatial bedroom, taking in the magnificent tapestries and paintings that adorned the walls. The very opulence of the room seemed to mock the figure who was being reduced to a parody of a man. All of Max's millions, only a tiny fraction of which he had spent on his own pleasures, were powerless to save him now.

As Violet rinsed out the cloth she looked at the ebony credenza festooned with photographs set in silver frames.

Here was a picture of Max at his first mine, holding a chunk of ore in his hand, his battered Panama—his trademark—askew on his head.

I was twenty then. Twenty when I was told I could never have children. I didn't know then who Max was. No one knew. . . .

A few months later that photograph was reproduced in every newspaper around the globe. It was the first glimpse at an anonymous figure who would soon become one of the wealthiest men in the world.

Another picture, taken about ten years later, showed Max on board the *Windsong*, a child of three or four clinging to his thigh with both hands.

That's when my Charlie died. I was so beside myself, I couldn't believe my grief would ever end. Then Max came to me and said I was going to America, to study to become the nurse I had always wanted to be. Did he know then he would need me now?

Carefully Violet rinsed out the cloth in the basin and patted dry Max McHenry's face, the skin wrinkled like crepe. She knew that Max's coma could last for years. At sixty-five he had the heart and constitution of a man half his age. As Violet checked the equipment one more time she made him a silent promise: She would stay by his side as long as there was hope.

But if he must die, then let it be when I'm beside him. The other nurses don't know him as I do. He will know if there's a friend beside him at the end.

Violet descended the staircase which opened on the serpentine hall that ran from one end of the house to the other, linking the various sections. When she reached the kitchen she pulled open the sliding door to the terrace. The echoes of the *balché* music calmed her.

Violet poured fresh water to make tea, and while she waited for the kettle to whistle tapped her foot to the beat of distant music. She felt no sacrilege in doing this. If this hadn't been her shift she would have been dancing in the streets. The *balché* was an affirmation of life, a celebration that dated back to the ancient Mayan rites intended to gain the favor of the all-powerful rain god, Chac. Now, as then, hens and turkeys were prepared for the feast, killed, cleaned, and wrapped in plantain leaves to be cooked in underground ovens called *pibs*. Women baked special cakes from corn dough and spices while the men brewed the traditional drink, the *balché*, from fermented maize, *balché* bark, honey, and water.

Over the centuries the *balché* festival had absorbed the music and dance of the other cultures that had taken root and flourished in the Angelines. The Indians, Carib blacks, and mestizos all contributed their music, dance, and costumes until the *balché* had grown to an extravaganza as wild and as colorful as New Orleans's Mardi Gras or Rio's *Carnaval*.

Violet listened to the throbbing music, the high pitch of horns and whistles carried on the manic backbeat of the conga and bongo, and imagined the revelers snaking their way through the streets of Angeline City. Come dawn, the parade would wind its way to Skyscape and the music would pulse beneath Max's bedroom window. For Angelinians, song and dancing and celebration were as powerful and moving as any prayer. There would be time enough for tears when death finally came.

Violet spooned leaves into a silver tea ball, dropped it into the pot, and poured the hot water over it. She sensed rather than heard the movement behind her. When she turned around she saw only a shadow, then caught the sound of a soft insistent whistle, like a mosquito buzzing by her ear. A fraction of a second later the frenetic beat of the *balché* seemed to explode in her skull.

Violet Lhuiller's killer stood poised over her as she crumpled to the floor, the tip of the iron bar in his hand bloodied. He didn't have to touch her to know she was dead.

The killer slipped out onto the terrace and came back carrying a jerry can in each hand and a bundle tucked under his right arm. He placed the cans beside Violet and moved off into the hall. When he reached the foot of the serpentine hall, the killer unwrapped the package containing two dozen candles. He lit one, let the wax drip onto the ironwood floorboards, and set the candle firmly into the congealing pool. He repeated this all the way along the hall until he had created a candlelit passage.

The killer went upstairs to continue his work. He entered Max McHenry's bedroom, turned off the oxygen, and ripped away the needle that fed intravenous solution into Max's thin vein. McHenry would now die slowly. If his weakened lungs didn't expire first, the smoke would eventually suffocate him.

When he returned to the kitchen the killer was breathing hard. From his pocket he brought out a screwdriver and, raising both jerry cans onto the counter, punctured their bottoms with a series of swift jabs. Holding a can in each hand well away from his body, the killer walked slowly through the hall, listening to the drip of gasoline as it spattered on the polished wood floor. He was especially careful not to let any gasoline touch the flames, at the same time making sure that the liquid ran all around the base of the candles.

The killer carefully examined his handiwork. The candles would take thirty minutes to burn down. When they did, Skyscape, so lovingly crafted from wood and mortar, would become an inferno. By then he would be far away.

The killer backed out of the hall, slipping through the doors in the kitchen. Then the bullfrogs, cicadas, owls, and nighthawks resumed their nocturnal litany beneath the music of the *balché*.

The air conditioner sucked in the raucous music as it labored to cool the humid night breeze. Andrew Stoughton was sitting in the familiar confines of his office at McHenry Enterprises, his long legs stretched out, feet on the desk. There was a large whiskey cradled in his lap. Tonight Andrew didn't have the slightest twinge of guilt about the paperwork that awaited his attention. He had left the demands of McHenry Enterprises far behind.

Andrew closed his eyes to the music, feeling the single-malt scotch work the tension from his belly, when suddenly he whirled around.

"Jesus, it's you! You scared the life out of me. Is anything wrong? Max?"

"I couldn't sleep," Rebecca said. "I saw your lights on and . . . I'm sorry I startled you."

Slowly Andrew relaxed, shaking his head at the state of his nerves as the antique clock above his desk struck one o'clock. Five hours earlier he and Rebecca had had supper on board the *Windsong*. They had eaten cold lobster and drunk white wine and for the first time in weeks Andrew had actually seen her smile. When Rebecca told him she would be sleeping aboard the vessel, Andrew seconded the idea. A night away from Skyscape, surrounded by water which would calm and soothe her, would do Rebecca a world of good. The waiting, the not knowing what would happen to Max, was taking its toll. A shallow furrow Andrew had never seen before ran across Rebecca's once-smooth forehead, while underneath the huge gray eyes the skin puffed out, as though filled with tears waiting to fall.

"Come and sit down," he said, offering her his chair.

As he brushed by her he caught her scent, Diorissimo by Dior, and felt her unrestrained breasts beneath the batik shift. The shy, coltish girl he had first met five years before had disappeared. At eighteen Rebecca was a woman complete.

Andrew perched himself on the edge of the desk, swung one leg over the other, and lit a cigar.

"Did the music keep you awake?"

Rebecca nodded. "I had forgotten how crazy the *balché* is. You can hear music for miles."

"And I'm forgetting my manners," Andrew said. "Can I get you anything—coffee, or"—he held up his glass—"whiskey?"

When Rebecca looked up at him, Andrew saw the slight ridge at the top of her nose where the cartilage had been broken after a fall from a horse. She shook her head.

No, I don't want coffee. I want to take your hand and press your fingers to my cheek, squeeze them so hard that you'll never get away. I want to feel your arms around me and your lips against my ear, telling me that everything will be all right. I don't want to be alone. . . .

In the three weeks since she had brought Max back to Sky-scape, Rebecca had tried to create some kind of regimen in her life. But all the things she loved—swimming and diving, riding through the endless trails on her Arabian mare—had become meaningless. In spite of the doctor's advice not to lose herself in her father's tragedy, Rebecca seldom left Skyscape for more than a few hours at a time. Wherever she went she carried the picture of him in bed, helpless. Like a magnet, this image always drew her back. She thought she could actually hear the respirator as it inflated his lungs. The sound was a continual reminder of her loss and she hated it. Yet she was terrified that she might one day enter the bedroom and not hear it.

Time lost its distinction. The days ran one into the next and seemed to stretch into infinity. Whenever Rebecca looked down that road she saw more of the same: empty, silent hours that trapped her as effectively as they had her father. Only Jewel and Andrew—and Bix with her daily telephone calls from Briarcrest— reminded her that she was not alone.

God only knows what I would have done without them.

"Are you sure there isn't anything I can get you?" Andrew asked, gently breaking the silence.

"Will you come to the house with me at dawn? The *balché* parade will have reached Skyscape by then. We can have breakfast and listen to the music."

"Of course. But morning's a long way off."

"I'll curl up on the couch," Rebecca said. "I'll be so quiet you won't even know I'm there. I won't disturb you while you work."

"I wasn't working," Andrew said heavily.

From the telltale Scots burr in his voice Rebecca knew he was exhausted. Without thinking she took his hand, her fingers gently massaging his palm.

In these past weeks Rebecca had had a chance to actually see what Andrew did for the company. Her image of him as the globe-trotting executive who traveled on private aircraft, lived in the finest hotel suites, and dined at the most exclusive restaurants vanished forever. The reality was a man who spent eighteen hours a day at his office, never more than an arm's length from the telephone. A man who juggled a hundred business options every day, made decisions affecting thousands of people, yet who still took the time to come to Skyscape. Rebecca was overwhelmed by Andrew's courage and confidence. Close to him she felt safe and protected. Without him she looked upon McHenry Enterprises with bewilderment.

Max can't die. If he's gone, I won't know what to do. I can't even pretend to understand any of this!

"Maybe it's best if we both get some rest," Rebecca started to say.

At that moment the telephone jangled sharply. For years to come Rebecca would remember Andrew's expression as he listened to the caller's words, his mild irritation dissolving into incredulity that in turn became fear. Before she could utter a word Andrew grabbed her hand and they were running out the door into the parking lot. It wasn't until the Jaguar had careered onto the main road leading out of Angeline City that Rebecca had a terse reply to the questions she had been hurling at him.

"There's a fire at Skyscape. A fishing trawler spotted the flames and radioed the coast guard. The fire trucks are on the way."

Rebecca braced herself against the dash and clung to the armrest as Andrew threw the car around the corners. Over the

scream of the engine and the squeal of tires she heard her heart
pounding. Every beat seemed to echo her silent prayer. *He's all
right! He's all right! He's all right!*

Rebecca smelled the smoke a half mile from the gates. As the
Jaguar leapt over a small hill she saw the sky lightening in the
east. But it wasn't the dawn. By the time they reached the stone
wall that ran along the perimeter of the property, flaming embers
drifted over the car.

The great house was burning, the flames an ugly yellow
serpent that seemed to run from one end to the other along the
ground floor. Rebecca jumped from the car even before it stopped,
stumbled, and began running across the vast expanse of lawn.
Suddenly her feet came out from under her and she felt herself
being swung around.

"Don't go any closer!" Andrew shouted. "Stay here and tell
the firemen I've gone inside to get Max!"

Before Rebecca could protest, Andrew flung off his jacket and
broke for the house. Rebecca stared up at the second story to her
father's bedroom. The windows were still dark and there didn't
seem to be any smoke. She began to pray for Max—and Andrew.

When the fire crews arrived, they were startled to find a young
woman standing in front of the house, her soot-covered face
thrust toward the flames. They were even more surprised when
she turned on them as they tried to lead her to safety. Then there
was the shattering of glass as a figure broke through the French
doors of the far wing. He was carrying something in his arms,
something wrapped in a sheet.

"Oh, God, no, please, no!"

Rebecca burst from the fireman's grip and streaked across the
grass, her momentum such that she almost collided with Andrew. As soon as she saw his eyes, watched the heaving chest
rise and fall, she shrank back.

"It's not him!" she whispered. "That's not my father!"

Gently Andrew lay the body at her feet. Before he could
stop her Rebecca flung back the sheet and saw her father's face,
the mouth gaping as though he were still trying to breathe. She
threw her head back and screamed, her cries rising into the
night. She cried out her father's name over and over again.

Gently, Andrew covered her hand with his and pried her
fingers from Max's face.

"No, please . . . I must be with him. He'll be all right as long
as I'm here."

With infinite tenderness Andrew laid the head of Max McHenry on the grass and covered it with a blanket. He drew his arm around Rebecca's shoulder and tried to force her to stand.

Like a dancer trying to execute an impossible move, Rebecca felt herself falling, fleeing the pain and terror of that monstrous image, the face that had once belonged to her father.

· 5 ·

Dawn of the third day after Max McHenry's death marked the end of the *balché*. By now the docks of Angeline City should have bustled with activity as the market stalls opened to receive fishermen returning with their bounty. Today the stalls remained shuttered. The boats, moored in the bay, rode lightly in the ebb tide. The town square behind the market, where fruit and vegetable sellers gathered, was deserted.

This morning Angeline City was silent except for the peal of church bells as its people, and Angelinians across the land paid their final respects to a man they loved as no other.

Rebecca had never worn black in her life. She hadn't thought of it as a color but rather a mood. She hated both. On the eve of Violet Lhuiller's funeral, held the day before, Rebecca had discovered she had nothing appropriate to wear. Jewel had had to stay up most of the night, sewing.

The dress and Rebecca's hair fluttered as the *Windsong* turned into the breeze, navigating the *quebrada,* the deep channel that linked the calm waters behind the reef with the open seas. The sun crested the horizon, creating a shimmering road of pink, gold, and orange for the vessel to travel upon. Rebecca felt the wind pushing the tears back into her eyes. Her hand came to rest on the casket beside her, seeking support that wasn't there anymore.

"This would be a fine place," Jewel said.

"A little farther out," Rebecca said, slipping her arm through Jewel's. "I don't want him to be disturbed. Ever."

"He will sleep the sleep of the just."

Together the two women watched as the waters beneath the *Windsong* passed through the spectrum of pale green to brilliant midnight blue, highlighted by the white, scythelike bow waves. When Rebecca judged they were well over the Great Trench, six thousand feet deep, she instructed the captain to stop.

Although her father hadn't been a religious man, Rebecca had agreed with Jewel that a minister should be present. As the elderly black Angelinian stepped forward, the rest of the mourners gathered in a semicircle behind the casket: Andrew, who had looked after every detail exactly as Rebecca had wished; Bix, whose frantic telephone calls Rebecca had finally answered and who had flown down immediately; Ramsey Peet, Max's best friend, attorney, and business adviser who had come in from New York.

Somehow Andrew had even managed to include the governor-general of the Angelines in the mourning party without his presence causing a scene. The short, corpulent Sir Geoffrey Smythe had arrived dressed in the trappings of his office: midnight-blue naval uniform laden with medals, ribbons, and ungainly braided shoulder boards, all topped by an oversize tricorn that kept sliding forward on his head. Rebecca knew that Max had had nothing but contempt for this pompous buffoon, and she was barely able to be civil when he murmured his whiskey-laden condolences. But, as Andrew whispered to her, Sir Geoffrey was the official representative of the Angelinian people, no matter how big an idiot he was. Protocol dictated that he be present.

When the last prayer had been uttered, two crew members, black armbands contrasting sharply against their white and gold uniforms, flanked the casket. Rebecca leaned forward and placed a single perfect orchid on the Angelinian flag, blue and yellow with a red shooting star in the upper left-hand corner.

"Amazing Grace, how sweet the sound . . ."

As Jewel's firm soprano filled the sky, the wind caught the words and carried them across the waves. Rebecca listened as the others joined in and at last she found her own voice. The beauty and finality of the old spiritual filled her with unbearable sadness.

When the last notes died away, the crewmen lifted one end of the smooth plank. With the flag rippling, the casket slid over the side. Rebecca scarcely heard the splash. As the *Windsong* got under way, she stared back, trying to burn into her memory exactly where her father lay, so that she might come out here and visit his invisible grave. Then she saw something that took her breath away.

As far as the eye could see the ocean was filled with boats, from the smallest dinghies used by island children learning to sail, to red, green, turquoise, and yellow fishing boats, to the

mammoth cruisers and motorsailors whose home registries recalled every port in the Caribbean.

Without Rebecca's having been aware of it, this flotilla had
silently followed the *Windsong*, maintaining a discreet distance.
Now craft after craft circled the place where Max McHenry's
body had been consigned to the deep. As they passed, the
mourners threw garlands over the side and soon the ocean was
ablaze with final tribute.

"Becky, are you going to be all right?"

Rebecca turned to Bix and managed a tiny smile.

"You've got sunburn," she said. "Your freckles are popping
out like crazy."

"Story of my life. Tell me you're okay."

"I'll be fine."

Bix looked deeply into her best friend's eyes, trying to divine
the truth for herself. For the last two days and nights she had sat
up with Rebecca, coaxing, cajoling, and sometimes brutally
forcing out the details of what had happened. When she had
finally broken through, Bix was overwhelmed by the torrent of
grief and grisly details that poured out. But she continued to prod
Rebecca until the last drop of poison had been secreted and her
exhausted friend had collapsed into a restless, tossing sleep.

Were it not for Jewel, who had been there with her, Bix would
never have considered leaving Rebecca.

"I'm so damn sorry, Becky," Bix whispered. "I'd stay if I
could but—"

"You've done more than enough," Rebecca told her. "I
wouldn't have made it without you."

The *Windsong*'s small tender which would ferry Bix and the
minister back to Angeline City bumped against the platform at
the vessel's stern.

"Promise me you'll call."

"I'll call. You get back and pass that Latin exam."

The two girls hugged each other. Abruptly Bix turned away
and made her way to the stern, where Andrew helped her into
the tender. Before he cast off the line she said fiercely, "Look
after her—and don't be such a damn fool!"

As the *Windsong* turned in a majestic arc and headed west
toward Angeline City, Rebecca retreated to her double stateroom
belowdecks. When she was six years old her father had had this
room redecorated just for her. The walls were done in peppermint-
pink fabric, matching the sofa and easy chairs. The accents—

dresser, vanity, and end tables—were dove gray. The Matisse etchings, all signed, all originals, were dramatized by matte-finished black frames.

As much as she loved the suite, Rebecca would have preferred it in blue and green, her favorite colors. Because she hadn't wanted to offend her father she had never told him that. Now he would never know.

Rebecca stripped off the black dress and flung it aside. She never wanted to look at it again. For twenty minutes she stood under the needle spray of the shower, eyes closed, praying that the icy water would numb her despair. There was so much to do, so much to learn. Mourning was a luxury that would have to wait until she was finally alone.

Dressed in navy-blue slacks with a wine-red sailor's jersey, Rebecca entered the main salon. The two men sitting by the Erté-designed coffee table rose as one. Both Andrew and Ramsey Peet were astonished at how composed Rebecca appeared. Her face, scrubbed clean and devoid of makeup, was radiant. Her hair, tied in a ponytail, gleamed in the indirect lighting.

Rebecca looked around at the salon with its rectangular double-glass windows, mirrored panels, and custom-designed glass sculpture showing the *Windsong* in full flight. Across the navy carpet, accented with bold beige strokes, was her father's desk, fully six feet across, its ebony surface sprinkled with telephones and buttons. Rebecca had no idea what the buttons were for.

"This was my father's favorite room," she said. "I thought it would be appropriate to talk here."

But that's not really the truth. Skyscape is destroyed. The offices in Angeline City are besieged by reporters. There is nowhere else.

Ramsey Peet leaned forward and nibbled on a wedge of fresh papaya from the arrangement Jewel had provided. He was a short slim man in his fifties with electric-blue eyes that were at odds with his easy, gracious manner. Rebecca recalled her father saying of Peet, "Don't be fooled by his bluer-than-blue blood or the fancy-pants Wall Street firm his father left him. Ramsey is a tiger. Only he eats the competition quietly, with the best table manners."

Ramsey Peet had been Max McHenry's attorney since he had poured his first ingot. Rebecca had known him and his wife, Lauren, for years. By the expression on his drawn features Rebecca knew her father's death had deeply affected the patrician New Yorker.

"Are you sure you're up to this?" Ramsey asked, tapping the foot-thick file on the coffee table.

Rebecca stared at the mountain of paperwork and shuddered in revulsion. Was this what a man's lifetime was reduced to? Instantly Andrew was beside her.

"It can wait, Rebecca," he said.

Rebecca's fingertips brushed his wrist. "I want to do it now," she said, hoping her voice was as firm as she imagined. "There isn't any better time."

Rebecca settled herself between the two men, conscious of their different smells. Ramsey Peet wore the same cologne Lauren had first bought for him ten years before, a crisp, masculine fragrance manufactured for the famous London barber, Truefitt & Hill. Andrew's skin smelled of sweat and the sea, and the resin from the boughs of Australian pines that had made up the wreaths.

"The first order of business is the will," Ramsey said quietly, removing a legal parchment from the top of the pile. "Max kept things very simple—for once taking the advice he paid me for. Besides a substantial bequest to Jewel, there are several other cash payments to individuals who had served him long and faithfully. I'm sure you'll recognize the names."

Rebecca scanned the sheet.

"Is there some way to help Violet's parents?" Rebecca asked. "I want to make sure they're financially secure for the rest of their lives."

"I can set up a trust for them," Peet said, scribbling hiero-glyphics with a gold CARAN D'ACHE fountain pen.

"And some kind of scholarship or fund, in Violet's name, for girls who want to study nursing."

"Leave the particulars to me."

Ramsey Peet returned to the will.

"After endowments to a variety of arts funds, charities, hospitals, and benevolent associations are accounted for, the bulk of the estate is yours. This includes all real property such as the *Windsong*, the jet, the Skyscape property, the two hundred thousand acres Max held throughout the Angelines, as well as the entire mining operation. Of course, everything is registered under the umbrella of McHenry Enterprises. Since there are no death duties in the Angelines, it's all free and clear, yours to do with as you wish."

"How much is all this worth?" Rebecca asked quietly.

"Taking into account the appreciation of the real estate holdings, I would say somewhere in the neighborhood of two hundred and fifty million dollars.''

Rebecca slumped back, looked from Ramsey Peet to Andrew, and uttered a strangled laugh.

"Two hundred and fifty million dollars . . . That's absurd! I can't imagine that much money!''

"Few people in the world can," Peet told her. "Nonetheless, that is the aggregate value of Max's holdings. Everything he built is now yours.''

"But I don't know anything about it!'' Rebecca cried. "I was never a part of what my father did. He . . . he never asked me if I wanted to know anything about all this.''

"That's the reason I wanted Andrew here," Peet said. "He knows better than anyone what McHenry Enterprises has been doing and the plans Max had for it.''

Andrew's tapered, flawlessly manicured fingers came together to form a steeple.

"Rebecca,'' he said. "The situation is not as complicated as it may appear. Max *was* McHenry Enterprises. He had a board of directors, certainly, but—with all due respect to you, Ramsey—it was a corporate convenience.''

"I should know," the attorney agreed. "I advised him to set up the tame board.''

"Max could do whatever he wanted with McHenry Enterprises,'' Andrew continued. "Take it in any direction he wished without having to answer to anyone. Everything you see around you—the offices, the employees, the thousands of files—that's the infrastructure Max set up to run the corporation.''

"Didn't you organize most of that?'' Rebecca interrupted.

"I helped out a little," Andrew said, waving his hand dismissively. "The point is, Max let the day-to-day matters run themselves. He had the best people. He had confidence in them and he let them do their jobs.''

Andrew paused. "What hurts me the most is that Max never had the chance to realize the full potential of what he had created. He didn't live to see his dream mature.''

"Did he tell you his dream?''

Rebecca's question caught Andrew by surprise. He thought he detected a note of envy in her words.

"Let me start at the beginning," he said carefully. "Max hired me because he realized that the foundation of his fortune, the gold mines, would begin to weaken over the next few years. A large percentage of the ore that was easy to get at had already been removed. What gold remained was proving hard to mine, making further development very costly.

"Up until this point Max had been reinvesting profits into operations. Whatever surplus was left went into two areas: land acquisition and Max's personal projects, the good works that he underwrote in the Angelines. But the producing veins were so rich, Max had too much capital lying idle, capital that could have been used to expand McHenry Enterprises when the gold finally ran out.

"I was brought on board not only to administer the present but also to plan the future."

"What did you suggest, Andrew?"

Andrew glanced at Ramsey Peet, who nodded encouragingly.

"Two major directions," he said. "In terms of diversification, I suggested that the company become involved in what is being referred to as high technology. Last year President Kennedy committed the United States to putting a man on the moon. This means billions of dollars will be poured into research involving computers, electronics, and other scientific areas. Because it supplies a strategic metal to American military contractors, McHenry Enterprises is in a unique position to become involved in this high technology. It's a question of examining the small computer and electronics firms that are popping up in California and Texas, seeing which ones have the greatest potential, buying them up, and developing them into a major contractor.

"The second area was more familiar to Max," Andrew continued. "Its possibilities intrigued him. This new technology I was talking about a moment ago will need new materials and manufacturing methods. Both require either new minerals or more of those we've already discovered: titanium, cobalt, platinum, bauxite, and a host of others. Max and I agreed that given its geology, the Central American isthmus was rich in these resources. My suggestion was to organize special teams of geologists, experts in their field, and send them out on expeditions. Max, who knew this region better than anyone, would have coordinated the effort.

"In this way," Andrew concluded, "McHenry Enterprises would have controlled both ends of the stick: We would have supplied the raw materials while at the same time developing the instruments that required these materials. Eventually, I saw us filling in the middle ground: shipping, refinement, even our own research division."

Rebecca couldn't help but feel the excitement that overtook

Andrew's voice. Twice he had caught himself and, remembering the circumstances, had tried to tone down his delivery. Each time his enthusiasm for the subject got the better of him.

He loves what he's doing, she thought. The company has gotten into his blood. Max couldn't have chosen better.

"What about McHenry Enterprises as it stands today?" she asked.

Ramsey Peet sensed Andrew's discomfort and answered for him.

"In the last few years, when Max tended to spend more and more time with his archaeological projects, Andrew assumed overall control. But Max never thought about his own death. He had a drive and will I've never seen in anyone else. He even had me convinced of his immortality. As a result, he didn't make any formal provisions for a successor, be he Andrew or anyone else."

The attorney paused. "My advice is to leave things as they are. Andrew has done a damn fine job as managing director. Your employees will work as hard for him as they did for Max. There's also the continuity to consider. Andrew has experience in dealing with your clients. He knows just how far to trust them and how to talk to them at the bargaining table. We don't want anyone getting the impression that McHenry Enterprises can be taken advantage of.

"As far as the archaeological digs are concerned, I guess Dallas Gibson could bring you up-to-date—"

Ramsey Peet realized that he no longer had Rebecca's attention. Her eyes had glazed over, her fingers became so tightly intertwined that the knuckles were white.

"I don't want to hear Dallas Gibson's name again," she said softly. "We'll talk about the excavations, and what to do with them, later."

In spite of repeated assurances by both Andrew and Ramsey Peet that the young archaeologist was blameless in her father's accident, Rebecca's conviction that Dallas was responsible never wavered. She had rebuffed his attempts to see her and left strict orders that he was not to be on board the *Windsong* with the funeral party. She hadn't the slightest intention of apologizing for her behavior at the hospital.

Rebecca turned to Andrew, aware that her heart was beating furiously. She was about to make her first decision as her father's heir.

"Andrew, I'd like very much for you to stay on as managing director," she said.

"Of course," he replied. "I'm grateful for your confidence, Rebecca."

"Ramsey, will there be any problem? As far as the board is concerned, I mean."

"None," the attorney assured her. "I think you've done the right thing, Rebecca. However, sooner or later we're going to have to elect a new president."

"What about you?"

Peet smiled. "I'm flattered. But I don't think so. It was Max's company, Rebecca. It bore his name. Your name too."

When she grasped what Peet was hinting at, Rebecca was overwhelmed.

Me? As president?

Rebecca thought back to that moment when, before she left Briarcrest with Andrew, she had changed out of her school uniform into traveling clothes.

I didn't realize then that one part of my life had ended and another begun . . . that I would never wear that uniform again.

"I want to learn," Rebecca said slowly. "I want to know everything about McHenry Enterprises, to try to understand what it is I belong to. I owe my father that."

"It would be my pleasure to show you," Andrew started to say.

He was interrupted by the captain of the *Windsong,* who entered the salon.

"Miss McHenry, gentlemen, Inspector Ainsley from the Angelines police has just come on board. He says the matter is urgent."

"Tell him to come in," Rebecca said. "Ramsey, Andrew, do you know anything about this?"

Both men shook their heads.

Although the doors to the salon had better than six and a half feet clearance, Inspector Robert Ainsley had to stoop. Beneath a gleaming shaven skull was a face that once might have adorned an African tribal mask, punctuated by eyes that glittered like chips of caramel onyx.

He was dressed in parade uniform: white linen jacket with black and gold shoulder boards, black trousers with a vertical slash of red along the sides, meticulously polished ankle-high boots. Rebecca noticed that on his right sleeve Ainsley wore a black armband.

"Forgive me for intruding on you like this, Miss McHenry," Ainsley said, his voice rumbling from deep within his chest. "My condolences on your loss—our loss."

"Thank you, Inspector," Rebecca said. "I'd like to introduce you to Mr. Peet, my father's attorney, and Mr. Stoughton, the managing director of McHenry Enterprises."

The men shook hands. Rebecca sensed the policeman's reluctance to speak.

"The captain said your business was urgent, Inspector."

"It also concerns you personally," Ainsley replied.

"Does it involve my father?"

"Yes."

"Then you may say whatever you want in front of these men. I have no secrets from them."

Ainsley studied his peaked cap lying on his lap, then looked up at Rebecca.

"Miss McHenry, you're aware that the police have been investigating the cause of the fire at Skyscape."

"Yes, I am," Rebecca said tightly. "Have you found out how it started?"

"We have part of the answer. A complete autopsy was performed on your father's body prior to its release."

Rebecca's open palm hit the smoked glass of the coffee table like a gunshot.

"Who gave you permission to do that!"

"I'm sorry, Miss McHenry," Ainsley replied. "We don't need anyone's permission when we suspect that death was caused by a criminal act."

"Criminal act?"

"More specifically, homicide."

"Inspector, as Miss McHenry's attorney, I suggest you explain exactly what you mean," Ramsey Peet cut in.

The huge man's shoulders slumped forward as though he were carrying a burden too heavy even for him.

"It was the fire marshal who alerted us," he said. "Traces of gasoline were found in the charred remains of the floorboards in the hall. This alone could be an indication of foul play and necessitated an autopsy. But then we found something else: residue of candle wax in the cracks of the marble inlay in the corridor. We're not sure yet how these two factors tie in, but I'm willing to stake my pension they do."

The policeman looked at Rebecca, trying to find a way to soften the blow.

"Please understand that under the circumstances we had to do the autopsy."

Rebecca nodded mutely and Ainsley continued.

"There is also an indication that Mr. McHenry was dead before the fire started."

"What are you telling us, Inspector?" Andrew demanded.

Robert Ainsley ignored the outburst.

"We recovered the oxygen tank beside Mr. McHenry's bed. Now, we know that during the rescue Mr. Stoughton would have removed the oxygen mask from Mr. McHenry's face as well as pulled out the intravenous feed needle from his arm. But Mr. Stoughton swears that not only was Mr. McHenry *not wearing* the mask at the time he entered the room, he never touched *the valve* on the tank. Yet when the firemen got to it, the first thing they noticed was that the valve *had been turned off*."

"What are you saying?" Rebecca demanded, her fists clenched on her knees.

"Your father suffocated to death, Miss McHenry," Inspector Ainsley said softly. "He, and Violet, his nurse, were murdered by a person or persons as yet unknown."

Rebecca moaned, shaking her head. Andrew took her into his arms, hugging her to his chest.

"But what about Violet?" he whispered. "What happened to her?"

"The killer left her to burn in the kitchen, Mr. Stoughton. Then he went upstairs and murdered Mr. McHenry. Before he left he poured gasoline along the hall and ignited it The blaze was meant to destroy the evidence of how both victims really died. Unfortunately for the killer, the fire never reached Mr. McHenry's bedroom. Max McHenry spoke to us from his grave."

· 6 ·

Even as Inspector Ainsley was boarding the *Windsong*, angry rumors swept the Angelines. Max McHenry hadn't died in an accident. Instead, an injured, helpless man had been brutally murdered.

Reporters, local and international, who had covered the McHenry funeral and had been ready to file their stories, were waiting for the chief inspector when he stepped off the police launch in Stann Creek Town on Chapel Key. Ainsley was not surprised at the reception. He himself had let slip that McHenry had been murdered. The press had sniffed scandal and conspiracy, unpacked their bags, and broken out the portable typewriters. It was all part of Ainsley's plan to use the press to get the greatest possible coverage so that maybe a witness would come forward.

"Is it true, Inspector? Was the killer a foreigner?"

"Where did he come from? Who was he working for?"

"Inspector, did you tell Miss McHenry that her father was murdered? What was her reaction?"

Wordlessly Ainsley plunged into the crowd. Reporters for the Angelines *Gleaner* immediately gave him a wide berth. Their out-of-town brethren, who didn't know any better, were left sprawling in the policeman's wake.

Ainsley jammed himself into the front seat of his car and roared away from the elegant marina. At Bye Street, Stann Creek Town's main thoroughfare, he turned left and headed toward the northern part of Chapel Key. As he passed the white Palladian columns of the Supreme Court building, he swore to himself that Max McHenry would have justice. Ainsley would have seen to that even if he hadn't been a policeman.

An orphan educated by Mennonite missionaries, Ainsley had lived in the Angelines all his life, never venturing beyond the Caribbean waters. Because of his physique he had begun working at the Angeline City docks when he was twelve years old.

47

Later he fished the seas and, in season, sweated fourteen hours a day in the cane fields. A quiet, godfearing boy-man, Ainsley was liked by everyone who knew him. Generous to a fault, he left his door open to anyone in need. It proved to be his undoing. When he was sixteen Ainsley, nicknamed Bones because he had once crushed a jaguar's skull with his bare hands, was arrested for allegedly raping a white girl.

Since the Angelines were then a British colony, English law prevailed. But where London had abolished the death penalty for all but the most heinous crimes, the hangman's noose remained as punishment for lesser offenses in the Angelines. The rape of a white woman by a black man was considered worse than murder.

Bones Ainsley had had neither the money nor the influence to retain a proper defense. No matter how strongly he pleaded his innocence, no matter the number of people who testified to his character, he would have gone to the gallows. Had it not been for Max McHenry.

Midas Max had talked to Ainsley and been convinced of his innocence. Within days the best attorneys and investigators in the Caribbean were on the case. Bones Ainsley never went to trial. The investigators discovered that the girl in question had tried to seduce him. When he rebuffed her she had set out to destroy him with lies.

Having to tell Rebecca McHenry that her father had been murdered was, Ainsley reflected, one of the hardest things he had ever done. At the end, when he watched her weeping silently, he was tempted to offer her the comfort of his promise to find the killer. But Ainsley did not know if he could keep his word.

Even twenty years after his vindication Bones Ainsley was hated by the ruling white community, the "wreckers." Controlling all the appointed posts in the judiciary and the civil service, having bought and paid for Sir Geoffrey Smythe's loyalty, and retaining their iron grip on the country's ruling political party, the wreckers had made only one mistake: They had agreed among themselves that the office of inspector of police ought to be an elected one, a token gesture of democracy to native Angelinians. What they had never dreamed of was that a black man would win the election. Or that he would be Bones Ainsley.

On the outskirts of Stann Creek Town, Bye Street became a coastal road, following the indentations of the key. The bustle of the capital gave way to the tranquil emerald paddocks bordered by white fences. In the distance Ainsley saw the first great houses, fanning out in a semicircle from the governor-general's mansion, that belonged to the oldest white families on the island.

As he drove past sculpted bushes and gardens bursting with bougainvillea, yellow elder, and allamanda, Ainsley felt the power and arrogance of the three-story gabled mansion that loomed directly before him. This was where Silas Lambros lived, whose granddaughter had tried to ruin Ainsley with her lies.

The gazebo stood in the center of the back lawn, overlooking the ocean. Inside, sitting very erect in a thronelike rattan chair, was Silas Lambros, waiting for the inspector to arrive. Lambros had known Ainsley was on his way to see him as soon as the policeman had landed in Stann Creek Town. He made it his business always to keep a finger on the pulse of Angelinian arteries, no matter how faint their beat.

Lambros poured himself another glass of Montrachet. The wine was one of few foibles in an otherwise ascetic life. At seventy-five his body remained lean and hard, toned by daily swimming and riding. His face reflected an island heritage the years in London could never erase. The walnut-hued skin was pulled tight across the cheeks, the high forehead and commanding jaw slashed by deep creases. But beneath the custom-tailored Savile Row suit, the hand-tooled shoes and subtle cologne, Lambros remained true to his lineage. The unmoving pale blue eyes belonged to a pirate.

His ancestors, whose bloodlines were a heady mix produced by British, Spanish, and Dutch intermarriage, had been the original "wreckers," deserters and pirates who had fled to the Angelines. Having established an outlaw empire, they prospered by luring unwary ships onto the reefs with false safety fires and plundering their cargoes. When London at last made peace with them in the eighteenth century, the wreckers became traders, running any goods that showed a profit, from rum to slaves. They paid lip allegiance to the Crown but cheerfully roasted British magistrates and governors whose view of the law didn't quite match theirs. By the early 1900s six families controlled all the shipping, fish trade, and cane production in the Angelines. At their head was the proud house of Lambros holding the jewel of the Crown: Tyne & Wear.

Tyne & Wear was the foundation of Silas Lambros's power. When Lambros had assumed the reins thirty years earlier the corporation already controlled the insurance company that underwrote all cargo leaving the Angelines as well as the banks that financed the ships. It held a monopoly of the country's sugar production and regulated the sale of the fishermen's catch.

Under Lambros's guidance Tyne & Wear began to expand, first to other Caribbean nations, where it swallowed up existing competitors, then across the world. By the early fifties it was doing business in thirty countries and its headquarters had been moved to London, appropriately housed in a building that faced both the stock exchange and the Bank of England.

However much Silas Lambros enjoyed London, he nonetheless retained his iron grip on the land of his forefathers. Tyne & Wear's contribution to the well-being of the Angelines was publicly acknowledged when the Crown ceded a vast tract of land adjacent to the governor-general's mansion so that Silas Lambros could build his new estate. In the same year Lambros was further honored when the Angeline Protestant Church he belonged to, modeled on the Dutch Reformed *kirk*, made him a deacon. Silas Lambros had achieved what his ancestors had only dreamed of: legitimacy.

"Inspector, what a pleasant surprise." Silas Lambros didn't bother to stand when Ainsley was shown in by the Welsh butler. "Sit down. A glass of wine, perhaps?"

"No, thank you, Mr. Lambros."

Bones Ainsley smiled to himself at how Lambros, for all the time he spent in London, still couldn't erase the rough islands cadence in his speech. It was as obvious as his loathing for Ainsley.

"Then you must be here in your official capacity."

"It's about the murder of Max McHenry."

Ainsley was not surprised when his words failed to crack Lambros's placid expression. Bluntness was a formidable weapon when dealing with most wreckers, who looked upon harsh reality as they would at something clinging to the sole of their shoe. But Lambros was different. Ainsley recalled stories that no one had seen Lambros shed a tear when his elder son, Nigel, whom he had worshipped, perished at sea. Nor had he hesitated to shield his other son from the subsequent board of inquiry by sending him into exile and forbidding his name ever to be mentioned in his house.

No, Ainsley thought, not even murder can touch what is left of Silas Lambros's soul.

"I wasn't aware that Mr. McHenry had been murdered," Lambros said quietly. "The fire was started by accident. Wasn't it?"

"The fire was set deliberately. Whoever did it thought the flames would destroy the evidence."

"And was the killer successful in his attempt?"

Ainsley understood that Lambros already knew the answers to both his questions. His informants in the fire department and the coroner's office would have taken the first possible opportunity to supply him the details.

He wants to know how much I know.

"No, he wasn't."

"Then I think this makes your job that much easier, Inspector."

"Mr. Lambros, where were you on the night of the *balché*?"

Lambros's eyes glittered, and Ainsley saw the whites in his nails as his hand tightened around the crystal goblet he held.

"I had a rather large party here, as I do every year. I can show you my guest list, if you like. Anyone on it would tell you I was here. You're not by any chance suggesting that I am under suspicion?"

"In a murder investigation a policeman must ask the obvious question: *Qui bono?*" Ainsley replied. "Who benefits from the murder or who had a motive to commit it? There was no love lost between you and Mr. McHenry."

"True," Lambros conceded. "But dislike for an individual is scarcely a motive for killing him."

"Your antipathy for each other was public knowledge, so much so that one of you would have had to be a fool to try to kill the other," Ainsley observed.

"I assure you I'm relieved to hear you say as much," Lambros said dryly.

"Nonetheless, Max McHenry was very popular among my people," the inspector said. "It is inconceivable to them—as it is to me—that any native Angelinian would have killed him. Because of these two facts people will be watching my investigation very carefully. They will expect quick results. They will ask questions if results aren't forthcoming. If people become angry, Mr. Lambros, everyone suffers."

"It is your responsibility to see to it they don't become angry."

"In order to do that I need your help." Ainsley smiled. "As one of our country's leading citizens, your influence extends into many areas. You hear and are told many things. If you happen to learn anything—however incongruous or seemingly unimportant—relating to Mr. McHenry's death, it would serve you well to get in touch with me. Promptly. That way I could assure everyone you're cooperating in my investigation."

Ainsley waited for his words to take effect, but Lambros seemed not to have heard them. Even in the midday heat and dressed in a suit, the unofficial emperor of the Angelines did not sweat.

"I appreciate your candor, Inspector," Lambros said without inflection. "Of course if I hear anything of consequence I will pass it along immediately. And I assume you will show me the same courtesy."

Bones Ainsley rose without answering the implied question. He had shown Lambros the velvet glove—asking for his cooperation in areas where Ainsley couldn't move freely—as well as the iron fist, the hint of what could happen to the peace of the Angelines if Lambros hid the truth. Now it was a matter of waiting and watching. And listening, for Ainsley had his own ears seeded inside the wrecker's castle.

"Ainsley!"

The word snapped like the tip of a bullwhip.

"Don't let color blind you," Lambros called out. "You can't be certain a native didn't murder the bastard."

"Almost certain," Ainsley replied. "I can be almost certain."

"How?" Lambros challenged him.

"It's not a question of who could have murdered Max McHenry but who would have dared to."

Streaming through the criss-cross slats of the gazebo, the sun created a diamond pattern of light and shadow across Lambros's face. The wrecker closed his eyes. He had expected Ainsley to serve notice. The policeman's threat only underlined his determination to find McHenry's killer. Ainsley, Lambros knew, was after revenge, not justice.

He would get neither. Silas Lambros knew that no matter how thorough the investigation, the murderer would never be caught.

· 7 ·

The truth about her father's death destroyed Rebecca's last reserves of strength. She had been struggling to come to terms with the tragedy at Skyscape and had succeeded in convincing herself that in a way the fire had been a merciful act. To have watched her father waste away day after day, month after month, trapped in a living death sustained by machines, would have been unbearable. When she buried him Rebecca believed the fire had freed them both.

Inspector Ainsley's shocking words had changed all that. Rebecca had nowhere to run from the fact that Max McHenry had been murdered. She had no way to live with it either.

The *Windsong* became her fortress. At first reporters tried to come out to the vessel to interview her. Those who managed to steal out on a boat were met by fishermen who had formed a protective circle around the *Windsong*. No amount of money could buy the silent, angry men who greeted unwanted visitors with razor-sharp knives and gaffing hooks.

After Ramsey Peet had reluctantly departed, unable to ignore the responsibilities of his New York practice, Jewel moved on board to care for her. She tried her best to make sure Rebecca ate properly and got enough sleep. But all too often the lovingly prepared meals went untouched, and in the middle of the night Jewel woke up to sobbing coming from the adjacent suite.

Rebecca spent most of her day indoors, seldom venturing onto the upper decks. For two hours every morning she forced herself to sit at her father's desk in the main salon and mechanically write out thank-you notes to people around the world who had sent their condolences. She also made an effort to answer the hundreds of letters sent by Angelinians. Many of these were written on scraps of paper, the writing style only semiliterate. There were even a few notes from schoolchildren, who had sent along sketches of her father. Rebecca was deeply moved by these simple yet sincere expressions of grief. They made her aware of how rich in friends her father had been and how deeply he had been loved.

Afterward, pleading fatigue, Rebecca returned to her suite and often slept through the afternoon. Such became the pattern for the next two weeks. Only in the evenings, when she knew Andrew or Inspector Ainsley was coming, did Rebecca feel any life stir within her.

Rebecca quickly formed a warm attachment to the huge policeman who returned to the *Windsong* every night for the first week. Jewel reminded her of how Max had staunchly defended Ainsley when he had stood unjustly accused and how the orphan's gratitude and respect had blossomed into affection. Rebecca noticed that Bones Ainsley had transferred his feelings for Max to her, and she immediately did away with the formalities between them.

Ainsley seemed to know everyone in the Angelines. He had talked with the stevedores and fishermen, spent time with the cab drivers and street vendors, questioned prostitutes and saloon keepers. He had driven out to the vast sugar plantations and spoken with the foremen, telling them to pass the word to their men. Bones Ainsley wanted to know if anyone had seen or heard anything unusual in the days preceding the *balché*.

To Rebecca it seemed that Ainsley had the whole country working for him. When she mentioned this the inspector replied, "There isn't a single Angelinian who doesn't share your pain. They all want to help. Don't you worry, we'll find the man."

Rebecca clung to this hope like a castaway to a piece of driftwood. She told herself that given everything that was being done, it would be impossible for the killer to escape. By the end of the second week, as Ainsley's reports became shorter and shorter, her faith waned.

"What about the wreckers?" she challenged Ainsley. "They hated my father. They had all the reason in the world to destroy him!"

"I've spoken to them," he told her. "Please believe me, if there's anything to be found there, I shall have it."

The anger in Rebecca's voice cut Ainsley to the quick. He wished he could tell her about the people he had among the wreckers. Deaf-mute waiters who worked in the exclusive Jockey Club had been taught to lip-read by the same Mennonite missionaries who had educated Ainsley. Cooks and maids were invaluable sources of the gossip that drifted between the ladies of the grand houses. At the marina, the boys who cut bait and prepared the rods on board the magnificent sportfishermen were ignored by the loud arrogant men who took time from their conversation only to curse their laziness.

There was little Bones Ainsley didn't know about what went on in the golden ghetto at the north end of Chapel Key. What had first puzzled and now disturbed him was that the wreckers, although they had shed no tears for McHenry, appeared as mystified—even frightened—by the murder as anyone else.

As October passed into November, Rebecca's physical condition deteriorated. In spite of Jewel's ministrations she lost weight at an alarming rate. Her golden skin paled and her hands trembled from exhaustion. She became susceptible to sudden chills and uncontrollable outbursts of crying. The only person who kept bringing her back from the edge of total collapse was Andrew.

Andrew had stayed aboard the *Windsong* that first night. The following day he was never far from Rebecca. He left her alone when he sensed she needed her own peace but materialized by her side whenever she faltered. Andrew screened all calls put through to the vessel, allowing only Bix and Ramsey Peet to speak to her.

As the days wore on, with each bringing more uncertainty than the previous one, Rebecca came to cherish the time Andrew made for her. She knew that he spent innumerable hours at the McHenry Enterprises offices, tending to the great corporation whose needs seemed insatiable. Yet he continually surprised her by snatching an hour to come out for lunch or for a brief visit after leaving the office late at night.

Each time she saw Andrew, Rebecca fell a little more in love with him. But the love was different now. It wasn't the schoolgirl infatuation she had carried for him during her years at Briarcrest. Rather, thought Rebecca, it's the beauty of seeing someone you love every day, talking to him about most inconsequential things, letting him hold you, even if the touch lasted only a few seconds.

It means belonging to someone.

Gradually the tension and anger over the killing of Max McHenry began to fade. Reporters packed up and left. People started thinking about Christmas and made plans for family reunions. Bones Ainsley stopped by only once a week, as though ashamed he had nothing to report.

Rebecca keenly felt the policeman's frustration. Ainsley was working simultaneously on two fronts. He had expanded his investigation into other Caribbean islands, hoping that his law enforcement contacts might come up with a lead in their own jurisdictions. But the endless queries produced nothing.

At the same time Ainsley devoted long hours to going over Max McHenry's personal and business affairs. The ruins of Skyscape were carefully raked in case a vital clue had survived the fire. With Ramsey Peet's cooperation, Ainsley had had Max's safety deposit box opened and the contents flown to the Angelines. A close inspection produced only personal souvenirs: an old rock hammer, probably the first Max had ever bought; an envelope with yellowing photographs of a family long dead; creased, soiled maps of the Yukon, Alaska, Australia, and northern Canada, all places Max had labored for years before his final expedition into the Angelines.

When the inspector gave these mementos to Rebecca, she quickly locked them away. She wasn't ready to deal with the memories of expeditions long past that Max had shared with her, images that had once made her feel so close to him.

Using Andrew Stoughton's intimate knowledge of both the man and the company, Ainsley pored over all the correspondence Max had had prior to his murder, examined the latest projects, and listed the names of those involved. Not one seemed pertinent to his investigation.

Together he and Andrew scrutinized the employee ledgers, concentrating on people who had been fired or who might have a grievance against Max. Even if the reasons for dismissal seemed innocuous, Ainsley tracked down the former employees and interrogated them until he was satisfied they were innocent.

The deeper he dug, the more Ainsley accepted that the notes and files in Max's Angeline City office had told him nothing. The private papers in the Skyscape library, which might have yielded a clue, had been reduced to ash.

Qui bono? Ainsley repeated to himself. Who would benefit from the murder of a man who was already in the grip of a coma and who would probably never recover?

Ainsley felt as though he were grappling with phantoms who mocked all his efforts to reach out and seize them. When he mentioned this to Rebecca one evening, she replied, "Yes, I hear them jeering at me as well."

*   *   *

One morning in mid-November, Rebecca came on deck to find Andrew already on board. She closed her eyes as he gave her a lingering kiss on the cheek.

"What brings you out here so early?" she asked, drinking in the sight of him. His eyes danced mischievously as he beckoned to one of the stewards, who brought Rebecca a dozen perfect long-stem roses, so fresh there was dew on the petals.

"Andrew, they're beautiful!"

"Did you think I wouldn't remember your birthday?" Andrew said, twisting the neck of a champagne bottle around its cork.

A fine mist erupted from the bottle. Andrew poured Rebecca a flute and raised his own.

"To a very happy nineteenth birthday, Rebecca." He smiled. "And many, many more."

Rebecca found herself crying, but for the first time in weeks she also heard the sound of her own laughter.

"Thank you, Andrew," she whispered. "Thank you so much!"

"I think there's something hidden in the flowers," he suggested.

Carefully Rebecca turned back the stems and discovered a slim jeweler's case nestled underneath. She lifted it out and looked at Andrew.

"Can I open it—right now?"

"Yes, right now."

Lying on the royal blue Tiffany velvet was a perfect golden sea horse, the size of her little finger. Its spine and tail were studded with tiny flawless diamonds and the eyes were two fiery pinpoint rubies. Speechless, Rebecca drew out the thin gold chain and the sea horse twirled in the sunlight.

Andrew undid the clasp and strung the chain around her neck. He stood back and looked at her in undisguised admiration.

"Beautiful. Even if I do say so myself."

It was all Rebecca could do not to fling herself into his arms.

"Thank you for remembering," she said softly. "It's the most wonderful thing you could have done for me."

Andrew pulled his chair closer to hers and covered her hand with his.

"Rebecca, I'll be going away for a little while."

He felt her tense and carried on quickly.

"I'm going only to Jamaica. A friend of mine has set me up in a villa near Montego Bay. I've been driving myself too hard. I know just how far I can push myself before my work suffers— and it's started to. I don't want you to worry about a thing. The people in the office know what has to be done. I've left a number where they can reach me day or night.''

"Will you be gone long?"

"A week, maybe ten days."

Why won't you take me with you?

Andrew handed Rebecca a slip of paper.

"This is the phone number. The houseman will be there when I'm not. He'll know where to reach me in case of an emergency."

You're going to meet a woman there!

"Rebecca, are you sure you'll be all right?"

"I'll be fine," she heard herself say. "I want you to have the best time, Andrew. You deserve it."

"The seaplane is picking me up at seven o'clock in Angeline City. I'll try to come by before I leave."

As she watched Andrew walk to the stern and disappear over the side into the waiting tender, Rebecca stifled the urge to run after him, call him back. Her fingers curled tightly around the sea horse. She couldn't believe he was really leaving her.

Jewel knew something was afoot when, for the first time in weeks, Rebecca not only finished her lunch but asked for a second helping. Jewel served it without comment, waiting to see what would happen next.

That afternoon Rebecca prowled the *Windsong* like a caged panther. She tried to read but gave up on Anna Karenina's tribulations after two chapters. She had enough of her own to worry about.

Unable to settle down, Rebecca changed into her swimsuit and for the next hour she swam around the *Windsong* in hard, long strokes, straining her unused muscles to the limit. Twenty minutes after she was back on board she was pacing again.

At half past six, when Andrew didn't show up, Rebecca asked the *Windsong*'s captain to move the vessel into the bay outside Angeline City. Rebecca arrived just in time to see the red and white seaplane park next to the dock. Through binoculars Rebecca watched Andrew, carrying an overnight bag, step nimbly from the dock into the hatch. A moment later the seaplane had chugged out of the bay and was taxiing past the *Windsong*. Rebecca watched it with stony eyes.

Have a wonderful time!

Rebecca disappeared into the dining room. Three strawberry margaritas later she could cheerfully have throttled Andrew Stoughton.

That evening Jewel prepared dinner on the barbecue on the upper deck. Surrounded by planters filled with hibiscus and oleander, the pungent odor of mesquite smoke teasing her nostrils, Rebecca watched as Jewel laid out enormous tiger shrimp on the grill.

"That's a very beautiful pendant," Jewel observed.

Rebecca flipped the sea horse carelessly. "I like your gift better."

Rebecca was wearing an island wraparound, knotted at one shoulder, the material blazing with huge hand-painted flowers. It had been Jewel's birthday present to her.

"Do you now?" Jewel asked laconically, adjusting her kerchief. "Or you sayin' that because your man went away?"

Rebecca licked the strawberry pulp from her lip. The margarita was delicious. She couldn't even taste the overproof rum.

"If he was my man he wouldn't have left me here alone," Rebecca said darkly.

Jewel's hearty laughter boomed over the spit and crackle of the fire.

"Child, you just bashin' yourself, 'cause you did nothin' to stop him."

"That's not true!"

"You remember my Benjamin?"

Rebecca nodded. Jewel's husband, a sailor, had perished at sea three months after he and Jewel had married.

"I never tell you Benjamin was married when we met?"

"No!"

"Well, he was. Randy fellow helped himself to trouble with a girl when he was younger than you. So he up and did the right thing. Wife ran off two years later anyway. Sometimes the right thing makes us miserable. What Mr. Andrew done was the right thing."

"How can you say that?" Rebecca cried.

"Child," Jewel said softly, "there is someone for each of us on this earth. No matter how much we have we are not complete without that person. That is to have love, to be complete. That is also the pain and ache, being incomplete. Benjamin was my man. I knew that as surely as the sun rises. So did he. Together we were complete. I had him for a little time, but I loved and was given love so much that I will be content for the rest of my days.

"Mr. Andrew loves you, child. I've watched him, I know. But to his way of thinkin' he did the right thing, goin' away by himself. No matter how much he wanted to take you with him.''

"But why is that the right thing—if he loves me?'' Rebecca demanded.

"Because he is a good, decent man. Don't you think I see how he looked at you or know about all the visits he paid you when you were away? Max knew too, yes, he did. And he was proud you attracted so fine a man. But Mr. Andrew loved Max like a father. He was more loyal to Max than anyone else who worked for him. Now Max is gone and Mr. Andrew is trying to help you, protect you, because he feels this is the right thing.''

"But why can't he just come out and tell me he loves me? If he does.''

"Because he doesn't want to take advantage,'' Jewel said. "Mr. Andrew is an honorable man.''

Rebecca's head was spinning, and not altogether from the margaritas. Was it possible? Could Andrew have been in love with her all this time?

"I fell in love with him the first time I saw him,'' Rebecca said, looking out at the ocean. "I wanted so much for him to like me back. He was always there for me when I needed someone. But at the same time I felt he was holding back, keeping me at a distance.''

"You were your father's daughter and he worked for Max,'' Jewel reminded her.

"Is that all it was?''

"For Mr. Andrew it was enough reason.''

"Now he's afraid to come to me because Max is dead and I'm mourning him.''

Rebecca jumped up and paced the deck.

"Jewel, my father—''

"Would Max think less of you because you can love when you still cry for him? No, child. I knew Max better than that. He grabbed on to life and whatever was in it. He would love you for the tears you give him, but after a time he would say, enough. There is a life ahead of you. Get on with it.''

Rebecca struggled to accept what Jewel was saying. She had to be sure. As though Jewel had read her mind, she said, "How will you ever know if you don't try? Give yourself time with him. It's the only way. Max would have blessed you both.''

"And you?''

"I think you best not let Mr. Andrew slip away. Men can be God's greatest fools and we women have to bring them around.''

Rebecca flung her arms around Jewel's neck. Five minutes later she was talking to the seaplane charter office over the radio-telephone.

The villa known as Tamarind lay nestled in the rich green hills overlooking Montego Bay. A low-slung, rambling affair crafted of timber and stucco, it had been a source of gossip among the locals since it was built in the thirties. No one knew exactly who owned Tamarind. The land had been bought from the estate of a deceased silent-film star; the construction had been left to local architects and contractors.

Throughout the years a number of visitors had stayed at Tamarind. When asked, they assured the taxi drivers and boat captains they hired that they weren't the owners. Because the same faces seldom appeared twice, the locals had no chance to pry further. Even the venerable houseman, Mr. Smith, who had been employed at Tamarind since it was built, wasn't privy to the identity of his masters. His pay was deposited directly into his account the first of every month, like clockwork, along with a generous allowance for household expenses. After three decades of faithful service Mr. Smith knew better than anyone that the house would never surrender its secret.

For the first time in months Andrew had slept a dreamless sleep. Although only two hundred miles away from the Angelines, this retreat seemed to be on the other side of the world. After the oppressive humidity of Angeline City the Jamaican breeze was a godsend, cleansing and soothing. Andrew awoke the next morning eager to welcome the day.

After a breakfast that consisted of a pitcher of grapefruit juice, fresh-baked banana bread studded with walnuts, and pitch-black coffee, he made his way to the dock where the rented sportfisherman waited. It wasn't until he was out on the water, sitting back in the Murray fighting chair watching the tip of his rod bounce lightly, that his thoughts were drawn back to Rebecca.

Andrew knew he had done the right thing by leaving when he did. Having worked like a Trojan all fall, he had made certain the Christmas deliveries were all on schedule. He had no qualms about being absent from the office.

Such wasn't the case where Rebecca was concerned. When he had first met her, a tall, leggy thirteen-year-old, Andrew had recognized something unique in Rebecca. It took him a while to define the attraction: Rebecca was devoid of artifice. She was as elemental—and at times unpredictable—as the ocean and land that had formed her.

He would have had to be blind and deaf not to notice Rebecca's feelings for him. There had been too many times when he had caught her, unaware that he was watching, looking at him with the eyes of a woman in need. When she touched him her fingers lingered, caressing him. When she spoke to him it was with an intimacy that brought out hidden meanings in her words.

Although Andrew realized what was happening, he never allowed Rebecca to see how close he had come to responding to her. There were times when temptation overwhelmed him. Yet for all the desire she ignited in him, Andrew always fell back on his iron discipline. Especially now, when she was so vulnerable. A wrong word, a careless gesture, and he would lose her forever.

At that instant the marlin struck, the reel singing as the line played out in a blur. Andrew gripped the rod's cork handle and braced his feet on the paddles. All his attention was focused on the fish when it made its first jump. He did not notice the red and white seaplane as it curved out of the sky into Montego Bay.

· 8 ·

Although Rebecca had met Andrew briefly when he had started working for McHenry Enterprises, it wasn't until she was leaving the Angelines that he came into her life.

When it had been decided that Rebecca, then thirteen, would go to school in California, Max McHenry had promised he would fly up with her and see that she was settled at Briarcrest. Having become a virtual recluse at Skyscape, Rebecca couldn't wait to leave the Angelines. The events at the school she had been attending in Stann Creek Town had shattered her, leaving her with a profound feeling of betrayal. No matter how often Max told her that what had happened hadn't been her fault, the hurt and shame wouldn't go away. Rebecca was able to live with them only by counting down the days to the hour when Max would fulfill his promise to her.

On the morning Rebecca was to leave, it was Andrew who showed up at the airport.

"There's been a cave-in at one of the mines," he said tersely. "Your father's working with the rescue crews. He asked me to fly up with you."

"But he promised!" Rebecca cried.

"For God's sake, girl!" Andrew snapped. "Men's lives are at stake! Now, get on that plane!"

Her eyes brimming with tears, Rebecca settled herself into a seat. Her father's promise had meant everything, yet he had gone back on his word, leaving her in the hands of a virtual stranger. Rebecca had never felt as alone or frightened in her life.

As Andrew buckled in beside her, Rebecca shot him a furious look.

Why hadn't he stayed behind, she thought to herself. After all, it was his job!

Rebecca waited for Andrew to apologize, but even before they were airborne, he had his briefcase open on his lap, his full concentration on the paperwork before him. During the flight neither said a word to the other.

When they landed at San Diego, Andrew silently ushered her through customs and into the waiting limousine.

He can't wait to get rid of me!

"That's not the way to Briarcrest," Rebecca said as the driver left Route 5 three miles before the turnoff. It was a minor but nonetheless sweet victory to have put Andrew Stoughton in his place at last.

"I know," Andrew replied. "I'd like to take you to dinner before dropping you off. There's a very good seafood restaurant in La Jolla."

Rebecca's mouth fell open.

From the outside the Captain's Table resembled an old barn, the wooden frame silvered by ocean salt. Inside was the most romantic room Rebecca had ever been in. Every table had a view of the pounding surf. The ceiling was draped in fishermen's nets, and on the tables, the silver service gleamed beneath red, blue, and green lanterns. The wine Andrew ordered came on ice packed into a polished bronze diving helmet.

Andrew ordered for both of them, but Rebecca didn't remember what she ate. She was too busy listening to Andrew, the stories and anecdotes he told her about his travels. He seemed to have been all around the world and knew the most interesting people.

"I owe you an apology for the way I behaved back there," Andrew said after dessert was served. "I know you'd rather have had Max bring you up. It just wasn't possible." He hesitated. "I'm especially sorry because I know why you're coming to Briarcrest."

Rebecca dropped a spoonful of baked Alaska in her lap. Andrew endeared himself to her by pretending to look away as she surreptitiously folded the mess into her napkin.

"Won't you tell me a little bit about yourself?" he asked. "After all, I hardly know you."

That was the last thing Rebecca wanted to do, but she couldn't get away from Andrew's steady gaze. Haltingly she began to tell him about Jewel and soon found herself going back to all the wonderful things they had done together. Her suspicion that Andrew was humoring her dissolved as she realized he was genuinely interested in what she was saying.

When the evening ended and the car brought them to Briarcrest, Rebecca was startled by the kiss on the cheek Andrew gave her.

"You're a very special lady," she heard him say. "One day you'll make some man very happy."

As Rebecca watched the car pull away she knew, with a thirteen-year-old's conviction, exactly who that man would be.

As soon as Rebecca stepped onto the dock in Montego Bay she panicked. She had made a terrible mistake by coming here. Andrew didn't want to see her. He had come to Jamaica to be alone—or alone with someone else. He would be angry with her for intruding on his privacy.

Rebecca looked at the seaplane. She was tempted to get right back in it and fly home.

There is someone for each of us on this earth. No matter how much we have, we are not complete without that person. That is to have love, to be complete.

There was nothing to go home to in the Angelines anymore. Hoisting her tote bag over one shoulder, Rebecca walked to the end of the pier, where a battered green and yellow taxi waited.

"Tamarind," she told the driver.

The taxi wheezed its way through the narrow streets of Montego Bay and onto the winding road cut into the lush Jamaican hills. In spite of herself Rebecca felt a peace and calm that was almost a physical ache. Everything that had overtaken her in the Angelines might as well have happened in another world. Here the terrible images that plagued her dreams—her father's ruined face, the charred, smoking skeleton of Skyscape, Inspector Ainsley's sorrowful expression when he had told her about the murder—had no place. It was as though she had stepped through a looking glass into another time, a place where nothing and no one could ever hurt her again.

It was because of Andrew, she knew. With him she was complete. And she loved him because he had made her feel this way at the very beginning.

In June, at the end of her first semester at Briarcrest, Andrew arrived to take her home.

"Can we have lunch at the Captain's Table?" Rebecca asked as the limousine whispered away from the school.

"Not today," Andrew replied. "We've got a busy schedule."

Rebecca did her best to hide her disappointment. Every day for the last five months she had treasured that wonderful evening she and Andrew had spent together. Each detail had become a precious moment she couldn't wait to relive. Now Andrew seemed to have forgotten all about it.

Rebecca tried to make conversation but he busied himself with his dreary paperwork, answering her in monosyllables. Obviously the last thing on his mind was one evening spent with a thirteen-year-old girl, Rebecca thought, bristling with self-contempt. How could she have been so stupid as to believe he'd remember?

It wasn't until they had been airborne for an hour that Andrew at last looked up from his work.

"Do you know what that is down there?" he asked casually.

Rebecca looked through the thin veil of clouds at the magnificent bridge that spanned the horseshoe bay.

"It can't be!" she cried. "That's the Golden Gate."

"I thought I'd surprise you." Andrew grinned. "I have some business in San Francisco. You might like to do some shopping while I'm away, then we can explore the city together."

Rebecca was so overwhelmed, she threw her arms around Andrew and kissed him hard on the lips.

"Easy now." He laughed, gently loosening her grip. "You'll give me whiplash."

Rebecca didn't care. She was sure she had felt his lips respond to hers.

The next two days were paradise for Rebecca. Andrew checked them into adjoining suites at the city's exclusive Sir Francis Drake Hotel near Union Square. After the limousine dropped Andrew at his appointments, the driver escorted Rebecca on a whirlwind shopping spree. She bought a gold pen and pencil set for her father and bolts of material for Jewel. When Andrew met her for high tea at the Cirque in the Fairmont Hotel she presented him with gold cuff links set in platinum.

Dinner in Chinatown was a unique experience. In a cramped room off a third-floor walkup Rebecca discovered such exotic dishes as cold hacked chicken, drunken shrimp, and orange beef. The sharp spices made her eyes water and at first her food seemed to have a will of its own until Andrew taught her to handle chopsticks properly.

Afterward they played tourist, walking through the Cannery to Fisherman's Wharf.

Completely exhausted at the end of the night, Rebecca nonetheless couldn't sleep. She kept thinking about the man in the next suite, the man she knew would one day be her husband. Rebecca had never been more certain of anything in her life.

*   *   *

As the taxi wended its way through the Devil's Grotto, caves carved out of the hills by the sea, Rebecca reflected how after San Francisco, Andrew kept popping into her life at the oddest moments.

When she summered with Bix in Newport at the end of her second year at Briarcrest, Andrew materialized to take them both to the America's Cup sea trials. When the school swim team won the national championship that winter, a huge bouquet was delivered to Rebecca in the dressing room. The enclosed card read: "Max and I are very proud of you. Love, Andrew."

Rebecca shared the flowers with the girls on the team but kept the card for herself, squirreling it away with her other mementos of Andrew.

Andrew never forgot her birthday, always sent her a unique Christmas gift—like the jade elephant from Hong Kong, hollowed out to accept coins—and seemed to call at the exact moment when Rebecca pined for him most. Yet as the years passed, Rebecca became more and more aware of the distance he carefully maintained between them. Sometimes Rebecca thought it was because of the fifteen-year difference in their ages. At other times she was convinced that he didn't love her, couldn't possibly love her—ever—and was only being thoughtful.

I guess I'm about to find out at last which it really is.

"Yes, miss?"

The man who opened the taxi door had to be at least a hundred years old—or so it seemed to Rebecca. His crinkly hair was the color of ash and the mustache was a bristle of pure silver. His face, like scarred ebony, was wrinkled in a kindly, curious expression.

"I'm . . . I'm looking for Mr. Stoughton," Rebecca stammered.

The ancient man's cocoa eyes regarded her thoughtfully.

"You be Miss McHenry."

Rebecca's heart leapt. Perhaps Andrew was expecting her after all! She smiled and said, "How did you know?"

"Everybody know you, miss," the houseman said somberly. "I was sorry when I heard about Midas Max. He was a good man."

Rebecca was touched but still disappointed. She had imagined Andrew leaving strict instructions to be informed the minute she arrived.

"Now you come in. My name is Mr. Smith. Mr. Andrew gone fishin'. Be back two, three hours."

With quiet dignity Mr. Smith insisted on carrying Rebecca's suitcase and led the way inside.

The split-level front room of Tamarind took Rebecca's breath away. Dominated by a single sheet of glass, it opened the house to the panoramic beauty of the Caribbean. The upper area was a study, whose centerpiece was an exquisite Louis XIV desk. Below was the sitting area, composed of three large sofas of rattan frame filled with batik-covered cushions. Gaily patterned rugs were scattered across cool rust-colored tiles.

"Is Andrew—Mr. Stoughton—expecting anyone?" Rebecca asked cautiously when the houseman reappeared. "I mean, does he have guests?"

"Mr. Andrew always come here alone," Mr. Smith said, revealing dentures the color of old ivory. "Would you like me to make some food for you?"

"No," Rebecca told him. "I'll go snorkeling on the reef."

It was the only way she would make it through the next three hours!

The marlin wasn't a world-record beater but at 1100 pounds it was a Caribbean giant. Andrew had had to battle the fish for five grueling hours. Twice it had almost thrown the hook, but Andrew had played it tenaciously, letting it run long and deep. The fish became more than a possible trophy. Its fight challenged every ounce of strength and cunning Andrew had to give. When the great blue at last surrendered, his hands were raw, his chest and shoulder muscles screamed for relief. Yet he couldn't remember the last time he had felt so intensely alive.

After the sportfisherman returned to Montego Bay, the requisite pennant flying from one of the Rupp outriggers, the fish was weighed and measured and the photographs were taken. Bone-weary, Andrew made arrangements to have it mounted and sipped congratulatory beers with the captain and dockside sailors. As the Caribbean sunset fanned across the waters, he jumped into his small outboard and started out for Tamarind's secluded cove two miles due west.

At first he thought it was a mirage caused by the late afternoon sun and his own fatigue. Andrew found binoculars in the scuba locker and focused the powerful lens on the lone figure in the blue and white runabout. The lens brought him so close he felt he could reach out and touch her.

Andrew watched as Rebecca stripped off her T-shirt, revealing golden breasts, ripe and perfectly tanned, the nipples a dark pink. She stepped out of her shorts, and, with a backward twist, was gone. The sun hit Andrew squarely in the eyes and he almost believed she had never been there at all.

Twenty feet below, she was an apparition gliding through a living dream of turreted castles, stair-step promontories, and temples encrusted with jewels of every shape, size, and color. Although Rebecca was swimming in the opposite direction, she immediately sensed another presence in the water. She turned around and, behind the mask, her eyes widened when she saw Andrew. For an instant shock overtook her. But she realized there was nowhere to run—not for either of them, not anymore.

Slowly Rebecca swam toward him, unashamed of her nakedness, her hair trailing behind her like some magic tail. She beckoned to him and took his hand and led him through her kingdom.

All along the outer wall of the reef, wavy-edged plate coral overlapped in pancake stacks that almost reached the surface. Staghorn formed a forest of stony trees, with tiny swallowtails darting among the trunks. Featherdusters brushed their arms and bellies as Rebecca and Andrew swam past. On either side sea fans weaved to and fro in the gentle current, as though beckoning them on, while curious queen angels came on patrol, sometimes swimming right up to plant a bumpy kiss on the plate of their face masks.

Andrew was bewitched by the moment. He didn't understand what had possessed him to steer his boat over to Rebecca's craft, strip off his clothes, and plunge in after her. He only knew that he was seeing a woman he had never set eyes on before. There was an invisible, almost mystical bond between Rebecca and the sea. In that perfect communion she shared with him Andrew saw a reflection of the love she held out to him. In this world she had come into her own, giving herself to him as no woman had ever done, weaving a seduction he was powerless to resist.

When his feet touched the sandy bottom, Andrew reached out and wordlessly drew Rebecca to him. Their masks dropped away and suddenly they were locked together, the ocean welding their bodies together with each wave. His hands held her face tightly, his lips upon her brow, eyes, cheek, and throat.

Rebecca clutched at him when Andrew's tongue plunged into her mouth. Her hand dropped beneath the waters to find him hard. She cupped his buttocks and shifted to open her legs. He lifted her like that, her legs around his waist, and walked her to the silken sheen of the beach, lowering her gently as his mouth roamed over her nipples, then down across her flat brown belly onto the slippery saltiness between her thighs.

Rebecca lost all control. She no longer knew whether it was the foamy surf that made her shudder or Andrew, whose tongue ignited her, making her hips arch up to plunge him deeper. The cries might have come from the birds or her own throat, the weight upon her from him or the Tyrian purple sky that seemed so very low.

Her legs shot up, her head whipping from side to side as he entered her. His lips were upon her ear, whispering a love so gentle that the pain dissolved, replaced by an urgency to return that love.

As the phosphorescence blazed across the reef, Rebecca strained herself against him, moving in time, letting him lead her into dimensions she could not describe. A single image burst upon her when she cried out: Her soul was separating from her body, drifting above them, smiling as it watched them dance like the waves on the ocean.

· 9 ·

I'm dreaming. None of this ever happened. I'll open my eyes and I'll be back in the Angelines.

Rebecca rolled across the huge bed and saw Andrew sitting on the edge, watching her.

"I'm not dreaming," she said huskily.

"Good morning, my love." He leaned over and kissed her gently. "Slept well?"

"Slept beautifully. What are you doing up so early?"

"It's almost noon."

"It's early!"

"There's some breakfast for us on the terrace. Why don't you get dressed and meet me out there."

Rebecca caught an edge to his voice. "Andrew, is everything all right?"

He looked back at her with that slightly crooked grin. "Everything's fine."

As Rebecca watched him leave, her heart withered. Something was dreadfully wrong and Andrew's lying to her was only part of it. When Rebecca looked down she saw she had drawn up the sheet to cover her breasts as though she were ashamed of being naked before him.

The day was glorious, with a blue sky that stretched out forever and no sign of the thunderheads that sometimes visited Jamaica before Christmas.

The breakfast Mr. Smith had prepared and served with quiet grace was a feast. There were omelets filled with sweet mango and fiery diced Scotch bonnet peppers, grilled ham, fresh sourdough biscuits, and a salad of endives with sour cream dressing. Blue Mountain coffee was kept piping hot in a samovar with its own tiny coal brazier.

Although the overpowering smell of the food, mixed with the

71

heady scent from the garden, made Rebecca's stomach growl,
she found herself unable to eat more than a few bites. She kept
asking herself why Andrew was so silent, almost remote. Rebecca went over every detail of their night together, trying to
find out what she could possibly have done wrong. True she was
inexperienced in love, but Andrew had been so patient and
considerate. He had touched and tasted her in places that made
her open herself to him completely. Straddling him, with his
fingers squeezing her nipples, she had watched his face explode
with pleasure as she glided above him.

Teach me! Teach me and I'll do anything for you!

No, it's not that, Rebecca decided. But the only alternative
she could think of made her blood freeze. Could Andrew already
have a woman? Was it possible that he was even secretly *married*?

Rebecca had never allowed the image of another woman to
intrude upon her daydreams about Andrew. In her mind he
belonged only to her.

*That's because you've never seen him with someone else! Do
you think he's been a monk all the years you've known him? Of
course there's been someone else for him while you were running around Briarcrest in that silly uniform!*

"Andrew, please tell me what's wrong!" Rebecca blurted out.

Andrew's green eyes brimmed with a sorrow that made Rebecca wince.

"I'm sorry," he said. "Please, walk with me."

He led her toward the beach and, taking her hand, guided her
into the surf until the warm water sloshed around their ankles.
His fingers intertwined with hers, and when he spoke he looked
straight ahead at some invisible point.

"I was born working class although my mother would roll
over in her grave if she heard me admit that," Andrew said.
"Dad was a clerk for Lloyds insurance, so in her eyes that made
us something better than the tradesmen and ordinary workers.

"During the war, like a lot of Londoners, my mother and I
stayed in the country. I was glad to be out of London, not so
happy about going to a huge old school where all the boys wore
uniforms and lived in terror of the prefects. When the emergency
was over, my mother figured out some way to have me stay
on."

"Didn't you like it there at all?" Rebecca asked, thinking of
Briarcrest.

"Not particularly. But if I hadn't attended I probably would
never have gotten the grant to Cambridge. Unfortunately my

father died during my second year. Since my mother couldn't work I had to pick up the slack. Ironically, during the post-war depression, the only place that would have me was Lloyds.''

''I'm sorry,'' Rebecca murmured.

''I didn't mind going to work but I damn well didn't like Lloyds. I never figured how my father put up with such a company for the better part of forty years. I lasted only two before moving on.''

Andrew stooped down to work a sand dollar out of the beach. He washed it off in the surf and gave it to Rebecca.

''It's considered a lucky charm in these parts, I'm told.''

Rebecca accepted his gift silently. Whatever Andrew was leading up to was costing him tremendous effort. Rebecca wondered if at the end she would feel the pain too.

''I then worked for the Severn Group, an international holding company that controlled a lot of mines throughout South America, Africa, and Australia. I became something of a trouble-shooter for them, checking out potential investments, examining ongoing operations, and making sure that graft was kept at a tolerable level.

''I was particularly good at weeding out thieves,'' Andrew mused. ''Anyway, my mother died while I was at Severn. Then I met your father and everything changed for me.''

They had reached the end of the property and climbed onto the wharf that ran thirty yards out into the cove. From the shack where the diving compressor, spare engine parts, and tools were kept, Andrew brought out a rough blanket for them to sit on.

Andrew lit a cigar and stared out over the almost motionless waters.

''I'm not sure what it was Max saw in me,'' he said softly. ''I know that at the beginning I was thrilled that out of all the people he could have chosen to help him run McHenry Enterprises, he offered me the job. Later I came to understand that he respected the work I had done—and more important, believed I could do better.

''Max was a very rare man. He backed his judgment by action and commitment. He gave me as much rein as I could handle, and when he thought I was getting in over my head he was there—with forty years of mining experience—to help.''

Andrew finally turned to Rebecca.

''Your father helped me become what I am today. But he did more. He offered me the chance to be a part of a family, to be

present cigar jammed into the corner of his mouth, an oversight Mr. Smith corrected as the minister arrived.

Rebecca was surprised when Andrew had told her about the minister.

"I'm old-fashioned, darling." He laughed. "I guess even an old agnostic like myself realizes that there are some things which must be blessed. You and this ceremony are two of them."

Rebecca silently blessed him.

The reverend, an anemic-looking young man with wire-rim glasses and a Pinocchio nose, belonged to the Angelinian Reformed Church and ministered to a small flock of worshipers in Jamaica.

Just like Andrew, Rebecca thought as she listened to the minister's nasal voice, to provide a bit of the Angelines even here.

Although it had been his idea that they get married at Tamarind, Andrew had later suggested that perhaps it would be better if they returned to the Angelines for the ceremony. Gently he reminded Rebecca of Jewel, who might feel slighted at not being able to attend.

"I love Jewel with all my heart," Rebecca had told him. "And somehow I'll make it up to her. But I don't want to go back now. I know it's absurd, but I feel that we're under some kind of spell. If we leave here we'll lose everything."

"Whatever makes you happy, my love," Andrew had whispered.

The next moment Rebecca heard herself saying, "I do," and Andrew was slipping a simple gold band on her finger.

It's done! I'm really Mrs. Andrew Stoughton!

Rebecca didn't want to let go of Andrew as he followed the minister's advice and kissed the bride. She savored his lips, letting all of him pour into her. Then she whirled around and dropped the bouquet into Mr. Smith's hands.

"Good luck!"

"If you would be so kind as to follow me, madam," the centenarian said with great aplomb. "The photographer is waiting."

Rebecca gasped when she saw how the front terrace had been transformed. A striped yellow and white tent had been erected over the flagstone. Behind it was a long table filled with a dozen dishes and two chefs ready to serve. Mr. Smith led Rebecca and Andrew to the single round table set in the tent, one side open to the ocean. He poured vintage Krug champagne and stepped back.

"To us," Andrew said.

"To us, always and forever!" Rebecca added while the photographer snapped away.

As she sipped the wine, Rebecca examined the Limoges setting and Georgian silver gleaming before her.

"Andrew, where did all of this come from?"

"I haven't the faintest idea," he said gravely. "But I suspect Mr. Smith is responsible."

Before Rebecca could corral Mr. Smith, the lunch was served. The elderly houseman started off the newlyweds with marinated salmon rolled around Beluga. This was followed by boneless stuffed quail served in orange sauce and a sherbet of black currants and Cassis to clear the palate. Next came lobster farci accompanied by two sauces, fresh artichoke hearts on a bed of radicchio, and pears in dry white wine with cinnamon for dessert.

"You're going to have a roly-poly bride if you don't stop this," Rebecca groaned, luxuriating in every morsel.

"We haven't gotten to the best part," Andrew said.

Rebecca gasped as she watched the chefs roll out a formal Victorian wedding cake.

"Oh, Andrew!"

As Mr. Smith handed her a long, elegant knife, Rebecca leaned across and whispered, "You're wrong, darling! This is only the second best part!"

After a two-day honeymoon, during which Rebecca made sure Andrew didn't even think about business, the couple returned briefly to Angeline City en route to New York.

Although Andrew offered to go with Rebecca to see Jewel, she insisted on dropping him off at the McHenry Enterprises office.

"You'll be impossible until you're satisfied it's all still here," she teased him.

The road took Rebecca past the ruins of Skyscape. She had steeled herself for this moment, but as she sped by the charred wreckage she suddenly braked and threw the car in reverse. Rebecca drove through the open gates and stared. The terrible emptiness she had lived with had melted away under Andrew's love. All that was left was rage.

"Be happy for me!" she whispered to a father she could never touch again. "I'm not alone anymore. Now I can promise you I'll find whoever did this. And when I do, he'll pay!"

Jewel's modest, cozy house, which she had insisted on keeping even though she had lived at Skyscape, was only a half mile down the road. Rebecca began to dread her decision of having come alone. It suddenly dawned on her how selfish she had been by not even telling Jewel of her marriage, much less asking her to attend. She owed her more than that.

Five minutes later, when she had screwed up the courage to show Jewel her wedding band, Rebecca was crying tears of joy.

"Can you forgive me for your not being there to give me away?"

"Child, what is there to forgive?" Jewel demanded, her moon face streaked with tears. "A beautiful thing happened, as it should have happened. Oh, Rebecca, I'm so happy for you! Now, tell me everything."

That evening Rebecca and Andrew were treated to another feast, this one of Angelinian fare lovingly prepared by Jewel herself. After they were alone in the extra bedroom, Rebecca snuggled up to Andrew and lay her head on his chest, listening to his heart beat.

"If you're ever unfaithful to me, your heart will tell me," she whispered. "Jewel's words of wisdom."

"Between the two of you I'm sure you'll keep me in line."

Rebecca poked him firmly in the ribs.

"Did you send the telegrams?"

"Both of them. I'd give anything to see Lauren and Ramsey's expressions when they hear the news."

"And Bix," Rebecca said dreamily. "God, I hope she can come meet us in New York."

Andrew shushed her by sliding his hand across her breast.

As soon as the McHenry jet cleared the Atlantic seaboard, Rebecca noticed the heavy cloud layer. When the Lear began its descent she saw the snow.

"Andrew, I don't know how to tell you this, but there's a snowstorm out there and since you were so distracting I forgot to pack any kind of coat."

Andrew glanced casually out the window then at his bride, who wore the same outfit she had been married in.

"So you did," he said, and went back to his papers.

Rebecca flashed him an angry look to no avail. How dare he be so unconcerned!

As soon as they cleared customs at Idlewild, Andrew steered Rebecca toward the VIP lounge on the second level of the terminal building. He spoke briefly to the attendant, and a moment later a man in livery hurried over, a large package tucked under his arm. Rebecca watched on in icy silence until Andrew opened the package. Nestled in the tissue paper was a full-length black sable coat from Neiman-Marcus in Dallas.

"Try it on," Andrew suggested, grinning. "I sent them your measurements but you never know . . ."

The fit was perfect. By the time they reached their limousine Rebecca had described to Andrew exactly how she was going to repay his thoughtfulness.

"I'm afraid there's one stop we have to make before the hotel," he said, disengaging himself from her kisses. "I promise it won't take long but I want you to be there. And please, don't say anything about our being married."

Mystified, Rebecca agreed.

As the car inched along Fifth Avenue, New York reached out and cast its spell over Rebecca. In the window of F.A.O. Schwarz, teddy bears dressed as elves were busy hammering out toys for a life-size Santa Claus. Saks had devoted two windows to a Victorian Christmas while Scribner's had an antique sleigh chock-full of books. The lions guarding the entrance to the New York Public Library slept under a coat of virgin snow, unmindful of the vendors hawking roasted chestnuts. At the corner of Forty-second Street shoppers laden with bags and boxes paused to listen to carols played by a Salvation Army brass quartet.

Rebecca thought it all so wonderful that she promised herself a walk with Andrew down Fifth. After she had bought herself some winter boots.

"We're here," Andrew said as the car glided up to the curb.

"Who are we going to see?" Rebecca asked as he took her elbow and guided her through the skyscraper's marble lobby.

"One of our biggest shippers," Andrew said grimly.

The offices of Star Lines were on the twentieth floor. Rebecca noticed that Andrew, at least, was expected. The pretty, dark-haired receptionist obviously remembered him from previous visits, and her Christmas kiss was a little too affectionate for Rebecca's liking. Yet that twinge of jealousy also made her glow.

He's my man!

Wendell Coltraine, owner of Star Lines, was a huge, fleshy man with a nose that looked as if it had been smashed in and a marked limp, the result of a college gridiron career.

"Andy, how are you? You look great! Terrible weather out there, isn't it? Who's the lucky lady this time? Gee, you're looking swell!"

"You're looking fine yourself, Wendell." Andrew smiled. "Rebecca, may I introduce Wendell Coltraine, president of Star Lines, which handles most of McHenry Enterprises' cargo."

Rebecca allowed Wendell Coltraine to pump her hand as though he were priming a well in the middle of a fire.

"Greattameetyou, Becky. Love the coat. The wife would kill for it! Can I get you folks some Christmas cheer?"

"Actually, I just stopped by because of your letter," Andrew said, examining the intricate model of a windjammer on Coltraine's desk. "I understand you want to cancel our cargo agreement."

"Well, Andy, you know how it works," Coltraine said genially. "Times change."

"You've been doing the shipping for McHenry Enterprises for over fifteen years," Andrew replied quietly. "In fact, it's because of our business that you've been able to expand the line."

"All true, Andy," Coltraine said, nodding his great wolf's head. "But old man McHenry is gone now. I can't keep shipping for you at the rates Max and I agreed on and still turn a buck. I got a family to think about, a kid to bring into the business."

"And a mistress to keep on East Seventy-ninth."

Coltraine's eyes flashed in anger, but he recovered immediately.

"Just a little bit of poontang, Andy. Didn't know you two were acquainted."

"We're not," Andrew said shortly. "I understand your position, Wendell, and appreciate your concerns."

"I knew you would." Coltraine beamed. "You sure you and the lady won't have that drink?"

"And I'll explain your reasons to Lewis at the next board meeting."

"Lewis who?" Coltraine blinked. "Explain what?"

"Lewis Stethem, the Undersecretary of State who's on the board of McHenry Enterprises," Andrew said flatly. "He'll want to know why our shipper's leaving us, and I'll have to tell him Star has grown too fat dealing with Cuba."

Rebecca was certain Coltraine was having a seizure.

"Now, see here, Andy, you can't go round stirring up that kind of talk."

"It's true, isn't it? I mean, if it's not, then you're free to sue for slander."

Coltraine tried to stare down Andrew but couldn't.

"Who else knows?" he demanded harshly.

"No one outside this room."

"What about the broad?"

"I wouldn't concern myself if I were you."

"Andy—"

Andrew cut him off at once. "It makes no difference to me that you ship for Fidel in the middle of an American embargo. Other people wouldn't be quite so understanding. But they needn't know as long as you continue to cargo for us."

"Me and Max go back a long way," Coltraine said piously. "You have my word, Andy. My ships will be there for you."

"I can't tell you how happy I am to hear that, Wendell. And by the way, have a very merry Christmas."

When they were alone in the elevator Rebecca confronted Andrew.

"What was that all about? Why did he want to leave us?"

"Coltraine's a jackal," Andrew said coldly. "He made his money off Max and now, with Max dead, he thinks he can renege on the deal."

"But can't we ship with someone else?"

"Not at the rates we've established. Besides, for what I have in mind McHenry Enterprises needs a guaranteed commitment to carry its cargo."

"Even if we have to blackmail people?" Rebecca asked.

"It's one of the more unpleasant aspects of doing business."

There was no apology in Andrew's voice.

As she walked to the car, Rebecca considered how much she had to learn from her husband. And about him.

The welcome they received at Lauren and Ramsey Peet's duplex penthouse on Park Avenue was everything Rebecca had imagined it would be. With the lights of New York providing a startling backdrop beyond the floor-to-ceiling windows, Rebecca felt as though she were floating above the city.

While Ramsey mixed the drinks, Rebecca told Lauren every detail of the wedding. When Bix arrived, cursing the snow that had delayed her flight by two hours, she had to repeat her story all over again.

"Are you happy, Becky?" Bix asked anxiously. "I mean truly happy?"

"Yes, undeniably, superlatively content!"

"Well, I guess all my nagging finally paid off." Bix grinned wickedly. She picked up Rebecca's hand and examined the plain gold wedding band.

"Hey, Andrew!" she called out. "Pretty chintzy piece of jewelry for the love of your life."

"Bix!" Rebecca whispered, horrified. "There wasn't time!"

"Oh, pooh! He should have bought a diamond years ago—just in case."

Andrew strolled over to them, nodding his head.

"Actually, Bix, for once I think you're right."

"Andrew, she didn't mean anything—"

Andrew gently pressed a finger against her lips and brought out a tiny velvet box.

"This might be more suitable."

The room stilled when Rebecca lifted the lid. Mounted on a gold band was a rose-pink pear-shaped diamond whose dimensions were easily as large as the tip of a lipstick. The main stone was surrounded by a necklace of much smaller though no less brilliant diamonds. Rebecca thought the arrangement resembled a tiny heart.

"Go ahead," Andrew said softly. "Put it on."

The fit was perfect.

Rebecca was at a loss for words. She could only stare helplessly into the face of her husband, her heart aching with love.

"This is from Lauren and me," Ramsey said.

The Peets' gift was a large Steuben glass sculpture, its etched motif showing two magnificent birds in a winged embrace.

"Black-crowned night herons," Rebecca murmured.

"That's right," Lauren said, squeezing her hand. "When they take a mate it's for life."

After toasts had been exchanged, Rebecca drew Ramsey away from the group.

"I'd like the board to pass a motion making Andrew president of McHenry Enterprises. I want him to have complete authority, the way Max had."

Ramsey Peet rolled the ash from his cigar.

"Somehow this doesn't surprise me," he said. "And I'll stand by what I said before: Andrew has done excellent work for the company. He's eminently qualified to lead it."

Rebecca thought back to the confrontation in Wendell Coltraine's office and silently agreed.

"However," the attorney cautioned her, "I think you must retain veto power over his decisions."

"What do you mean?"

"You're the McHenry, Rebecca. Regardless of who's president, it's still your company, and ultimately your responsibility."

"But I don't know anything about it!"

"On board the *Windsong* you said you wanted to learn and Andrew agreed to teach you. I want you to promise me you'll keep your end of the bargain."

Rebecca was deeply touched by the lawyer's concern.

"I will, Ramsey. I promise."

"Then I'll have the board ratify Andrew's appointment by the first of the year."

As the two couples and Bix prepared to leave for the theater to see Diahann Carroll in *No Strings*, Ramsey Peet found a moment alone with Andrew.

"Are you planning to set up home in the Angelines?" he asked casually.

Andrew shook his head. "Eventually yes. But we'll be staying on in Jamaica for at least a few months."

"But Skyscape—"

"Didn't Rebecca tell you?" Andrew asked, surprised. "She's made up her mind. Skyscape will not be torn down or even touched. She wants it to remain exactly as it is, a charred wreck, until Max's killer is apprehended. It's her way of showing that no matter what, she will never forget."

· 10 ·

The next two months were the most peaceful Rebecca had had since Max's death. Her love for Andrew became the rock upon which she was determined to build a new life.

After Christmas dinner with Lauren, Ramsey, and Bix, the newlyweds returned to Tamarind. Andrew took advantage of the hiatus in business between Christmas and New Year's to set up a schedule that would permit him to stay in Jamaica three days of the week. When he was making arrangements with the seaplane charter to ferry him between Tamarind and Angeline City, he was appalled by the cost. The next day Rebecca bought the service, agreeing to keep the current management and pilots.

"It's a small price to pay to have you home for dinner," she told Andrew.

After a quiet New Year's celebration, highlighted by Ramsey's telegram confirming Andrew's appointment as president of McHenry Enterprises, Andrew returned to his rigorous schedule. He left Tamarind at dawn on a Monday and returned late Thursday afternoon. Over the weekend, when he wasn't on the telephone, he quizzed Rebecca on the work he had left her.

Andrew had mapped out a study course for Rebecca that covered every aspect of the company her father had founded. As she plowed through the material, Rebecca learned about the principles of mining, smelting, and refining. She could recite the total gross weight, in troy ounces, that had been produced by the world's leading gold countries—Canada, South Africa, and Russia—and how the market was regulated by supply and demand. She memorized the industries that required bullion for their operations and was challenged to come up with innovative ways McHenry Enterprises could capture different markets.

The more Rebecca immersed herself in her studies the closer she felt to her father. Knowing what she did now, it saddened her that he had never shown her his world.

Sensing her melancholy, Andrew said, "Max would be very proud of you, darling. All you needed was the chance to become involved."

And she loved him all the more for those words.

When Andrew came home, Rebecca made sure he forgot about the office. They whiled away the days on the ocean, diving, fishing, and simply enjoying each other's company. At least twice a month Jewel came and Tamarind was filled with heavenly smells from the kitchen as she and Mr. Smith traded recipes. In the evenings Andrew took Rebecca dancing in Montego Bay or Kingston and on more than one occasion, when the night was simply too beautiful to let go, they stayed over at a hotel.

Sunday afternoons had their own particular schedule. As owner of McHenry Enterprises, Rebecca retained the authority to approve all major decisions affecting the corporation. Andrew had carefully explained where he proposed to take the firm in the first quarter of 1963, and Rebecca had given him her wholehearted approval. It was time for McHenry Enterprises to expand, and she was convinced the small computer and electronics companies Andrew had targeted for buy-outs were exactly the right acquisitions.

"It will mean going outside for money," Andrew warned her. "But I've arranged financing with a London-based consortium at very good terms."

"What about the Walker Bank?" Rebecca asked, referring to the New York house her father had always dealt with.

"We're talking about a credit line of over three hundred million dollars," Andrew replied. "The Walker can't handle that figure. Besides, right now the British banks are clamoring for business. We'll never see these kinds of rates again."

Rebecca examined the draft proposals.

"Has Ramsey vetted these?"

"Here's his letter."

Ramsey, writing on the gold-embossed letterhead of Peet, Burroughs, and Calhoun, firmly endorsed Andrew's proposals.

It couldn't be better, Rebecca thought, and signed the agreements giving Andrew the power to go ahead with the acquisitions.

But she was wrong. As excited as she was about embarking on the new course Andrew had charted, Rebecca found everything eclipsed by what she learned six weeks later.

The first signs were innocent enough. During her morning swim, Rebecca tired after only a quarter hour in the water. When she came out she found the sun oppressive—even though she was shivering.

It's a bug. If I look after it now, I'll be fine when Andrew arrives.

Rebecca slept that entire afternoon. At dinner she couldn't take more than a few bites of Mr. Smith's famous ceviche. Those she managed to swallow came right back up in the middle of the night. The next morning Rebecca awoke feeling nauseated. Her entire body ached as though someone had beaten her with a rubber mallet. When Mr. Smith came in with breakfast, Rebecca pulled the sheet over her head.

"Leave me alone," she mumbled, burrowing into her pillow.

That afternoon a doctor from Montego Bay arrived. He was a short, stout man with the gentlest hands Rebecca had ever felt. Dr. Honoré de Grise assured Rebecca that in his sixty years of practice he had seen everything there was to the human body.

"But not mine," Rebecca groaned. "Can you cancel the next few days of my life?"

Dr. de Grise clucked to himself as he took Rebecca's temperature and peered into her nose, ears, and throat. The thin wooden spatula with which he depressed her tongue caused her to gag.

"How much longer do I have to live?" Rebecca asked.

"At least seventy years," de Grise pronounced. "However, to be more precise, I would have to conduct some tests in my clinic. Preferably right now."

The tone of his voice told Rebecca that de Grise wouldn't take no for an answer. For the first time she experienced a pang of fear. What if there really were something wrong with her? Rebecca reached for whatever clothing was at hand.

The physician called first thing the following morning, waking her out of a restless sleep.

"I am pleased to tell you that you will live," he announced cheerfully.

"For the first time in your sixty years of practice you're wrong!"

"Not at all. In fact, given your superb physical condition, you can have as many more children as you wish."

"Many more! Does that mean . . ."

The moment she realized she was pregnant Rebecca felt energy pour into her. She tried to come to grips with the enormity of what was happening to her. She felt as though she had boarded a train whose destination was a mystery. Certainly at the very end she would become a mother. But what would happen to her during the journey? How would her body change and, with it, her emotions? The awe and wonder and fear of her condition tugged Rebecca in a dozen different directions simultaneously. Especially where Andrew was concerned.

Rebecca wanted so badly to tell Andrew, who was in New York, but couldn't summon the nerve. She knew intuitively that he would make a fine father. But did he want a child right now, when he had so much work ahead of him? Was he ready to accept a new being into their lives at a point when they were still discovering each other?

The questions plagued Rebecca until Mr. Smith, who was strictly supervising her new diet, offered a solution.

"When is Mr. Andrew back?"

"In five days."

"Then you rest now and do everything the doctor told you. When I know for sure Mr. Andrew be back, I tell you. Then you go and tell him to his ear he is a daddy."

Rebecca marveled at his wisdom.

Having decided to hold on to her secret, the hardest thing Rebecca had to do during the next week was not to tell Andrew her news when he called. She found herself jabbering away about the most inane things in an effort to stay away from the subject and couldn't understand why Andrew became suspicious.

"Are you sure everything's all right, Rebecca?" he would repeat.

"Everything's fine, darling. Please, hurry home. I miss you terribly."

"Monday can't come soon enough. I'll call you the minute I get back to Angeline City."

No, I'll see you when you're there!

Rebecca prepared for her trip to Angeline City with a field marshal's attention to detail. She called the seaplane charter service and made the pilot promise his craft would be ready first thing in the morning. Arrangements were made for a large comfortable car to take her into Montego Bay. She telephoned Jewel, and with great effort casually told her she and Andrew would be on board the *Windsong* Monday night. Would she join them for dinner? Finally Rebecca got Dr. de Grise's solemn word that an hour's plane ride wouldn't harm the baby at all. In fact, he would probably enjoy it. Rebecca had already decided her firstborn would be a boy.

Monday morning arrived with a basket of butterflies in Rebecca's stomach. Convinced that something would go wrong, she prowled the house, working herself up into a feverish state. Mr. Smith was visibly relieved when the Angeline City airport called to say that the Carib-Air flight from Miami would arrive on schedule and yes, Mr. Stoughton was on board.

Having changed her clothes three times, finally settling on comfortable loose-fitting slacks with a wildly painted *guayabera*, Rebecca finally left the house. In spite of Mr. Smith's repeated assurances that she looked enchanting, Rebecca felt bloated.

I'm going to get so fat, Andrew will hate me!

All during the trip to Angeline City, Rebecca held on to his gold sea horse.

As soon as the plane docked, Rebecca telephoned the McHenry offices and learned Andrew was having lunch at the Perch. She left at once.

One of Rebecca's favorite restaurants, the Perch was located at the end of Angeline City's public beach, well away from the harbor. Its dining room was built on stilts over the water, and at night the floodlamps drew in thousands of tiny baitfish that boiled the water whenever a crust of bread was thrown to them. Rebecca loved the roughhouse company of the sailors and dockers who frequented the Perch late at night along with their ladies and with whom her father had often broken bread. By day the patrons were just as interesting—businessmen who swore by Ole the proprietor's blackened redfish and hot iron lobster.

Rebecca arrived at the Perch as the dining room was filling up. She slipped by the people waiting to be seated and glanced around for Andrew. She spotted his white mane immediately and was about to call to him. Her voice died in her throat, when suddenly the woman sitting across from Andrew reached out and caressed his cheek. It was Celeste Lambros.

"Miss Rebecca, you okay?"

The anxious words wheezed by Ole, the mountainous proprietor, jolted Rebecca into the present. She looked around her frantically and realized that somehow she had backed out of the dining room and was now leaning against the bar.

"I'm fine, Ole, really," she managed to say.

Suddenly Rebecca was conscious that everyone around her was staring at her. With the image of Celeste searing her mind, she began to walk the length of the bar, her steps quickening until she was running, bumping into people but oblivious to their exclamations.

Andrew will notice, she thought frantically. He'll hear the commotion and come after me.

Rebecca prayed Andrew was only a few steps behind her, ready to sweep her into his arms and explain everything. When Rebecca at last reached the street, gasping for breath, she turned around. No one had followed her.

Rebecca stumbled into a taxi that had just dropped off passengers, and told the driver to take her to the docks. The pilot, who was completing the refueling of the seaplane, was ordered to take off at once.

Sitting in the last seat at the rear of the craft, her knuckles pressed hard against her teeth, Rebecca fought back the panic that threatened to overwhelm her. She realized now she had made a mistake by running. Andrew was her husband! She had had every right in the world to walk up to him and demand to know what was going on. Undoubtedly Andrew would have had a very good explanation for being with Celeste.

The problem, Rebecca thought, *is that I can't imagine what it might be.*

But you love him and trust him! How can you believe he would hurt you when all he's shown you is love?

Rebecca desperately wanted *not* to believe that. She remembered the first time Andrew had brought her up to Briarcrest, how he had quietly apologized for shouting at her.

I know what you've been through, Rebecca, why you're coming here.

Rebecca was convinced, by his tone, his eyes, that Andrew had heard or been told of what had happened at Miss Potter's.

If he knew, what was he doing with Celeste? What could she possibly be to him?

The questions plagued Rebecca all the way to Montego Bay. She wept as much on their account as because she realized that by running, she had allowed Celeste to humiliate her once more.

· 11 ·

When she was eleven years old Rebecca had gone as far as she could in the local school at Angeline City. The question of where she should study next caused one of the few running arguments she had ever had with her father.

The Angelines boasted the finest private girls' institution in the Caribbean, just across the water in Stann Creek Town. Rebecca had visited the school once and fallen in love with it.

On the face of it there was little about Miss Potter's that Max could object to. The school had exacting standards. Its tutors were first-rate, culled from the best applicants from around the world and drawn to Stann Creek Town by generous pay and an attractive way of life.

But while the school might have abided by the letter of antisegregationist laws, it did not honor the spirit. Ninety percent of the two hundred girls enrolled were white. The elite were from the wreckers' families, including Silas Lambros's grand-daughter, Celeste. The second, and largest tier, consisted of girls from the prominent white families of other islands. On the bottom rung were the twenty black, Indian, and mulatto girls brought in from every island in the Caribbean on scholarships awarded by the school in open competition.

Such a blatantly racist structure infuriated Max, but when he tried to explain it to Rebecca she refused to knuckle under.

"I'm an Angelinian," she insisted. "I'm no different from any of the other girls."

But Max's fears ran deeper. He nursed a hatred of all things having to do with the wreckers. Over the years he had boycotted their banks, shipping lines, warehouses, and stores. He had spurned invitations to their houses and avoided their exclusive preserve, the Jockey Club, like the plague. In his own inimitable way, Max had made it clear he loathed their policies and preju-

89

dices. For all his wealth and power, he would never become one of them. Nor would his daughter.

To avoid the parochial attitude entrenched in Stann Creek Town, Max had sent Rebecca to a public school in Angeline City. There, he had proudly watched her grow up among children who were native Angelinians. But Max was already cheating. Rebecca was very bright and her schooling was being supplemented by private tutors for a few hours each day at Skyscape.

I'm an Angelinian. I'm no different from any of the other girls.

Rebecca was right, Max thought. She was Angelinian. But he had taken her across the Caribbean and to the United States, shown her places and introduced her to people who were light years away from the simple life in the Angelines. Max knew that while Rebecca would always call the Angelines home, she would soon be able to sample whatever the world offered. That was something Max rejoiced in.

But Rebecca was also different in another way. Stann Creek Town, Max feared, might well teach her that.

Max had many alternatives to Miss Potter's. He could send Rebecca away to any one of a dozen schools in the United States that would be eager to take her. There was only one problem: Max wasn't sure he could stand being separated from his beloved daughter.

Rebecca, on the other hand, couldn't deny the magic of Stann Creek Town, so different from the frontier atmosphere of Angeline City.

The houses along Bye Street were in the grand tradition. Each was at least two stories high, with a front porch and side veranda; the shutters and posts were a gleaming black and green set off by white sidings. The lawns were flawlessly cut, the gardens radiant with a hundred different flowers.

Along the wide promenade, with its carefully cultivated lawns, strolled women in gaily colored skirts and dresses, their hair done in the latest styles. In restaurants and cafés, jacketed waiters presented tea and scones on silver service while the conversation drifted on the feathery notes of a string quartet. In the evenings tall young men, their faces burnished by the sun, walked ladies across Regent Park, the fragrance from the flowers as heady as, Rebecca imagined, the whispered endearments must have been.

"But where will you live?" Max demanded, seizing any excuse not to give in to Rebecca's pleas.

"In the dorms with the rest of the girls," Rebecca answered sweetly.

Max was horrified.

"An apartment," he countered. "I'll get a nice place for you and Jewel. Nothing grand, say a dozen rooms—"

"Father, I have to live in the dorms. It's the rules!"

Max was beside himself. When he went to Jewel for support she sided with Rebecca.

Jewel told him gently, "I know what you're afraid of, Max. But you can't protect Rebecca forever. Stann Creek Town is part of the Angelines. It's hers to explore and learn about. That's something you can't change."

Max knew when he was beaten.

"It's a bloody conspiracy is what it is."

Rebecca ran up to her father and kissed him.

"Please don't be afraid, Father," she whispered. "I'm not leaving you. I'll never leave you."

When Max crushed her body against his, Rebecca knew she had won.

Miss Potter, who had arrived in Stann Creek Town in 1925 to found the school, was still headmistress over thirty years later. A diminutive, peppery Scotswoman, she gave truck to no one, regardless of social standing. Any opinion she might have had about her black students was kept strictly private. In her eyes, when a girl had bested the hurdles set by her—a written and oral entrance examination, a personal interview, and an interview for her parents—she was on equal footing with the rest of her classmates.

Unfortunately Miss Potter had never been able to instill that sense of tolerance in some of her charges. Prejudice, as she had learned over the years, came from the mother's milk.

Once their child entered the school, even the most influential parents had no say over any aspect of life or behavior within the brick walls. Many were pleased that Miss Potter strictly forbade child-parent communications during the term. Daughters known to be petulant, stubborn, or downright unmanageable reappeared at Christmas break as chastened, polite ladies. Of course there were exceptions.

Celeste Lambros, whose curly blond hair, pouting lips, and ripe figure often graced the social pages of the *Gleaner*, was three years older than Rebecca and that much further ahead in school. She was the acknowledged leader of the wreckers' daughters.

Content with their own company, they studied just enough to pass into the next grade. Their reward for such an effort was hours of gossip about the boys at St. Michael's on the other end of the island, exchanges about the latest London and New York fashions, and incessant speculation as to whether or not virginity was something to be taken seriously these days.

Without intending to, Rebecca became the rallying point for the scholarship girls. She mixed with them easily, as though they had been friends for life. Like herself, these girls excelled in sports and as a team were virtually unbeatable.

The white girls who could never hope to enter Celeste Lambros's charmed circle formed different attitudes toward Rebecca. Some tried shamelessly to cultivate the friendship of the McHenry heiress. Others, whose middle-class prejudices against Rebecca's scholarship friends had been ingrained in the cradle, coldly avoided her.

The scholarship girls studied harder than the other students, and to keep up with them Rebecca found herself excelling in history, geography, and Latin, perfecting her Spanish and moving along nicely in French and English literature. Algebra she could have lived without.

The first year at Miss Potter's passed without incident, and until Christmas the pattern of the second was identical. That year Rebecca, who had turned thirteen in November, pleaded with her father to be allowed to attend the school's Christmas ball. After much huffing and puffing—and scrutinizing the morals of the young rakes at St. Michael's, who would be the escorts—Max finally consented.

Next to the cotillion, the Christmas ball at Miss Potter's was the event of the Stann Creek Town social calendar. Because she had had little contact with boys during school terms, Rebecca was surprised and delighted by the number of invitations that flowed into Skyscape. Almost every boy at St. Michael's was ardent in his pursuit to have her on his arm.

Her friends found merit in every potential escort while Max, upon hearing the prospect's name, promptly entered into character assassination. At the end of two days of heartbreaking debate Rebecca threw up her hands.

"This is supposed to be fun!" she cried.

With that she accepted the invitation of a childhood friend, Thomas Berry, a black Angelinian and scholarship student at St. Mike's whose father was a foreman at one of the McHenry mines.

On the evening of the ball Max at last admitted to himself—if to no one else—that his daughter was growing up. One look at Rebecca in her pale orange gown set off with a white sash, her hair piled high and studded with tiny diamonds, was enough to convince him. His eyes were glazed with tears when he realized just how much like her mother she looked.

The dance was held at the Jockey Club, a marble and mahogany edifice that smelled of polished leather, aromatic tobacco, and aged port. Its ballroom was magnificent. The robin's-egg-blue walls, dark gleaming hardwood floors, and cornices carved with heroic feats from Greek mythology took Rebecca's breath away. The light from six brilliant chandeliers illuminated the great oil paintings of wreckers, governors, and monarchs long dead. At the far end of the room, on a gallery framed by an ornate lattice grill, was the orchestra.

Rebecca remembered every detail of the evening. The hours slipped by unnoticed, some in the arms of Thomas Berry, who proved to be a good dancer, others at the tables, where eight couples did their best to act adult and not wolf down the delicacies from the fabled club kitchens. Even the trips to the powder room were an adventure, a chance to gossip about tragedies and raptures on the dance floor.

"Might I have this dance?"

Rebecca turned to look at Emmett Simpson, son of the club president. Emmett, eighteen, was tall, with pure, swept-back black hair and laughing blue eyes that melted one's resolve. She hesitated not only because she was taken by his presence but also because it was common knowledge that Emmett Simpson was Celeste Lambros's beau. He was one of the few boys from whom Rebecca hadn't received an invitation.

"I don't bite, you know—contrary to what you might have heard." Emmett laughed.

Before she knew it Rebecca was in his arms, gliding along the floor. His scent teased her, and as he guided her he brushed her breasts with his chest. Rebecca heard little of what he said to her and murmured replies that made no sense. Above her, the chandeliers were spinning, blending the dancers into a mad kaleidoscopic collage.

Then the music stopped.

"Would you and your escort care to come over and sit with our crowd?" Emmett asked, his eyes riveted on Rebecca.

"I . . . I don't think so," Rebecca replied, catching a glimpse of a furious Celeste. "I'd better get back."

But Emmett would not release her. He leaned forward, his breath warm on Rebecca's ear.

"Please, I'd really like you to come."

Rebecca shook her head but didn't move away.

"Can I call you at home during the holidays?" he persisted.

"All right," Rebecca said, and broke away just as Celeste materialized at Emmett's side, a proprietary hand on his arm.

"Somewhat immature for your tastes, isn't she?" Celeste demanded, watching Rebecca's retreating back.

"Not really," Emmett said thoughtfully.

"Don't be so beastly." Celeste pouted, slipping her arm through his.

The next moment they were with their friends, laughing at some joke Emmett had made. But beneath the sparkle in Celeste's eyes, the green-eyed monster winked. Celeste wasn't about to forgive or forget this intrusion into her preserve.

By the time the new term began, the image of Emmett Simpson faded from Rebecca's mind. He had telephoned three times over the holidays but Rebecca had refused to accept the calls. She had felt wonderful in his arms. But Emmett belonged to Celeste and he didn't have to live at Miss Potter's. Rebecca reasoned that not seeing him was a small enough sacrifice if it kept the peace. As matters turned out, she was wrong.

A few days into the new term Rebecca, who was late for class, dashed across the playing field as a shortcut. The grass was sodden from the night's thunderstorm and muddy where the earth was raw. But she would rather have wet shoes than deal with Mr. Sergeant's glacial rebuke for being late for Latin class.

Running across the field, Rebecca almost reached the front steps, when she collided with Celeste Lambros, flanked by five of her friends.

"Have a good time at the ball?" Celeste demanded, blocking Rebecca's way.

"It was fine," Rebecca answered breathlessly. "Look, I'm going to be late for class."

Celeste stood her ground.

"Did you see Emmett over the holidays?" Celeste's voice was bitter.

"No, of course not!"

"But he called you, didn't he?"

Rebecca looked at Celeste's smirking friends, who had formed a ring around both girls.

"Didn't he?"

"Yes," Rebecca said quietly. "But I didn't see him."

The shove Celeste gave Rebecca wasn't too hard, and Rebecca wouldn't have lost her balance had she not been tripped from behind. She fell backward into the mounds of earth that bordered the flower beds. Before she could stand up, the other girls had her arms and legs pinned.

Although Rebecca was easily the strongest of them all, she had no chance against four. Celeste knelt down beside her and scooped up a handful of muddy earth.

"How was that nigger you were with, Rebecca?" she asked softly. "Did you let him touch you? Is it true what they say about them, that they're as big as stallions?"

"Let me go!" Rebecca screamed.

Her head whipped to one side as Celeste slapped her across the face. The next thing Rebecca felt was cold mud being scraped across her forehead.

"We know why you love niggers so much, Rebecca," Celeste crooned, rubbing the mud into Rebecca's cheeks. "Because your mother was a little Indian slut, wasn't she? Something your father found in the jungle and then *presto!* nine months later a little booger baby lands on his doorstep. You look white, Rebecca, but you're really as black as the ace of spades. Aren't you?"

Rebecca squeezed her eyes shut as the mud being slapped on her face mixed with hot tears. She didn't know how long she lay there. When the rain started again, Rebecca stumbled to her feet and slowly gathered up her books. Still in shock, her ears ringing with Celeste's evil words, she slowly pulled open the doors to the school, her footsteps leaving muddy tracks along the pristine linoleum. When she reached her classroom, Rebecca walked straight in, puzzled why one of the girls screamed as soon as she saw her.

That afternoon the *Windsong* steamed alongside the pier by the school. Max McHenry, still wearing his miner's jacket and boots, his battered Panama jammed on his head, strode into the administration building like the fifth horseman of the apocalypse. Fifteen minutes later he came back out, his arm around Rebecca, holding her close.

"It was all my fault!" Max swore under his breath. "I should never have allowed you to go to that damned school in the first place!"

"No," Rebecca whispered. "I wanted to go there. I . . . I thought I belonged. . . ."

Rebecca's voice caught and she began sobbing, not because of the way she had been humiliated but because the beautiful image she had of her mother had been desecrated. Throughout the years, everything Max had told her about Apho Hel had almost made her mother a living person. Time and again Rebecca demanded that her father retell the stories, and each time she felt proud to be a part of a royal priestess's lineage. Now she wanted just to escape, taking the broken pieces of her dream with her.

That was one wish Max granted instantly. Several weeks later Rebecca was on her way to California.

Because she wasn't expected, Rebecca had to telephone Mr. Smith to come and pick her up at the pier. By the time the elderly houseman drove up she had regained a semblance of composure.

"Did my husband call while I was away?" Rebecca asked as soon as Mr. Smith got out of the car.

Rebecca was convinced that Andrew must have called her the minute he arrived in Angeline City. But by then Rebecca was on her way. Since Mr. Smith had been sworn to secrecy about her departure, Andrew couldn't have known she would be in Angeline City. So he had gone ahead and . . .

And what?

"Mr. Andrew didn't call," the houseman said, concerned. "Miss Rebecca, are you all right? Did Mr. Andrew come back safely?"

Rebecca's head swam.

"Yes, he came back safely," she repeated numbly. "Please, take me home."

He never bothered to call! He went straight to the office and from there to the Perch, to Celeste. Or did he even stop at the office?

Rebecca felt the uncertainty eating away at her like a cancer. When nausea washed over her she realized that she wasn't the only one who was suffering.

This can't be happening! I won't let anything hurt my baby.

Rebecca vowed to call the McHenry offices as soon as she arrived at Tamarind. If Andrew wasn't there she'd demand that someone go out and find him immediately. Then she would ask him what he had been doing with Celeste Lambros.

Having made her decision, Rebecca sat back and watched the

scenery flash by below the mountain road. She clasped her hands over her belly and tried to put everything else out of her mind, concentrating on the child inside her.

It will be all right, she promised him, willing herself to believe that as well.

They were less than a mile from Tamarind when Rebecca heard the horn blasts behind the car. Twisting around, she saw a powerful black car gaining rapidly. Mr. Smith immediately edged his vehicle closer to the side of the narrow road, leaving more than enough room for the other driver to pass.

"Crazy man!" He shook his head as the black sedan came abreast. "Kill himself driving like that."

Rebecca started to say she agreed with him, but her words were lost in the grinding screech of metal hitting and bouncing off metal. She felt the car shudder and swerve violently as Mr. Smith fought to keep them on the road.

The second hit threw Rebecca heavily against the door. Dazed, she scrambled onto the seat and stared in horror at the cruel, impassive face of the anonymous driver.

"Who are you?" she screamed. "Why—"

Vainly Mr. Smith tried to accelerate out of the way, but the black car caught up easily and broadsided him. For a few seconds the two vehicles raced side by side, as though welded together. Seeing the hairpin turn materialize ahead of him, Mr. Smith jerked the wheel to try to stay on the road.

"Get down, miss!"

Rebecca heard the houseman's scream and the crackle of the splintering barrier at the same time. With its engine howling, the sedan flew off the turn, sailing into the shallow ravine below. It hit the underbrush on all four tires, throwing Rebecca hard against the roof. She saw the windshield disintegrate into a fine spiderweb as the sudden jolt flung her against the front seats.

The sedan was suspended on the incline, as though clinging to the side of the hill. Then inexorably gravity pulled it over and it rolled to the bottom, turning over three times before coming to rest, its wheels spinning crazily to the sky.

When the killer in the black sedan looked over the edge he saw a woman's limp, bloodied arm hanging out from one of the windows. He was quite satisfied with his work.

· 12 ·

The light seemed very far away, only a pinprick really, but it was so bright, Rebecca squeezed her eyes shut.

"Come now, let me have a look at you."

The voice was somehow familiar but she couldn't place it. The light was closer now and appeared to be dancing like a firefly. As Rebecca's blurred vision focused, she saw the face of Dr. Honoré de Grise swimming before her.

"The car . . ." she cried weakly.

"Shh," he soothed her, rubbing her hand. "You're in my clinic at Montego Bay. You remember it, don't you, Rebecca? That's where I examined you."

"My baby . . . The car after us . . ."

"You're safe now," Dr. de Grise whispered. "You're going to be all right. I want you to rest."

Rebecca felt the prick of the needle and her cry echoed back to her from the blackness.

"How long have I been here?"

Rebecca was sitting up in bed. The small room was washed in sunlight. On the table beside the bed was a vase bursting with black-eyed susans.

"Two days," Dr. de Grise said. "You've slept through most of them. How do you feel?"

Rebecca glanced at her bandaged arm. Her body ached as though she had been beaten, and there was a shooting pain in her left hip. Her mouth was dry from the sedatives, but her mind was clear, alert.

"As though somebody tried to kill me," she said quietly.

"You're an incredibly lucky young woman," de Grise said. "The cut on your arm is the worst of it. The bumps and bruises are the result of your having been thrown around in the back of the car. Thank God the front seats were high.

They were what kept you from being hurled through the windshield."

Rebecca remembered the fractured spiderweb glass.

"Mr. Smith . . . ?"

The physician shook his head. "He died instantly."

Rebecca covered her mouth with her hand and hunched forward, crying silently. Dr. de Grise let her grief flow. He prayed that she wouldn't ask about the baby. Not yet.

"The police are waiting to question you," de Grise said. "I told them they could see you as soon as you were up to it."

There were two of them, the constable in charge of the Montego Bay station and a detective from the Criminal Investigation Division in Kingston. Rebecca told them what had happened on the road and did her best to describe the man who had been driving the other car.

"You have been in Jamaica for some time, Mrs. Stoughton," the detective said. "Have you seen this man before? Was there anything familiar about him?"

"Nothing at all. Believe me, I would have remembered."

The detective made notes on everything Rebecca had done and everywhere she had been since arriving in the country.

"We'll start by questioning the people you came into contact with," he said. "They might be able to come up with a name for the man you described."

"How did I get here?" Rebecca asked him.

"Some farm workers saw what happened on the road. They pulled you out of the car. Unfortunately they didn't get a look at either the driver of the other vehicle or the license plate number."

The detective paused. "Do you have any idea why someone would do this to you?"

Rebecca shook her head.

"I've notified Inspector Ainsley in Stann Creek Town," the officer said. "He assured me of his complete cooperation. And he said he would talk to a friend of yours, Jewel, and tell her you are all right."

"Thank you."

Dr. de Grise came back into the room and gave the policemen a pointed look.

"One last thing, Mrs. Stoughton," the detective said. "We've been trying to contact your husband in Angeline City. There seems to be no one at the McHenry offices. I called your vessel, but he's not there either. Is there anywhere else Mr. Stoughton might be? Out of the country perhaps?"

*Andrew was in Angeline City! I saw him with Celeste. He must
have heard what happened . . . Why isn't he here?*

"Mrs. Stoughton?"

Rebecca noticed that the detective was looking at her keenly.

"My husband is in New York on business," she whispered.
"He should be returning today."

"Then I'll see to it he is contacted as soon as he arrives. In the
meantime there will be an officer outside your door at all times.
Rest assured, whoever did this won't get a second chance."

Dr. de Grise finally insisted the officers leave.

"I want you to rest now," he said, preparing a sedative.

As he slid in the needle de Grise heard Rebecca's cold, empty
voice.

"My baby's dead, isn't he?"

"There was nothing I could do," the physician said gently.
"When they brought you in you were hemorrhaging so badly, I
had to perform the abortion."

"Was my baby already dead?"

De Grise nodded.

"And it was a boy, wasn't it?"

"Yes."

Rebecca slept into the late afternoon. When the nurse appeared with her dinner she also brought a small suitcase.

"Dr. de Grise had some fresh clothes brought down from
Tamarind," she said, hanging up the skirt and blouse. Under-
wear and a pair of flat sandals went into the dresser. "They'll be
right here for you when you're ready to go home."

As she picked at her food, Rebecca's thoughts returned to the
clothes. Slowly an idea formed. When the nurse came back for
the tray, Rebecca was feigning sleep. As soon as she was gone,
Rebecca slipped out of bed and took several tentative steps. Her
hip was still badly swollen, but if she could walk the stiffness
out of it she'd be all right. Her arm was the worst. It throbbed
incessantly if she held it by her side; the pain shot right up to her
shoulder. She would need to fashion a sling.

Rebecca opened the closet door and examined the clothing. It
was fine for what she had in mind. There was only one drawback. After Rebecca checked the pockets she realized she had no
money. Her purse and everything in it must be locked away
somewhere in the clinic.

There had to be a way around that too.

*   *   *

At four o'clock the next morning the only sound in the corridors was the slapping of ivory dominoes against wood. The nurse and the policeman on duty were sitting opposite each other, fingers flashing across the pieces, intent on the next move. The nurse slapped down a blank domino blocking his next play.

"That's three games!"

"Again," the policeman replied, turning the dominoes on the blind side and mixing them up.

The nurse hesitated. Dr. de Grise had left explicit instructions that his patient be checked every two hours. Earlier the nurse had looked in on Rebecca McHenry and found her sleeping peacefully. The sedative she had given the poor girl was working just fine.

"You runnin' off without letting me get my money back?" the policeman demanded with a wolfish grin.

The nurse sank back in her chair. She was superstitious enough to believe that if she left the table now, her luck would break. And after she took this handsome man's money she wanted to raise the stakes to sexual favors.

When light began to fade the black into purple and the purple into a timid pink, Rebecca was at the pier in Montego Bay.

It had taken her over an hour to walk the mile from the clinic to the bay. Each step had been excruciating until she found herself a rough, gnarled branch and used it as a makeshift cane. Her arm was strapped into a sling she had fashioned out of a pillowcase.

Rebecca knew that the easiest way for her to get to the Angelines would be by seaplane. But as soon as the duty nurse realized she was gone, the alarm would go out. The police could always order a plane back to Montego Bay, and that Rebecca would not risk. She had to get back to the Angelines. There would be no rest for her until she found Andrew and had answers to the questions that were tormenting her.

Rebecca moved along the pier until she came to the sportfisherman which, in another lifetime it seemed, Andrew had chartered for his marlin run. Careful to maintain her balance, Rebecca stepped over the gunwale. The smell of coffee mingled with that of freshly cut bait.

"Who's there?"

The skipper, who had been Andrew's best man, emerged from belowdecks. Rebecca thought the cigar clamped in his jaws was the same one he had nursed at her wedding.

"Mrs. Stoughton! What you doing here?" He looked closely

at her. "Jesus in heaven, you supposed to be in the hospital. I heard—"

"I need you to take me to Angeline City," Rebecca said, collapsing on the white plastic-covered cushions.

She straightened out her leg, which was throbbing badly, and massaged her thigh.

"Now?"

"Right now."

"I can't be doin' that," the captain protested. "Look at you. You need to be in the hospital!"

"I need to be in Angeline City."

"But I have a charter—"

"I'll pay you whatever you want when you get me there."

The captain sat down beside her. "Oh, missus, it's not the money. You wouldn't do well on the trip. The seas are running rough."

"Captain, my husband is missing," Rebecca said. "I'm asking you—pleading with you—to take me across."

The skipper stared at her and shook his head.

"Doctor know you're gone?"

"No."

"Then we'd best be off before he does. On one condition."

"Name it."

"You go below and rest. With this sea we'll be lucky to make Angeline City in six hours."

The trip took eight and Rebecca threw up three times. By the time the sportfisherman cleared the channel into Angeline City harbor, she was running a fever and sweating profusely. The aspirin the captain fed her did nothing for the fierce pain in her arm and hip. As Rebecca drifted in and out of consciousness she cursed not having taken some painkillers from the clinic in Montego Bay.

When Rebecca felt the vessel bump against the tire-lined wharf, she staggered to her feet, making for the hatch. She found her way blocked by a giant figure.

"Rebecca, you are a damn fool!" Inspector Bones Ainsley said, shaking his head. "What did you think you were doing running off like that? Dr. de Grise has been beside himself."

"I left of my own free will," Rebecca said weakly. "There's no crime in that."

"None in stupidity either!" Ainsley retorted. "Come on, let's get you out of here."

Rebecca leaned heavily against Ainsley as he helped her off the boat.

"How did you know where to find me?"

"As soon as the police in Jamaica told me you had disappeared, I knew you were coming back here," he replied sourly. "It was only a matter of finding out how."

"I have to pay the captain," Rebecca protested as Ainsley, a firm grip on her elbow, walked her toward his car.

"Later. Right now you're going to the hospital. Where you belong!"

Rebecca dug in her heels. Summoning the last of her strength, she gripped Ainsley's shoulder and forced him to face her.

"The Jamaican police told me they hadn't been able to contact Andrew," she said as calmly and reasonably as she could. "I know he's here because I saw him at the Perch a few days ago."

Rebecca drew a deep breath. "I want to find my husband, Bones."

She did not miss the pain that flickered in the policeman's eyes.

"You know where he is, don't you, Bones? Please, please take me to him."

Bones Ainsley realized he had given too much away. Nonetheless he stubbornly shook his head.

"It won't do you no good now—" he started to say.

"Bones!"

The desperation in Rebecca's voice cut him to the quick. Bones tenderly laid his hands on Rebecca's shoulders.

"He took the *Windsong* out to Chapel Key," he said softly, as though not wanting anyone else to hear him. "It's berthed at the Lambros dock."

Abruptly Rebecca turned her face away from him, staring hard as though the very force in her eyes would stop the tears. It didn't.

"Then that's where we're going too," she whispered.

The police helicopter Bones Ainsley radioed to pick them up arrived ten minutes later. The flight to Chapel Key took less than five minutes. Ainsley had the pilot land on the pad adjacent to the governor-general's residence, where a police car was waiting for them.

"And what do we have here?" Ainsley growled, braking the car in front of the gates of the Lambros estate.

Another police vehicle was parked off to the side of the road, two constables lounging against it. Both snapped to attention as Ainsley extricated himself from behind the wheel.

Rebecca strained to hear what was being said but Ainsley deliberately kept his back to her, effectively screening the words of the other officers. Then she saw his shoulders slump and his face become an expressionless mask as he faced her. Rebecca felt herself being weighed, judged, as though Bones Ainsley were wrestling with some terrible decision.

"What is it, Bones?" Rebecca called to him, getting out of the car.

Then she heard it—soft lovely music drifting over the tranquility of the estate. For an instant she smiled because she recognized the Mendelssohn theme. Just as abruptly the smile dissolved. Rebecca uttered a sharp cry and ran through the gates.

She kept on running even though her lungs were being seared by her raging breathing. She ran oblivious to the pounding of feet and Ainsley's shouts behind her. With every step she took the music became louder, more majestic, so utterly final.

Rebecca staggered around the back of the grand house and suddenly stopped short. There, on the flawless back lawn, was a small gathering of the preeminent wrecker families dressed in their finery. The gazebo where they sat was decorated with pink roses and flowing satin bows. And the string quartet was just launching into another chorus of the Wedding March.

Horrified, Rebecca watched as the newlyweds turned to face their well-wishers. Through the rice and confetti being showered upon them, she saw Celeste Lambros, gowned in flowing white, step down from the gazebo.

At her side was the groom, Andrew Stoughton.

PART TWO

NEW YORK CITY
EUROPE
THE ANGELINES
1963

· 13 ·

The next morning, like a drunk suffering from a blackout, Rebecca couldn't remember anything about getting back to Angeline City or what had happened afterward. She knew only that the day before had not been a nightmare. The front page of the Angelines *Gleaner* carried a large photograph of Andrew Stoughton with his new bride.

"How are you feeling?"

Rebecca looked up at Ramsey Peet standing in the doorway of Jewel's kitchen. She rushed into his arms and hugged him fiercely.

"What's going on, Ramsey? What's happened? What are you doing here?"

"Shh, one thing at a time," Peet said, leading her back to the table.

In the corner Jewel stood over the stove, making herbal tea. When she brought the pot, Rebecca saw her hands trembling.

"Drink it, girl," she whispered. "It'll do you good."

Rebecca looked from her to Ramsey and pushed the cup away. *"What is going on?"*

"I flew down last night," the attorney explained haltingly. "As soon as Inspector Ainsley called . . ."

"And?"

"Rebecca, I want you to listen very carefully to me," Peet said. "I haven't had time to examine all the facts, but from the material I've seen, Rebecca, Andrew filed to have your marriage annulled two days before he left for New York—"

"That's impossible!"

"Rebecca, listen! You were married by a minister of the Angelinian Reformed Church. According to its laws, a marriage can be declared invalid if one party discovers the other to be of mixed ancestry . . . nonwhite. From the papers he's filed Andrew claims that you never told him your mother was Mayan. He presented your birth certificate as evidence to the church elders and was granted an annulment. His subsequent marriage to Celeste Lambros was perfectly legal—''

"That's not true!" Rebecca cried, jumping to her feet. "Andrew knew who my mother was. And he's still my husband! I was carrying his child! I was the only one he loved. . . . He told me. . . .''

Jewel caught Rebecca before her legs gave out from under her. She clasped Rebecca's head to her bosom, rocking her, stroking her hair.

Both Jewel and Ramsey had been shocked when Bones Ainsley, after talking with Dr. de Grise, had told them about Rebecca's pregnancy and subsequent miscarriage. In their eyes it made Andrew Stoughton's actions even more despicable.

"I'll send for a doctor," Ramsey offered.

"No need," Jewel told him, her voice breaking. "I can care for her. The worst is over with."

The attorney shook his head. "I wish to God it were."

An hour later the reporters who had managed to find out where Rebecca McHenry was began calling. At first Jewel was polite, telling them Rebecca wasn't speaking to anyone. When the reporters kept calling back, she took the receiver off the hook.

Undaunted, an enterprising few decided to come out in person. Jewel greeted them with an ancient Purdey shotgun which, as she demonstrated, was in perfect working order.

That evening Inspector Ainsley made it known that anyone caught near Jewel's house would be arrested for trespassing. He put teeth into his order by stationing a car at the top of the dead-end road that ran from the beachfront property to the blacktop highway leading to Angeline City.

What Ainsley didn't make public was the fact that he would be spending his nights on a cot in the screened lanai of Jewel's home. Someone had tried to murder Rebecca McHenry in Jamaica. Whoever it was had failed and might just try again. Ainsley fervently hoped that would be the case. Because if he caught the driver of that car, he would almost certainly have the man who had murdered Max McHenry.

To us.
To us always and forever.
That was my wedding toast, Rebecca thought.

Time ceased to have any meaning for Rebecca. She drifted between semiconsciousness and deep sleep during which those two sentences danced like phantoms in her head.

Where is Andrew? Why isn't he here for me? That's right. . . . Andrew is my husband but he's married to Celeste. . . .

And she would laugh hysterically until she was screaming and Jewel would rush into the bedroom to hold her. . . .

Once, Rebecca awoke, got out of bed, and calmly walked into the front room. She picked up the telephone and dialed a number. When the operator told her the line had been disconnected, Rebecca hung up and dialed again. And again. And again.

How very odd. Andrew didn't say anything about disconnecting the line to the house where he used to live. He must be at the office.

There was no answer at the McHenry Enterprises office in Angeline City, either. When Jewel at last appeared, driven home from the market by one of the police officers who had been watching Rebecca, she found the receiver off the hook and Rebecca sitting by the telephone like a statue. Jewel did not leave the house again.

The fever-induced delirium lasted over a week. Sometimes Rebecca was perfectly lucid and protested when Jewel insisted on feeding her herbal medicines. There were other periods she never remembered, when sweat poured off her and Jewel had to bathe her in alcohol, or when chills seized her, making her shake uncontrollably. The only mercy was found in sleep.

On the ninth day the fever broke. That morning Rebecca convinced Jewel to take her for a walk along the beach. The sun and salt air were the sweetest tonic she could have asked for. When they returned home, Rebecca asked to see the previous week's newspapers.

"I threw them out," Jewel told her without a hint of apology.

"Then I will go into the *Gleaner*'s office in Angeline City and get the back issues."

Jewel sighed at the determination in Rebecca's voice. The girl would do just that, and Jewel didn't want her anywhere near Angeline City. She went into her bedroom and fetched the newspapers.

The photograph of Andrew with Celeste hadn't changed or disappeared. And it still had the power to cleave Rebecca's heart. But the next day's headline stunned her.

"What is this?" she demanded.

Rebecca flipped through the front pages of the papers, skimming the headlines. Each was a variation of the first one she had read: MCHENRY ENTERPRISES BOUGHT BY TYNE & WEAR.

Suddenly Rebecca remembered that Ramsey Peet was here. He had flown down because Bones Ainsley had called him. Or had he come for a different reason?

Forcing down her panic, Rebecca said to Jewel, "Please find Ramsey. Tell him I have to talk to him at once!"

In his quarter century of law practice Ramsey Peet had never witnessed a more cunning or ruthless act of piracy than the one Andrew Stoughton had committed against Rebecca and McHenry Enterprises.

Peet was staggered as much by the brilliant execution as he was by the magnitude of the crime. The giant fraud Stoughton had perpetrated reminded the lawyer of Winston Churchill's description of Russia: a riddle wrapped in a mystery inside an enigma. Even now, after his own protean efforts in the Angelines, those of three juniors and a half dozen financial investigators working out of New York, Peet knew he had pieced together only a general picture of the theft.

The worst of it is that Stoughton will probably get away with it.

The realization shamed Ramsey Peet. In large measure he had been the architect of this horror. Whenever Peet recalled his glowing endorsements of Andrew Stoughton, he saw just how deeply he had betrayed Rebecca.

Ramsey looked carefully at the woman seated opposite him. Rebecca appeared thinner, her complexion sallow from her bout with fever. Although her eyes were clear, there was a stillness about her that troubled the lawyer.

"This is only a preliminary report," Peet said, watching the light in the screened lanai cast a glow on Rebecca's features. "I don't have all the facts yet—"

"Ramsey, please," Rebecca interrupted gently. "No equivocation. Just tell me the truth."

I suppose that's all that's left, Ramsey thought sadly.

"As far as I can tell, Andrew must have been planning this maneuver for years," he said. "The key to it was the small computer and electronics companies he had targeted for buy-outs.

"As managing director Andrew had the power to enter into any negotiations on behalf of McHenry Enterprises. He was very methodical. First, he lined up a number of companies for takeover. Second, he came up with a dollar figure needed to buy them out. Third, he went outside for financing.

"The last was necessary because the total amount needed was three hundred million dollars. All McHenry assets came to only two hundred and fifty million."

Ramsey Peet took a deep breath.

"Andrew pledged these assets with the Foster-Swann Bank of London in return for the necessary working capital. What no one knew then was that Foster-Swann was—and is—controlled by Tyne & Wear."

Rebecca blanched.

"Go on," she said softly.

"Andrew did exactly what he said he would. He bought those small companies on behalf of McHenry Enterprises. But he paid enormous sums for operations that had no assets.

"Those companies were little more than shells. On paper they had all sorts of potential; in reality very few would have panned out. There were never any firm defense contracts, imminent technological breakthroughs, or promising development programs."

"But I saw the financial reports and the development statements," Rebecca protested. "Those companies were sound."

"Only according to Andrew's interpretation, which was all we had."

Rebecca closed her eyes.

"What is their net worth?"

"All told, maybe five million."

"Andrew bought five million dollars' worth of assets for three hundred million?"

"The acquisitions were all legal," Peet told her. "The contracts are binding."

"But isn't that fraud?"

"It's bad business judgment," Peet said, the words stinging him. "You can't put a man in jail for that."

"What happened next?"

"After the companies were sold to McHenry Enterprises, Foster-Swann immediately called in its three-hundred-million-dollar loan. Of course the assets of the newly acquired firms didn't come anywhere near that amount, as Foster-Swann knew they wouldn't. So Andrew had McHenry Enterprises default, as he must always have planned for it to do. Within hours Foster-Swann had a writ to seize all McHenry assets in order to recover their loan."

"That's when they closed the McHenry offices . . ."

"And had the legal right to do so. Through Foster-Swann, Silas Lambros and Tyne & Wear control everything that once belonged to you—the mines, the land, the *Windsong* . . ."

"How could Andrew—"

The words died in Rebecca's throat when she realized she had given Andrew the power to do anything he wanted. She had offered it to him on board the *Windsong* the day she had buried her father, then again in New York when she had asked Ramsey to have the board ratify Andrew's powers. She had begged Andrew to take the keys to the kingdom and he had obliged her.

"Ramsey, how could Andrew have been plotting to destroy McHenry Enterprises when all these years he's been so loyal to Max? What motive could he have?"

"I have investigators going through Andrew's employment records right now," Peet replied. "So far there's nothing to suggest a connection to Lambros or the wreckers. Don't forget, Rebecca, Max himself would have thoroughly checked Andrew's background before bringing him into the company. If he had even suspected Andrew of divided loyalties, Max would have thrown him out immediately. Naturally my investigators will keep digging. . . ."

Rebecca recalled what Andrew had told her about himself that morning on the beach in Montego Bay, before he asked her to marry him. His story had been so simple. So poignant. Such a lie?

"I won't let Andrew or Lambros or anyone else steal what is mine," Rebecca said.

This was the moment Ramsey Peet had been dreading.

"That's going to be very difficult to prevent. It's taken me days of legal maneuvering to obtain access to only a fraction of the records we need. The power Silas Lambros has over the Angelinian government and judiciary is extraordinary. The courts are forcing us to file a separate motion for every scrap of paper we want. They can drag their feet on each request. In the meantime McHenry Enterprises can be plundered—"

"What do you mean?"

"Right now Tyne & Wear can do anything it wants with your company—sell off part of it, drain the assets, or use it as collateral. What I'm telling you, Rebecca, is that there might be nothing left for us to get back."

"Even though Andrew deliberately created this situation?" Rebecca demanded.

"We can't prove that," the attorney answered. "We have no

tangible evidence linking Andrew to Tyne & Wear prior to his having approached their bank, Foster-Swann. We can't prove conspiracy, at least not yet, on the part of Silas Lambros. Our only hope is to somehow find a connection between those small companies and Tyne & Wear.''

The attorney paused.

"Given the thought and planning that went into this scam, it's possible that years ago Tyne & Wear set up these companies. It funded them just enough to make them *appear* viable concerns, like an elaborate Trojan horse, designed for one purpose only: to make us believe we were seeing something that didn't exist.''

Rebecca held up her hand.

"In Jamaica Andrew showed me a letter, written on your office stationery, with your signature. In it you stated that you had vetted all the companies Andrew proposed to buy.''

"I never wrote such a letter!'' Peet said, his eyes blazing. "Andrew never sent me any detailed analyses of those companies. Do you still have that letter?''

"Andrew showed it to me then put it away. I never saw it again.''

Rebecca watched the color drain from Ramsey Peet's face.

"I swear to you I never wrote that letter,'' he said. ''That's one thing I don't have to forgive myself for.''

He paused, staring at her with haunted eyes. "I worked with Max for twenty years. He trusted me implicitly and I betrayed that trust. When you needed me most I wasn't there.

"After you and Andrew were married I had to go to Europe and the Orient on business. Things became complicated. The deals took longer to bring together than I had anticipated. The workload was staggering. . . . Rebecca, I neglected you. Whenever I called the office I was told you were fine. There wasn't any reason to suspect something was wrong.''

Rebecca came to him and gripped his hands.

"Was Andrew aware that you would be away?''

"I mentioned it to him in passing,'' Peet admitted, then added bitterly, ''Given the fact that everyone around the office knew Andrew, it would have been very easy for him to get hold of my itinerary, find out where I was and how long I expected to be gone.''

"Just as easy as it would have been for him to take a few sheets of your office stationery, forge your signature, and convince me that you were being kept up-to-date,'' Rebecca said.

"If we had that letter, we could prove fraud, forgery, and a half dozen other charges," Peet said. "But it was meant to be used once—on you. By now it's cold ashes. If we ask for it, Andrew will deny it ever existed. His word against yours."

Rebecca traced a finger along the thin welt on her left arm. Her body had all but healed. Now it was only her heart that was breaking.

"Ramsey, you've got to find Andrew for me," she said. "I have to talk to him face-to-face. He's the managing director of McHenry Enterprises—"

Rebecca stopped when she saw the attorney shake his head.

"My office received Andrew's resignation a few hours ago. It was dated, with the hour and the date notarized, precisely the same time as the Foster-Swann Bank called in the loan."

"He . . . he walked out? Just like that?"

"Andrew put as much distance between himself and McHenry Enterprises as he could," Peet said. "He was counting on being long gone by the time you heard anything, which is why he arranged for his resignation to be delivered only now. What spoiled his plan was the fact that you saw him with Celeste Lambros."

"And you don't know where he is, do you?" Rebecca said dully.

"No. Nor do we have any recourse against him. We can't ask Ainsley to arrest Andrew, because he hasn't committed any crime. He's been unscrupulous, unethical, and a bandit. Ironically that doesn't make him a criminal."

Rebecca pushed the stack of newspapers across the table to Peet.

"I'm not the only one Andrew's trying to destroy. Tyne & Wear is closing some of the mines, Ramsey. They're throwing thousands of men out of work. I can't let them trample over the Angelines like this."

"Rebecca—"

"First thing tomorrow I want you to arrange a meeting with the chief minister," Rebecca continued. "We'll fight this thing any way we have to!"

Rebecca did not read the resignation in Peet's eyes.

Just as well, he thought. There will be time tomorrow to tell her the rest.

At eight o'clock that evening the governor-general of the Angelines, Sir Geoffrey Smythe, summoned Inspector Ainsley to his office in Government House.

Scion to one of England's oldest families, and now in his early seventies, Sir Geoffrey had once divided his time between the ancestral home in Suffolk and his seat in the House of Lords. When his rabid speeches against socialism and the decline of the Empire became too much of an embarrassment even to his fellow peers, it was recommended to King George VI that Sir Geoffrey be appointed to the vacant post of governor-general of the Angelines. Not only would the Lords be spared Sir Geoffrey's diatribes, but the post carried with it a generous stipend, something which Sir Geoffrey, like so many of his class, badly needed to make noble ends meet. The man who had made the suggestion had been Silas Lambros.

For the last twenty-two years Sir Geoffrey had made certain that the will of Silas Lambros and the Crown were one and the same and that their will was done. He lived among the wreckers and looked upon the rest of the country with benign unconcern. This indifference toward a people he ostensibly was responsible for had earned the governor-general Ainsley's contempt.

"This deportation order must be executed at once," Sir Geoffrey said, pointing to a thick envelope on the blotter atop his Chippendale desk.

Ainsley tore open the envelope, wondering who had managed to offend Silas Lambros. It wouldn't be the first time the governor-general had decreed a Lambros competitor an undesirable.

"The order concerns Rebecca McHenry," Sir Geoffrey said. "You're to deliver it to her attorney, Ramsey Peet. And I want you to be at the airport in the morning to make sure she gets on the first plane out."

Ainsley stared at him in disbelief.

"You can't be serious! Miss McHenry is a citizen—"

"Was a citizen," the governor-general corrected him, relishing the words.

"What do you mean?" the policeman demanded. "What have you scheming bastards done to her now?"

"Don't say something you'll regret, Inspector," Sir Geoffrey warned. "Rebecca McHenry holds dual citizenship, American and Angelinian."

"What of it?"

"This is permissible until the age of nineteen," the governor-general said silkily. "At that time the individual with dual status must renounce one in favor of the other. You might recall that Miss McHenry turned nineteen last November. The ninety-day grace period for her to apply for full citizenship has lapsed. Therefore she may be deported.''

"That's a technicality!" Ainsley roared.

"That's the law! One which you are obliged to uphold."

Ainsley couldn't believe what he was hearing.

"But you must show just cause!"

"So we have," Sir Geoffrey told him. "Not that it's any of your business, but Miss McHenry is, for all intents and purposes, destitute. She has no fixed residence, no source of income to support herself, no employment permit."

The governor-general smiled. "In short, she has no reason to stay here any longer."

It took all of Ainsley's self-control not to physically erase Sir Geoffrey's smug expression.

"Haven't you done enough to her?" he asked. "Doesn't Lambros have everything he wants? For God's sake, this is her home!"

"I'll expect your written report testifying to her departure one hour after the plane leaves," Sir Geoffrey said.

As he watched Ainsley's retreating back, Sir Geoffrey called out: "And, Inspector, be sure to bring me her Angelinian passport after it has been stamped by immigration. She has an American passport that will allow her to enter the United States."

"Can the son of a bitch do it?"

Ainsley turned to Jewel. "Forgive me for cussin'."

Ramsey Peet pushed the documents across Jewel's kitchen table.

"In a word, yes. The paperwork is flawless. I could fight it, of course. And, given six or seven months, win. But there's no point."

"No point?" Ainsley glowered.

"Not to Rebecca's staying here," Peet said heavily. "Ten days ago she had a husband, was pregnant by him, and had everything to live for. All that's gone. I know she can't believe that yet, much less accept it. Nonetheless it's true. You know what's happening out there, people whispering about her, laughing at her, some even holding her responsible for what's happened to McHenry Enterprises. How long do you think she can endure this?"

Jewel laid a hand on Ainsley's forearm.

"Man is right," she said softly. "People don't understand how she suffers. The Angelines is no place for her now."

"What do you plan to do?" Bones Ainsley asked.

"There's a jet on its way from Miami. We'll leave at dawn. I want to spare her as much embarrassment as possible."

Ainsley put his arm around Jewel as she wept.

"Lauren and I will look after her," the attorney promised, "try to help her come to terms with what's happened. . . ."

"What about Stoughton and Lambros?" Ainsley demanded.

Ramsey Peet hesitated. "The first thing Tyne & Wear's people did was strip all bank accounts. Then they rerouted accounts receivable into Foster-Swann. I'll fight Lambros as long as I can. I owe Max that much. But the resources . . ."

Rebecca was lying in bed, her eyes wide open in the darkness, listening to their conversation through the half-open door to her room. Each word she heard jabbed her like a tiny dagger, and she fought not to cry out. It was monstrous, she thought. What kind of people were Silas Lambros and Sir Geoffrey Smythe that they would throw her out of the land where she had been born? And why wasn't there anything anyone could do?

Rebecca rolled over on her side, her fingers digging into the pillow. The loss of her baby and Andrew's double treachery had robbed her of the last of her strength. There was nothing left with which to challenge Lambros and Smythe. At least not now.

I'll fight Lambros as long as I can . . .

We'll fight, Rebecca silently promised. She needed time to understand fully what had been done to her and then to find a way to redress the injustices heaped upon her. And not only for herself. She had to fight for everything her father had done and believed in. For the way he had lived and the way he had died.

· 14 ·

Silas Lambros stood behind the green-tinted glass of the control tower at Angeline City airport, surveying the lone jet parked on the runway. He had arrived an hour earlier and watched the plane being refueled. He had observed the crew make their customary walkaround. Every detail became indelibly etched in his mind. Silas Lambros had waited years for this moment, and he intended to savor it to the fullest.

When he saw Rebecca McHenry appear on the tarmac his triumph was complete.

"Good riddance!" Lambros muttered, loud enough for the two controllers to pretend they hadn't heard him.

As Rebecca, flanked by her attorney, Bones Ainsley, and a black woman he assumed was the McHenry housekeeper, walked slowly toward the private aircraft, Lambros thought how much more satisfied he would have been had that been Max McHenry himself leaving the country.

Of all the competitors he had ever faced, men whom he had matched wits against, lied to, cheated, and destroyed, Lambros had to admit that the toughest had been McHenry. What he would never admit was that one day McHenry might even have bested him.

Thirty years earlier, when McHenry had crawled out of the jungle, Lambros didn't even know who he was. That soon changed. McHenry had scraped together the last of his pennies to register his claims. Because he had nothing left with which to begin mining, he came to Lambros's Island Royal Bank for a loan. The bedraggled prospector never got past the front door.

But Lambros was a cautious man who never underestimated anyone. McHenry's claims and geological reports were quickly checked out. The results told Lambros that all he had to do was wait until the claims expired, as they in due course would, and he could re-register the richest lodes in the Angelines in his name.

Two days before the expiration date McHenry snatched the fortune away. Somewhere he had gotten the money to retain his claims and start a legitimate mining operation. The feud was born.

From the very beginning Silas Lambros believed their differences were as irreconcilable as they were profound. McHenry was an American who cared little for heritage and tradition and even less for allegiance to the Crown. His contempt for the manners and mores of the wreckers was made painfully clear when he refused to do business with them. He made a fortune from the earth but instead of dissipating it, poured it back into the land and became richer still.

Lambros considered that had McHenry been just another lucky panhandler, he would have eventually made a mistake that would spell his ruin. Instead, McHenry became a threat. Not only did he live among native Angelinians and share his wealth with them, he came to be loved by them. Moreover, he bought thousands upon thousands of acres of land as quickly as he could, and from anyone who would sell.

While other wreckers continued to ignore McHenry, Lambros saw him for what he was: not only an affront but, in the very near future, a challenge to the very order of life Lambros held dear. His death had become inevitable.

"Good morning, Silas."

Lambros did not turn around. "Yes, it is, isn't it?"

Andrew Stoughton slid his sunglasses into the breast pocket of his tan suit. He stood beside his father-in-law, his green eyes fixed on Rebecca embracing Jewel.

"Touching," he said dryly.

Lambros smiled faintly. There had been times he had wondered if Andrew would have the stamina and courage—and yes, faith—to carry out what had been asked of him. To live a lie for five years, be a spy in the heart of the enemy's camp, was no small task. But Andrew had succeeded beyond his wildest expectations. It was uncanny, Lambros thought, how he had played the seduction of Rebecca McHenry, not over weeks or months, but years, binding her to him with threads she never suspected were being woven. And then to have eloped! A masterstroke worthy of a wrecker!

"Did you enjoy your honeymoon in Nassau?" Lambros inquired, watching Rebecca McHenry board the aircraft.

"It was splendid. Celeste sends you her love."

Andrew was also watching Rebecca. At that moment it seemed

she was staring right at him as though she knew he was in the tower. That was absurd. The dawn sun had glazed the tinted windows with an opaque sheen.

Andrew felt no remorse or pity for Rebecca. He had been Silas Lambros's chosen instrument to destroy McHenry. How he was to accomplish this had been his business. From the minute he had noticed Rebecca's infatuation with him he knew that he, in turn, had found his own instrument.

Thinking back, Andrew marveled at the beautiful symmetry of his deception. Every move he had made, from that first dinner at La Jolla to risking his life to carry Max's body out of the burning house had served to bind Rebecca to him. Step by step he had coaxed her toward him. And she had come, bringing with her the McHenry fortune.

There had been only one moment of doubt, in Jamaica, after they had married. Andrew realized that as Rebecca's husband he had enormous power. If he went to Rebecca and confessed that during his years with Max he had been secretly working for Tyne & Wear, maybe, just maybe, she would forgive him. If she did, then her vast wealth and influence, coupled with his own position in McHenry Enterprises, would shield him from Lambros's wrath and retaliation.

If, if, if . . .

Having thought it through, Andrew had decided there were too many unknowns. Rebecca could have reacted in completely the opposite way. She could have stripped him of the McHenry Enterprises presidency as easily as she had given it. His confession might have broken her trust, destroyed her love—everything he had so carefully built up. If she had turned on him, he would have had nothing left.

Andrew could not afford to trust in love. He had made the mistake of doing so years before and had almost been ruined. For him, love was a weapon, one he had learned to wield expertly.

The only mistake we're making, Andrew reflected, is letting her go.

Andrew knew how much Silas Lambros prided himself on not underestimating his adversary. That pride was blinding him now. Andrew's five years with McHenry had given him a unique understanding of the man—and an appreciation of his influence. Max was gone but he had died a martyr's death. This only added to a name that already held great power over Angelinians. It was a name Rebecca shared.

However weak she appears to us now, we have to consider her potential threat, Andrew thought. You can't allow an enemy's child to live. The ancients slaughtered children not out of cruelty but fear.

Andrew marveled at how a man of Lambros's insight and perception could be so myopic. It was a chink in the armor that one day might prove invaluable.

As the jet began to roll down the runway, Andrew Stoughton and Silas Lambros left the control tower. They walked along the perimeter fence and out the gate to where Lambros's open-air carriage waited.

The sight of the carriage, gleaming black with gilt pinstripes and red leather seats, never failed to make Andrew smile. Drawn by two handsome quarterhorses in shiny harness, it had once belonged to a second cousin of the Queen of England. Andrew thought it suited its present owner, head of the first family of the Angelines, perfectly.

The liveried servant helped Silas Lambros up, and Andrew sat beside him.

"Silas, I've gotten back the reports on those computer companies I told you I'd check on," he said over the clip-clop of hooves. "We have some excellent prospects."

Silas Lambros dropped his hand on Andrew's shoulder, the gesture friendly, the grip ironlike.

"Andrew, don't spoil my little moment. I told you before, I haven't the slightest interest in computers or electronics or the rest of that fairy tale you wove for McHenry."

"What I spun for McHenry might have been a fairy tale," Andrew replied, stung at being patronized. "But what I learned while doing that tells me we can't ignore this new high technology. The future—"

"Will be what I say it will be," Lambros told him, his eyes glittering. "You have brought me what I wanted: McHenry's land and the mines The only thing I have to know is how many are still producing and for how long. After the gold is exhausted we'll talk about your pretty toys."

Silas Lambros regarded his son-in-law carefully.

"You have done marvelous things, Andrew. Don't overreach yourself. Never forget where you started from or the obligation you still owe me for having gotten you out of there. The fact that you are married to Celeste changes nothing between us."

Andrew curbed what he truly wanted to say.

"I'm sorry, Silas. As you say, there will be another time."

Lambros patted his arm, then asked, "Ainsley hasn't been asking you any more questions regarding that incident in Jamaica, has he?"

"He has no reason to. I was in Angeline City when the . . . accident occurred. I was in a very public place, seen by a lot of people."

"Of course," Lambros said. "I just didn't want Ainsley upsetting Celeste by coming to the house." He paused. "It was an accident, wasn't it, Andrew? In spite of what everyone is saying? There isn't any connection to you or to Tyne & Wear?"

"As far as I'm concerned, that's exactly what it was."

Andrew looked away, staring at the gaily colored storefronts that lined Bye Street but seeing neither them nor the people who turned to watch the carriage's stately procession. He was grateful the sunglasses masked the contempt in his eyes.

You hypocritical bastard! thought Andrew. Since the day I nailed your first double-dealing vice-president I've been doing your dirty work for you. You sent me to more hellholes to deal with more scum than I want to remember. Now that I've murdered for you, all you're worried about is your precious name and company!

Andrew tried to calm his raging anger. He shouldn't have been surprised by what Silas Lambros had hinted at. Deep in his heart he knew that when it came to protecting his family and interests, the old wrecker would sacrifice anyone, including his own son-in-law.

You never had the guts to bloody your own hands, Andrew thought grimly. In all the years McHenry was a threat to you, you couldn't bring yourself to eliminate him. No, you waited for someone like me, someone you could talk to over and over again about the need to destroy McHenry, never giving direct instructions but always hinting, insinuating. . . . And I was perfect for you, wasn't I? Someone who was beholden to you. Someone who, if caught, could never point an accusing finger at you because no one would take the word of a tainted, ex-Lloyds man over that of the mighty Silas Lambros!

As the ornate carriage swept through Stann Creek Town on its way to the wreckers' golden ghetto, Andrew carefully considered the balance between what had been paid and what was due.

Silas Lambros had reimbursed him handsomely, by way of a block of Tyne & Wear stock, for Max McHenry's death. Andrew reckoned he could have demanded as much again had his man not failed to kill Rebecca on that winding coastal road in

Jamaica. But it wasn't enough. Not the stock, nor the power within the company, not even Celeste. The old wrecker had refused to part, would never part with the one thing Andrew truly coveted: his freedom.

But that, too, will be mine soon.

Over the years, Andrew had ferreted out a weakness in Silas Lambros, created by a loss he had never recovered from. Slowly, carefully, Andrew had exploited it. A measure of his success lay in the fact that within Tyne & Wear he was already regarded as the undisputed heir apparent. Because Andrew had made certain there were no other contenders, all that remained was to have the old wrecker crown him.

That, too, will happen, Andrew thought. Sooner than he thinks!

Because there was something about Andrew Stoughton his master never suspected: Andrew had a higher loyalty to others than he had to Silas Lambros. Those to whom this allegiance belonged had already helped him silently, unobtrusively. At the right moment Andrew would use them to free himself once and for all.

When Jewel had awakened that morning she had discovered Rebecca gone. Frantic, she had raced outside, where she saw Rebecca standing knee-deep in the outgoing tide, silhouetted against the gray light of a new day.

"It's all right," Rebecca called to her. "I'm not going to do anything silly."

After reaching the beach, Rebecca saw Jewel's distraught expression and embraced her.

"I'm sorry I frightened you," she said. "Last night I heard everything. I know I have to go."

"Oh, child!" Jewel whispered.

"Shh," Rebecca said. "There's nothing you can do. Nothing anyone can do. Not right now. Come walk with me. There's so little time left."

Arm in arm, the two women walked along the packed wet sand in silence, their touch conveying thoughts and feelings words could never express.

Everything I've loved and held dear has been snatched away. The man I trusted and gave myself to betrayed me. My father's enemies have at last succeeded in destroying his work. There's nothing more they can take away from me. . . . That in itself must be a kind of strength.

As she watched the dawn strike color into the ocean, Rebecca felt her senses heighten. Every scent, every sound, seemed new and vital, as though she were experiencing it for the first time. She let it all flow into her, aching to take as many memories with her as possible. No matter how long her exile lasted or where she was destined to spend it, the memories would always be her link to the Angelines.

"We should be getting back," Rebecca said.

She felt something warm at the base of her throat and fingered the sea horse Andrew had given her. The sun had warmed the gold, the light glinting off the diamonds. Rebecca curled her palm around the sea horse and squeezed tightly.

"It's time," she repeated softly.

When Ramsey Peet arrived he was surprised to see Rebecca packed and waiting. Her set expression told him no explanations were needed. At the airport Rebecca handed her passport to a silent Bones Ainsley, who escorted the party to the jet. As she mounted the steps to the cabin door, Rebecca turned around and looked at the control tower. For an instant, because of a freak change in the light, she saw Andrew Stoughton standing there.

Weren't you satisfied in ruining me completely? When you held me in your arms and made love to me, was it hate, not love, that fueled your passion? Was it you, Andrew, my love, who tried to have me killed on that road in Montego Bay? Was it you who murdered my father?

But how could you have killed him when you were with me that night? How could you have hated him so much, when you risked your own life to bring him out of the flames? The same way you loved and hated me . . .

At that moment Rebecca understood why she had allowed Andrew to do what he had done to her. She had grown up, safe and inviolate, in the security of a world her father had created. Even Briarcrest, where, under Bix's tutelage, she had matured quickly, was a self-contained universe. Her experience with boys had been fleeting—a lark. No one had ever taught her what it meant to fall in love with a man, how to weigh the truth in his words and judge the honesty in his eyes. Andrew had deceived her so well because she had given him her trust, her entire being, without even thinking that she should hold back something in order to protect herself.

And she wasn't the only one on whom he had practiced his duplicity.

Before she disappeared into the plane's cabin, Rebecca said to Ainsley, "Please, whatever happens, don't forget Max."

Seventy miles to the northwest, in the foothills of the Maya Ridge, Dallas Gibson helped his Indian workers load the last of the camp's gear onto the barges that would take the cargo downriver.

The closure of the archaeological digs at Pusilha had come one week ago, with the arrival of a Tyne & Wear representative who informed Dallas of his company's takeover of McHenry Enterprises. Dallas, who had heard nothing about the cataclysmic events in Angeline City, had been stunned. He immediately radioed Tyne & Wear offices in Stann Creek Town and was told that the McHenry foundation that had been financing the digs had been dissolved. Not only was there no money to continue, but the land on which the excavations were going on now belonged to Tyne & Wear, which had no interest in archaeological explorations.

As the tents were broken down, the equipment catalogued and stowed away, Dallas surveyed the place he had given five years of his life to. Scattered across the jungle floor were monoliths and altars, some fallen over and cracked, others still erect, their surfaces carved with human figures, animals, inscriptions, and reliefs. Here a part of a staircase jutted out from the undergrowth; there a stone monument in the shape of a mythic creature or long-forgotten deity.

From the moment he had set eyes on Pusilha, Dallas had been entranced by its beauty. An entire civilization had flourished here with artists, painters, sculptors, warriors, and a ruling elite of noblemen and priests whose work a millennium had failed to erode. It was, Dallas had thought, like coming across the wreck of an ancient vessel, shorn of masts and rigging, the name effaced, the crew missing so there was no one to say who the ship had belonged to, where she had been headed, or what had caused her destruction.

For Dallas, Pusilha breathed life into a world he had only dreamed about.

Who is going to protect it when I leave, Dallas asked himself as he stood at the foot of the sacrificial *cenote*.

Realizing that Tyne & Wear was indifferent to the fate of Pusilha, now partially excavated and a tempting, vulnerable target for any thief and fortune hunter, Dallas did what he could to insure that the ruins would not be plundered. He moved all the

recently excavated relics, along with the delicate field instruments, to the museum in Angeline City. Using the last of his
own money, he hired some of the Indian workers to guard the
site, promising to return as soon as he could.

Back in Angeline City, Dallas immediately went to see Bones
Ainsley. Familiar with the archaeologist's reputation and knowing how close he had been to Max, Ainsley told him about what
had happened to Rebecca McHenry. Dallas was shocked.

"But doesn't she have any recourse? Surely Stoughton and
Tyne & Wear don't believe they can get away with it!"

"They do and they have," Ainsley said with quiet finality.

"The hell she must be going through," Dallas murmured.

"At least she has someone to look out for her," the policeman
said. "Leaving was the best thing for her right now. There was
nothing anyone here could do for her."

Dallas regarded him thoughtfully. "That's not altogether true."

Storing his equipment and jungle clothing with Jewel, Dallas
flew to Miami the next morning and then on to Washington. By
late afternoon he was luxuriating in the oversize tub in his suite
at the Hay-Adams opposite the White House while a tailor made
final alterations to his new suit. At eight o'clock in the evening a
limousine picked him up and took him to the Senate dining
room.

Sitting in a deep, red leather chair in the lounge, Dallas sipped
his manhattan, ignoring the mildly curious looks his deep tan and
weather-coarsened features drew from senators, and more speculative glances from the women on their arms.

"Senator Gibson, sir," the white-jacketed waiter announced.

Dallas rose and faced the tall, broad-shouldered man with
swept-back silver hair and hazel eyes.

"Hello, Dad. It's great to see you."

The senior senator from California shook his son's hand firmly.

"It's very good to see you, son. I understand you have a little
problem."

· 15 ·

Where am I?

Rebecca awoke with a start, her eyes darting around the room. For an instant she didn't recognize the flower-patterned wallpaper or lace curtains over the windows. This wasn't her bed or her room. And why didn't she hear Jewel moving about in the kitchen?

Feeling groggy, Rebecca stumbled over to the window and tried to open it. Claustrophobia welled inside her. She needed open space, to hear the waves breaking on the shore and see the limitless vista of the sea.

The windows wouldn't budge. They were hermetically sealed against the din of New York. Then Rebecca remembered she was in Lauren and Ramsey's apartment high above Park Avenue. And she remembered why.

Rebecca ran for the shower. She had promised herself she wouldn't cry. The hot stinging water almost made her keep her promise.

The bathroom in the guest suite was filled with everything from toothbrushes to crystal jars and flagons of delicately scented powders and expensive perfumes. The closet held three new outfits, including a spring coat. Rebecca chose a navy-blue skirt, matching it with a yellow cashmere sweater and accenting that with a wine-red Hermès silk scarf. She added a dash of Chanel as the final touch.

She looked at herself in the full-length mirror and thought she saw a stranger standing there. Only when she slipped on the golden sea horse did she remember the long flight from the Angelines, during which she had sat wrapped in silence; Lauren's long, hard embrace when she met her and Ramsey at the airport; the quiet, reassuring words spoken to her during the ride to Manhattan.

127

"Honey, I know it's hard," Lauren had said. "But I don't want you to worry about a thing. This is your home for as long as you want to stay. Things will work out. You'll see."

Yes, they will work out, Rebecca thought. *And I know exactly where to start!*

Rebecca was relieved to find that Lauren had gone out. She had her coffee in the breakfast nook overlooking the gray skyline of the city. The clouds were so low they seemed oppressive. Rebecca recalled another time, when the sky had been brilliant with stars and this home had been alive with laughter . . . and Andrew was slipping the rose-diamond ring on her finger.

It was time to go.

April had roared into the city like a lion, with cold rains that froze the remaining snow into black-pitted gray hulks and created slush puddles that made a mockery of waterproof boots. After a jolting cab ride down Broadway, Rebecca wrapped her sable coat tightly around herself and wandered through the maze of streets in the financial district until she found the Walker Bank.

Because it was a commercial bank, the Walker had neither tellers nor wickets. Under an ornate vaulted ceiling which would have been more appropriate in a cathedral was an array of cherrywood desks staffed by subdued middle-aged men. Their conversations with each other and on the telephone were carried out in murmurs, like those between a priest and penitent.

"Can I help you, miss?"

The guard who had materialized beside her was resplendent in a gray uniform with gleaming silver buttons.

"I . . . I'd like to talk to someone about the McHenry account," Rebecca said.

"I'm sorry, but we don't handle individual portfolios."

"McHenry Enterprises, in the Angelines," Rebecca added.

The guard's eyebrows rose like two caterpillars.

"I see. If you'll wait here a moment, please."

Rebecca watched the guard approach one of the wraiths behind a desk and whisper something. The banker looked up at Rebecca, blinked, and reached for the telephone. As Rebecca glanced around the floor she saw others staring in her direction.

"Will you follow me please, miss?" the guard said.

Nervously Rebecca fell in behind him, registering the curious looks that followed her.

What's wrong with them? Why are they looking at me as though I'm some sort of freak?

The treatment continued beyond the glass and mahogany panels that separated the main floor from the working area. Rebecca threaded her way past desks manned by elderly women with blue-rinsed hair who looked up from their ledgers as she passed them.

This was something out of a Dickens novel!

The guard stopped before a brilliantly polished door, knocked twice, and opened it. Rebecca was expecting to meet someone approximately two hundred years old but instead found herself looking at a young man standing behind a barrister's desk, both hands in the pockets of his exquisitely tailored navy blazer. She guessed him to be about thirty, with high, sharp cheekbones, a slim, tapered nose, and coal-black curly hair that matched his eyebrows. The eyes were startling in their color, reminding Rebecca of a hue Monet had described as cathedral blue.

"Miss McHenry?" he said, coming round the desk. "My name is Eric Walker. My father was Bartholomew Walker. He worked with Mr. McHenry for many years. May I say, it's a pleasure to meet you after all this time."

Before Rebecca knew it, Eric Walker had escorted her to a chair, offered a cup of coffee, which she declined, and returned to his seat behind the desk.

"I was very sorry to hear about your father," the banker said gravely. "Equally sorry at not having been able to attend the funeral. However, my father was very ill at the time and it was impossible for me to leave. He, too, passed away recently."

Rebecca murmured her regrets.

"I'm also aware of what's been happening with McHenry Enterprises," Eric Walker said. "I think it's an atrocious situation. I'm sure Ramsey Peet will work it out for you."

"Mr. Walker, I'm living in New York for the time being," Rebecca said quickly. "I've come to you to discuss the status of my father's accounts with the bank."

"You realize that all McHenry Enterprises accounts have been taken over by Tyne & Wear," Walker said. "In fact, they have all been closed."

"I'm very much aware of that," Rebecca answered coldly. "It's the personal accounts I'm interested in."

Rebecca was confused by his surprised then speculative expression.

"You must be referring to the special account your father opened with us when you were in California," Eric Walker said, reading from a file. "Well, it seems it's still active."

Rebecca's heart soared. Andrew and Tyne & Wear might have raided the corporate assets, but they wouldn't have been able to touch her father's private account. This money was crucial to her since it would finance her fight against the raiders.

"How much is there?" Rebecca asked eagerly.

"As of today, fifteen hundred twenty-one dollars and thirty-seven cents," the banker said, offering her the statement.

"Fifteen hundred dollars!"

The figures swam before Rebecca's eyes.

"But this was my father's personal account!"

"Miss McHenry, I'm sorry, I thought you understood that this account was a courtesy the bank extended to your father," Eric Walker said. "When you were attending Briarcrest we were authorized to deduct fifteen hundred dollars a month from the corporate portfolio, channel it through Mr. McHenry's personal account, and forward the amount to you."

Rebecca remembered. Max had insisted on the arrangement even though Rebecca had tried to convince him she couldn't possibly spend that much at Briarcrest. However, the accumulated amount had come in handy during holidays and when she summered with Bix.

"But what about the money my father would have kept for his own use?" Rebecca demanded.

"Like most very wealthy individuals, your father didn't require cash," Eric Walker explained. "Whatever he needed he could sign for. The bills were forwarded to us for settlement. There was no reason to keep large amounts liquid when they could be invested."

"And that's all there is? I mean, he didn't have anything more anywhere?"

The banker shook his head. "At least not with us."

Rebecca stared blindly at the columns of figures and finally closed the folder.

"Can I have the money?"

Eric Walker was about to tell her that this was one account which, probably because of its infinitesimal value, had been overlooked during probate. By all rights he should turn it over to Ramsey Peet for audit. Yet he was moved by the shame and embarrassment of the woman sitting before him.

"The remaining amount was to have been drawn by you in October of last year," he said. "We sent the check to Briarcrest but by then you must have been in the Angelines. Who knows what happened to it by now. Technically, I suppose I can release the full amount to you.''

The banker paused. ''Would you like to wait for the cash or shall we send out a check?''

Rebecca's cheeks burned.

''I'll take the cash if you don't mind.''

When Eric Walker left the office Rebecca slumped in her chair. If there was no money, how would she pay Ramsey for all the work that had to be done in the fight against Tyne & Wear? The legal fees—to say nothing about those from investigators, with all their related expenses—would be enormous.

How am I going to look after myself?

''Here you are, Miss McHenry.''

Rebecca's hand trembled as she took the proffered envelope and jammed it into her purse.

''If there's anything else I can do for you—'' Eric Walker started to say.

''I don't think so,'' Rebecca whispered.

As she walked through the maze of desks into the open court, the hum of commerce ceased. The only thing Rebecca heard was the staccato echo of her boot heels on marble, slow at first, then mounting quickly in a drumroll as she ran from the bank.

Rebecca walked all the way back to Park Avenue. She fought the crush of pedestrian traffic in the financial district and kept jumping back from the curb to avoid being drenched by taxis hitting the puddles at the corners. When she reached lower Fifth Avenue, even the sable coat couldn't protect her from the bitter wind streaming down from the north.

No matter how foul the weather or loud the traffic she couldn't drive that single thought from her mind.

I have no money! No wonder they all stared at me in the bank. They knew who I was—and precisely what I wasn't worth!

The pity in Eric Walker's eyes had been the worst.

As she continued her dogged walk uptown, it slowly dawned on Rebecca that she was never meant to know the exact nature of her circumstances.

The first thing Tyne & Wear's people did was strip all bank accounts. . . . I'll fight Lambros as long as I can. . . . But the resources . . .

What Ramsey had meant was that there were no resources. Everything belonging to her father had been tied up, one way or another, in the company. He took whatever he needed, when he needed it.

As for herself, Rebecca realized she had never asked where the monthly allowance sent to her at Briarcrest had come from. Money had never mattered.

Her teeth chattering, Rebecca finally hailed a cab to take her the rest of the way. When she opened her pocketbook to pay the driver she looked closely at the crisp twenty-dollar bills. They might as well be play money.

As the cab pulled away, Rebecca looked up at the Peets' penthouse duplex atop the prewar building, distinctive because of its curved-glass solarium. Now she understood what that warm, cozy guestroom, and everything that came with it, really were: charity.

Rebecca was determined to sit down with Ramsey and have him explain exactly how much money she had—or didn't have. Unfortunately the attorney had gone to Baltimore and wouldn't be back until the end of the week.

In the meantime Rebecca found her days full, thanks to Lauren. Refusing to take no for an answer, Lauren swept Rebecca off to the Metropolitan Museum, followed by lunch at the Carlyle. The next day they visited the Guggenheim. When the weather warmed they took the Circle Line cruise around Manhattan, then strolled down Fifth Avenue, shopping for spring outfits. Despite her protests, Rebecca ended up with lingerie, hose, slacks, skirts, and blouses from Bloomingdale's. Bergdorf's supplied a stunning ice-blue cocktail dress, while Ferragamo provided the pumps and slippers. Toilet accessories were added to Lauren's bill at Elizabeth Arden, following a delicious head-to-toe pampering.

Rebecca understood that Lauren was only trying to keep her busy, prevent her from dwelling on the past. Yet with every dollar that was spent on her, Rebecca's humiliation grew. On the afternoon she was to meet Ramsey it exploded.

Rebecca could not wait for him any longer. Each day that slipped by was a day wasted. She was frantic to know what he was doing for her and how she could help him. Over everything hung the shame of taking his money.

When she telephoned him Friday, Ramsey agreed to meet her as soon as he arrived in the city. He suggested she wait for him at his club, the Gotham.

Rebecca arrived at the Gotham a half hour early and was shown into the Chinoiserie, the club lounge where women were admitted. The room was decorated with artifacts brought back by members who had been to China. As the steward showed Rebecca to Ramsey's table she admired the medieval warrior's suit of armor, priceless silk rugs, and fragile Ming vases that gave the lounge a comfortable clutter. Rebecca slipped into the red-leather banquette behind a three-panel screen depicting a hunting scene and ordered a glass of red wine.

Because it was the middle of the afternoon the Chinoiserie was virtually empty. Voices tended to carry and Rebecca heard her name very clearly.

"You know, I saw the McHenry girl only yesterday, lunching with Peet's wife."

"The daughter of that bullion millionaire who was killed in the Angelines?"

"The same."

"Incredible story, that. A couple of months after the old man dies she ups and marries Andrew Stoughton, who then proceeds to sell the company out from under her, lock, stock, and barrel. Poor girl doesn't have two cents to rub together."

"What's she doing in New York?"

"Somebody had to take her in. The way I hear it, Ramsey was damned negligent in handling her affairs. I suppose he felt so guilty he had no choice but to look after her."

There was a pause, the sound of clinking ice cubes, then the same voice carried on.

"Did I tell you? I thought there was something fishy about Ramsey's sudden departure to the Angelines. I checked around and heard Tyne & Wear was about to take over a major. Got my hands on as much of their stock as I could."

"Do well on it?"

"Stock jumped thirty points the next day."

"Talk about a killing! How come you never told me—"

Rebecca listened in horror, not realizing that the conversation had stopped abruptly.

They know. . . . They're laughing at me. Everyone knows!

She snatched up her purse, ready to run, when she heard a third, vaguely familiar voice.

"I think you've said more than enough, gentlemen. And I use the term very loosely!"

Rebecca saw Eric Walker standing a few feet away, positioned so that he could see her and the two anonymous speakers at the same time.

"You owe Mr. Peet's guest an apology."

Rebecca stared coldly at the two men, ignoring their mumbled apologies. When they had beaten a hasty retreat, Eric Walker sat down beside her.

"Miss McHenry, I can't tell you how sorry I am."

"Does everyone know?" Rebecca cut him off.

"Certainly anyone in the financial world. That includes most of the club members."

"Do most of your club members brag about the money they've made from other people's misfortunes?" Rebecca demanded angrily.

"I can't condone their behavior," Eric Walker told her quietly. "But in this city fortunes are made and lost every day. I guess the callousness comes with the territory. It's a sort of protection against the day it happens to them."

"It's cruel!"

Eric Walker had nothing to say to this. It was cruel, and Rebecca McHenry was so vulnerable and lovely that he wanted only to take her in his arms and comfort her. Except that she was waiting for Ramsey Peet and his own date was staring at him from across the room, growing more irritable by the minute.

She can wait, Eric thought.

"Would you like me to stay with you until Ramsey arrives?"

Rebecca shook her head. "I'd like to be alone if you don't mind."

As he rose she added, "Thank you for having been there."

"I only wish it had been under better circumstances. Perhaps I can call you when you're settled."

Rebecca looked at Eric Walker and realized just how handsome a man he was. There was a self-assurance about him that was comforting. Rebecca froze when she realized that Andrew had had that same quality.

"I don't think that's a very good idea," she said.

"If there's anything I can assist you with, please, don't hesitate to call," Eric said as he left.

The quintessential gentleman, Rebecca thought. Another man would have said "help." Eric had chosen "assist." She appreciated the distinction—and his consideration.

Rebecca couldn't help but replay in her mind the conversation she had overheard. She had never considered the pain Ramsey was living with because of what had happened in the Angelines. When she recalled his admission of having neglected her affairs—and she had done nothing to reassure him—she was ashamed.

Other things began to fall into place as well. For the past week

Lauren had been giving her her undivided attention. Rebecca had heard Lauren on the telephone canceling other dates and appointments, excusing herself from social commitments. She had thought Lauren had only been showing her kindness. Now Rebecca understood there was another reason. Lauren was protecting her from the whispers and pointed stares of New York society, the kind of talk Rebecca had overheard today, the kind of looks she had gotten at the Walker Bank.

She's deliberately cutting herself off from her own life because of me.

When Rebecca noticed Ramsey enter, his face breaking into a warm smile as he saw her, she realized it wasn't charity he and Lauren were showing her. It was love. But the kind of love she could not accept from them. The cost was too great. Rebecca got up. She still had to talk to Ramsey—and now Lauren as well. But not in the Chinoiserie. Not with greedy, malicious ears on the other side of the screen.

On the way up Park Avenue Rebecca rehearsed exactly what she was going to say. Once she walked into the Peets' apartment she never had the chance.

"Lady, you are number one on my shitlist!"

The throaty voice, blazing green eyes, and flowing red hair made Rebecca's heart jump.

"Bix!"

The two girls raced to each other.

"If you're so overwhelmed to see me, how come you didn't call me sooner?" Bix demanded.

"Things just happened so quickly," Rebecca stammered.

"Come on, Ramsey." Lauren laughed. "Hop into the shower then take me out for dinner. These two need time to get reacquainted."

As soon as the Peets departed, Bix put on a pot of coffee, found Ramsey's private stock of cognac, and helped herself to his hand-rolled Egyptian cigarettes. With everything in its proper place she sat Rebecca down in the formal living room.

"Tell all!" Bix commanded.

Over endless cups of coffee Rebecca poured out her heart to her best friend. Bix smoked and listened, pausing only to hurl another epithet whenever Andrew's name was mentioned.

"What do you plan to do now?" she asked when Rebecca finally ran out of steam.

As shocked as she was by what had happened to Rebecca, Bix

knew the last thing Rebecca needed now was consolation. She was wounded, grievously so, but she had to get back on her feet, start moving forward. Somewhere.

"I don't know," Rebecca confessed. "I can't stay here. I've got to find a place to stay, get some sort of job. . . ."

Suddenly Rebecca grabbed Bix's arm.

"What are *you* doing in New York?"

"*I* have a job," Bix said smugly.

"Where?"

"In a bucket shop."

Rebecca shook her head. "In English, please."

"A bucket shop is a travel wholesaler specializing in super-cheap air tickets and hotel packages," Bix explained. "This place is affiliated with a dozen student travel offices on college campuses. The amount of business they send us is unbelievable."

Bix paused. "There's an opening for a bright young lady conversant in romance languages. The job pays one hundred dollars a week, and if the qualified party is interested, she can share a Village apartment with yours truly. The rent is one twenty-five a month."

Rebecca was uncertain. A hundred dollars a week sounded like so little—until she remembered that right now the sum total of her worldly goods was just over fifteen hundred.

"What have you got to lose, Becky?" Bix asked quietly. "You know you can't stay here. And I'm sure as hell not going to let you wallow in self-pity. That's exactly what Mr. Andrew Bastard Stoughton would like."

Bix saw her friend hesitate. "You can't change overnight what's happened, Becky. You have to give Ramsey time to see what he can do. You need time to decide what you can do. Give yourself a chance. Please . . ."

One of the hardest things Rebecca ever did was tell Lauren and Ramsey she was leaving. To their credit, the Peets heard her out without interruption, a courtesy that made her words feel like lead.

"Please don't think I'm being ungrateful," Rebecca said desperately, unaware that she was repeating herself for the third time. "You've already done so much that I can't repay you for— "

Ramsey Peet held up his hand.

"There is nothing to repay," he told her. "Neither Lauren nor I ever wanted you to feel that what we were doing was out of pity or charity."

The attorney paused, swirling the whiskey in his heavy crystal glass.

"I suppose I should have told you about your father's personal finances. I didn't see the point in doing so while we were still in the Angelines. I guess I was waiting for the right moment, not realizing that there is never a good time for this sort of thing." He smiled wanly. "I seem to be making my share of mistakes where you're concerned, don't I?"

"Ramsey, don't say that!"

"We were hoping that you might consider college in the fall," Lauren said wistfully. "Any one of a dozen places would have you."

"That's not the place for me," Rebecca said. "I have to start looking after myself, paying my own way."

Ramsey caught an undercurrent to Rebecca's words and looked at her keenly.

"There's something else, isn't there . . ."

"Andrew and Silas Lambros made me a victim," Rebecca said. "If I keep thinking of myself as one, then that's what I'll remain. Instead, I plan to repay the favor—somewhere, in some way, in full!"

"Do you really mean that?" Peet asked.

"I swear it!"

"Then perhaps you'll allow me to make a few suggestions," he said with a secretive smile.

· 16 ·

"Got two tickets to Madrid?"

"Madrid is gone. I can give you Tangier or Valencia."

The gangly Harvard sophomore turned to his girlfriend.

"Where the hell's Valencia?"

"On the east coast of Spain," Rebecca told him. "A TWA charter leaves Idlewild on June fourteenth. If you're doing the Med, there's a ferry from Valencia to Ibiza and another to Majorca."

"Who needs Madrid?" the girl said enthusiastically. "We'll take it!"

Rebecca slapped two tickets on the counter and began filling them in.

"I'll need your passports."

She scribbled out the flight details on IATA stock, checked the expiration date on the passports, and made a note of the numbers on their student identification cards.

"That will be ninety-nine dollars per."

The student handed over two one-hundred-dollar bills. Rebecca gave him his change, snatched one flyer from each of the five piles beneath the counter, and slipped them into a folder.

"All the information you need is in here: addresses of youth hostels and the American consulate, American Express emergency numbers, travel insurance forms, and the ferry schedule from Valencia. Have a great trip. Next!"

The girl beside Rebecca tapped her on the shoulder and pointed to the clock. It was five to twelve. Rebecca wondered where the morning had gone. She must have processed fifty tickets on her own. There were four other counselors working the counter and still the foyer was jammed with students.

"It's going to be a long day," the girl told her. "Go get some lunch. Bix is waiting for you at the Buffalo Roadhouse."

Rebecca needed no encouragement. She slung her oversize

handbag over her shoulder and slipped out the back way. The June sun felt terrific on her face.

Rebecca came out of the alley onto Bleecker Street and saw that the line in front of GoSee, made up of students from all over the northeast, stretched halfway down the block. While she waited for the light to change on the corner of Seventh Avenue, she heard herself laughing out loud. Three months earlier she would have considered that a miracle.

"What is this place?"

Two days after she had moved from the Peets' apartment, Bix took her down to where she worked. Rebecca felt as though she had walked into the Marquis de Sade's private salon in the Charandon asylum. In front of her was one large room, partitioned off by a counter near the front door and rows of shelves that divided the working space into three separate areas. The place was bedlam, with telephones ringing off the hook, people yelling at one another across old scarred desks, and papers flying.

"It used to be a bagel factory," Bix told her, squeezing through a knot of clamoring students.

"This is known as the pit," she said as they pushed their way into the central working area. "You can see where the ovens used to be. All the shelves and stuff are original. Torrey varnished everything and made them into pigeonholes."

At least Rebecca understood where the sweet smell of dough came from. Gazing around, she wondered if this was what it would be like to live inside a loaf of bread.

Bix dragged her over to a desk in the center of the melee. Its occupant had both feet stretched out on the desktop, one battered cowboy boot crossed over the other. His weathered jeans and red-plaid workshirt—sleeves rolled up to reveal deeply tanned arms—matched his quiet Texas drawl. Beneath curly chestnut locks were the blackest eyes Rebecca had ever seen.

"Come on, honey, you know your people can't use those seats. Give a poor Panhandle boy a break and assign them to me."

He jammed the receiver between his ear and shoulder and winked.

"Give *me* a break!" Bix muttered. "If she falls for that downhome bull . . ."

"I knew you could do it, babe," the man said softly. "Sure I'll come down personally and sign the paperwork. Later."

"I don't believe it!" Bix groaned. "Becky, this is Torrey Stewart, president, janitor, and resident lady-killer of GoSee International. Torrey, this is Becky."

Torrey bounded to his feet and pecked Bix on the cheek.

"Don't bother with her," he told Rebecca. "Bix gets jealous when I lay on the charm. By the way, that was Pan Am. We just picked up another three hundred seats in August."

"You have all the charm of a sidewinder," Bix retorted.

"I understand you want to work in this fine establishment." Torrey laughed, sweeping his arm across the chaos. "Know anything about the travel business?"

"No," Rebecca said, "but I speak Spanish and French—"

"Great! We'll start you off on this stuff the Spanish tourist office sent over."

He guided Rebecca toward the shelves groaning with stacks of folders and brochures.

"The material they translate isn't any good to us," Torrey said. "That's all your usual if-it's-Tuesday-this-must-be-Belgium tour crap. What we have here is the stuff they produce for their own students—cheap hotels, hostels, deals on rail passes, where to eat, which beaches are okay for skinny-dipping—that sort of thing. Naturally none of this ever gets translated except by yours truly."

"You want every page translated?" Rebecca asked, horrified by the thick piles of manuals and brochures.

"No way. Read through it. Pick out the pertinent details and draw up a one- or two-page summary. When that's done, I'll show you the French stuff. That's really amazing!"

Dazed, Rebecca watched as Torrey swung an arm around Bix and led her away. For a moment she stared at the ancient Underwood typewriter.

What do I have to lose, she thought, and picked up a brochure that waxed eloquent on the toilet facilities of a hostel near Barcelona.

During the first week Rebecca had grave doubts about her ability to survive within GoSee International, much less function. The frantic pace of the pit left her stunned. The endless cacophony produced by a dozen voices shouting into telephones —to say nothing of the mob beyond the counter—made concentration impossible. The interruptions were constant, with counselors hurling questions at her about Spanish train schedules,

French customs allowances, and once, an earnest query about yak treks in Nepal.

Now she understood why the telex codeword for GoSee was "hectic" and the cable appellation "kaos."

Rebecca marveled at how Bix, working two desks away, tuned out the din and concentrated on the Mediterranean islands bookings. Once in a while Torrey would drift by, the calm eye in the center of the hurricane, glance over her shoulder at the copy, and offer encouragement.

"You're doing great. In a couple of weeks I'll put you on the airline reservations desks."

Rebecca cringed.

At six o'clock each evening the madness ceased as mysteriously as it had erupted ten hours earlier. In the post-work bull sessions, held over beers at the Buffalo Roadhouse on Seventh Avenue, Rebecca got to know the other counselors.

"We call them counselors because they're not certified travel agents," Torrey confided.

"You're certified," Bix murmured.

"Certifiable," Torrey corrected her.

The counselors were all college students, most from NYU. It was their second season with GoSee and they considered themselves veterans. A chubby, bespectled anthropology major was a whiz at ferreting out airlines that had empty space on their Atlantic runs. A coed from Boston had the director of the Italian tourist board wrapped around her little finger. A Queens College senior had relatives on the staff at the University of London. As a result GoSee had first crack at whatever dormitory space was available.

Rebecca was fascinated by Torrey Stewart. The son of a Texas sharecropper, he had learned to fly crop dusters in his early teens. Having gone through Baylor on a scholarship, Torrey had been able to pocket the money he made working part-time for a dusting service. That stake enabled him to open GoSee.

"The first generation of Americans to travel—I mean on a large scale—were the guys in the war," Torrey explained. "They were working-class or middle-class kids who wouldn't have gone outside their neighborhoods had it not been for the army. Now their kids are growing up. They'll be the biggest travelers in American history. And I'll send them wherever they want to go. The key is to get 'em young."

The airlines and foreign tourist boards felt the same way. Instead of flying with empty seats, Pan Am, TWA, and others were just as happy to sell block seats at discount prices or even to lease an entire aircraft. The tourist boards were only too willing to provide information on the glories of their particular countries.

They all see the same thing, Rebecca thought. Once students are bitten by the travel bug they'll be back for more—when they're making money and can afford a better style of travel.

"After a long cold winter there's nothing like a hot Mediterranean beach," Torrey was fond of saying. "Thank the Lord for this rotten climate!"

Rebecca had to agree. More than three quarters of all reservations were for the resort strips in Spain, Portugal, France, and Italy.

As much as she loved exploring the small Village restaurants, Rebecca usually declined to join the group for dinner. For the first few weeks evenings were reserved for homework.

The sublet Bix had ferreted out belonged to a college professor and his wife whom Bix herself had dispatched to France for a three-month bicycle tour via GoSee. The Perry Street apartment occupied the entire second floor of a four-story town house. Its two bedrooms, separated by the living room and kitchen, and— Rebecca considered herself blessed—a thoroughly modernized bathroom, guaranteed each girl her privacy. There was even a small garden in back that the tenants shared.

While Bix worked her way through the jazz and folk clubs that seemed to sprout throughout the Village like mushrooms after a night's rain, Rebecca cracked the books. She read everything about the travel industry she could get her hands on. Most of the material came from Torrey Stewart's personal library, built up over the years. Rebecca delved into the arcane mysteries of air travel, reservations systems, charters, and the strict regulations that governed the trust accounts in which clients' money was held. She worked her way through the history of travel agencies, beginning with the world's two oldest establishments, Thomas Cook and American Express. In perusing the back issues of the industry bible, the weekly magazine *Travel World,* Rebecca learned about the horror stories as well as the successes of the agency business. There were accounts of hotels that didn't live up to their billing and some that didn't exist at all, of tourist groups destined for Lourdes ending up in Morocco, and of kickback deals between the international hotel chains and the big wholesalers.

The more she delved into the industry the more fascinated

Rebecca became. Without having set out to, she quickly brought herself on par with the other counselors working at GoSee. Torrey carefully noted her diligence and moved her from the translation desk to the airline reservations phones, and then to the travel planning group. Rebecca proved herself at each level, absorbing the experience of others and building on her own.

The first week in June, just as the crush hit GoSee, Torrey said to her, "Congratulations, darlin'. You're movin' on up to the front lines."

Rebecca stared at the sea of bodies pressing against the counter. "And for that I should thank you?" she asked.

The Buffalo Roadhouse was a Greenwich Village landmark. Outside the front door was a cone-shaped mound of asphalt, two feet high, that bubbled and smoked continuously. The Roadhouse owner had discovered that the steam was caused by a faulty vent. He built the miniature volcano over the fissure to draw the city fathers' attention to this oversight by their municipal road crews. Instead, the volcano became a Village legend.

Rebecca waved to the bartender and threaded her way through the lunch crowd to where Bix and Torrey were sitting. Torrey rose, pecked her on the cheek, and ordered another round of drinks.

"How's life in the trenches?" he asked.

"We're doing very nicely without you," Rebecca said archly.

Torrey accepted the repartee in good humor. For the last two weeks Bix and Rebecca had effectively been managing the operation while Torrey had disappeared into the wilds of LaGuardia Airport in Queens working on the last leg of training on the DC6's.

"Well, soon you, too, will be released," Torrey said, his eyes twinkling. He glanced at Bix. "Should I tell her, or do you want to?"

"Please, I wouldn't think of stealing your thunder," Bix replied. But Rebecca could sense her friend's excitement.

"Since things are going to start windin' down in September—and you gals have been working so hard—I figured that maybe the three of us would skedaddle to the Old World and play tourist for a while."

Rebecca's heart leapt in anticipation. She knew Bix was thinking the same thing: This could be the trip they had planned but that had never come to pass. There was one drawback.

"It sounds fantastic, Torrey. But I don't know if I can afford—"

"Everything except pocket money is on the house," Torrey said. "Hell, we've pushed through so much business this season we deserve a break."

He paused and added with mock seriousness, "Besides, it's our responsibility to do a spot check of all the places we've been sending folks."

"Oh, Becky, please say yes!" Bix cried.

Rebecca looked at the two of them.

"Are you sure I won't be a fifth wheel?"

It was no secret to anyone, least of all Rebecca, that Bix and Torrey had become lovers. For all intents and purposes, the Perry Street apartment was Rebecca's even though Bix continued to pick up her share of the rent.

"We want you to come," Torrey said quietly. "Not only will it be good for you but you'll learn more by being on the road for a couple weeks than in months of reading brochures."

Rebecca's eyes glistened, "You're on!"

"Great! Tonight we'll go out to the Seville, gorge ourselves on paella—"

"I can't," Rebecca interrupted. "I have to see Ramsey."

Torrey was about to try to persuade Rebecca otherwise, when Bix squeezed his thigh.

"How about meeting us for drinks afterward, at the Brasilia?"

"Around ten?"

"Ten is great!"

Throughout lunch they talked eagerly about possible itineraries. After Rebecca left, Torrey said, "What's with her and that lawyer? She's started spending almost as much time there as she does in the office."

Bix patted his hand. "Don't strain yourself thinking. Becky knows what she's doing."

And she wished she knew what that was.

On her way downtown Rebecca stopped off at the newsstand outside the entrance to the subway. The elderly black who was familiar with her routine plucked off copies of the *Times, Wall Street Journal,* and *Barron's,* as well as a half dozen British and continental magazines, some of them straight gossip sheets.

"One day you gotta tell me how the *Journal* and *The News of the World* fit together," he groused good-naturedly.

"As soon as I make the connection you'll be the first to know," Rebecca promised as she slipped the papers into her shoulder bag.

Bracing herself in the rocking IRT car, Rebecca took out *Barron's* and quickly skimmed the pages. Over the months she had become an expert speedreader, training her eye to search out a dozen key words in the stories. She found one of them in a three-inch article buried on page thirty-six. Rebecca dog-eared the page, finished her reading, then tore the page out.

Even at seven o'clock in the evening there was still activity at 12 Wall Street, the Federal-style building where the firm of Peet, Burroughs, and Calhoun had its offices. Rebecca signed in at the security desk in the lobby and took the old-fashioned, ornate elevator to the third floor. As she walked through the reception area and down the hall, she observed junior partners sitting behind their desks, shirt-sleeves rolled up, whispering into their telephones. Some of them would not go home until midnight.

As Rebecca passed by she exchanged brief greetings or acknowledged the wave of a hand. By now everyone knew who she was; they were surprised if they didn't see her at least three times a week.

Ramsey Peet's office befitted his station as a senior partner and founder's son. The fruitwood inlay of the desk gleamed of lemon oil and polish. Beside the island formed by three large sofas was a huge globe mounted on a pedestal. It was Ramsey's version of Greek worry beads. Whenever he was pondering the imponderable, the lawyer would sit on the sofa and idly spin the world.

The one thing that made the office truly distinctive was the complete absence of any law texts. There wasn't one legal tome to add an erudite clutter to the surroundings. Instead, oils and bronze statues by Frederic Remington highlighted the walls.

Rebecca settled herself on the butter-soft leather sofa and, while waiting for Ramsey, quickly went through the rest of the newspapers and magazines. None of the key words leapt off the pages. Rebecca returned to the article she had clipped and reread it carefully, making a mental note of the file it was destined for.

Like a good detective, Rebecca didn't overlook a single clue, even if at the time it appeared incongruous or meaningless. Over the last few months she had managed to bring together a number of intriguing facts about her quarry by piecing together information from disparate, seemingly unrelated sources.

"You'd never make a poker player, Rebecca. From your expression I gather you've found another nugget."

Ramsey Peet swept into the room, kissed Rebecca lightly on the cheek, and fumbled with his key ring.

"I presume you want the files."

"Please."

Ramsey withdrew four thick files from the locked cabinet and set them out on the coffee table.

"I have a couple things to finish up next door," he said. "Will you be all right for a few minutes?"

"Fine, Ramsey. Go ahead."

Rebecca arranged the files before her and looked at the bold title on each flap.

TYNE & WEAR
SILAS LAMBROS
CELESTE LAMBROS
ANDREW STOUGHTON

She opened the Tyne & Wear file and carefully slipped in the clipping from *Barron's*.

Know your adversary, Ramsey had counseled her. Get as much information on him as you can. What are his strengths, his weaknesses, his foibles and habits? Keep track of his movements. They will tell you not only what he's doing but will give you an indication as to what he's thinking.

Although the idea to start files on Andrew Stoughton and the others had been Ramsey's, Rebecca had insisted that she be involved in examining and interpreting the results of the ongoing investigation into exactly how Andrew had engineered the massive theft.

At first Ramsey had been reluctant to agree. Rebecca had no formal training in corporate organization or banking procedures.

"I'm not going to hold you up," Rebecca had assured him. "Just let me know when new material comes in so we can go over it together."

They held their sessions on the Monday night of each week. Then Monday and Tuesday. Then three times a week. And finally weekends as well.

Ramsey Peet was amazed at how quickly Rebecca absorbed the material, at the questions she posed and the suggestions she offered. He couldn't fathom the reason for this until one evening he overheard the office cleaners talking about how mercilessly Peet, Burroughs, and Calhoun drove their students. When Ramsey demanded an explanation the black woman turned on him.

"What about that poor girl you got workin' in the basement?

She be there 'bout every night. Lord, sometime I find her sleeping on the books when I leave!''

Not having the slightest idea what they were talking about, Ramsey Peet hurried down to the library to see this phantom for himself. What he found was Rebecca, surrounded by texts on the fundamentals of economics, business management, international financing, and currency transactions.

The nights Rebecca didn't spend on Wall Street were devoted to further research. In the cavernous holds of the New York Public Library, Rebecca found rare books that covered the wreckers' history from their inception. More recent works, dealing with the economic history of the Caribbean, brought Tyne & Wear into sharper focus. Although there was no history of the company per se, Rebecca discovered reams of material in books related to the sugar trade. The looting, spoilation, and outright piracy carried out by Tyne & Wear and others against Caribbean nations shocked her.

Information on the Lambros family was, as Rebecca quickly discovered, much sparser. She found the reason in several references in the London *Times*: in the last twenty years any journalist who dared to write an exposé of the family had been slapped with a libel suit. Even when the defendants managed to have the support of their publications, the verdict was always the same. The house of Lambros, employing the highest-paid legal gunslingers available, triumphed. It didn't seem to matter that the awards for damages were far below what the action must have cost. Silas Lambros was sending a clear message to interlopers: the family would go to any lengths to protect its privacy.

But there was the other side of the coin. Silas Lambros was, to a degree, a public figure. His movements were watched and reported by the financial press; speculation about mergers, buyouts, and new enterprises abounded. In a few instances Lambros had even deigned to give what purported to be a ''frank and in-depth discussion.'' The fawning tone of such pieces turned Rebecca's stomach.

Rebecca had to steel herself when she finally traced the old buccaneer to the present day and began to encounter references to her father. Yet for the thousands of words that had been devoted to Tyne & Wear's buy-out of McHenry Enterprises, there wasn't a single quote directly attributable to Silas Lambros. That he did not trumpet his victory told Rebecca more about the character of the man than any biography could have revealed.

If the head of the family eschewed the limelight, the same couldn't be said for his granddaughter.

Although more than six years had elapsed since the ugly incident at Miss Potter's the mere thought of Celeste Lambros made Rebecca's skin crawl. Nonetheless she persevered, concentrating on a single moment frozen in time: Celeste gowned in white, a bride, on Andrew's arm.

Celeste Lambros's life was an open book. She had been the darling of society and gossip columnists from Miami to New York. Rebecca came across story after story about Celeste's escapades among the rich and powerful prior to her marriage to Andrew. *Keyhole,* a notorious scandal magazine, linked her name to that of innumerable movie stars, athletes, and wealthy bachelors.

Nor were Celeste's conquests confined to the United States. European magazines showed pictures of Celeste dancing with a French count, raising a glass of champagne on board a Greek shipping magnate's yacht, and sunbathing topless on the Italian Riviera.

The paparazzi were no less attentive after her marriage. Rebecca couldn't help but wince when she saw pictures of the couple coming out of a West End premiere or ducking into a fashionable London nightclub. Andrew was being touted as the wunderkind of Tyne & Wear who had just established himself in the company's London headquarters. Celeste's parties at their Eaton Square residence were all the rage. One British gossip speculated at length on the rumors of Celeste's being pregnant. His impeccable source was "someone very close to" a nurse who worked part-time for a Harley Street physician whose offices were in the same building as those of Celeste's doctor.

Ludicrous though the story was, it drove home a brutal point. One day Celeste Lambros would have the baby that should have been hers.

The thought of what her unborn child could have been was all Rebecca needed to steel herself when she turned her attention to her former husband.

Ironically the one thing Rebecca knew for certain about Andrew was that he had been the father of her child. Of the three people she was investigating, he was the most elusive, a man who had made himself into a ghost.

The duplicate personnel file on Andrew Stoughton provided by Ramsey Peet held no surprises. The man was obviously a brilliant executive with a flair for organization and for getting the best work out of the people under him. Andrew had streamlined the McHenry offices in the Angelines and invested in new business and communications equipment that made for greater efficiency. Far from being a desk-bound pencil pusher, he had traveled into the field, familiarizing himself with the mining operations from the ground up. Later, he had proven himself a tough negotiator with the people McHenry Enterprises did business with.

Something I can vouch for, Rebecca thought, remembering how Andrew had handled Wendell Coltraine, the Star Lines owner who had wanted to renege on his contract.

Realizing she would have to dig further back, Rebecca had asked Ramsey Peet to obtain Andrew's employment record while he had been with the Severn Group plus whatever information was available on his schooling. That was when the trail began to disappear.

The Severn Group had been mothballed shortly after Andrew had come to McHenry Enterprises. Its various companies had been sold off to interests that hid themselves behind numbered or name-plate companies in Lichtenstein and Panama. The directors were nowhere to be found.

Andrew's two years at Lloyds were also shrouded in mystery. Employment records had vanished from company archives. Supervisors and executives whom he had worked under had only a vague recollection of the man. Coworkers had either moved on or couldn't really remember him.

Andrew's schooling was also a dead-end track. The registrar at Kings College, Cambridge, recalled Andrew having been a student, but it seemed that his records had been misplaced. Since Andrew had never completed his studies at the university, there had been no great concern about the oversight.

The private school which Andrew had told Rebecca he had attended during the war had been torn down ten years earlier. Its records had been traced to a London warehouse, but nothing had been found pertaining to Andrew Stoughton.

Who are you? Why have you gone to such trouble to erase the past?

If Andrew's history was little more than a shadow in a cave, his present was almost too normal. Like Silas Lambros, Andrew avoided the media where he or Tyne & Wear was concerned. Social events were another matter. Rebecca found plenty of stories about Andrew sitting on the board of this charity or that hospital. He was photographed at ground-breaking ceremonies for a new orphanage and was seen at the opening night of the Royal Ballet. His rather predictable social circle, mostly captains of industry, was leavened with a sprinkling of the titled.

The feeling that beneath this pristine existence Andrew was hiding something continued to haunt Rebecca.

Ramsey Peet returned with an accordion file under one arm.

"Sorry about the delay," he apologized. "We're handling a West Coast movie studio merger and getting a clear picture of the assets is next to impossible. These people could convince you *Gone With the Wind* still hasn't turned a profit!"

The attorney drew out memoranda from the file and spread it across the coffee table.

"This is the most recent information on those computer and electronics companies," he said.

For the next hour Ramsey elaborated on the intricate web of shadow companies Andrew Stoughton had bought on behalf of McHenry Enterprises. The law firm's investigators had trekked across the southwest and California, putting each company under a microscope. Leases were examined and signatures compared. Where employment records were available, they were seized and the individual employees tracked down. Court orders forced the banks doing business with the companies to open up their deposit and withdrawal records. Payroll tax deductions were checked with the IRS field offices in every state.

Rebecca listened carefully as Ramsey explained how each company had operated within the strict confines of the law.

"Stoughton made sure every *i* was dotted and every *t* crossed," he said. "So far there's nothing to suggest Tyne & Wear had anything to do with these companies. There isn't a single irregularity that points to conspiracy."

"What about the initial funding for all these firms?" Rebecca asked. "Is there any way to trace the start-up capital to Tyne & Wear?"

Ramsey shook his head. "In each case we've followed the money to an off-shore haven. Once we got to the Bahamas, Grand Cayman, or Switzerland we ran into banking secrecy laws. There's no way to prove that the money came from Tyne & Wear or that Stoughton had anything to do with arranging its flow into these companies."

And that's as far as we can go, Rebecca thought.

To understand exactly how Andrew had stolen McHenry Enterprises had involved hundreds of hours on Ramsey's part. The disbursements to associate firms and investigators must have run into the tens of thousands of dollars, every penny of which was absorbed by Ramsey. And the knowledge gleaned had only led them down blind alleys.

"Our next step should be taken in London," Ramsey was saying. "I want to know more about Foster-Swann, possibly prove a connection between it and Stoughton before he negotiated the loan—"

"No, Ramsey."

The attorney looked at her blankly.

"What do you mean?"

"That Andrew has covered every step, every angle. We've started to tilt at windmills."

For an instant she glimpsed the objection he wanted to make. Instead, Ramsey turned away, pushing his fingers through his hair.

"I won't give up," he said stubbornly, yet he was unable to keep the resignation from the edge of his voice.

"I'm not suggesting we do," Rebecca told him. "But we're not going to get inside Tyne & Wear by storming the gates."

Peet glanced at her, intrigued. "Any alternatives in mind?"

Rebecca tapped the files she had compiled.

"The answer lies in here, in the past. This is only the tip of the iceberg, Ramsey. We need every scrap of information on Andrew and Silas Lambros we can get our hands on. We have to find their weakness and exploit it."

The attorney shook his head. "Given who Lambros and Stoughton are, that's going to be very difficult. Remember how far we *didn't* get into Andrew's background."

"It's the only way," Rebecca insisted. "And we have to do this so quietly, they won't have a clue as to what's going on. We have to lead them to believe that we've given up, exhausted ourselves."

"The process could take years," Ramsey warned her.

"Time," Rebecca replied softly, "is something I have more than enough of."

The attorney thought about what Rebecca had said, then asked, "Why the change of tactics? Why do you want to concentrate entirely on Andrew and Silas Lambros?"

"What is the one thing that had to happen for Andrew's scheme to work?" Rebecca asked in turn.

Ramsey hesitated, stung by the coldness behind Rebecca's question.

"Max had to die."

"And who are the only two men who could have seen to it that he did?"

"Stoughton and Lambros. Except they both had iron-clad alibis as to their whereabouts at the time of the fire. In fact, you yourself vouched for Andrew."

"I've thought about this a great deal, Ramsey," Rebecca said slowly. "It's true that I told the police Andrew was with me when Skyscape was set on fire. But I wasn't with him that long before the fishing boat saw the flames and radioed for help. Andrew said he had been in his office all night. Neither I nor anyone else had any reason to doubt him. But what if he *hadn't* been there? You remember what Bones said about the wax in the floorboards? It could have come from candles. . . ."

"What are you getting at, Rebecca?" Ramsey demanded.

Rebecca looked steadily into Ramsey's eyes.

"That somehow Andrew could have gone to Skyscape, set the fire, and returned in time for me to find him at the office. I think Lambros and Andrew conspired to kill Max and Andrew was the one who actually committed the murder."

"Do you realize what you're saying?" Ramsey whispered.

"More than you think," Rebecca said, turning away. "If I'm right, then I made love to my father's murderer. I married him then let him destroy everything. But even that wasn't enough for Andrew. He had to try to kill me as well."

Martin Fletcher was an international tax specialist, a full partner in Peet, Burroughs, and Calhoun, and an associate of Ramsey Peet. He was a short, plump man with a baby-pink cherubic face, thick lips, and a hairpiece that tended to shift around on his scalp. When Martin Fletcher was nervous his palms sweated profusely, which was the reason Andrew Stoughton didn't shake hands.

The two men were standing at the counter of the Golden Lion, a pub on Dean Street in Soho, an area of London none of their associates would ever venture into. Which was exactly why it had been chosen.

Martin Fletcher's business took him to London frequently. After office hours he had become good friends with many young men. Andrew Stoughton had photographs showing just how intimate these friends were.

"Listen, I told you Peet has given up," Fletcher said in his high-pitched voice.

"There's no need to attract attention, Martin," Andrew said smoothly. "You're quite sure?"

"Absolutely. Peet has paid off the associate firms he was using, as well as the investigators. Christ, I should know—I'm the one who handles the company books!"

"And what about Miss McHenry?"

"I haven't seen her around in—what? a couple of months. I'm telling you, Andrew, they're through beating their heads against the wall. You've got nothing to worry about."

Andrew considered this but did not comment.

"Do you know what she's doing now?"

"She's still working for that hole-in-the-wall travel outfit in the Village," Fletcher said derisively. "Peet told me she's coming over to Europe mid-September with the guy who owns GoSee and his girlfriend. A little R&R for the three of them. That should convince you she's given up."

Andrew filed away this nugget and drained the last of his whiskey. He knew Fletcher didn't have anything more for him.

"Oh, by the way, Martin, did I introduce you to Charles?"

Andrew stepped away from the bar so that the tax specialist could get a good look at the tall blond man who had been standing beside him. Martin Fletcher took one glance at the young Adonis and felt his palms dry up.

"I'm sure you two will be very happy together," Andrew murmured as he took his leave.

A single thought pursued him as he walked out of the bar.

Like hell she's given up!

· 17 ·

The Pan Am flight to Paris was unlike anything Rebecca had ever experienced. Crammed into the DC8's last thirty seats, which Torrey had purchased as a block, were students from across the United States. Wearing army surplus jackets and sprouting feathery beards, boys from San Francisco carried on intense discussions about Allen Ginsberg's poetry with West Coast girls wearing Indian-style bandannas and loose-fitting embroidered blouses. Crew-cut jocks from the Midwest exchanged bawdy stories of the past year's conquests, then turned their attention to young ladies clutching oversize guide books to Paris museums.

Jammed into a window seat, Rebecca gave silent thanks when, somewhere over the Atlantic, the duty-free liquor had finally killed the excited chatter. After the cabin lights were extinguished, she felt Bix shift in her seat so that her head was nestled against Torrey's chest.

"You okay?" Torrey whispered, stroking Bix's hair.

Rebecca gave him a quick nod and smile and gazed out the window, where the crescent moon, riding low in the heavens, looked like the trough of a guillotine.

Stop being so morbid! she scolded herself. But when she reflected on the last two months she had to admit there was little to cheer about.

Ramsey had embarked on a low-key campaign of reaching out to friends, colleagues, and associates who at one time or another had done business with Silas Lambros. Playing on the fact that everyone in the business world knew of his role in the Rebecca McHenry fiasco, he adopted the demeanor of someone who was still groping to understand what had happened. His mournful, slightly bewildered air worked exactly as he had hoped: first came expressions of sympathy, then the professional gossip on Lambros and Tyne & Wear. With the patience of gold panners,

Ramsey and Rebecca sifted through these secondhand stories, innuendos, and rumors in search of valuable specks of truth.

The process was arduous and for the most part inconclusive. Rebecca was appalled by the brutal tactics Lambros had used to capture rival companies or secure contracts, tactics that reminded her time and again of how he and Andrew Stoughton had stolen McHenry Enterprises. But in these cases, just as in hers, Lambros had pushed ruthlessness and manipulation only to the legal limits, stopping short of going over them.

Confronted by example after example of successful piracy, Rebecca realized there was little hope of uncovering a sin in Lambros's business dealings that could be used as an effective lever.

The matter of Andrew Stoughton was even more disheartening. Not only had Ramsey's initial queries into his background proved fruitless but Andrew now enjoyed the cloak of secrecy provided by Tyne & Wear. By following Celeste's never-ending affair with the press, Rebecca was at least able to keep Andrew in sight. To try to penetrate the core of the man, she had no choice but to use a painful alternative.

Rebecca's reconstruction of her life with Andrew began with the first time she saw him, on the trip to California. The task was daunting not only because of the memories it evoked. All the mementos she had of Andrew, and, most important, her diary, had been destroyed in the Skyscape blaze. Letters, small gifts, birthday cards, photographs—these were memory triggers that could have brought a past event to life.

Nonetheless Rebecca spent hours dredging her memory for names and places, things they had done together, promises that had been kept and those that were broken. You were his wife! she kept telling herself. What were all the little question marks about his behavior you overlooked or chose to ignore? When he whispered in his sleep, was it fatigue talking or a confession? Try to remember the conversations you overheard, the little discrepancies in his explanations for being away. . . . Where had he been going, on what pretext?

By September Rebecca was exhausted. She felt like a woman with two lives, one in present-day New York, the other a past life she scarcely recognized anymore, hard though she tried to make sense of it. The process was tearing her apart and she had nothing but reopened wounds to show for it.

"I'm glad you're leaving tomorrow," Ramsey had told her. "If you weren't I would put you on a plane somewhere myself.

Give me your word of honor you won't even think of what
we've been doing.''

It had been an easy promise to make.

Rebecca glanced over at Bix, her head nestled in Torrey's
shoulder, and felt a pang of envy. There were a lot of couples on
the plane. Even the students who were traveling alone and who
came from different schools shared a certain camaraderie. They
had sung the same songs, shared the same classes, struggled
through the same texts. At that moment Rebecca felt herself far
removed from them, as though she were standing outside and
looking through a window at a party she would never be invited
to join.

Rebecca couldn't define what it was that made her respond to
Paris, only that she fell in love with the city instantly and with
all her heart.

While Torrey made the rounds at the Ministry of Tourism,
Rebecca and Bix threw themselves into exploring the city. After
breakfasting on croissants and café au lait at a sidewalk table on
the rue Sufflot, they followed the winding cobbled streets of the
Latin Quarter, stopping at curio shops, antiques dealers, and
antiquarian bookstores. They walked along the Left Bank of the
Seine, cut through the maze of streets below St. Germain, and
crossed the river at the magnificent Pont Alexandre III to find
themselves in the heart of the chic Right Bank.

After a martini at the Ritz bar, they window-shopped along the
rue St. Honoré, watching as gilded women stepped from limou-
sines or sports cars to be greeted deferentially by doormen at
Chanel, Lanvin, and Balenciaga.

"One day that's going to be you, kiddo," Bix said.

"I couldn't afford to buy a scarf from these people!" Rebecca
replied.

"Mark my words . . ."

As they walked on, Rebecca looked over her shoulder at the
stunning silk creations in the artfully decorated window. A pang
of regret and envy shot through her. Once, she could have
walked in and bought whatever she wanted in any of these
stores.

One day! she promised herself.

The girls' days generally ended in Montmartre, where Torrey
joined them to watch the sun set across the city from the vantage
point of the majestic Sacré Coeur. After taking in the jazz clubs
near the Moulin Rouge they finished off the night with bowls of

hot thick onion soup, served in the cafés of Les Halles, the city's market quarter.

As sorry as Rebecca was to leave Paris, she was excited when they stepped off the famous Disque Bleu express at the Marseilles railroad station and picked up their Volkswagen camper for the drive along the sun-drenched coast toward Spain. What Rebecca had missed most living in New York was the constant presence of the sea. For the next ten days she would sample the beaches at Palamós, Barcelona, Tortosa, and Denja, luxuriating in the warm salty waters of the Gulf of Valencia.

The itinerary Torrey had mapped out for the trio included the islands of Ibiza and Majorca, destinations chosen by many of the students who had traveled with GoSee. Rebecca was amazed by the sight of thousands of young people bronzing themselves.

"This reminds me of a rookery filled with basking seals," she exclaimed as they carved out a tiny plot for themselves on the beach. "Where do they all stay?"

The few hotels and pensions Rebecca had seen in San Antonio, Abad and Tagomago wouldn't have held a tenth of the number.

"That's the down side of traveling on a shoestring," Torrey told her. "Unless you can afford to stay at a posh resort or are lucky enough to get a room in a hotel in town, you camp out on the beach."

Torrey was absolutely right. As night fell, hundreds of tents mushroomed up from the sand. The songs drifting around the campfires were sung in German, French, Swedish, Norwegian, and Dutch.

"I guess there's not much difference between our winters and theirs," Bix remarked, ogling a pair of Danish boys wearing a deep tan and little else. "By Christmas they'll be as lily-white as their buns are now."

"I love your attention to detail," Torrey commented dryly.

"If we can send Americans to Europe in the summer, why can't we give them Mexico or the Caribbean during the winter, when they're sick and tired of the snow and cold," Rebecca thought aloud.

"A whole mess of reasons," Torrey said, rolling on his stomach. "Number one, kids can't afford the glitzy places like Acapulco or Nassau. Two, nobody in Mexico or the islands is geared up to offer cheap vacations. Don't forget that students save all year just to get here for the summer. They're not likely to spend that money for a Christmas vacation or at spring break—no matter how cold the northeast becomes.

"Three, there's the problem of amenities. When kids come to Europe they're willing to do without some of the creature comforts of home. If worse comes to worst they'll pool their money and send one person to get a room in a decent hotel. Then twenty will pile in and keep the bathtub in use all night. You're not going to find that in the Yucatan or the islands where good hotels are located only in the major centers."

In her mind's eye Rebecca saw the miles of unspoiled beach so common in the Angelines and other Caribbean islands. Some were so deserted that if she had returned to them a week or two after her visit, she would have found only her own footprints, undisturbed. Yet many of these beaches were close to freshwater springs and were cooled by trade winds that kept the insects away.

Rebecca decided that Torrey Stewart might be an expert on European travel but he had a lot to learn as far as his own backyard was concerned.

After a week on Ibiza and Majorca, Rebecca, Bix, and Torrey got the camper back on the road. They followed the coastal road through Cartagena en route to Málaga and finally Gibraltar. After sightseeing the Rock they would board a plane for Lisbon and from there, one of the last charters home to New York.

Before leaving, Rebecca had gone over her itinerary with Lauren and Ramsey. Along the route she dutifully stopped off at American Express offices to check for messages although she never expected to find any waiting for her.

While Bix and Torrey enjoyed a glass of wine at one of the cafés in Málaga's Botanical Gardens, Rebecca strolled the two blocks to the travel bureau. As the clerk leafed through the stacks of general delivery telegrams, Rebecca loaded up on the brochures set in wooden sleeves along the walls. Getting whatever information she could on new places had become second nature to her.

Rebecca's eyes widened when the clerk passed her a yellow envelope. Quickly she tore it open and stifled a cry as she read the telegram inside.

JEWEL VERY ILL. COME HOME SOONEST. RAMSEY.

The telegram had been sent four days before.

· 18 ·

Her eyes red-rimmed from lack of sleep, Rebecca stumbled off the TWA Lisbon–New York flight in a daze.

"You made record time," Ramsey Peet said as he met her outside customs and shepherded her toward the upstairs lounge at Idlewild. "Fourteen hours from Málaga to New York."

"It feels more like a hundred and fourteen," Rebecca groaned, recalling her frantic attempts to make all the connections. "Torrey worked miracles. Somewhere in Málaga and Lisbon there are two very angry passengers who got bumped."

When Ramsey asked the lounge hostess for a table, Rebecca said, "Let's stand. If I sit down again I may never get up."

Rebecca gulped down her first ginger ale and ordered a second. Steeling herself, she asked, "Any change in Jewel's condition?"

In Málaga, Rebecca had somehow managed to find a clear overseas line in Spain's otherwise archaic telephone system. Her conversation with Ramsey, shot through with static and third-party interruptions, had been just long enough for her to learn Jewel was in the hospital in Angeline City.

"It's her heart," Ramsey said. "Five days ago she collapsed in the street. Bones Ainsley told me the doctors discovered Jewel has a congenital heart disease. The walls of her heart are paper-thin. Nothing can be done to treat her condition or reverse the damage. All she can do is rest and take it as easy as possible."

Ramsey didn't add the doctors' last comment: that another attack would probably be fatal.

Rebecca gripped Ramsey's forearm.

"I must go to her. There has to be a way you can get me back into the Angelines!"

"I applied to the Angelinian government for a temporary visa on compassionate grounds," Ramsey said. "They started giving me the runaround, when yesterday this arrived for you. From the

159

office of Senator Gibson no less. You didn't tell me you had friends in such high places."

Puzzled, Rebecca opened the large manila envelope. The first thing that slid into her hand was an olive-green Angelinian passport.

Rebecca was stunned. "Is it . . . real?"

"Looks perfectly valid to me," Ramsey told her, smiling. "All you have to do is sign it."

"But how—"

"There's a flight leaving for Miami in twenty minutes," Ramsey added. "I've booked you on it as well as the CaribAir connection to Angeline City."

Distracted, Rebecca waved away the stewardess, then apologized when she realized the woman was only asking her to fasten the seat belt. Rebecca returned to the documents in her lap, unable to believe they were real.

The covering letter bore the seal of the United States Senate. Beneath it was the name of Senator Lewis Gibson emblazoned in raised gold type. The tone of the letter was cordial but neutral. The senator offered his congratulations that the misunderstanding between the government of the Angelines and Rebecca McHenry had been resolved. Period. No explanations, no embellishments.

The accompanying letter to Senator Gibson from the Angelinian Minister of the Interior was a masterpiece in understatement. The minister had concluded that the government's depriving Rebecca McHenry of her citizenship had been a premature action. Upon reviewing her case, the minister noted that certain properties thought to have been a part of McHenry Enterprises in fact belonged to the personal estate of Maxwell McHenry. As Miss McHenry was the sole heir, she was entitled, by the law of succession, to enjoy the benefits of this estate, to wit: Windemere and Tongue Keys, the vessel *Windsong,* and the property designated as Skyscape on the Angelinian mainland.

As an afterthought the minister added that he was including Miss McHenry's new passport.

Rebecca read the letter through a half dozen times before she believed it was true. Each time she could almost hear its writer gritting his teeth as he penned the words.

It's not a dream. I'm going home. I'm really going home!

But who in the world is Senator Lewis Gibson and why did he do this for me?

*   *   *

In spite of her fatigue Rebecca was still apprehensive as she waited her turn at Angelinian customs and immigration. Part of her was convinced that all this was some grotesque joke.

In fact, the black Angelinian behind the counter did examine the passport carefully. But when he stamped it, a wide smile broke over his face.

"Welcome home, miss."

They were the sweetest words Rebecca had ever heard.

"I'm happy to second that."

Rebecca whirled around.

"Bones?"

Rebecca raced toward him, flinging her arms around his neck.

"When Mr. Peet told me you were arriving I thought I had better come see this miracle for myself," the giant policeman said.

"Then why are you wrinkling your nose?"

"Because you need a bath!"

"You certainly know how to sweet-talk a girl." Rebecca laughed.

"There are ladies who would vouch for that," Ainsley agreed solemnly.

Without her asking, Bones Ainsley drove Rebecca straight to the hospital. Rebecca sat back in the front seat, breathing deeply of the island scent. It had been only six months, yet she felt as though she had been away a lifetime.

"I'm sorry I have nothing to tell you about your father," Bones said softly. "I've done everything I could . . ."

"I know," Rebecca said.

Suddenly she turned to him. "Bones, if she's gone I won't have anyone."

And there was nothing the policeman could say to that.

The hospital room threw Rebecca back in time. It was identical to the one in which her father had lain, and it brought back memories that made her shiver.

Rebecca closed the door behind her and slowly approached the bed where Jewel lay, her dark moon face at peace, the gold tooth glinting as she drew long, even breaths. Rebecca reached for Jewel's hand, and their fingers intertwined.

"So glad you're back, child."

Jewel spoke the words without opening her eyes but her grip tightened.

"Jewel . . ."

"Hush, now. I won't be havin' any cryin' or long faces."

"No crying," Rebecca promised.

"So that Mr. Gibson brought you back to me like he promised. . . . Ah, he's a fine man. . . . You'll sit with me awhile. . . ."

"Yes, I'm right here. I'll always be here now. . . ."

Rebecca felt Jewel's grip relax as she drifted off to sleep. For a long time she sat like that, in the chair beside the bed, watching Jewel, praying to a God she wasn't sure existed . . . and remembering.

To Rebecca, Jewel was part of her consciousness, someone without whom the world she knew as a child would not be complete.

The first six years of Rebecca's life revolved around Jewel and life as it was lived by the native people of the Angelines. Every morning after Rebecca had had her swim she got dressed and scrambled onto her donkey. With Jewel walking ahead, the three of them set off up the winding trail that led from the beach to the road for Angeline City.

Rebecca never tired of the wonders around her. From the Angeline foothills came the mountain people, their beasts burdened with sacks of charcoal, coconut, cane, tree stumps to be used for building boats, and joints of meat from cattle or goats butchered that morning. Donkeys brayed greetings to their cousins who were climbing up from the shore, their backs heavy with fish, lobster, seaweed, and palm fronds for thatching.

As the two parties merged on the road to Angeline City, Rebecca saw mothers with babies strapped across their breasts. They walked in that peculiar island gait, bodies thrust forward, chatting with one another in singsong voices as their bare feet stirred the dust. Farmers who worked the *milpas*—small plots of land—joined in, trussed chickens slung over one shoulder, a sack of mangoes over the other. Squealing piglets tethered to one another were herded along, followed by temperamental goats. Peddlers bearing such delicacies as calves' tongues hanging from a string or enormous platters piled high with cassava bread also joined in.

Angeline City fascinated Rebecca. Here, thousands of voices mingled in the streets, a heady mixture of Indian dialect that confounded the ear, black patois only the initiated could understand, as well as Spanish and English. Jewel taught her each one.

In the fish market Rebecca learned to identify the bounty of the sea. Snapper, shark, yellowtail, ray, turtle, conch, and grou-

per were laid out before her on beds of ice. Adjacent to the fish
stalls was the spice market which filled her head with dizzying
scents. Wizened women, whose cackling laughter sometimes
frightened Rebecca, muttered incantations while grinding roots,
bark, and dried flowers into potions for long life, luck in money
or marriage, potency, or cures for barrenness.

When they returned home Jewel and Rebecca swam in the
shallow reefs. It was Jewel who taught Reecca the names of
the little fish in the pond and showed her the hiding places of the
crabs, mangrove oysters, and shy octopuses. Together they caught
lobster for their lunch and later Rebecca gathered fallen coco-
nuts, bringing them back to Jewel, who split them over a spike
imbedded in the sand and peeled away the husks. The husks
went into making a fire in which the lobster was baked; the nut
was cut up by machete into chunks of delicious dessert.

Later, when Rebecca was going to school, Jewel told her
stories about the Angelines. She explained how all the different
people who had come here had found peace and plenty and lived
in harmony with one another. At school Rebecca met white
Mennonite children, mestizos, Kekchi and Mopan Indians, Cre-
oles, and black Caribs. She grew up with a fierce pride in her
country, without understanding that such a thing as prejudice
even existed.

That she learned about only later. . . .

Rebecca awoke with a start. For an instant she was confused
by the moonlight that swathed the room. Then she saw Jewel and
remembered where she was.

I turned my back on my own people, she thought, remembering her dream. When Celeste humiliated me, I blamed not only
her but the whole of the Angelines. I never stopped to think that
she was only one person. I forgot about all my friends, everything that I loved, had grown up with. All because Celeste made
me think I wasn't as good as she was. I, not anyone else,
allowed her to destroy the image I had of my mother . . . the
image I had of myself.

When Jewel was able to leave the hospital, Rebecca brought
her home to the beachfront house and moved into its spare
bedroom. Although the house was as neat as a pin, Rebecca
scrubbed down the floors, dusted everything in sight, and washed
all the linen. She went to the market and carted back enough
food for a siege. When the doctor failed to arrive promptly for

Jewel's examination, Rebecca telephoned the hospital demanding to know where he was. She was still on the phone when the physician appeared at the front door.

"I'm not some helpless old woman, and I won't be havin' you treat me like one!" Jewel complained. "Thank the Lord Bones is comin' for you today!"

"Is there something you need?" Rebecca said anxiously.

"No," Jewel replied pointedly. "He's takin' you into Angeline City."

The road to Angeline City passed the boundaries of Skyscape. Rebecca observed the familiar landmarks as they drove by. At the last minute she turned to Ainsley and pointed toward the gates sagging from their moorings in the stone columns.

The neglect was obvious. Wild grass, two feet high, grew lush between the palms and Australian pines that had once been surrounded by an emerald carpet. The gardens were choked with brush, and what remained of the foundation was slowly being cracked apart by weeds and vines. Some of the charred timbers had toppled; others remained stark against the sky like black, rotted teeth. There was an eerie silence to Skyscape, broken only by the crash of surf below the cliff and the keening of the wind as it roamed the ruins.

"I've seen enough," Rebecca said abruptly. "Let's go."

It was the same place but not the same. The minute Rebecca stepped into the dusty streets of Angeline City she couldn't shake the feeling that something profound had changed.

"What are all the boats doing in the harbor?" she asked Bones as they walked along the edge of the piers.

Angeline Bay was dotted with fishing boats that should have gone out to sea at first light.

"The fish processing plant Max built has been closed," he told her. "Lambros and the wreckers say there's no market. Truth is, the men now bring their catch to the wreckers' factory. Lambros pays them all right but then freezes the catch until he gets the price he wants. If anyone brings in more than Lambros can hold, the catch rots."

As they passed the labor exchange in the town square, Rebecca saw groups of men standing around, smoking and talking quietly. She recognized some of them as miners.

"Lambros shut down half of the mines when his managers

told him the ore was too expensive to remove," Bones explained. "Word is, the rest will close pretty soon too."

"But that doesn't make any sense!" Rebecca said. "Every dollar he invested would come back to him three times over. What's the point of throwing these men out of work?"

"They are the lucky ones," Ainsley replied. "Every morning they come here and wait for Lambros's trucks to pick them up and take them to the cane fields. There's more money for the wreckers in sugar than in gold."

"What about the miners who couldn't leave their villages to come here?"

"They are the unlucky ones."

The more Rebecca saw, the greater the difference became between the memories she had of the Angelines as a child and the stark reality before her. There was a lethargy in the air, a sense of quiet resignation that bordered on despair. In the open-air markets, where good-natured haggling produced a kind of carnival atmosphere, the mood was sullen. Women picked through the produce carefully, and sellers refused to bargain.

Sometimes Rebecca noticed people pointing at her, whispering among themselves.

"Do they blame me for what's happened to them?"

"No," Ainsley said. "Everyone knows how much you lost. They look at you because they remember how good Max was to them. They wonder if you can help them. Because you're a McHenry."

Rebecca felt deeply ashamed. All this time she had been consumed by her own troubles and grief without realizing that there were thousands of people suffering. Her people, the Angelinians, were also paying for the crime Andrew Stoughton had committed against her.

"What else has been going on, Bones?" she asked.

The policeman's reply drew a graphic portrait of callousness and malign neglect. Funds had been suspended for the schools Max had built. With no way to pay the teachers, classes were cut back to half a day. In some districts they were canceled altogether.

Clinics that had been established around the mining camps closed their doors. There was no money to pay the doctors much less fly them into the camps.

The fields of experimental farms Max had encouraged lay fallow. Where once a man could grow enough to feed his family for a year and still have a harvest left to sell, he now labored on the huge collective plantations administered by the wreckers' overseers.

The scholarship fund set up to enable gifted Angelinians to study abroad had been terminated, the money siphoned out. There would be no more chances for people like Violet Lhuiller to realize their dreams.

When Rebecca thought back to that kind nurse who had ministered to her father, she began to comprehend the toll Lambros's greed had taken. No one would ever be able to calculate how much promise and hope had been destroyed.

That, Rebecca thought, is the true measure of Lambros's cruelty.

As if he had been reading her mind, Bones said, "You don't know what the Angelines were like before Max came here. But if Lambros is allowed to have his way, you'll see it for yourself. The man is taking us back."

They boarded Ainsley's yellow and white runabout and went out to the *Windsong*.

"You might as well see her now," Bones said. "But don't expect her to be the same."

Rebecca feared the worst when she realized Bones was heading for the ships' basin at the far end of the harbor, where derelicts waited to be cannibalized then cut up for scrap.

"Goddamn them!"

Dirty and dilapidated, with a thick crust of barnacles on her underbelly, the *Windsong* was hardly recognizable. Her teak decks were bleached from lack of oil and the brass fittings were pitted green. Exposed to the elements, the interior was awash with rain and dirt, the carpets and furniture completely ruined.

"Our august governor-general used her as his private party palace," Bones said bitterly. "Until, that is, he ran her on Claw Reef and left a portion of the hull on the coral before managing to get her off. It's a miracle she's still afloat."

Rebecca clenched her fists.

"I'll have her repaired," she said. "One day she'll be exactly as my father built her!"

Bones Ainsley aimed the runabout for the open sea, moving through the *quebrada* north along the coast. Twenty minutes later Rebecca sighted the two keys the Angelinian government had so magnanimously returned to her.

Lying a mile off shore, Windemere Key was shaped like a boomerang, with a lazy curve of beach almost three miles long.

The interior was hilly, with an old lighthouse at the highest elevation. As the runabout bobbed a hundred feet from the beach, Rebecca could hear the screeches and squawks of the parrots and toucans in the dense foliage.

Rebecca climbed up on the runabout's bow and sat looking at the Garden-of-Eden landscape stretched out before her.

"Turn it around leeward," she said at last, not moving.

Bones Ainsley swung the boat north. For the next three hours he expertly steered in whatever direction Rebecca indicated, guiding the runabout through the *quebradas,* into the shallow coves, and along the fringe of the crescent-shaped beach. He ran it up on to the silver sand and walked with her along the deserted stretch, watching as every so often she plunged into the thick growth. Ainsley was puzzled as much by her silence as by her behavior.

"Tide's moving out," he told her as she emerged from the jungle. "We'd best be off."

Rebecca stared at him. "What did you say?"

"The tide's going out," Ainsley repeated.

"It's the perfect name," Rebecca murmured as she walked by him, lost in her thoughts, like a sleepwalker.

"Do you want to see Tongue Key?" Bones asked her when they were in the runabout.

"There's no need. Let's get back to Angeline City."

Rebecca settled herself in the stern, watching Windemere and its paradise of sand and jungle recede in the distance. Looking at the scimitar-shaped beach, she recalled another place, another time: the coast of Spain, with its tens of thousands of bodies crammed on the beaches of the Costa del Sol.

Windemere only needed the people.

On the way through Angeline City, Bones Ainsley stopped at the hardware store.

"Something Jewel wanted me to show you," Bones said, getting out of the car.

Mystified, Rebecca followed him inside. Ainsley greeted Sam Meat Pie, the proprietor, and walked through the store. Rebecca followed him as he climbed the back stairs to the second-floor offices.

"Bones," she started to say.

Ainsley stopped in front of one of the offices and pointed to the cardboard sign tacked to the door. Rebecca gasped when she read the handwriting.

DEPARTMENT OF ARCHAEOLOGY, FIELD OFFICE
UNIVERSITY OF CHICAGO
DALLAS GIBSON, SUPERVISOR

"I've arranged for someone to take you to him tomorrow," Bones said. "Now I guess we better head back so Jewel can tell you all about him."

· 19 ·

Rebecca's journey lasted almost a full day. At dawn she boarded a launch which took her up the Angelinian coast, north to the mouth of the New River. There she transferred to a barge that plied its way upstream until the river disappeared into swampy shallows. The last two hours consisted of a bone-jarring ride in an ancient Willys Jeep along a road built of railway ties.

The intense heat of the rain forest produced a greenhouse effect, and the bugs grew bloated on her thickened blood. It was more penance than she had bargained for. Yet the deeper she penetrated the jungle the more quickly the centuries seemed to slip away. Rebecca recalled the times when Max would take her along on some of his expeditions into the interior. Then, too, she had felt, in a way she couldn't articulate, that she was really coming home.

"Welcome."

Dallas Gibson looked exactly as Rebecca had remembered him, dressed in jungle fatigues topped off with that old Australian slouch hat. His face was even more weathered than she remembered. His chestnut hair curled over his jacket collar, and his soft hazel eyes studied her thoughtfully.

Rebecca recalled the agony in those eyes when Dallas had tried to explain her father's accident. How he hadn't defended himself when she had vented her fury on him, accusing him of being responsible for what happened to Max. . . . How she had never told him how wrong she had been.

"You're probably exhausted," Dallas said, helping her out of the Willys. "It's only a couple hundred yards along the trail to the excavations. Supper is on."

Dallas took the lead, moving swiftly and surely along what Rebecca assumed was a path. She couldn't see it and took care to follow his steps exactly. After innumerable twists and turns

Dallas came to an abrupt halt. When Rebecca reached his side she found herself looking into a shallow valley that cradled a ruined empire.

"Pusilha," Dallas said softly. "This was your father's discovery. Later on it became his life."

Rebecca was overwhelmed by the majesty of the spectacle before her. In the dying afternoon sun the buildings, many of them still partially covered by vines and brush, rose from the earth like glittering palaces.

"Would you like to walk through some of the city?" Dallas asked.

They began at the Ball Court. Shaped like a capital *I*, it was two hundred seventy-two feet long, ninety-nine wide, and was flanked by sloping tiered walls. Here the traditional Mayan game of pok-a-tok had been played; two teams of young men tried to put a hard rubber ball through a stone hoop set on its side and imbedded high in the stone walls around the court. At the top of the walls Dallas pointed out the small temples that were being cleared of undergrowth. These were the vantage points from which nobles started the elaborate rituals prior to the games, viewed the contest, and oversaw the concluding ceremonies.

"In some eras of Mayan history these ceremonies included the sacrifice of a single male from the losers' ranks," Dallas told her. "These fellas didn't take defeat lightly."

As they crossed the Great Plaza, Dallas explained the significance of the Castle, a four-sided pyramid seventy-eight feet high, dedicated to the worship of Kukulcan, the Plumed Serpent.

"The Castle is incontrovertible evidence that the Mayan astronomers had a sophisticated way to measure time. On the spring and fall equinoxes, March twenty-first and September twenty-first, on the dark side of the ninety-one-step staircase, a series of triangles can be seen forming an undulating serpent. It descends in March and ascends in September. This is an indication of just how precisely the Mayans not only built the pyramid but how carefully they chose its location."

Dallas took Rebecca across to the Temple of the Jaguars and Platform of the Eagles and showed her how slowly and painstakingly archaeological excavation had to proceed. Beneath a huge statue of the reclining god Chac Mool, he ducked into a tunnel lit only by a string of pale yellow lights. Moving past large straw baskets used to carry out dirt, Rebecca stepped into a series of subterranean rooms.

"The first find of its kind," Dallas said, his disembodied voice floating in the gloom.

He shone a flashlight on the stone benches, drainage troughs, and hearths that surrounded a rectangle that was a ritual bath.

"I've long suspected that certain ceremonies required purification rites," he said, playing the light over walls inlaid with perfectly preserved inscriptions. "Now I'm sure of it."

"How many people lived here?" Rebecca asked as they made their way outside.

It seemed unbelievable to her that Pusilha, which was equivalent in size to a small town, could have existed in the middle of such dense jungle.

"This may give you an idea," Dallas replied, and helped her up the steps of the Castle.

To the north, in an area half the size of a football field, Rebecca saw a mammoth plaster-lined trough, only partially excavated.

"This was the central reservoir, supplemented by bottle-shaped underground pits called chultuns as well as an elaborate drainage and aqueduct system. Judging by the reservoir's size, we estimate Pusilha's population to have been around thirty thousand people."

As the last light fled the sky, Dallas guided Rebecca to one of three bunkhouse-style dwellings on the perimeter of the excavations.

"It's not much as far as labs go but it's enough for field work."

In the makeshift laboratory-storage vault, Rebecca saw the treasure trove Pusilha was yielding. There were jade mosaic masks, part of funerary offerings, the eyes and mouths inlaid with shell and pyrite. The inscriptions on a jade jar offered clues to the identity of the nobleman who had commissioned it. A vaulted sepulcher, removed intact, had yielded ornaments, vases depicting court scenes, and mythological tableaux, as well as a polychrome ceramic censer.

As she touched each piece Rebecca felt the ghosts of Pusilha slowly coming to life. Running her fingers over the embossed inscriptions, she heard, somewhere in the core of her being, the ritual incantations of the craftsmen as they labored. Here, as the howler monkeys greeted the night with screeches, Rebecca sensed the presence of men and women whose images recalled her mother and whose blood flowed through her veins.

Dallas guided her to the adjoining bunkhouse and there introduced her to the six-man team that comprised the archaeological field unit of the University of Chicago.

"I managed to convince the university that to abandon Pusilha after all the work that had gone into it would be sacrilege," he explained. "Fortunately there were those in the department who had been following Max's efforts and supported me. With the funding we've hired fifty more Indians to help with the digs."

Dallas ladled out stew into an aluminum pan and Rebecca, who hadn't eaten since morning, devoured it. As the archaeologists turned in for the night, she found herself alone with Dallas.

Rebecca clamped her hands around the chipped enamel cup.

"I came because I wanted to apologize," she said in a low voice. "That day at the hospital, everything I said . . . ."

Rebecca hadn't known just how deep the trust and relationship between Dallas Gibson and her father had been. While she was on her way to California, Dallas was headed for the jungles to oversee the excavations at Pusilha which, according to Jewel, Max considered the most important project of his entire life.

"It was a terrible time for you," Dallas said, his hand resting on Rebecca's shoulder. "I can understand why you thought the accident was my fault."

"Then why did you help me?" Rebecca demanded. "Why did you go to your father and tell him how Andrew Stoughton had stolen everything. . . ."

Dallas rose and lit another oil lamp.

"Your father meant a great deal to me," he said slowly. "He was an extraordinary man, not because of what he possessed or had achieved but because of his compassion and sensibility. What happened to you after he was murdered was a travesty. I owed it to him to try to help."

"Why was this place so important to my father?" Rebecca asked suddenly.

Dallas looked at her quizzically. "Max didn't tell you anything about Pusilha?"

Rebecca shook her head. "I knew he funded archaeological digs around the Angelines but I never suspected he was so involved in them."

"Yes, he was," Dallas told her. "Especially this one. Rebecca, it was here at Pusilha that Max met your mother, Apho Hel."

For the tribe that dwelled in the most southerly shadow of the Maya Mountains, near a place it called Pusilha, the coming of the year 1943 held no significance. These true descendants of the Maya continued to measure time and seasons as their ancestors had, dividing both into *tuns, katuns, baktuns,* and *pictuns.* They knew little of the great holocaust that had overtaken the world, and existed as had their forefathers: hunting the jaguar, boar, and snake in the jungle, fishing in the streams, taking maize from the land, and trading with middlemen who brought the pelts and skins out of the rain forests.

The tribe was a remnant, an ever-shrinking island in the midst of an encroaching sea called progress. Some of the young men had been given leave to work in the mines a white man had opened near Pusilha. The conditions were strict: They were not permitted to live in the camp but each night had to return four miles to the village. Those who left the village for the towns were never allowed to return. Women who succumbed to the overtures of the traders or hunters were banished. The tribe fiercely guarded its solitude, allowing marriage only within itself or the half dozen remaining tribes scattered throughout the wilds of Guatemala, British Honduras, and the Angelines. Only in this way could survival be guaranteed, the purity of the bloodlines preserved.

There was one woman who stood apart from both the men and women of her tribe. She was called Apho Hel, after the sister of Pacal, who had ruled in Palenque between the years A.D. 615 and 683.

Apho Hel was considered a true descendant not only of the Maya but of the Olmec, who preceded them. Like her mother and all the females of her line, she was the custodian of her people's history, passed down orally from generation to generation. She was a symbol of the tribe's purity, her blood to be mixed only with that of a youth of similar lineage when she reached her seventeenth birthday, which fell this year. She would bear children until another female was born in order that the link joining present, past, and future be maintained.

It wasn't only tradition and its responsibilities that set Apho Hel apart from the other women. Unlike most Mayans, Apho Hel was tall. Her bold and adventuresome spirit bore none of the submissiveness found in her sisters. Because she ventured from the foothills, Apho Hel knew more about the world beyond her village than most men did. She roamed the mountains and valleys, watching as each year the roads cut deeper and deeper into her forests. She saw her tribesmen journey into the mining camps, some to fell trees for new roads, others to disappear into the pits. By night she sat under a sky whose stars were blotted out by the crimson fires from smelters and open hearths which turned rock into liquid and liquid into gold.

Apho Hel understood better than anyone in her tribe that the days of isolation were almost at an end. As the woman who was a living memory, she sensed that the tragedies of the past were about to return in a different form but with no less virulence.

Once, the Maya had only nature to contend with: droughts, hurricanes, and outbreaks of pestilence. Her people had endured these and persevered, slowly returning to prosperity. But then came the Spaniards, with their swords, horses, and priests. The soldiers taught the Maya what it meant to be slaves, to be worked to death for gold. Their priests desecrated temples, burned the ancient codices, and tried to destroy that bond between the people and their gods.

They had almost succeeded. Because of her standing, Apho Hel alone was privy to where the last buried cities were to be found. On certain feast days she made pilgrimages to them, journeying many miles to stand before altars and monuments scarcely visible in the jungle growth to offer prayers to the gods of her ancestors.

The jungle had beaten back the Spaniards and in time covered the remains of glory beneath an impenetrable canopy. But neither her mother nor her forebears could have imagined that one day men would find ways to penetrate even the densest rain forest, moving slowly but inexorably toward the last untouched remains of a once-great civilization.

Apho Hel understood that as soon as the roads reached Pusilha her tribe would have to retreat still deeper into the forests. One by one men would give up hunting and trapping and enter the mines. Bereft of their men, the women would turn to the white and black men, the Indians and mestizos who came as workers and overseers. Her tribe, and all the others scattered throughout the rain forest, had no protection—from anyone, against anything that might be done to them.

Even in the face of such circumstances, survival might have been possible for another generation or two. But there was something as insidious as the encroachment from without that was attacking the tribe from within.

As the numbers of her people dwindled, intermarriage among the ones remaining multiplied. The effort to keep the strain pure caused offspring to be born blind, with gross deformities, or to die within a few hours of birth. Although the priests claimed such aberrations were the will of the gods, Apho Hel had seen too many tragically impaired children born to brother and sister or father and daughter to believe them. Having been promised to a first cousin, Apho Hel shuddered in revulsion when she imagined what her own sons or daughters would look like if they survived.

This fear weighed heavily upon her as she entered her seventeenth year. As the day of her marriage drew near, Apho Hel understood that the ways of the past could not help her or her people any longer. A miracle was needed.

It was from the men who labored in the mines that Apho Hel first heard of the white man who stood apart from others by virtue of his strength and skills. It was said that he worked as hard as any laborer, from dawn until dusk, that he placed himself among men, not above them.

No one was ever beaten at the mines where the man called Max ruled. His workers lived in dry huts, their bellies full, their pockets heavy with the reward for their labors. Yet this was a man whose riches were too vast to be counted, who had taken out more gold from a single vein than Pacal had had removed in his entire reign.

Intrigued by such tales, Apho Hel one day slipped close to the mines to see the man leaving the camp. As she followed him into the jungle her trepidation grew. The man called Max seemed sure of where he was going, moving swiftly over trails Apho Hel had thought only she knew. To her horror the man did not pause until he reached the ruined city of Pusilha three hours later.

Apho Hel had seen what had happened to the other great Mayan cities throughout the country. The white explorers came and, using Indian laborers, peeled back the protective layers of jungle growth to expose the ruins. The tombs were opened and their treasures removed. Whole walls inlaid with hieroglyphics and frescoes were cut from temples and rolled away. Monuments, statues, and altars were ripped from their pedestals and carried off until finally nothing but gaping holes and yawning crevices remained, to be populated by snakes and scorpions, like some dusty skull.

But this man was different. Apho Hel watched as he walked slowly about the ruins, hacking away at the undergrowth where it obscured a pillar or obelisk so that he might examine the piece more carefully. There was a reverence to his labor, a respect for what he stood in the midst of. Apho Hel sensed it in the careful way in which he ran his hands over the ancient stone, fingers tracing the outlines of hieroglyphics she knew he could not interpret.

For many days Apho Hel returned to Pusilha, each time expecting that the man had brought someone with him. But the man always returned alone.

Apho Hel remembered stories from an earlier time, when one of her ancestors had been called upon to save her people from catastrophe. This priestess had found her answer in the form of a stranger whose intercession had ultimately prevented a tragedy. Could it be the past was repeating itself?

Apho Hel spent many days among the ruined temples seeking the answer. When she was certain of what she must do, she revealed herself to this new stranger called Max, waiting for him by the sacred *cenote* where priestesses long-dead had murmured their incantations to the god Itzamna.

"As his mining empire fanned out deeper and deeper into the jungle, Max became fascinated by the stories of lost Mayan cities told to him by the Indian and mestizo workers," Dallas Gibson continued. "He traveled to the excavations at Altun Ha, Tikal, and Chichen Itza, spending weeks among the monuments, learning what he could from the archaeologists working there.

"Max soon discovered there was a good reason that so few cities had been unearthed. The scholars should have thought like prospectors, concentrating on where the gold and precious stones for the temples would have come from. He was convinced the cities had to have been built near the mines so that the material could be easily transported to the finished sites. He put his theory into practice and found Pusilha."

"And Apho Hel," Rebecca murmured.

She was intoxicated by Dallas's narration. Every word was like another lamp being turned on, its glow illuminating a little more of a mysterious past.

"Do you know what happened to Apho Hel after she met my father?"

Dallas nodded. Sensing his embarrassment, Rebecca reached out and touched his hand.

"Please, you must understand how much this means to me."

"Your mother was an exceptional woman," Dallas said. "She was of pure blood and already promised in marriage to a cousin. Yet she knew that inbreeding would only hasten the destruction of her people, whose life, customs, and heritage were already being threatened. When she met Max she realized he was the one person who could not only insure her lineage but also preserve her history. In defiance of custom she gave herself to your father so that their child would bind him to her. You are the continuation of Apho Hel's line, the cord to her immortality and that of her race.''

Rebecca's mind was spinning. Why? Why hadn't Max ever told her this?

As though he divined her question, Dallas carried on.

"Several weeks after your father met Apho Hel she disappeared. Max was beside himself. He did everything in his power to try to find her but she and her people had vanished.

"Eight months later, at Skyscape, Max was visited by two members of Apho Hel's tribe. They told him they knew of his relationship with Apho Hel and how she had betrayed her responsibility to her people. They said Max would never see her again. Before they left, they gave him the baby, illegitimate in their eyes, that she had delivered.

"Max couldn't believe what was happening. He pleaded with the Mayans to tell him if the woman he loved was alive. He promised them anything they wanted if only they would bring her to him. He was told to forget Apho Hel had ever existed."

"But he never did," Rebecca whispered, remembering the life-size portrait of the woman in her father's library. "Even after he knew she was dead."

"Dead? Max never had any reason—"

Dallas stopped himself but realized he had already said too much.

"Never had any reason for what?" Rebecca demanded.

Dallas shook his head. "Look, maybe there were things Max never told me—"

"*Never had any reason for what?*" Rebecca repeated fiercely. "Tell me, Dallas!"

He stared up at her, his eyes full of apology.

"To believe she was dead," he whispered.

Dallas's words flew on the sparks and smoke of the fire. When Rebecca looked up at the sky she saw embers disappearing into the night, extinguished.

Gone . . . Just like everything I've believed for all these years. Everything Max wanted me to believe . . .

The enormity of what Dallas had revealed left her in utter confusion. She no longer knew what was true. . . . Except that in the midst of chaos a new hope was being born. That her mother might still be alive somewhere. That she was not alone.

"Please tell me the rest, Dallas," Rebecca said, and added, "It's not your fault Max kept this from me. But if I know as much as he told you, maybe I can understand why."

"There isn't much more," Dallas said softly. "All I can tell you is that Max continued to search for Apho Hel until the day he died. He would disappear into the jungle for weeks at a time, never telling anyone where he was going. He didn't even take guides. He never gave up hope of finding Apho Hel. He was possessed by the dream of someday bringing her home to her daughter."

Rebecca remembered her father's haunted expression when he had shown her Apho Hel's portrait for the first time, how his voice had cracked when he had told her who Apho Hel was.

How many other nights, countless nights, like that had there been? How many hours had he spent sitting in front of that image, alone, remembering, planning, hoping . . . ?

And every time he looked at me he must have suffered because he saw her reflection. He told me she was dead because he didn't want to share the pain of hope with me. . . .

"There's one last thing," Dallas said. "The reason Max spent millions of dollars on archaeological digs. It wasn't only because of his love for the Angelines and the desire to preserve a priceless heritage. He did it for Apho Hel. When they were lovers he promised her that the cities of her people would never disappear, that he would always protect them. He swore to her that they would always stand in the sun."

When Rebecca heard these words, the final lamp in that dark corridor flickered and came to life. Her destiny, which had always been out of reach somewhere in the shadows, was at last revealed.

"There's something I want to show you," Dallas said.

He went into one of the bunkhouses and returned with a small chamois bag which he handed Rebecca.

"Open it."

The five jade pieces poured into her hand, the flames setting the green stones ablaze. Rebecca carefully examined the inscriptions on each one.

"Max was carrying these when he came out of the jungle . . . just before his accident," Dallas explained. "I found the bag in the *cenote*, after Max was on his way to the hospital. I know I should have given it to you but—"

"Do you have any idea what the inscriptions mean?" Rebecca interrupted him.

Dallas shook his head. "I've never seen anything like them. I don't know where he could have found them. Was there any reference to them in his private papers?"

"None that I've come across," Rebecca said. "But since he spent so much time at Pusilha, wouldn't they have come from here?"

"Perhaps," Dallas said slowly, hefting the jade. "If you don't mind, I'd like to hold on to these and continue working on the inscriptions. I might come across a clue that will help me decipher them."

"I hope so," Rebecca said fervently. "I think the stones were very important to Max. And I think I know why—"

She paused and looked at Dallas.

"There's one more thing I have to know. Did Max let anyone know that he believed Apho Hel might still be alive? Possibly Jewel?"

"Jewel might have guessed at what Max was doing, but I'm sure he never told her, or anyone else, outright."

Rebecca nodded. She had thought as much. Jewel would have accepted the story of Rebecca's mother being dead. Just as she herself had . . .

Rebecca looked past the flames at the golden city below her, sparkling under the brilliance of the floodlights.

"And so it will!" she whispered.

Dallas drew closer. "Will what?"

"Apho Hel's city. It will always stand in the sun. I promise!"

· 20 ·

Jewel was quick to notice the change in Rebecca when she returned from Pusilha, the heightened sense of purpose and excitement. She wondered what had happened between Rebecca and Dallas Gibson.

"Tell me about Max's first strike," Rebecca said at supper the next evening.

"Lord, I tol' you that story hundreds of times!" Jewel protested.

"Then one more time won't hurt, will it?"

Jewel laughed. The tale was the cornerstone of Max McHenry's legend. Having made six expeditions into the interior, Max was broke. Nonetheless he was convinced that one more attempt would take him to the eldorado he knew had to be there. The only person who had had any belief in him, and who had advanced the money to finance his dream, had been Jewel.

Max believed in himself, in his instinct, thought Rebecca.

"That's exactly what I have to do," she finished aloud.

"Do what, girl?" Jewel asked.

Rebecca reached for Jewel's hand and held it tightly.

"Have the courage of my convictions," she replied enigmatically.

The next morning Rebecca wrote a detailed letter to Ramsey Peet outlining her plan. She closed by asking the attorney to check several points of Angelinian law for her. This wouldn't be a problem since Ramsey, because of his long association with Max, had a complete set of Angelinian legal texts in New York.

Another letter was sent to Bix and Torrey, specifying exactly the kind of information she needed from them.

Rebecca spent the first two weeks of October shuttling between Jewel's home and Windemere and Tongue Keys. She covered every square foot of the two islands, surveying the beachfront, checking for freshwater springs, measuring the depths of the *quebradas* that ran between the coral necklace of reefs.

She made notes on the vegetation, discovering banana, pawpaw, coconut, and plantain growing wild. Two hundred yards offshore she found hundreds of colonies of spiny lobster.

Rebecca became a familiar face in the Angeline City Registry Office. Mystified clerks dug through the records of the Ministry of Economic Affairs that dealt with the registration of merchants and promotion of industrial development. From the Ministry of Works and Utilities Rebecca got copies of statutes pertaining to island planning, development of beaches, water, sewage, and road requirements. Publicly available documents gave her a breakdown of all the hotels and guesthouses in the Angelines, the gross income taken in through tourism, and the places from which the visitors had come.

When Rebecca had as much information as she needed, she invited Bones Ainsley to dinner. Over blackened redfish she outlined her plan to the policeman and Jewel.

"Well, what do you think? Will it work?"

Ainsley, who had listened carefully to Rebecca, referred to some of her research.

"You don't need to refresh your memory, Bones Ainsley," Jewel said gravely. "Why don't you just go ahead and tell her."

Rebecca's heart sank.

"Maybe I didn't explain the details clearly enough," Rebecca started to say.

"You explained enough," Jewel told her. "Now you listen to the man."

"It can work!" Rebecca said, ignoring her. "The only thing that's missing is—"

"Of course it will work," Bones said easily, leaning back and drawing on his pipe.

Rebecca stared at him blankly. "What did you say?"

"It will work," Bones repeated, and cracked a slow smile.

"You're not just saying that, are you?" Rebecca demanded suspiciously.

She looked from Bones to Jewel and saw the truth in their expressions.

"My God, you're not!"

The day before she was to leave for New York, Rebecca received a telephone call from Norris Darling, a prominent Angelinian attorney in Stann Creek Town.

"It's about your properties, Miss McHenry," Darling explained. "Specifically the two keys, Windemere and Tongue, as well as the land outside Angeline City. I happen to have a party interested in buying them. Would it be convenient for you to meet me at the Jockey Club to discuss the matter?''

"No, it would not," Rebecca told him shortly. "But I will see you at the Perch in Angeline City, one o'clock sharp.''

When Rebecca told Jewel about the call she said, "He's a wreckers' boy, that one. Whatever he wants to see you about, it can't be good for you.''

"Maybe we can turn the tables," Rebecca said thoughtfully.

Norris Darling was a Carib black, tall and debonair, who proudly displayed the trappings of his association with the wreckers: three-piece London-tailored suit, gold cuff links and tie clip, and an ostentatious watch. Yet these accouterments couldn't hide his fawning, sycophantic character, which, Rebecca suspected, had been instrumental in his appointment.

"It's so good of you to see me on such short notice," Darling began.

"My time is limited," Rebecca replied curtly.

Mildly flustered, Darling plunged ahead.

"I have a client, a recluse actually, who is seeking some very private property. He's seen aerial photographs of the two keys and thinks they suit his requirements perfectly. He's prepared to make a generous offer.''

"And just who is this client?" Rebecca asked.

"Ah, he insists on anonymity, Miss McHenry. However, I can assure you of his financial rectitude. You'll have your money deposited to the financial institution of your choice.''

"Really? What about Skyscape? Why does your client want it?''

"He feels it would be the perfect location for his daughter's home," Darling replied smoothly. "She's going to be a bride soon.''

"How wonderful. What kind of price are you talking about?"

"I'm authorized to offer twenty thousand dollars," Darling said reverently.

"Mr. Darling!" Rebecca exclaimed. "That certainly indicates your client's financial rectitude. I presume you mean U.S. dollars.''

Darling wet his lips. The Angelinian dollar was worth only twenty cents U.S.

"Of course.''

"No deal.''

Darling blinked rapidly. "I beg your pardon?"

"Both of us know the properties are worth a lot more than

that,'' Rebecca said with a shrug. "Unless your client is prepared to go higher . . .''

"I might convince him to go to twenty-five thousand," Darling said cautiously.

"Don't insult me!" Rebecca snapped at him. "I know what Silas Lambros can afford!''

"Mr. Lambros isn't the sort—''

Norris Darling clamped his mouth shut. His fawning expression dissolved into hostility.

"Isn't the sort to what?" Rebecca asked softly, her eyes boring in his. "Tell me, Mr. Darling, why did he send a messenger boy? Is he afraid to come to me himself?''

"You had better take what he's willing to give you," Darling hissed.

"Are you threatening me?" Rebecca said clearly.

Ole, the owner of the Perch, moved his three-hundred-pound bulk over to their table.

"This fellow bein' a problem, Miss McHenry?" he rasped.

"He's just leaving," Rebecca said, never taking her eyes off Darling. "You can tell Silas Lambros that nothing of mine is for sale—to him or anyone else. Not now, not ever!''

As she watched Darling beat an undignified retreat, Rebecca realized her skin was crawling. Lambros wouldn't stop here. This had been only the opening shot.

Norris Darling had no choice but to report the result of his conversation with Rebecca McHenry to his principal. It was a task that caused him to gnaw his cuticles raw.

"I wouldn't be too concerned," Andrew Stoughton said, speaking from London. "I expected as much. You didn't give her any indication I was the buyer?''

"None," Darling assured him hastily. "She immediately assumed it was Mr. Lambros.''

"You did well, Norris," Stoughton told him. "Continue to keep an eye on her. We'll have what we want in a week or so.''

After he hung up, Andrew Stoughton made an entry in his private diary, reminding himself to cable the Angelinian Ministry of Revenue in six days.

Rebecca, Andrew reflected, should have taken the offer. He had instructed Darling to go as high as fifty thousand dollars for the properties. Not that he had really believed Rebecca would accept. The point of the exercise had been threefold: Rebecca would have been expecting some kind of reaction on the part of

Tyne & Wear to her return to the Angelines. The offer to buy her out was an indication her presence had not gone unnoticed.

The ploy also had the advantage of distracting Rebecca, lulling her into a false sense of security by letting her think the properties belonged to her free and clear.

Finally, by not denying that Silas Lambros was behind the offer, Norris Darling had turned Rebecca's assumption into a hard certainty in her own mind. Which meant that she would be on guard against the wrong person, at the wrong time.

Andrew made some swift calculations and reckoned that by the end of the following week Windemere and Tongue Keys as well as Skyscape would be his for the princely sum of $208.47.

The council of war was held on the last Wednesday of October. Because the date coincided with Torrey Stewart's birthday, everyone agreed to meet at the Rio Grande, a restaurant on West Tenth Street off Sixth which specialized in southwest cuisine.

Rebecca had flown in five days earlier. Returning to the familiar haunt on Perry Street, she had divided her time between Bix and Torrey, and Lauren and Ramsey. She argued her case before them, listened to their criticisms, and prepared detailed rebuttals. She carefully noted suggestions and quickly tracked down additional information. Her conviction that she was right grew with every question and challenge thrust at her.

Then why am I sitting here quaking in my boots, she thought, watching the others devour baked beans, cornbread, Rebel Fire chili, and the Rio Grande's specialty, spit-roasted pig. The climax of the evening came when the waiters wheeled out Torrey's birthday cake, shaped like a bottle of Lone Star beer.

"I want to thank y'all for the good times," Torrey said after blowing out the candles. "Even my momma would have been proud of the chow.

"But now there's something more important than a birthday we got to discuss."

He looked at Rebecca.

"Rebecca here has spent days trying to convince me of her scheme. Truth is, I had some doubts. But not anymore. Becky, darlin', you can count me and GoSee in on this."

Before Rebecca could react, Bix reached across and grabbed her hand.

"Me too!"

"Lauren and I have discussed this at length," Ramsey said from the other side of the table. "There are a great many pitfalls, but if anyone can get around them, it's you, my dear. You have our wholehearted support—and this.''

He passed Rebecca an envelope and winked. ''Go ahead, open it.''

The check was for fifty thousand dollars.

''I can't accept this, Ramsey,'' Rebecca said, unashamedly wiping tears from her eyes.

''But, honey, you need working capital,'' Lauren objected.

Rebecca glanced at the curious faces around her.

''I have it,'' she said. ''The irony is that without knowing, Andrew Stoughton provided it.''

The next morning Rebecca was early for her appointment at the august premises of Creighton and McLean.

Tucked between La Vieille Russie and a philatelic dealer on Fifth Avenue, the shop occupied an unparalleled position among New York's great jewelry houses. Far smaller than either Tiffany or van Cleef and Arpels, it catered to a clientele that considered the Big Two to be patronized by the hoi polloi. C & M creations were unique, each one commissioned by a particular individual for a specific occasion. Unlike its competitors, the firm made no attempt to carry midrange stones. Its buyers scoured the world for only the very best, and often the largest, examples of any particular gem. Ariel Creighton, the firm's cofounder, personally greeted Rebecca when she was announced by the husky young man dressed in the C & M uniform, a morning coat.

''It's so good to see you, my dear,'' he said, bowing slightly. ''Come, let us sit.''

Ariel Creighton, all five feet of him, moved off like a penguin with a shock of white hair. As she followed, Rebecca glanced at the glass display cases. Each one held only three stones, a universe of exploding color set in distinctive arrangements.

Rebecca couldn't help but smile at the trompe l'oeil. Many years ago, when she had been here with her father, Max and Ariel had chuckled over the fact that each gem was only a replica—perfectly executed—of the true stone held in the vaults below the street. The ''ghosts,'' as they were called, were so flawless that clients were almost always surprised that the stone they examined and the one they took delivery of weren't one and the same.

Creighton ushered Rebecca to an oxblood leather wing chair in his domain in the back half of the store. The ancient Persian rugs, illuminated paintings by Dutch masters, and beveled-glass lamps combined to form the impression of an aesthete's den rather than an office where hundreds of thousands of dollars changed hands over a few discreet words.

"I must say, my dear, you're looking exceptionally well."

Rebecca accepted the compliment with a smile. A long-standing McHenry customer, Creighton had been one of the first to send his condolences when Max was killed. Discretion—plus his friendship with Max—were the reasons Rebecca had chosen to come to him.

"Ariel, I have a delicate matter to put to you," Rebecca said.

Teddy-bear eyes sparkled behind rimless glasses. "I'm intrigued."

Rebecca removed a jeweler's case from her purse and placed it before the dealer. As Creighton opened the lid the reflection of the rose-diamond ring Andrew had given her cast its glow over his glasses.

"A marvelous example of the Type Two A," he said, not touching the stone yet totally lost in appreciation of it. "I would guess the band at five hundred fifty nanometers. The amount of manganese is exceptional and so, therefore, is this particular hue of pink. I don't believe I've ever seen anything quite like it— which, of course, surprises me."

Creighton closed the lid gently, as though regretting to have to eclipse such a brilliant creation.

"I want to sell it," Rebecca told him.

Ariel Creighton pursed his lips.

"I can tell from the setting the gold used was Max's," he said at last. "Are you sure you want to part with it?"

"This wasn't a gift from my father."

"I see," Creighton said. "Nonetheless it would be highly unusual for me to purchase something that has already been sold once. Even a gem as tempting as this one."

"I appreciate that. But who else can do justice to it?"

Creighton inclined his head. "You have obviously inherited Max's talent for *le mot juste*. I will give you thirty-five thousand for it, in cash, immediately. The offer stands for"—he checked the ornate Lefarge clock behind him—"the next sixty seconds."

Rebecca couldn't believe what she was hearing.

"It's got to be worth more than that!"

"Yes, I'm quite sure it is," Ariel Creighton said, not taking his eyes off the sweep of the second hand. "But not to me."

Rebecca felt her head spinning. She hadn't bothered to have the ring appraised elsewhere and consequently wasn't sure how much it would fetch. The thought never entered her mind, because of Creighton's long-standing business relationship with Max. She knew that it had cost Andrew far more. That night at the Peets' apartment, when Andrew had presented it to her, Ramsey had taken her aside and advised her to make certain the ring was insured. Lloyds had underwritten a policy of $100,000.

"Why are you trying to cheat me?" Rebecca asked at last.

"If that is how you feel, you're perfectly free to take the piece to another house," Creighton told her. "After all, my dear, business *is* business. Nothing personal, you understand."

For an instant Rebecca was tempted to take him at his word. But she needed the money now and there was no guarantee that she would get a better offer anywhere else—or receive the cash immediately.

Business is business.

Wendell Coltraine's face flashed into Rebecca's mind. The head of Star Lines had also wanted to cheat her by getting out of his contract with McHenry Enterprises. But then she had had Andrew beside her. Andrew, who had used blackmail to make Coltraine see the error of his ways.

If I'm going to survive, I'll have to recognize the thief who hides behind the three-piece suit, impeccable manners, and years of so-called friendship.

"Give me the money."

The jeweler's case disappeared off Creighton's desktop in a blur, replaced by stacks of crisp banknotes.

"Sign the bill of sale, please."

Rebecca scrawled her signature, eager to get away from the man.

"You wouldn't be interested in parting with that piece, would you?" the jeweler asked, looking covetously at the sea horse.

Rebecca was tempted. Once, the sea horse had been her continual reminder of Andrew, a talisman that protected her from evil. Now she continued to wear it without really understanding why.

It's different, Rebecca thought, fingering the diamonds along the spine. *It reminds me of everything that's happened, of things that I'll never allow to happen to me again.*

"It's not for sale," she said coldly.

Ariel Creighton laughed softly. "My dear, *everything* is for sale, sometime or other."

*   *   *

As he had promised Rebecca, Bones Ainsley was keeping tabs on Norris Darling. The policeman's eyes and ears across the city monitored the dandy's activities and reported faithfully every day. As soon as a pattern became apparent, Ainsley made a few inquiries himself.

For several days Ainsley puzzled over the lawyer's frequent visits to a particular government office. He spoke with the clerks in the department but according to them, what Darling wanted to know about Rebecca McHenry's properties was information in the public domain. With all the reports in front of him, Ainsley spent hours trying to discover the reason for Darling's behavior. The fact that it seemed so innocent made it suspicious.

Early one morning Ainsley made the connection. Using the authority of his office, he instructed the long distance operator to free a circuit and connect him to New York. In the Peets' apartment the maid answered, telling Ainsley no one was at home. Ramsey Peet's secretary informed him the attorney was in conference at another firm.

"Then you had better give me *that* number!" Ainsley thundered.

As the secretary searched for it, Ainsley agonized that it might already be too late. Given the time difference between New York and the Angelines, he didn't think there was any way Rebecca could avoid the silent but deadly trap Andrew Stoughton had laid for her.

Norris Darling arrived at the Registry Office in Angeline City at a quarter to five, fifteen minutes before the end of the working day. He could have come earlier, but since he knew Rebecca McHenry was still out of the country, he had enjoyed a leisurely lunch followed by a memorable siesta in the company of his new secretary.

If Darling needed to salve his conscience, all he had to remember was the contents of Andrew Stoughton's cable. An Angelinian property owner had until five o'clock today to pay any property taxes that were in arrears. If Rebecca McHenry didn't show up by then, her properties automatically went on the auction block. However, according to Angelinian law, if a third party paid the back taxes the minute the time limit expired, the property reverted to him. Stoughton had made it very clear Darling was to be that third party.

At precisely five o'clock, just as the clerk was closing the wicket, Darling stepped up, slipping his papers beneath the grill. He had gone over them three times, making certain every detail was in order. Andrew Stoughton's reaction to incompetence was as merciless as it was legendary."

"But the taxes have been paid," the clerk said.

Norris Darling smiled confidently. "Why don't you check again? They couldn't have been paid."

"You tell that to the lady over there."

Darling looked over his shoulder at the plump black woman wearing a yellow kerchief. In the middle of her smile he saw a gold tooth.

Jewel walked over to him and held up a receipt for taxes paid on behalf of Rebecca McHenry for Windemere and Tongue Keys as well as Skyscape. The registrar's stamp was dated four thirty-seven, eight minutes before Norris Darling had come in.

"You give this to your bossman," Jewel said sweetly, cramming a telegram into Darling's breast pocket.

Too stunned to stop her, Darling grabbed the yellow flimsy addressed to him.

NOT THIS TIME. R.M.

PART THREE

————————————————————

NEW YORK
THE ANGELINES
LONDON
1963–1970

· 21 ·

Norris Darling's attempt to buy her properties out from under her infused Rebecca with a sense of urgency. Even though there were a hundred and one questions and details that had to be answered and looked after, Rebecca was determined to go ahead with the first phase of her plan. Darling's ploy was a clear signal of just how offensive Silas Lambros and his collaborator, Andrew Stoughton, found her presence to be. Rebecca had no doubt the two men were determined to run the last of the McHenrys out of the Angelines once and for all.

The sooner my vision becomes reality, Rebecca thought, the harder it will be for them to stop me!

The day after she received Jewel's confirmation that the property taxes had been paid, Rebecca made an appointment with Eric Walker. This time her reception was markedly different.

The gray-uniformed doorman had obviously been told to expect her. When he ushered her past the rows of wizened Dickensian scribes, not one pair of eyes took any notice. Only Eric Walker's warm smile and the faint concern peeking out from behind the welcome in his eyes hadn't changed.

"It's good to see you again, Rebecca," he said, taking her hand in both of his and holding it a fraction longer than politeness dictated.

"You too," Rebecca answered.

She remembered how Eric had intervened on her behalf at the Gotham Club, shaming the two members who had been gossiping about her. She felt that same aura of protection and concern envelop her now. Eric Walker, she decided, was a comfortable man, whose self-assurance invited trust and confidence. Rebecca was sorry she had refused his invitation to meet over lunch, insisting instead that they talk in his office.

"There's still time to change your mind," Eric said, running a hand through his coal-black curly hair.

"About what?"

"Lunch."

Rebecca laughed and blushed at the same time.

"Maybe after we've finished."

The banker spread out his hands in mock resignation.

"My shareholders thank you for keeping my nose to the grindstone. How may the Walker Bank assist you?"

There it is again! That old-fashioned courtesy.

"I want to open an account," Rebecca said, reaching into her handbag. "With this."

She placed a manila envelope with the Peet, Burroughs, and Calhoun logo on Walker's desk. The banker frowned, hefted the envelope, and noted the wax seal bearing the law firm's imprint.

"Cash?"

"Cash."

"You didn't by any chance break into Ramsey's piggy bank?"

"Not quite!"

"Your word's good enough for me," Eric said, depressing a lever on the intercom and speaking to his secretary. "Marjorie, would you bring in the standard new account forms, please?"

He turned to Rebecca. "I assume the account will be in your name."

"No, McHenry Enterprises. Ramsey Peet will have the articles of incorporation and the rest of the paperwork delivered by the close of business today."

Eric Walker didn't take his eyes off her as he instructed his secretary what name to type in.

"Would you mind telling me what this is all about," he asked quietly.

"I'm bringing McHenry Enterprises back to life," Rebecca said, signing the papers and handing the secretary the envelope.

"Intriguing," Eric commented. "But what do you propose to do with it?"

Rebecca took a deep breath and began.

At first she had been reluctant to discuss the details of her venture with anyone except the people closest to her. Ramsey Peet had persuaded her otherwise.

"A good banker is one of the underpinnings of any sound business venture," he had counseled her. "Ideally he should be someone you've worked with before, a man with enough influence to get things done yet one who can make time for you when necessary. You may be small potatoes now, but if you succeed, the services he can provide will be indispensable.''

Ramsey drew up a short list of a half dozen candidates, all of whom held senior positions in New York's leading banks.

"Flexibility and Caribbean connections will be important to you.''

Rebecca scanned the names but none made an impression on her.

''What about the Walker Bank?'' she suggested. ''Max worked with them for twenty years. The Walker may not be as large as the ones you've mentioned but at least there's a past association.''

Rebecca didn't add that it was Eric's gallantry that had sparked the suggestion.

Ramsey Peet thought the matter over, made several phone calls, and got back to Rebecca the next day.

''It seems that Eric learned his lessons at his father's knee, and learned them well. He's kept all the top-flight people Bartholomew brought in. There's a modernization program under way and the bank is moving into the international arena. Walker stock is beginning to simmer, which, given how conservatively bankers view these things, means that it's a solid investment. I think you just might have found your niche.''

Rebecca silently seconded that opinion. There were times her project seemed so frail, she felt as though she were walking on eggshells. She needed the power of a New York bank to counter whatever obstacles Silas Lambros's Island Royal Bank might throw her way. Money would have to be moved swiftly and on schedule, with a minimum of red tape. Given the paltry sum she had to work with, every penny had to be made to count. There was no margin for error.

Even after she had worked out in her own mind that Eric Walker was the man to deal with, Rebecca found herself being very circumspect when talking to him. She didn't go into any detail as to how or why she had gotten the properties in the Angelines. She didn't mention the long discussions she had had with Ramsey, Torrey, and Bix about her project.

''Basically it's a very simple plan,'' Rebecca said, forcing herself to downplay her enthusiasm. ''The Angelines don't have much of a hospitality industry. Most of the hotels and guesthouses on the mainland cater to businessmen. There's nothing for the average tourist who wants to explore the outlying keys. As these government figures indicate, the number of non-business visitors is rising steadily. I think a small resort—eight to ten *palapas* to hold sixteen to twenty people—would fit the bill perfectly.''

Eric Walker, who had been listening thoughtfully, leafed through the supporting documentation Rebecca handed him.

"I take it the keys have enough water to support something like this and are accessible from the mainland?" he asked.

"Right on both counts."

"What about staff?"

"That won't be a problem. All I need is a cook, bartender, a couple of girls to clean the *palapas* and do the laundry. Besides managing the place, I can pitch in wherever needed. Things like game fishing, snorkeling, or diving can be subcontracted."

"How long will it take you to build the resort?"

"Four to six months," Rebecca told him. "I'll lose time because of Christmas and New Year's. January is the green season in the Angelines. The rains will slow things down."

Eric Walker clasped his hands behind his head and leaned back.

"I'm still not sure exactly how the Walker can help you," he confessed. "By the sound of it there isn't any U.S. connection with the project. Wouldn't you be better off with a local bank—" He caught himself just in time. "Or with a branch of the multinationals?"

"I won't deal with any of the island banks or the multinational subsidiaries," Rebecca said flatly. "Both are subject to government regulation—and interference."

"How will you pay your employees if not through a local bank?" Eric objected.

"The same way my father—with your father's help—paid his. When Max set up McHenry Enterprises he and the Walker Bank arranged for all employees to be paid by checks drawn on the Walker in New York. The bank sent out letters to every local bank where employees had their personal accounts, guaranteeing the amounts and asking that the checks be considered as good as cash. The Angelinian banks agreed and forwarded the checks to New York for payment.

"I'm asking you for the same kind of arrangement."

Eric Walker got out of his chair and thrust his hands deep into his trouser pockets.

"That arrangement was feasible—for both parties—only because of the volume of money involved," he said, pacing across the Bokhara rug. "Your father's payroll was over two million dollars a month. In large part it was the sheer numbers that gave the Walker the necessary clout to convince Angelinian banks to play along.''

"And Max's accounts were what allowed the Walker to become a force in Caribbean financing!" Rebecca said sharply.

"Point," Eric said quietly. "It's not my end that I'm worried about. I'll do whatever I can to help you. It's the Angelinian banks that have to be convinced to go along."

The turning point had been reached. Rebecca had walked into this meeting knowing that if she was going to have the protection she needed, the Walker would have to go to bat for her. Without a firm non-negotiable request from the Walker to honor its checks, she would be left at the mercy of local banks and therefore vulnerable to Silas Lambros.

"Eric, I know we're talking paltry figures," Rebecca said, trying to keep her desperation in check. "But what do you have to lose? I'll keep the full thirty-five thousand on account here. You can charge me the going handling fee—''

"What happens when the money runs out?" Eric interrupted. "We haven't discussed a line of credit using the value of your properties as collateral."

"That's because I'll never put my holdings up as collateral!" Rebecca told him. "Either I'll make do with what I have or else, when the last penny is gone, you can close the account!"

Her voice, the set expression on her face, revealed to Eric the depth of Rebecca's determination. Part of him wanted to give her anything she wanted. But he could no more do this than he could sweep her into his arms.

For the first time ever, Eric Walker cursed the discipline and caution that had been so deeply ingrained in him. Yet as much as he wanted to, he couldn't go against them. With a few phone calls he could get the Angelinian banks to bend to his will. The Walker had more than enough outstanding favors that could be called in. But obligations, not money, were a banker's real currency, to be used judiciously, at the right moment, for the right purpose. How could he possibly convince his board that a $35,000 investment on a highly speculative venture with no collateral justified asking for favors?

Rebecca was keenly aware of the struggle going on behind Eric's composed features. It was reflected in his eyes, in the slight pursing of his lips and the telltale finger-combing of his hair. She had come here knowing she would have to convince the banker to help her, but without telling him everything about her project. As attracted as she was to Eric Walker, Rebecca could not extend him her full trust. The deal would be done on her terms or not at all.

"Can you give me a day or two to think about this?" Eric asked finally.

"Of course," Rebecca said, getting to her feet.

There was an awkward silence as they formally shook hands. For an instant their eyes locked and each waited to see who would suggest they go out for lunch. A heartbeat later the opportunity vanished.

"Did you hear what I said?"

The cool voice, with an impatient edge to it, drifted across the terrace to the sea wall. Andrew Stoughton's head never moved, but his eyes, concealed behind sunglasses, shifted from the file in his lap to his wife.

Celeste Stoughton, née Lambros, reached the end of the pool and with a lazy flip disappeared beneath the diamond-blue water, surfacing to breaststroke in the opposite direction. The flash of her tanned buttocks and breasts shimmering in the water aroused Andrew. When her legs opened and closed in perfect rhythm, he imagined the delight between them and grew hard. Whatever faults Celeste had, failure to excite him was not one of them.

That had been the case since the first time he had seen her, in London, when Celeste had just turned sixteen. Andrew, twelve years older and fully aware of the affect he had on women, had been shocked by the electricity that passed between himself and Celeste. Usually it was he who casually threw the charge, jolting his victim into glazed submission.

A less experienced man—and in the next year Andrew was to see plenty of them—would have been reduced to a puppy with its tongue hanging out. Instead, Andrew affected a bland, bored expression around Celeste, as much for his own protection as to infuriate her.

Celeste reacted exactly as Andrew had expected. Using every ounce of brazen sexuality that her blue eyes, blond hair, and ripe figure commanded, she cut down a swath of lovers to get to him, making sure that Andrew saw how the victims suffered.

This is what I can offer a man, she showed him by example. *And this is what happens when I take away what he's tasted.*

Andrew received such messages with an ironic, mocking smile. He continued to play the elusive prince in Celeste's erotic fairy tale until he sensed she was ripe for his next move. One night, after a victory celebration dinner at Silas Lambros's Eaton Square residence, he allowed himself to be caught.

The dinner had been intimate, that is to say, only ten couples. The next youngest man to Andrew at the table was twenty years his senior. The women, discreet, well-maintained mistresses of the Tyne & Wear board members, were scarcely out of their teens. Only Andrew had come alone, making veiled apologies about a companion suddenly taken ill. Celeste pounced on the bait.

Andrew left immediately after dinner. As he drove his Aston-Martin to his apartment off Marble Arch, he noticed the head-lights behind him. Andrew entered his mews flat, leaving the front door unlocked. Thirty seconds later he heard it open, close, and the latch fall.

There were no preliminaries. Andrew caught Celeste by the wrist, swinging her hard against him. His lips and hands were everywhere, igniting her while at the same time stripping her naked. Andrew carried her to the bedroom and threw her roughly onto the lynx spread. Before Celeste knew what was happening she was spread-eagle on the bed, her wrists and ankles bound to the posts by four silk scarves. A fifth served as a blindfold.

Her helplessness serving only to heighten his excitement, Andrew roamed over Celeste's body with icy passion, probing with fingers, lips, and tongue until everything was blotted out by Celeste's quivers and cries. When he at last took her it was with pent-up savagery, the fear and thrill of which left him spent.

It was over as suddenly as it had begun. One by one Andrew undid the knotted scarves and without so much as a backward glance went into the bathroom. Under the pounding hot water he wondered whether his gamble had paid off. Even though he knew from Lambros's own lips that Celeste was a wild creature, if she told her grandfather about tonight there would be no tomorrow for Andrew Stoughton. But if she didn't . . .

A full ten minutes passed before the door to the shower cabinet slid open and Andrew saw Celeste standing there, arms across her breasts, shaking, her hair tangled with sweat. There was a rivulet of dried blood along her thigh.

Andrew turned off the water and stepped out of the cabinet, never taking his eyes off her.

"Kneel," he said coldly.

Celeste hesitated, then slowly lowered herself, her fingers gripping his buttocks. Tentatively she began to make love to him, then more quickly, until he threw back his head and squeezed his eyes shut.

The gamble had paid off.

Celeste could tell by the bulge in Andrew's bathing briefs what he was thinking. Sunglasses couldn't hide that. She curled up beside the chaise longue on the hot flagstones and slipped her hand underneath the elastic. She remembered their first time as vividly as she knew he did. But in quite a different light. Oh, yes, to this day Andrew believed that he had forced himself on her, subdued and subjugated her. What he never suspected, even after many repetitions, was how much she enjoyed it. Because with every submission she drew him that much closer to her. The prisoner was the real master.

Celeste knew all about Andrew's London conquests, which had made him all the more attractive. But she caught and responded to something far more primitive in him than physical beauty and a bedroom track record that London society reveled in gossiping about. In Andrew, Celeste recognized a kindred spirit whose physical appetites were a reflection of a deeper hunger, the hunger of a predator. He was the kind of man who would let nothing stand in the way of what he wanted. Amorality, coupled with a lust for power, was the real aphrodisiac.

For a year Celeste worked singlemindedly to wear Andrew down. She flaunted her lovers before him, knowing that Andrew could not have cared less about the men yet couldn't help but be intrigued by the girl who toyed with them. She made certain he saw how her grandfather doted on her and demonstrated the power of persuasion she had over him. The messages were unmistakable: together we can do great things—if you're the man I think you are.

Celeste shivered when she remembered the night he took her. For those few hours, as he used her body at will, she reveled not only in his lovemaking but in the delicious realization that she held his fate—along with his balls—in the palm of her hand. A few words to her grandfather and Andrew would be ruined. Or else she could give herself to him, and with her the power that would make Andrew an unrivaled force within Tyne & Wear.

Celeste had accurately predicted her grandfather's response when she announced that Andrew was her lover. Silas Lambros looked at her steadily and commented, "You could have done worse."

Two weeks later he made it worse.

Celeste returned from a whirlwind tour of London dressmakers who specialized in trousseaus to find Andrew packing. When he told her what Silas Lambros had ordered him to do, Celeste was enraged. She flew to the great house on Eaton Square and used every artifice she could to change her grandfather's mind. Neither tears nor entreaties nor threats touched Silas Lambros.

"I want Andrew inside McHenry Enterprises so that I can destroy the bloody prospector once and for all," he said flatly. "The future—no, the very survival—of Tyne & Wear hangs in the balance. As a wrecker you have to understand that sacrifices must be made."

As far as Celeste was concerned, sacrifices were for other people. Yet nothing she did changed her grandfather's mind. In fact, the harder she tried, the sterner his admonitions became.

"You will not see Andrew once he's gone. You won't go near him. He can't be associated with Tyne & Wear or anyone connected with it. Too much time and money has been spent creating falsehoods for McHenry to accept. But it's not enough to fool McHenry once, get him to take Andrew on. The deception has to be played out for as long as it takes. One slip on Andrew's part—or yours—and he'll be finished."

Silas Lambros paused. "And that would displease me mightily."

A few months later Celeste read about Andrew's appointment to McHenry Enterprises in the *Financial Times*.

Celeste might have been able to heed her grandfather's warning had it not been for Rebecca McHenry. It was bad enough that Andrew was three thousand miles away in the Angelines, worse that whenever she visited Stann Creek Town, Celeste didn't dare contact him. Then she heard the whispers in the wreckers' coterie about the dashing McHenry executive, Andrew Stoughton, being involved with Midas Max's daughter.

Celeste spared no effort or expense in substantiating these rumors. She realized that while Andrew might not have bedded the McHenry heiress yet, he was methodically working in that direction, all in the name of undermining McHenry Enterprises. It was then that Celeste remembered the ball at the Jockey Club, where Rebecca had flirted with her date. Later, Celeste had taught her the price of poaching. It seemed that Rebecca needed another lesson.

All of Celeste's promises to her grandfather went out the window. Risking everything, she began telephoning Andrew at the McHenry offices in Angeline City, agreeing to stop only if he would meet her during his frequent trips to the United States. International hotels became their refuges, the king-size beds of the suites a sexual battleground. Celeste called on every wile she had perfected. Sometimes she played the cringing beggar, allowing Andrew to use her as he would. Other times she deliberately kept him waiting or missed assignations entirely. It was as much a punishment as a ruse.

Celeste never expected Andrew to throw his responsibility to Silas Lambros away just to be with her. She would have been contemptuous of him if he had. Yet the closer Andrew became to Rebecca the more risks Celeste demanded they take. Every time she and Andrew stole a few hours Celeste gloated at Rebecca's ignorance. When Andrew told her he had made love to Rebecca, Celeste demanded every detail from him. Then she walked out on him.

As Andrew was getting ready to play his last card—by marrying Rebecca—Celeste confronted her grandfather.

"When Andrew's done with that little slut, I want to marry him—immediately!"

Silas Lambros agreed. "The moment Andrew delivers McHenry Enterprises, his marriage will be annulled. I promise you that."

Celeste took her grandfather at his word. Although she and Andrew managed to see each other twice in the two months he was Rebecca's husband, Celeste writhed under the resentment that for the first time, Andrew actually belonged to the woman she despised. But her greatest triumph came not when she and Andrew stood before a minister. The real victory had been celebrated a few days earlier when the two of them met publicly for the first time at the Perch. Andrew hadn't noticed Rebecca enter the dining room, nor her shocked expression when she realized who was sitting with her husband. Celeste had.

Celeste continued her lazy caresses, squeezing Andrew and feeling him shiver.

"You didn't hear a word I said, did you?"

"Not a word."

"It's time for us to get back to London, darling. I'm missing the best part of the Season. We've been here over a month and I'm bored to distraction."

Andrew grunted. He knew just how much Celeste relished being one of the luminaries of London society. Although only twenty-two, her social graces had been honed in the cradle. The power that came with being Silas Lambros's granddaughter, along with her innate understanding of the London pecking order, made invitations to Celeste's dinner parties hotly sought after. It was a skill Andrew admired and appreciated, mainly because he had little patience for social obligations.

"We can't go back just yet," he said.

Abruptly the caresses stopped.

"And why not?"

"Because I'm not quite done here."

Celeste grabbed the file lying on his chest. She didn't have to open it to know what it contained.

"It's the McHenry bitch, isn't it? You've been thinking of nothing else since we got here."

Celeste snatched away her husband's sunglasses.

"I think you're obsessed with her!" she whispered. "Look into my eyes and tell me I'm wrong!"

Andrew's gaze did not waver.

"She's nothing to me."

Never taking his eyes off Celeste, Andrew reached out and reclaimed his sunglasses.

"Nothing," he repeated before slipping them on.

But even as he watched Celeste's anger dissolve, Andrew wondered if that was really true.

After Norris Darling's failure to buy Rebecca's properties for the price of back taxes, Andrew had redoubled his discreet surveillance of her. Rebecca was up to something, that much he knew for certain. Despite Silas Lambros's conviction that McHenry's daughter wasn't a threat, Andrew knew that Rebecca had powerful allies in Ramsey Peet and Senator Gibson of California, and, in the Angelines, Inspector Ainsley. The bringing together of allies always came before some kind of bold move. This morning Andrew had learned what that was going to be.

"If you're so keen on London, why don't you go back," Andrew suggested to his wife. "I'll follow as soon as I can."

"And when will that be?" Celeste demanded sarcastically.

"I'm not sure. A week, perhaps two."

Celeste stood up, her breasts swaying before Andrew's lips.

"Are you sure I can't change your mind?"

"No."

As he watched his wife storm off, Andrew reached for the file. He reread the confidential memo Eric Walker had drafted to Ramsey Peet. Walker had agreed to use his bank's influence in the Angelines to have local institutions honor McHenry checks drawn on the Walker in New York. The memo ended by mentioning that the Walker Bank would be happy to arrange a line of credit once the resort became operational.

She's doing exactly what Max once did, Andrew thought, recalling how McHenry had refused to deal with the local Angelinian banks and instead paid his employees through New York.

The memory of the old prospector made Andrew uneasy. Silas Lambros had been a fool in dismissing Rebecca out of hand. He didn't appreciate to what extent she was her father's daughter. Celeste was a little closer to the mark. She recognized Rebecca as a rival, but she was too blinded by jealousy to see the real threat.

You should have died in Jamaica. If you had followed Max to the grave, I would have been free of you. . . .

Instead, Rebecca had survived the accident he had arranged for her. Even after she had been thrown out of the Angelines she had found her way back. Now she was on the verge of gaining a foothold.

Andrew realized that Rebecca was far more cautious now. Another accident would be hard to arrange, even more difficult to execute successfully. Yet he had no choice but to move against her. He had destroyed Max McHenry and stolen his empire because it had suited not only Lambros's purposes but his own. The old wrecker had been too gratified by the victory to see that it was also Andrew's opening salvo against him, the first move toward what Andrew saw as his final goal: control of Tyne & Wear.

But as long as Rebecca was in the Angelines, as long as she traded on the magic of the McHenry name, Andrew realized he would have to keep looking over his shoulder. Rebecca wanted revenge. The fact that she had few resources, at least for now, didn't change his perception of her as a threat. Once upon a time Max McHenry had had nothing either. Andrew swore he would not permit Rebecca to come between him and what he believed would be his greatest achievement.

Andrew jotted down several points he wanted to include in his message to Martin Fletcher, the tax lawyer who had furnished him the copy of the memo from Peet's office. Among them was a directive to Fletcher to find out exactly where or from whom Rebecca had gotten her money.

It was very important that Andrew know as much as possible about Rebecca's intentions. The more he knew, the warmer the welcome he could give her.

· 22 ·

"Ah, Miss McHenry, I'm terribly sorry but the permits you applied for to build your hotel are unavailable."

Rebecca shot to her feet, towering over the Angelinian Minister of Tourism. The Honorable Leslie Ball was a mulatto, with a rooster's puffed-out chest and accompanying strut. His face was dominated by a large beak nose and glasses whose bottle-thick lenses lent him the countenance of a squinting turtle. This hybrid appearance had earned him the nickname "turtlecock," and cartoonists had a field day drawing caricatures of him, something Ball glowered about in public but secretly enjoyed immensely.

"What do you mean, they're unavailable?" Rebecca demanded, leaning on Ball's desk with both palms. "My attorney in New York received confirmation from his Stann Creek Town affiliate that the filings had been completed satisfactorily."

The Honorable Leslie Ball carefully licked his forefinger and turned several pages in a file marked THE TIDES.

"Let us go over this, shall we?" he suggested amiably.

Rebecca opened her own dossier and began snapping out papers.

"On October thirteenth of this year I, through my attorney, applied for a permit to build a lodge on Windemere Key, which is wholly owned by me," she said. "Along with the application I filed a separate claim under the Hotels Encouragement Act which would refund me all customs duties paid on materials imported to construct and equip the resort. Your office has examined the particulars—guest facilities, amenities, estimated cost and location—and approved them."

Rebecca slid the sheets toward the minister without breaking stride.

"McHenry Enterprises submitted a separate request that the resort known as The Tides be exempt from all real property and other taxes for ten years from the date the facility opens. This is

205

also in keeping with the Act. Furthermore, we sought, and were given, exemptions from real property taxes in excess of fifteen dollars for every bedroom in the hotel for the next ten years of operation.

"Finally, my company requested, and received, a tax-exempt status on all hotel earnings for twenty years from the opening date. This status also exempts the corporation from direct tax—and I quote the Tax Act—'on or against dividends declared in respect to its indebtedness for the same twenty-year period.' "

Rebecca passed him these papers, littered with enormous wax seals from various departments of the Angelinian government.

"I'm ready to proceed, Mr. Minister," Rebecca said. "Are you?"

The Honorable Leslie Ball fussed with the paperwork, peering down at the seals and signatures from a height of two inches.

"Well, this is certainly all in order," he announced, his dentures rattling like dice. "Except for one minor point."

Rebecca's fingers curled into her palms, her nails biting flesh. Bones Ainsley had warned her to expect something like this.

"It doesn't matter who signed the papers. If the turtlecock decides he wants to change the rules, that's exactly what he'll do."

"And what would that point be?" Rebecca asked tightly.

"At one time the Hotels Encouragement Act included small resorts of the kind you propose, that is to say, a minimum of ten rooms or twenty-person occupancy," the Honorable Leslie Ball said.

"At one time?"

"The ruling was changed yesterday. The Act now applies only to hotels that offer twenty rooms or a forty-person occupancy."

"There was nothing in the legislative proceedings about this!" Rebecca said hotly.

"The Act was amended by an order-in-council. As you're well aware, Miss McHenry, such orders are not required to be printed in the newspapers."

Rebecca knew this to be true. An order-in-council was the equivalent of a U.S. executive order. The Angelinian chief minister, in cooperation with his cabinet, had the power to amend or modify any piece of legislation he wished. Later, if Parliament objected, the order could be revoked. That, Rebecca was certain, would not be the case here.

"But my filings were accepted before the order-in-council went into effect," Rebecca protested.

"Ah, but they were not presented for my signature until this morning," the Honorable Leslie Ball pointed out. "Pity, all this work and expense gone to waste simply because of a date."

"If I have to pay duty on the materials I need to build the resort, I won't be able to go ahead," Rebecca told him.

"I'm sorry, Miss McHenry, but the law is clear. Your project doesn't fit within our exemption parameters. Of course, an argument could be made that the date on the papers is incorrect."

Rebecca knew what was coming.

"Just how persuasive would this argument have to be?"

The turtlecock scribbled something on his notepad and turned it so Rebecca could read the writing. When she saw the figure, $5,000, she was sickened.

"My cousin, Alvin Ball, is an attorney who has much experience in these matters. If you were to see him by the close of business today, I think he would facilitate matters."

And if I don't, I'm stopped before I can begin!

"Please tell your cousin to expect me in two hours. I trust a letter of credit telexed from the Walker Bank will suffice."

"Admirably, Miss McHenry, admirably. May I say how pleased I am to welcome McHenry Enterprises to our family of entrepreneurs." He paused. "We'll be watching your progress with great interest."

I bet you will!

Rebecca left Government House and walked across the street to the Stann Creek Town post office. She booked a long distance call to New York and waited fifteen minutes before the operator indicated her party was on the line.

In a clipped tone Rebecca told Eric Walker exactly what had happened and what she needed. The banker was furious.

"You can't give in to this kind of blackmail! I'll talk to Ball myself, or the chief minister if necessary—"

"Eric, there's nothing you can do," Rebecca said. "I appreciate your concern, but there's no way out. I can't afford to wait."

It sickened Rebecca to have to say those words. Five thousand dollars represented a precious fifteen percent of her operating budget. She could have done so much with that money.

"Are you absolutely sure there's nothing I can do?" Eric asked once more.

"Just send that telex."

"The son of a bitch will have it within the hour. Tell him the money will be transferred to any account he wants."

"Thank you, Eric."

There was a pause on the line.

"Please, look after yourself down there," he said. "Call if you need anything, anything at all."

On the ferry back to Angeline City, Rebecca took comfort in Eric's words. By the time she reached the mainland she had dismissed all thoughts of the Honorable Leslie Ball and the bribe he had extracted from her.

Keep moving ahead. Don't look back. Don't hesitate. Once you have the permits they can't stop you.

Rebecca had no idea how wrong she was.

The next day, after she received the permits, magically backdated twenty-four hours before the order-in-council, Rebecca left for Windemere Key. The surveyor and engineer had been working on the key for a week and their job was almost complete.

Rebecca studied the surveyor's report carefully and was elated.

"Because of the key's elevation and rock formation you have more than enough water in the earth itself," the surveyor explained. "However, I would suggest a backup system of concrete cisterns built into the hill to trap rainwater."

The engineer concurred. "With the cisterns you have an emergency supply. If one set of pumps breaks down, the backup kicks in automatically."

Rebecca examined their estimates for the cisterns. Even though the cost was higher than she had expected, the concept was sound.

"Put them into the plans."

The surveyor and engineer then walked her around the perimeter of the property, describing how far up the beach the *palapas* had to be built, how high off the ground the structure had to stand, and how deep the supporting pillars, set in reinforced concrete, had to be sunk. They explained where the drainage and plumbing routes had to be dug, what kind of below-ground electrical system was best, and the kind of generator needed to supply the power.

Surrounded by cahoon palms, and trumpet and banana trees, their scent leavened by wild ginger, Rebecca could scarcely believe that she would be able to bring a hint of civilization to such unspoiled beauty.

"The only reason you can," the surveyor told her, "is that the trade winds and the natural drainage keep the insects away. Except here."

On the exact spot Rebecca intended to place her central *palapa*, with its dining room, bar, kitchen, and a small office, was a swamp. The brackish water reeked of decay, and the buzz of mosquitoes and flies all but drowned out the calls of the yellow nap parrots and scarlet macaws.

"How did it get here?" Rebecca cried. "I went over every square foot of this key and this wasn't here before!"

"The green-season rains are worse than usual," the surveyor told her. "In a way it was just as well they came now, because they showed us where the ground was silt. You're going to have to drain this area and fill it in before building anything on it. Even if you change the setting for the *palapa* you'll still need to spray once every two weeks. If you don't, it will be a breeding ground for disaster."

The insects eating Rebecca alive were proof of that.

"I'll fill it in," Rebecca said grimly.

The engineer and surveyor looked at each other skeptically. Obviously no one had told this woman that there wasn't a barge big or strong enough to transfer a bulldozer from Angeline City to Windemere Key.

"We'll do it by hand!"

"Are you crazy, girl?" Jewel demanded. "Do you know how long that would take?"

"There's no other way," Rebecca said stubbornly. "I can't leave the swamp there."

Dust motes danced through the shafts of November sunlight as the two women walked through the streets of Angeline City.

"I'll get more men, that's all," Rebecca said confidently. "A dozen working on drainage and land fill will get the job done in a week."

"If they survive!" Jewel muttered darkly.

"Oh, they will. You just mix enough of that potion of yours."

Across the square from the fish market was the labor exchange, a branch of the employment bureau. Here unemployed or part-time workers gathered in the early morning, scanning the posted sheets for whatever jobs were available. The offerings were always for manual laborers, either in the cane fields, fishing boats, or loading docks. In the spring and fall, when most of the harbor repairs were done, there was a demand for carpenters as well.

The exchange wasn't open yet. About thirty men, ranging from teenagers to grandfathers, stood around in small groups, talking quietly, smoking, and drinking coffee dispensed from a cantina shack. As soon as they spotted Rebecca, conversation ceased.

What have I done now, Rebecca wondered.

Then all at once they surrounded her, thrusting questions at her in Spanish and Creole. To a man they knew that a McHenry was back in the Angelines to build some fabulous new hotel.

At first Rebecca was surprised by the reception, but then she remembered how things worked in the Angelines. The minute the Honorable Leslie Ball's cousin had expedited her hotel permits, his secretary had whispered the news to her nephew, who had passed the news, in strict confidence, to his brother, who had told his wife, who had then gone to the market. . . . And so word had gone out, like a trickle of water that became a torrential river, with the news that Rebecca McHenry had returned—for good.

Unfortunately, Rebecca thought, trying to answer as many questions as she could, rumor had exaggerated the truth until these laborers thought she was going to build the Taj Mahal. Still, she was grateful for the response. It meant a great deal more to her than simply the availability of skilled hands and strong backs.

The manager of the labor exchange rang the old ship's bell outside the door to indicate the office was open. He waded into the throng, graciously greeted Rebecca and Jewel, and escorted them inside.

"A moment, please," he said, smiling nervously. "I have an announcement for the men."

Rebecca glanced at Jewel and saw her own concern mirrored in the creased moon face. Looking out the window, she saw the manager gesticulating wildly as he addressed the men. When he noticed Rebecca, his motions became even more frantic. The laborers, on the other hand, had become sullen, some even angry.

The manager came back in, mopping his face with a red handkerchief the size of a tablecloth.

"Forgive me for keeping you waiting," he rattled off in Spanish. "Instructions, orders . . ." He shrugged his shoulders in resignation. "Now, how may I be of service to you, Señorita McHenry?"

"I need three dozen men," Rebecca told him. "Half for general labor, to clear jungle and fill in swamp, the rest experienced tradesmen." She handed him a list with the particulars. "I'll guarantee employment for at least sixty days."

Rebecca saw that the manager only pretended to read the list. It was his teeth that were moving—not his eyes—as he nervously chewed his lower lip.

"I'm afraid, señorita, I cannot help you," he said at last. "I have no craftsmen such as you require. The men you see out there are all going elsewhere."

"If that's the case, what are they doing standing around?" Rebecca challenged.

"Señorita, please . . ." the manager stammered.

"The truth is that they don't have anywhere to go for work, isn't it?" she carried on, her anger rising.

The manager flinched.

"Are you calling me a liar, señorita?"

"Worse. I'm calling you a coward! Who put the fear of God into you—Lambros?"

The manager scrapped together what was left of his self-respect.

"I think it would be best if you go, señorita. There's nothing for you here." He paused and added in a whisper, "I'm sorry."

When Rebecca and Jewel came outside, the men turned away, their eyes downcast. For an instant Rebecca was tempted to reach out to them and tell them no one had the right to stop them working for her.

"You'll do more harm than good," Jewel counseled her. "It's not you they're afraid of."

"But I need them!"

Jewel gripped her arm and led her away.

Jewel took Rebecca home and made her swear not to leave until she returned. At dusk Rebecca heard the rattle of an ancient flatbed truck as it bumped its way down the road. Jewel climbed out, followed by a dozen men who had been riding standing up on the bed.

"The best I could do for one day," she said.

Rebecca waded among the men, shaking hands and thanking them.

"Where did you get them all?" she demanded, embracing Jewel.

"No great secret," Jewel said, smiling broadly. "I knew these fellows when they worked for Max. They haven't had a regular job since. I tol' them you'd put rice and beans in their bellies and pay them."

Jewel lowered her voice.

"Bones is goin' to try to round up some more. When word

gets out, you can believe Lambros will be madder than the March hare. You'd best move them to Windemere soon as you can."

One of the men broke away from the group and came over to Rebecca. He was in his late teens, with a delicate oval-shaped face and thick black hair.

"Pardon, señorita," he said shyly. "But I have an uncle who might be of service to you."

"Then you talk to him as soon as you can. We can use anyone who's willing to work."

"No, señorita, I don't mean like that," the youth explained hastily. "My uncle is a foreman in the sawmill near Angeline City. You need good strong logs, fresh wood to build your hotel, sí?"

"Sí."

"He tells me he will help you how he can. His name is Eduardo Martinez."

Rebecca's eyes glistened. "What is your name?"

"Miguel, señorita."

"Miguel, I want you to tell your uncle I'm very grateful. I'll give him a list of what I need just as soon as I can." Rebecca kissed him on both cheeks. "Thank you!"

That night Rebecca went to sleep in peace. She had only a third of the work force she needed, but it was a start. Tomorrow she would get more men. And to have a source for ready-cut logs and planks was a godsend. It would save weeks of cutting down, treating, and finishing the trees of Windemere to build the *palapas*.

Perhaps, just perhaps, she had surmounted the obstacles set in her way.

The next morning, while the stars and crescent moon were still descending toward the horizon, Rebecca slipped the mooring lines of Bones Ainsley's cruiser, the *Mardi Gras,* and set course for the *quebrada* that would lead her to the open sea.

On board were fifteen workmen, the dozen Jewel had brought yesterday as well as three who had shown up during the night. They sat along the vinyl seats on the lower deck, drinking hot coffee laced with rum. In the center of the deck, strapped down and covered with canvas, were crates stuffed with equipment Rebecca had purchased by special order in Angeline City: power saws and jacks, studs and hooks, large canvas tents which would

be their shelters, propane cylinders for the lamps, and portable
stoves.

Once in a while Rebecca looked back at the scene on the deck,
fixing every detail in her mind. The exhilaration and anticipation
filled her with a dizzying ache. She couldn't help but recall
the stories Jewel had told her about Max, his struggles in those
early days to equip and provision his expeditions, the hardships
he had faced in the jungle, the disappointments and defeats he
had had to live with before his first strike. Rebecca felt she
was following in her father's footsteps, that somewhere on the
wind she could hear his voice encouraging her, his eyes watching
over her.

By the time the sun broke the horizon, all the equipment had
been off-loaded. The tents were pitched, cots, cooking utensils,
and tinned provisions broken out and stored. After the shovels,
pickaxes, spades, and axes had been distributed, Rebecca stripped
down to cutoff jeans and a T-shirt. She rolled up a twenty-gallon
drum and pried its lid open.

"I'm sure you all know what this is." She gasped as the
stench hit her.

The drum was filled with a black tarlike pitch, its rank odor a
cross between rotting wood and dead fish. It was the same
concoction Jewel had made for Max when he had gone into the
jungle. Rebecca took the older woman's word that no bug or
mosquito would come near a piece of skin covered with it. The
smell alone would kill them.

Rebecca took a deep breath and plunged her arm into the
muck. Cringing, she applied it to her exposed skin, then closed
her eyes tightly while she smeared her face. Watching her, the
men laughed, then stepped up one by one to cover themselves.

Tackling the swamp proved a more daunting task than Rebecca had imagined. First, drainage had to be hollowed out to
allow as much stagnant water as possible to flow away and be
absorbed by the earth. While four men using chainsaws mowed a
corridor through the trees, Rebecca and the others began digging
the channel. By the time the sun was directly overhead, they had
gone less than sixty feet.

"Don't you worry none," Jewel said laughing, as she ladled
out broiled fish and beans onto Rebecca's tin plate. "That jungle
won't grow back faster than you cut it down."

Jewel and the wives of two of the men had come out on
another boat, whose skipper had towed back Bones Ainsley's
Mardi Gras. At first Rebecca had been firmly opposed to Jew-

el's being on Windemere Key, fearful that the primitive conditions would exacerbate her heart condition. Jewel pooh-poohed her arguments and went her own way. Rebecca consoled herself with the thought that at least this way she could keep an eye on her.

Lunch was a hasty affair. Even though most Angelinians observed the siesta hour, Rebecca and her men disappeared into the jungle. Foot by painful foot the trench was dug, deepened, and finally completed just before nightfall. Toting her shovel over her shoulder, Rebecca staggered out of the jungle, her muscles screaming for relief. With the last of her strength she scrubbed off the noxious pitch and, at Jewel's insistence, took a few mouthfuls of dinner. Around the bonfire the women had built, men sat eating, talking, and passing the rum bottle. Rebecca wondered where they got the energy. Determined not to be outdone, she grabbed the bottle and recklessly took a long swallow. Rebecca acknowledged the cheers and sat in for another round. The third time the bottle came around Rebecca leaned back to empty it. The liquor raced down her throat and she swore she heard a soft explosion. At the same time as she reached forward to give the bottle away she began to keel over backward, unconscious before her head touched the sand.

Filling in the swamp took ten days of grueling labor. The only time Rebecca wasn't helping with the task was the morning she went to the sawmill to meet Eduardo Martinez. The strapping foreman promised delivery of the wood she needed at below market price.

"But I must have full payment now, señorita," he said apologetically. "It takes a little grease for the men to cut down the extra trees."

Rebecca wrote him a check on the spot.

"I want you and your family to be among my first guests," she told him.

"You are very kind, señorita. It would be a pleasure."

Rebecca gave her team a well-earned, much-needed holiday after the last shovelful of dirt had been thrown over the swamp. She and Jewel returned to the house outside Angeline City, where Rebecca luxuriated in a long hot bath. When she looked at herself in the mirror, all she saw were blisters, calluses, and hard, tense muscles. It's all worth it, she repeated to herself. If Max could do it, so can you!

The only piece of bad news Rebecca had to deal with came

from Bones Ainsley. As Jewel had feared, Silas Lambros had used his enormous influence to dissuade other laborers from working for her.

"He's made it clear that anyone who works for you will never hold a job, if he can help it."

"Then I'm putting out a message of my own," Rebecca said. "Anyone who comes to work for me now will have first shot at whatever job is available once The Tides is on stream!"

Rebecca's counteroffer yielded only seven additional men, giving her less than two thirds of the workforce she needed.

"It'll be all right," she told Jewel. "We're going to save a lot of time and money because of Eduardo Martinez's wood. We'll be able to start building the *palapas* as soon as we get back."

Rebecca returned to Windemere Key to find that her men had built a makeshift dock from the beach into the deeper part of the lagoon. Now, instead of the cargo being transferred from boat to boat, the barge carrying the wood could off-load on shore.

By noon, when there was still no sign of Eduardo Martinez, Rebecca began to fret. At last one of the men shouted, pointing to an approaching vessel. Thirty minutes later the barge, piled high with mahogany trunks as thick as a man's waist and planks that still smelled of resin, nudged the dock. Rebecca slipped on heavy gloves and workboots and joined the daisy chain for the off-loading.

The first hint that something wasn't right came when the barge captain cast off as soon as the last bundle had been taken off. Rebecca had intended to ask him to stay for the evening meal but thought that he was just eager to get back to Angeline City and eat with his family.

The second signal was stronger. With tin snips one of the men snapped the metal ties binding the planks. He lifted the top boards and examined them closely, finding them in excellent condition. Then he saw what lay underneath.

"Señorita!"

Rebecca raced over to the bundle and glanced down. The planks along the second tier were riddled with wormholes. Under the light Rebecca could see thick white maggots digging in and out of the fiber.

"Oh, no!"

Grabbing the tin snips, Rebecca went from bundle to bundle, cutting the ties, throwing off the top layer of planks and examining the rest. Each case was the same: The timber was infested.

"Take the chainsaw and cut that piece in half," Rebecca told one of the men, pointing to a mahogany trunk.

As the serrated blade chewed through the bark into the pulp, an evil smell rose from the wood. When the log broke in two, Rebecca saw that its interior was honeycombed. The mahogany had been destroyed by termites.

"Miguel!"

But the young worker with the innocent eyes and dazzling smile who had told Rebecca about his uncle, the sawmill foreman, was nowhere to be found. None of the men could remember coming out with him.

"What do we do now, señorita?" someone asked her.

Rebecca's anger choked her words. She was thinking of how Eduardo Martinez had cheated her, of the money she had, like a fool, handed over to him without even asking to see her consignment. Money that would have disappeared by now because Angelinian banks had been instructed to honor McHenry checks immediately.

"Tomorrow we begin to cut down the trees we need," Rebecca said, fighting to keep the despair from her voice. "But first we do this!"

Rebecca seized a gallon tin of kerosene and began sprinkling the liquid over the bundles and logs. She grabbed one of the torches and ignited the joke that had been played on her.

For a long time Rebecca sat on the beach listening to the pop and crackle of her folly. She remained like that after the men had gone to bed and even Jewel had turned in. All the while her fingers toyed with the golden sea horse that caught and reflected the flames.

At dawn, when the lumber had been reduced to a pile of smoking ash, Rebecca went into the sea and swam hard for an hour. She was in the makeshift shower about to wash off the salt when she heard the throb of distant diesels.

The vessel was too far out for her to identify either the name or the faces of the men who were on the foredeck. There were at least a dozen of them. Rebecca, who knew every vessel in the Angeline City harbor, didn't recognize this one.

Never taking her eyes off the boat, Rebecca looped the binoculars around her neck, leaving both hands free. Walking toward the pier, Rebecca slipped two shells into Jewel's ancient shotgun, which she had brought with her from the tent. She reached the end of the dock and raising the gun with one hand, pointed the barrels at the approaching vessel.

Let them come!

· 23 ·

There were fifteen men on the deck of the sorry-looking fishing boat whose engine belched and wheezed and finally died with a prolonged shudder. They all resembled each other: short, squat frames with slabs of muscle across the chest, oval-shaped faces with broad, flat noses and rich jet-black hair that shimmered in the dawn. They were Mayans, and behind their passive dark eyes Rebecca discerned glints of surprise and curiosity.

"Hey, lady, put that damn blunderbuss away! I come in peace."

A California drawl cascaded from the wheelhouse. Rebecca looked up to see Dallas Gibson leaning over the railing, his Australian slouch hat pushed back on his hair, his eyes glittering against his customary deep tan.

"What on earth are you doing here?" Rebecca cried.

"What does it look like? I'm rescuing you!"

"Seriously, I heard you could use a little help so me and some of the boys here decided to lend a hand."

Dallas and Rebecca were standing side by side watching the Mayans unload the tools and supplies they had brought. Rebecca was still bewildered. She hadn't seen or spoken to Dallas since her visit to Pusilha.

"Who told you I was here?"

"I heard you were setting up shop but had a few labor relations problems," Dallas said, grinning.

"Dallas!"

"Okay, okay! This is the woman who made me do it," he confessed, giving Jewel a big hug as she waddled up to him. "She's a witch."

Rebecca's laughter, as Jewel bussed Dallas on the cheek, masked her uneasiness. She was overwhelmed by his generosity but at the same time felt that it obligated her even more to him.

217

Dallas had prevailed upon his father to use his influence in having her Angelinian citizenship restored. Dallas had been the one to fill in the crucial missing pieces of her father's life—and Apho Hel's. Now, like magic, Dallas was here to help her build The Tides.

Why does he keep popping in and out of my life?

"What about the excavations at Pusilha?" she asked him. "Aren't you needed there?"

"The University of Chicago has changed its priorities," Dallas told her. "The archaeology department was going to fund a major excavation at Machu Pichu in Peru. At the last minute the Peruvian government opted for a team from the University of Santiago. I managed to convince the powers-that-be that Pusilha was a much more important dig to begin with. We have thirty men there now. Pusilha is in good hands."

Rebecca was startled to discover how glad she suddenly was that he had come.

"Your trip must have been exhausting. Can I interest you in some fresh hot coffee?"

His smile embraced her.

"I'd love that."

Rebecca quickly discovered that Dallas's experience in the field was of enormous help to her. Together they went over the surveyor's and engineer's ground plans and design for the *palapas*. Dallas approved the first and had a number of suggestions for the dwellings.

"I don't know if I can afford it," Rebecca said after hearing him out.

"The additional material will increase the cost," Dallas admitted. "But the result will be that much stronger and safer."

Rebecca weighed the expense against the benefit and decided he was right.

"Since we're going to be here for a while, wouldn't it be better to put a roof over our heads rather than live in tents?"

Again, Rebecca saw his point but this time raised an objection.

"I can't afford to build bunkhouses."

"It's not as though it will be a waste of time or money," Dallas said reasonably. "Things will be much more comfortable for all of us, and when we're done, you can convert the bunkhouse into a storage hut—or even use it for overflow."

"I don't know—" Rebecca said, then stopped.

"Give me forty-eight hours."

"You're on."

Rebecca went back to her own work, a job as dirty and physically exhausting as the filling in of the swamp had been. Although Windemere had long stretches of beautiful sugar-white beach, these were broken up by patches of mangrove that flourished in the shallow waters. There was only one way to get rid of the growth: first, the thin-trunk trees had to be chopped off at the water level and dragged away. Then the roots themselves had to be wrested from the sandbars. Dividing her men into teams of three, Rebecca led them into the shallows. Soon the air was filled with the sound of whistling machetes and the crack of wood as the blades rose and fell.

Laboring in waist-high water under a hot November sun, the men tired quickly and needed frequent rest intervals. On the beach they examined one another's legs for leeches and scraped them off with razor-sharp knife blades.

Rebecca hadn't realized that cutting away the tops of the mangrove was the easy part. To get at the roots meant going underwater, yanking and pulling until the roots came loose. Every foot of clearing was dearly paid for by aching lungs, scarred hands, and burning skin.

At the end of the second day in the mangrove Rebecca staggered out of the water and beheld a mirage. At the foot of the jungle was a long rectangular *palapa,* complete in every detail.

"Ready for occupancy," Dallas announced.

Rebecca was so overwhelmed by the sight of this, the first building of The Tides, she didn't notice how heavy Dallas's voice was.

"It's beautiful!" she cried, running her hand over one of the ceiba pillars. She threw her arms around his neck.

"Show me the inside!"

That was when she felt his tears upon her cheek.

"Dallas, what's wrong?"

"It just came over the shortwave radio," he whispered. "President Kennedy's been shot. . . . ."

Dallas's grief, her own disbelief, the job of seeing the first building which made The Tides a reality, the awful sensation of loss—these were the contradictory emotions that served to freeze the moment in Rebecca's mind.

But the tragedy in Texas made the world only pause, not stop.

After a day of mourning, most of it spent huddled next to Dallas, listening to the grim details over the shortwave radio, Rebecca led her men back into the mangrove. As November passed into December and the days were counted off to Christmas, the clusters of trees along the shoreline began to disappear. By noon of the twenty-fourth, the last day of work for a week, better than half the clearing had been done. The mangrove which had been piled up on the beach and left to dry was set ablaze. When the wood had been reduced to fiery coals, the Christmas barbecue got under way. Rebecca had bought small presents for each of the men and handed these out while the roasting chickens crackled and spit over the flames. The rum jug was broken out and passed around, followed by the singing of native Christmas carols. By the time the charter boat arrived to take Rebecca's workers to the mainland, no one wanted to leave.

Rebecca spent Christmas Eve on Windemere Key with Jewel, Bones, and the Mayan workers who had stayed behind. Dallas had left to spend a few days with his family in California. Their farewells had been tentative, the air between them charged with unspoken promises. The minute his dilapidated vessel was out of sight, Rebecca felt very much alone. It was as though Dallas had taken his laughter and strength with him, leaving behind only their echoes.

Rebecca elected to spend the night of the twenty-fourth on board Bones's vessel. Dragging a thin mattress onto the roof of the pilothouse, she lay on her back, staring at a sky blazing with stars.

The gentle rocking of the boat, the soft lapping of the waves, the awesome spectacle of the universe above her, filled Rebecca with a deep peace. At that moment all the trials and hardships she had faced—and those that still lay ahead—melted away. When she looked back over the last eight weeks, she couldn't believe how far she had come. But she didn't think about The Tides and the one bunkhouse that was the beginning. Tonight she remembered all the people who had reached out and given of themselves to help her. Without them, none of what she had would have come to pass.

Yet, when Rebecca considered her good fortune, she couldn't steer her thoughts away from the price that had been extracted for it. The wind, cooling her tears, made her realize she was crying. Rebecca looked inside herself and realized that for all she had, there were deep and empty recesses in her soul. As Christmas Eve passed into Christmas Day she walked through these barren rooms, touching the memories of a man she had loved like no other, feeling the stir of a child whose life had been torn from her womb. There was no anger in her this holy night, only an aching loss that showed her how alone and incomplete she was.

When Rebecca was finally lulled to sleep she never knew that her hands were clasped on her belly, as though they were cradling the child that had once grown within her.

Rebecca awoke on Christmas Day to the sound of men singing. Rolling over on her stomach, she saw the Mayan workers in the shallows down the beach, hacking away at the mangrove. With a groan she got up, squinting against the brilliance of the morning sun.

"Merry Christmas!" Jewel and Bones called up to her from the foredeck. " 'Bout time you got up, girl. The work's awaitin'!"

There seemed to be no end to the work either.

Even when her men returned after New Year's it took two full weeks to weed out the rest of the mangrove. After the last pile of wood went up in flames Rebecca turned her attention to clearing the area where the *palapas* would stand. She had intended to chop away the brush and cut down the larger trees. Dallas Gibson offered an alternative.

"If you cut down the palms, you'll be losing the natural shade," he pointed out. "Wouldn't it be better to work around the trees?"

Rebecca chided herself for not having thought of this.

"Another thing," Dallas said. "I don't think it's a good idea to cut the brush."

"Why not?"

"No matter how close to the earth you cut, you're still going to leave spikes. That might create problems when guests start running around in bare feet."

"That means we have to pull everything up by the roots!"

Dallas grinned. " 'Fraid so."

He walked off to supervise the felling of trees for the *palapas*, leaving Rebecca to stew.

The clearing of the land took another month, but Rebecca had to admit that the result was well worth the effort. The towering palms not only provided shade, but once the *palapas* were in place they would appear to be a natural part of the landscape.

Although Rebecca spent most of her time clearing brush, she made a point of watching Dallas and learning from his experience. She followed his Mayan workers into the interior, where they selected and chopped down Caribbean pines. Trimmed of their branches, the logs were hauled into the ocean, where the salt water killed the insects. Once the bark was softened, it was stripped from the trunk. The log was beached to dry, then treated with insecticide and preservative. After two coats of shellac it was ready to be used.

Rebecca was astonished at how quickly and efficiently the Mayans worked. Dallas divided his men into two teams, sending one up into the hills to build the cisterns, while the other continued to prepare the materials for the *palapas*. Once the logs that would serve as the supporting pillars and posts were ready, the Mayans began chopping bundles of swamp grass for the roof padding.

By the middle of February, Rebecca's men had rebuilt the temporary dock, turning it into a full-fledged pier that jutted fifty yards into the sea. Day after day the *Mardi Gras* returned to Windemere, off-loading large plates of tin sheeting and hundreds of bundles of bamboo. The sheeting was carried to the site where the *palapas* would stand; the bamboo was treated in salt water and sprayed, then the thin stakes were woven together to form panels to cover the interior *palapa* walls. Rebecca's blistered fingers were testimony to the painful fact that over a thousand such thin reeds had to be joined together to complete one section.

By March the pace of work quickened, as though everyone were eager to put together the individual components they had been working on. When Rebecca returned from Angeline City with bags of concrete, her men set to mixing the powder and pouring the mixture into forms. One by one the treated posts were sunk and the skeletal frame emerged. Ropes and pulleys were used to lay the crossbeams. When these were in place, the tin sheets were hoisted and hammered fast. The floor, made from planed, dense ironwood, was laid in, and bamboo panels covered the plywood sheeting.

Rebecca carefully photographed the progress. In the evenings she made copious notes on how the building was coming along, where shortcuts could be made, and which details could be attended to upfront, to save time later on. It was also at night that Rebecca did her bookkeeping. Every few days another check had to be written to cover expenses ranging from the diesel fuel the *Mardi Gras* burned to the kegs of nails and other hardware the construction fed on. As her reserves in the Walker Bank dwindled, Rebecca fought off panic. The construction of The Tides was becoming a race, not against time, but against her own bank account.

· 24 ·

April rains had come and gone, washing London of its filmy winter dirt and grime. Across the city parks May was in full bloom. Women had shed their overcoats in favor of bright spring dresses, and even the usually dour streets of the financial district were alive with color.

In Silas Lambros's office at Tyne & Wear headquarters, Andrew Stoughton looked out at the female traffic surging below. There were a thousand different faces in the crowds, but he saw only one.

"I've examined your reports on Rebecca McHenry's little venture and I'm still no closer to understanding your concern."

Andrew turned around, his hands braced behind him on the window ledge.

"She's managed to build her resort, Silas," he said, trying to keep his voice level. "Even with the odds against her."

"She has a collection of shacks!" Lambros replied contemptuously, tossing the aerial photographs across the desk blotter. "Who do you think would stay in a place like that?"

"I'm not sure. But she must have an idea. Otherwise she wouldn't have gone ahead with it."

The old wrecker sighed and gripped his son-in-law by the shoulder.

"Andrew, I went along with your little scheme to stop Rebecca McHenry. You asked me to use my influence with Leslie Ball and the others, and I did. Believe me, I haven't lost any sleep over the fact that she hasn't packed up and left.

"Look out there. See the pace, the momentum of the City. *That's* where your mind should be. On our business. Not on some godforsaken spit of sand in the Caribbean.

"You know, Andrew, I've noticed Celeste hasn't been in the best of humor lately. She's turned waspish. I haven't seen her like that since you were working for McHenry."

Lambros paused before sliding his point home. "She tells me it's on account of your obsession with the McHenry woman. Is she correct, Andrew?"

"It's not an obsession," Andrew said coldly. "It's concern. I'm concerned that after everything we've done, we still haven't gotten her out of the Angelines."

"Andrew, listen to me," Silas Lambros counseled. "There is nothing Rebecca McHenry can do to harm us. Unless, of course, we allow ourselves to see threats that aren't there. Let the fool woman play at running a hotel. You yourself told me she's down to her last few thousand dollars. And she hasn't even outfitted the place yet! The fact that she has Eric Walker on her side is meaningless if her account dries up. Then she'll see how quickly those who've helped her will last."

"I can't help but feel that she's going to pull through this, Silas."

"Celeste was right, you know," Lambros said, his tone hard. "This woman has gotten under your skin."

"I don't want to spend another five years of my life fighting a second McHenry," Andrew told him, matching the older man's inflection.

"And I don't like to see my chief executive ignoring company business while he chases phantoms!" Lambros snapped. "Nor do I like the way his behavior is affecting his wife!"

That's really what this summons is all about, Andrew thought. Silas Lambros could not have cared less about Rebecca McHenry. The veiled accusation that Andrew had been neglecting company affairs was equally groundless. It was Celeste who was the real subject of discussion—and probably the instigator of this meeting as well.

"If you really feel Rebecca McHenry is a threat to us, tell me how you propose to deal with her," Lambros said, his tone leaving no doubt that he was humoring Andrew.

Andrew had his argument prepared and quickly laid out the particulars.

"That seems a bit drastic, don't you think?" Lambros commented.

"Do I have your permission to go ahead?" Andrew asked, ignoring the question.

"On one condition. From this moment on I don't want you to give Rebecca McHenry another thought. If this is what it takes to exorcise her, so much the worse for her. But as of now, Andrew, she doesn't exist for you."

Andrew took a deep breath.

"Thank you, Silas."

"You can show me your thanks by taking Celeste to dinner at the Café Royal. She's been saying that the two of you never go out anymore."

"I will, Silas. Tonight."

Andrew was barely able to control himself as he walked to his office. He closed the door and instructed his secretary to hold all calls. Having locked himself in the bathroom, he fumbled in his vest pocket for the antique snuffbox, and his trembling fingers snatched two of the white pills that scattered across the veined rose marble surrounding the basin. Andrew threw his head back and tossed the pills down his throat. He swallowed hard and leaned forward, both arms taut against the sink. He squeezed his eyes shut, waiting for the potent tranquilizer to take effect.

The medication was one of Andrew's deepest secrets. Celeste had no idea he took it; Silas Lambros had never been allowed even to suspect that at certain moments Andrew could not do without it.

Andrew had discovered he was prone to severe manic attacks years ago, while he had still been a troubleshooter for Tyne & Wear's shadowy affiliate, the Severn Group. The doctor in India who had treated him had been alarmed because the illness gave almost no warning before it struck. When he had asked about blackouts, losses of memory, and fits of physical rage, Andrew had calmly lied. He had almost convinced himself that the mornings he had woken up in some filthy hotel room or alley, had been a part of someone else's experience.

Andrew had paid the Delhi physician handsomely, not only for his treatment but for the name of an associate in London. The medication that filled the snuffbox did not come from Harley Street but from a hole-in-the-wall office on the fringe of Golders Green.

Slowly the thunder and rage that had engulfed him subsided. From a tiny compartment in his billfold Andrew withdrew a telex, the edges worn from having been handled so many times. The message had been sent by Martin Fletcher, who had finally solved the riddle of where Rebecca had gotten her start-up capital for The Tides.

The bitch sold the ring I gave her!

Andrew never believed Rebecca capable of such a thing. He had always considered her a high-strung creature, ruled by her emotions, who would have thrown or given the ring away on the spur of the moment.

Andrew stared at the words of the telex, not really seeing them. He didn't have to. They were seared in his mind, a constant reminder of how he had been used and tricked. Maybe, just maybe, he might have been able to smother the rage brought on by what Rebecca had done to him. But Silas Lambros had chosen that precise moment to rake him over the coals about Celeste, to remind Andrew of just how easily he could make him jump at the snap of his fingers. That had been too much. . . .

Andrew waited until he felt the drug taking effect. He scrubbed the sheen of sweat from his face and looked at his reflection with dead eyes that were like ice chips. At that moment he didn't know which of the two he hated more: Rebecca, who had managed to humiliate him so completely, or Lambros, who had long ago fashioned the golden chain that still kept Andrew bound to him.

Andrew Stoughton had been born working-class, on the other side of the world from the glory of Eaton Square and Tyne & Wear. His mother doted on him, nicknaming him "Prince Harry." His father was as gray a figure as the ledgers he kept so faithfully for Lloyds.

May Stoughton never acknowledged her husband's station in life. She lived on airs, in a fantasy where she was a lady, with a son who deserved only the best. Too late did Andrew learn that his father had worked himself to death to pay for toys and treats an ungrateful young boy constantly demanded, which were grabbed for the instant they appeared, used, and discarded within a fortnight.

Andrew Stoughton had been educated at a minor public school, Beardsley Hall, a luxury the family could ill afford. Eventually Andrew discovered the price his mother had paid. After the war, when London children were being sent home from the refuges in the countryside, May Stoughton connived and plotted to keep her son enrolled at the boarding school. The cruel whispers about his mother sleeping with the headmaster hounded Andrew mercilessly.

George Stoughton passed away when his son was in his second year at Cambridge—failing brilliantly. A poor boy among rich Yankees and titled snobs, he turned to gambling to keep his poverty at bay. With his winnings Andrew bought endless rounds of drink, toasting those whose money he had taken, unaware that

at the same time as they accepted his desperate largess they had
nothing but contempt for him.

Andrew's reputation for holding illicit card games, spread
throughout the university by losers who wanted quick and easy
revenge, came to the administrator's attention. When his father
died, Andrew was one step from expulsion. George Stoughton's
passing gave Andrew the excuse he needed to leave. He never
realized he was the only one who believed it.

At Lloyds the reality of the world his mother had tried so
desperately to protect him from descended upon Andrew with a
vengeance. The work in the Maritime Division hall of ledgers
was tedious beyond belief, the people around him infected with a
pallor that ate into their souls. As the months wore on, Andrew
realized that he would have to change his fate or else surrender
and permit it to grind him into dust.

Salvation came in the form of a junior executive Andrew
bumped into at the local pub. He had been at Cambridge during
Andrew's years and unlike his fellows had actually won money
in the midnight games. The two began to meet regularly for
lunch and it wasn't long before Andrew was introduced to others
who had gone from a university straight into the company's
management positions. Soon Andrew was receiving invitations
to country homes and parties in the West End, where the women
and wines were equally exotic.

At twenty-three Andrew had already enjoyed his share of
sexual favors, but it wasn't until St. John's Wood and Knightsbridge
opened up to him that he realized the power he had at his
command. Undeniably handsome, with a roguish quality that
first attracted then fascinated, Andrew discovered that the daughters of Harley Street physicians and Middle Temple barristers
were bored by men who were nothing more than overgrown
schoolboys. It wasn't long before the staff of Claridges recognized him—if not his ever-changing companions—instantly.

Andrew never thought of himself as using women. He drove
their MGs or Aston-Martins, drank their fathers' claret, and
accepted gifts of jewelry and clothing. What he gave back was
something these women had never before had from a man: a
sympathetic ear.

It was a measure of Andrew's prowess—and innocence—that
even when he gently wound down a relationship, the girl involved never felt slighted but had only glowing tributes for him.
Each felt that Andrew truly cared about her, which was the truth.
It was just that he cared about himself more.

Andrew's reputation with women earned him a grudging respect and admiration from the young turks at Lloyds. Flattered by their attention and knowing full well that since he had tasted the succulent life he could never again go back, Andrew began to push his newfound friends for information on stocks and bonds. He didn't have much to invest but felt he had to start building his fortune somewhere. He was a young man in a great hurry.

After his first year at Lloyds, Andrew was approached by one of the young turks to buy in on a venture the group was sponsoring. Since he didn't have sufficient capital, the group was willing to finance his share—if he could make a few discreet but vital changes to certain maritime files.

In spite of the glittering opportunity to make more money in one stroke than his father had earned in his entire career, Andrew balked. For the first time in his life he felt he was moving dangerously out of his depth. Although he wanted desperately to believe he was equal to his well-heeled, well-connected friends, Andrew's working-class antennae warned of danger. Continually pressed to make up his mind, taunted by some who hadn't wanted him in on the deal in the first place, Andrew was racked by indecision. Had he read his classics at Cambridge a little more carefully, he might have recognized the temptation sent his way for what it was.

Her name was Teresa and she was a glacial, ephemeral vision that drifted through the society columns of London papers. She was also the sister of one of Andrew's would-be partners.

Teresa, who had never given Andrew a second glance, descended on him with all the power of her raven-haired beauty and unattainability. Using tiny smiles and intimate caresses, she wove a web of fantasy around Andrew, making him her consort in London society. She also made it very clear that as much as she loved him, she could never marry a poor man.

Andrew swallowed the golden bait and never felt the hook. With visions of a magnificent society wedding dancing in his head, he agreed to file certain papers in the Maritime Division ledgers to seal his fate with his new friends.

The Greek merchantman the group had ostensibly "bought" was insured by Lloyds. In due course reports of her capsizing and sinking were confirmed and the claim forwarded for settlement. But a sharp-eyed investigator noticed certain discrepancies, which in turn led to others. Eventually it was discovered that the ship in question had been lying on the bottom of the

Mediterranean for ten years. When the dust had settled, the paperwork revealed that Andrew Stoughton, wittingly or otherwise, had insured a ghost.

Throughout the internal investigation Andrew stubbornly maintained his innocence in the affair, but his replies to the interrogators' questions were unconvincing. Andrew refused to implicate his friends. He felt duty-bound to keep them out of the investigation, to prove to them and Teresa that he was worthy of belonging. Only when the threat of dismissal became one of criminal prosecution did he surrender their names.

Andrew never doubted his friends would stand by him. During his suspension from Lloyds he tried frantically to contact them. But no one answered his calls and he was politely but firmly turned away at the doors of their homes. The worst of it was Teresa's silent disappearance.

Andrew sweated out the time before the inquiry hearing in his tiny bed-sit. When he was at last summoned he was devastated to find he was the only accused. The inquiry counsel informed him that the merchantman he had insured was owned by a series of nameplate companies stretching between Panama and Hong Kong. The true owners were impossible to trace. Since his was the only signature of record, he alone would be prosecuted on the fraud and extortion charges.

Dismissed from Lloyds and warned not to leave London, Andrew watched his golden world, which had been so tantalizingly near, crumble. In a fit of rage he stormed into a West End party only to find his friends laughing at him and Teresa in the arms of another man. Andrew, on the brink of madness, saw not his friends but the beautiful Teresa as the betrayer. At that moment Andrew, who had truly believed he had found love, began to nourish a deep loathing and contempt for all women. All the misery he left in his wake over the years had not even come close to erasing the indelible memory of that first humiliation.

The drug had him now. He could feel its thousands of tiny chisels digging away at his psyche, loosening the coils of madness that trapped his brain. Andrew glanced at his watch. Only three minutes had elapsed, certainly not long enough for his secretary to become suspicious. He ran the taps again, filling the basin and plunging his face into the icy water. He held it there for as long as he could.

Lloyds had kept Andrew dangling on the hook of uncertainty for almost two weeks. He would wake up sick with anticipation that the final, inevitable act would be played out that day. He had thought of running but made himself believe that that was exactly what they were waiting for, for him to add to the already incontrovertible evidence of his guilt. So he waited, alone in that miserable bed-sit, ears straining for the pounding of feet on the stairs, the rap on the door, the constables staring at him with contempt.

The nightmare came true but not in the way Andrew had expected. Instead of the police it was Silas Lambros who had appeared. Dazed, Andrew had listened in silence as the legendary head of Tyne & Wear explained that he had induced Lloyds not to prosecute. In return, he expected Andrew Stoughton to start work the next day as a clerk in the conglomerate's financial division. Silas Lambros made it clear Andrew had no choice in the matter. If he should do anything to displease his new master he would find himself enjoying the hospitality of Wormwood Scrubs prison.

The old bastard would have had me chained for life, Andrew thought, toweling his face. If I hadn't seen my chance at redemption for exactly what it was: a prison with walls as thick as those of Wormwood Scrubs. But I can't settle with Silas, not yet. . . .

Carefully, Andrew checked his appearance in the mirror. There wasn't a hair out of place, nothing to indicate the torturous passage he had just survived. As he stared at his reflection, he saw the terrified face of the lovely Teresa, her knuckles white on the steering wheel, her eyes darting wildly between the road ahead of her and the impassive expression of the driver in the car beside her. She was screaming, wrenching the wheel to steer him off, accelerating in a vain attempt to escape. Until the road suddenly disappeared and the white convertible sailed over the precipice near a remote Swiss village whose name wasn't even on the map.

Andrew remembered how stark Teresa's black hair had been against the white of her car. Rebecca would look the same way in her final seconds, helpless, paralyzed, utterly defeated. And like Teresa, Rebecca would realize, in those final seconds, the terrible price for the small victory she had won.

· 25 ·

"I still don't believe it!"

Dallas loved the ring of wonder in Rebecca's voice. She reminded him of a child catching the first glimpse of the presents under the tree on Christmas morning.

Dallas had found her walking the grounds at twilight, looking around herself as though seeing The Tides for the first time.

The ten *palapas* were all up, set in a rough semicircle behind a row of vegetation that separated them from the beach. Each hut had a veranda and was positioned so that the trade winds swept through the screened windows, cooling the interior. On the decks were lacquered stumps of ironwood that served as small tables. Large spikes had been driven into one of the supporting pillars and the frame, waiting for hammocks to be strung between them.

The partially finished interiors were identical: a built-in bed frame, closet, cabinet, and desk. Large fans were suspended from the peaks of the roofs.

"It still looks bare," Rebecca admitted. "The chairs, bedding, and decorations will add the color."

Rebecca moved from one *palapa* to the next, examining each in detail. She loved the sweet cloying smell of the wood, the airiness provided by the steepled roof, and the sense of peace and privacy that made each hut its own little world.

"If I were to come here, I wouldn't want to leave," Dallas said.

Set apart from the dwellings was the largest *palapa*, four times the size of the others. The ceiling rose thirty feet at the crown, giving the enormous room a vaulted effect. Divided by a wall of bamboo, the left-hand side was an open-air dining room with reed shutters that, in bad weather, could be dropped at a second's notice and firmly tied down. On the right was a built-in bar and a semicircular area for the lounge.

Behind the dining room was the kitchen, barren except for the pipes and electrical outlets jutting from the floor and walls. Beside it was the pantry. To the left of the bar a small area had been roughed out for Rebecca's office.

Rebecca walked slowly through the *palapa,* running her hand over the wood surfaces as though reassuring herself that everything was real. At the entrance to the kitchen she paused, watching Dallas as he leaned against the molasses-colored railing of the veranda and lighted a cigarette.

He's given me six months of his life without asking for anything in return. Why? What can any of this mean to him?

Rebecca had never expected Dallas to stay for as long as he had. At first she thought he'd leave after the mangrove had been cleared. Then she expected him to be gone once the heavy work of cutting and treating the logs had been finished. When the time came to dig the ditches and lay the pipes, surely he'd sail off. But he hadn't.

As the weeks passed, Dallas Gibson had become a familiar part of the self-contained universe on Windemere Key. Rebecca found it reassuring to hear his voice first thing in the morning, talking to the men as they broke bread and papaya. Dallas's skilled organization quickly gained the workers' respect. Although Rebecca's team from Angeline City and the Mayans from the interior of the country were worlds apart, Dallas soon had them working side by side. Instinctively he knew just how far and how hard he could push the men. Thinking back, Rebecca remembered how many times her own decisions about the schedule had been the result of an observation Dallas had made.

Yet for all his influence over the workers, Dallas never usurped Rebecca's authority. His suggestions were never made in front of the men. Whenever there was a difference of opinion, Rebecca prevailed.

Yet there was another side to this man who loved to play dominoes around the fire and captained the Mayans in soccer against Rebecca's men. Sometimes Rebecca glimpsed his private moments, when he sat at the water's edge with a Mayan, listening intently, drawing figures in the wet sand with a stick. Several times Rebecca had gone to that spot before the tide erased the drawings. She stared at them for a long time but couldn't decipher the hieroglyphics. She never asked him to explain them to her.

There was the Dallas Gibson who, at dusk, took his vessel off the reef for an hour's fishing, a solitary figure outlined against the horizon. He could be seen coming down the hill at dawn

234 PHILIP SHELBY

while everyone was still asleep. Why he went up there and what he found—if anything—Rebecca never knew.

Watching him smoke his cigarette, content in the silence that had enveloped the two of them, Rebecca wanted to know more about this scholarly man who appeared so self-contained. Sometimes, when she felt his presence so keenly, she looked around to find his gaze locked on her. Rebecca wished he would come to her and hold her and tell her all the silent things that swam behind those hazel eyes.

He still feels responsible for Max's accident, Rebecca thought. *The words I spoke at Pusilha weren't enough. Maybe he doesn't even believe I've forgiven him.*

Rebecca took a tentative step toward Dallas. In spite of the gratitude she felt, and the undeniable physical attraction, Rebecca found it difficult to trust him completely. Whenever her loneliness threatened to get the better of her, when she ached to feel Dallas's body beside hers, Rebecca always looked at her sea horse. Sometimes the temptation to rip it off and fling it into the ocean was overwhelming. Yet she couldn't bring herself to do it. The pendant was a reminder of her promise to Max, one day to avenge his death and see to it the guilty were punished.

What kind of life does that condemn me to?

His touch, unexpected yet so gentle, startled her.

"Let's walk," Dallas said.

He slipped his arm around her waist as though it were the most natural thing in the world. Wordlessly Rebecca fell into step with him, conscious of their hips bumping lightly as they walked to the beach and toward the cove. It felt so right and so good, she wished they could go on like that forever.

When Dallas spoke his voice was soft, reflective. He looked straight ahead at the moonlit silver beach and spoke of things as though the events he described were unfolding directly before him. He told Rebecca of his boyhood in San Francisco and his first trip to Mérida in Mexico, where he had climbed the Mayan ruins with his father.

"I didn't want to go home," Dallas said. "I would have been happy to stay there for the rest of my life."

The fascination with Mayan culture and lore found its natural expression in archaeology. From high school Dallas had gone directly to the University of Chicago, one of the country's leading schools in the field. He finished his undergraduate degree in three years and his master's in eighteen months. His fieldwork in Egypt under the world-renowned Dr. Emil Shulmann guaranteed him early admission to the doctoral program. Dallas had been halfway through his field research in the Angelines when he had met Max.

"Max opened up the world of the Maya to me. He knew more about their civilization than most experts. It wasn't until later, when he told me about Apho Hel, that I realized I could help him."

Dallas studied every scrap of information Max had culled on Apho Hel's tribe. Because Pusilha had obviously held a special significance for Apho Hel, he used it as his base. As the excavations proceeded, Dallas spent exhausting hours deciphering hieroglyphic inscriptions and codes, searching for the one clue that would tell him where the tribe had gone. On the slimmest of leads he trekked through the jungle to authenticate his findings, each time plunging deeper into the rain forests, discovering Mayan sites no one had even suspected might exist. His findings created intense excitement in the archaeological world, but the fate of Apho Hel and her people remained as elusive as ever.

"Pusilha is the key," Dallas said. "I know if we dig deep enough, we'll find a clue to her disappearance."

Rebecca took his hand and made him face her.

"One day, when I can take Max's place and help you, will you find her for me?"

Dallas ran his fingers through her thick sable hair and slowly drew her mouth to his.

"I promise you I'll find her."

With that kiss Rebecca felt his love pour into her. As she trembled under the passion of his touch she became aware of something more, a feeling she had never experienced with Andrew: that someone not only loved her but truly cared for her.

There is someone for each of us in this world.

Jewel's words shone with the radiance that was all about her that night, and Rebecca couldn't believe they weren't true.

"We'd better be getting back," Rebecca said.

They had been standing like statues, made alabaster by the moonlight. The tide had crept up but they were oblivious to the warm water swirling around their ankles. Reluctantly, with final lingering touches, they parted.

"When are you leaving for New York?" Dallas asked as they walked toward the lights.

"In two days. I don't think anyone will be moving tomorrow."

Dallas laughed. "That much is guaranteed."

Rebecca had planned a huge dinner for everyone after the last nail had been driven in. Jewel had gone to Angeline City and returned with the makings of a magnificent feast, the centerpiece of which was a whole pig, now roasting luau style in a covered pit dug on the beach. She had also brought back enough rum to sink a battleship.

"What about you?" Rebecca asked.

"The men will be heading back to Pusilha. I'll go with them—unless you haven't made arrangements for someone to look after the place while you're gone."

Silently Rebecca chided herself for not having thought of this. She couldn't leave The Tides unprotected.

"I don't know," she said.

"Let me work out some arrangement with Bones to have food and other supplies brought out," Dallas said gently.

Rebecca cupped his face in both hands.

"You've already done so much for me—"

Dallas pressed a finger against her lips.

"Then let me stay and see this through to the end. Believe me, the worst that can happen is the Mayans taking all my money in poker."

"I'll be back as soon as I can," Rebecca promised.

Dallas looked into her eyes and said, "I'm counting on it."

· 26 ·

New York in May, with its warm, breezy days and comfortably cool nights, acted like an elixir on Rebecca. She felt its effect the minute she spotted Lauren and Ramsey Peet outside the gate at LaGuardia.

Lauren embraced her, then held her at arm's length and exclaimed, "Rebecca, I don't recognize you at all!"

Rebecca grinned, suddenly very conscious of Lauren's chic opposite her own faded denims, much-scrubbed blouse, and beaten sneakers.

Ramsey Peet knew that his wife hadn't been referring to Rebecca's clothing. There was a difference in her and the exterior was only a hint: the tiny furrows on a once smooth forehead, the sharp lines between the sides of her nose to the edge of her lips. The rest of the difference lay in the gray eyes, lighter now, Ramsey thought, but also more distant. Cautious, probing eyes to match a confident, even commanding, voice.

"You've nothing planned for this afternoon, have you?" Lauren asked, and, without waiting for a reply, carried on. "That's good. You can have my appointment at Miro's. I don't know how you could have abused that lovely skin of yours. And your hair! Tell her, Ramsey."

"You're beautiful," Ramsey said, chuckling.

Nonetheless Rebecca spent the afternoon at Miro's, New York's most exclusive spa. Following a thorough scrubbing in a Japanese bath, her body was handed over to a Swedish woman with the strength of a Clydesdale whose sausagelike fingers managed to loosen and relax every muscle built up on Windemere Key.

"If I had to guess, I'd say you were either a ballerina or a construction worker, lady," the Swede muttered in pure Brooklynese as she refined her torture.

"I think . . . I want . . . to see . . . my lawyer," Rebecca gasped.

"Hey, that's good!" The Swede chortled and continued to punish a trapezoid muscle.

When Lauren returned for her she brought Rebecca two new outfits: a raw silk pants suit by Balmain and a breezy spring dress from Suzy Prentiss of London.

"Now, that's the Rebecca I remember," Lauren said approvingly as the makeup artist finished with her.

After the ordeal with Tina the Terrible, Rebecca had wanted to call it quits. Yet she hadn't felt this pampered and relaxed in months. To hell with feeling guilty. She deserved this!

Suddenly she wished very much that Dallas could see her.

"Where are we off to next?" she asked, slipping into the Peets' limousine.

"I thought we'd have tea at the Plaza before heading home. Dinner isn't until nine. Bix and Torrey are meeting us in Chinatown. They can't wait to see you."

As the driver navigated the traffic up Sixth, Lauren chatted on about how well Torrey's business was doing and the charming Village brownstone he and Bix shared.

"I thought of asking Eric Walker to join us. There's still time to call him."

Rebecca shot her a pointed look.

"Don't you start being a matchmaker," she warned. "That's Jewel's prerogative."

She ignored Lauren's exaggerated pout.

The reunion with Bix was everything Rebecca had imagined it would be. As they worked their way through such exotic fare as turegake chicken, camphor- and tea-smoked duck, and abalone with mushrooms, the two women breathlessly caught up with each other's lives.

What it all comes down to, Rebecca thought, feeling the glow of Bix's radiance, is Torrey. Every woman needs a man to make her feel wanted.

Torrey's attentiveness toward Bix, his gentle teasing when she got carrried away on a pet peeve, the minute touches and caresses, spoke volumes.

As she was thinking about this, Rebecca heard Ramsey say, "I understand you saw quite a bit of Dallas Gibson in the Angelines."

Rebecca flushed. "Yes, I did."

She immediately changed the subject, but the brief silence around the table told her everyone had noticed the evasion.

By midnight Rebecca had had every detail of the building of The Tides coaxed out of her. The pictures had all been passed around, and final shots of mai-tai, a clear, fiery Chinese liqueur, thrown back. Rebecca hugged Lauren and Ramsey, telling them not to wait up for her. She and Bix would probably stay up all night talking.

The Perry Street brownstone was markedly different from what Rebecca had remembered. When the building had gone co-op, Torrey had bought the second-floor walk-through apartment and left the interior decorating to Bix. Large free-form sofas covered in corduroy, Navajo throw rugs, Indian brass planters, and framed prints by Warhol and Roy Lichtenstein gave the living room a warm, easy feel.

"Well, ladies, I'm sure you've got a lot of jawin' to do," Torrey said. "I'm going to sack out."

"You're getting old," Bix muttered, but still returned his kiss passionately.

"He loves you very much, doesn't he?" Rebecca said.

"Of course," Bix said airily. "What's not to love?"

When she brought coffee from the kitchen and settled herself against a pile of thick wool cushions, she added, "Next to you, he's the best thing that's ever happened to me."

Bix waited to hear if Rebecca would break the silence. When she didn't, Bix said, "Talk to me, Becky."

The words came haltingly at first, like timid woodland creatures, then faster, until Rebecca had no way of stopping them even if she wanted to. Every secret fear she had carefully hidden away rushed out.

Rebecca told Bix about the bribe she had had to pay to obtain her license, the difficulty in getting workmen, the way she had been cheated over the lumber. She described the state of fear she had lived in, waiting for something else to go wrong. She spoke of the grueling hours and how often she had almost given up because no matter how hard she worked, the dream kept receding instead of coming closer.

By the time Rebecca finished, Bix was seeing quite a different picture from the one Rebecca had drawn over dinner, filled with breathless adventure and amusing anecdotes.

"But you've done it!" Bix told her over and over again. "The Tides is real now. No one can take it away from you."

"It may be real but it's far from finished," Rebecca replied. She explained how much equipment was still needed and the astronomical prices it fetched in the Caribbean. "There's no way I can afford to buy it down there, even secondhand."

"Do you have a list of what you need?"

Chewing on her lip, Bix studied the papers Rebecca handed her.

"No problem," she announced cheerfully.

"I see," Rebecca said dryly. "You're going to pull it all out of a hat, are you?"

"A very big hat. Don't make any plans for the day after tomorrow."

Bix refused to elaborate and changed the topic.

"You want to tell me about Dallas?"

Rebecca was tempted. Dallas had kept drifting in and out of her mind since she had left the Angelines. The thought of him warmed her and the memory of his kisses added an extra beat to her heart. Still, she wasn't exactly sure how she was going to bring him into her life—if at all. Deliberately Rebecca had forced herself not to anticipate, to dispel the dreams. Dreams could be dangerous, fatal, like creatures whose tentacles made one helpless. A victim.

"So how about it?" Bix persisted.

"There's nothing to tell."

Bix looked keenly at her friend and nodded.

"Okay. You know and I know I'm going to worm it out of you before you leave."

Not this time, Rebecca thought, and using Bix's tactics, sweetly asked her if she was pregnant or merely putting on weight.

Two days later Bix rented a car and she and Rebecca drove out to Orient Point on Long Island. There they boarded the ferry that plies the choppy Atlantic waters between the Point and New London, Connecticut.

"New London has one of the largest navy bases in the country," Bix informed Rebecca as they drove up to the gatehouse.

"Where did you get these?" Rebecca asked, examining the visitor's pass a Shore Patrol officer handed her.

"You're forgetting Daddy is an admiral."

The size of the New London complex staggered Rebecca. There were miles of piers, lined with battleships, destroyers, frigates, and tenders. Bix had to reduce her maniacal driving speed to a crawl to avoid hitting the sailors and officers who hurried along the narrow streets. She stopped before a huge warehouse surrounded by a cyclone fence and informed the shore patrol they were expected.

"Well, this is it," Bix said as the quartermaster, clipboard tucked under one arm, escorted them inside.

Rebecca gazed around, bewildered. As far as she could see, there were crates of machinery and equipment set on pallets, stacked forty feet high.

"We've got everything from turbines to nail files," the quartermaster told them. "You might want to use this map. It'll tell you where to find what you're looking for. Otherwise you could spend a week in here and get plain lost."

Judging by the cavernous dimensions of the warehouse, Rebecca believed him.

While Bix fiddled with the starter on the electric golf cart, Rebecca asked quietly, "Bix, what is this place and what the hell are we doing here?"

"This, my dear, is the largest surplus warehouse on the East Coast. And if we can't find here what you need for The Tides, then we're in big trouble. You take the map and navigate. Hang on!"

As they raced down the alleys between the towering crates, Bix explained that the navy always ended up with material it couldn't use on either its ships or shore bases. Twice a year it auctioned off this surplus. The buyers ranged from institutions to individuals.

"The spring selloff is next week," Bix shouted as they careened around a corner. "We're getting a head start."

They spent all afternoon in the warehouse, dashing from one corner to the next with Rebecca matching her list against the quartermaster's map. She found everything she could possibly need to outfit The Tides: mattresses and bedding once consigned to officers' quarters in Subic Bay in the Philippines; an entire kitchen—still crated—that had been earmarked for Pearl Harbor; generators, lanterns, and electrical equipment that was supposed to have gone to Rota in Spain.

"How much is all this going to cost me?" Rebecca wondered aloud when she and Bix were done.

She had less than five thousand dollars left and needed a fifth of that to lay in provisions at The Tides. She also had to consider the cost of shipping to the Angelines.

"Why don't you make an offer?" Bix suggested casually.

Rebecca checked the price list only to discover that the navy intended to start the bidding on the material she wanted at double what she could afford to pay. Three times Rebecca went over the inventory, cutting corners where she could. Still the total defeated her.

"It's no use," she said miserably.

"Give me a figure, Becky," Bix said patiently.

Rebecca scribbled down her offer and Bix walked off to the quartermaster. Ten minutes later she was back.

"Write out a check for the full amount," Bix told her.

"What?"

"Don't ask questions, just write the check!"

Stunned, Rebecca filled in the amount and watched Bix disappear. She returned with a triumphant smile, flourishing a stamped bill of sale.

"Compliments of the navy, Becky. Our own version of a little foreign aid. Now go kick Silas Lambros's butt!"

Three months later, at the end of August, Rebecca was standing on the edge of the largest wharf at Angeline City harbor, anxiously scanning the horizon. It was already nine o'clock in the morning and the vessel she was waiting for should have arrived at dawn.

The ninety days since she had left New York had passed in a whirlwind. Rebecca returned to Windemere Key and, calling six men back to work, began to put the finishing touches to the resort.

Where each *palapa* had once been separated from the others by a stretch of beaten dirt, there was now a grassy carpet, accented by shrubs and flowers with such exotic names as angel's trumpet, plumbago, and match-me-if-you-can. Avocado pear, passion fruit, and granadilla trees dotted the paths while chalice flower and queen's wreath vines decorated the exterior of the central *palapa*.

The interior of the huts had also been transformed. Jewel's craftsmen had fashioned strong cane chairs and coffee tables. In each room was hung a painting, bold and primitive, by a local artist, and over each bed was a decorative wall hanging. The straw floor mats, with their unique designs, added the final accent.

When she wasn't working on the refinements to The Tides, Rebecca set about organizing the last step of her plan. She took hundreds of photographs of her property and scrutinized each one with a critical eye. If they were not exactly what she wanted, she went out and took more. In the evenings she studied the brochures produced by Caribbean resorts and hotels, breaking down their ad copy, determining which was the most effective, then writing her own. The results were sent to Bix and Torrey at GoSee. Suggestions and comments went back and forth in the mail until everyone was satisfied. In Bix's last letter Rebecca learned that the artwork and copy had gone to the printer. The finished product would be waiting for Rebecca when she arrived in New York, after everything was ready at The Tides.

If that damn boat ever gets here! Rebecca thought.

Shortly before lunch the merchantman *Baltimore,* on lease to the U.S. Navy, was made fast at the dock. Rebecca raced on board to speak to the captain. She let out a huge sigh of relief when the cargo manifest matched her own bill of lading.

"How soon can you unload?" Rebecca asked. "I've got men ready for the transfer."

The captain smiled and pointed to the merchantman's crane which was already hoisting pallets from the hold to the dock.

"Your stuff is first off—by special request from Admiral Ryan."

Rebecca planted a big kiss on the captain's cheek and shot down the gangplank. Her ship had come in.

· 27 ·

By mid-September, when the season had changed from green to gold and burnt orange, Rebecca returned to New York. She was in the familiar but, this being the end of the day, silent offices of GoSee International, sitting on a packing crate in the storeroom.

"How many of these did you have printed up?" she asked Torrey, waving a four-color brochure for The Tides.

"Ten thousand," Torrey said laconically.

"What in God's name am I going to do with ten thousand brochures? Do you realize how much it will cost to mail them?"

"Hold on, Becky," Bix said. "First of all, it was cheaper to print this many. Second, you'll go through them before you know it. And third, no one's mailing anything. We're going to deliver these."

Rebecca eyed her warily.

"Bix, what have you dreamed up now?"

"Actually it's the same principle Torrey used when he was starting out. There's a northeast phenomenon that students have been savvy to for years called the driveaway plan. People who are moving or going on vacation and want to use their car in, say, Florida or the Carolinas don't always drive there. They give their car to an agency, which in turn hands it over to reasonably upstanding citizens like ourselves to deliver it. The company provides expense money for gas plus a small fee. The most important thing to us is the ridiculous amount of time they allot to get the car to a particular destination. For example, a whole week from Boston to Miami. Since we could do that distance in less than thirty hours of nonstop driving, do you realize the number of places we could hit in between?"

"And if we get a big sedan, we can take as much material as will fit," Rebecca said, her eyes gleaming.

"Nothing less than a station wagon," Bix agreed.

"What are we waiting for?"

*   *   *

During the next four weeks Rebecca and Bix went as far north as Bangor, Maine, west to Chicago and Green Bay, south to Atlanta, and right up the Atlantic seaboard. There were even three forays into Canada at Montreal, Ottawa, and Toronto.

Armed with Torrey's guide listing all American universities and colleges, they chose cities which were either university towns or hubs for several colleges in the vicinity. Having selected the area, Bix had arranged for driveaway cars through GoSee. If they were lucky, the final destination also had a large student population.

Once they arrived on campus Bix headed for the student travel center. Using a letter of introduction from Torrey, she cajoled the directors to take hundreds of brochures and made them promise to mention The Tides when they advertised in the student paper. She explained the best way to get to the Angelines and left sample sheets of airline fares and schedules. On occasion she sweetened the pot by promising the director a personal tour of the Angelines if he brought a group down.

Rebecca went around to the dormitories and pinned brochures to any bulletin board she could find. She left pamphlets with every club and society on campus and prowled the lecture halls in search of corkboard. She walked into sorority and fraternity houses and talked to as many members as she could. She even slipped into faculty clubs. Her weapons were the stapler and thumbtack and she used them ruthlessly.

Wherever possible, the two women slept on campus or in cheap rooming houses that catered to students. They ate in student cafeterias and used the athletic facilities for a quick shower and change of clothing. Then it was back into the car or van and an all-night drive to the next stop.

The pace was grueling but Rebecca's enthusiasm never flagged. With each campus they struck, she became more and more convinced that she and Bix had chosen the right approach. She was overwhelmed by the large number of students concentrated in a relatively small area. Here was a population that lived in the cold for six months of the year, to whom sun and sand was a faraway, often financially impractical dream. The best they could hope for was a few days in a crammed room in Fort Lauderdale during the madness of spring break. Well, now they had a choice. If only one half of one percent of these students made the effort to get a cheap flight from Miami to Angeline City, they could spend a whole week in her paradise for the niggardly sum of twenty dollars a day, including food. All drinks were advertised for one dollar. The sun, the beach, the ocean were thrown in gratis.

But they've got to know The Tides exists!

This was the thought that kept Rebecca going when she felt she couldn't drive another mile on a gloomy rainswept turnpike or stomach one more greasy-spoon meal. Somehow, when she and Bix compared notes at the end of the day, she managed to forget her exhaustion and discomfort.

When they returned to New York in October, Torrey showed them the reservations system he had worked out. Another phone number had been added to GoSee's line. Torrey's people would take the reservations, bank the deposits, and handle flight particulars. After sending the client a confirmation notice and voucher, GoSee would call Rebecca, who would meet the plane in Angeline City and ferry the people over to Windemere.

"You're sure everything's ready on your end?" Torrey asked over lunch the day Rebecca was to fly back.

Even the delicious seafood salad at the Plaza's Oyster Bar failed to tempt Rebecca. She was too nervous to eat.

"All the kitchen equipment was installed and checked out. The bathroom fixtures all work. The generator puts out more than enough power and the cisterns are full. The *palapas* are ready—only the beds have to be made. I've even got cartons of toothbrushes and extra towels."

Rebecca smiled weakly. "The only thing that's missing are the people."

Torrey grinned and pulled out a pink check from his wallet.

"Well, you're going to have at least two. This came in while you ladies were still on the road. Figured I'd wait till now to give it to you, send you off on a high note."

Slowly Rebecca read the name of the payee on the check: GoSee—and in brackets, The Tides.

Opening day for The Tides was the last Thursday of November, the beginning of the Thanksgiving weekend. The more days she crossed off the calendar, the more impossible Rebecca became to live with. She knew it but there was nothing she could do about it.

It was Jewel who bore the brunt of Rebecca's frayed nerves. When the two women went into Angeline City to interview cooks and maids, Rebecca subjected each applicant to a barrage of questions, often leaving her on the verge of tears.

"You're not looking for a chef to run the first minister's kitchens!" Jewel hissed as another chastened applicant withdrew.

"No, I want someone better," Rebecca told her. "I'm not going to settle for second best!"

Jewel finally conspired with Dallas Gibson to keep Rebecca away while she hired the kitchen and cleaning staff.

When the time came to provision The Tides, Rebecca haunted the markets, rejecting almost everything offered to her.

"Your people sure goin' to lose a lot of weight down here," Jewel said.

Rebecca saw the wisdom in Jewel's observation and promptly put in her orders. Jewel was mortified.

"Where do you plan to store all this?" she demanded, pointing to the crates of fish and hanging carcasses Rebecca had bought.

"In the freezer?" Rebecca said hopefully.

Jewel rolled her eyes and trundled off to cancel the order.

There was a host of what Rebecca saw as last-minute glitches. Once, in the middle of the night, she woke up Jewel.

"I just realized the glasses haven't arrived!"

"They'll be here soon enough," Jewel groaned.

"But what if they're not!"

"Then folks'll drink beer out of the bottles like everyone else and we'll use plastic cups."

Rebecca thought this sounded reasonable.

"Will we have enough ice?"

Whatever problems Rebecca had—or thought she had—lack of reservations wasn't one of them. By the middle of November, Thanksgiving weekend was sold out and, according to Bix, reservations over the Christmas–New Year's period were coming in. An early winter storm that had dumped a foot of snow throughout the northeast was doing wonders for business.

If the yellow confirmation slips from GoSee weren't enough to convince Rebecca, the November statement from the Walker Bank did. For the first and only time since the McHenry Enterprises account had been opened the precipitous slide in the balance had stopped.

On November 24, two days before The Tides' official opening, Rebecca returned to the mainland. She went around Angeline City and picked up the employees Jewel had hired. Back at Jewel's house, she carefully went over their responsibilities one last time. In the evening, just before the markets closed, she supervised the transfer of food, liquor, and beer to the waiting barge. Everyone would spend the night at Jewel's. The next morning, before dawn, Rebecca would drive them to the barge, which would sail immediately. There would be no chance of anyone being left behind. Rebecca herself would spend the night on the vessel, close to her provisions, the shotgun within easy reach. If Silas Lambros had any surprises for her, this was the time he would play his hand.

On Windemere Key, Dallas Gibson made his final walkaround. He had done this every night since Rebecca's departure even though he knew that he and the three Mayans who had stayed behind were the only people on the key. For Dallas, The Tides was more than just a collection of *palapas*. It was an extension of the woman he ached to hold again, and he was determined to protect it as though it were made of her own flesh and blood.

By the fire on the beach Dallas took a cup of coffee with his men, then disappeared into the bunkhouse. For the longest time he lay on his side looking out the window at the open sea, imagining that the lights of passing ships belonged to Angeline City. Then he fell asleep and dreamed of Rebecca.

The three intruders moved in single file out of the jungle that covered the center of Windemere Key, stepping cautiously into the clearing. Beneath the moon the beach was a diamond-studded cape, highlighted by the black swell of ocean. A fire was burning brightly on the sand, casting wavering shadows of the three men who sat around it, smoking and talking softly, their rifles set up against one another in a pyramid.

The leader of the marauders knelt by a post of one of the *palapas* and took in the scene. It was exactly as he had been told to expect. The men guarding the resort were obviously not anticipating any trouble. Weeks of boring duty had eroded their wariness, making them easy prey.

The leader whispered to his men. The instructions of the man who had hired them had been specific: There was to be no killing. As he watched his two attackers melt into the night and circle toward the fire, the leader removed the cloth between the bottles strapped to his belt and let the glass clink together. The alien sound sent birds winging from their roosts in the palms.

As expected, one of the three Mayans rose to investigate. As soon as he was far enough away from the other two, the attackers pounced. The leader took down the third man himself, clubbing him viciously behind the ear. A few minutes later the unconscious guards were trussed up, gagged, and tied around a palm trunk.

The leader moved out onto the beach and surveyed the silent empty *palapas* while his men removed a dozen bottles, their necks stuffed with rags, from a knapsack. The odor of gasoline drifted in the air. As soon as the wicks were lit, the homemade bombs would become lethal incendiaries.

Thrown inside a *palapa*, the gasoline would explode, the flames feeding on the dry wood, bamboo, and thatch. The Tides would become a gigantic inferno, burning to the ground in minutes. No one could stop the destruction even if they wanted to. And that was exactly what the man who had hired them had demanded.

The leader flicked open an old Zippo lighter and ignited the wick. With a casual toss he sent the bottle sailing through the large barracklike *palapa*. Within seconds tongues of flame appeared at the windows.

"Let's do the rest," the leader said. "I have something warm waiting for me in my bed."

The others laughed and began to move among the *palapas*. One of them lit a wick and was about to toss the bomb into the dining area of the central *palapa*, when he felt something terribly hot slam into his shoulder. The incendiary traveled only a few yards, exploding harmlessly on the sand.

"I've been shot!" the attacker groaned.

The second gunshot hit one of the bottles lined up by the knapsack. As soon as it exploded, the others went off like dynamite charges.

By this time the leader was prone on the sand. He had been assured there would be only three guards. Where had the fourth come from?

The leader saw the wink of a flash from a muzzle and trained his rifle on the spot. One of his men was down, his incendiaries destroyed. Unless he got this fourth man—and quickly—he would have to retreat. His principal had told him in no uncertain terms that neither he nor his men could be captured. There could be no clues as to who had attacked The Tides.

So be it! the leader thought savagely, pumping rounds into the area where he had seen the flash. First I kill this *puerco,* then I finish the job!

His inducement was five thousand dollars, payable upon evidence that The Tides no longer existed. The leader wasn't about to let such a fortune slip through his fingers.

First light didn't appear until the barge was at the *quebrada*, the channel between the reefs which paralleled Windemere. Also, the wind was blowing away from the key. For these two reasons Rebecca had no hint that anything was amiss. Only when dawn spilled over the horizon did she see the lazy column of smoke rising from the interior.

"Bones, tell the captain to stop and lower the Zodiac."

While Bones Ainsley winched the rubber raft into the water, Rebecca slipped below and got Jewel's shotgun. Mechanically she loaded it, her fingers trembling as she tried to keep down the panic that was tearing her apart. On deck she plunged through the men and women she had brought with her and who were now standing along the rail, transfixed by the evidence of destruction.

"Let me go alone," Bones said to her. "If anyone's still there—"

"I want to see for myself who it is," Rebecca cut him off. "Don't argue with me, Bones. Not on this."

Rebecca jumped into the Zodiac and, gripping the bow lines, pulled hard until the nose of the rubber raft was raised from the water. She braced herself as Bones opened the outboard's throttle and kept her eyes riveted on the beach for any movement.

As the Zodiac raced toward shore the wind changed direction. The smell of charred wood and foliage sent a shiver of terror through Rebecca. She never realized she was whispering aloud, repeating over and over again, "Please, let him be safe!"

A giant fist clutched Rebecca's heart as the Zodiac veered and she glimpsed the smoldering ruins through the trees and brush.

"No, damn it! No! No! No!"

Rebecca leapt from the Zodiac as soon as it reached the shallows. Holding the shotgun waist-high, she plowed through the surf onto the beach, staggering toward the trail that led to the *palapas*. Suddenly her feet caught on something and she almost fell.

Rebecca spun around, staring down at what she had tripped over. Horrified, she sank to her knees and, throwing the gun aside, began to dig furiously. By the time Bones reached her, Rebecca had pulled Dallas Gibson's torso from the sand. His head lay in her lap, an ugly, blood-encrusted gash along the temple.

Rebecca looked up at Bones and the policeman flinched at the anguish in her face. Then Rebecca's head fell forward and her hair settled like a shroud across Dallas's silent features, muffling her sobs.

· 28 ·

The funeral was held on the last day of November, in the private plot of the hilltop cemetery overlooking San Francisco Bay. The winter fog crept among the assembly like an uninvited mourner.

With the exception of Rebecca, the interment was restricted to family. At the funeral home Rebecca had seen the hundreds of people, luminaries from the world of politics, entertainment, and business, who had crammed the chapel to pay their respects. They would all be at the Gibsons' Pacific Heights mansion afterward.

Rebecca stood behind Senator Lewis Gibson, who was flanked by his wife and two daughters. As the minister's final words drifted away, Dallas's mother stepped forward and placed a single, perfect white rose on her son's coffin.

Rebecca waited until the immediate family had filed by to pay their condolences, then stepped forward. After the senator escorted his wife and daughters to the lead limousine, he came back for her. The tranquility of the afternoon was broken by the roar of motorcycle engines as police outriders led the vehicles from the cemetery.

"I hate wakes," Lewis Gibson said suddenly as the second car in the procession glided away. "It's barbaric to have strangers intrude on your grief when all you want is to be left alone with it."

Rebecca understood what he meant. In spite of a guilty conscience, she hadn't been able to bring herself to attend Dallas's wake. There was pain she couldn't hide, yet was so private she cherished it like some fragile talisman that would be shattered if she allowed anyone to glimpse it.

It was the same feeling she had had when she had buried Max.

Rebecca felt Lewis Gibson's strong, weathered hand cover hers, thinking how much it felt like Dallas's, and wished there was some way she could help him.

Dallas's murder and the events that followed had brought her and Lewis Gibson close together. They had shown Rebecca just how alike father and son had been.

"I'm sorry I can't stay," was all she managed to say.

"I don't want you to. We all have our peace to make . . . alone."

The motorcade followed the highway back to the city. By prearrangement the car carrying Rebecca and Lewis Gibson peeled off at the airport exit ramp, taking two police escorts with it.

"You've been a great help to me," Lewis Gibson said. "Your being here made me understand why Dallas was very happy with you, what you meant to him."

The senator passed Rebecca a letter written on blue onion skin.

"It's on the last page."

In his last letter home Dallas had told his father everything about The Tides. His words were full of energy and enthusiasm. Then Rebecca came across her name.

I know you and Mom have been worrying about my not getting married. I guess until I found Rebecca marriage didn't mean a whole lot. I had never known what it was like to love a woman so completely. Rebecca is someone I never believed existed—or at least, that I would ever find. Do you think she'd have a guy who spends his time poking around in history?

"Oh, God, yes," Rebecca whispered, remembering their fleeting hours on the beach. The gentleness of his touch and kiss, the embrace which made her feel loved but not possessed, the restrained passion—those had all been part of Dallas's promise not to demand what she, then, had been unable to give.

Rebecca fought back tears she thought had all been cried. In life Dallas's feelings for her had begun to fill the void of loneliness in which she had been existing. In death they were cruel. Not only did they show Rebecca what she had lost, they were a bitter reminder of the responsibility she bore for what happened.

"He also left this for you," Lewis Gibson said, passing Rebecca a small weathered chamois bag with leather drawstrings.

Rebecca opened the sachet and five brilliantly polished jade stones poured into her palm.

"Do they mean anything to you?" Lewis Gibson asked.

"Not really."

Rebecca looked at the inscriptions on the stones. Had Dallas ever interpreted those strange markings? She curled her fingers around the stones.

"I should never have let him stay on Windemere," she whispered. "If I had thought ahead—"

"What happened to Dallas wasn't your fault," the senator said sharply. "Dallas was there because he wanted to be. No one could have known what would happen. I won't have you blaming yourself."

"I'm not sure I can promise you that."

"I can promise you one thing," Lewis Gibson said, his voice cold like a tomb. "I intend to find out who murdered my boy."

Rebecca said nothing. She remembered Lewis Gibson's frantic arrival in Angeline City, the terrible scene in the hospital morgue, where he had wept over his son's body, the icy control he had displayed while Bones Ainsley reconstructed the grim events.

Bones reckoned there could have been only four attackers.

"The Mayans told me they were ambushed one by one," he explained. "My guess is that Dallas had already gone to bed. When the *palapa* he was sleeping in was torched, he somehow made it out and fought back. At this point he had the element of surprise. The attackers weren't expecting any more resistance. He was able to shoot down three before they could set fire to the rest of the buildings. The fourth man managed to wound him but Dallas must have kept firing back, preventing the lone survivor from completing what he had come to do. When he made a run for the boat they had come in, Dallas followed and tried to stop him. The fact that the boat was still there when we arrived means he got them all."

At that point Bones had paused.

"Your son was shot three times. He was bleeding badly but he continued to fight."

This account of Dallas's heroism was cold comfort to Lewis Gibson. He couldn't understand why the dead killers hadn't been identified. Bones tried to explain that nothing had been found in their clothing and that no one in either Angeline City or Stann Creek Town knew who they were. He held out little hope that anyone from the interior would recognize them from their descriptions.

To Rebecca, the conclusion brought back horrible memories of the impassive face of the driver who had run her off the road in Jamaica. He, too, had never been identified or caught.

In his grief Lewis Gibson had cut a swath right up to the first minister's office, demanding action, threatening the devastating consequences he could inflict on the Angelines. Rebecca had let his fury flow. When he had exhausted himself, she had quietly convinced him that to punish an entire country was not the way to insure justice.

"Use your influence to help Bones," she urged. "He's the best chance we have. If it turns out the killers didn't come from the Angelines, Bones will start looking in the other islands. That's when he may need you."

But as the limousine drew up in front of the terminal building, Rebecca was convinced that not even Lewis Gibson's far-reaching powers would give him the answer he sought so desperately. The target that night hadn't been Dallas but The Tides. And ultimately Rebecca herself. The people who wanted to destroy her were beyond the reach of even a man like Senator Gibson.

I'm the only one who can bring you vengeance. And I will, for your son, and for myself.

"Rebecca, are you all right?" Lewis Gibson asked anxiously.

"I'm fine . . . fine."

Rebecca slid out of the car, struggling to regain her composure.

"Let me walk you to the gate," the senator insisted.

"Lewis, I'm okay, really. It's just that you never know when the finality of it all will hit you. . . ."

She stood on her toes and kissed him quickly on the cheek.

"I won't forget what happened on Windemere," she whispered. "I promise."

But as Rebecca walked swiftly down the concourse, followed by a skycap carrying her bags, another thought entered her mind.

How many more people will suffer because of me and what I'm trying to do?

At that moment Rebecca almost wished The Tides had burned to the ground. She might have yielded to the temptation to walk away from the Angelines once and for all, start a new life somewhere far away from all this death and loss. But she couldn't. The Tides had survived. A man who had meant more to her than she had realized had died protecting her dream.

Even though Dallas's death diminished her, Rebecca understood that now she had yet another murder to avenge. She also realized that at last, she had her enemies placed in their proper perspective. Andrew was the ultimate threat because he wouldn't rest until she, too, was dead. But Andrew was hiding behind

Silas Lambros and Tyne & Wear. To get to him, Rebecca would
first have to settle accounts with the old wrecker.

And that's just fine, she thought grimly, handing her ticket to
the agent. Because he still has something that belongs to me!

The love and trust Dallas Gibson had breathed a frail life into
was extinguished with his death. To lessen the pain of his loss,
Rebecca hid his memory away, returning to the familiar emptiness she had existed in after Andrew's betrayal, an emptiness in
which there were no dreams. Only The Tides was real. Only The
Tides, if it survived and prospered, could become the weapon
she needed. But in order to survive, it had to be protected.

As soon as Rebecca landed in the Angelines, she went to Sam
Meat Pie's hardware store and purchased a pair of rifles and a
shotgun. The two constables Bones had stationed on Windemere
couldn't remain there indefinitely. Rebecca knew her bartender
and handyman were crack shots. The shotgun, a model identical
to the one Max had taught her to use, would remain in her
quarters, out of sight but always loaded and instantly available.

Rebecca arrived on Windemere Key just before the next group
was to fly in. Because there was no telephone on the island, she
had no idea what had happened during that first, crucial week.

"They played until all hours of the morning," Jewel told
Rebecca. "Ate us out of house and home and drank every last
bottle of beer we had."

Jewel's pride at The Tides' success was muted by sadness.
She had been shocked by the violence on Windemere and had
mourned Dallas Gibson, whom she had affectionately adopted
into her Angelinian family.

Going over the receipts in her tiny office, Rebecca thought
that nothing less than an orgy had taken place. The cashbox was
overflowing with crumpled Angelinian and American bills. The
liquor and food stocks were almost depleted. As Rebecca examined the accounts, Jewel told her how successful the barbecues
and boat trips onto the reef had been.

"These children would have stayed forever if they could."

Rebecca was thrilled but she cautioned herself not to be too
optimistic. According to Bix's reservation sheet, the three weeks
until Christmas were lean.

"Well, we have time to restock and clean up a bit," Rebecca
said. "There won't be more than six people on the next plane."

The next morning Rebecca went into Angeline City for provisions. By midmorning Bones's *Mardi Gras* was loaded and wait-

ing to take on the arrivals from CaribAir's Miami flight. Rebecca had expected a half dozen. When she got to the airport, there were twenty excited, very pale faces looking for her.

In a flash Rebecca was on the phone to Torrey.

"Where did you find them?" she demanded. "And more to the point, why didn't you warn me?"

"They're all grad students who've finished their course work and are working on their theses." Torrey laughed. "There are more on the way. Think you can handle them?"

"You bet!"

That week, during which Rebecca was run ragged by her guests, brought about significant, if impromptu, changes in the day-to-day life of The Tides. Rebecca quickly realized that to maintain some kind of order, her guests had to be kept busy—which meant organizing things for them to do. Some were content to lie on the beach all day, but most were curious about this paradise they had been dropped into. Rebecca organized expeditions into the interior of Windemere and hired guides to take groups scuba diving off the reef. Noticing that her guests tended both to turn in late and to sleep late, she changed the meal schedules to suit their hours. Dinner became a nightly barbecue and was moved to nine o'clock, when the cocktail hour finally petered out. Somewhere Rebecca found a volleyball net and strung it up between two poles at one end of the beach. In the afternoons, when the sun had beaten down even the most enthusiastic sportsman, she discovered a demand for paperbacks with which to while away the hours.

Every night Rebecca made copious notes about her guests' likes and dislikes, what they expected and what surprised them, the things they needed and those they could do without. At the end of the second week she had a list of improvements she meant to attend to immediately.

The only real worry facing Rebecca was Jewel. Now that she had experienced firsthand how hectic the pace of The Tides could be, she felt guilty about having left Jewel all alone that first week.

"I won't have you running after them or spending all your time in a hot kitchen," she told her. "I need you in Angeline City, where you can talk to Bix and Torrey direct and let me know via the shortwave what to expect."

Jewel refused to budge.

"Keepin' busy is doin' my heart a world of good," she

informed Rebecca tartly. "Besides, I love these children. They make me feel young."

No matter how hard Rebecca tried to persuade her, Jewel would not leave. In the end Rebecca relented. It was true: The students loved Jewel and immediately adopted her as a kind of den mother.

Ironically, it was money that turned out to be Rebecca's biggest problem. There was too much of it. By Christmas week she had stacks of currency squirreled away in a makeshift safe in her office. Idle money, as Ramsey had taught her, was a sin.

"I don't want to bank it in the Angelines," she told Eric Walker. "It's nobody's business how well The Tides is doing."

Eric came up with an immediate solution.

"There's a special bonded courier flight that leaves Stann Creek Town for Miami every Monday morning. Take the cash to the Brinks office at the airport. They'll count it, seal it, and give you a receipt. Make sure you keep enough for expenses. I'll process the rest into your account and take out short-term ninety-day notes."

Rebecca thought this a sound solution. Nonetheless she telephoned Ramsey and got a second opinion.

"Do it," he advised her, rattling off the current rates. "The Walker's offering you a quarter point more than the competition. Slowly it will add up."

That Monday Rebecca, accompanied by Bones Ainsley, went to the Brinks office in Stann Creek Town airport. She watched as the money was counted and the receipt made out.

"Is something wrong?" the security clerk asked, noticing that Rebecca was frowning at the receipt.

"No, nothing."

When she and Bones were outside, Rebecca let out a giant whoop. Even though she had counted and recounted the money, it wasn't until now that the realization sunk in: The Tides had been netting over a thousand dollars a week.

Incredibly the deluge continued. Not only did reservations keep The Tides full, but people without bookings showed up, hoping to find a vacancy. The demand for space was so great that Rebecca partitioned the bunkhouse where she and Jewel lived into three rooms, squeezing the two of them into the smallest one.

"I think you're on to something," Torrey said in his usual understatement when he and Bix came down in February.

Torrey examined Rebecca's operation with a critical eye. Acting on his suggestions, Rebecca organized shopping and sightseeing excursions into Angeline City. Instead of paying a day rate for the barge that brought her provisions, she worked out a three-month lease, thus cutting her expenses. Contracts with local fishermen provided her guests with the opportunity to do some deep-sea fishing.

"A lot of the girls seem to have come down in twos and threes—and are unattached," Bix observed. "Maybe there's a way you can get them to mix more easily with the guys? . . ."

Rebecca hired an Angelinian trio to play Fridays and Saturdays, and the bar receipts trebled. The music, a mixture of rock and island ballads, was so popular that Rebecca hired the band until spring.

"Maybe we should change our marketing for next season," Rebecca mused, watching couples cling to each other on the dance floor. "Sun, sea, and sex."

"You want to go that route," Torrey agreed. "And you better start thinking expansion."

Rebecca was already three steps ahead of him.

"Maybe you should think about buying an old DC-six and starting a charter service between here and Miami."

As much as she hated to, Rebecca closed The Tides after Easter, the beginning of the off season in the Caribbean.

"Don't stop taking reservations and deposits," she told Bix over the phone. "And make sure that everyone knows we're going to have sixty rooms come Labor Day."

In a rare moment Bix was speechless.

"What do you plan to do, go high rise?" she asked at last.

"You'll see."

Late spring and summer was a frenetic period for Rebecca. Although her account at the Walker was healthy enough, the kind of expansion she had in mind wouldn't have been possible without the cash flow resulting from the deposits GoSee made.

By the end of June, The Tides had grown from ten to twenty-five *palapas*. Simultaneously construction had started on Tongue Key, a half mile to the south. Rebecca found herself racing between the two islands, supervising the clearing of land, making sure that building supplies arrived on schedule, ferrying everything from extra tools to iced tea to her workers.

At the same time, Rebecca purchased an aged but seaworthy catamaran, affectionately dubbed the *Manatee*. Not only did that reduce her transport costs, but she had the means to ferry her guests to and from Angeline City as well as provide them with a live-aboard vessel for day trips to the reefs.

The third week in August, Rebecca traveled to New York. She and Bix went to Long Island City to pick up a second printing of Tides brochures as well as posters Rebecca intended to use as giveaways on campus.

"I want one in every dorm on campus, stuck on the wall right over the desk. When some poor student is tired of burning his eyes out over economics or history, I want him to look up and see just how close paradise is."

Both Eric Walker and Ramsey Peet thought the posters were a novel, effective idea. However, both men were concerned with the way Rebecca had gambled her first season's earnings on expansion.

"You're not leaving yourself much of a safety net," the banker told her. "With the extra expenses—staff, provisions, maintenance, and sundries—your reserves will be depleted."

"Don't you think you're moving a little too quickly?" Ramsey added.

"The Tides is booked from Labor Day straight through until the middle of October," Rebecca reminded them. "We expanded our advertising to include newsletters of major companies. As a result, we've reached the secretarial and clerical workers who can't afford the expensive resorts but who can take their one- or two-week vacations just about any time they want. They're going to be a steady source of cash.

"Besides," Rebecca added. "That's how Max built McHenry Enterprises—by pouring profits into development."

Rebecca didn't tell them that it was the memory of Dallas Gibson that fueled her almost headlong desire to expand The Tides. The larger and more established her dream became, the more difficult it would be for Andrew Stoughton to hurt her. And the sooner she would have something to fight back with.

After Labor Day Rebecca and Bix left to repeat their colleges blitz of the previous year. This time, however, Rebecca discovered that the editors of campus papers were eager to see her. Almost all had heard about The Tides and wanted not only the promotional material but to interview her and do a feature on this unique resort.

"I can't believe it," Rebecca said to Bix as they headed for Chicago in their driveaway car. "We've covered only half the territory and we're almost out of material!"

"Not to worry," Bix told her. "I telephoned Torrey and he's

going to air-freight more brochures into O'Hare. Meanwhile, the phone's been ringing off the hook. A lot of calls from the west coast and Texas.''

"How on earth did they hear about me?"

"You've got the most precious advertising in the business, Becky: word of mouth.''

Bix paused, then added. "Of course, the fact that I had GoSee do a mass-mailing before we left might have something to do with it.''

The Labor Day to Christmas season of 1965 exceeded Rebecca's wildest dreams. The resorts on both Windemere and Tongue were full, with only a few days in which a *palapa* or two stood vacant. The slack Rebecca had expected in late October and early November never materialized. Word of mouth had brought The Tides to the attention of recent graduates who, having begun their careers the previous spring, saw an opportunity for a cheap, idyllic vacation. Recognizing the potential of this new market, Rebecca tooled up a newsletter and instructed Bix to send copies, along with brochures and posters, to as many alumni offices as she could.

By this time Rebecca had streamlined the resorts' operations. Having seen how enthusiastically her guests had responded to having their days organized, Rebecca made sure that there were enough activities to keep them occupied until they dropped. New arrivals mingled over welcome cocktails and were given a list of all The Tides had to offer. Rebecca made it a point to greet her guests personally, coax the shy ones out of their shells, introduce the singles to one another, and politely but firmly put the fraternity boozehounds in their place.

Besides the usual activities, Rebecca introduced theme nights such as a masquerade dance, suppers consisting entirely of a particular island's cuisine, and excursions to the breathtaking Pyramid waterfalls in the lush rain forest outside Angeline City. Just as Rebecca had expected, her guests tended to pair off after a few days. Passion and romance blossomed quickly as the sun and sea melted inhibitions. On some mornings, when she took her constitutional along the beach, Rebecca saw a dozen pairs of arms and legs protruding under blankets on the sand. At that moment she couldn't help but envy the entwined figures.

Rebecca also found a marked difference in the attitude toward her in Angeline City. The people who, from the very beginning, had defied Lambros and supported her were now joined by others. Merchants and tradesmen came forward, hoping to get lucrative supply contracts. There was no longer any shortage of workers, either to help with expansion or to run The Tides. Everywhere she went Rebecca was greeted warmly. There wasn't a door closed to her, a service that wouldn't be performed, or a favor not granted.

This is the way it must have been for Max, Rebecca thought as she plunged through the markets, haggling good-naturedly before placing her orders.

But for all the good fortune coming her way, Rebecca never let her guard down. Bones had warned her that Silas Lambros would try to seed spies among her staff to keep him abreast of what was happening at The Tides. The policeman suggested a hiring policy to stop such infiltration attempts cold. Any applicant who was not vouched for by people Rebecca trusted or whose references were suspect would automatically be checked by Bones for any connection to the old wrecker.

Rebecca added only one modification to Bones's plan: She insisted that those applicants also be screened for any possible relationship to Andrew Stoughton.

"Have you spoken to Ramsey or Eric Walker about this?"

Torrey dipped his sunglasses to get a better look at a bikinied coed who was sashaying toward the beach.

Bix kicked him under the table. "Keep your mind on your work."

"Of course," Rebecca said airly. "I took out options on those properties."

"You mean Ramsey and Eric actually encouraged you to put money down?" Torrey asked, incredulous. "Becky, Jamaica and Cancún aren't the Angelines. What the hell do you know about those places? The people and customs are different. There are a zillion new laws and codes you'll have to follow. Raw materials aren't the same. Most of all, you don't have people you can work with over there."

"I know The Tides will do well in both places," Rebecca told him. "Jamaica has either first-class hotels or guesthouses and small inns. Mexico's Yucatan Peninsula has even less to choose from. Now is the best time to go in, before some smart operator decides to copy The Tides. We've been open nearly a year and a half, and it's amazing no one's done it yet."

Torrey glanced at the facts and figures Rebecca had presented him with.

"It's an awful gamble," he said, unconvinced. "Can't you carve out another place here in the Angelines?"

Rebecca didn't dare confess that she had also placed money down on a stretch of beachfront property thirty miles north of Angeline City, in a place she had dubbed Palm Cove.

"You're going to have a real problem with air connections," he said at last. "Assuming you can get these places started, how are you going to bring in the people?"

The commercial airline route and schedule charts Torrey had brought with him illustrated the lack of suitable air links between gateway cities such as Miami, Houston, and New Orleans and points south.

"There wouldn't be a problem if GoSee were to buy one of those DC-sixes you keep talking about."

Torrey pushed his sunglasses down his nose and stared at Rebecca.

"No way," he said, shaking his head. "Uh-un, I'm not going into the charter service."

"There, there, pet," Bix cooed, patting his hand. "You don't have to do anything you don't want to. But why not have a look at the bookings for The Tides—straight through the summer?"

Torrey, who hadn't seen the latest reservation figures, was flabbergasted.

"Who in their right minds would want to come here in the *summer*?" he mumbled.

"Just think of all the commissions," Bix said coyly.

"And the profits from a charter service," Rebecca added.

Torrey backed away. "No. I'm not letting the two of you gang up on me. I came here to bake my bones, not to get involved in some crazy scheme to ferry kids to paradise."

Rebecca and Bix watched him stomp off into the surf, then looked at each other.

"Will he do it?"

"Of course he'll do it," Bix said confidently. "He just doesn't know it yet." She looked at Rebecca. "You *have* talked this over with Ramsey and Eric?"

"You've got to be kidding!" Rebecca said in mock horror.

"Rebecca, why didn't you come to us first?"

Ramsey Peet placed his hand on the Indian subcontinent and spun the large globe until, either by design or accident, it stopped at Mexico.

"The opportunity was there," Rebecca said. "I took it."

"Well, at least you used our associate firms in Mexico City and Kingston to handle the paperwork," he said gruffly. "If you do go ahead and exercise the options, the documentation is in order. Unless I can talk you out of it, that is."

"I don't know about that, Ramsey," Eric Walker said slowly.

He glanced up from the sheets in his lap and glanced out the window, where a freak March hailstorm was grinding Manhattan to a standstill. On his left Rebecca, her golden skin exuding warmth and vitality, seemed like a creature from another planet. The plaid wool skirt and bulky sweater seemed out of place on her.

"The sale prices look pretty good," the banker observed. "Obviously there're enough resources to support the kind of operation Rebecca has in mind: labor pool, building materials, food supplies. And she's right about one thing: There isn't another resort like this anywhere in Mexico or Jamaica."

"I'm not sure of the political stability in those areas, particularly Jamaica," Ramsey objected.

"The people there need jobs," Rebecca said. "That's what I'm going to provide. Besides, I've been to both places with Max more times than I can remember. I still know people there."

"You're going to have to keep an eye out on currency fluctuations," Eric told her. "Right now you'd be working with a favorable exchange rate. If you buy the land and sign the building and supplies contracts quickly, you could be saving a bundle."

Rebecca shot him a grateful look.

"What about the cash flow, Eric?" Ramsey persisted. "Isn't this going to deplete the account substantially?"

"Normally I wouldn't advise a client to put so much of her own capital into a single project. But Rebecca's not your ordinary businesswoman. We couldn't talk her out of the original expansion of The Tides when there was a real chance of her losing everything. Her position is far stronger now."

"Even if everything else falls into place, success hinges on being able to get the people into those places." Ramsey refused to retreat from his position as devil's advocate. "You've told us about the charter agreement with GoSee, but I don't see Torrey's paperwork."

"He's looking after it right now," Rebecca said hastily. "The aircraft has been examined and approved. As soon as the FAA processes the application, I'll get you copies of the license."

Ramsey Peet sighed and slapped his hands on his thighs. He looked at Rebecca with a whimsical smile.

"What the hell. Let's do it. I could never talk Max out of anything either."

"Has the FAA really approved the plane?"

They were seated across from each other at Lutèce. The blue, gold, and white decor of the famous restaurant was set off by glittering candelabra, but as far as Eric Walker was concerned, Rebecca was the focus of the room. She wore a simple cornflower-blue dress shot through with silver thread. Her bronzed arms were unadorned, the effect softened as the light caught the golden downy hairs. Her mane lay across one shoulder like a docile, gleaming sable and her eyes, framed by scimitar brows, regarded him mischievously.

"Let's just say that Torrey's been convinced to put the application in. You know how thorough he is. The certification won't be a problem."

Rebecca had had reservations about accepting Eric's dinner invitation. Now she was glad she had allowed Lauren to cajole her into it. Eric knew how to put her at ease. Everything he did, from sending flowers to having his driver pick her up, to the introduction to Lutèce's owner, had been effortlessly graceful. Yet Rebecca sensed that Eric was showing off just a tiny bit for her. She was pleased that he considered her so special.

The evening stirred memories, though, that cast a pall on its brilliance and that inadvertently detracted from the impression Rebecca knew Eric wanted to make on her. Over cocktails a number of people stopped by their table to pay their respects. It was, Rebecca thought, power acknowledging power, with carefully cultivated words whose lightness spoke volumes. The homage reminded Rebecca of long-ago Christmas parties, when Max had been the recipient of so much flattery. It also brought back memories of another man who had only to walk into a room to hold it in the palm of his hand. Andrew Stoughton had had this same power, and what he had done with it made Rebecca wary.

"You're a million miles away."

Rebecca looked up guiltily. "I'm sorry."

Eric's fingertips brushed the top of her hand.

"Don't worry about Torrey and the plane. I'm sure Bix will see to it he comes through."

They both laughed at that.

"Did I tell you that the Walker has decided to expand into the Angelines?" Eric said casually.

"No!" Rebecca exclaimed. "When did this happen?"

"Today, as a matter of fact. The board unanimously approved my plan to set up a branch in Angeline City."

"Eric, that's wonderful."

"It will certainly make things easier."

As The Tides revenues poured in, Rebecca found herself spending a small fortune on bonded couriers who carried her surplus cash to Miami. Still, she had refused to deposit a penny in banks subject to Silas Lambros's influence. All that could change if the Walker came in.

Throughout dinner Eric described the plans he had for the new branch; The Tides had been critical in getting the necessary approval.

"You're becoming a force to be reckoned with. I'll be the first to admit that I intend to use your account as a drawing card for business."

"By all means." Rebecca laughed, then added, "Just remember the lock Silas Lambros has on the islands."

"Lambros won't be there forever," Eric said gently. "He is the past. You are the future."

He paused. "And I hope you'll permit me to share it."

Although she tried not to, Rebecca shrank from his words. There was every temptation to become involved with Eric. Now that the Walker was coming to the Angelines, there would also be the opportunity. It was something she would have to guard against. Rebecca dared not allow Eric, or anyone else, a glimpse at the woman who was forming behind the facade of success.

Eric accepted the message Rebecca's silence conveyed. He reached out and gently pried her fingers away from the sea horse.

"Maybe when you no longer need this," he said, toying with the ornament.

Rebecca looked into his brilliant blue eyes and the temptation to laugh away his words died. She had never told Eric who had given her the sea horse or what it symbolized for her. But that didn't mean Eric couldn't have found out from Ramsey while, being a perceptive man, noting Rebecca's obsession with the ornament.

"Maybe. But I can never ask you to wait. I can't give you promises."

Because there are others I've already made.

· 29 ·

Over the next few years Rebecca learned that timing is everything.

Torrey had predicted the young people of the sixties would become the most adventurous travelers in American history, and he had been right. The Stars and Stripes could be seen on backpacks throughout Europe, North Africa, Central and South America, and the Far East. Fueled by an insatiable curiosity, backed by a dollar that was the prince of currencies, millions of college-age Americans took to the road. At some point in their travels that road took them through The Tides.

The groundwork Rebecca had done during her college blitz was paying enormous dividends. The Tides had gotten a well-deserved reputation as a safe, inexpensive haven where the weary traveler could find rest and relaxation. With the growing philosophy of free love, the resorts became even more attractive. Since Rebecca's beaches were all on private property, there were no restrictions on nude sunbathing. The practice that had once scandalized middle-class Americans visiting St. Tropez became commonplace on the sun-drenched sands of Mexico, Jamaica, Antigua, and the Angelines.

Rebecca seized every opportunity that came along. The minute Torrey's charter service proved a success, she became his partner in two other aircraft. Anything that was remotely related to The Tides, from the shipping of supplies to providing guest services, was looked upon as a potential profit center. By the end of three years' operations, the new McHenry Enterprises had a fleet of flattop dive vessels to take scuba divers and snorkelers to the reefs. Local musical talent competed for contracts while gift shops expanded from a single counter to full-fledged designer boutiques.

And the money continued to pour in. Under the careful direction of Ramsey Peet and Eric Walker, Rebecca invested in the stock market, making enormous profits from exactly those companies Andrew Stoughton had told her were the key to the future: high-tech computer firms.

As Rebecca's coffers swelled, so did her reputation throughout the Caribbean. Seeing hard evidence that local economies blossomed whenever a Tides resort opened, ministers of tourism began making discreet queries to Ramsey Peet, offering incentives and tax advantages. Driving a hard but fair bargain, Rebecca was able to lock up prime beachfront land for future development.

One factor invariably helped Rebecca win a bidding war with competitors. Wherever a new Tides was opened, a second, purely goodwill project was initiated. On Grand Cayman her resources opened a turtle farm so that fishermen could repopulate depleted stocks. On the Yucatan Peninsula thousands of dollars were earmarked to fund local archaeological digs. Of course the Angelines remained the greatest beneficiary. Rebecca waged a long and bitter fight against the wrecker-backed government on an issue she refused to let die. When the government finally acquiesced, a national referendum was held. Fully two thirds of all Angelinians voted to have Pusilha declared a national park, inviolate to development. They also agreed that the preserve should bear the name of the man who had devoted so much of himself and his expertise to it: Dallas Gibson.

When Dallas's father learned of Rebecca's memorial, he immediately funded a series of scholarships for deserving students of archeology at the University of Chicago.

While the wreckers continued to ignore Rebecca, the vast majority of Angelinians came to revere her. Of all her contributions, none was better received than the training center she had opened in Angeline City. The Tides was continually hungry for staff. Instead of bringing seasoned personnel from Europe or the United States, Rebecca created her own special course to develop senior and middle management as well as train basic staff. Since The Tides was a unique concept, the technique proved a success. Angelinians worked easily with one another and Rebecca found that the center was soon producing as many graduates as her resorts could handle. These she then sent out across the Caribbean to train the local labor force.

"You been doin' so much, time you did something for yourself."

Rebecca turned to Jewel and gripped her hand. They were sitting in the screened lanai of Jewel's home, the only place Rebecca felt truly comfortable.

"Time to get yourself a man," Jewel added slyly.

Although the years had caused her to slow her pace a little, Jewel remained the roving spirit of The Tides, turning up here and there to attend to this and that. Half the time even Rebecca didn't know where she was. Nonetheless she remained the inveterate matchmaker and had been carefully building a mountain out of Eric Walker's frequent visits—which Rebecca insisted added up to nothing more than a molehill.

"As my next project, I've decided to restore the *Windsong*," Rebecca said, changing the subject.

Jewel shook her head in exasperation and closed her eyes. The rocker creaked softly.

"What about Skyscape?"

Bones Ainsley had removed the briar pipe from between his ivory teeth and sent the words on a cloud of pungent blue haze.

Rebecca wondered if the smoke hid the terrible anger she felt flashing in her eyes. Not a month went by that she didn't return to that scene of devastation. Although hardly any part of Skyscape remained standing and the jungle had reclaimed the once-pristine grounds, Rebecca saw Skyscape only as it had once been. A split-second later that image would be replaced by the roar of flames.

"Not yet," she said softly. "Not as long as Lambros holds what is mine."

"In time you'll get back what he stole from you," Ainsley said.

Ah, Bones, but that's only the half of it!

In her mind the roar of the flames had been replaced by the cold, cruel laughter of Andrew Stoughton.

Rebecca looked deeply into Bones's onyx eyes.

"Tell me about Ramon Fuentes," she said softly.

At that moment Bones Ainsley understood that only one thing would ever satisfy Rebecca.

· 30 ·

Sometimes the nightmare came upon him during a storm, sometimes after he received a coded telex from his father. Tonight, the light drizzle that had blanketed London had become a raging thunderstorm. He had sat in bed for hours, watching the forks of lightning. Every crackle made him flinch. Even when he could no longer keep sleep at bay, his entire body quivered whenever thunder reared up out of the clouds, and the nightmare, a quarter century old, snaked toward him.

Justin Lambros had been sixteen years old on that February morning, eight years younger than his brother Nigel.

Age was the least of the differences between them. Nigel was tall, with a golden mane and a bronzed, well-muscled body. He could handle any type of vessel or woman with equal skill, was gracious, charming, or witty as the situation dictated. He was also Silas Lambros's favorite, sharing his father's passion for everything Tyne & Wear represented, the heir apparent who had already demonstrated how thick his wrecker's blood was.

Justin Lambros shared none of his brother's features or characteristics. Born late into the marriage, his mother had died bringing him into the world. That, as Justin would learn over the years, would be only one of many things his father would never forgive him for, never forget.

All the Lambros clan were fair-skinned and fair-haired; Justin had a Mediterranean olive complexion and jet-black hair that betrayed a Spanish or Portuguese ancestor somewhere in the family's bloodline. All Lambroses were accomplished sportsmen—sleek, fit men who easily mastered the competition. Even as a child Justin had tended to run to fat. Lacking coordination and athletic skills, he preferred the gentler pursuits of music, painting, and lepidoptary, which were looked upon with contempt by his father and elder brother.

Yet Justin loved them fiercely and tried desperately to live up to their images. Shamed by his failures, he redoubled his efforts, smiling at the taunts and criticisms hurled at him. It was never their fault, always his. He was the one who was different, who had to prove himself.

It was this need for acceptance that brought Justin out on the *Bollinger* that afternoon in February.

Nigel had christened the forty-one-foot Chris-Craft presented to him on his twenty-fourth birthday the *Bollinger* because of the champagne that had been consumed on the occasion. Although Justin had struggled through a power squadron course, he had never been permitted even to board the vessel. Why Nigel had relented on that particular day Justin never knew. Perhaps it was Nigel's preoccupation with the blond Lufthansa flight attendant he had brought in from Nassau, or the amount of wine he had consumed over the al fresco lunch on the bridge. Whatever the case, when Justin had appeared at the dock with the new fishing tackle, Nigel had waved him aboard.

The day was peerless, with a brisk wind blowing out of the east. The *Bollinger* swept along as though in flight and Justin, who sat next to the craft's skipper, Ramon Fuentes, scarcely noticed that Nigel and the girl had disappeared belowdecks.

Of all the employees on the Lambros estate, Justin felt closest to the weatherbeaten captain who had been in the family's service since Justin could remember. It was Fuentes who, when Justin was learning to sail, had taken him under his wing. He taught the boy the secret of navigating by the stars and how the phases of the moon affected the tides. Under his patient guidance Justin learned to smell a change in the current or winds and align his craft with the elements so that vessel and sea worked in tandem, never against each other. Justin loved him for this.

When the *Bollinger* was halfway out to the fishing banks off Chapel Key, Fuentes, who had been carefully scrutinizing the horizon, tapped Justin on the shoulder.

"Take the wheel," he said, and, before Justin could object, disappeared.

The light tremor from the wheel both frightened and intoxicated Justin. The sheer power flowing into him made him want to shout.

"Amusing yourself, little brother?"

Nigel's voice startled him. Justin flinched and was about to step away from the wheel, when Nigel clapped him on the back.

"Ramon says a storm's coming up. What do you say?"

His brother's weight on his shoulder and the slur in his voice told Justin that Nigel was drunk.

"We should head in."

"I say we keep going."

Nigel swept an arm across the sky and sea, blue on cobalt.

"Nothing! I think Ramon's been into the grog!"

Justin knew he was wrong. Ramon never drank.

"Unless, of course, you don't think you can handle the *Bollinger*."

The girl, giggling and weaving, collided with Nigel. She had heard Nigel's question and was watching Justin with a challenging expression. Justin raised his eyes to Ramon, who shook his head.

Maybe he is wrong, Justin thought. There's been no storm warning on the radio. The horizon is clear.

Justin scanned the sea as though trying to divine its intention from the rocking motion of the swells.

"Oh, Christ, give me the wheel!" Nigel said. "I thought you had more guts than this."

Justin was amazed by his own next words.

"You go below and have something to eat. I'll get us out to the banks."

Justin set his gaze firmly on the sea ahead of him. He felt very pleased about his decision, yet he dared not turn around to meet Ramon's eyes; the disapproval in them seemed to burn the back of his neck.

The storm was the kind nicknamed "the cat" by Caribbean sailors and fishermen. It wasn't born in the stratosphere, where radar could detect its growth, but in the winds that skimmed the waters, swirling and gathering momentum. The first hint that it was forming came from the lengthening waves, followed by rolling whitecaps and gathering swells.

Justin noticed all these things, and although Ramon had taught him to recognize "the cat," he chose to ignore them. This was his moment of triumph. He imagined the lavish praise Nigel would heap on him when they returned home, the respect he would gain in his father's eyes.

"The cat" reared out of the water just as the *Bollinger* was in the middle of a serpentine *quebrada* that led into the fishing banks. The water, which had been a pale green, indicating shallow draft, suddenly became milky. Justin's sense of the depth under the keel vanished as the first brutal gusts tore into the vessel.

Suddenly Justin was fighting for control. The *Bollinger* rolled, then pitched into an onrushing trough, only to be hoisted up, shaking like a stallion on its hindquarters. Wildly Justin looked around for Ramon, who was scrambling to his side.

"No, let him do it!"

Justin whirled around and saw Nigel weaving his way toward him, dragging the terrified girl.

"You keep the wheel, damn it!" he roared. "Let's see what stuff you're made of!"

"I can't hold her," Justin shouted.

As if to underline his words, the wheel spun out of his grasp and the *Bollinger* pitched viciously to the right. The sickening grating of coral on fiberglass tore through the savagery of the storm.

Out of the corner of his eye Justin saw Ramon crawling toward the wheel. He struggled to his feet and made a grab for it, and the wooden handles slammed into his wrist. Justin felt the bones crack and a red haze of pain drifted across his eyes. Suddenly he was detached from everything that was happening. Ramon and Nigel were being tossed around in the cockpit like pinballs, neither managing to reach the wheel. The *Bollinger*, rudderless, was at the complete mercy of "the cat."

Desperately Justin clawed his way to the wheel.

My responsibility! I was at the wheel! My responsibility.

Then a mountainous wave swept over the vessel, sluicing torrents of water across the decks. Just before he blacked out, Justin saw his brother and the girl, intertwined as though in a parody of lovemaking, carried off the *Bollinger*. For an instant they disappeared into a green wall of glass. Then their bodies were flung away as carelessly as a terrier discards a rat, landing broken and bleeding on the hard, glittering coral whose teeth now held the boat fast.

The nightmare he dreamed always ended there. In reality that part had been the least savage. As he did every time it seized him, Justin woke with a start and staggered into the bathroom. The scalding water drumming on his flesh, punishing him, was the only release.

Neither Nigel's body nor the girl's was ever recovered. While Justin lay in the Stann Creek Town clinic recovering from his wounds, his father continued to search the waters long after there was any hope left. The currents, twisted by "the cat," could have taken the bodies in any one of a dozen different directions. The fish would have done the rest.

Silas Lambros had neither visited Justin at the clinic nor spoken so much as a word to him until the funeral. When the marble slab bearing Nigel's name had been set among the weathered headstones that marked the resting places of his wrecker ancestors, Justin reached out to his father. Silas Lambros flinched from the touch, as if brushed by something repulsive.

"You will leave the Angelines as soon as possible," he said in a stony voice. "You will finish your education in England and then I shall find you suitable employment. You will make no attempt to contact me. Is that clear?"

"Father—"

"Is that clear?"

The words cut into Justin like daggers. Although his world had been circumscribed by his having been born into a wrecker family, Justin felt a deep love for the Angelines and its people. In spite of his background, he was untainted by prejudice and was proud to count many black people as friends. He could not believe his father intended to exile him from everything he held dear.

"There is a maritime hearing into . . . into the accident—" he said, then broke off.

"I will handle the inquiry."

"But what about Ramon? I have to speak up for him, tell the commission that what happened wasn't his fault."

"What happens to Ramon is none of your concern."

His father's words had an ominous ring to them.

"Father, please, don't send me away!" Justin whispered. "I couldn't bear it—"

"You can and you will!" Silas Lambros said fiercely.

"What about Celeste?" Justin managed to say.

He adored Nigel's small daughter. At eighteen Nigel had run off with the wife of a Bermudian banker. He tired of her as soon as Celeste was born, and the Lambros influence had painlessly eased the woman out of his life.

"Celeste is my responsibility," his father snapped. "She will become what Nigel was. And what you can never be!"

The echo of these last words stung Justin. He raised his face to the full force of the shower to wash away the tears. Stepping out of the stall, he toweled briskly, combed his thinning hair and began to dress. His comfortable Mayfair flat seemed oppressive. He needed to walk, to hear the birds in the park, to see another human being who might, out of charity, offer him a good-morning smile.

His father had been a man of his word. Justin was almost forty-one and had spent a quarter century in exile, first in an English boarding school, then at Cambridge where, to overcome his homesickness, he turned to painting. The first efforts, watercolors, were crude, but his work came to the attention of a don who recognized the raw, vivid imagery of the islands that leapt off the canvas. Under his tutelage Justin learned discipline and technique. Most important, he realized his own limitations. He would never be another Gauguin, but he nonetheless breathed life into that part of him which had never left the Angelines.

It was still very early in the morning. The sounds of Mayfair came only from the birds rustling in the centenarian oaks and the rattle of bottles in the milkman's basket. As he walked across the quadrangle, Justin still couldn't believe that the role he would play in the life of Tyne & Wear later on had been thought out so exactly by his father. Or had it? Because everything had fallen into place so neatly. Too neatly.

After Cambridge, Justin drifted into the London art scene. He had several exhibitions and critics had been impressed by his work. But Justin did not capitalize on his mild success. Using his mother's maiden name, Prescott, he had been able to draw a veil over the past. He lived comfortably but not extravagantly and was careful to avoid those circles familiar with the Lambros family. To come into the public eye now meant to court possible disaster. He didn't want people to know who he was. Such knowledge meant questions. And questions would ultimately lay bare the guilt and humiliation he had tried so hard to bury.

Justin now refused offers to exhibit. He continued to paint because it was as necessary to him as breathing. But the canvases remained in his studio, carefully hidden away from everyone, a private world he retreated into late at night to drink in the color and memories.

To fulfill that need to remain in touch with other artists Justin opened up his own gallery. Because of his gentle and under-standing personality, painters flocked to him. With a discerning eye he cultivated those in whom he saw true talent and politely dissuaded dilettantes. He advanced money on an artist's word and became as much a father confessor as agent to his clients. Because of his uncanny ability to judge the eclectic mood of collectors in the fifties and sixties, the Prescott Gallery became one of the most successful in London.

Standing before it now, set in a brick-paved mews with a wrought-iron sign over the door, Justin was aware of pride, and even love. It had been his greatest creation—until the day it had been stolen from him.

Over the years Justin had come to assume his father would never contact him. The monthly stipend deposited into his bank account was as close as he ever came to the man who had virtually disowned him. Then one day, without warning, his father had appeared in London and told him what he must do.

Justin had listened in silence, unable to believe what was being. asked—no, demanded—of him. His father brooked no argument. He made no attempt to heal the wounds inflicted a decade earlier. He simply issued his instructions and left. That day the Prescott Gallery became tainted.

No one knew how his creation had become corrupted and Justin steeled himself not to see it in that light. Instead, every day he struggled to instill more beauty into it, to make it a place where dreams were realized for some, where others found peace in that beauty. In the end he, too, found a small measure of that peace.

It was at that moment that he saw her—or more properly, her reflection. Justin didn't understand how he had missed her. She had been standing in front of the plate-glass window, one hip slightly cocked, three fingers on her lower lip. She had been absolutely still, a part of the landscape. Then she turned around and the sable mane shimmered in the fine morning light. The deep gray eyes met his and she smiled, as though just for him.

· 31 ·

The journey that brought Rebecca to the Prescott Gallery in London in the spring of 1970 had begun six months earlier and four thousand miles away.

As the Tides' influence and prestige grew, so, too, did Rebecca's stature in the Angelines. When the sixties drew to an end she felt confident and financially secure enough to plan her opening moves against Andrew Stoughton.

Rebecca knew she could not challenge Andrew directly. He had all the resources of Tyne & Wear at his disposal, resources that dwarfed those of The Tides. If Andrew even suspected Rebecca was on the offensive, he would crush her.

I have to take him from the blind side, thought Rebecca. *Get to him through Tyne & Wear, weaken the company and so weaken what Andrew has to work with.*

Ironically, it was Silas Lambros's insatiable greed for land that proved to be the key.

Even before he had made his play for the McHenry holdings, Silas Lambros had been master of vast tracts of Angelinian land. Through publicly available records Rebecca learned that much of this acquisition had taken place after Sir Geoffrey Smythe's appointment as governor-general. She was all too familiar with the rumors that still circulated beneath the veneer of Angelinian democracy: that Lambros had paid Sir Geoffrey millions to use his influence in the British Parliament to have Crown lands converted into common holdings, holdings which Tyne & Wear promptly bought up through its dummy corporations registered in Grand Cayman and the Netherlands Antilles. However, the rumors remained just that. Because of Lambros's iron grip on the government, no investigation had ever been undertaken. Proof of any collusion between Lambros and Sir Geoffrey, if it existed at all, had been buried long ago or destroyed altogether.

From her intensive research of Silas Lambros, Rebecca knew

277

that the wrecker would have covered his tracks completely. Given the memory she had of the governor-general, the man who had been so pious on the morning of Max's funeral then had signed her deportation order a few months later, Rebecca wasn't sure that was the case with someone as vain and arrogant as Sir Geoffrey Smythe.

On her first trip to England, ostensibly to study the feasibility of opening a European office, Rebecca took a room in a small Knightsbridge hotel and spent hours poring over Debrett's *Peerage, Who's Who,* and other records detailing British nobility. From Sir Geoffrey's social activities and club memberships Rebecca formed a mental picture of the man. She then drove out to the small town of Bury St. Edmunds, to the ancestral seat of the Smythe clan, Abbot's Yew.

Telling the locals she was an American history student, Rebecca spent a week in the village. Warming to her obvious interest in the magnificent castle, the usually taciturn villagers confided in her. Loyalty to the Smythes, and Sir Geoffrey in particular, ran deep. Generations of people in the shire had depended on the manor for their livelihood. Smiling politely and encouraging them, Rebecca listened carefully to everything they said. As the paeans became more and more flowery, she lost her initial guilt about seeking out information under false pretenses. Obviously there was a side to Sir Geoffrey these innocent farmers and tradesmen had never seen.

A single theme dominated the conversation and it became Rebecca's next stepping-stone. No one in Bury St. Edmunds quite understood how Sir Geoffrey was able to maintain a palatial residence such as Abbot's Yew, especially given the hard times other noble and far wealthier families had fallen upon. Since the end of World War II astronomical British taxes had virtually destroyed the holdings of the peerage. Many had been forced to sell their estates to foreigners or, if that was unpalatable, handed them over to the National Trust, which converted the grand homes into tourist attractions. Only the wealthiest families and those with holdings outside of England could afford to maintain their ancestral seats. How the Smythes, who had never been in that league, managed was a mystery.

Although Rebecca wanted to get inside Abbot's Yew to investigate further this strange state of affairs, she didn't dare visit the house on one of the weekly public tours for fear that Sir Geoffrey might spot and recognize her. Nevertheless she felt she knew it intimately from the villagers' descriptions of the forty grandiose rooms, the ballroom where Edward VIII and Mrs. Simpson had danced, and the chapel that dated back to the time of William the Conqueror. Strolling along the periphery of the estate, Rebecca noted the rolling acres of farmland worked for Sir Geoffrey, the paddocks and stables with their prize examples of horseflesh, and the discreet purr of hand-tooled automobiles as they wended their way along miles of private road.

Sitting in the local pub, coyly named the Spotted Dick after a character in a Dickens novel, Rebecca sipped her yeasty, warm ale and agreed that it was indeed a mystery how Sir Geoffrey continued to maintain his lordly way of life.

" 'Tain't no mystery at all," a voice from the end of the bar broke in.

"Now, Maggie, don't you be starting up with that silly talk of yours," the publican warned.

The big, raw-boned woman with the bright-red complexion of an inveterate drinker snorted in disgust.

"I worked me a few years for old Sir Geoff," she told Rebecca in a loud, grating voice. "Got to love those pretty pictures. Then one day my favorite was up and gone, just like that! When I asked, all innocent, what happened to it, the squire told me to mind my own business."

"What do you think happened?" Rebecca asked her.

"Why, Sir Geoff sold it, of course!" Maggie answered smugly. "Sold it to keep the tax man from the door."

A collective groan went up from the men lined up against the bar.

"You know that doesn't make any sense at all, Maggie," one of them said. "All of us been in the squire's house. There ain't nothing missing off his walls. You wonder how they're still standing with all the pictures on 'em."

"Oh, there are still plenty of pictures," Maggie agreed, nodding her head sagely. "They just ain't the same ones."

She turned to Rebecca with a conspiratorial wink.

"You see, dearie, the very next day, after my picture was gone, I look up and see another one hanging in the same place. Ugly thing it was, all crazy faces and the like. I asked myself why Sir Geoff would have such a thing in his house, but before I know it, it's gone too. So I says to the squire, casual like, it's a good thing you sent that one back to the cellar or wherever you keep the rest of your pictures."

Maggie lit another unfiltered Players and shook her head.

"Well, I tell you, my lovely, did Sir Geoff snap at me! Told me where the pictures came from was none of my business—"

"That's why you were sacked from Abbot's Yew," the publican interrupted angrily. "You got a long nose, Maggie, always poking it where it don't belong. And if you keep at it, my girl, I'll be asking you to leave." He glanced at Rebecca and added, "No one needs to be hearing your rumormongering."

The threat of banishment effectively silenced the gregarious Maggie, who glowered into her beer.

"There's nothing to what she goes on about," the publican assured Rebecca. "I happen to know, from Sir Geoffrey himself, that he often loans paintings to museums. That's what has been confusing old Maggie."

Rebecca nodded as though in agreement. From the background she had gleaned on Abbot's Yew she knew that its art collection wasn't extensive. The Smythes had concentrated on antique furniture and tapestries and had some of the finest examples of Bayeux weave in the country.

No, the amount of money Sir Geoffrey needed every year for taxes couldn't be raised by selling off a minor Pre-Raphaelite. Rebecca was convinced that the only way the former governor-general of the Angelines could continue to fund his life-style was through a connection with someone who was truly wealthy. Someone like Silas Lambros who had wanted and could pay generously for the one thing Sir Geoffrey had had the power to give: Angelinian land.

Somewhere, Rebecca thought to herself, a devil's bargain had been struck. And because Abbot's Yew needed a constant infusion of capital, the link between the two men still had to be in place. Whatever it took, Rebecca was determined to find it.

Over the next two years, in spite of the grueling pace The Tides set for her, Rebecca snatched whatever time she could to study Tyne & Wear's senior management as well as individuals in companies the conglomerate did business with. She read all the business and financial papers she could get her hands on, searching for any mention of Silas Lambros. She drew up a master list of the men his name was most frequently linked with and studied them as well. Then she tried to cross-reference the association with Sir Geoffrey Smythe.

Rebecca was searching for the conduit who had to exist between Lambros and the former governor-general, a man in whom both the wrecker and Sir Geoffrey had absolute trust, who would be responsible for siphoning Tyne & Wear moneys into Sir Geoffrey's accounts. For a long time Rebecca thought that the identity of such an individual might be obvious: Andrew Stoughton. But there was a compelling argument against him. Assuming that Sir Geoffrey had received millions from Lambros, this placed the wrecker in a potentially indefensible position. If the rumors could be substantiated, then Silas Lambros stood to lose everything. Not even the power of Tyne & Wear would be able to shield him from an investigation by the British Parliament and eventual public censure. Therefore the go-between would have to be someone heavily indebted to Lambros, someone over whom he exercised absolute control or who was compromised himself. For all the loyalty Andrew Stoughton had shown Lambros, Rebecca could not believe the old wrecker would hand his ambitious son-in-law the sword of Damocles to hold over his head.

Who then? The deeper Rebecca dug, the more quickly she eliminated potential candidates.

If only Lambros had a son! A blood relation would be Silas Lambros's obvious choice.

The thought of offspring reminded Rebecca that not even Silas Lambros was immune to tragedy. She dug out the accounts of Nigel's death at sea and slowly reread them. A small voice in the back of her mind kept prodding her on, hinting that she wasn't seeing something that was right in front of her.

Rebecca perused the newspaper accounts of Nigel's accident and the minutes of the maritime board of inquiry. The haste with which the board had reached its conclusion was almost indecent: In less than seventy-two hours its members had decreed that the accident had been caused by the negligence of the craft's skipper, Ramon Fuentes—this in spite of Fuentes's persistent denials.

Her curiosity piqued, Rebecca turned to the clippings dealing with the aftermath of the board's inquiry. Ramon Fuentes had been found guilty. His master's license was revoked and he was facing criminal charges, when he suddenly disappeared. In the intervening years no trace of the man was ever found.

At the same time, Justin Lambros, who had been on board the *Bollinger* that fateful afternoon but who had never been called upon to testify, departed for England. As far as Rebecca knew, Silas Lambros's younger son had never set foot in the Angelines since.

Rebecca felt the tingle of excitement along her spine. So there was a son in England. Not only a man bound to Lambros by blood but someone over whom Lambros had absolute control. Reading between the lines of the board's report, Rebecca discerned Lambros's influence. He had protected his son, shielding him from the board, then sent him away. The fact that Justin was his son would have changed nothing. Rebecca knew Silas Lambros well enough to believe he would use anyone, including his own blood, however and whenever it suited him.

Could Justin be the key she had been searching for? To find out meant working on two fronts. Rebecca had to find Ramon Fuentes. He alone knew exactly what had happened that afternoon. But she also had to track down Justin Lambros.

As soon as Rebecca had the opportunity to do so without arousing suspicion, she flew to London. Within forty-eight hours she had met with a man who had come highly recommended and outlined exactly what she needed. Substantial money changed hands, the agreement was sealed with a handshake, and Rebecca was winging her way back to the Caribbean.

In the comfort of the Pan Am 707 first-class seat, Rebecca began to think of the best way to enlist Bones Ainsley's cooperation. She was certain that Ramon Fuentes, if he were still alive, was somewhere in the Caribbean. The difficulty in getting to him lay in the fact that no one had seen him for almost twenty-five years. There was good reason for this. A warrant was still outstanding for his arrest, the charge manslaughter.

"It took some doing, ma'am, and far longer than I had anticipated. Not finding him, of course. That was relatively easy. Making the connection you asked about was quite another matter."

Rebecca was sitting very still, her back straight against the floral print cover of the Queen Anne chair. She did not hear the hard, freezing rain as it sluiced down the beveled windows of the Connaught Hotel. Her concentration was focused entirely on the man opposite her. Almost three months had passed since her initial trip to London. In the interim she had heard nothing. Then, a scant forty-eight hours ago, the carefully worded telegram she had built her hopes upon had arrived, summoning her across the Atlantic.

The man lifted his hands, turning his palms toward the flames. He was short and squat, with a doughy face punctuated by dark, seemingly lifeless eyes, like raisins set in a gingerbread man. He was clean-shaven, his mud-brown hair carefully combed across the breadth of his skull. He hadn't bothered to unbutton his navy-blue overcoat, frayed at the collar and cuffs. The soles of his wingtips were worn on the outside edge, betraying a slightly pigeon-toed gait.

Alan Ballantyne might have been an undertaker's assistant, a civil service clerk, or one of those curious, middle-aged bachelors of indeterminate means. He was about as memorable as a conductor on a London double-decker bus, which was precisely the effect Alan Ballantyne, as one of England's most successful—and expensive—detectives, had taken pains to cultivate. For twenty years he had been in the service of Scotland Yard and had ended his career as chief inspector before opening his own investigative agency.

"I want to see him," Rebecca said softly.

Ballantyne inclined his head and reached for a well-worn but equally well-cared-for briefcase. He withdrew an accordion file and passed Rebecca a glossy eight by ten photograph.

Rebecca's anticipation was so great, the photo almost slipped through her fingers.

When she looked at the face in the picture she was sure there had to be a mistake.

"This can't be him!"

"The family resemblance is somewhat weak," Alan Ballantyne conceded.

Over the past months Rebecca had formed a mental composite of Justin Lambros. She imagined he would have his father's strong jaw and commanding nose, his brother's laughing but very cold eyes, the same swept-back hair. The man in the photograph was the exact antithesis. A prominent double chin spilled over the shirt collar. The fleshy nose was accented by well-fed cheeks, and the eyes were buried under swarthy brows.

"I assure you, Miss McHenry, that is Justin Prescott," the detective said. "Born Justin Lambros, in Stann Creek Town, the Angelines, younger son of Mary and Silas Lambros. With your permission I shall dispense with the history of his education in England, which began at the age of sixteen, and move directly to what pertains to your inquiry. You might want to read the details at your leisure. They are all in my report."

Ballantyne slid a one-inch-thick dossier onto the coffee table. Rebecca nodded but didn't look up from the photograph. Even though there was nothing of the wrecker in this face, it still belonged to a Lambros. She could learn to hate it easily enough.

"As I mentioned," the detective continued, "determining the subject's true identity and whereabouts wasn't a problem. You yourself told me he was a Lambros. With that in mind I surveyed Foster-Swann's client roster—the bank controlled by Tyne & Wear—and sure enough came across a Justin Prescott. Since Prescott was the mother's maiden name, I was certain I had the right man. Nonetheless I verified my finding through two independent sources.''

Rebecca put the photograph aside. She wondered just what kind of resources this innocuous little man had that he could "survey" a bank's client list.

As though he had read her mind, the detective offered her a ghost of an answer.

"Odd how people who wish to remain anonymous invariably indulge in a foolish idiosyncrasy—like banking at a family-owned institution.''

"What does Justin Lambros do at Tyne & Wear?" Rebecca asked. "What's his connection to Sir Geoffrey Smythe?''

"Miss McHenry, did I say that Mr. Lambros is employed by Tyne & Wear?''

"No. But he must be associated with the company—''

"Then you know something I do not. My inquiries have led me to conclude, beyond any doubt, that Justin Lambros has absolutely no connection with Tyne & Wear whatsoever.''

"That's impossible!'' Rebecca cried. "He's Lambros's son! And if, as you said, Justin and Sir Geoffrey Smythe know each other, there has to be a connection!''

"There is, Miss McHenry. But it's not what you think. Justin Prescott, as he's known in London, is the owner of a modest but quite reputable art gallery—''

"Wait!''

Rebecca leapt out of her chair, fists clenched. Art gallery . . . The reference echoed painfully in her mind until suddenly she brought it together . . . with Abbot's Yew. Sir Geoffrey Smythe. Bury St. Edmunds. The Spotted Dick pub. Maggie! Sweet, beautiful Maggie, the cleaning woman who had worked in Abbot's Yew for twenty years . . . and knew every picture that hung on its walls. Works of art which she insisted were there one day and gone the next. Being sold off to pay taxes. Through Justin Prescott's gallery! Maggie, whom everyone in the town had written off as a drunk, had unwittingly stumbled close to the truth!

"Mr. Ballantyne,'' Rebecca said, her voice trembling, "this is terribly important. Is Sir Geoffrey a frequent visitor to the gallery?''

"Exactly, Miss McHenry," the detective said, handing her the report. "It would appear that there is a strong connection between Sir Geoffrey and the gallery. I think you will find the report quite interesting."

The detective was wrong. The report wasn't interesting. It fascinated Rebecca. As she read through it, pieces of the puzzle began falling into place. At the same time, the next stage of her plan took shape.

Thirty minutes later Rebecca closed the file.

"We're ready to proceed, Mr. Ballantyne."

The detective smiled. "I am, as always, at your service."

Rebecca had intended to speak to Bones Ainsley the minute she was back in Angeline City. But as soon as she walked into her office the floodgates opened. For a full half hour Rebecca sat speechless as her secretary rattled off the emergencies that required her immediate attention. If that wasn't enough, as soon as the managers of the various Tides resorts learned Rebecca had returned, the phone was ringing off the hook. Office staff kept running in with urgent questions or thrusting pink message slips at her.

"Enough!"

Rebecca instructed the switchboard to hold all calls. She shooed away her staff and told her secretary to bar the door for one hour—no exceptions. Rebecca went through the message slips, determining the priority in which they would be answered, took a deep breath, and reached for the phone.

The first call was to Bix in New York.

"Oh, Becky, I'm so glad to hear from you. How was London?"

"There are possibilities," Rebecca said carefully.

As far as Bix knew, Rebecca had returned to England to pursue the idea of opening a European office. Rebecca hated misleading her best friend but didn't dare confide her real intentions to Bix. This was something she had to do alone.

"How's your own project coming along?" asked Rebecca.

For the last two years Bix and Torrey had been deeply involved in the anti–Vietnam War movement. However, both realized that there was more to do than march on the Capitol or demonstrate in the streets of Chicago. Bix made time to help out in the offices of an influential New York senator who vehemently opposed the war while Torrey channeled some of GoSee's profits toward private rehabilitation and counseling centers that were springing up all over the country.

"You should see what it's like here, Becky. A lot of guys are coming home. . . . They're so badly broken up, emotionally and physically. They need places where they can get away. We do what we can but a lot of destinations we offer don't have any facilities for the handicapped. It's not fair."

No, it isn't, Rebecca thought.

"Listen, Bix," she said. "Maybe there is something we can do."

Quickly Rebecca outlined her spur-of-the-moment idea.

"If you can set up a special package for the vets, I'll look after my end."

"That sounds great!" Bix said enthusiastically. "But what about the cost?"

"Let me worry about that."

"Becky, you're really something. Thank you!"

"I'll let you know when the facilities are ready. And you call me as soon as you hear from Torrey."

Rebecca buzzed her secretary and asked her to make two appointments, one with the chief physician of rehabilitation at the Angelines City hospital, the other with the landscape architect who had molded the grounds for The Tides.

"Would you also get the number of a hospital supply firm in Miami."

The doctor would advise her exactly what she could expect when dealing with young, handicapped guests. The architect would lay out the necessary boardwalks and ramps and oversee the construction of special bathing facilities. Rebecca vowed that unlike other resorts, The Tides would welcome handicapped men and women, regardless of the cost.

By the end of the day Rebecca had cleared most of her desk. A simmering labor dispute in Jamaica had been satisfactorily ironed out. In Palm Cove, the generators for the water filtration units had finally been installed. On Windemere Key carpenters had delivered a special bed just in time to accommodate a seven-foot client.

Midnight had come and gone by the time Rebecca finally closed up shop.

The next morning Rebecca arrived at Bones Ainsley's apartment over the police station. Even though Bones rose early Rebecca had made certain she was there before he woke up. As always Bones's door was open. Rebecca let herself in, put on coffee, squeezed fresh orange-mango juice, and slipped the raisin bread into the oven. A few minutes later she heard the shower.

"You're going to make someone a fine wife one day," Bones said, swooping down to hug her.

He peeked into the oven at the raisin loaf, then looked at Rebecca.

"What are you having for breakfast?"

Rebecca waited until Bones had demolished the bread and was on his third cup of coffee before she let the light conversation between them drift away. The policeman sat back, arms crossed, and regarded her solemnly.

"You want to know about Ramon Fuentes," he said flatly.

The first time she had asked him about the ill-fated captain, Bones had taken Rebecca at her word: that she had a very good reason for her question. He hadn't demanded to know why she wanted background on Ramon Fuentes, although he had his suspicions. These were heightened when Rebecca had asked him to try to locate the man.

"You've found him, haven't you?"

Bones nodded. "Now you must tell me why he is so important to you."

Rebecca had been dreading this moment. She had prayed that Bones wouldn't press her for an explanation.

"Bones, can't you just tell me where he is?"

"I'm sorry," he said gently. "Ramon is still a fugitive. The people who have helped me locate him have stopped short of telling me exactly where he is. Because I don't want to know. If I did, I would be obliged, as an officer of the law, to bring him back to stand trial. I believe Ramon is innocent, but he wouldn't have a chance against Silas Lambros. Lambros's grief runs deep. He would see to it that Ramon spent the rest of his life in prison."

"What if I told you that I could prove Ramon is innocent— providing I can get to him?"

Bones looked at her keenly.

"What could you possibly know about something that happened when you were just a babe?"

"More than you think."

"I'm sorry, Rebecca," the policeman said. "But before I allow you to become involved in something that might tempt justice, I have to know why you're so interested in Ramon Fuentes."

Rebecca didn't miss the finality in his words. Ramon Fuentes was crucial to her plans. Yet if she shared them with Bones he might try to stop her, thinking he was protecting her. Rebecca

realized she had to take that chance. She could not bring herself
to lie to Bones Ainsley.

"I think you had better have another cup of coffee," she said,
and started to tell him exactly what she had been doing in
London.

Bones Ainsley smoked an entire pipe while listening to Rebecca's account.

"Are you absolutely certain you want to go ahead with this?"
he asked finally.

"You've seen what Lambros has done to me," Rebecca said,
her voice devoid of emotion. "I have to do this. Not only for
myself and The Tides but for Max . . . and Dallas."

It was an argument Bones could not rebut. Nonetheless he
played his final card.

"It's going to be difficult for you to live with yourself afterward. You're not made of the same stuff as Lambros—thank
God! Please, think about this."

She wrapped both hands around his enormous fingers.

"It can't be any more difficult later than it is already," she
whispered. "And if I do nothing, how can I *ever* live with
myself?"

· 32 ·

British Honduras was one of the most beautiful countries in Central America, with lush, tropical rain forests, rainbow-misted waterfalls, and unbroken stretches of virgin coastline. For the jaguar hunter, lepidopterist, and ornithologist, British Honduras was paradise. But like paradise, it had its dark underbelly.

Peter Town was a legendary hideaway for thieves, men on the run, and those who wished, for one reason or another, to disappear off the face of the earth. No man had ever been rendered up to the law. The outcasts who had retreated here had formed their own rules of conduct, the first being that once a man had been accepted into the fraternity he would never be betrayed by it to outsiders.

Peter Town had been built at the mouth of a sluggish, muddy river and stood a scant five inches above sea level. As Rebecca walked along the dusty street she almost gagged at the stench from what the locals sourly referred to as the "nine o'clock parade"—the open sewers, nothing more than hollowed-out troughs, that lined both sides of the street. Every twelve hours at nine o'clock, water flooded the troughs, washing away the human waste into the bay.

Rebecca crossed the main square, bounded by the post office, a bank, and an L-shaped park. Already the homeless had carved out their space along the dead brown grass and underneath the ziricote trees, whose leaves dripped a thick milky syrup. Rebecca kept her eyes on the ground, careful to sidestep the bodies. Even an accidental touch could result in a knife flashing out.

At the other side of the park Rebecca waited as a jeep carrying British marines rolled by. The soldiers, here to protect the country in its continual border dispute with Guatemala, gave her only a cursory glance. Rebecca was grateful she had listened to Bones's advice about how to dress. Peter Town was no place for a clothes horse. Rebecca's old ankle-length skirt and loose peasant blouse allowed her to blend in with the surroundings.

She heard the music as soon as she entered the docks. Here the streets were almost completely dark, with only pools of light from tavern doorways to illuminate the way. Again, Rebecca stayed in the middle of the street, avoiding the alleys, where mongrels foraged among crates of garbage, and the inky doorways between the sputtering neon signs of the sailors' clubs. She had to walk the length of the street before she found the Toucan.

The interior of the club was much as Rebecca had imagined it would be: a long bar to one side, where a dozen men stood drinking, a haphazard collection of tables and chairs, and an ancient jukebox wheezing out a salsa beat. The air was thick with tobacco and ganja, cheap perfume, and whatever was mixed in with the sawdust strewn across the rough-planked floor.

The low conversation didn't break as Rebecca walked toward the end of the bar, but she knew that all eyes were upon her. From the tables she heard the throaty laughs of the whores as they exchanged opinions on this lost lamb who had wandered into their territory. The men watched her progress in the mirror that ran the length of the bar. Twice Rebecca felt grasping fingers squeeze her backside but ignored them, noting the hilts of knives strapped to belts.

Rebecca looked up and down for the bartender and gasped when he popped up directly in front of her like some maniacal jack-in-the-box. She noticed the platform behind the bar and the reason for it: the bartender was a dwarf.

"And how may I be of service to you, pretty lady?" the man cackled, his normal-size head far too large for the rest of his body.

"I'm looking for someone."

"And it isn't you!" one of the drinkers bawled out, drawing laughter from the others.

The dwarf snarled at them, then magically his features were transformed into an unctuous smile.

"Yes, pretty lady, and who are you looking for?"

"Ramon Fuentes."

The dwarf didn't miss a beat. "I have never heard of such a man, and believe me, I know *everyone*."

Out of the corner of her eye Rebecca noticed that several of the drinkers were now staring at her.

What have I gotten myself into?

Rebecca slipped one hand into the folds of her skirt, her

fingers seeking the handle of the knife strapped to her thigh. "I will wait," she said, controlling the trembling in her voice. "A beer, *por favor*."

The dwarf skittered off. He plunged his arm into a cooler lined with ice blocks and withdrew a beer. He slammed the green bottle down without bothering about such niceties as a glass.

"Who is the man you want to see?" he demanded suddenly.

"Ramon Fuentes," she said clearly.

The dwarf looked at her solemnly, then threw back his head and brayed. At the same time, Rebecca saw bemused smiles down the bar.

"What is Ramon Fuentes to you, *chita*?"

Rebecca found herself staring at one of the ugliest men she had ever seen. His face was deeply scarred by what must have been a severe case of chicken pox. The nose was broken and twisted to one side. The thick zapata mustache failed to conceal a harelip.

The man's hand moved in a blur, catching her wrist between his thumb and forefinger, causing Rebecca to cry out as pain shot through her arm.

"Now, *chita*, will you tell me why you come for Ramon?"

Rebecca felt her legs turning to jelly. If she didn't answer, this man would kill her. That much was evident from his toneless voice and the soulless, unblinking eyes riveted on her.

"Are you Ramon?" Rebecca managed to say.

Instantly the grip on her wrist tightened.

"Bones Ainsley told me where to find you!" she gasped.

Her arm, numb from fingertips to elbow, dropped by her side.

"Bones . . ." the man said softly. "It's been a long time since I heard his name. Tell me, *chita*, why did he send you to me?"

"To tell you that you can finally come home," Rebecca whispered.

Ramon Fuentes had been on the run every waking day of twenty of the last twenty-five years. Fleeing the Angelines only hours before the warrant for his arrest was issued, he had stolen away on a vessel bound for Panama. There he had managed to get a job as third mate on board a fourth-rate tramp steamer going through the canal.

At thirty Ramon had already been at sea half his life. Yet suddenly his years of experience counted for nothing. A wanted man, he didn't dare produce his master's certificate, necessary to secure the captain's position he had trained long and hard for. As a result Ramon had to take whatever work was available—cook, washer, mate, or, when he found himself between ships, manual laborer. It was a bitter blow to his self-respect, which eroded a little more with each passing year.

Over the next two decades Ramon Fuentes ventured into every major port in the world as well as a host of backwaters. He watched copper and sulphur being poured into his ore carrier at Gladstone on the Australian east coast and unloaded the same cargo in Yokohama. As a crane operator he handled teak in Bangkok, rice in Colombo, cotton in Bombay, and oil-drilling equipment in Dubai. He plied the Mediterranean, weathered the fearsome storms off the Cape of Good Hope, and spent months in the bone-numbing cold of the North Sea.

With each new ship and crew his despair became more and more profound. Wrenched from his native land, living each day among strangers, Ramon buried his homesickness and anger in the bottle. The scars on his toughened body were souvenirs from a thousand fights in a thousand bars. The only time he permitted his true feelings to show was in the privacy of squalid, dockside hotel rooms where, lying awake in the darkness, he dreamed of the Angelines and wept.

"Then one day, I don't remember how, I found myself in Belize. Here I finally stopped running. I had managed to save a little money and bought a fishing boat. Now I have this house and a little hidden away . . . in case I have to run again."

The two of them were sitting on the porch of Ramon's small house, set on the beach on the outskirts of Peter Town. The hours had flown by as Ramon told his story, and Rebecca saw the first glimmer of dawn break over the horizon. Even though he had reduced a full bottle of mescal by half and had accepted Rebecca not only as Bones's friend but Max McHenry's daughter, Rebecca noticed Ramon's eyes remained alert, sometimes glinting with suspicion.

"You're never going to have to run again," Rebecca promised him.

"So the McHenrys can still work miracles, eh?" Ramon laughed.

"According to Bones, the statute of limitations on the charge against you—manslaughter—hasn't run out," Rebecca said. "If you go back, you will have to stand trial for that as well as evasion of justice."

"Why don't you ask me to bring along the rope for them to hang me," Ramon demanded venomously.

"Because nobody's going to hang," Rebecca replied quietly. "I've read the commission transcripts about the accident on the *Bollinger*. I know it wasn't your fault."

Ramon rose and leaned against the veranda railing, staring out at his mistress, the sea.

Rebecca persisted. "You've paid with twenty years of your life for something that wasn't your fault. You can go home—if you want to."

Ramon looked at her sadly. "The only man who can help me is Justin Lambros, and he disappeared years ago."

"I've found him."

Ramon was stunned. "You . . . you found him? Where?"

"In London. He's been living there under a different name." Rebecca paused. "He is the key to your coming home."

"But will he help?" Ramon demanded. "Why should he go against his father now, when all these years he's been silent?"

"Because I'm going to force him to do so," Rebecca said coldly.

Ramon scrutinized Rebecca's face.

"You can do this, can't you?" he said rhetorically.

"With your help."

Ramon looked at her for what seemed a very long time, as though weighing the consequences of his next words. "If you help me, I will be in your debt forever," he said at last.

"There are no debts between friends," Rebecca told him. "Besides, I will be getting something out of this. But first I have to know exactly what happened on the *Bollinger* that day. The truth, Ramon, all of it."

When Rebecca returned to the Angelines she found a message from Alan Ballantyne buried in the pile of memo notes. Trying to concentrate on her work, she fretted away two hours until it was seven o'clock in the morning in London. The detective came on the line at once, sounding as though he had been up for hours.

"There was an interesting development several days ago," Ballantyne said. "Sir Geoffrey Smythe sold a painting, a Seurat, through a Zurich gallery. Fortunately I was able to determine that this particular picture had been in his collection for only three months."

Rebecca wondered what kind of connection Ballantyne had used to get *that* particular information.

"It seems that Sir Geoffrey had obtained the Seurat from the

Prescott Gallery," the detective continued, "at a ridiculously low price, if the records are accurate."

"You managed to see the gallery ledgers?" Rebecca asked, incredulous.

"I have a photocopy of the bill of sale," Ballantyne said dryly. "At any rate, Sir Geoffrey sold the painting for roughly ten times the amount he had paid for it—much closer to its true value."

"Do you know where the Prescott Gallery obtained the Seurat?" Rebecca asked, her heart pounding.

"As a matter of fact, I do."

When Ballantyne told her, Rebecca gasped. The final piece of the puzzle had been found. It fit perfectly.

"The Prescott Gallery doesn't usually deal in major pieces like that, does it?"

"Not at all. I've seen a few minor Picassos and a Miró, but nothing more impressive."

"I think we're going to see another treasure appear quite mysteriously," Rebecca said. "When it does, I want you to call me right away."

"It will be my pleasure, Miss McHenry."

Rebecca's head was spinning. She was close, very close, to springing the trap. Now came the hardest part: waiting for another painting to come into the Prescott Gallery. Rebecca knew that this could easily be a matter of months. Justin Lambros, Sir Geoffrey Smythe, and the mastermind who stood behind them were all careful men. But as long as the former governor-general needed the money, another transaction must be in the making. In the meantime the final details of her plan had to be set in place.

Even Alan Ballantyne was surprised when his source within the Prescott Gallery informed him that a Klee valued at half a million American dollars was scheduled to arrive within the week. The detective reckoned that Sir Geoffrey, who had spent the last month in Monte Carlo, had either had a string of very bad luck at the tables or else his latest mistress was proving extremely expensive.

Ballantyne waited until he had a copy of the Lloyds insurance bill in his hands before calling his client in the Angelines. After his conversation with Rebecca McHenry, the detective telephoned a second party, to whom he had been relaying every bit of information he had obtained for Rebecca.

Every time he spoke with this person Alan Ballantyne felt sickened. Throughout his career he had acted as a man of principle. His record at Scotland Yard had been sterling, his reputation for discretion legendary. When he had left the force, such a reputation had gone a long way in establishing him as a preeminent investigator. Yet at the core of all the hard-earned accolades lay a gigantic lie.

Ten years ago Alan Ballantyne's wife, a beautiful, fragile woman he worshipped, was stricken with multiple sclerosis. Knowing all too well the hellish conditions in the public institutions where the chronically ill were confined, the detective spent his life savings to keep her in a private clinic. When that money was gone, he sold their modest home in Paddington, moving himself into a one-bedroom flat. Six months later he took out a loan against the next three years of his salary.

Still it wasn't enough. Every time Ballantyne visited his wife, who was incontinent now, unable to feed herself, and scarcely able to recognize him, he prayed for God to put her out of her misery. Although the doctors had quietly discussed with him the option of euthanasia, the detective couldn't bear the thought of being the one to sanction mercy killing.

So Alan Ballantyne continued to pay. When the banks refused further financing, the police force's credit union lent him the amount accrued in his pension plan. That melted away in less than six months. Alan Ballantyne knew he had only one place to turn to: the criminals he had been so successful in putting away behind bars.

The approach was extremely cautious, the deal agreed upon in the shadows of a Soho nightclub. The day after a shipment of heroin from Marseilles arrived in London, Alan Ballantyne was given thirty thousand pounds—enough, he reckoned, to pay for his wife's care until she died.

The next day, when he went to the hospital, he was told she had passed away in her sleep. The doctor had tried to contact the detective but the Yard hadn't been able to locate him. Alan Ballantyne hadn't shared the number of the Soho club with anyone.

The men who had given him the money refused to take it back. They had pictures of Ballantyne accepting payment and that was their lock on him. The chief inspector took the only course available to him: He resigned.

Out of Scotland Yard, Alan Ballantyne was worthless to the underworld. He had almost forgotten that the photographs of his one indiscretion existed at all—until the day a certain man called on him at his Kensington office. The man had brought the pictures with him and assured Ballantyne he would destroy him with them unless the detective performed one service. Ballantyne had a new client, Rebecca McHenry. The man wanted to know why she was so interested in Sir Geoffrey Smythe. Everything the detective passed on to the Angelines was to be copied and sent to a London post office box.

Alan Ballantyne knew he had no choice. Only a man with phenomenal power could have induced London's major heroin dealer to part with the damning photographs. Such a man could destroy him without blinking—and would. So the detective did what was necessary. Every time he spoke to Rebecca he ached to tell her that she was in terrible danger. Yet he could no more bring himself to save her than he could save himself.

· 33 ·

Justin Lambros fumbled for his keys as he walked toward his gallery. The girl standing before the window hadn't taken her eyes off him and her smile was as dazzling as ever.

"Good morning," Justin stammered sliding the first of two keys into the lock.

"Good morning," Rebecca said. "I'm lucky you came along."

"Well, we really don't open until ten o'clock," Justin started to say. As he was trying to fit the second key he dropped the entire ring.

"Clumsy of me . . ." he muttered, blushing furiously.

"I do it all the time." Rebecca laughed.

Justin opened the second lock and pushed the door open.

"May I come in?" Rebecca asked hopefully.

Justin knew he had made a mistake. As soon as the second lock had been turned, a silent alarm had gone off in the central offices of a private security firm. Unless he telephoned in the appropriate code word in sixty seconds, the firm would assume a robbery was in progress—after which all hell would break loose.

The prudent thing to do was to ask the girl to wait outside. Justin knew if he did that she would feel offended and leave. That's the way his luck with women always ran.

"Yes, please come in," he said, hurrying toward the back of the gallery. "I'll be just a moment."

Rebecca stepped inside, closing the door behind her. From Alan Ballantyne's detailed description of the gallery, she knew exactly where Justin had gone and why.

The interior was what she had expected. The walls, running forty feet lengthwise, were sandblasted brick. Track lights and recessed spotlights were strategically placed to illuminate the paintings in the most effective way. In the center of the room was an island consisting of gray velvet couches, and several chairs and coffee tables. All the furniture had modern but very simple lines. Even the potted ficuses and ferns had been chosen so as not to detract a client's attention from the paintings.

Rebecca walked the length of the gallery, her heels echoing off the gleaming hardwood. She cast an appreciative eye over the paintings on the wall—an eclectic offering ranging from the frenzied universe of Jackson Pollock to the pop art of Andy Warhol. She did not see the Klee nor had she expected to. That, as the detective had told her, would be in the special viewing room next to the office.

"It's gorgeous," Rebecca exclaimed, looking at the Cubist rendition of a madonna with child mounted on an easel.

Justin Lambros hurried in, surprised that this lovely creature had somehow discovered the viewing room. Only favored clients knew it existed.

"I never thought this particular piece would go on the market," Rebecca said breathlessly. "How much are you asking for it?"

"I'm afraid it's spoken for, Miss . . ."

"Templeton," Rebecca said, giving him the name she had adopted for the occasion. "Have you really sold it?"

"I'm afraid so."

"There's no chance of changing your mind?"

"None, Miss Templeton," Justin said, his regret genuine. "By the way, my name is Justin Prescott. I own the gallery."

Rebecca shook his damp hand and turned her attention to the painting.

"If it really is spoken for, perhaps I could come to a satisfactory arrangement with the owner."

"It's gallery policy never to disclose the identity of our clients. However, if you would like to leave your name and address in London, I'll certainly pass it on. Should the buyer entertain the idea of selling, he can contact you directly."

"That would be wonderful," Rebecca said. "I've always loved Klee and with my divorce settlement I'm looking to indulge myself. After all, I deserve it, don't you think?"

At the reference to her single status Justin's hopes soared.

"I'm sure you do," he said fervently. "Perhaps I can show you some other fine examples—"

"Oh, that's so sweet of you, but my morning is completely booked," Rebecca said apologetically. "However, I would love to attend an exhibit if you have one in the near future. You can reach me at the Connaught."

"As a matter of fact, there's a showing of a new artist—

terrifically talented—next week," Justin said in a rush. "Would you consider coming as my guest?"

"I'd love to. And perhaps I can ask you for a small favor."

"Anything."

"Even though the Klee is gone, do you think it might be possible for me to view it—privately, I mean? I can spend hours looking at his work."

"I would be more than happy to arrange that," Justin said gallantly. "When would be a convenient time?"

"Tomorrow morning?"

"Splendid. I'll look forward to it."

"As will I," Rebecca promised him.

Rebecca hadn't doubted Justin Lambros would grant her request. Alan Ballantyne had told her Sir Geoffrey was still out of the country, not expected back for ten days to two weeks. That, Rebecca figured, would be more than ample time to complete what she had come to do.

Rebecca had been telling the truth when she had said that her morning was going to be busy. At ten o'clock she met with the travel organizer of the British National Union of Students to discuss organizing charter flights between London and the Caribbean. Traditionally the English favored the cheap resorts in Spain, North Africa, and the Greek islands to get away from the bone-chilling British climate. However, the travel bug had crossed the Atlantic and Rebecca was given an enthusiastic reception.

Buoyed by the possibilities of tapping into this new market, Rebecca lunched with two British Overseas Airline Corporation executives. She walked away from the three-hour repast with pages of facts and figures related to the leasing of BOAC jets.

The next morning Rebecca appeared punctually at the Prescott Gallery. She had dressed carefully for the occasion, choosing a smart jade-green pants suit by Givenchy, the perfect accent to her golden skin and sable hair. A light Burberry coat, with oxblood gloves and matching purse from Hermès, completed the outfit.

That Justin Lambros was glad to see her was an understatement. He almost fell over himself in greeting her and fussed over her until, mercifully, a customer arrived. While Justin attended to business, Rebecca sat in the viewing room, staring at the Klee but not really seeing it. She didn't much care for the artist's work, considering it derivative, but had read up on his life and influence in order to support the illusion she had created. Her

homework paid off when Justin, having finished with his client
and entrusted the shop to his two assistants, hurried into the
viewing room to be with her. Rebecca waited a whole hour for
him to screw up the courage to ask her out to lunch.

Rebecca played Justin Lambros very carefully. She knew that
she could wrap him around her little finger without his ever
being aware of what was happening, but that wasn't the effect
she wanted. Justin Lambros had to believe that he was the one
who had courted and captured her.

After their first lunch Rebecca regretfully but firmly turned
down his invitation for dinner the next evening. The same afternoon a mammoth bouquet of flowers was delivered to her suite
at the Connaught. Rebecca waited twenty-four hours, then called
to thank Justin and agreed to meet him for tea at the Savoy.

By the evening of the exhibit Justin was calling her every day.
Rebecca shopped carefully for the occasion, choosing a dove-
gray evening dress made of silk that molded itself to her body,
black silk pumps, and a sable jacket from Dior. When Justin
picked her up in a white Rolls-Royce, his gaping expression told
Rebecca her preparation had been more than justified.

She had expected Justin to show her off and he didn't disappoint her. Introducing her as a visitor from San Francisco, he
quickly trotted out the few details Rebecca had given him about
her fictitious background. Soon she was the center of attention,
drawing admiring glances from the men in the room and venom-
ous looks from the artist, whose night of triumph this was
supposed to be. In spite of the homage being accorded her,
Rebecca was careful not to encourage flirtatious advances. Except for brief visits to the ladies' room, she never left Justin's
side.

As the days went by, Rebecca found her life in London
divided into two distinct parts. By day she was the entrepreneur,
meeting with travel wholesalers and agents, real estate agents
and bankers. At night she slipped into her Templeton persona.
She always made it a point to meet Justin at the gallery, just
before closing. She insisted on spending at least a few minutes
with the Klee which, after three weeks, still hadn't been moved
from the viewing room. By now, Rebecca knew, the painting
should have been delivered to Sir Geoffrey Smythe. That it
hadn't been told her she had succeeded in making Justin believe
it was the drawing card that would always bring her back to him.

When Rebecca had begun her campaign against Justin, she
had felt only contempt for the man. What Justin had done—or

allowed his father to do—made him a coward in her eyes. Another man, even if he had had the excuse of youth, might have tried in later life to correct the injustice he had helped create. Neither Justin's gallantry nor his obvious infatuation softened her outrage.

Completely unaware of her true feelings, Justin pursued Rebecca shamelessly. They met every second day and had dinner at least three times a week. Rebecca allowed Justin to take her to West End plays and for boat rides on the Thames on Sunday afternoons. They browsed the flea market in Portobello Road, played tourist at the Tower of London, and rowed the gaily painted boats on Hyde Park's Serpentine.

Because of Justin's natural shyness, Rebecca never had to worry about his trying to take her home. He remained the perfect gentleman, seeing her to the lobby of the Connaught and at most, having a nightcap with her at the bar. But for all her deft orchestration, there was something Rebecca had neither anticipated nor was able to control.

From the beginning she had encouraged Justin to talk about himself. Not only did she want to steer him away from questions about her fictitious past, but anything Justin said about himself might prove valuable later on. It was a tactic Rebecca was coming to regret.

At first Justin had been predictable, recounting his life in London, how and why he had started the gallery. When he spoke of the artists he had found and brought to public attention, it was with a quiet pride, not proprietary arrogance. As was his nature, he downplayed his successes and dwelt on failures, on artists and works that deserved but never got recognition. When he talked like this, Rebecca sensed a different person emerging from behind the exterior man who was likely to spill champagne on her dress or step on her ankle while rushing ahead to open a door. This was a thoughtful, considerate individual who took others' fortunes—or lack of them—to heart, always wondering if there wasn't something more he could have done.

Rebecca found it more and more difficult to see Justin as a means to her particular end. In spite of her determination to keep her image of him as the enemy, she was drawn in by his honesty and compassion, the way in which he held nothing back. Or so Rebecca thought, until one afternoon Justin asked her to come to the gallery to see something very special.

Rebecca loved London Sundays when, in the morning, the streets were deserted and the roar of traffic was replaced by the peal of church bells. She chose to walk the two miles between the Connaught and the Prescott Gallery, taking pleasure in stretching her legs, pausing occasionally to window-shop. On the spur of the moment she bought café au lait for herself and Justin from a French-style bakery.

Rebecca saw Justin through the plate-glass window. As he ushered her inside, thanking her profusely for the coffee, Rebecca couldn't restrain a smile. Justin was wearing his idea of casual Sunday dress: tweed slacks, yellow cashmere sweater over a pink shirt, argyle socks, and loafers.

Justin guided her to the back of the gallery, his inconsequential chatter a measure of his nervousness. As he opened the door to the viewing room, Rebecca, who had been mildly intrigued by the invitation, was stunned. The Klee was gone. In its place were twenty paintings, each on an individual easel. They were all landscapes, boldly conceived and executed, their brilliant colors striking the viewer head-on. Rebecca flinched before the power contained in the works. Her surprise became anguish when she recognized the backgrounds.

"This is my secret life," Justin was saying. "For all we've talked about, you don't know where I really came from or where, in my heart, I still live. These are all landscapes of a place called the Angelines, where I was born."

Justin reached out and tentatively covered Rebecca's hand.

"I would like to tell you about it, what it means to me and why."

Rebecca didn't know how long she sat there, her eyes moving from painting to painting, drinking in this reflection of one man's love. She scarcely heard Justin recounting his boyhood in the Angelines, how deeply he felt for its beauty and people. The canvases spoke more eloquently than words ever could.

"I know I don't have much talent," Justin said at last. "I can paint only what I feel."

He paused. "I've never shown these to anyone. There has never been anyone I have loved enough to trust them to."

"They're very beautiful," Rebecca managed to whisper.

When she saw the joy break over his face, Rebecca realized she had made a terrible mistake.

"I have to go."

Scooping up her purse, she walked swiftly out of the viewing room. She heard Justin calling after her, his voice cracking with bewilderment and despair. Rebecca began to run. She knew she had to get away from him, the man she hadn't seen until that moment. If she failed, she would never be able to go through with the final scene of the script she had so carefully written.

For the next three days Rebecca shut Justin Lambros out of her life, instructing the hotel switchboard to screen her calls and not to put his through. The hotel, whose perennial guests included the wealthy and famous who regularly checked in under pseudonyms, guarded her privacy with complete discretion.

Rebecca threw herself into her work with a passion, trying to fill every waking hour. But at night, when she tossed restlessly in the oversize bed, Justin's pain-filled expression continued to haunt her. In her dreams she heard him recounting the life he had left behind in the Angelines. His sad, faraway voice touched a familiar chord in her, the one that had vibrated so painfully when she, too, had found herself an exile.

It's not the same! she kept telling herself fiercely. He didn't say a word about what forced him to leave the Angelines. For all his concern about the people, he never once thought of breaking with his father.

Yet all the reasoning in the world couldn't change the fact that Rebecca now saw Justin as someone quite different from the man she had so carefully manipulated. In his own way Justin Lambros was as much of a victim as she was.

Finally, when she realized her resolve was crumbling, Rebecca took the step that committed her, irrevocably, to seeing her plan through.

For the last three days Justin Lambros had acted like a man possessed. Dumping his responsibilities at the gallery on his assistants, he thought of nothing but Rebecca. Two sales that had required painstaking effort fell through because there was no one to lead buyer and seller through the final delicate steps of negotiation. A showing by an artist who had at long last consented to be represented by the Prescott Gallery turned into a shambles when Justin failed to appear. But the worst thing the assistants had to deal with was the wrath of Sir Geoffrey Smythe who, having returned from the Continent, was screaming for his Klee. Neither the painting nor the gallery owner could be located.

After that terrible scene in the viewing room, Justin had sequestered himself in his studio in Southwark on the south side of the Thames. It was a refuge no one knew about. At first Justin agonized over the reason for Rebecca's incredible behavior. Time after time he replayed what he had said, desperately trying to figure out why his words had caused such a reaction. The harder he tried—and failed—the more frantic Justin became. For the first time in his life he had shared his innermost thoughts and feelings with another human being. He had prayed that this woman who had suddenly transformed his life would understand just how precious these revelations were to him. Instead, Rebecca had obviously found them repellent.

Why?

When he couldn't fathom the answer, Justin laid siege to Rebecca. He bombarded the Connaught switchboard with calls, pleading with the operator to put him through to Miss Templeton's suite. In the face of the Connaught's intractable policy of protecting their guests' privacy, he resigned himself to leaving messages.

When Rebecca failed to return his calls, Justin sent telegrams, supplementing these with flowers. Finally he found a messenger service that would deliver his texts verbally. As a last resort Justin began to haunt Carlos Place, hoping to catch Rebecca coming or going. One morning, after spending two hours on the sidewalk, his patience was rewarded. Justin caught a fleeting glimpse of Rebecca sweeping through the glass doors. He bolted from his post, but too late. Oblivious to his shouts, Rebecca disappeared into the hotel's limousine and was gone, leaving Justin panting in front of a beefy doorman who regarded him suspiciously.

Justin returned to his refuge unbowed. In the privacy of his atelier he unwrapped the burlap that protected his last hope of ever seeing this woman again. Justin was sure that whatever he had done to disgust Rebecca, it couldn't be so awful as to make her forget the Klee. For that painting, if nothing else, she would come to him.

Early on the morning of the fourth day a telephone call proved Justin right. What he should have asked himself, but did not, was how Rebecca had managed to get the number of his studio, a number which was unlisted.

She was sitting in profile in the shadows of the dimly lit suite. Justin could see the graceful curve of her neck, the even rise and fall of her breasts as she breathed. She hadn't bothered to answer the door. At the desk they had told him he was expected. The door to the suite had been unlocked.

"Rebecca . . ."

"Come in, Justin."

Her voice seemed so remote, as though she were speaking to him from one end of a very long corridor. Clutching the burlap-wrapped canvas he had brought with him, Justin crossed the room. When he was standing in front of her, and she refused to look up, he thought he would faint.

"Rebecca, I have to know what happened," he blurted out, unable to help himself.

Finally she looked up at him and her eyes mocked him.

"Does the name McHenry mean anything to you, Justin?"

"Max McHenry?" *But what did—*

"I'm his daughter."

Rebecca watched him pale and drove on mercilessly.

"Is that the Klee, Justin? Did you bring it for me?"

He nodded miserably.

"What makes you think I would accept anything from a Lambros?"

Justin's head snapped up, and his eyes widened in disbelief.

"Oh, Justin," Rebecca said, laughing softly. "Don't you realize I know everything about you? Everything. Were you going to sell that painting to me instead of to Sir Geoffrey? Wouldn't that have displeased your father immensely? After all, your little gallery is just a front, isn't it?"

"No," Justin stammered. "It's not like that at all. You don't understand—"

"Oh, but I do. After twenty-five years you still jump when your father tells you to. He's corrupted you so thoroughly, you've come to believe your own lies."

The contempt in her words made him flinch.

"I didn't have any choice," Justin whispered.

"Just as you never had any choice about testifying for Ramon Fuentes?" Rebecca demanded harshly. "You made a choice all right. You destroyed an innocent man!"

"I would have changed everything if I could have!" Justin cried. "I tried to find him! I swear I did! But I couldn't . . . and then it was too late."

"No, it isn't," Rebecca told him, reaching for his hand. "It's never too late. You see, Justin, I have found Ramon for you."

Justin Lambros turned around fearfully. Despite himself, he uttered a strangled cry when he saw Ramon Fuentes coming toward him, like some hideous apparition the sea had finally rendered up.

· 34 ·

Silas Lambros flicked the intercom switch and barked irritably at his driver.

"Turn on the heat, man! I'm freezing to death back here!"

Although a surge of warm air flowed from the vents almost immediately, the head of Tyne & Wear huddled deeper into the corner of the seat, tightening the scarf around his neck.

Silas Lambros had been traveling nonstop for sixteen hours. A private jet had ferried him from Stann Creek Town to New York, where, after a two-hour delay, he had boarded a commercial liner for London. The journey was nightmarish. The first-class cabin, usually sedate, was filled with members of a rock band who had guzzled down the complimentary champagne, then proceeded to work their way through the liquor reserves. The captain had finally had to intervene, threatening to use restraints.

Things were no better at Heathrow, where a baggage-handlers strike forced passengers to wait until airline representatives had unloaded the luggage in a hangar. To add insult to already grievous injury, a jam-packed Air India flight had touched down minutes before, its passengers choking the customs and immigration booths. By the time Silas Lambros was met by his driver he had wished a thousand deaths on Sir Geoffrey Smythe for inflicting this hell upon him.

As the great car sped through Bury St. Edmunds, the wrecker watched Abbot's Yew materialize through the haze of the gentle spring rain. Once more he mentally replayed Sir Geoffrey's hysterical ramblings, trying to find some clue as to what had happened. The former governor-general of the Angelines had demanded that Lambros come to London immediately. Something terrible had happened—something that affected their "common interest," as Sir Geoffrey had put it. They were both in terrible danger.

Silas Lambros knew exactly what Sir Geoffrey had been referring to. He had tried to calm down the peer but Sir Geoffrey was beyond reason, his desperate pleas an indication that he no longer had any control over the situation.

Silas Lambros had told him to shut up and not say a word to anyone until he arrived in Abbot's Yew.

As the limousine wended its way along the drive, Silas Lambros remembered the day, so long ago, when he and the then-bankrupt peer had struck their bargain. Both had realized the risk they were taking. Should their arrangement ever be uncovered, even the enormous gains each had made wouldn't be able to protect them from British government retribution. Yet the plans had been worked out so carefully, there wasn't the slightest risk of exposure. Proof of this was the fact that, in spite of rumors, the arrangement had continued to work for more than twenty years.

So, after all this time, what had happened? Silas Lambros asked himself.

The question had gnawed at him throughout his journey. Any answer he came up with only made him shudder.

The library of Abbot's Yew would have done justice to either the British Museum or any one of London's distinguished gentlemen's clubs. Recreating the interior of a medieval monastery, it had a vaulted ceiling and arched leaded windows. The walls were lined with built-in bookcases, the shelves glowing from leather-bound volumes. A stepladder on wheels stood next to the glass cabinets housing the rare-book collection. The ascetic effect was broken by a single desk and two wing chairs set at angles in front of it.

Sir Geoffrey Smythe slumped forward, elbows on the leather blotter, his sagging face in his palms. His eyes were lightly closed as he listened to Justin Lambros's voice.

"I had the wheel of the *Bollinger* when Ramon Fuentes warned me about the storm. It was my decision whether or not we should head back into port. I knew that we should turn around, but then Nigel came on deck . . . and he laughed at me for wanting to return. I shouldn't have listened to him. He was drunk and had no idea of the danger we were in. But I couldn't bear the thought of humiliating myself in front of him, so I stayed on course. . . .

"The storm hit us without warning . . . just like a 'cat' does . . . as Ramon knew it would. Nigel and his girlfriend were on the pilot deck. Nigel was acting like a madman, screaming at me to maintain course. When the first big wave hit us I was knocked away from the wheel. I remember breaking my wrist in the fall, then my head hit something, and for a moment I lost consciousness. The next thing I remember is Ramon trying to regain control of the *Bollinger* but it was impossible. Another wave hit us and I saw Nigel and the girl thrown over to the railing. Ramon was struggling with the wheel when the boat pitched. I heard screams and saw the girl clutching Nigel. . . . He was trying to throw her off. The next instant they were gone. The wave carried them off together. . . . Nigel had tried to get away from the girl in order to save himself . . . and failed. I don't remember anything after that.

"What happened on board the *Bollinger* that day was entirely my fault. I should never have been at the wheel. If I had listened to Ramon, perhaps my brother and the girl would still be alive. . . ."

The words trailed off, replaced by labored rasps, like those of a drowning man struggling for air.

"I should have spoken up for Ramon Fuentes at the board of inquiry. Instead, I remained silent . . . and ruined the life of a man who had never shown me anything but kindness."

There was a pause, then Justin's deadened monotone once again broke the silence of the library.

"My father sent me away after that. He worshipped Nigel and refused to believe my account of what had happened. He would not permit Nigel's memory to be sullied. Like a coward, I gave in to him.

"Years later, when my father had helped Sir Geoffrey Smythe become governor-general of the Angelines, he visited me in London. My father and Sir Geoffrey had worked out an arrangement whereby Crown land in the Angelines would be transferred into common holdings. Sir Geoffrey would use his influence in the House of Lords to bring this about. He would tell my father in advance what parcels would become available so that Tyne & Wear could buy them up. In return, my father agreed to provide Sir Geoffrey with enough income to maintain Abbot's Yew.

"I and my gallery played a major role in this agreement. Because of the need for absolute secrecy, there could be no connection between my father and Sir Geoffrey. In order to get the money to Sir Geoffrey my father arranged for me, through the gallery, to buy certain paintings from the Lambros collection at ridiculously low prices. These masterpieces were then sold to Sir Geoffrey at a fraction of their market value. The point was that no one could question the legitimacy of the transaction. The Prescott Gallery had a receipt from my father for the paintings; Sir Geoffrey had a bill of sale from us, proof of what he had paid.

"The key to the plan lay in the next step. Sir Geoffrey would hold on to the painting for a few months, then go to Zurich, where a broker would introduce him to a private collector who wanted the piece. At that point Sir Geoffrey would sell it for fair market value. Something he had acquired for a few thousand pounds brought him a hundred times that amount.

"And because the transaction was made in Switzerland, Sir Geoffrey never declared any taxes on his windfall. . . ."

Hearing the crunch of tires on gravel, the master of Abbot's Yew stirred from his reverie. He gazed up at the oil portraits of his ancestors, stern, unforgiving faces that stared at him from across the centuries. Everything he had done had been for them, to preserve the heritage they had entrusted him with. Now, because of one man's tortured conscience, he stood to lose not only his home and lands but the respect that had always surrounded his family's name.

Sir Geoffrey could imagine what would happen. There would be questions in both houses of Parliament. The government, already an enemy of the peerage, would delight in a major investigation. The press would feed off the scandal, dragging centuries of service and achievement through the gutter. There would be nowhere to hide, not from public contempt, not from those polite, cold-eyed inspectors from Inland Revenue who would appear at Abbot's Yew with the authority to pry into every corner of his life.

It can't be allowed to happen, Sir Geoffrey thought. But the horrible truth was that his fate was no longer in his hands.

Sir Geoffrey Smythe watched Rebecca McHenry punch the rewind button on the tape recorder, mesmerized as the spool containing Justin Lambros's damning confession became a blur.

For the first time in his seventy-five years Silas Lambros truly felt his age. Upon arriving at Abbot's Yew he had expected to be shown into his usual suite, have a bath drawn for him, and fresh clothing laid out. Instead, Plender, Sir Geoffrey's cadaverous manservant, had taken him directly to the library.

Silas Lambros gasped when he saw Rebecca. For an instant he was spun back in time, imagining that it was Max McHenry who was sitting there. His surprise became fear when he noticed the tape recorder. Lambros's first thought had been, what has this fool told her? Now he had heard the tape, and he knew that Sir Geoffrey had had nothing to do with the course of events. The betrayal had been committed by his own blood. That, more than the result of his son's confession, rankled Silas Lambros.

The wrecker had demanded to hear the tape twice. Not that he had missed anything the first time. It was a way of buying time in which to examine all possible consequences. And find a way to go on the offensive.

"Are you aware of the criminal penalties for blackmail?" Lambros asked at last.

"I haven't asked you for anything," Rebecca answered coldly.

"Really, there's no need for threats—" Sir Geoffrey spoke up.

"Shut up," Lambros said, not bothering to look at the peer. "This is all very interesting," he continued. "But what, in fact, do you have? The ramblings of a man obviously on the verge of a nervous breakdown. None of what is on that tape is verifiable. The tape itself is no evidence at all—"

This time it was Rebecca who interrupted.

"If there was only the tape, I would agree with you. I've had a notarized transcript made."

She tossed Lambros a sheaf of papers, the cover stamped with a notary public's seal.

"That's your copy. You'll note Justin's signature on the last page. As for actual proof of what you and Sir Geoffrey have been doing, I have copies of the bills of sale for paintings the Prescott Gallery bought from you then sold to Sir Geoffrey. Notarized, of course. I also have the name of the broker in Zurich who is prepared to testify in an English court that he acted as intermediary between Sir Geoffrey and other buyers. The Swiss, as you well know, keep meticulous records."

"But my dear girl," Lambros protested delicately. "It's obvious my son is not a well man. Heaven knows what induced him to create this fantasy."

Lambros paused, a smile baring his teeth.

"Perhaps even you did. But assuming the contrary, I'm certain I can find doctors who will testify to my son's enfeebled condition. Which, of course, leaves you nowhere."

"What kind of man are you?" Rebecca asked in disbelief. "How can you sit there thinking of ways to crucify your own son so that the truth remains buried? Well, this time it won't be. You ruined Ramon Fuentes's life. You used—and destroyed—Justin—"

"And you, my dear, are so pristine? You, of course, didn't use Justin for your purposes."

For an instant Rebecca faltered. Justin's horrified expression upon seeing Ramon Fuentes swam before her eyes. She saw his wild stare as he realized how cleverly she had seduced him, holding out the promise of things she never intended to give.

Yes, she had used Justin and in the end he had crumbled, no longer able to live with the shame his father had consigned him to. Seeing Ramon Fuentes, the man he hadn't had the courage to speak up for, shattered the delicate illusion Justin Lambros had spun for himself: that of a man unjustly exiled from the land he loved. The final blow came when, under Rebecca's relentless questioning, Justin admitted that had Ramon Fuentes not shielded him during the investigation, charges of negligence on the high seas resulting in death would have been brought against him. In such a case not even his father's influence would have been enough to protect Justin from a certain guilty verdict.

Rebecca explained to Justin there was only one way he could make amends for the past. He had to clear Ramon Fuentes so that the captain could go home. When this was done Rebecca told him how her patrimony had been stolen by Andrew Stoughton and Silas Lambros. She described the cruelty of Sir Geoffrey Smythe and her own exile. Then she spelled out the details about the arrangement between Silas Lambros and Sir Geoffrey, praying that Alan Ballantyne's information had been accurate.

It was. Not once did Justin Lambros correct her.

"What do you want me to do?" he had asked finally.

"Put all the details of your father's dealings with Sir Geoffrey on tape," Rebecca said, not daring to breathe. "After that I'll have a notarized transcript made."

"What will you do with it?"

Rebecca looked steadily at him.

"I'm going to get back what is mine. Nothing more, nothing less. I don't want to hurt anyone—"

She didn't realize how callous the words were until she heard them with her own ears.

Justin smiled wanly at her.

"Did you care at all?" he asked her.

There was nothing in his voice except innocent curiosity. When Rebecca hesitated, he said, "That's all right. It doesn't really matter."

Rebecca wanted to tell him he was wrong, that it did matter, that under different circumstances . . . She stopped, realizing that she was only lying to herself.

Justin was watching her but it wasn't his face Rebecca saw. Instead, it was Dallas and her father.

"I'll give you what you want."

And then Rebecca understood what Bones had meant about consequences.

"And just what do you think is yours, Miss McHenry?" Silas Lambros demanded.

"The land and the mines you and Andrew Stoughton stole from me."

"Really?"

"Silas, for God's sake, listen to her!" Sir Geoffrey shouted. "She can ruin us!"

"Don't be a fool!" Lambros retorted contemptuously.

But the peer wouldn't be stopped this time.

"Supposing you were to get this land back," he said. "What then?"

"Nothing. The evidence I have remains in a vault. It's my insurance that neither of you will double-cross me—or have anyone else try to do so."

"Do you expect us to believe that?" Lambros demanded.

"I expect you to believe that I will take everything I have to the Home Secretary, the Solicitor-General, and the newspapers. Of course, if you think I'm making all this up, you can launch a libel suit against me. I'm sure the media will find that very interesting."

"What guarantee do we have that you will keep your word?" Sir Geoffrey asked quickly.

"Exactly that," Rebecca told him. "My word."

"Surely you don't expect to get all this merely for the price of your silence," Lambros said.

"Not at all." Rebecca smiled. "This has to be a legitimate sale, so there are no complications later on."

"And what figure did you have in mind?" asked Lambros, sensing that all might not be lost after all.

"One pound. Or about two forty at today's exchange rate."

Plender had been in the peer's service longer than anyone could remember. The household staff that he supervised had long ago forgotten his first name and referred to him, as did everyone in Bury St. Edmunds, as Plender. He was considered a cold, aloof man of indeterminate age, with no relatives or any life outside of Abbot's Yew. It was exactly the image Plender had gone to great lengths to cultivate.

Long ago Plender had discovered that his most onerous duty was to continually hide his contempt for his employer. In Plender's opinion, Sir Geoffrey Smythe was nothing more than a bloated, pompous leech. When the manservant expressed this sentiment to his lover, the younger man, who worked for a London wine merchant, came up with a scheme that alleviated Plender's disgust.

In the years that Sir Geoffrey Smythe served as Her Majesty's representative in the Angelines, Plender was virtual master of Abbot's Yew with full authority to make sure the ancestral seat was maintained exactly as Sir Geoffrey would have wished. Plender saw to this with a vengeance. He authorized extensive repairs to the main house where none were needed, sent carpets and furniture out for cleaning that was never done, commissioned landscape architects, surveyors, and interior decorators for studies that were never put into effect. All the people involved were either his friends or those of his lover. None had any scruples about providing duplicate bills.

Over a period of ten years Plender had managed to skim off over two hundred thousand pounds from the operating budget of Abbot's Yew. This money, safely on deposit in a Madrid bank, was his nest egg. Part of it would buy him and his lover a villa on Ibiza. The balance, judiciously invested, would provide a comfortable income for the rest of their lives.

Plender and his lover had thought the scheme out very carefully. They amortized their theft over years to avoid detection. For the same reason, they agreed that work traditionally done by local tradesmen couldn't be given to London firms. That was the surest way to get tongues wagging.

So how had he done it? Plender wondered for the umpteenth time as he walked briskly from the Charing Cross train station to the Strand Place Hotel down the street.

The bane of Plender's existence, who could not only destroy his idyllic dreams of Ibiza but also land him in jail, was waiting for him at the hotel's busy bar. Alan Ballantyne acknowledged the manservant's arrival by ordering him a pink gin.

The detective had never told Plender how he had discovered the embezzlement or why any had been suspected in the first place. Plender had been mortified when Ballantyne had quietly told him which bank in Madrid held the money—as well as the current amount. Only then had Ballantyne assured Plender that he wasn't interested in exposing him, as long as the manservant did one thing: report all visits by Silas Lambros to Abbot's Yew and the substance of any conversations that took place between the wrecker and Sir Geoffrey. To facilitate this, the detective had provided Plender with a highly sensitive miniature tape recorder which the manservant was to secret in Sir Geoffrey's library, where business discussions were held, prior to Silas Lambros's arrival.

Plender, who knew better than to ask this taciturn man the whys and wherefores, proved himself very adept at handling the equipment.

Rebecca had given Silas Lambros forty-eight hours to transfer the title of the land stolen from her. Whenever she recalled the wrecker's stunned expression at the mention of the price she had set, Rebecca laughed to herself. Both Lambros and Sir Geoffrey had been so taken aback that neither had tried to stop her when, after dropping her bombshell, she had swept out of Abbot's Yew.

In spite of her victory Rebecca was certain that the war was far from over. Even though she had Silas Lambros boxed in, he would use every minute of those two days to try to find a way to weasel out. Rebecca would have expected nothing less. That was why she wasn't surprised to learn that Lambros had contacted the journalist with whom Rebecca intended to meet. Rebecca smiled. The Fleet Street veteran would tell Lambros only as much as he himself knew at this point: He would be interviewing the head of McHenry Enterprises for a piece on The Tides phenomenon. Of course Lambros would immediately realize that Rebecca could hand the journalist a juicier story than that. He would also be reassured, by the newspaperman's ignorance, that Rebecca was keeping her word.

Nor was Rebecca surprised when the wrecker installed himself in one of the prime suites at the Dorchester instead of retreating to his palatial home. During the rites of spring Celeste ruled at Eaton Square, holding one party after another. The Dorchester, on the other hand, was fabled for privacy. All suite telephones were direct dial, eliminating the possibility of someone listening in on the switchboard. There were also telex facilities as well as bonded messengers available twenty-four hours a day.

Rebecca had calculated that the net worth of her land had, because of the now-defunct gold mining operations, dropped to a hundred million dollars, less than half its value when Max was alive. Even so, Silas Lambros didn't dare go to the board of

Tyne & Wear and explain why, all of a sudden, the giant conglomerate had to sell sixty percent of its Angelinian holdings. Too many questions would be raised for which there were no suitable answers. The only thing Lambros could do, given his position as chairman of Tyne & Wear, was conclude the sale on his own authority and present the board with a fait accompli. That meant he would have to cover the hundred million out of his own pocket.

Rebecca had made a careful accounting of the wrecker's assets. As wealthy as Lambros was personally, he would have to call in every debt and favor owed him. Rebecca could just imagine the flood of telexes and calls that were pouring in and out of the Dorchester suite.

And he has to gather his capital discreetly, Rebecca thought.

It would be tricky enough for Lambros to explain to the board members why the sale had gone through without their knowledge. If they ever learned that Silas Lambros had placed himself on the brink of financial ruin in order to close the deal, the old wrecker would be utterly destroyed.

Rebecca had expected Lambros to do one other thing, and he hadn't disappointed her. Upon his return to London, Silas Lambros had gone immediately to the Prescott Gallery. Rebecca knew Lambros would want to confront Justin, demand explanations, and see if there was any way he could use his son to stop Rebecca. This, Rebecca considered, was the most dangerous juncture of her plan. If Silas Lambros brought enough pressure to bear on Justin, he might retract everything.

Rebecca knew that even under those circumstances the release of Justin's taped confession would be more than enough to cause scandal and official inquiry. But she would also be compelled to drag Justin into the public spotlight to explain why he was changing his story. The thought that this might happen sickened Rebecca. What she had already done to Justin was something she would have to live with for the rest of her life. Yet she realized she could not falter now. If Justin bowed to his father, she would once more force him to look into Ramon Fuentes's eyes and dare him to retract his previous statements. Deep in her heart Rebecca could not believe Justin had the strength to rebuild the illusion she had shattered.

Half the allotted time was gone. Rebecca remained sequestered in the Connaught suite, unable to concentrate on anything but Silas Lambros's frantic movements around London. Alan

Ballantyne, her eyes, ears, and legs on the street, reported faithfully every few hours.

"There's been an interesting development," the detective said when he telephoned just after midnight. "The subject"— Ballantyne never referred to Lambros by name—"paid a visit to a converted warehouse in Southwark. I later learned this is Justin Lambros's studio. He wasn't there nor, as I have reported, was he at the gallery. He isn't at his flat either. In fact, no one seems to know where he is."

Rebecca answered the detective's unspoken question.

"I haven't seen or heard from him."

"Then it's quite possible he's gone to ground," Ballantyne said. "Perhaps he doesn't want *anyone* to find him."

An uneasy feeling stirred within Rebecca, but she shrugged it off as nerves. Justin Lambros must have heard about or anticipated his father's arrival in London and bolted. Whatever sympathy Rebecca had felt for Justin evaporated in the face of this final act of cowardice.

"Don't worry about him," she told Ballantyne. "If Lambros can't find him, so much the better. And there's nothing Justin Lambros can do that will affect me now."

Silas Lambros was not a man who hid behind illusions. He saw the evidence his own son had provided Rebecca McHenry for exactly what it was: damning. How this woman had managed to get it didn't concern him at the moment. From her icy composure and the dispassion with which she had presented the facts Lambros knew Rebecca would carry out her threat to use the material at her disposal.

Nor did the wrecker waste time berating Sir Geoffrey Smythe. The former governor-general had always been a weak man, easy to manipulate, even easier to corrupt. Had he been otherwise, he never would have struck his bargain with the chief of Tyne & Wear.

Clever bitch! Lambros thought grimly. First she got what she needed out of Justin, then she confronted Smythe, who must have toppled like the weakling he's always been. If he had any backbone, he would have put her off until I could get there.

As it was, Silas Lambros had walked into a situation from which there was no retreat. Justin had already collapsed. At the first hint of public scandal Smythe would crack and tell everything in the hope of receiving clemency from a government prepared to carve him apart. That meant he, Silas Lambros,

would bear the brunt of the investigation. Which might just be
enough for his enemies on the board of Tyne & Wear to muster
their forces and do away with him.

The fact that outsiders might gain control of an entity he
considered a family trust rankled Silas Lambros. For that reason,
and that reason alone, he had instructed his Swiss banker to
begin transferring, as discreetly as possible, one hundred million
dollars, almost his entire personal fortune, from Zurich to New
York.

Once the financial arrangements were under way, Silas Lambros
turned his attention to try to find a way to thwart Rebecca
McHenry. He considered asking Andrew Stoughton for help but
rejected the idea. How many times had Andrew warned him
about the McHenry woman? And how often had those warnings
fallen on deaf ears? The ignominy was too much for Lambros to
bear. When the "sale" of the lands became public, Andrew, and
perhaps others on the board, would suspect that something wasn't
right. But as long as Tyne & Wear had a hundred million to
show on its books, no one would dare ask embarrassing questions. Silas Lambros intended for matters to stay that way.

The one person who might provide a means to forestall or
even abort what was about to happen was Justin. Silas Lambros
would have made a deal with the devil himself to find out where
his son was. But no matter where his private investigators looked
or what financial incentives they had been instructed to offer,
Justin was not to be found.

As the chimes of the clock struck the forty-seventh hour, Silas
Lambros felt his last hopes fade. The time for reprieve was past.

For all the implications and money involved, the terms of the
sale were so simple that they could have been handled by a law
clerk.

Rebecca had seen to it that the most experienced international
property lawyer in London drafted the document. She had gone
over it with him twice, questioning anything that she did not
fully understand. The attorney had indulged Rebecca. Not only
was his meter running, but if this beautiful, intense woman
was satisfied with his work, then more could be in the offing.
The lawyer had heard whispers in the financial community
about the intention of McHenry Enterprises to expand into the
Mediterranean.

The signing took place in the Dorchester suite. Shortly before
Rebecca was to arrive, Silas Lambros's attorney finished reading

the agreement. He had not seen it before and now he was desperately trying to marshal his thoughts.

"Mr. Lambros, sir . . ." the attorney began. "I really must protest! Surely this figure of one pound cannot be accurate. Is there something here that I am not privy to? Are you under any kind of duress?"

Silas Lambros silenced the young man with his gaze. He had personally culled this particular not-too-bright, overly in debt, sycophantic specimen from the cavernous holds of Tyne & Wear's legal department. For exactly all those qualities.

"Do you wish to suggest I am also senile and incompetent?" Lambros demanded coldly.

"No, sir, not at all—"

"Given even your modest legal talent, can you see anything untoward with this document?"

"No, sir—"

"Neither do I!"

It was, as Silas Lambros had expected, a duplicate of the one Rebecca McHenry had so thoughtfully had delivered the evening before for his examination.

"Then I suggest we get on with it. And I needn't remind you that should you ever, even in your dreams, speak of what happened here today, I will have your balls for bookends!"

The young attorney displayed excellent self-preservation instincts.

"In that case, sir," he said in a low voice, "we are ready to proceed."

It was, Lambros later reflected, a measure of his character that he was able to be civil to Rebecca McHenry. He affixed his signature to the deed of sale, watched as the lawyers witnessed and testified to it, and actually held in his hand the certified check for one pound. He looked at it for a very long time, aware that both representatives were holding their collective breaths, still unable to believe what was transpiring. Only Rebecca McHenry seemed unconcerned.

"Is something wrong?" he heard her say.

"Not at all," Lambros murmured, carefully folding the check. He began to walk to the bedroom, then turned around.

"You are a person of your word, are you not?"

Rebecca returned his gaze just as fiercely.

"I hope you are too."

*   *   *

At two o'clock the following morning most of London was asleep. But there were exceptions.

In her suite at the Connaught, Rebecca was sitting at a marble table, its surface covered with papers, notes, and ledgers. The moment she had arrived from the Dorchester she had stripped, immersed herself in a long, hot bath, and, wrapped in the hotel's flowing terry-cloth robe, sat down to work. Six hours later she was completing a rough draft of exactly what she would do with the land that was suddenly hers.

In spite of the mild breeze billowing the curtains, a fire was blazing in the hearth. When Rebecca poured herself a cognac, the neck of the decanter tinkled nervously against the snifter. She had hoped the work would exhaust her. Yet the minute she stepped away from the table, her concentration was broken.

I should be out celebrating, she thought. I should have called Bix or Ramsey . . . somebody, and told them what's happened. Instead, I want to go home and forget all this.

Over and over Rebecca told herself she had achieved the impossible: Not only had she bested Silas Lambros, but in doing so she had also gotten back what had been stolen from her.

In the only way possible.

But was that true? Had there been no other way except by using Justin Lambros . . . even after she could no longer hate him?

As she sat huddled in the darkness, Rebecca yearned to reach out to someone, to hear comforting words and feel strong arms protecting her. In a way she could not define, she had taken an irrevocable step forward. In the process, something had been lost, leaving her less than she had been before.

In his suite at the Dorchester, Silas Lambros lay awake in the darkness, his mind turning over the details he had been working on. The chairman of the Zurich bank, who had stayed in his office long after business hours, had informed him that the hundred million dollars had been electronically transferred to the Tyne & Wear account in New York. Lambros had chosen New York because that was where Rebecca McHenry had her corporate account. As he would explain to the board, it was logical for the purchase sum to go to a bank in Wall Street.

Within the hour New York was on the line. The hundred million had arrived and been credited to the Tyne & Wear account. All references to Zurich had been destroyed. A phony paper trail had been established linking the transfer to the Walker

Bank. Lambros made a mental note to come up with a suitable reward for the bank's vice-president who had handled the matter.

Now, he thought, it's a matter of getting it back.

Silas Lambros had no plans yet. From experience, he knew his revenge would be months, perhaps even years, in the making. There was a great deal he had to learn about The Tides before striking at Rebecca McHenry.

Fifteen floors below Silas Lambros's lavish suite, in the bowels of the hotel, a nondescript man in a black trench coat trudged up the employee's staircase to the ground floor.

Alan Ballantyne had let himself in during the shift change. When he came to the administration offices he found the door to the night manager's cubbyhole open. The detective stepped inside and saw three keys on the desk. He placed a bulky manila envelope beside them and stepped into the corridor. A moment later he came back inside. The envelope, filled with five thousand pounds in worn notes, had disappeared. The keys were still on the desk.

A moment later the detective had used one of them to open the steel-lined door to the safety deposit box room. Quickly he found the box whose number corresponded to that on the other two keys, inserted both, and turned them at the same time. The heavy panel swung forward.

Alan Ballantyne withdrew the box, set its contents on the table, and adjusted the gooseneck lamp. It took him less than two minutes to photograph every page of the sales agreement Silas Lambros had personally deposited there less than six hours earlier.

· 36 ·

The boardroom of Tyne & Wear was a study in burled walnut, Lalique chandeliers, and Baccarat crystal. Immortalized in oil, the stern faces of wreckers long dead gazed down on the eight men seated around the twenty-foot table, as though ready to pass judgment on their arguments and decisions.

It was a room Silas Lambros felt eminently comfortable in—as well he should have. The men before him represented some of the most powerful industries in the world: Rolls-Royce, Westminster Bank, Lloyds, Continental Fidelity Insurance, among others. They had been asked to sit on the board of Tyne & Wear—and each had eagerly accepted—because of what Tyne & Wear could offer their companies. And vice versa. But none could deny that in this room Silas Lambros was *primus inter pares*, first among equals, just as he had been for the last four decades.

As Big Ben tolled noon, Silas Lambros opened the meeting.

"Gentlemen, I must apologize for Andrew's absence. I have tried to find his whereabouts but without success. I suggest that to avoid wasting time—and not to slight the chef—we begin."

There were several appreciative chuckles and nods. It was common knowledge that Tyne & Wear's executive kitchen served the best fare in London, prepared by a chef Silas Lambros had lured away from Paris's fabled Tour d'Argent.

"What I am about to disclose to you represents a major coup for the company," Lambros carried on. "Usually a transaction of this caliber would have been brought before the full board for consideration. However, in this one instance, I have acted unilaterally."

Lambros paused, gauging the mood of the room. Arbitrary action was not something these men merely disapproved of, they saw it as a personal affront. But in this case their expressions ranged from neutrality to curiosity. The wrecker knew he had them.

"As you are well aware, the company has extensive holdings in the Angelines, raw land and defunct mines, neither of which is producing revenue. It is my pleasure to announce that through a series of secret negotiations I have effected the sale of these questionable assets to McHenry Enterprises—"

Lambros allowed himself a dramatic pause of three heartbeats, then slipped in the best part.

"—for one hundred million dollars cash."

Twelve blocks away, in the narrow confines of Fleet Street, Andrew Stoughton sat fuming in the backseat of his Rolls-Royce. A double-decker bus had collided with a delivery van and traffic was hopelessly snarled. Even the Rolls's heavy-duty glass windows couldn't keep out the din.

Andrew checked his watch. The board meeting was already under way. He reckoned Silas Lambros would deliver his statement as quickly as he could without raising suspicion and then ask for a vote of confidence. Andrew calculated he had twenty minutes at best. And he hadn't moved a foot in the last five.

Andrew scooped up the papers lying beside him and threw open the door. With the startled chauffeur calling after him he sprinted, like a broken-field runner, through the chaos of Fleet Street.

"And in conclusion I would suggest that this infusion of capital will allow the company to take advantage of certain opportunities in the aerospace and defense industries. I look forward, gentlemen, to your counsel as to how best to proceed."

Silas Lambros pretended to sit down, then straightened up, as though remembering a minor oversight.

"In spite of the fact that our young colleague is still not here, I ask that the board vote on a motion of confidence regarding this sale."

Lambros noticed the members looking at one another. Uncertainty hung in the air, as though they all were privy to something he was not. Lambros's stomach knotted.

"Gentlemen," he said graciously. "If you have any questions—"

At that instant the door swung open. Andrew Stoughton, breathing hard, his gray suit stained black from fresh newsprint, burst in. Ignoring his father-in-law's startled expression, he went around the table dropping a copy of the *Evening Standard* in front of each member. He slapped the last copy before Silas Lambros.

"I have only one question, gentlemen," he said, looking hard into Lambros's disbelieving eyes. "Does our august chairman's account regarding the indiscriminate sale—no, giveaway—of our Angelinian assets match the facts presented here, for the whole world to see?"

Rebecca hadn't been able to fall asleep until dawn. Even though it was one o'clock in the afternoon, when she finally heard the insistent knocking at her door she thought she had slept for only a few minutes.

"Terribly sorry to have disturbed you, madam," the assistant manager, complete in morning coat and carnation, apologized. "This package was delivered a few minutes ago. The gentleman insisted it is a matter of the greatest urgency."

Rebecca squinted at the handwriting but didn't recognize it. She mumbled her thanks and, tossing the plain-wrapped package on the escritoire, disappeared into the bathroom. Ten minutes later, her face scrubbed, teeth brushed, and most of the fog in her head gone, she cut the strings binding the mysterious present.

The newspaper's headline screamed out at her in twenty-point type: DEAL OF THE CENTURY! McHENRY BUYS TYNE & WEAR CARIBBEAN ASSETS FOR £1!

Rebecca slumped back in the chair, her head spinning. Deliberately she averted her eyes from the headline and forced herself to read the first few paragraphs of the story. When she realized the reporter knew exactly what had transpired, she read the rest.

Rebecca couldn't believe it. Every last detail was spelled out. It was as though someone had gotten hold of the actual contract between her and Lambros and paraphrased the clauses. The one relating to the purchase price was set in bold type.

The sidebar stories gave background on herself and The Tides as well as on Silas Lambros. There was intense speculation as to what the so-called "sale" really meant. Surely Tyne & Wear hadn't parted with property and going concerns valued at approximately one hundred million U.S. dollars without getting anything in return. Had there been some kind of under-the-table deal? If so, what was McHenry Enterprises' end of it? Why weren't Tyne & Wear stockholders apprised of the agreement, considering the terms involved?

Rebecca shook her head as though trying to dispel a bad dream. The one question the reporter hadn't answered concerned his source. Rebecca couldn't believe that Lambros would have had anything to do with the disclosure. It would—and most probably already did—spell his ruin. Certainly she had kept her word. . . .

Rebecca snatched up the telephone and convinced the manager to open her safety deposit box at once. She waited on the open line, reading through the article again, hoping to find a clue as to the leak. When the manager came back on, he assured Rebecca that the document she had placed in the box last night was still there.

Rebecca instructed him to hold all her calls without exception, until further notice. She flipped back to the front page, thinking hard. All hell was breaking loose right now. She would be swamped with calls from the media and hadn't the faintest idea what to say to them. She had to find out who had had the paper delivered. If she knew that—

Then Rebecca saw it, a slip of white paper clipped to the top of the page near the masthead. Her eyes blurred with tears as she read the single sentence.

WHY DID YOU DO IT?
JUSTIN

Thirty minutes later Rebecca swept through the lobby of the Connaught. She froze when she saw the reporters and photographers crowded outside the doors. Before she could think of another way to leave, Rebecca heard the telltale Klaxon of a British police car. Seconds later a white Rover screeched in front of the hotel and two beefy constables pounded into the lobby. Rebecca heard her name being mentioned and saw the clerk pointing at her.

"What is it?" she demanded as the officers flanked her. "What's happened?"

"We are in need of your assistance, ma'am," one of the constables said. "It is literally a matter of life and death."

"I don't understand—"

"Do you know a Mr. Justin Prescott, ma'am?"

"Yes . . . yes, in fact, I was on my way to his gallery—"

The constable squeezed her arm gently, as though to comfort her.

"I can assure you that's not where he is at the moment."

At ground level the wind had been gentle, barely stirring the new buds on the trees. A hundred and fifty feet up, among the cables and girders, it whistled fiercely, changing direction without warning, jerking his body from side to side.

Just like "the cat," Justin thought. As he shifted to get a better stance, the serrated edge of the cable cut even deeper into his already bleeding palms.

Looking down through his legs, Justin saw that traffic on London Bridge had come to a standstill. People were gaping at him, some shouting for him to hold on, others pleading that he come down. Justin couldn't hear everything they were saying because the wind snatched away the words.

But there was no mistaking the braying sound of the police siren. Justin took a deep breath and moved farther along the girder.

He wouldn't have made it up here had it not been for the construction scaffolding erected so that workers could wash the iron with acid. He had watched the cleaning for two days and had chosen his moment carefully. As soon as noon struck on the union clock the workers began climbing down from their posts. When the last man was down Justin had thrust a briefcase into his hands and scrambled up the ladder that led to the catwalk.

They had tried to stop him, of course. When Justin yanked out the pistol he had brought with him, the men retreated and prudently called the police. Justin had kept climbing and hadn't looked back until he had reached the top of the span where it met the tower itself.

From the vantage point he could see all of southeast London and, across the river in Southwark, columns of thick, black smoke. The converted warehouse where he had had his studio and lived his secret life was an inferno. By now his paintings were nothing but ash, the brilliant, savage colors reduced to a uniform black. Soon the same blackness would cover his life.

The wind whipped hair into his eyes. Justin heard the tinny echo of a megaphone and a commanding policeman's voice telling him to hold on. Help was on the way.

Justin threw back his head and laughed. Once, maybe, he would have accepted help. But he was beyond it now. If Rebecca had just stepped out of his life as unexpectedly as she had come into it, he could have lived with the rejection. All the women he had ever known had been with him for the wrong reasons—his money, his gallery, his desperate eagerness for companionship. When they had gotten what they wanted, they left. Had Justin allowed himself to love any one of them, he would have been a broken man many times over.

He had thought Rebecca was different. Justin had sensed a terrible hurt somewhere inside her and this vulnerability had made him open up to her. He had thought that by sharing his innermost hopes and fears with her she would realize that she could trust him, perhaps even love him. The possibility of such love, the fact that he believed that after all these years he might actually find it, stripped him of his armor.

But she, like the others, had come to him only to use him. Had it been for money or favors, he might have lived with the deceit. But Rebecca had come to destroy, and her revelations had made him bleed. He had told her everything she wanted to hear, signed the papers she placed in front of him. Her cruelty and her power over him lay in how precisely she had destroyed his illusions, about the gallery and about himself, the man who had never stopped running, never stood up for himself, who had been living his life at the expense of another man's.

Then, when she had what she needed, she had broken her promise to him and ruined his father. Revenge was what she had wanted all along.

Justin looked down and saw a policeman moving carefully up the catwalk. Below, standing in a knot of blue uniforms, was a woman.

Someone had bothered to read those few pages after all, thought Justin. The police, thinking she could sway me, brought her to me.

Justin was glad Rebecca was here, to see and feel just how he was going to punish her.

"Everything's going to be all right," the policeman called to him, crouching, coming closer with every step.

Yes, it will.

When Justin released his grip on the cable he felt a great weight lift from his shoulders. The wind seemed to hold him aloft for an instant, then he was spinning through the air, the earth and sky tumbling madly before his eyes. The last, and sweetest, sound he heard was Rebecca's scream.

PART FOUR

• ─────────────────────────── •

HONG KONG
NEW YORK
LONDON
CAYOS DE LA
FORTUNA

1970–1971

· 37 ·

The Choy Brothers shipyard, located between the Star Ferry Pier and Poor Man's Nightclub, was definitely *not* on the must-see list of Hong Kong attractions. The mile-long stretch of diesel-stained concrete piers, corrugated metal warehouses, and loading cranes was a world away from the breathtaking vista below Victoria Peak or the serenity of the Tiger Balm Gardens.

The chauffeur opened the door of the Choy Rolls-Royce and Rebecca McHenry stepped into a wall of stifling heat. November 1970 had broken all existing temperature records. Rebecca wondered if she wasn't slightly mad to have come to the crown colony this time of year. But then, nothing could have held her back once she had received Lu Choy's telegram.

Immediately Rebecca felt her beige safari-style suit, specially chosen because it was loose-fitting, wilt and cling to her like a second skin. The yellow and red scarf, worn headband-style around her forehead, was damp to the touch.

By contrast, Rebecca's host seemed unaffected by the autumn steambath. Lu Choy was standing before the massive sliding doors to the warehouse. He was a short, rotund man, giving one the impression of a wise, bespectacled panda clad in exquisitely tailored sharkskin. His face, textured like ancient calligraphy, seemed ageless. Not even the carefully manicured hands, constantly tugging at a wispy beard, betrayed his years.

"Welcome, Wahbecca," Lu Choy murmured, his voice like wind chimes in a gentle breeze. He bowed, then offered Rebecca a cool, dry palm.

"You honor me with your greeting," Rebecca answered, observing the customary Chinese courtesy.

"It is you who hono' me," Lu Choy said, panda eyes dancing. "Please pe'mit me to show you my humble place of wo'k."

That, Rebecca thought dryly, has to be the understatement of the year.

331

Since the turn of the century the Choy family had ranked among the world's foremost shipbuilders, deftly incorporating ancient skills with every innovation that came along. As the doors to the four-story warehouse rolled back, Rebecca saw no less than seven yachts, each over one hundred feet long, in various stages of construction, lined up along the length of the shop. Walking past the massive wooden struts that held the hulls, she marveled at the intensity of the labor around her. Perched on scaffolding, beetling their way into the framework, were hundreds of workers, each one concentrating on his task with single-minded ferocity. At the stern of each vessel, mechanics were supervising the installation of the mighty engines that would breathe life into the ships. On the opposite side of the warehouse, Choy designers were hunched over slabs of plywood supported by sawhorses, studying the interior layouts, matching exotic woods, metal fittings and trims, carpeting, and upholstery fabric to the individual client's specifications.

Rebecca followed Lu Choy toward the darkened end of the warehouse. The master shipbuilder snapped his fingers and lamps glowed. Beneath a giant overhead crane, with the girdle snugly in place around her hull, the *Windsong* materialized like a ghostly apparition.

"She's magnificent!" Rebecca exclaimed.

The battered wreck, mothballed for five years in the Angelines and shipped to Hong Kong eighteen months earlier, had disappeared. In its place was a gleaming new vessel. She retained the sleek racing lines Lu Choy and Max McHenry had designed for her thirty years earlier, but now the stern had been lengthened and reinforced to support a helipad and a new superstructure. An antifouling paint that secreted a chemical film to protect the hull against barnacles gleamed below the waterline, while blue, golden brown, and crimson sparkled along the trim.

"She is my maste'piece," Lu Choy said proudly.

"You've performed a miracle," Rebecca told him, looking up at the panel above the pilothouse.

Lu Choy followed her gaze to where, according to Rebecca's instructions, the name had been inscribed.

"Wahbecca, I am cu'ious," the shipbuilder said. "What is the meaning of that symbol?"

Beside the *Windsong*'s name was a hand-painted rendition of the golden sea horse Rebecca wore around her neck. She studied it carefully and was satisfied the artist hadn't missed a single detail.

"It is a reminder, Lu Choy," she said.

"It is also a symbol of good luck," the Chinese observed.

"Not for everyone."

The Pan Am 747 began a steep climb as soon as its tires cleared the runway at Hong Kong's Kai Tak airport. The jet made a sweeping curve, giving the passengers a panoramic view of the Crown Colony, before settling on a northeasterly course for the continental United States.

Seated by the window in the upper-deck first-class cabin, Rebecca watched Victoria Peak recede in the distance. She reached down to withdraw a folder from her briefcase.

"Champagne, Miss McHenry?"

Rebecca smiled wanly at the flight attendant. "No, thank you."

"Oh, for heaven's sake, don't be such a stick-in-the-mud," Ramsey chided her. "You've just launched a two-million-dollar vessel. Celebrate!"

Ramsey, who had been in Hong Kong on business, had joined her at the Lu Choy shipyards. Afterward he had spirited a reluctant Rebecca to the Nefertiti, Hong Kong's premiere supper club. After dinner, and over her protests, they had ended up at the Ship of Fools in Kowloon, where the attorney had kept her on the disco floor until five in the morning.

Rebecca's leg muscles were still tender from the experience, and the thought of more champagne made her dizzy.

"Precisely because it is a two-million-dollar investment, Ramon wants me to okay his crew selection," Rebecca told him.

Upon her return to the Angelines, Rebecca had handed Justin Lambros's notarized statement to the attorney general. In less than a month Ramon Fuentes had been completely exonerated and returned to his home a free man. A few days later Rebecca offered him command of the new *Windsong*. Ramon accepted without a second thought.

Before Rebecca had left for Hong Kong, Ramon had provided her with a list of prospective crew members. According to the etiquette of yacht management, both master and owner had the power to hire and fire. However, the experienced owner always deferred to the captain's recommendations.

Since the *Windsong* had been refurbished to serve as Rebecca's floating corporate headquarters and her range had been increased to allow her to spend more time at sea, she required no less than nine full-time crew members: the master, chief, and second mate, chief engineer, his second, a radio engineer, a chef, and two stewards who could double as mates. From the curriculum vitae of the men on the list, Rebecca was certain Ramon had sought out only the very best. Besides extensive experience, his most important criterion was dedication. Ramon expected Rebecca to pay top dollar but in return he would guarantee men who worked as required. Tending a vessel the size of the *Windsong*, whether at sea or in port, was not a nine-to-five job.

Rebecca chuckled to herself when she glanced at the chef's name and credentials. She could have sworn he was happily employed on board the *Sea Cloud*, a majestic schooner built for J. P. Morgan that now operated as a deluxe charter vessel. Whatever the reason for his discontent, Rebecca could find no fault with the sample menus. They all sounded deliciously exotic.

"It seems Ramon has everything under control," she said, making a note to call her captain from the West Coast and closing the file.

"You're going to have the most talked-about boat in the Caribbean."

"Vessel, Ramsey. The *Windsong* is a vessel."

"And what's this?"

The attorney leaned over to pick up a paper that had fluttered away from the file. The creased, worn edges aroused suspicions; the signature sealed them.

"I thought you told me you had gotten rid of this," he said quietly.

Rebecca reached for Justin's letter to her, the one he had brought with him that day to London Bridge.

"No, Rebecca. It's over. I won't have you punishing yourself."

Rebecca uttered a sharp cry as Ramsey tore the frail paper in half.

"What Justin did had nothing to do with you," the attorney continued as he ripped the paper apart again. "He was emotionally unstable, a condition he had his father to thank for."

Rebecca watched, mesmerized, as Ramsey methodically tore the letter she had been carrying for the last six months. He had seen it once before, when she had come to New York. He had made her promise to destroy it.

But I couldn't. I don't know why, but I couldn't!

Clenching the shreds in his fist, Ramsey stood up.

"Excuse me while I go and get rid of this."

Rebecca had fled from London as quickly as she could, away from the press which hounded her as unmercifully as her own mind, which constantly replayed Justin's leap. As before, she had found shelter in the Angelines and there, with them, the madness of what had happened receded. But her promise to herself never to speak of how she had gotten back her land was worthless. The story was too juicy for the media to put to rest. For the sake of her sanity Rebecca had gone to New York and told Ramsey everything. In spite of his understanding and support, she did not feel purged. It was as though Justin, with that letter, had bound her to him with an inextricable guilt. Every time she reasoned that she was not at fault she remembered her last sight of him and the chains became tighter than ever.

As he settled back in his seat, Ramsey asked the flight attendant for two glasses of champagne.

"I figured that with all the work you've been doing on Tides II, you had put the ghosts to rest. Instead, you've been wallowing in self-pity."

The color drained from Rebecca's face, as though he had struck her.

"How can you say that?" she whispered. "You weren't there—"

"Damn right! If I had been there, I would have made my peace, gone to a chapel to say a prayer for a poor, tormented soul, and gotten on with my life."

"That's callous!"

"That is survival, Rebecca! I remember your telling me that you would never be a victim again. Well, take a good look at yourself. You've been carrying that letter around for months, flagellating yourself with it every chance you get! What would you call that kind of behavior?"

Ramsey paused, then ordered gruffly, "Drink your champagne."

Much to her surprise, Rebecca did.

"You didn't goad Justin into suicide," Ramsey carried on, reaching around to pluck the champagne bottle from the trolley. "You weren't responsible for his death because he didn't really kill himself. Justin Lambros was murdered.

"Drink your wine!"

Rebecca gulped down what was left. Ramsy was refilling her flute before she could withdraw it.

"What do you mean, murdered?" she asked weakly.

"By whoever leaked the details of your deal with Lambros. Since it wasn't you, and it certainly wasn't Lambros, that leaves only one other person, doesn't it? The same son of a bitch who killed Max. The same one who had Dallas murdered. You yourself put the finger on him."

"Andrew . . ." Rebecca whispered.

"Your champagne is getting warm!"

Rebecca threw back the wine greedily.

"Just look at what he did to Lambros as soon as news of your deal hit the street," Ramsey said. "News which—and I'll stake my last dime on this—he himself leaked."

"But how could Andrew have found out about the deal?"

"Do you think you're the only clever one, tracking down Ramon, then Justin, then setting up that confrontation?"

They were well into the second bottle and Rebecca was still hurling questions. How could Andrew have gotten to the papers, either at the Connaught or the Dorchester? Had he bribed the management, or was it possible one of the two attorneys had been made an offer he couldn't refuse? How had Andrew convinced a skeptical Fleet Street that the document was valid?

Ramsey Peet had no answers, but he kept fueling Rebecca's questions, focusing her attention on Andrew Stoughton.

"The bastar'," Rebecca said, unaware that she had slurred the epithet.

Not being a drinking woman, Rebecca had no idea how fiercely alcohol could concentrate one's thoughts. She saw Max lying helpless in the huge bed, his life sustained by machines. The image changed to one of dancing flames and Skyscape burning. Rebecca remembered her screams as Andrew ran in to save Max, how warm the grass felt beneath her feet. . . . She remembered how the sea had been strewn with flowers at Max's funeral and how, desperate and alone, she had flung herself into Andrew's arms . . . only to discover that their idyll in Jamaica would become a nightmare in which two people would die, the gentle Mr. Smith and her unborn child.

Andrew, who had betrayed her by stripping McHenry Enterprises, and who had sealed his duplicity that day at the Perch with Celeste . . . Andrew, who had had her thrown out of her native land and had torn down everything Max had created . . . Andrew, who had recognized the threat of The Tides and had Dallas murdered when he had tried to defend the dream.

No matter where I look I always find him there. No matter what I do I can't get beyond his shadow, a shadow that eclipses everything it touches.

Rebecca began to cry softly. She wept for Justin, who, like

Dallas, should never have become involved in this madness. Afterward, the tears became cold and pitiless. Rebecca drifted into sleep lulled by a phrase that kept repeating itself over and over in her mind: Revenge is a dish best eaten cold, very cold.

Rebecca slept throughout most of the eleven-hour flight to Los Angeles. Even so, she landed with a splitting headache and a feeling that her mouth had been a parade ground for the Russian army. Without Ramsey's help she never would have made her connection to San Diego.

"I don't want to go," she moaned as the attorney checked her bags through.

"You'll be fine," Ramsey said, patting her hand. "I've booked you a day room at the local Howard Johnson's. You have about two hours to recuperate."

"I'll pay you anything to take my place."

"Now, Rebecca, it's a media event. The press wants to see the glamorous, exciting Rebecca McHenry. Not some old fogey."

"An old fogey who managed to close the Ship of Fools," Rebecca muttered under her breath.

At the gate she flung her arms around the attorney.

"Thank you," she whispered. "For the talking-to, for being there."

"Knock 'em dead!" Ramsey said cheerfully.

"If I look the way I feel, they'll think *I'm* dead!"

The twin-engine commuter craft lurched and heaved its way into San Diego. Grateful to be on the ground, Rebecca gathered up her luggage and took a cab to the hacienda-style Howard Johnson's. She gulped down two aspirin, showered, and, while dressing, made mental notes on her room. There was absolutely no way The Tides could benefit by copying the typical American motel style.

The Tides field office was strategically located in a shopping mall between the University of California at San Diego campus and the affluent suburbs that had sprung up north of the city. As she rounded the corner in the blissfully air-conditioned arcade, Rebecca stopped dead in her tracks. Strung across the entrance to the office was a huge banner reading: NUMBER FIFTY AND STILL GOING STRONG!!!

"There she is!"

Before she knew what was happening, Rebecca was surrounded by the office staff, led by a youthful, bearded manager whose houndstooth sport coat seemed incongruous with his ponytail.

"Welcome, Miss McHenry, it's great that you could make it!"

Rebecca blushed as the hot spotlights came on. She found microphones thrust at her, reporters shouting questions.

"Listen!" she called out. "Please, everyone, listen. I . . . I never expected anything like this. Come inside and I'll answer any questions you have."

In spite of the chaos behind her, Rebecca surveyed the office with a critical eye. The shades were white, gold, and blue, reflecting The Tides motif. Behind a long undulating counter, covered in rust fabric, were the agents' work stations. Along the opposite walls were Lucite jackets chock-full of brochures on every Tides property. The walls were alive with neatly framed posters of spectacular sunsets and idyllic beaches carefully cropped so that the stylized "T" in the Tides couldn't be missed.

Shaking hands and exchanging greetings with her staff, Rebecca stepped up to the makeshift podium the manager had prepared.

He grinned when she asked him why the press was here. "Just a little surprise."

Nervously Rebecca smoothed her crème caramel silk jacket and faced the reporters.

"First of all, I want to say I never expected this kind of reception. I thought the opening of the fiftieth Tides travel office was going to be a quiet affair." She glanced at the manager. "I couldn't have been more wonderfully wrong.

"I really had nothing more to say than to wish my staff the best of luck. I felt that the San Diego outlet would become one of the most successful in the Tides chain. Now I'm sure of it."

Rebecca paused, then smiled.

"However, there is an announcement I was going to make in a few days in New York. Under the circumstances, it seems appropriate to make it now.

"The Tides is undergoing a major expansion program."

Rebecca waited until the exclamations of surprise died down.

"The new resorts will be known as Tides II. They will be completely different from the *palapa*-style accommodations you're all familiar with. Tides II will be a self-contained, full-service resort, offering superior single-cabin rooms set around a beautiful free-form pool. Every type of amenity will be provided in the all-inclusive price.

"This type of resort is geared to the young, single, or married professional who is looking for an up-scale, hassle-free vacation.

Those of you who have experienced The Tides know that our reputation is built on the people who look after our guests. Tides II will provide an even greater range of services. The staff will give each client individual attention. We're going to expand the kitchen and bar services, upgrade the sporting activities, and offer in-depth tours for those who wish to explore the countryside.

"Finally—and this is a first as far as all-inclusive resorts are concerned—several Tides II operations will have what we're calling kiddie clubs. These resorts will have special counselors to look after children between the ages of two and twelve, organize their meals and activities, and see to it that by the end of the day they're too tired to even want to see their parents. This way married couples can enjoy themselves without worrying what their children are up to."

Before questions drowned out her words, Rebecca managed to add that a formal announcement and a detailed press release would be sent out the following week. For the next half hour she fielded reporters' queries, gave a three-minute television interview, and promised to appear on two local radio shows. Just as she thought the impromptu conference was winding down, the manager stepped up beside her.

"Ladies and gentlemen, Miss McHenry confessed she was surprised by the reception we gave her. Well, that was just the beginning. Not only is this the opening of the fiftieth Tides travel office, it is also the opening of the first in Europe!"

He motioned at two agents, who rolled up a television. The manager placed a phone before Rebecca and checked his watch.

"Any second now," he said.

Puzzled, Rebecca stared at the hissing snow on the screen. At the same instant, the picture came on and the phone rang.

"That's for you," the manager said.

"Becky, is that you? Can you hear me?"

"Bix! Yes, I can hear you. You're supposed to be in London."

"I am in London. Can't you see?"

Rebecca glanced at the television screen, which now showed Bix surrounded by eager faces. The camera pulled back and she recognized the interior of the Tides London office. Rebecca almost dropped the phone.

"How did you manage this?" she gasped.

"Oh, just a little satellite magic," Bix said. "Welcome home!"

While Rebecca was wondering what to say next, the pony-tailed manager stepped in and briefed the media on the satellite hookup between The Tides offices. He put Bix on a conference speaker so that everyone could listen to the details of the London launching. Five thousand miles apart, bottles of champagne were opened simultaneously. Rebecca and Bix toasted each other. Both women knew they were on the verge of tears.

"Now for the finale," Bix announced.

The television went blank, then flickered, and a huge blimp swam majestically on-screen. Its electronic message was flashed for the entire city to see.

THE WHOLE WORLD COMES TO THE TIDES!

Everyone in the office was transfixed by the spectacle. The cheers erupted when the camera on the blimp sent back pictures of nighttime London, complete with the neon extravaganza of Piccadilly Circus. As the blimp turned, the Thames and the lights of its bridges came into focus. In the midst of the celebration, no one noticed that the smile had faded from Rebecca's lips. Nor did they see her lips move silently when, as London Bridge materialized, she remembered Ramsey Peet's words to her and at last made her peace with Justin Lambros.

· 38 ·

When Rebecca arrived in New York, Bix and Torrey insisted that she settle in their home on Perry Street. Rebecca had jumped the gun by announcing Tides II in San Diego. There was so much work to be done, she didn't have time to worry about getting an apartment.

The past summer and fall Rebecca had visited each of the fourteen locations where a Tides II resort was under construction. The pace had been frenetic and, because of the scope of the operations, there had been more snags and delays than she had anticipated. Nonetheless, after London, the nonstop activity was a tonic for her. She went from Cabo San Lucas on the tip of Mexico's Baja peninsula to the sleepy village of Ixtapa on the Pacific coast to Caribbean islands known only to the cognoscenti—Dominica, Nevis–St. Kitts, Anguilla—observing the progress, encouraging the construction crews, and making last-minute changes and additions.

Rebecca knew she wouldn't have the resorts ready for guests for the winter season. That didn't bother her because she and Bix had worked out a marketing campaign that revolved around a summer launch. Rebecca believed the southern latitudes were seen exclusively as winter retreats. She was determined to change the perception—or misconception. Tides II would open their doors in late June, when school was out. The advertising would focus on the special introductory rates, which had been carefully set with an eye to what the Catskills, Green Mountains, and Rockies were charging. Rebecca was more than willing to sacrifice her profit margin for the one thing Tides II needed for a successful launch: word-of-mouth publicity.

While Rebecca had worked the field, Bix had set up the infrastructure in New York. The Tides had long outgrown its space-sharing arrangement with GoSee. Bix had found offices in a prewar building on lower Fifth Avenue, renovated them, and then moved the entire operation. Thousands of letters had been mailed out announcing the new Tides headquarters. Telex machines linked the fifty field offices, and a nationwide toll-free 800 number was secured from Bell. By the time Rebecca returned to New York, the only thing she had to do was decorate her own office.

Rebecca was eagerly looking forward to Bix's ideas on how best to promote Tides II. Because of the resorts' upscale positioning in the market, Rebecca had to introduce—and, more important, sell—the concept to travel wholesalers, the big agencies such as American Express, and the independent retailers. Without the endorsement and firm support from the travel industry—which could make or break a new venture—Rebecca knew she faced an uphill battle.

The ever-shortening Manhattan days disappeared one into the other. Rebecca found herself waking in darkness, trudging the seven long blocks in the snow and slush to the office, and not leaving until the clubs in the neighborhood were starting to fill up. Whenever she felt the hours bearing down on her, she would walk into the reception area and gaze at the model of Tides II for Cabo San Lucas. The architect had managed to capture the essence of what the three-story, L-shaped hotel, with its lagoon-style swimming pool surrounded by sixty-foot palms, was to be: a world unto itself. Each time Rebecca saw the model her sense of purpose was renewed, the ache to make her dream a reality just as great as it had been when she had seen Windemere Key that first time.

In the weeks before Christmas, Rebecca wrote and rewrote ad copy and held conferences with artists and designers who presented layouts for her approval. She breakfasted at the Regency with the marketing barons of American Express and nibbled lunch while airline charter vice-presidents swilled martinis and tried to overcharge her on block seats. Dinner was always reserved for the sharp-eyed, three-piece-suited men from the travel wholesalers who ate little, drank less, and said almost nothing until the moment of decision.

A week before Christmas, when everybody who was traveling was either en route or booked, and the industry let out a collective sigh of relief, Rebecca had the deal she wanted from Amex, agreements from three of the four airlines that flew her routes, and three of five wholesalers. It was, she considered, kicking off her shoes and wriggling her toes along the radiator, not a bad beginning.

"Hello? Anybody home?"

Rebecca started, unaware that the evening shadows and falling snow outside the windows had lulled her to sleep. Her first thought was: Burglars don't announce their arrival.

Eric Walker, his curly black hair dusted with melting snow, peered into her office.

"This is your friendly neighborhood banker checking to make sure his favorite client hasn't wasted away on him."

"What have you gone and done?" Rebecca exclaimed, relieving him of the two bags he was carrying. "It smells delicious."

"If you can't go to the Chung King Dynasty, the Dynasty comes to you."

"But how did you know I'd be here?"

"I called your private line and got a busy signal."

Rebecca cleared the coffee table, arranged paper plates and plastic forks left over from other deliveries, and ladled out the steaming Chinese food.

"I'm starving!" she groaned, devouring a spring roll.

"With the kind of schedule you're keeping, I'm not surprised."

There was no recrimination in Eric's words, but Rebecca still felt guilty. As Tides II had moved from the drawing boards to actual construction, she and Eric had spent weeks together, working out the financial arrangements, setting up connections with local banks, haggling over exchange rates. Eric had matched her hours, working day and night when circumstances dictated, making certain that there were no clever loopholes in the fine print.

After the financing had been hammered out, Rebecca had left for the field. Whenever she returned to New York and Eric called to invite her for dinner, there was always another wholesaler to woo or a conference that couldn't be postponed.

After everything he has done for me, I should have made the time, Rebecca thought.

"Have you decided what you're doing over the holidays?" Eric asked as they picked at the last morsels of lotus shrimp.

"I haven't really thought about it," Rebecca told him. "It depends on Bix and Torrey."

"Well, here's something to consider. I have a chalet in Stowe. It's beautiful in the Green Mountains this time of year. I'd very much like the three of you to spend Christmas with me up there."

Rebecca was stunned by the invitation. She had assumed she, Bix, and Torrey would spend Christmas together, either in the Angelines with Jewel or in New York with Lauren and Ramsey.

"I don't expect you to say yes or no right away," Eric said gently. "But think about it, talk to them, and let me know."

He paused. "I think it would do you a world of good to get away from the work. Who knows, you might even come to like the snow as much as you do the sun."

"I think I would, too," Rebecca said softly.

Eric's chalet turned out to be a sprawling five-bedroom custom-designed house nestled on a rise with dramatic views of Stowe village and Mount Mansfield. It had a forty-foot indoor swimming pool, a sauna, whirlpool, and outfitted exercise room.

"This is sinfully delicious," Bix groaned, stretching out in the oversize Jacuzzi. "I can't believe we've been here a whole week."

"Most of which you seem to have spent in this tub," Rebecca kidded her.

A few minutes later Rebecca and Bix emerged from the whirlpool, bikinis clinging to their pinkened skin. Eric and Torrey let out appreciative wolf whistles.

"You must have some kind of hormonal imbalance," Bix muttered, slapping away Torrey's hand. "Always horny!"

"I never heard you complain before."

Rebecca and Eric laughed as the lovers disappeared in the direction of their bedroom.

"Give me a minute to change and I'll meet you on the balcony?" Rebecca asked.

"Not on my account." Eric grinned.

"You're worse than Torrey," Rebecca said over her shoulder and gave her hips an exaggerated wiggle.

Later, when they were seated on the cantilevered balcony, looking across a Christmas-card-perfect scene, Rebecca said, "I don't think I've been this relaxed in months. It's wonderful, Eric, thank you."

"Believe me, the pleasure is mine."

And it was. To be with Rebecca outside a working environment meant discovering a whole new woman. Eric taught her to use snowshoes and to cross-country ski, and together they tramped the property, catching glimpses of rabbit tracks and laying out salt licks for the deer. He cooked huge country-style breakfasts that Rebecca then walked off in Stowe village, where they explored the arts and crafts stores. Evenings were spent in front of the huge fireplace, playing backgammon and listening to the crackle of logs and the whisper of the wind. Sometimes, when the mood struck, they made it a foursome with Bix and Torrey and went dancing at Topnotch, the exclusive resort farther up Mountain Road.

Rebecca cupped the mug of hot chocolate in both palms that Eric handed her and stared at the sun igniting the mountains. She sat in silence, conscious of the presence of the man next to her, his scent and relaxed posture. Out of the corner of her eye she saw his face in profile, the strong jaw and slightly crooked nose, one eye squinting against the setting sun, creating a tiny fan of creases. At that moment Rebecca wanted to feel him on top of her, her arms clutching his back, her legs holding him a prisoner.

"Rebecca, are you all right?"

Her eyes, wild, locked on his. Then she realized he had asked her something, reached across and taken her hand, and she had seized it.

"I'm fine," Rebecca lied. "Just thinking about home." She worked her hand free and searched desperately for something to say.

"Are you going to be away a lot in the New Year?"

"Enough so that I won't be able to enjoy this," Eric replied, swinging his arm across the vista.

Rebecca nodded silently. In the last five years the Walker Bank had grown tremendously. Not only had it followed The Tides across the Caribbean, it was now an international force, with offices in European capitals and the Middle East. Eric had once joked that he was spending more time in the seats of aircraft than in the one behind his desk.

"We're looking seriously into South America at the moment," he said, then added, "which means I'll be able to spend more time in New York."

Rebecca didn't mistake the hidden message in his words.

"There's a meeting of the Organization of American States on Contodora Island the end of January," she told him. "You might consider attending."

She felt his fingertips on her cheek. "The booking has already been made," he said.

In spite of the hearty beef bourguignon, the velvety Bordeaux that accompanied it, and the after-dinner liqueurs, Rebecca found she couldn't sleep. Long after everyone had turned in she prowled the dark house until finally, throwing a ski jacket over her nightgown, she ventured onto the balcony. The sky was as magnificent as any she had ever seen in the Caribbean, the stars

so brilliant they reminded her of their ancient Arab description:
The stars are the eyes of Allah.

What do you see that I don't? What do you know that I don't?

The still cold created billowing clouds around her mouth and
she wondered if she really saw shapes in the mist, the way her
mother's ancestors witnessed visions in smoky fires. Suddenly
she understood how weary she was, but not from the pace of her
life or the demands upon her. She was tired of being alone, of
not having another human being she could turn to for comfort,
who would hold her and shelter her for just a little while so she
could sleep undisturbed, protected. The fear she had lived with
since Andrew's betrayal had paralyzed her. It had held her back
from accepting what Dallas had offered and now, he, too, was
gone.

Two fat tears slid down her cheeks.

I won't live this way! I can't live this way!

Only when she returned inside did Rebecca feel how cold she
was. Shivering, she walked quickly but deliberately to Eric's
bedroom. Inside, she saw him sprawled on his belly, one arm
outstretched as though reaching for something . . . or someone.
The ski jacket dropped to the floor followed by the nightgown.
Shivering, Rebecca drew back the duvet and without hesitation
slipped in beside him. He started at her cold flesh.

"Don't say anything," she whispered. "Just hold me and
warm me and let me sleep with you."

Eric shifted so that she could spoon her body into his. His arm
embraced her and his breath warmed the back of her neck.
Rebecca never remembered when it was that she stopped shivering.

The next morning Bix and Torrey had to make their own
breakfast.

· 39 ·

"I think I went into the wrong profession."

Rebecca looked over at Eric, who was lying in the chaise longue, his eyes closed against the glare of the sun, a lazy smile on his lips. The ten days on Contodora Island before the conference had been a fountain of youth for him. The sun had burned away the Manhattan pallor; a steady regimen of swimming and tennis had shed extra executive pounds. Their lovemaking, a frantic coupling, had eased into a languid, exploratory rhythm.

"Whatever do you mean, sir?" she asked coyly.

Eric shifted and pointed to the fifteen-story Hilton behind them, complete with a two-tier swimming pool, and overrun by a thousand delegates to the conference of the Organization of American States.

"I should have gone into partnership with you on The Tides."

"That," Rebecca said emphatically, "is not The Tides and never will be. In fact, it looks remarkably similar to the Hilton in the Bahamas."

"Or in Dubai," Eric added.

They laughed at the same time, their fingers intertwining.

"I love you," Eric said.

"I love you too."

Each time Rebecca spoke the words she believed they were as true as they were ever going to be.

Bix and Torrey hadn't said a word about the dramatic change in Rebecca and Eric's relationship. Nor did the new lovers offer any explanation. What had happened seemed so natural and right that all four simply accepted it. Dancing in Eric's arms at the Topnotch New Year's Eve ball, Rebecca thought it was an auspicious way to ring in 1971.

In spite of Torrey's initial reluctance, he and Bix stayed in Stowe while Rebecca and Eric drove back to Manhattan. With a few days' grace before the January sell-off madness erupted, Rebecca contacted Eric's real estate agent and spent the rest of the week combing the Upper East Side addresses he had provided. Her good fortune was running strong. On Seventy-first off Fifth was a duplex apartment that had just been cleared by the probate court. The heirs were relocating to Malibu and were eager to sell. Rebecca clinched the deal over drinks at the Carlyle.

Over Eric's protests Rebecca also decided to move into the Carlyle while her new home was being painted and decorated. She loved Eric's elegant apartment only six blocks away but didn't feel comfortable with the idea of moving in for less than the month the refurbishing would take. Privately she admitted to herself that she didn't want to rush her relationship with Eric. They were two independent people who still had a great deal to learn about each other. One day, when the time was right, Rebecca was certain they would live together. But it would be because their love and understanding of each other, not circumstances, dictated that they should.

In spite of Eric's obvious reluctance to accept it, the arrangement worked wonderfully. With their days full, Rebecca and Eric made time in the evenings to see each other. Rebecca was thrilled that Eric took nothing for granted. When they had seats to the von Karajan performance at Lincoln Center, the Walker Bank limousine materialized beneath the Carlyle canopy. Afterward, ignoring Rebecca's pleas of an early morning meeting, there was a supper at the Russian Tea Room. During the week Rebecca never knew whether the next knock on the door would usher in a client or a messenger bearing a bouquet and handmade chocolate truffles.

A week before she and Eric were scheduled to leave for Contodora Island, Rebecca received a personal telephone call from the secretary general of the Organization of American States. The Ecuadoran, who was also the foreign minister, came graciously to the point.

"Miss McHenry, as you know, we have delayed announcing who our guest speaker will be."

Rebecca knew. She had been surprised to receive an invitation at all. The OAS was primarily a political forum where the countries of the northern and southern hemispheres sat down to discuss issues of mutual interest, principally trade, finance, and tourism. The fact that the invitation mentioned that a guest speaker would be named at a later date had scarcely registered.

"I am not sure that you are familiar with how the choice is made," the Ecuadoran carried on smoothly. "Each member state puts forth a candidate from a prepared list. As soon as one attains a majority, we have our speaker. However, this year something quite extraordinary happened. You have been chosen by an overwhelming vote to address the conference."

"*I beg your pardon?*"

The Ecuadoran took her literally and repeated his words.

"But I didn't know my name was even on the list!"

"That is the truly extraordinary part," the Ecuadoran admitted, as though he, too, were utterly confounded by the turn of events. "Your name *wasn't* on the list. You became a write-in candidate."

"Going so soon, my love?"

Rebecca had gathered up her lotion and paperback. She took Eric's palm and pressed it to her lips.

"I must have my massage, get my hair done, and all those other things if I'm to look my best tonight."

"You never look anything less," Eric whispered, nuzzling her behind the ear.

"And you shouldn't start something we can't finish!" Rebecca gasped, squirming away.

"Rebecca!"

She stopped and turned back to him.

"I'm very proud of you, darling. You deserve everything coming your way."

The gala opening night of the conference took place in a multitiered amphitheater open to the stars. The tables, set in a semicircle, were all lighted by candles in tall, tulip-shaped glass lamps. The head table was at the bottom of the amphitheater. Whenever Rebecca looked up, she felt she was on some kind of ancient stage.

Rebecca was seated between the Brazilian foreign minister, the conference chairman, and a government minister from Chile, a diminutive man with a slightly off-kilter toupee and roving hands. Even before the entree was served, Rebecca had twice had to slap away his advances on her thigh.

Although she held her own in the light conversation that circulated up and down the table, Rebecca was nervous. During the cocktail reception before dinner she had had a chance to meet almost all the delegates who had nominated her as speaker. To a person they had congratulated her and immediately remarked that it would be wonderful if The Tides expanded into their regions. There were both subtle and not so subtle hints that a great deal of money would change hands under the table in return for preferred consideration.

Wait until they hear my speech, Rebecca thought wryly.

The seating was arranged in such a way that the most important guests were closest to the head table. These included the ministers and their mistresses—Rebecca was hard pressed to see a woman over twenty-five in their company—the presidents and CEOs of the major hotel chains, the bankers and tour representatives. Farther away were the second-string executives who would do the spadework on any agreements that might be struck. Near the top were the industry scroungers who had begged, borrowed, or stolen an invitation.

As she picked at her crème brulée, Rebecca focused her concentration on Eric, who was sitting a few tables away. No matter how hard she tried, she couldn't distract him from his conversation with the president of Chase Manhattan. As her gaze shifted, a face suddenly struck her. The man was staring directly at her, his dark eyes so penetrating they frightened her. Rebecca thought he looked about thirty-five. His dinner jacket stretched across a swimmer's chest. His face was bronze as only the sun and sea could make it. The jet-black hair was combed back, emphasizing the high cheekbones, aquiline nose, and thin, hard lips.

Rebecca's gaze was riveted as much by his unwavering stare as by the fact that the man seemed oblivious to the whispered conversation earnestly directed at him by the others at the table. Clearly he was the center of attention—and he didn't give a damn.

Who is he?

Rebecca searched her mind to try to match a name to the face but couldn't. She was certain she had never met or been introduced to the man. Yet there was an undeniable familiarity to him, like that of a face in a fading photograph.

And what does he want from me?

Rebecca was so mesmerized she almost missed her introduction by the Brazilian. When she rose to the applause she desperately searched for reassurance in Eric. But her eyes returned to the intense dark-eyed man.

Rebecca adjusted the microphone and cleared her throat. At first her voice sounded tentative, but as she got into the body of her speech her confidence rose. She told the delegates that in the next twenty years tourism would become a major economic factor in their countries. As jets shrank the world and travel was made more affordable, millions of people would be eager to explore the places they had only dreamed about.

It is our responsibility to insure that the people of the host countries benefit from the newfound wealth, Rebecca told the assembly. The higher the percentage of the tourist dollar that goes into the local economy, the greater the overall benefit. In addition, corporations seeking to do resort business should contribute goodwill projects to the community. The closer and more harmonious the relationship between the people and entrepreneurs, the better the result for both.

Rebecca spoke for twenty minutes, driving home point after point, using The Tides to illustrate what she meant. When she finished there was deathly silence in the amphitheater.

Oh, my God, I've alienated every last one of them.

The chairman of American Airlines rose to his feet.

"Young lady," he said grimly. "In the last twenty years no one has ever lectured me like that. You say what we all know but don't have the balls to say. My hat's off to you!"

His lone applause echoed throughout the assembly. Then, one by one, table by table, they rose to give her a standing ovation.

"You were spectacular!" Eric exclaimed.

After what seemed an interminable wait, he had managed to work his way through the crush surrounding Rebecca. He spirited her away from the amphitheater toward the ballroom, where the dancing would soon begin, and steered her into a deserted corridor. Rebecca wasn't sure she was breathless from his kiss or the headiness of the accolades.

"I was terrified up there," she confessed.

"This is one meeting the Organization of American States won't forget," Eric predicted. "Those were the movers and shakers out there, the people who make the decisions. You shook them up."

"I certainly hope so!"

Suddenly, she thought of Silas Lambros and the economic stranglehold Tyne & Wear once had on the Angelines. The situation was much better now, but there was still a long way for her own country to go.

"What's wrong, darling?" Eric asked, noticing the shadow darken her features.

"Nothing, my love. I just realized how much I still have left to do."

"Not tonight," Eric said firmly, taking her elbow. "I insist on the first dance."

"I wouldn't have it any other way."

The evening was whirled away under a canopy of tiny diamond-bright stars. The ballroom had been transformed into a 1930s nightclub, complete with a floor show of leggy girls, crooning singers, and music that ranged from cotton blues to samba to big-band favorites.

Rebecca enjoyed every minute of it. At the beginning she danced twice with Eric, then lost count of the number of partners. She was so flushed with excitement that she laughed out loud when the Chilean minister placed his hand on her left cheek instead of on the small of her back. Rebecca was about to brush it off when, suddenly, the Chilean was gone. In his place was the dark-eyed man who had seemed to look right through her.

"My name is Anthony Fabrizzi," he said quietly. "I thought if I remained polite much longer, I would probably never get to dance with you."

Before she could say a word, Rebecca felt herself gliding away from the throng, guided by Anthony Fabrizzi's expert lead.

"By the way, I liked what you said—and how you said it."

"Thank you . . . Mr. Fabrizzi," she managed to say.

Fabrizzi . . . Fabrizzi . . . Rebecca had heard the name before. Where?

"I make it a point never to do business at such places," Anthony Fabrizzi said as though he hadn't heard her. "However, there are always exceptions." He looked at her, eyes unblinking. "I'm even sorrier that it has to be done at this particular moment, because you are a very beautiful woman and I am as attracted to you as you are to me."

Rebecca froze in mid-step.

"Please, the music hasn't stopped yet," he said.

In spite of her shock, Rebecca found her feet moving in time to his.

"I represent the Polaris Group. Is the name familiar to you?"

"No! I mean yes," she corrected herself, angry because she was caught off-guard.

Rebecca made the connection. She knew the senior executives of all the major hotels and chains and made a point of following their careers. But Polaris was no ordinary operation, and its chief executive, Anthony Fabrizzi, was an industry anomaly. Unlike most CEOs, who, at heart, were born salesmen, the head of Polaris was a retiring, shadowy figure. Rebecca could not recall ever having seen a photograph of him. Anthony Fabrizzi never gave interviews, and in industry journals he was always quoted through spokesmen.

"Yes, I've heard of the Polaris Group," Rebecca said, more calmly this time. "But I resent your arrogance—"

"Polaris is prepared to make an offer of one hundred million dollars for The Tides."

Her anger exploded so quickly, Rebecca never had a chance to be astonished.

"Get away from me!"

The music was loud and the dancers so caught up in themselves that no one paid any attention to Rebecca's words. Anthony Fabrizzi's arms were still tightly around her and Rebecca pushed ineffectually against his chest.

"I'm very glad you said that, Rebecca," he told her, oblivious to her struggle. "To show you I mean you no harm, I am going to tell you something that is known to only five people in the world. One of them is the President of the United States."

"What are you talking about?"

As soon as she said this, Rebecca realized that without being aware of it she had lowered her voice. She felt Anthony Fabrizzi's warm breath in her ear. The words he murmured were beyond belief, yet he spoke them as calmly as if he were giving road directions.

"That can't be true," Rebecca whispered.

She looked into those fathomless dark eyes, searching for the lie.

"I assure you it is. I trust you not to divulge what I've told you to anyone and to make your own decision. I'll see you again, soon. Thank you for the dance."

Her lips were crushed under his and then he was gone, like a magician's illusion. Rebecca searched for his retreating back, then realized she was standing alone in the middle of the floor, the object of curious looks from dancers gliding by. She forced herself to walk toward the tables.

"Darling, you're shivering! Is everything all right?"

Rebecca started when Eric came up behind her. She stared at him uncomprehendingly, then at last said, "I just met Anthony Fabrizzi."

Eric's mouth tightened. "I saw him tonight as well. Anthony Fabrizzi is Mafia. He's poison, Rebecca. Stay away from him!"

February and March slipped away before she noticed they were gone. After Contodora, Rebecca found herself deluged with invitations to speak at regional conferences. Tourism ministers from a dozen Central and South American countries became insistent suitors. Rebecca felt she had wandered into a mine field. If she accepted one invitation and rejected another, the outcry was heard all the way to the *Windsong*.

On board her yacht, anchored halfway between Palm Cove and Angeline City, Rebecca continued to monitor the progress of Tides II. It had been difficult to leave Eric and New York but, as Rebecca had explained to her unhappy lover, she had little choice. From where the *Windsong* was berthed she could be at any one of the Tides II sites in a few hours. The helicopter was always on standby and the Lear was on call in Angeline City.

But there was another, equally compelling reason that Rebecca had wanted to get away from New York: the words Anthony Fabrizzi had whispered in her ear.

At first Rebecca had tried to dismiss him. She wanted to believe that he was, as Eric had said, poison. The memory of his strong arms, the dark, penetrating eyes, and the animal musk that surrounded him conspired against her.

It hadn't taken Rebecca long to come up with details on the Polaris Group. Registered in the Bahamas, the corporation operated a number of hotel-casinos around the world, from Las Vegas to Bangkok. Each property was unique in design and exclusive in terms of clientele. The Polaris Group catered strictly to high rollers. The price of admission to the tables was one hundred thousand dollars. Players with credit of half a million or more received total comp.

It was, Rebecca conceded grudgingly, a brilliant marketing scheme. The Polaris hotels were as far removed from the nickel-and-dime action of Las Vegas as Tides II was from Howard Johnson.

And Anthony Fabrizzi had not only come up with the scheme but continued to run it.

On the surface Anthony Fabrizzi appeared a model citizen. Unlike other crime figures, his life was an open book. A Harvard graduate, he had seen early service in Vietnam and had distinguished himself in the field. After two years with Polaris he had been touted by the hotel industry as a whiz kid. Everything he touched turned to gold. The gaming commissions in all the countries Polaris had interests in had given him a clean bill of health. The U.S. Attorney's office charged with enforcing the RICO statute—Racketeer Influenced Criminal Organizations—had yet to find any connection between Polaris and organized crime.

Except one, Rebecca thought.

Anthony Fabrizzi was the only son of Michele Fabrizzi, undisputed Mafia lord of the eastern seaboard. No matter how pristine the son was, he would always walk in his father's shadow.

What can I possibly mean to him?

The question haunted Rebecca. She realized now that it had nothing to do with The Tides. The more she thought about the offer made to her on the dance floor, the more convinced she became that it hadn't been serious. It was as though Anthony Fabrizzi had made it for form's sake, knowing she would refuse.

As though he would have thought less of me had I even considered it.

Is that why he told me the rest, Rebecca wondered, because I had passed some sort of test?

"I am going to tell you something that is known to only five people in the world. One of them is the President of the United States. . . ."

Rebecca still couldn't believe the words were true. Because if they were, they heralded the most cataclysmic economic decision of the century. Millions would lose but a few, if they acted, would gain enormously.

Over the last two months Rebecca had been awfully tempted to share her knowledge with Eric. It pained her that, for a reason she couldn't fathom, she wasn't able to do so. *Perhaps,* she thought, *Anthony Fabrizzi knows me better than I think. He made me promise not to share the information with anyone. He must have known about my relationship with Eric. He wanted to see which was stronger, that or my word. . . .*

The fact that she hadn't gone to Eric hadn't prevented Rebecca from making discreet inquiries. Couching her questions in vague hypothetical terms, she put them to Ramsey Peet and his friends in the banking community. Their response was unequivocally negative. Sources in London and Zurich echoed the sentiment. The only hint that Anthony Fabrizzi's words might have any substance at all came from the most unlikely source. Over dinner with a member of the Saudi royal family who had extensive investments in the Americas, Rebecca casually mentioned the topic. The prince had smiled and replied enigmatically, "Sometimes all is *not* Allah's will. Men, too, can influence the course of their lives.''

Into bankruptcy! Rebecca thought grimly.

It hadn't taken Rebecca long to figure out why Anthony Fabrizzi believed his revelation was important to her. Obviously he had done his homework on her assets.

And if what he says is true, then I would be a fool to pass up the opportunity!

Rebecca did some detailed calculations. She discovered that if she were to commit funds to this new project, there wouldn't be enough money to insure the operation of Tides II until the resorts began to pay their own way. No matter how she juggled the figures they still came out in the red.

At that point Rebecca was glad to be isolated aboard the *Windsong*. She was up at all hours of the night, prowling the decks, sometimes playing backgammon with the watch officer until dawn. The more she tried to put the idea to rest, the more insistent it became in her mind. It was as though Anthony Fabrizzi had, by a few words, created a vampire against whose tantalizing promises she had no defense.

When she wasn't thinking about not doing the project, Rebecca was furiously drawing up estimates and working out timetables for it . . . just in case. By early April she conceded that it was now or never. Time would make the decision she could not make for herself.

Am I really being the fool? she asked herself, staring at the calender that read April 1, April Fool's Day. *What do I have to base a decision on except the whispers of a Mafia godson and the Cheshire smile of some Arabian sheikh? I must be crazy even to be thinking about it! I can just imagine what Ramsey would say. . . . And Eric!*

The decision was made. Calmly Rebecca reached for the phone and instructed Ramon to steam for Angeline City.

News that the McHenry gold mines were being reactivated spread like brushfire throughout the Angelines. Those who did not believe it were silenced when the engineers and surveyors arrived. Word went out that men were needed to clear the jungles around the mines and restore the roads so that construction crews could get in.

Rebecca had expected a barrage of telephone calls as soon as the press got hold of the story. She wasn't disappointed. Ramsey demanded to know whether she had broken the bank at Monte

Carlo or simply taken leave of her senses. Eric, in London on business, was terrified that she was being blackmailed. Her accountant threatened to commit suicide if the project wasn't scrapped immediately.

To each, Rebecca gave a quiet but strong reply.

"Talk is cheap. Everyone who listened to me at Contodora seemed to agree with that. Well, I'm putting my money where my convictions are—in the hope that Hilton, Sheraton, and the rest will do the same. I don't have to explain to you what this project means, in economic terms, to the people of the Angelines."

"What are you really up to?" Bix asked when she called.

"I wish I knew," Rebecca confessed, and left it at that.

Toward the end of the deluge there arrived a telegram which both elated and depressed Rebecca.

> YOU ARE DOING THE RIGHT THING. YOUR TRUST
> MEANS A GREAT DEAL TO ME.
>   ANTHONY

The fact that Anthony Fabrizzi's was the only note of encouragement buoyed Rebecca. But *was* she doing the right thing, or had her instinct erred in trusting the words of a total stranger?

At least I have an audience, Rebecca thought wryly. The whole world is watching.

Although she was unaware of it, there was one person who was watching far more keenly than the others.

· 40 ·

The great house on Eaton Square did not acknowledge the arrival of spring. The upstairs windows remained shuttered. Downstairs, heavy curtains draped the panes like shrouds. Those who had business at the house—the postman, delivery men, and the nurses—came and went as quickly as possible. Even the families in the neighboring mansions shrank away, unconsciously crossing the street whenever they approached the house. It was as though they knew it jealously guarded a tragedy which, if they came too close, would touch them as well.

Inside, Celeste Lambros moved swiftly through the silence. She ascended the right-hand side of the grand double staircase and hurried to the end of the corridor to the master suite. She had been downstairs, eating a salad the cook had prepared for her. Her movements had been mechanical and she had tasted nothing. She ate only because in the last year she had lost weight at an alarming rate. Her doctor had threatened to hospitalize her unless she followed the diet he had prescribed. Celeste, aware that the cook reported faithfully to the doctor, knew he wouldn't believe her if she told him she could subsist on hate alone.

The nurse had just completed giving her patient his sponge bath. Celeste averted her eyes until her grandfather was dressed and the covers had been pulled over his frail body. The nurse left without a word. She knew what was about to happen.

"I'm back, Grandfather," Celeste said brightly, settling in the comfortable chair beside the bed. "I ate everything, like a good girl, so that mean Dr. Pritchard doesn't have any excuse to send me away."

Celeste paused, and her voice rose half an octave.

"And I have some very interesting news for you. It concerns Rebecca McHenry. I do think she's finally made the mistake we've been waiting for. Are you ready?"

358

As Celeste began to explain, Silas Lambros continued to stare up at the ceiling. He saw neither the dusty chandelier nor the watermark that stained the plaster. He didn't see or hear his granddaughter or even sense her presence. The world as he had known it had erupted that day in the Tyne & Wear boardroom, leaving the wrecker, whose ancestors had lured so many to their deaths, on the silent, frozen shoals of catatonia.

It had been an act of fate that Celeste had witnessed the horror at all. She had stopped by Tyne & Wear to remind her grandfather not to plan anything for the weekend. She expected him to react gruffly, saying there was too much work to be done, but in the end, relent. It was a charade they enjoyed playing every year just before his birthday.

Celeste was waiting in Silas Lambros's office at the opposite end of the floor from the conference room, when her grandfather's secretary stumbled in, crying. Precious seconds were wasted to calm the hysterical woman, who babbled on about Mr. Lambros collapsing. Celeste pushed her aside and ran. Her grandfather was lying on the floor, curled up like a baby, his body seized by a violent trembling. He looks so small, Celeste thought, mesmerized. Almost insignificant . . .

Andrew was on his hands and knees beside him. When she rolled him over, Celeste saw the whites in her grandfather's eyes and the thin streams of spittle running from his lips.

"You're killing him!" Celeste screamed.

She jumped on his back, clawing at his face. Andrew swung his arm, hitting her across the cheek.

"I'm trying to prevent him from choking!" Andrew shouted, ripping away the tie and top buttons of her grandfather's shirt.

Celeste didn't believe him then; she didn't believe it when the other board members finally pinned her into a chair and the ambulance emergency team arrived. She didn't believe it because she had seen the newspapers on the conference table and read the headlines. When she saw the cold triumph in Andrew's eyes as her grandfather was wheeled away, she knew what had happened in this room. And who was responsible.

After the stroke Silas Lambros lapsed into a catatonic state from which he never recovered. Celeste, who was by his side during the two-week confinement, saw her world crack and shatter when the physicians and psychiatrists told her that the condition was irreversible. At that moment she felt naked and vulnerable, something she had never before experienced. However turbulent her life had been, she could always rely upon the refuge provided by her grandfather, retreat behind the wall of money, power, and influence. All that, as she quickly learned, had dissolved like a mirage.

No sooner had she moved her grandfather from the hospital into Eaton Square than Andrew appeared. Without asking, he went upstairs and for a long time stood over the husk that was Silas Lambros. Celeste thought she saw the grim expression soften. She had no way of knowing that Andrew was reflecting on a colossal irony: Nine years earlier he had watched another seemingly indestructible man reduced to a parody of his former self—Silas Lambros's enemy, Max McHenry.

"We have to talk," Andrew said abruptly, and turned away.

As she followed him down the staircase Celeste caught herself staring at Andrew's broad back.

Does he have any feeling at all for this house where we first met? Does he have any feeling for me?

Celeste and Andrew had been living apart for over a year. Their estrangement had not come about because of Andrew's affairs. Celeste had known he was cheating on her, indiscriminately, indiscreetly. She had guessed it from the whispers of her closest friends, had seen it in the glint of a girlfriend's eye, smelled it in Andrew's skin when he slipped into bed beside her, his crotch still damp from whatever woman he had just left.

Celeste could have fought his infidelity body for body; she had been powerless against his indifference. She had realized that by his affairs Andrew was telling her he no longer cared what she thought, that he no longer needed her power, that he had used her and now was leaving her behind. The separation, when it came, had been a banal anticlimax.

For the first time since Silas Lambros had been struck down, Celeste was furious with her grandfather. Over the years, without realizing it, he had come to depend heavily on Andrew. In his eyes Andrew was the reincarnation of Nigel, the son he had built his empire for. It was this myopia that Celeste hadn't been able to tolerate. Time and again she had warned her grandfather that he was losing control of Andrew. Andrew was forming his own allies, both within and without Tyne & Wear. Using the company's worldwide resources, he was building his own fiefdom. Silas Lambros had only laughed.

"I know things about Andrew that would destroy him overnight. So long as I'm alive he is mine!"

Now, Celeste thought bitterly, *you are neither alive nor dead but Andrew is a free man. Because you never shared what it was you knew about him.*

Proof of just how great that freedom was had come when, only three days after Silas Lambros's stroke, Celeste's lawyer had informed her that Andrew had filed for divorce.

"Your attorney spoke quite eloquently for you," Celeste told him when they were in the drawing room.

Andrew extracted a cigar from a leather folder.

"I'd rather you didn't," Celeste said coldly. "The smell hangs on for days, and besides, you won't be staying long enough to finish it."

Andrew inclined his head. "As you wish. What I came to discuss is the appointment of the new chairman," he said. "Since there are no surviving Lambroses—"

"Except me!"

"Of course, Celeste. Believe me, I hadn't forgotten you. But I don't think you want to run Tyne & Wear."

"What if I do?" she demanded.

"You don't have enough votes on the board to qualify."

That, Celeste admitted, was true. She might be the last of the clan, but she knew nothing about the workings of the company her name stood for, and everyone was aware of that.

"Who do you think is qualified?"

"I am."

"Never!"

"Think about it," Andrew said reasonably. "I know Tyne & Wear better than anyone else. Silas made sure of that. I also have the unanimous support of the board."

"Not mine!" Celeste's eyes flashed. "You're forgetting one thing: the founder's shares. Grandfather transferred them to me two months ago. With them, I can block anything you or the board try to do."

So that's where they went, Andrew thought to himself. For weeks he had been trying to find out what had happened to the founder's shares. They represented the ultimate power in the company, a full thirty-five percent of the voting stock. Whoever held them could either control the destiny of Tyne & Wear or make life very difficult for those who tried to.

"The founder's shares can be very effective—if used properly," Andrew said. "For the good of the company you should use them to help me. Otherwise, Celeste, I'll fight you. Between my fourteen percent and what the other board members hold we can challenge you in a proxy fight. I think you have some idea of how devastating that would be for the company.''

Even with her limited knowledge of business Celeste knew Andrew was telling the truth. She had seen her grandfather go after companies that had refused to be taken over and the fierce battles that had followed for the stockholders' votes.

"Look," Andrew continued. "I don't intend to strip Tyne & Wear, run it into the ground, or sell it off to someone else. I want to carry on what Silas started. And you know I can do it. That means you get to keep the life-style you've been accustomed to because sure as hell, after what Silas did, his estate is worth nothing.''

Again Celeste had no choice but to face the truth. When power of attorney over all her grandfather's assets had been transferred to her, she realized how little cash there was. To maintain Eaton Square and other properties, to provide her grandfather with the care he needed, to live as she believed she should always live, Celeste had only the founder's shares to rely upon. If their dividends ever dropped, as they would in a proxy fight, the wolves would start circling the door.

"I'll speak with my lawyers," Celeste told him. "You'll have my decision by the end of the week.''

Andrew rose. "No later, Celeste. The longer the company appears adrift, the more nervous the stockholders become.''

"At the end of the week!" Celeste repeated tightly, and rang for the butler to show Andrew out.

The lawyers had the answers to her questions within forty-eight hours. They were exactly what Celeste had expected, but she made Andrew wait until Friday.

"I want to make one thing very clear," she said when she spoke to him that morning. "If I discover that anything is being done behind my back or that you're taking Tyne & Wear in a direction I don't agree with, I will fight you.''

"Fair enough," Andrew agreed.

"I also want to know when the next board meeting will be held.''

"Planning to attend, are you?''

"I'm the only Lambros you've got, Andrew. You need me more than you know!''

Celeste hung up and regarded the silent instrument.

And I need you, she thought, at least for a while. I will eventually destroy you, but you will not be the first. Sweet

Rebecca McHenry, who drove Justin to suicide and destroyed Grandfather, must pay for what she's done. The bitch will bleed and she will also give me what I need to fight you.

"A year has passed since I made that vow, Grandfather," Celeste said dreamily. "There were times I thought I wouldn't be able to carry it out. The bitch seemed perfect, without a flaw. But I found the weakness, Grandfather. I waited so long but she finally made that one mistake. Soon, very soon, we will have what is ours!"

Celeste reached out and caressed her grandfather's forehead, the skin dry as papyrus. She leaned over and kissed him and looked fondly into his sightless eyes. She was the last in a line of great wreckers, and she would make him very proud.

· 41 ·

The wedding wasn't the most extravagant the Angelines had ever seen but for sheer joy and exuberance it couldn't be matched.

Having delegated her responsibilities in Tides II, Rebecca threw herself into the preparations. The *Windsong,* where the actual ceremony would take place, was decked out in bunting. Colored lights were strung along the superstructure and furniture in the main salon was shifted to make room for the altar and guest seating.

The food was prepared under the supervision of the *Windsong*'s chef. Jewel looked after the seating arrangement and native quartet while Rebecca made sure the speedboat pilots knew exactly where and when to meet incoming guests. On the morning of the wedding, great bouquets and floral arrangements were put in place, their scent permeating the entire vessel.

Although the day was a brilliant blue and everything was ready, Rebecca couldn't dispel her nervousness. She was constantly on the phone to the bridge for an update on sea and wind conditions. The office of the charter company that was jetting down guests assembled in Miami assured her the plane would arrive on time. Rebecca even tested the small organ, playing a few chords of the Wedding March.

Finally, at two o'clock on May 3, the ceremony began. Standing by the entrance to the salon, Rebecca peeked inside at the expectant faces. Then the organ struck up and she heard Bix mutter, "Here goes nothing!"

In her flowing white gown edged with silk rosettes, and a train held by two giggling cousins, Bix started to move down the red carpet. Admiral Ryan, decked out in dress whites, held her arm with paternal pride. To the side of the altar stood Torrey, fidgeting in his dove-gray morning coat and cravat, his eyes as wide as those of a child on the first day of school. Rebecca, the maid of honor, was in tears even before the vows were exchanged.

The ceremony was brief, as both Torrey and Bix had wanted. As soon as the final words were spoken, the newlyweds started up the aisle, laughing as rice and confetti rained down on them. Bix saw Rebecca in the semicircle of bridesmaids and, with a whoop, threw the bouquet. The flowers sailed high over the stern, and for an instant it seemed as though the bouquet would go into the water. Rebecca felt her shoulder bumped and at the last instant the bouquet dropped into her outstretched hands.

Flushing, she turned to Eric.

"That's not fair!" she laughed. "You knocked them right into my hands!"

"All is fair in love," he whispered.

Rebecca clutched the bouquet to her breast, wondering if this was the way it was meant to be.

The next day, amid tears, hugs, and kisses, Bix and Torrey set off for a honeymoon at the Tides II property in Ixtapa. The resort was fully staffed but wasn't scheduled to open for another ten days. Bix and Torrey would have it all to themselves.

As she watched the Lear rise over Angeline Bay, Rebecca felt a profound melancholy settle within her. She recalled the times she and Bix had joked and laughed about marriage; the pendulum would swing from the firm belief that they would remain single forever to excited speculation about the right man. In spite of Bix's devil-may-care attitude toward Torrey, Rebecca knew that she cherished and was fiercely protective of him. But even though she knew the marriage had been inevitable, Rebecca couldn't quite grasp the reality. She sternly told herself she wasn't losing her friend. But her heart whispered that something profound had changed and that in a way she couldn't articulate, she had been left behind.

Immediately after the wedding the Windsong was restored to her usual order. The next morning, when Rebecca entered her office in the main salon, the memorandum for the day's agenda had already been laid out on the table by her secretary. What she couldn't account for was the concern in Eric's and Ramsey's expressions.

"Somebody die?" Rebecca asked lightly.

In her dark blue jeans, bright orange T-shirt, and bare feet set in Topsiders, she radiated a casualness that contrasted sharply with her advisers' attire.

"Not yet," Ramsey said. "But the patient isn't doing so well."

Eric looked up from the ledgers and computer printouts and added, "I'm afraid he's right."

Rebecca settled herself between the two men.

"All right. What is the problem?"

"Quite simply, you're running out of money," Eric told her. "The gold-mining operations are draining your reserves more quickly than we had projected. Right now, if you start extracting ore in sixty days as we hope, it will take at least a year for the mines to break even."

Eric shook his head. "You don't have that much time. Because of the cut rates established for Tides II, you'll have to carry the resorts until October. Cash flow from The Tides is off by five percent, which means you can't look there for help."

"What about the investment portfolio?" Rebecca asked.

"If you were to liquidate everything—and I mean everything," Ramsey said, "that would still leave you short. And, given the market, it's a lousy time even to consider doing that."

Rebecca examined the bottom-line figures. She had overextended herself badly. The reorganization and reopening of the mines had exceeded initial estimates but she had plunged ahead. She dared not believe that her intuition had been folly.

I need three more months! By August, what Anthony Fabrizzi said would happen should have come to pass. . . .

"And if it doesn't?" she said.

"If what doesn't, Rebecca?" Eric asked.

"I'm sorry, I was just thinking aloud. How much longer until we need an infusion of capital?"

"No more than thirty days," Ramsey told her. "But you can't wait that long. It'll take weeks to put together bridge financing."

Rebecca took a deep breath and looked at both men.

"Where do we get it?"

"If you put up the investment portfolio as collateral, we can get about a third of the amount," Eric said, looking decidedly uncomfortable. "The rest—"

"Either you put up The Tides stock you hold or else you go public," Ramsey finished bluntly. "I'm sorry, Rebecca, but I don't see any alternative."

She had known it would come to this but the words still terrified her. The idea of allowing strangers to have even the slightest control over her vision was repugnant.

"I can't do that!" Rebecca said. "I would be giving up everything I've fought to get."

"No, you wouldn't, Rebecca," Eric explained gently. "Ramsey and I have calculated that you would retain at least sixty-five percent control. We reckon that if we issue the stock at between five and six dollars, the market will immediately push it up to twenty-four or twenty-five. Given your reputation and especially the publicity after Contodora, that isn't unrealistic. As soon as we feel the price has topped out, the Walker will lend you the balance of the amount you need based on the market value of the sixty-five percent you control."

Rebecca thought about this for a moment.

"But if for some reason the stock drops, I stand to lose a great deal—almost everything."

"As soon as Tides II comes on-stream, you can step into the market and buy back the outstanding shares," Eric told her. "Tides II is your virtual guarantee that the price of the stock won't just hold but will probably go up."

Rebecca twisted a loose strand of hair around her finger.

"I don't know," she said hesitantly. "It seems to be happening so fast. . . ."

"If you wait any longer, the consequences could be even worse," Ramsey said. "Something would have to give, either Tides II or the mining. Either alternative could hurt you badly."

"How much time do I have?"

"No more than a few days," Eric told her. "Even so, we'll all be working overtime to make sure the well doesn't run dry."

Rebecca barely slept the next two days. She sequestered herself in her office in the main salon and reviewed every facet of The Tides' financial position. Ramsey and Eric had been right: There was no way out.

The only avenue Rebecca hadn't explored was Anthony Fabrizzi. She needed reassurance that what he had told her was still accurate and on schedule. She finally called the Polaris Group headquarters in New York, only to have a personal secretary tell her Anthony Fabrizzi was out of the country. No one was to know where or for how long.

Damn you! Rebecca thought, fighting back a sinking feeling. It was as though she had, like a fool, stepped into a riptide and was being swept along by forces far beyond her control. She wished she had been candid with Ramsey and Eric from the very beginning. Together they would have had her committed before letting her deal with someone like Anthony Fabrizzi.

The evening before she was due to leave for New York

with her answer, Rebecca had a solitary dinner on the pilotdeck. Ramon and the senior officers were in Angeline City enjoying a well-deserved shore leave, and there was only a skeleton crew on board. The arrival of the helicopter came as a complete surprise.

Anthony Fabrizzi jumped down from the copilot seat and walked swiftly toward her.

"We have to talk."

No greeting, no explanations.

When Rebecca had shown him into the main salon, she said caustically, "Nice to see you again, Mr. Fabrizzi—I think."

Anthony Fabrizzi stared deeply into her eyes, his own expressionless, as if shuttered against emotion.

"I understand you're running out of money," he said.

Rebecca felt as though he had slapped her.

"Is that why you're here?" she demanded. "To make another offer for The Tides? Up the ante?"

In spite of her fury, Rebecca couldn't hold back the despair welling inside her. If he knew she was being pushed into a financial corner, he also knew why. Was that the reason he had come here, to take personal pleasure in springing a trap he had set for her?

"We have a lot to discuss," Anthony Fabrizzi said. "I would appreciate a drink."

Silently Rebecca indicated the bar in the corner.

He's not going to take a damn thing from me! she swore to herself. I'll see him in hell first!

As though he had been reading her mind, Anthony Fabrizzi turned to Rebecca, glass in hand.

"You'll be needing one too."

Three hours later the crew was surprised when Rebecca ordered that Ramon and the officers be brought back to the *Windsong* as soon as possible and the vessel swung into the wind immediately. They were further amazed when they saw her escort her mysterious visitor to the pad, then, without a word, abruptly turn away. The gentleman slipped into his seat and the helicopter was airborne. Rebecca disappeared into her suite with explicit instructions not to be disturbed.

When he returned to the communications center, the radio officer found a message waiting to be sent immediately. It was for Eric Walker in New York and contained only two words: GO AHEAD.

*   *   *

It seemed to Rebecca that never in her life had she signed so many forms. There were the underwriters' affidavits and asset declaration forms, Securities and Exchange Commission papers, and the Standard & Poor rating sheets. She had meetings with the board of the Walker Bank and huddled with Ramsey's corporate law gurus until the small hours of the morning.

"If I have to sign my name one more time, I'm going to invest in an AutoPen," Rebecca groaned, referring to the instrument that reproduced signatures perfectly.

She felt Eric's fingers undo the terry-cloth belt and slip the bathrobe from her shoulders.

"What are you doing?"

"You're tense," Eric whispered, kneeling behind her on the bed.

Rebecca felt his fingers go to work on the knotted muscles between the shoulder blades, and her head slumped forward.

"That's so good!" she exclaimed.

Eric had been at her side throughout the ordeal of paperwork. He had been there for her in the small hours of the morning when, unable to sleep, she had watched the spring dawn break over Central Park. He seemed to know exactly when she needed his touch and when solitude was the only answer. He didn't protest when she missed dinners at his apartment or forgot that he was coming to hers. But behind such consideration Rebecca discerned an unspoken question, one which Eric's self-control prevented him from blurting out: Would she take him to be her husband? Rebecca understood that it was the reply, not the question, that he feared.

The day The Tides stock went on the New York Stock Exchange under the trading name of Suncorp, Eric took her to a special restaurant called The Trap, outside Montauk. A plain, barnlike place with checkered tablecloths and wine served by the liter, it specialized in lobster. By the end of the evening Rebecca had almost succeeded in forgetting that there was a world beyond The Trap. The booming Atlantic that pounded the granite below made her feel she was aboard a ghost ship headed for a mysterious destination.

In spite of the chatter at nearby tables, Rebecca had been quiet the whole evening. She stared at other couples in the room, envying them their whispered conversations, the squeeze of two hands across the table, the long dreamy silences or excited chatter.

I don't know how much longer I can go on like this, she thought.

And yet Rebecca knew she had no choice. Everything she had achieved could not eradicate what remained of Skyscape, the charred skeleton which, if not for its modern lines, might have been mistaken for Mayan ruins in the thick clifftop jungle. Nor could she forget Dallas Gibson, who had died trying to help her. Behind them, somewhere in the mists of time past, stood the man responsible for the twin horrors. A man she still had to face, who had to pay so that she could not only make amends but live without fear.

Because of all she owed, because she needed the strength to carry on, Rebecca reached out and took Eric's hand.

"Yes," she said softly. "I will marry you."

Eric Walker entered the foyer of his apartment building in a daze. If asked, he couldn't have told anyone what had happened that evening, what he had eaten, or how he had gotten home. Only Rebecca's words echoed in his mind. They had been so unexpected, so unbelievable, that he had, like an idiot, asked her to repeat them. When she did, he knew he wasn't dreaming.

Eric Walker had been very careful not to pressure Rebecca on the subject of marriage. He had dropped broad hints but, having received no encouragement, had thought they had fallen on stony ground. Then tonight!

Eric remembered asking Rebecca over and over again if she was sure. She had cupped his face while he was driving and whispered yes each time. At that point he bemoaned the fact that he didn't even have a bottle of champagne at home with which to celebrate.

"No matter, darling," Rebecca had whispered. "I want you to take me home. We've both made a big decision tonight and I think it would be better if we were alone."

Eric didn't dare disagree.

"Is everything all right, Mr. Walker?" the security man asked anxiously.

Eric Walker looked at him strangely. "Of course, Charlie. How would you like to come to my wedding?"

Eric ignored the man's gaping expression and sailed into the elevator. By the time he reached his front door he was humming an early Beatles tune to himself. He did not give a second thought to the fact that the lights were on in the apartment. But he smelled the perfume immediately.

"Well, my love, you look as though you not only swallowed the canary but the whole aviary," Celeste Lambros said. "Don't tell me you finally popped the question and the little bitch said yes?"

· 42 ·

The irony haunted Eric Walker: If Rebecca hadn't made such a success of The Tides, the Walker Bank would never have expanded through the Caribbean. If that hadn't happened, perhaps he would never have had to betray the woman he loved.

During the bullish sixties Eric had wanted the Walker to branch out into the international arena. His only stumbling block was the board of directors. His father, Bartholomew Walker, had surrounded himself with hard, conservative men. When he learned that his illness was terminal, he bestowed upon them extraordinary powers regarding the bank's day-to-day operations. Eric might have assumed the title of president but his capacity to make independent decisions was severely limited.

For several years Eric had chafed under the board's thumb. When he wanted the bank to be at the leading edge in financing new technology, his proposals were unanimously dismissed. Ventures that bore the slightest whiff of speculation were voted down. Only the fact that the Walker had thirty-five thousand dollars of Rebecca McHenry's money had induced the members grudgingly to lend their support to The Tides.

The success of The Tides should have given Eric the power to force the board to listen to him. Instead, its members kept him on as tight a leash as before, their policies unswervingly conservative. Eric had gained little stature for this coup. His salary and profit-sharing percentage did not reflect the volume of business he was bringing in. Other bankers his age, with far less prestigious titles, were raking in three times his paycheck and bonuses. It was this loss of face before his peers that finally pushed Eric over the edge.

Arbitrage—the buying and selling of currencies—is one of the most harrowing games played on the market. The dollar may open strongly in Zurich but be down two points in London an hour later. By the time New York opens, it may be up, only to

372

drop again when Tokyo comes on line. The people who speculate on a currency's value are like air traffic controllers juggling half a dozen planes trying to land on the same runway at the same time. Unlike their counterparts in the tower, arbitragers can make a lot of money in a matter of hours. But when a plane crashes they are among the victims.

Eric had always been fascinated by arbitrage. He studied the financial markets and, without telling anyone, indulged in some mild speculation with his own funds. He never mentioned that he always won and just as quickly put those winnings on another ride of the currency roulette wheel. Like the gambler who converts five dollars into five hundred, Eric became convinced of his infallibility. If his Midas touch could change ten thousand dollars into forty thousand, what could he do with an even bigger stake?

That question was Eric's first step on the road to embezzlement.

In a modern bank Eric would have found tampering with clients' funds much more difficult—so much so that the risk of exposure might have dissuaded him. But now the Walker's antiquated accounting procedures and first-generation business machines worked in his favor. As an officer who had access to every nook and cranny of the bank, Eric could pick and choose his victims at leisure. Nonetheless he did exercise some caution, lifting funds from those accounts that had little or no activity in them or whose funds were locked in long-term. He also faithfully replaced the money as soon as he had made his killing, knowing full well that it was there whenever he needed it.

Until there came the time when he gambled and lost. A sudden decision by the British government to devalue the pound cost Eric tens of thousands of dollars in less than five minutes. His subsequent scramble to divest himself of pounds no one wanted ran the losses into six figures.

No matter. The cookie jar was still there. Confident he would recoup his losses, Eric withdrew another stake and returned to the game. In the next three weeks he was successively burned by the Swiss franc, Japanese yen, Iranian rial, and even the lowly Canadian dollar. By now the corporate account he had been raiding was down over a quarter of a million dollars. As soon as he touched it again, the invisible alarms sounded.

"So you and Rebecca are going to be married," Celeste murmured, savoring the words.

She sat back on the white, silk-covered sofa, tucking her feet underneath her, and patted the cushions beside her.

"Why don't you come here and tell me all about it."

The joy of the past few hours dribbled through Eric's fingers like sand, something he would never quite recapture.

Eric had never suspected that the last corporate account he touched had been rigged. Having taken the money, he was on his way to place his buy/sell orders, when a large, purposeful gentleman intercepted him and steered him toward a limousine that was idling before the doors of the Walker Bank. Eric recognized Celeste Lambros at once.

Celeste hadn't given him a moment to think about what was happening. In a harsh, clipped voice she explained that she knew all about his arbitrage losses, the accounts he had plundered, and, more specifically, how much he had taken from his last victim. When she mentioned the name of the man behind the corporate veil, Eric blanched.

"Of course," Celeste had continued over the purr of the car's engine, "you do have alternatives. First, you will put back the money you were going to use today. Later, I'll give you what is necessary to balance the account. I will also not disclose to this party that you tried to rob him. You see, darling, I need you whole."

Like any amateur thief, Eric wasn't thinking of how or when Celeste had discovered his embezzlement. He saw only that she had the power of life and death over him—and she was offering him life.

"In return, I want you to tell me everything, everything, about Rebecca McHenry."

"That's all?" Eric gasped.

"For now, darling, for now."

That had been four months ago, just after Eric and Rebecca returned from Vermont, after he had made love to her for the first time. . . . And of course that wasn't all. It was only the beginning.

During the next several weeks Eric felt as though he were on the Inquisition's rack. Celeste demanded to know everything about Rebecca McHenry, from the vaguest plans for the future to the minutest details concerning Tides II. She questioned Eric on finances, political allies and enemies, the fiscal state of The Tides travel offices, even on Rebecca's health. At first Eric had tried to generalize. But he soon discovered that Celeste already had answers to many of her questions. Whenever he prevaricated, she unsheathed the threat of exposing him.

With every interrogation Eric's self-esteem diminished. He tried to convince himself that what he was telling Celeste really couldn't hurt Rebecca. How could Celeste be a threat after the losses she had suffered? But there was more in store. Celeste began to take a great interest in his intimacy with Rebecca. She demanded he tell her how they made love, how often, and where. Eric burned with shame as the words came from his mouth, yet he dared not stop them. He still believed the nightmare would end.

For a while it actually did. About the time Rebecca became involved in reopening the gold mines in the Angelines, Celeste suddenly vanished. At first Eric was not relieved, only cautious. As weeks passed without a word, he began to think that she had actually set him free. Realizing that he might have only this one chance, Eric began to court Rebecca even more fervently than before. That he had been weak did not, in his eyes, diminish the love he felt for her. Moreover, if he could convince Rebecca that they belonged together, he would be free of Celeste forever. Celeste would think twice about blackmailing him if he had the power of The Tides behind him. If Celeste dared to make public accusations, Eric was certain he could convince Rebecca that they were fabrications. After all, once the money had all been returned, no one would be any the wiser.

As Eric walked toward Celeste, this last thought changed his initial fear of seeing her in his apartment into anger.

"What do you want?" he said shortly, standing before her.

"Oh, my! The mouse that roared. Sit down, darling. Being overbearing doesn't become you. Now, tell me, when is the big day?"

"We haven't set a date—"

"But you will let me know, won't you?"

"What business is it of yours? You've got what you wanted. You're not holding a gun to my head anymore—"

"*I* might not be, darling," Celeste said icily. "But I'm not so sure about my friend."

Eric followed Celeste's gaze to where the man stood, his hands folded in front of him like a graveside mourner.

"What you did not know, Mr. Walker, was that the last account you attempted to embezzle happened to belong to a company I control," Anthony Fabrizzi said.

*   *   *

Only after Eric had swallowed half the double scotch Celeste had poured for him did he manage to stop shaking. Sitting on the ottoman opposite his nemesis, he stared at her in disbelief.

"You swore you would never tell anyone," Eric said hoarsely, his voice catching as much on fear as on the whiskey. "You said if I gave you what you wanted that would be the end of it."

"I'm afraid Anthony was very persuasive," Celeste said.

Eric watched as she rubbed the back of her neck against Fabrizzi's fingers. It was a blatantly sexual gesture. *How could she have discovered it was his account I was using?* Eric thought wildly. *What kind of deal has she struck with Fabrizzi?*

"But Anthony's talents have nothing to do with what we're here to discuss," Celeste said. "Unless, of course, you prove obstinate."

Eric kept silent. He had to find out what was going on. The best way to do that was to keep Celeste talking.

"Of course, you won't," Celeste said, uncurling herself and coming over to the window.

"Look out there, Eric," she said, gesturing at the lights of Manhattan. "That's what you have to lose. Not only what you've gained so far but everything that's possible for you to have. Think about that while you listen to me.

"You know, I'm very happy you're marrying Rebecca. It shows me just how much trust she has in you. That's very important, trust. . . . Because what you will make sure of is that she signs over her stock as collateral for the loan she needs."

The fact that Celeste knew about The Tides going public didn't surprise Eric. The news had traveled all over the financial world. What he didn't understand was the special meaning the offering had for her.

"I can't tell you how important it is for you to do this—for us, and yourself," Celeste said. "Because when the stock hits what we believe is its peak, something will happen that will cause the bottom to fall out of it."

The crystal old-fashioned glass made a dull thud as it hit the carpet, spilling ice cubes and watery scotch across Eric's wingtips.

"You can't be serious!" he whispered. "You don't have the means—"

"We have the means, Mr. Walker," Anthony Fabrizzi said, breaking his silence. "Believe me, we do."

"As soon as the stock plummets, you, as a prudent banker, will have all the reason in the world to call in your loan," Celeste carried on as though oblivious to the interruption. "And that's what you will do. When you have the stock, I shall inform the board of the Walker Bank that I am interested in purchasing it. Given the option of holding on to paper that's not going to get them their money back or giving it to me at fifty cents on the dollar, they will take the fifty cents. Of course once I announce I have purchased the stock on behalf of Tyne & Wear and intend to clean house, its value will skyrocket.''

"But why?" Eric pleaded, looking from Celeste to Anthony Fabrizzi. "Why are you doing this to her? It's monstrous!"

"Really?" Celeste shot back. "And what about everything she's done to my family? You fool, Eric! You really don't know what Rebecca was doing in London all that time, do you?"

Eric stared at her incomprehensibly. Of course he had heard about the bizarre suicide of a man who turned out to be Silas Lambros's younger son and of Lambros's subsequent stroke at the Tyne & Wear board meeting. He knew Rebecca had been in London during that time; it was then she had bought back her father's holdings in the Angelines. But what could Rebecca have had to do with Justin Lambros's death?

What was she hiding from him?

Eric saw the truth in Celeste's cold rage. Somehow Rebecca had been involved. Had Celeste been acting alone, Eric might have been able to dismiss her as a raving, distraught woman. But not after she had convinced Anthony Fabrizzi to help her.

Fabrizzi . . . Where does he fit in, Eric thought, trying to marshal his arguments. Celeste was consumed beyond reason with the thought of revenge. But if he could make Fabrizzi see how insane all this was . . .

"Mr. Fabrizzi," Eric said. "I don't know what you have to do with any of this—"

"What I have to do, Mr. Walker, is directly related to what you have forced me to do," Anthony Fabrizzi said coldly. "It was your greed that brought you here, nothing more. What kind of man are you, that you now dare ask help from someone you stole from?"

Eric's face burned. "Mr. Fabrizzi—"

"Don't humiliate yourself any more than you already have," Celeste snapped, disgusted. "Rebecca should have known better than to say no when Anthony—"

"That's enough!"

Fabrizzi's voice snapped in the room like a whip, but it was too late. Eric stared from one to the other, realization dawning on him at last.

Contodora . . . It had all begun that night at Contodora. He remembered Rebecca coming off the dance floor in a state of shock. She had asked him who Anthony Fabrizzi was and he had told her. Later, when pressed, she had told him Fabrizzi had shown an interest in buying The Tides, but had seemed to accept her refusal. She had never mentioned the man again.

"You wanted to buy her out, didn't you?" he said aloud, looking at Fabrizzi. "That night, at Contodora, you told her you wanted The Tides and she told you no. But you were going to get them one way or another, weren't you?"

Anthony Fabrizzi's cold silence and Celeste's triumphant smile were all the confirmation Eric needed.

"The point is, Mr. Walker," Fabrizzi said, "you are going to do exactly as we tell you. You do have one alternative: to go to Rebecca McHenry and explain how you've been selling her out all this time, that she's about to marry a thief and a coward, a man who professes love but is continually betraying her—"

"Stop it!" Eric shouted. "I don't want to hear it! I . . . I'm not like that . . . I didn't . . ."

Eric slumped forward, his head buried in his hands.

"Of course you're not that kind of man," Fabrizzi said pitilessly, and walked from the room.

· 43 ·

"You've been awfully quiet all this time."

The Caribbean sunset warmed Rebecca's face as she and Jewel walked along the deserted beach on Windemere Key. The place where The Tides had been born was empty of people except for the tradesmen who, having come out to do the annual repairs and face-lift, had already finished for the day.

"It's good to be home," Rebecca said, stepping lightly to one side to avoid a scurrying hermit crab. "I'm sorry I didn't come sooner."

"Pay it no mind," Jewel said, patting her arm.

In spite of everything that was going on around her—or perhaps because of it—Rebecca had suddenly come to a dead halt. She had explained to Eric that she needed to step outside of what was happening, to try to gain some perspective. She had also been working herself into a frenzy. Her physical and emotional strength were dangerously low.

"Everything's been set in motion, darling," she had told Eric. "I need this time to get away, and it's been ages since I've seen Jewel."

Eric had objected much more forcefully than Rebecca had expected, saying that he needed her too. But he knew her well enough to understand he couldn't change her mind. True to character, Eric had taken the time to drive her to the airport. After the jet lifted off, the flight attendant presented Rebecca with a bottle of champagne and a card from him, saying how much he already missed her.

In the calm waters of the lagoon Rebecca felt the grit and grime, the tension and worry, peel away like dead skin. The biggest decisions she had to make were what to have for dinner and when to get up in the morning. And Jewel was always there to talk to.

At first Rebecca didn't think that Jewel had changed at all.

But the more time she spent with her the more differences she noticed. Jewel's walk was a little slower now, her speech likewise. Sometimes she would end a sentence abruptly, as though she had forgotten its conclusion, then pick up the same thought a few minutes later. There was also a serenity to her, an aura of peace. Rebecca found it immensely comforting.

"I'm not going to leave you alone for this long again," Rebecca said suddenly. "I promise."

"Oh, girl, girl!" Jewel laughed, her voice ringing over the wheeling, squawking gulls. "You're never too far away from me. Not in my heart. Besides, I got more people than I know what to do with!"

That much, Rebecca knew, was true. A year ago she had had a small bungalow built for Jewel on Windemere so that she wouldn't have to travel so much between the key and Angeline City. Gradually the bungalow became her second home, and while Jewel now did very little work at The Tides, she still enjoyed filling in here and there and gossiping with the young people.

The two women came to a giant palm trunk, half buried in the sand, and rested.

"It's hard to believe this was where it all started," Rebecca said, staring out to sea. "It seems like such a long time ago."

"It was a long time," Jewel said. "Not in years maybe but in yourself."

A silence descended between them, broken only by the onrushing tide as it ran up the sand, the foam crackling, hissing, finally receding.

"You came here to heal yourself," Jewel said. "But there is more, so tell me."

"Never were one to beat around the bush, were you?" She grinned.

"Don't be talkin' disrespect to your elders," Jewel huffed.

"Okay," Rebecca said. "If that's the way you want it." She paused then finished. "Eric and I are getting married."

For an instant Rebecca honestly thought Jewel was going to keel over.

"Oh, Lord, that's so fine," Jewel whispered through her tears. "So fine!"

When Rebecca returned to Manhattan, Bix immediately invited her and Eric over for the first barbecue of the season.

"Torrey would have been grilling in the middle of winter if

I'd let him," Bix told her. "So don't say you can't come. It's been ages since we've seen the two of you. Besides, Lauren and Ramsey will be there."

When Rebecca told Eric about the impromptu party, he agreed that it would be a fine occasion to tell their friends the good news.

The day couldn't have been more perfect. The May rains had scrubbed the air of winter and June was ushered in with brilliant sunshine. In one corner of the tiny Perry Street garden Torrey was standing over the barbecue, turning steaks that Rebecca thought must have been cut from a mastodon, not a steer. Ramsey was over by the makeshift bar, pouring indiscriminate amounts of tequila, lime juice, and triple sec into a blender for frozen margaritas. The aroma of blooms mingled with that of grilled pepper-studded meat.

"You folks are really quiet today," Torrey called over from the barbecue.

Rebecca, reclining in a chaise longue, peered over the rim of her sunglasses, first at Torrey then at Eric.

"Think we should tell them?" she whispered.

Just then Torrey called out. "So what gives?"

"Attend to your cooking, husband!" Bix admonished him, walking by and whacking Torrey on the butt with a spatula.

"Nag, nag, nag!" Torrey muttered. "Take it from me, Eric. Everything changes mightily once you've been to the altar."

Rebecca and Eric convulsed in laughter.

"You think I'm going to tell them?" Eric said. "After he was decent enough to warn me off? You've got to be kidding!"

"Swine!"

"All right," Lauren said firmly. "Something's up and we must know what it is. Ramsey, shut off that infernal machine and bring the margaritas. We'll get them smashed if we have to!"

As soon as everyone was holding a thick, salt-rimmed goblet, Lauren said, "Well, we're waiting."

Rebecca prodded Eric, who shyly made the announcement. Immediately the barbecue became a celebration.

Throughout the meal Rebecca was inundated by questions from Bix and Lauren. Had she chosen a designer for her wedding dress? Did she and Eric prefer a civil or religious ceremony? How many guests did they plan to have and where was the reception to be held? And what about the date?

"We're going to wait until August," Rebecca said firmly. "Once The Tides stock offering is over with."

Bix, who had expected Rebecca to choose the Angelines as the site, was surprised when her best friend asked Lauren if she and Ramsey would lend them their Long Island estate for the ceremony.

"Not that there are going to be a lot of people," Rebecca explained. "Both Eric and I want an intimate wedding. But it's so beautiful by the Sound in August. I can't think of a nicer place."

Dabbing her eyes, Lauren agreed at once.

Meanwhile, the men huddled with Eric, offering words of masculine wisdom on how to circumvent the follies of marriage.

"Pretend you know exactly what she's talking about even if you don't have a clue," Torrey said solemnly.

"And agree with her," Ramsey added. "It's a small price to pay to keep the peace."

"But don't let her keep you from the boys," warned Torrey. "You've got to be your own man."

The afternoon rolled along on laughter and jokes. As she fielded questions about where they would honeymoon and sidestepped sly innuendos about children, Rebecca noticed Lauren and Ramsey holding hands. Bix had brought her chair next to Torrey's and had her head on his shoulder, holding his arm above her breasts.

As the party wound down, Rebecca excused herself and went inside. A few minutes later Bix, who came in with a tray of dirty dishes, heard the sound of smashing glass in the bathroom. She knocked anxiously on the door, called Rebecca's name and, hearing no reply, entered.

Rebecca was leaning heavily against the counter, her head bowed, her face deathly pale. On the floor was a flagon of perfume she had brushed from the shelf below the mirror. The odor of sickness made Bix gag.

"Becky . . ."

"I'm all right," Rebecca whispered, running water and splashing her face.

"Are you . . . pregnant?" Bix asked softly.

Rebecca looked up, her gray eyes glistening.

"No, it's nothing like that . . ." Thank God, she added silently.

"Honey . . . honey, are you awake?"

Bix rolled over, the water bed sloshing gently beneath her. She stuffed two oversize pillows behind her back and stared out at the moonlit room drowning in shades of blue. Beside her, Torrey lay on his back, his eyes closed, his breathing deep and regular.

"I'm worried about Rebecca," Bix said. "And it's not just her being sick today."

Bix curled a finger around a strand of hair and tugged it thoughtfully.

"She loves Eric, I know she does. Hell, maybe it's just my imagination! Maybe it's all the work and tension from that damned stock offering—something she never wanted to do in the first place."

Across the room a clock ticked, its luminous dial creating a nebula in the darkness.

"Eric's changed too. I ran into him a few times when Rebecca was away. He's lost weight. He smiles too quickly. He doesn't look me in the eye. He's damn nervous about something, and it isn't marriage. It's as though there's something more to The Tides going public than anyone knows—or is willing to talk about."

Bix chewed her lip, thinking. She was startled when Torrey spoke in the gloom.

"You're right, babe," he said softly. "There's something about him that bothers the hell out of me. I can't put my finger on it but I think you and I better ask a few discreet questions. I don't want Rebecca walking off a cliff."

Bix slid beside him, huddling against his shoulder, draping her arm over his chest.

"Thank you," she said. "I thought I was the only crazy one in the family."

As Torrey stroked her, Bix felt an uneasy sleep wash over her. Images of Rebecca flitted through her mind. And the man in the background was not Eric but Andrew Stoughton.

From the port of Cartegena, Colombia, a rusting tramp freighter weighed anchor at high tide. The *Santa Maria*'s captain steered cautiously through the harbor channel. When he was in open water he set a northeasterly course that would take him around the coast of Venezuela then straight north into the Caribbean.

The freighter's manifest indicated that the ship was carrying bananas, sugar cane, and coffee. A detailed inspection of the ship would have confirmed this. The log read that the freighter was going to make half a dozen stops in various Caribbean ports to take on Miami-bound cargo. Again, nothing appeared amiss.

The holds were half empty and could easily accommodate the extra consignments. If for some reason the *Santa Maria* was intercepted by the Coast Guard, the officers would have no cause to board it. Its record, as well as that of its captain, was clean. That the vessel flew the Panamanian flag, was registered to a holding company in Nigeria which in turn was controlled by a nameplate firm in Luxembourg was standard operating procedure in the gray world of Caribbean shipping.

Only those who knew exactly what they were looking for and where to find it would have known that the freighter was a contraband carrier. The captain was confident he wouldn't encounter such men. Had any ever existed, they were dead by now. Those who did know the *Santa Maria*'s secrets were his employers.

All banks have safety deposit boxes. The Swiss Financial Alliance has crypts.

Below its comparatively modest tower on the corner of Park Avenue and Forty-eighth Street, carved out of the Manhattan bedrock, are immense temperature-controlled vaults. Swiss by conception and design, they hold everything from priceless works of art to a perfectly preserved replica of an Egyptian pharaoh's barge—the difference being that the replica, which had somehow found its way out of a royal tomb, was carved from solid gold.

The Swiss do not concern themselves about such details. Nor do they ask why such treasures should be hidden away from the world. Instead, they charge by the square foot for crypt space and deduct the annual rent from their clients' accounts.

The requirements of the Polaris Group were not extravagant: Anthony Fabrizzi's valuables fit neatly into a two-foot-square locker. It was privacy and security that had made him choose the Swiss Financial Alliance crypts.

All clients who had business in the crypts were shown up to a special room on the second floor of the bank. If their valuables were such that they could not be moved, a bank executive and an armed guard accompanied the principal downstairs via elevator. Anthony Fabrizzi merely gave the managing director, a frequent guest though never a gambler at Polaris's Bangkok resort, the magnetic card to his box and waited for a guard to bring it up.

Anthony Fabrizzi leaned across and lighted Celeste's cigarette. He watched carefully as, after a single puff, she tapped nonexistent ashes into a crystal tray.

"Oppressive, isn't it?" Celeste said, glancing around the room.

The paneling was dark walnut, the furniture of heavy Gothic design that might have come from a Bavarian castle—and probably did. Thick patterned curtains blocked out natural light which the chandeliers and lamps couldn't emulate.

"Perhaps," Anthony Fabrizzi agreed. "However, it's for our own privacy. Even if the curtains were drawn, the reinforced glass has been treated so that no one can look in—or listen in. We can say anything we want in this room without fear of consequence."

Celeste regarded him through the haze of smoke. In his conservatively cut three-piece pinstripe, Anthony Fabrizzi appeared as though he belonged there. Until one looked closely at the eyes, which seemed never to blink, or listened to the voice and heard the menace beneath what one had thought was only quiet authority. To touch Anthony Fabrizzi was to run a finger over a razor.

The security guard wheeled in the lead box, returned the magnetic card, and quietly departed. Celeste watched as Anthony Fabrizzi delicately inserted the card into a slot and the door clicked open. How many times had she imagined those fingers running over her body, caressing her, parting her and exploring? She dreamed of scissoring her legs around that trim waist, of digging her nails into the muscular back. . . . She dreamed of it now, unaware that her nostrils were flaring lightly and her tongue ran behind her teeth as though straining to break free.

It wasn't that she hadn't made her intentions clear. Quite the opposite. She had all but gone on her knees before him. Celeste flushed when she remembered how, over dinner, she had indulged in one of her fantasies. Suddenly Anthony had said, "I appreciate the thought and I'm honored. But regrettably I don't mix business with pleasure."

The height of charm, Celeste thought. To turn humiliation into flattery.

Anthony Fabrizzi handed her a cable.

"The ship sailed three hours ago. These are the coordinates for her present location. Please call the marine operator and have her patch you through."

Celeste understood that Anthony expected her to follow his instructions. When they had become partners he had kept her abreast of the minutest developments on his side of the operation. He expected her to question and challenge his arrangements, and she had. Both understood this was the laying of the foundation for trust and respect. This was business.

Celeste gave the marine operator the name of the vessel and the coordinates. The operator advised her that the relay might take some time since the vessel might not be monitoring the necessary frequency. Celeste asked her to have the Cartagena operator try anyway. Three minutes later Celeste had the captain on the line. She gave him the code word and he responded immediately with the countersign.

"We seem to be well on our way." Celeste smiled. "As long as that wreck doesn't break down."

"The superstructure looks like shit," Anthony Fabrizzi said flatly. "But the engines are brand new. She'll get to where she's going on time."

In her mind Celeste pictured the *Santa Maria*'s course. She would curve around Punta Gallinas on Colombia's Guajira Peninsula and make Oranjestad in the Netherlands Antilles her first port of call. From there she would head northeast to Speightstown, Barbados, then turn northwest to Saint John's, Antigua, and Virgin Gorda in the British Virgin Islands. At length the vessel could dock at Kingston, Jamaica, then proceed straight across to Angeline City, her final destination.

In each venue the *Santa Maria* would take on legitimate cargo. In each she would leave something behind that wasn't on the manifest, a poison that would blight The Tides resorts that had blossomed in each of those regions.

"Have you notified your people?" Anthony Fabrizzi asked.

Celeste nodded. "They'll be waiting for the *Santa Maria*."

She looked for the slightest hint of doubt or concern in Fabrizzi's eyes but saw neither. This second part of her plan to destroy Rebecca McHenry and The Tides rested solely in her hands.

When Celeste had heard that Rebecca and Eric Walker had become an item, she immediately canvassed her New York friends for details. Over drinks at the Waldorf and tea on the manicured lawns of Westchester County estates, she threaded together bits of gossip like pearls on a string. The bliss which the two lovebirds seemed to have, by all accounts, found, nauseated Celeste. She had almost wished she had never asked about them in the first place when the wife of an investment banker innocently dropped a bombshell.

"Charlie tells me Eric's been losing dreadfully on the money markets," she said. "Good thing he latched on to Rebecca when he did. The boy's just about in the poorhouse."

Intrigued by this piece of dirt, Celeste changed her tack, focusing her questions on Eric's financial status. She was soon convinced that Eric was in fact a hairsbreadth away from an embarrassing, if not calamitous situation.

If that's the case, why is he still in the market?

The fact that Eric continued to play—and lose—at arbitrage led Celeste to suspect that all was not well at the house of Walker.

Celeste might never have been able to lift the veil covering the embezzlement had it not been for one crucial factor. Several years earlier Silas Lambros had been instrumental in averting a scandal that would have ruined the career and reputation of a man currently sitting on the board of the Walker. Celeste called in the favor and explained exactly what she wanted.

"You're asking an awful lot," the board member told her. "Besides, if Eric is pilfering accounts to cover his losses, I'm duty-bound to report it."

"Of course you are," Celeste replied. "But only to me."

The board member shook his head. "Too much of a risk. If someone ever found out I hadn't warned the bank's controller, I'd be out on my ass."

Celeste had sweetened the pot by adding a huge amount of cash, almost all her personal reserves. When the board member demanded her as well, she had had no second thoughts about giving him all the sex he could handle—and then some. Three weeks later, when she was presented with evidence of Eric's malfeasance, Celeste thought the price had been cheap.

"He's been one sly son of a bitch," the board member said as he and Celeste lay in the king-size bed of a St. Regis suite. "If you hadn't put me on to him, he might have gotten away with it."

Celeste ran her fingers through the curly gray hairs on his chest.

"Show me everything."

"I thought I already had." The man laughed.

Celeste ignored the remark and flipped through the stapled photostats, scanning the rows of dates and figures.

"What does this mean?"

"To trap a thief you have to think like one," the board member said. "These are the Walker's long-term deposits, most of them from estates set up for little old widows. They're clients

388 PHILIP SHELBY

who have been with the bank for years and never bother to look at statements. Whoever does their accounts wouldn't care if money was being taken in or out. They'd simply assume the bank was moving the funds around to get the best possible interest rates. As you can see, Eric has been dipping generously into some of them and the shit will hit the fan if the money isn't replaced by statement time.''

"What about these?" Celeste asked, running a long fingernail along a shorter column of figures.

"That's where our boy is asking for a whole pack of trouble," the board member said, propping himself up on one elbow, his hand straying over Celeste's breast. "These are the corporate accounts of what we call shadow firms. They're owned by so many holding and nameplate companies that no one can figure out where the real control lies. Except"—he tapped his finger over a name—"this one."

"Polaris?" Celeste asked.

"Eric made a bad mistake when he helped himself to this one. He probably doesn't know who controls it."

"Please don't keep me in suspense," Celeste said dryly.

"Anthony Fabrizzi."

"Fabrizzi?" Celeste asked, puzzled. "Not the Fabrizzis the papers write about?"

"The very same, my love," the board member said, nuzzling her.

He groaned as Celeste let the pages drop from her fingers, quickly finding his penis and squeezing it. As any man would have, he mistook the gleam in her eye for something it most certainly was not.

Having sharpened the hooks she would use on Eric, Celeste had waited for the right moment. Eric had told her about Anthony Fabrizzi's offer to buy The Tides. Now another crucial piece of information had fallen in her hands: Eric Walker had unwittingly rifled an account belonging to one of Fabrizzi's companies.

Celeste had realized that she couldn't move against Rebecca by herself. Her money was all but exhausted. Even if the funds had been available, she didn't have the necessary connections to implement the second half of her plan. Anthony Fabrizzi did.

Celeste had arranged a meeting with Fabrizzi and shown him evidence of Eric's embezzlement. That, she reflected, had been the most terrifying moment of the whole plan. Anthony Fabrizzi was a man who went his own way. With a single phone call he could make Eric Walker disappear off the face of the earth. Nonetheless Fabrizzi had heard her out.

"So why shouldn't I nail his sorry ass to the wall?" he asked her.

"Because if we join forces, we can have what we both want—The Tides. Besides, don't you owe me something for having told you how Eric's been stealing from you?"

"What do you have in mind?"

"If you help me take The Tides away from Rebecca McHenry, I'll be able to force my ex-husband out of Tyne & Wear. As soon as I've done that, you get forty-nine percent control of The Tides."

"The Tyne & Wear board wouldn't want me as a partner," Anthony Fabrizzi replied.

"The board wouldn't have to know. This would be our private agreement."

Anthony Fabrizzi considered the offer.

"I think we can work something out," he said quietly.

The delicious irony had come when even Rebecca cooperated—unwittingly. When she heard about Rebecca's intention to reopen the gold mines, a move that would strap her financially, Celeste realized it was time to strike.

"My grandfather has been doing business in the Caribbean all his life," Celeste told Fabrizzi when they met again. "There isn't a harbor master or dock steward that isn't in his debt. I've called in the markers, Anthony. All my people are waiting for is your cocaine."

"What happens then?" Fabrizzi asked her.

"They will hold on to it until the ship has made her last delivery in the Angelines," Celeste told him. "By then it should be a matter of days before McHenry signs the last authorization and The Tides goes public. As soon as that happens, the cocaine is planted in the resorts and the police in each jurisdiction are notified."

"A coordinated bust," Fabrizzi concluded. "One strike after another. Arrests, panic among the guests, total shutdown."

"And The Tides stock falls through the floor," Celeste said softly.

"You're assuming that as soon as Tyne & Wear announces it will buy the stock, its price will rise dramatically," Fabrizzi observed. "A hell of a gamble."

"It will happen," Celeste said firmly. "You needn't worry about it."

"I don't have to worry," Fabrizzi said delicately. "I'll be holding collateral."

The clock striking the hour broke Celeste's reverie.

"If you don't mind, I'd like to get on with this," Anthony Fabrizzi said.

Celeste knew what he was asking for. She took a large sealed envelope from her purse and pushed it across the table. Anthony Fabrizzi tore open the flap and Celeste's founder's shares spilled onto the polished veneer.

Celeste's lips tightened as she watched Fabrizzi shuffle through the shares. This, her birthright, was what she had had to mortgage in order to get his help. Because not only had Anthony Fabrizzi used his contacts to procure the cocaine and arrange for its shipment, he had also paid for it.

Celeste had bridled when Fabrizzi had demanded the shares as collateral.

"The cocaine you're supplying is worth only a fraction of their value," she had protested hotly.

"Of course it is," Anthony Fabrizzi had replied coldly. "Then there's my time and effort to consider."

"Even so!"

Fabrizzi had spread his hands out, palms up, and given a tiny shrug.

"If you have the million in cash . . ." he said slowly.

But she didn't have it and they both knew it. Celeste had no choice but to agree that the founder's shares would remain in Fabrizzi's possession, safely hidden in the crypts until she paid him back—with dramatically increased Tides stock.

It wouldn't be all that bad, Celeste had reckoned. They would be partners and, if she had her way, a great deal more as well.

Anthony Fabrizzi locked the shares away and phoned the guard.

"I believe this calls for a celebration," he said.

"What did you have in mind?" Celeste asked softly.

"Dinner at my apartment. I'm trying out a new chef for one of my hotels."

"Sounds delicious."

"I've asked Eric to join us," Anthony added. "When it comes this close to the wire, his type always needs reassuring. My driver will pick up both of you."

Celeste pouted then sighed. Anthony was right, as usual. Eric needed to have his hand held. But there was always later.

*   *   *

The photographer had once been employed by the FBI and had achieved a reputation as the best photo surveillance specialist in the business. However, he discovered that on the public market his talents commanded ten times the money the Bureau paid him. A client such as Anthony Fabrizzi was even more generous.

Having been told exactly what was needed, the photographer stationed his understudy on the street near the front doors of the Pierre. When the Fabrizzi limousine pulled up to the curb, the understudy quickly snapped Eric Walker helping Celeste Lambros from the car. The next frames caught the couple in profile as they swept past the uniformed doorman.

Inside, the photographer was waiting. He got two shots of the man talking to the woman, his head inclined toward her. From that angle it seemed as though they were about to kiss. Another one caught the woman's hand grazing his cheek. That she was reaching for a bit of lint on the shoulder of his suit didn't matter. To the untrained eye the gesture was unmistakably intimate. A final few frames froze the couple as they entered the elevator. Who would know that this particular bank of cars serviced only the residents who had apartments in the hotel?

The photographer left the hotel, picked up his understudy, and hailed a cab to take them to his Village studio. Mr. Fabrizzi had said he wanted the photographs by that night. That he would pay five thousand dollars on delivery was no small inducement.

· 44 ·

Although everyone had a different explanation for it, there was no doubt that the shell Rebecca had retreated into after her return from the Angelines finally cracked and fell away. Lauren Peet, who was busy looking after the wedding details, blithely put it down to prenuptial jitters.

"You should have seen me after Ramsey proposed!" she told Bix. "I was a wreck!"

Ramsey and Eric thought that it was worry over the Tides II launching.

"Just wait until the first resort opens," Eric predicted. "Rebecca will be fine."

On August 1, Bix flew down for the grand opening of Tides II in Ixtapa and found herself confronted by a totally different person. In spite of the frantic pace Rebecca had been keeping, Bix had never seen her looking better.

"Isn't this wonderful?" Rebecca exclaimed as they strolled through a lush tropical garden lit by fat Japanese lanterns. The resort was filled with the first paying clientele as well as guests and representatives of the Mexican government. Rebecca graciously acknowledged their compliments, thrilled and satisfied that her hard work was being recognized.

"Are you sure you can handle six more nights like this?" Rebecca teased her best friend.

The Tides II openings were staggered by two-day intervals, giving Rebecca and Bix enough time to get to the next resort, make sure there were no last-minute glitches, and rest a little.

"I think I can stand the pace," Bix replied airily, helping herself to another rum and Coke. Then her tone became serious. "Are you sure everything's all right, Becky? Really?"

"It is, Bix, believe me," Rebecca whispered, hugging her.

Bix remained unconvinced. Because Rebecca had been spending all her time on location these past few weeks, Bix had filled

392

in for her at The Tides headquarters in New York. She had had plenty of opportunities to spend time with Eric and had used every one of them. But like Rebecca, Eric had seemed cheerful and open, excited as much by the Tides II launches as he was by the thought of Rebecca's return.

Either you're the best damned actor I've ever seen or else I'm really barking up the wrong tree, Bix thought.

Yet she couldn't shake the premonition that something was wrong, even though neither she nor Torrey had been able to find out anything about Eric that would substantiate their suspicions.

From Ixtapa, Rebecca and Bix flew to Guadeloupe, where the French governor held a reception in their honor and one of his ministers made a naked pass at Bix.

"He offered to show me the Paris position," Bix reported after they were on their way to Nevis-St. Kitts. "As though he didn't notice the wedding band!"

"The French see that as a challenge." Rebecca laughed.

By the end of the last opening, home in the Angelines, both women were exhausted.

"What do you say we park our fannies on this little ol' boat for a few days." Bix sighed, lying back in the *Windsong*'s open-air hot tub.

"Just what I had in mind," Rebecca agreed. "Although before I surrender myself, I better call Eric."

"Everything still okay with the offering?" Bix asked casually.

"August fifteenth is the big day."

Less than a week away, Bix thought, watching Rebecca disappear into the forward compartments. And not a word from Torrey . . .

Andrew Stoughton couldn't believe that a single woman would be so difficult to find—especially one like Celeste, who left a paper trail of bills and receipts wherever she went.

Although he knew Celeste was in New York, Andrew had had no luck reaching her at the Waldorf, Celeste's favorite stopping place in the city. While waiting in London for his calls to be returned, he had tried a number of mutual acquaintances. It turned out that they weren't even aware Celeste was in Manhattan. At wit's end, there was nothing Andrew could do but stew. With good reason.

For the last three months Andrew had been negotiating a deal that would make Tyne & Wear's shipping division the sole carrier for Europe's largest construction firm. The deal was worth tens of millions in profits, yet it was being opposed by the board on grounds that the construction company was rumored to be partially controlled by the Italian underworld.

Andrew had worked hard to overcome the board's objections. Ever since Celeste had helped him become chairman of Tyne & Wear, Andrew had sworn to put his imprint on the company. He didn't give a damn about the board's old boy niceties, which dictated what sort of people its members condescended to do business with. He was determined to expand the company and increase his stature any way he could. Besides, Andrew had already assured the principal of the construction company that the deal would go through. He was well aware of the consequences if he reneged on his promise.

As long as Celeste voted her founder's shares with him, Andrew knew he would win. So far she always had because she understood the benefit to her. Celeste had agreed to vote with him on this issue as well. But twice Andrew had had to cancel board meetings because Celeste had left messages that she wouldn't be able to attend. If she failed to appear this third time, Andrew knew his opposition would force a vote—one which he would most certainly lose.

So where the hell is she?

Andrew watched the relentless sweep of the clock's hands toward nine o'clock. The board members would be arriving at any moment. Andrew gritted his teeth as he imagined their quiet smiles of triumph.

Ten minutes later Andrew began greeting the men as they entered. All declined his offer of tea as well as his suggestion that they begin with the minor business on the agenda.

"There really is only one piece of business we're all interested in, Andrew," the chairman of Continental Fidelity Insurance, leader of the opposition, said dryly. "I see that Celeste hasn't graced us with her presence," he added with heavy sarcasm.

"I'm sure she'll be along in a moment," Andrew said smoothly, fighting to keep his anger down. He didn't know if Celeste was even in the country.

As the clock struck the half hour, Andrew had no choice but to call the meeting to order. Tabling the vote, he cursed Celeste and vowed that one way or another she would pay for this.

"Sorry I'm late, but the traffic from Heathrow was horrendous."

Wearing a gray linen suit, set off by a brilliant red blouse and matching wide-brimmed hat, Celeste sailed into the room as though nothing were amiss.

"Gentlemen, would you excuse us for a moment?" Andrew said.

He rose and took Celeste's elbow, guiding her none too gently to the private office behind the boardroom.

"Where the hell have you been?" Andrew hissed.

"Busy, darling. Frightfully busy."

"Doing what?"

"That is none of your concern."

"It is when you jeopardize my plans!" Andrew exploded. "Has the vote been taken?"

"Not yet, but—"

"Then I will thank you to stop shouting at me," Celeste said coldly. "I told you you would have my vote and I'm here to exercise it. Don't make me change my mind."

With Celeste present the expressions of the men around the table changed markedly. Their confidence in any easy victory became resignation. As long as Celeste voted her founder's shares with Andrew, there wasn't a thing they could do to stop him. Bowing to the inevitable, several members deserted Continental Fidelity and voted with Andrew, implicitly telling him that they expected future considerations for this show of loyalty. But Celeste's vote was still crucial.

"I cast my vote with the chair," Celeste said, nodding toward Andrew.

"I assume this means you are committing your founder's shares to the vote," the Continental Fidelity chairman said.

"Of course."

"And you are still in possession of those shares?"

Celeste's temper blazed. "Just what are you implying?"

The head of Continental Fidelity blinked in surprise.

"Miss Lambros, the question was merely a formality, to have it in the minutes. If you'll recall, we have to ask you whether you still control the founder's shares."

"No one else will ever control them," Celeste said tightly.

"I think Miss Lambros is tired from her journey," Andrew intervened. "In any event, I believe the motion is carried?"

There was no dissent. Celeste declined to stay for the remainder of the meeting and excused herself. Seizing the opportunity, Andrew saw her out, then went immediately to his office.

You don't have them! By God, something's happened and you don't have them anymore! Andrew's fingers trembled as he dialed the number.

Can you be wrong? Did you misread something?

He didn't think so. He remembered all the minute nuances that Celeste couldn't control when she lied, the slight change in the timbre of her voice, the anxious way her eyes flitted from one object to the next, like tiny creatures desperate to escape.

And she almost lost control. What would she have done had they caught the lie and forced her to produce the shares?

Alan Ballantyne answered on the third ring.

"Mr. Ballantyne, what kind of connections have you in New York City?" Andrew asked without preamble.

"Excellent ones, Mr. Stoughton. Scotland Yard works very closely with the police department of that particular city."

"My former wife has been spending quite a bit of time there recently. I've reason to believe she lost or gave away something of great value to her. I would be very grateful if you could provide the details."

"Can you tell me where Miss Lambros was staying?"

"At the Waldorf. I also suspect that financial people are involved, perhaps a banker. I'm not certain, of course, but this may help you."

"Possibly," the detective replied. "I shall leave directly, Mr. Stoughton, and contact you as soon as there's anything to report."

"Time may be of the essence," Andrew advised him.

"It always is, Mr. Stoughton," Alan Ballantyne said gently.

Rebecca and Bix returned to New York on August 11. By that time Alan Ballantyne had been in the city for several days.

When she learned that Eric had to go to California on business, Rebecca had toyed with the idea of flying out there but decided instead to spend the time at The Tides head office, catching up on work that had piled up in her absence.

Bix, who had barely unpacked before the phone rang, wished she had never arrived. The caller was Torrey, and he had something to show her.

Alan Ballantyne could not complain about his own fortune. Upon arrival, he had gone directly to the New York police headquarters where a colleague was waiting. The British detective and the American lieutenant, a hulking bear by the name of Martin Essenheimer, had once worked on an international jewel robbery together. They had become close friends, sharing a passion for salmon fly fishing and chess, which they played through the mails. Essenheimer listened to Ballantyne's request, made a few phone calls, and arranged to meet the Englishman after his shift ended.

Within forty-eight hours Alan Ballantyne had the numbers of all the places Celeste Lambros had called from the Waldorf. He had then matched the names and discovered that the majority had been to Eric Walker, both at his bank and home, and to Anthony Fabrizzi at his private number. There was also one call to the Swiss Financial Alliance bank group.

"Interesting playmates your lady runs with," Essenheimer growled. "Wonder what the connection is?"

Alan Ballantyne was having similar thoughts.

"Martin, what usually brings an allegedly reputable banker and a man of questionable circumstances together?" he asked.

The lieutenant thought for a moment and answered with his own question.

"Who is the lender of last resort when an allegedly reputable banker—as if there are any of those—fucks up royally or goes dirty?"

"My thought precisely," Ballantyne said. "Is there any way we can find out if Mr. Walker has fallen into either category?"

The answer came in twenty-four hours later when Essenheimer's colleague in the Federal Reserve's economic intelligence unit unearthed a nugget.

"Looks like our boy has been taking a beating on the currency markets," the lieutenant observed.

"But he's managed to cover his losses," Ballantyne murmured.

"Courtesy of you-know-who. According to Washington the Walker Bank is clean. No one's been cooking the books or scamming accounts."

"When was the last audit performed?"

"Several weeks ago."

"So there's nothing to say the money, if it had been misappropriated, couldn't have been replaced before the audit."

Essenheimer shrugged. "Nothing we could prove."

"Perhaps that's not important," Ballantyne suggested. "Perhaps Miss Lambros and Mr. Fabrizzi are the principals in whatever is going on."

The lieutenant grinned. "I can definitely help you out on that score."

"Do tell?"

"Everybody and his brother has had wiretaps and surveillance on Fabrizzi to try to get something on him. We've gone one better.'' Essenheimer dropped his voice confidentially. "And if one word of this gets out—''

"Martin, you know me better than that," Alan Ballantyne protested, knowing his friend was only going through the motions.

"We managed to get a guy on the inside of that Swiss cheese pile on Forty-eighth. He can tell us what Fabrizzi and the broad were doing there.''

"That's splendid," Ballantyne said politely. "But how does that give us anything of substance?''

"The guy also has a duplicate magnetic card to Fabrizzi's safety deposit box.''

Even Alan Ballantyne was impressed.

Five days after he had dispatched Alan Ballantyne to New York, Andrew Stoughton received a telex with lists of numbers. It was signed F.S.

Retrieving the serial numbers of the founder's shares from the Tyne & Wear vault, Andrew matched them against the numbers on the telex. There were no discrepancies.

Within the hour Andrew was on the line to the detective. The substance of that conversation convinced him to be on the next plane to New York.

"I can't believe it! What is that bastard doing on the town with her?''

The photograph in the *New York Post*'s gossip column was, for a change, exceptionally sharp, the faces unmistakable: Eric Walker and Celeste Lambros. They were stepping into an elevator. Beside them was a bellboy outfitted in a jacket emblazoned with the Pierre's logo. As if that wasn't enough, the columnist identified the hotel in a saucy comment about Eric Walker's upcoming marriage to Rebecca McHenry, ending it with a coy question about his relationship to Celeste Lambros.

Torrey pushed the newspaper across the kitchen table.

"I found it in my office. One of the kids must have left it there. Do you think Rebecca knows about this yet?''

Bix shook her head. "She never buys the *Post*.''

Torrey turned his chair around so that his arms were folded across the back, the legs straddling the seat.

"What do you want to do?''

"I'd like to put Mr. Eric Walker in that chair and ask him what the hell is going on!''

"About Rebecca," Torrey said gently. "Do we show her this?''

"Jesus, I don't know!" Bix cried, running both hands through her red mane.

"Maybe it's nothing at all," Torrey suggested lamely. "I mean, they might have done business at one time or another . . ."

"You don't believe that any more than I do," Bix snapped.

You're right on that, Torrey thought to himself.

"The Tides stock offering goes for Rebecca's final signature in four days," Bix said, thinking aloud. "Two weeks later she and Eric are getting married. So what the hell is he doing skulking around hotels with Celeste Lambros?"

"The stock offering isn't the issue," Torrey said. "Ramsey is handling the paperwork. If Eric was trying anything funny, he would have been nailed by now."

"I know," Bix said miserably. "Maybe we should talk to Eric first . . . before we say anything to Rebecca. Oh, Torrey, I can't bear to have her hurt again! Not after what Andrew did to her."

Bix admitted to herself that it was all too easy to find instances that redeemed Eric, like the Christmas the four of them had spent at his chalet and the good times they had shared with Lauren and Ramsey at the Perry Street apartment. Bix had been moved by Eric's attentiveness toward Rebecca, how gently and thoughtfully he had treated her.

He couldn't have staged his behavior, Bix thought. She recalled Rebecca's telling her about Eric's coming to her rescue at Ramsey's club. That had happened before the two of them had ever become involved. Since then, Rebecca had reveled in the attention Eric paid her. It was the little things that told a woman she was loved, the flowers and telephone calls, surprise visits and small presents. . . .

If I show Rebecca the photograph and it turns out that Eric has a perfectly reasonable explanation, then things will never be the same between us. I will have hurt her so badly she'll never trust me again. . . . But I have to do something!

Torrey put his arms around his young wife and hugged her tightly.

"This thing is tearing you apart and I won't have that," he said. "We'll try to get hold of Eric right now. If we can't, I'll fly out to the coast and talk to him there."

Bix looked up at him. "I want to be wrong about this. Please tell me I'm wrong."

In the end Torrey did fly to Los Angeles to try to find Eric. Although Bix, using Rebecca's name, had pried Eric's whereabouts and itinerary from the banker's personal secretary, it was impossible to get hold of him. Eric was never at the Beverly Hills Hotel and always seemed to have just left a meeting when Bix finally got through to his associates. None of her calls was ever returned.

"I don't like it," Bix said three days before the stock signing.

"Not another word, honey," Torrey said, and left that same evening.

While she waited for Torrey's call, Bix hovered over Rebecca. She spent most of her time at The Tides head office and, because of their men's absences, the two women had lunch and dinner together. Rebecca's carefree attitude convinced Bix that her friend hadn't seen the *Post* gossip piece. Even Eric's being away didn't faze her. Bix's carefully worded questions about what Eric was doing brought only vague replies about some kind of venture with West Coast banks.

She doesn't suspect a thing! Bix thought, drumming her fingers as she waited for Torrey to call. When he at last did, there was nothing to cheer about: Eric had left Los Angeles for Sacramento for talks with state officials. Torrey was heading up there but he wasn't optimistic about reaching Eric before he had to return on the fourteenth.

There was nothing Bix could do except watch helplessly as the hours ticked away. Finally, on the morning of the fourteenth, after a sleepless night, she decided she had to talk to someone else about this, make an eleventh-hour attempt to find a way to avoid hurting Rebecca. Her last hope was Ramsey Peet.

"Hi, Bix," the receptionist greeted her brightly. "We were wondering where you were. Why don't you go right in? I'll buzz Mr. Peet's secretary that you're on your way."

Puzzled, Bix walked swiftly down the corridor, oblivious to the rattle of typewriters behind mandarin-orange partitions.

"You just missed them," Ramsey's secretary said, smiling up at her.

"Missed who?"

"Why, Rebecca and Eric. They left a few minutes ago—"

"Where's Ramsey?" Bix shouted.

The secretary shrank back. "In his office—"

Bix ran toward the double doors and barged in.

"What the hell was Eric doing here?" she demanded.

Ramsey Peet started to rise from his chair.

"He came in from the West Coast earlier than expected," the

attorney said testily. "The paperwork for the stock offering was ready for Rebecca to sign—which she did. She and Eric are probably out celebrating. Bix, what's gotten into you—"

"She *couldn't* have done that," Bix said. "Where are the papers?"

"Bix, she did," Ramsey told her pointedly. "I was a witness, for heaven's sake. As soon as we were done, a bonded courier took the papers to the Walker Bank vaults."

"Jesus Christ!" Bix screamed, her fury making Ramsey flinch. "Do you realize what we've let her do?"

· 45 ·

"What do you call this place again?"

"Cayos de la Fortuna. Actually it's part of all the little keys you see out there known as Cayos Cochinos."

"Hog islands?"

Rebecca laughed, looking out at the coral formations that were little more than specks in the ocean surrounding the largest, the teardrop island of Cayos de la Fortuna.

"Legend has it that Cortez and other conquistadors tried their hand at farming here. Until Henry Morgan came along and made it a pirates' den."

"Aha!" Eric said with a glint in his eye. "So we have buried treasure and buccaneers' ghosts for company. Those thieves must have had it pretty good to afford one of these."

The sweep of his arm encompassed the long red-tiled terrace that overlooked Half Moon Blight and the low-slung hacienda-style house Rebecca had brought him to last night.

"Thieves generally do," Rebecca said. "At least for a while."

The previous afternoon, as soon as the papers had been signed, Rebecca had taken Eric directly from Wall Street to LaGuardia. When Eric had laughingly protested that he didn't even have an overnight bag, Rebecca told him all he needed was his passport. Eric, like most international businessmen, always carried his passport.

From the airport they had taken the dinner flight to Miami, connecting with a Tanhasa flight to La Ceiba on the Honduran coast. A boatman had been waiting to ferry them across to Cayos de la Fortuna.

"What other surprises do you have in store?" Eric had asked, eyes dancing mischievously as Rebecca led him through the elegant home carved from native stone and mahogany.

"You'll see tomorrow," she had promised him.

"Whose place is this anyway?" Eric asked, watching Rebecca bring out a tray of coffee and hot, sticky rolls.

"Just a friend's," she replied.

"Someone you met at Contodora?"

Rebecca had mentioned that Cayos de la Fortuna was a private island. Eric was aware that many Central and South American politicians had little hideaways like this one, financed through the generosity of the poor taxpayer via the national treasury.

Eric relaxed, enjoying the smell of fresh coffee mingling with the flowers that grew in a riot along the edge of the terrace. He had returned from the West Coast a day early because of all the messages Bix and Torrey had left for him. A sixth sense had warned Eric that they were harbingers of bad tidings. He had become convinced of that when Torrey's last calls had originated in Los Angeles. It might have been a coincidence that this sudden interest in him had surfaced on the eve of the stock offering, but Eric wasn't about to gamble. He had flown back to New York on the first available flight, surprised Rebecca, and, much to his relief, realized nothing had changed. She hadn't said a word when he had suggested that they complete the paperwork immediately.

So it had been done. His soul empty, Eric had watched the woman he loved lose everything with a few strokes of the pen he himself had handed her. He had imagined he would have a last minute change of heart, that he would wrench the pen away and tear up the offering. He had seen himself confessing everything, making her understand how he had been trapped and how, in the final moment, he had chosen to sacrifice himself for her . . . and earn her forgiveness.

But none of that had happened. Eric's only thought had been of Celeste. When would she drop her bombshell, and what form would it take? Not that it really mattered. He would stand by Rebecca. In the maelstrom that followed, when everything was lost and she had been deserted, he would still be by her side. Her dream would be gone but somehow, over the course of a lifetime, he would make it up to her. And she would never know, never even suspect he had been responsible for her downfall.

Eric shifted in his chair, suddenly aware that Rebecca had been studying him. He smiled at her then, reaching for his cup, and noticed that she had set out a third seating at the table.

"Are we expecting company?"

Rebecca pointed to a dot in the sky. Eric heard the faint hum of the engine as the seaplane curved out of the sky, made a perfect landing outside the reef, and throttled carefully toward a waiting boat.

"Bix and Torrey?" Eric asked.

Rebecca shook her head. "A surprise."

A few minutes later Eric watched with mild interest as a man jumped off the boat onto the dock and moved swiftly up the wooden steps from the beach to the house. From the briefcase he carried Eric presumed he was some kind of messenger.

"Don't tell me you had work brought down!" he protested.

Rebecca didn't answer. When she greeted the man Eric looked at him more carefully. There was something familiar about him. . . . Of course! He was the Walker security messenger who had ferried the stock papers from Ramsey Peet's office to the bank.

"Fancy meeting you here," Eric said, getting to his feet.

The man didn't acknowledge him. He unlocked the handcuffs that bound his wrist to the attaché case handle. With a second key he opened the case itself.

"No, it's not possible!" Eric exclaimed, the color draining from his face. "Rebecca, what's going on?"

Rebecca didn't bother to look up as she went through the stock certificates and loan agreements she had signed in New York.

"What the hell are you doing here?" Eric demanded, moving closer to the security man.

A gun materialized in the messenger's hand.

"Please, Mr. Walker, step away from Miss McHenry and the briefcase."

Eric responded to the command immediately, then grew red with rage.

"You stupid son of a bitch!" he screamed. "Who do you think you're giving orders to? You work for me!"

"No, Eric," Rebecca said, her voice so dead and pitiless that Eric winced. "He works for the Treasury Department. I think we had better go inside now. There's something I want you to listen to."

"Goddamnit, Tony, I want some answers!"

The cabin cruiser pitched and rolled in the heavy seas off La Ceiba. Celeste, who loathed the ocean, felt her insides churn. Beside her, Anthony Fabrizzi stood at the controls, seemingly oblivious to the rough waters.

"Very soon, Celeste. Very soon, I promise."

Celeste collapsed on the vinyl seat, gripping the railing for support. Her face was pale and her hair was plastered against her forehead, soaked by sea spray. Her body trembled, as much from fear of the water as exhaustion. But she knew that even if she had gotten some sleep last night, it wouldn't have made any difference.

The nightmare had erupted early last evening after Celeste had sequestered herself in her Waldorf suite. She had ordered a light dinner from room service and settled down to hear from her people in the Caribbean. As soon as Eric Walker had called to say that Rebecca had consigned her stock for the loan and that the loan was going through, Celeste had telephoned Anthony Fabrizzi, asking him to transfer the cocaine.

The first call, from the Netherlands Antilles, had come in exactly on time. But the message wasn't what Celeste had expected. The shipping agent who had served Tyne & Wear for years was hysterical. He was calling from the police station in Oranjestad, babbling on about having been arrested for drug possession. He demanded Celeste help him . . . or else.

Celeste had barely had the time to collect her thoughts, when the phone rang again. It was the insurance agent in Speightstown, Barbados. Armed with warrants, the police had broken into his offices and found three kilos of cocaine in his safe. The agent was beside himself. He had a wife and family to think of, a reputation to protect. What was Celeste going to do—

Celeste hung up on him. Her nerves screamed when the phone sounded again.

The news was the same each time. In Saint John's, Antigua, on Virgin Gorda, in Kingston, Jamaica, and in Angeline City, her contacts were being arrested one by one, sometimes only minutes after taking delivery of the drugs. There were impassioned pleas for help, demands for attorneys and money, and once, a veiled threat.

Knowing the police might be listening in on the other end, Celeste immediately distanced herself from her callers. Her expressions of surprise and dismay were genuine enough, given the magnitude of the catastrophe. But they were couched in terms that suggested she had no idea what was going on. Slipping into the role of the good Samaritan, Celeste promised each caller she would do her best to help. She knew she had to offer something, even false hope, to these desperate people who, because of their association with Tyne & Wear, believed she would look after them. Otherwise, Celeste thought grimly, they'll sell me down the river to try to save themselves.

Shortly after two o'clock the next morning Celeste had finally calmed down enough to call Anthony Fabrizzi. He had already heard of the intercepts.

"I want you to be at Newark Airport in thirty minutes," he had told her. "Don't ask questions, just be there. We have business to look after."

As the cabin cruiser sliced through the calm waters surrounding Cayos de la Fortuna, Celeste wondered exactly what that business was. On the flight down, despite her anger and entreaties, Anthony Fabrizzi hadn't uttered a word.

After the boat was made fast and they were on the dock, Celeste gripped Fabrizzi's arm.

"What are we doing here!" she shouted. "What is this place?"

"Please, Celeste, come with me."

"I'm not taking another step until you tell me what you intend to do about this fiasco!"

"What I intend to do?" Fabrizzi asked quietly. "Why should I do anything?"

"You were responsible for the shipment—"

"And I lived up to my end of the bargain. I got you your cocaine, I arranged for the delivery. My people performed, Celeste. Yours were arrested."

"That doesn't mean anything!" Celeste cried. "You were running the operation. You were responsible. No, Anthony, you're not walking away from this. You've failed. And I want my founder's shares back."

"No, Celeste," Fabrizzi said, his voice so gentle it cut her. "I think you're laboring under a misconception. I repeat: I have kept my part of our bargain. You, it seems, have run into some shit-poor luck. But that doesn't mean you get your shares back. After all, they were collateral. And that, my dear, is what business is all about."

For the first time since she had set eyes on Anthony Fabrizzi, Celeste realized what it was she had found so attractive about him: Deep down he terrified her.

"Tried to do? What did I try to do? Rebecca . . ."

Conscious of the security man standing at the edge of the terrace, Eric tried to keep his voice low. From Rebecca's grim expression he realized she didn't believe a word.

"Rebecca . . ." he tried again.

Rebecca showed Eric the newspaper photo of him and Celeste in the Pierre.

"Was Celeste your lover, Eric? Is that why you wanted to ruin me? For her?"

"No, it wasn't anything like that!" Eric exclaimed. "You don't understand—"

"You didn't embezzle for her either?" Rebecca pursued him relentlessly. "No, you didn't. That much I know. You were probably in way over your head by then."

Suddenly Rebecca gripped Eric's face; her eyes, flashing with tears, were only millimeters from his.

"You've got to tell me, Eric!" she said. "After everything you promised, swore to me . . . why? When you were in trouble, why didn't you come to me? Why did you have to steal . . . then run to her?"

He was able to meet her gaze.

"Does it really matter?" he asked. "Don't you understand, I would have stood by you—"

"Don't give me that crap!" Rebecca struck out at him, stepping back. "Have you no feeling at all? Can you imagine the pain I've been living with all these months?"

Eric's mouth fell open. "Months . . ."

"I've known since the day I sent you instructions to go ahead with the offering," Rebecca told him. "That's when the hurt began, Eric. That's how long I've been carrying it.

"I had to lie to people I loved, Eric. I had to create falsehoods which they not only believed but participated in. Like our wedding . . . And I had to play the charade myself, every waking hour of every day. The pain, Eric . . . if you only understood what you made me do."

"All the times we made love, was that part of the charade too?" Eric suggested cruelly. "Are you really saying you felt nothing?"

"I did love you," Rebecca said softly. "I had learned to love you because of everything we had shared. Because I believed in your decency as well as your love for me. But you couldn't trust my love. You couldn't find the courage to use it to explain how deeply in debt you were, that you needed my help. Instead, you deceived me and, to save yourself, would have allowed Celeste to ruin me. I have nothing but pity for you."

Eric stared out to sea for a moment, then spoke without turning around.

"You still need me, Rebecca. Without me The Tides—

everything you've built—is gone. Forever. The Walker has an agreement with you and you need its money."

"What about Celeste's plans to ruin the value of my shares?"

Eric stiffened but he did not lose control. There could be no holding back now.

"I'm your one hope of convincing Celeste to stop her madness—"

"You can't, Eric, and you know it!"

"Then I'm the only one who can help you rebuild," he said, looking hard at the federal agent. "No one can prove embezzlement. My position is secure. Yours isn't. Even if you tried to unload the gold-mining operation, you couldn't raise enough money to salvage The Tides. The gold blinded you, Rebecca. All those do-good projects—"

"No, it hasn't," Rebecca said softly. "I guess you haven't heard the news."

Rebecca went inside the house and reappeared with a battery-powered tape recorder. Snapping in the cassette, she said, "The announcement was broadcast two hours ago. You shouldn't have any problem recognizing the voice."

Eric Walker listened with growing astonishment as the President of the United States, Richard Nixon, made the declaration that effective immediately the historic link between gold and the dollar was being broken. No longer would investors be able to convert dollars into gold at the fixed rate of thirty-five dollars to the ounce. The President solemnly assured his audience that such a move would have no effect on the international monetary system created by the Bretton Woods Conference of 1944. In fact, the very opposite was true. . . .

You fool! Eric screamed silently. *What have you done?*

But he knew the answer to that already. Freed from its link to the dollar, gold would skyrocket, depreciating the dollar as it climbed higher and higher. Among the millions who would suffer Eric saw his own, suddenly anonymous face. And on the other side of the mirror stood Rebecca, with the golden mountains her father had discovered and which, with a few words, had suddenly become Midas's dream.

"Tony, please," Celeste gasped. "Wait a minute."

The climb up the steep incline to the house had exhausted her. Leaning against the terrace railing, Celeste felt her head spinning, as much from Anthony Fabrizzi's words as from breathlessness. What Fabrizzi had said about not returning her shares could not be true. She couldn't believe that the awful finality in his voice, which had thrilled her when it had been directed at others, had been meant for her. Celeste fought back her panic, calling upon all the wiles that had served her so effectively in the past. She moved closer to Tony, slipping her arm through his, her fingertips caressing his hard bicep.

"Darling," she said in a low, husky voice, speaking so that he would feel her breath in his ear. "You're frightening me and I know you don't want to do that."

Gently, as though he were leading a child, Fabrizzi disengaged her arm and guided Celeste to the table. He looked back at her, then walked away to the opposite end of the terrace.

"Nobody wanted to hurt you, Celeste," a voice said behind her. "You've brought this on yourself."

For an instant Celeste's face betrayed her. Her lips parted, the cheeks sagged. Her eyes became huge in wonder and rage. Then it was all gone, replaced by the cold, haughty wrecker's expression bequeathed to her by her ancestors. Slowly Celeste turned around and faced Rebecca.

At that moment both women knew they were remembering the same thing: that scene at Miss Potter's, where, so many years ago, one had heaped humiliation upon the other. It was the first time since then that they had been face-to-face.

Celeste looked at Rebecca, the realization dawning on her.

"Tony was always with you, wasn't he?" she said softly.

"Always."

Rebecca came over and sat opposite Celeste. The fear and resentment this woman had created in her evaporated. An adolescent nightmare had at last been seen for exactly what it was—nothing.

"You should never have tried to ruin me, Celeste," Rebecca said. "There was no cause, not after everything you and your family have done to me. But you couldn't pass up the opportunity, could you? You knew of my relationship with Eric and saw it as a means to get to me. Then you discovered his embezzlement, found a way to blackmail him, and forced him to work with you to destroy me.

"When you learned that at Contodora I had spurned Tony's offer to buy out The Tides, the next piece fell into place. If you could convince him that by helping you he could get a piece of The Tides, you would have a necessary ally. You needed his contacts so you reached out and poisoned him too. At least, so you thought . . .

"What you never even suspected, because your vanity blinded you, was that he might have a greater loyalty."

Celeste looked at the man who had returned to Rebecca's side. Her eyes, like those of a schoolgirl who had just been jilted, explored his impassive expression. There was belief and disbelief, hatred and sorrow.

"I would never have betrayed Rebecca," Anthony Fabrizzi said. "I went along with you only to protect her. To be sure you couldn't hurt her I had to take away your only weapon. That's why I demanded these."

From his jacket Anthony removed the founder's shares and handed them to Rebecca.

"You can't do that!" Celeste cried hoarsely.

She reached across to snatch the papers but Rebecca caught her wrist, forcing it back on the table.

"My having the shares was also my proof to Rebecca of what you were planning against her," Anthony Fabrizzi continued. "You see, she understood that you would never, never surrender them . . . unless it was to achieve something only they could buy. Such as her destruction."

"Tony was also responsible for that photograph of you and Eric at the Pierre," Rebecca said. "He had it taken, made sure the *Post* ran it. All to convince me that you and Eric were in this together . . ."

Rebecca paused.

"I know you won't believe this, Celeste, but after what happened to Justin and your grandfather, I never intended to hurt you any more than you had already been hurt. Suddenly everything you had done to me, especially where Andrew was concerned, didn't matter. The Lambroses had paid enough for the suffering they had inflicted on me.

"But for you it wasn't enough, was it? Maybe it could never be enough . . ."

Celeste started to laugh, softly at first, then with hysterical abandon.

"You bastard!" she gasped, shaking her head at Anthony Fabrizzi. "You were the one who tipped off the police as soon as the deliveries had been made!"

"That's right, Celeste." There was no remorse, no apology in his voice.

Celeste's hand snaked out, gripped Rebecca's forearm.

"You've got to give me back the shares!" she shouted. "I'm

ruined without them. My grandfather's care . . . I won't be able to help him.''

"You'll find a way, Celeste," Rebecca told her quietly. "You always have. But you will never see the shares again. Once, you helped steal what was mine. Now I am serving notice to Tyne & Wear: As long as I hold the founder's shares, no one, ever, tries to hurt me again!''

"You're *giving* her the shares?" Celeste cried.

"They belong to her much more than to anyone else." Anthony Fabrizzi shrugged. "Including you, Celeste."

Her eyes were blazing like those of a trapped animal.

"You think you're so clever, the pair of you," Celeste raged. "Well, it seems you've overlooked a little detail. You have Eric's money. He can call that loan in any time he wants. I'll force him to call it! Yes, I can do that because I know everything about him. . . .''

Celeste's voice died when she saw Eric appear, a tall, purposeful-looking man at his side. One look at his beaten expression crushed Celeste. His words were unnecessary, but he spoke them anyway.

"It's over, Celeste. There isn't any way out."

Eric turned to Rebecca. "What happens now, to me and Celeste?"

"I think you had better ask the gentleman beside you."

The federal agent who had posed as the bank security courier cleared his throat.

"Mr. Walker, the United States Treasury Department has issued a warrant for your arrest based on a complaint made by Mr. Fabrizzi of the Polaris Group. Mr. Fabrizzi has proven to our satisfaction that you have been engaged in systematic tampering with his company's account. Our investigation also shows irregularities with other accounts. Do you wish to hear the specific charges at this time?"

Eric shook his head. "That won't be necessary."

"Are you willing to return voluntarily to New York or do you wish to petition the Honduran government for asylum against extradition?"

"Would it do any good?" Eric asked.

The agent smiled thinly. "I don't believe so, sir. I doubt whether the Hondurans would want to antagonize our government by letting you stay here. Even if they did, I would still find a way to get you out, with or without your cooperation."

The agent's tone of voice left no room for doubt.

"I believe you would," Eric said.

He rose and looked at Rebecca. For a moment it appeared as though he would say something. Then he drew back his shoulders in a last effort at dignity and walked by her without another glance.

Anthony Fabrizzi leaned forward and helped Celeste up.

"I will take you to La Ceiba," he said in a low voice. "The plane will fly you back to New York. Go to your grandfather, Celeste. Care for him. Stay very silent and never come back to the Caribbean again. Whatever happens to your people will happen. There's nothing you can do for them—except pray that not one of them ever gets out of prison to find you."

· 46 ·

For a long time Rebecca stood on the terrace looking out to sea. She watched Tony's cruiser disappear in the direction of La Ceiba, then, an hour later, caught a glimpse of its silhouette on the horizon as it returned. Rebecca wasn't thinking of what had happened this day. Over the months she had replayed the scenario in her mind, directing the characters' movements, choosing their lines, and polishing them over and over again. In the end the confrontation with Eric and Celeste had held no surprises. It was in the past before it had ever come about.

But there remained questions that weren't part of the script and that were still unanswered. Rebecca moved to the patio table and shuffled through the founder's shares that now belonged to her. At least that was what Tony had said. But why would he have given her something so valuable, something that without his help she never would have obtained? Why should she have them when he could do so much with them? Was there a final, unknown price he had yet to extract from her?

Rebecca grimaced at the thought. She had learned that there was always a price. To try to find the answers she thought back to that day Tony had arrived unannounced at the *Windsong* and the words which, at first, had seemed too cruel.

"My finances are none of your business!" Rebecca snapped, watching Anthony Fabrizzi come over to her, drinks in his hand.

"Take it," he ordered, passing her a glass.

Anthony Fabrizzi settled himself beneath the sculptured glass rendering of the *Windsong* in full flight and looked up at her.

"They are because you believed what I told you at Contodora," he said. "You went ahead and on my word committed what turns out to be everything you have."

The uneasiness Rebecca had felt in his presence tightened into panic.

413

"Are you telling me you were wrong?" she asked. "That the move to free gold from a fixed dollar rate—"

He shook his head. "It's not that at all."

Relief and confusion flooded Rebecca.

"Then I don't understand."

Anthony Fabrizzi wet his lips with the bourbon and set his glass down.

"By now you must have checked me out pretty thoroughly," he said, his eyes boring into hers.

Rebecca nodded stiffly.

"I would have been surprised if you hadn't," he continued. "Don't you think I knew a great deal about you a long time before Contodora?"

"What do you mean by that?" Rebecca demanded, her skin crawling at the thought that someone had been spying on her without her being aware of it.

"It all began when Andrew Stoughton stole everything your father left you," he replied. "Like so many other people, I was intrigued by how he had done it."

Rebecca winced, remembering that humiliating conversation she had overheard between the two members of the Gotham Club.

"It was only later that I became interested—no, fascinated—by the woman who had been the victim," he added gently.

As she continued to listen, Rebecca didn't know what to think. Obviously Fabrizzi had been watching her, quietly, from a distance. He knew all about her return to the Angelines after a fraction of her property had been restored to her, the months of grueling work she had put in on Windemere, the attempts to stop her that culminated in the murder of Dallas Gibson.

"I almost intervened at that point but I knew that then you would have told me to go to hell. You wouldn't have accepted help from anyone."

"But you had never met me much less spoken to me," Rebecca said. "What was I to you?"

"At first I didn't know the answer to that myself," Anthony Fabrizzi replied quietly. "But there was something about you that wouldn't let me go. I felt I knew you, had always known you. I watched the way you refused to let the world beat you down, and it was all I could do not to help you. I watched you gamble time and again and held my breath until I was sure you had won. I saw what you did to Justin Lambros and I realized that you were no more an ordinary woman than I am an ordinary man. We are two of a kind, yet there's a difference. Part of you was charmed, as though you could do no wrong. The other part, which ached to love and trust, was always vulnerable, always choosing the wrong way . . . or the wrong man.''

Rebecca looked down and saw that without being aware of it she had finished her drink. Anthony Fabrizzi's words had cut too close to the heart, making her feel naked before him. She was shocked, and a little afraid at just how easily he had opened up her life and drawn all the right conclusions.

"This is all very interesting, Mr. Fabrizzi," she said, cursing the tremor in her voice. "And I suppose I should be flattered. But I still don't know what it has to do with my financial position."

"It has everything to do with it," he replied. "And with Eric Walker."

Rebecca's eyes shot up at the mention of Eric's name.

"My relationship with Eric Walker is none of your business!" she snapped.

"But his with Celeste Lambros is."

Rebecca stifled the cry in her throat. Very deliberately and without a word she got up and poured herself another drink.

"I think you had better explain that," she said, leaning against the leather padding of the bar.

Anthony Fabrizzi obliged. In a voice devoid of emotion he told her how Celeste Lambros had come to him with evidence that Eric Walker had rifled the Polaris account in order to cover his arbitrage losses.

"My company wasn't the only one he stole from," Fabrizzi added. "The list is quite distinguished."

He tossed a sheaf of papers onto the coffee table.

"Would you like to have a look?"

Rebecca stared at the papers with loathing. By all rights she should throw Anthony Fabrizzi and his lies out right now. Yet she felt a reluctant confidence in him. Behind his cold manner, she suspected, was a man who understood how painful the truth could be.

"No," Rebecca managed to say. "It's obvious you have more to tell me."

"My first reaction was to burn Walker," Fabrizzi continued. "But I realized that Celeste Lambros wouldn't have brought his embezzlement to my attention without having an ulterior motive. After all, we hadn't met before that day. As it turned out, she did. Celeste wants to use Walker against you—and needs me to help her. If I back her up, Walker will have no choice but to play along.''

"But what does she want?" Rebecca cried.

"Revenge. For what she believes you did to her grandfather. She wants Walker to convince you to go public so that she can destroy the value of the shares and force Walker to call in your loans, effectively ruining you."

"She can't do that!" Rebecca said, furious. "The Tides is solid—"

"If I help her, it can be done," Anthony Fabrizzi replied. "And right now, because of your gold commitment, you're not that solid."

Rebecca shivered at the quiet finality behind his words.

"How?" she asked. "How do you think you can do this?"

When Fabrizzi explained about the cocaine, Rebecca felt sick. Yes, with him, Celeste could triumph.

"And what do you get out of it?" she asked at last.

"A piece of The Tides. A very large piece."

"Just what you wanted from the very beginning, at Contodora," Rebecca said bitterly.

Recklessly she threw back her drink and almost gagged.

"Well, I guess you've said all you've come to say. Now, why don't you get the hell out!"

"Isn't there a question you want to ask?" Anthony Fabrizzi suggested.

"I don't want to say another word to you!"

"Such as why I'm telling you all this?" he finished.

She had asked the question, and that had been the beginning of another story which had left her even more confused about this enigmatic man called Anthony Fabrizzi.

Rebecca heard the soft rumble of engines and moved back to the parapet to watch Tony tie his boat at the dock. As he straightened up, he saw her and waved.

I still don't have the answers.

Rebecca remembered how silent the *Windsong*'s salon had seemed after she had finally asked the question Tony wanted to hear.

"We're going to turn the tables—on both of them."

He explained how Celeste, in spite of her hold on Eric, didn't have the money or the connections either to buy the cocaine or to plant it in The Tides.

"I'm going to tell Celeste that I'll finance the deal and ship the drugs if she puts up her founder's shares as collateral."

After he explained what the shares were and how he intended to use them, Rebecca had asked, "But why should you give them to me at the end? I will have done nothing."

"That's not true. For the next several months you're going to have to live with a man you know is out to save himself by cheating, and ultimately ruining you. Neither Eric nor Celeste can have the slightest suspicion of what we're doing. For me it will be easy. But you have to ask yourself if you can go through with it. Once we start there won't be any chance for second thoughts."

Rebecca had pointed to the evidence of Eric's malfeasance.

"How can you be so sure he'll sell me out?" she had demanded. "Why shouldn't I confront him right now, get him to admit what he's done, and help him instead of . . . of doing something like this?"

"Because he's already cheated you by not admitting his involvement with Celeste. Because if you tell him, you'll never be certain in your own mind as to exactly the kind of man he is."

At this point Tony paused, then drove home the final nail. "Because if you have the founder's shares, neither Celeste nor Andrew Stoughton will ever be able to hurt you again."

From that moment on she had no choice. The poisonous seeds had been planted. God, how she wished they would rot! But they didn't because Tony tended them so carefully, telling her about Eric's capitulation to Celeste the very same evening Rebecca had said she would marry him. She had known then that love had nothing to do with this anymore . . . if it ever had.

"Rebecca, are you all right?"

She felt Tony's hands upon her shoulders, his fingers slipping across the warm skin beneath her sable mane. Gently she shook him off and stepped away.

She had thought the deceit ended with Justin's death. She had sworn then that she would never do anything like that again. Tony had taught her otherwise with pictures and reports, and she'd hated him for that. . . .

"Will the British government extradite Celeste to stand trial in the islands?" Rebecca asked without turning around.

"I doubt it. Celeste was smarter than to commit to paper any of the arrangements she made with her people. It's their word against hers. And she's still a Lambros."

She sensed him moving closer and squeezed her eyes against

the tears, wishing that it would all be over at last. Suddenly she turned and faced him, holding the founder's shares between them.

"Are you really giving these to me?" she demanded.

"Of course," he said, perplexed.

"Then you've got to tell me why, Anthony. I have to know!"

He stood back from her, arms folded across his chest.

"There were times this could have ended differently. I even prayed it would. I prayed that Eric would find the strength to be honest with you. Because I knew you would forgive him and maybe, just maybe, be happy with him after all. But it didn't work out that way, and now you hate me more than you hate him."

Tony paused. "I don't have to tell you why you need the founder's shares. You're alone again, and waiting out there for you is Andrew Stoughton, a killer. He's not going to rest until one of you sleeps with the fish. To defend yourself, to have something you can use against him, you need those." Anthony Fabrizzi gestured at the shares in her hand. "With that you're going to finish the fight once and for all. And it's your fight, not mine. If I kept the shares and used them to help you, I would appear to control your destiny. And you could never love a man who holds such power over you."

Anthony Fabrizzi reached out and cupped Rebecca's cheek.

"Go now and do what you must. You'll tell me when it's time."

As she watched him walk away, Rebecca felt a cold dread envelop her. She looked down at the shares and wanted nothing more than to fling them into the sea. They filled her with a foreboding she could neither ignore nor understand.

PART FIVE

CAYOS DE LA FORTUNA
LONDON
THE ANGELINES
1971–1972

· 47 ·

Rebecca left Cayos de la Fortuna and Tony's house that same afternoon. She wanted to get away from this place, so beautiful yet made so ugly by what had happened. Even though she had known for months of the conspiracy against her, a tiny part of her had steadfastly refused to believe it.

It's true, she thought. *It's not love that's the last to die. It's hope.*

When Rebecca returned to her co-op in New York, she immediately called Bix. It took a half hour to reassure her friend that she was all right and that nothing had happened to The Tides. She asked Bix and Torrey to come over the next morning, then telephoned Lauren and Ramsey and went through the whole explanation again.

By the time she was through, Rebecca was beyond exhaustion, in a manic state that kept her moving restlessly around the apartment. Neither the hot Jacuzzi nor a stinging shower could calm her. Whatever music she chose grated on her nerves. Whenever she closed her eyes she felt the walls and ceiling moving in on her, threatening to suffocate her. The pain of what had been done to her was not the worst of it. What was to come haunted her, keeping her company through that hot August night until dawn spilled over the horizon. It was a new day, but Rebecca didn't see any difference between it and the one that had passed forever.

They arrived together, probably, Rebecca thought, by design. Everyone was smiling. Bix and Lauren rattled on about how gorgeous the apartment, with its dominant blue, green, and white decor, looked. Ramsey and Torrey exchanged anecdotes about having to work in a deserted Manhattan in the middle of August.

The eyes gave them away. Rebecca couldn't mistake the silent questions, the scrutiny as she was measured, evaluated, and judged.

They're only concerned about me, she thought. *They only want to help.*

There was fresh orange juice and coffee on the two-inch-thick kidney-shaped glass table, the centerpiece of the room. Rebecca led them over to the aquamarine sofa and love seats and watched silently as they poured for themselves.

"You know why I asked you to come here this morning," she said. "I'm sure that Eric's embezzlement is already old news in New York."

The collective silence confirmed what Rebecca had already taken for granted.

"I know you've all been worried about me," she carried on, trying to keep her voice firm and clear. "I can't thank you enough for the love you've shown me. It makes what I have to say that much more difficult. . . ."

Rebecca told them everything, how she had been warned of Eric's treachery by Anthony Fabrizzi, how she had kept that warning to herself and thereby betrayed the people she loved most.

"I was afraid that if you knew what Eric was up to, you might not have been able to keep up the charade," she confessed. "As long as you believed everything was fine, so did Eric. That was why I felt we had to become engaged."

Rebecca paused. "But that doesn't change the fact that I wasn't truthful with you . . . or how ashamed I am."

In spite of the protests, Rebecca continued on swiftly, recounting Celeste's role and the way in which she had planned to destroy The Tides. She concluded with Eric's arrest and Celeste's banishment from the Caribbean.

"At least I've saved you the postage of those wedding invitations, Lauren," she said, trying to make light of the matter.

Blinking back tears, Lauren shook her head. "Not to worry."

Slowly Rebecca's friends surrounded her, hugging and reassuring her. Yet the comfort she sought from them seemed to disappear before it ever reached her, like life-giving rain that evaporates before it touches the parched earth. Rebecca was beginning to realize the truth of Bones Ainsley's warning: Her double life and her secret battle against Eric's treachery had changed her more than she would ever have believed possible. The girl who had been so devastated by her father's death, so bewildered and afraid of the legacy he had left her, was only a dim memory.

"I suppose, as the allegedly hardheaded one among us, I get

to ask the sixty-four-dollar question," Ramsey said. "What do you intend to do now?"

"There's some unfinished business," Rebecca said, her voice glacial. "I want every dollar I have out of the Walker as soon as possible."

"I'll see to it first thing tomorrow," Ramsey promised grimly. "The Walker won't know what hit them."

Rebecca noticed Bix's pained expression. "What's wrong?"

"I know how you feel and I don't blame you for wanting to get out of the Walker," Bix said. "But Eric's actions have already hurt the bank. The Walker has become a major bank due mainly to The Tides. If you pull out, Becky, the big accounts are sure to follow. Even an institution the size of the Walker might not be able to survive that kind of run. If the bank collapses, thousands of innocent people will be hurt."

Bix searched her friend's impassive face for some reaction.

"Closing your account won't punish Eric any more than he's already been punished," Bix finished quietly. "You can't hold everyone responsible for what he did."

Rebecca was tempted to dismiss Bix's words out of hand. She never wanted to hear the Walker name again, much less see it every day on checks or memoranda. Yet Bix was right: If she went ahead and withdrew her money, other people would end up paying for Eric's crimes.

"What's your opinion, Ramsey?"

"Bix has a point," he said shortly. "The Walker board has been frantically telling Wall Street that Eric was the only bad apple in the bunch. They point out that a federal audit has accounted for every penny.

"However, I wouldn't blame you a bit if you pulled out. The Walker leaves a bad taste in my mouth too. On the other hand, if you want financing in the future, I can go in there and guarantee you the lowest rates in the country."

Rebecca thought about this. The Walker's credibility was on the ropes. If a major depositor like The Tides walked, many would follow. Rebecca thought back to all the employees she had met during her many visits to the bank. Most of them were older men and women who had been working there since Eric's father had opened for business. They and the clients who trusted them would be the real losers.

"Get the best deal you can out of the Walker, Ramsey," Rebecca said.

"Count on it."

"Becky, there's something you're not telling us," Torrey said gently, speaking for the first time.

Rebecca saw Bix throw him a dirty look and laughed sadly.

"You're too perceptive for your own good, Torrey Stewart. But you're right."

Rebecca hesitated. "Telling all of you the truth was hard enough. Now I have to face Jewel."

She's the only family I have. . . .

These words, spoken to Bones so many years ago, were just as true today. When Rebecca thought of how happy Jewel had been when she had told her about the wedding, she couldn't imagine there were words kind or soft enough to explain what she had done.

But I have to be the one to tell her! Rebecca said to herself. *I can't let her hear it from someone else or the newspapers.*

Long after her company had gone, Rebecca continued to wrestle with the question. A dozen times she picked up the phone, only to discover her mouth dry, the words gone.

Not over the phone, she decided at last. *I have to do this face-to-face.*

An hour later Rebecca had made the necessary arrangements. She was on her way out the door when the telephone rang. Rebecca paused, then muttered, "To hell with it!" and kept on going. It wasn't until she arrived in Angeline City that she realized how insignificant her resolution had been.

"She never knew a thing, Rebecca. I swear it. She went to sleep one night and never woke up. I took her to the hospital, but there was nothing the doctors could do. The next day her heart just gave out."

Rebecca and Bones Ainsley were the last two mourners. They were standing in the small cemetery outside Angeline City on the bluffs where the wind blew in from the sea.

"Why didn't you call me sooner?"

"Because I knew what you were already going through," Bones said.

"You still should have called me!" Rebecca cried. "It wasn't fair, Bones—"

"Fair to whom?" the policeman asked quietly. "Don't you think I knew what kind of state you were in after everything Eric Walker did to you? In that condition, what could you have offered Jewel? Your being here would only have torn you apart."

Rebecca realized he was right. She could not have endured watching Jewel die. Eric had left her a husk, with nothing left to give. In a way, Rebecca thought, Bones had shown her a great kindness. Now she could make her own peace with Jewel, in her own way.

The policeman placed his arm around Rebecca's shoulder and led her from the white limestone headstone. He guided her over to a giant malelucca tree and fished out his briar pipe.

"We had best wait awhile," he said, indicating the serpentine line of cars, buggies, and people that jammed the narrow hillside road.

"There were so many who loved her," Rebecca whispered, blinking back tears. She looked up at him. "You told me the truth, didn't you, Bones?" Rebecca said hesitantly. "She never knew about Eric . . . about . . . anything."

"You have my word. The news reached the Angelines when she was already in the hospital."

Rebecca leaned against the weathered white bark. She had told Bones everything that had happened, everything that she had planned, somehow, to tell Jewel.

"I still don't know if I would have found the strength," Rebecca confessed. "The last thing in the world I wanted to do was make her unhappy."

Suddenly Rebecca couldn't stand it any longer. With a hoarse cry she flung herself into Bones's arms, burying herself in his massive chest.

"Oh, my God, Bones," she sobbed. "I wasn't with her at the end. I wasn't there and now she's gone. . . ."

· 48 ·

The bastard was a gentleman to the end. Celeste had to grant Anthony Fabrizzi that much when, stepping from Polaris's Grumman jet in Newark, she found a limousine waiting for her. At least she would be spared the breathtaking vistas of New Jersey during the ride to Manhattan.

Settling herself in the back of the car, Celeste lowered the bar and popped open a half bottle of Perrier Jouet. It wasn't her favorite but under the circumstances it would have to do. In spite of the repeated offerings from the stewardess, Celeste hadn't dared touch a drop during the long flight from Cayos de la Fortuna.

The speed and totality with which her world had collapsed almost overwhelmed Celeste. But not quite. She had her grandfather's wrecker blood and, on the verge of ruin, did not look back at what had happened, but instead tried to find a way to contain the damage, regroup, survive. As the Grumman winged northeast Celeste forced herself to concentrate on her options. She quickly discovered there were very few.

As much as Celeste hated to admit it, there was no hope of getting back her founder's shares from Rebecca McHenry, at least not in the foreseeable future. Her grandfather's disastrous attempt to cover personally the cost of the sale of Tyne & Wear's Angelinian holdings to Rebecca had all but bankrupted the Lambros family. The few surviving investments, now under her control, yielded a paltry forty thousand pounds a year. Taxes on her properties, upkeep, and staff devoured most of that. A little income trickled in from estates in Scotland and Australia, but this was hardly worth mentioning. The bottom line remained unchanged: For all intents and purposes Celeste considered herself destitute.

And that wasn't the worst of it. So far she had been very lucky. Everyone on the board of Tyne & Wear, including An-

426

drew, took for granted that she still had the founder's shares, because it was unthinkable that she should ever part with them. But sooner or later circumstances would arise that demanded she produce them. The minute she couldn't, Andrew would throw her off the board—and to the wolves.

Celeste shivered and quickly refilled her flute. The wolves . . . Their faces belonged to her friends and acquaintances, people she had known all her life. They sat next to her at Covent Garden or on any one of innumerable committees she chaired. As different as they were, they shared one common characteristic: They could smell blood for miles and they would turn away from her—or on her—in an instant.

So what do I have to lose? Celeste thought bitterly.

The way of life she had taken for granted no longer existed. Andrew had already begun the process by destroying her grandfather; the society she had once ruled would finish it. The key was to survive—and to come out with enough to start a new life, to build the foundation for a new revenge.

For generations the Lambroses had maintained a palatial but little-known residence in the town of Ouchy, a discreet distance from Geneva. The Swiss would welcome her money. In turn the money would buy her protection from any kind of repercussions her plan inevitably brought. It would also care for her grandfather for the rest of his days.

As the limousine sped into Manhattan, Celeste settled the issue in her mind. She knew intimately many men in London, young and old, all equally foolish and rich. When she returned there she would line them up like little ducks all in a row. Waving the tantalizing promise of a huge but suitably mysterious project in which she and the founder's shares played the principal role, she would worm her way into their greed, their pants if need be, and finally into their pocketbooks. The entry fee to play in this nonexistent game wouldn't be too high. She didn't want to raise any suspicions. But the amount she would get from each one would add up to a golden one million pounds, a truly worthy going-away present, hers to enjoy and use once she was safely within the fortress of the Alps.

But only if the McHenry bitch doesn't move first!

That Rebecca might immediately tell the world she had Tyne & Wear by the balls was the only fly in the ointment. Her intuition told Celeste Rebecca wouldn't act so quickly. It wasn't her way. Still, as the limousine swept along Park Avenue toward the Waldorf, Celeste reached for the telephone and dialed BOAC.

*   *   *

"The key for suite twenty-four hundred," Celeste told the desk clerk.

When he handed it to her, she added, "Please have my bill ready first thing in the morning. I'll also need a car at nine o'clock to take me to Kennedy Airport."

"Going somewhere, are we?"

Celeste whirled around to find Andrew Stoughton beside her. Before she could utter a word he took her elbow and led her across the cavernous lobby to the hotel's legendary Peacock Alley.

"You've been a very busy girl," Andrew said once they were seated and had ordered drinks. "I've been waiting for you for days. No one seems to know where you've been."

Celeste ignored the implied question.

"It's nobody's business," she replied tartly. "Including yours."

Andrew shook his head, chuckling softly. But his eyes were very cold.

"Seems that one of your friends has come to a rather ignominious end," Andrew said. "Eric Walker?"

"I don't know what you're talking about."

"What about Anthony Fabrizzi?" Andrew suggested, sitting back in the padded booth. "Know him?"

"No. And furthermore I resent—"

"Show me the founder's shares, Celeste."

Beneath the seemingly polite request was a hard demand.

"Don't be absurd, Andrew," Celeste snapped. "I don't carry them around with me."

"Then they must be in London," Andrew said, sipping his campari and soda. "What a coincidence that you're leaving on tomorrow's flight. So am I. We can go directly from the airport to Coutts Bank."

"Andrew, what kind of game are you playing?" Celeste demanded, adding just the right pinch of world-weariness to her voice to indicate he was boring her.

"You always were the consummate actress," Andrew said. "I mean that as a compliment. But I know you too well, Celeste. At the last board meeting, when you were asked about the shares, you lied. You didn't have them. And you didn't show up for the previous meetings because you were over here, scheming with your new playmates."

Andrew tossed a sheaf of papers on the tiny table.

"Go ahead, look at them."

He knows everything, Celeste thought wildly as she leafed through the telephone records of her calls from the Waldorf, the numbers matched to Eric's and Anthony's names. There was also a three-page typed summary of her movements around New York, including the time she had been at the Swiss Financial Alliance.

"Andrew, you're beneath contempt," Celeste said, pushing away the papers with the tip of a fingernail. "I ought to sue you for invasion of privacy."

Andrew laughed. "Nice try, Celeste. But not good enough. The shares aren't in London, are they?"

Quickly Celeste considered her options. If she stuck to her story, it was only a matter of time before Andrew would know for certain she was lying. As chairman of Tyne & Wear he had the power to demand that she prove she was in physical possession of the shares. She couldn't stop him there.

But there might be another way.

"No, I've moved the shares."

"Yes, I know you have," Andrew said softly. "To Anthony Fabrizzi's safety deposit box at the Swiss Financial Alliance. What I want to know is why."

She was a good actress but not in this league. Celeste's involuntary gasp gave her away.

"How did you find out?" she asked.

Andrew dismissed the question with a wave of his hand.

"Just tell me whether or not you have access to that box," he said. "If you do, fine. If you don't . . ."

Celeste understood the implications. Her mind was racing to try to find some way to turn this impending disaster around. There seemed to be only one course of action open to her, fraught with the risk that she could lose everything here and now. Yet the longer she waited, the more vulnerable she would appear.

Celeste felt giddy, as though she were teetering on the edge of an abyss.

"I don't have the shares, Andrew," she said at last.

She was gratified by his stunned expression and took courage from it. Obviously Andrew was frightened that so large a piece of Tyne & Wear could be in hostile hands, with the potential to cause him untold grief.

"Who does?" he said at last. "Fabrizzi?"

"No, not Tony."

"Then who!"

Celeste sat back in her chair, toying with her string of pearls.

"That's still none of your business," she replied silkily.

"Damn you, Celeste!"

He lunged at her, knocking over their drinks.

"Making a scene, are we?" Celeste mocked him, holding her ground. "We are in public, darling."

Andrew fought to control his anger as the waiter cleaned up the mess.

"Enough games," he said once they were alone again. "Who has the shares?"

"They're important to you, aren't they?" Celeste said. "After all, whoever has them can make life hell for you. Maybe even challenge you for control of the company . . ."

Andrew maintained his stony silence.

"All right, Andrew," Celeste said at once, her voice brittle. "In return for telling you who has the shares I want a guaranteed annuity, for the rest of my life, of half a million pounds."

For a moment Andrew said nothing.

"You've been swindled, haven't you?" he said, wondering. "Someone turned the tables on you, got inside your defenses and literally stole the clothes off your back. You've forfeited everything. . . . Celeste, I never thought you could be that stupid."

Celeste ignored the insult.

"I want that agreement in writing."

"Oh, you do? And why on earth should I give it in the first place? You've got nothing! You're no more a threat to me than old Silas."

Celeste flinched at the callous reference to her grandfather.

"But you've got to know who has the shares, Andrew," she said softly. "Otherwise you won't know what to expect, from what quarter, for what reason. You're very, very vulnerable at the moment, darling."

"Don't you think that I'll be hearing from whoever has them soon enough?"

"Of course you will. You just have to wait for them to line you up in their sights. For that matter, why don't you just slash your wrists."

For the first time Celeste saw Andrew's confidence waver. She pounced on the opportunity.

"There's only one question you have to ask yourself, darling. Is it worth it for you to jeopardize everything you've built for a measly half million pounds a year? If you maintain control over Tyne & Wear, that amount is a drop in the proverbial bucket."

Celeste paused. "Think of it as long-term insurance."

Andrew finished his campari, swirling the ice at the bottom of his glass. Inside, he was seething at her latest bid to control him. Yet Celeste was right. He could not escape the fact that not knowing who constituted the threat, or from what quarter it would come, were tremendous disadvantages. Possibly even lethal. Nor was there any doubt about the threat. Tyne & Wear was too tempting a takeover target for anyone holding thirty-five percent of the shares.

Andrew signaled the waiter for a telephone. Ignoring Celeste, he spoke with a senior partner of the law firm Tyne & Wear used in the States.

"We have a meeting in the Wall Street district," he announced, getting to his feet. "You'll get your annuity. But I'm warning you, Celeste, if I find out you've lied to me . . ."

"Never, darling," Celeste said, hiding her smile behind downcast, seemingly contrite eyes.

Ninety minutes later, after the documents had been executed, Celeste told Andrew who had the founder's shares. She couldn't hide her satisfaction as she watched his expression change from incredulity to rage.

"Shall I get you a glass of water?" Celeste asked solicitously. His skin was so mottled that for an instant she thought he might collapse then and there.

"You must learn to take better care of yourself," she advised with mock concern. "Otherwise that bitch will be the death of you."

· 49 ·

Rebecca did not return to New York after Jewel's funeral. She telephoned Bix from the *Windsong* and asked her to look after the head office. She would remain here in the Caribbean, checking on the Tides II resorts personally. There was also something else she had to do.

The day after the funeral Rebecca went to Jewel's little cottage on the mainland, the place she had considered her real home for so long. She walked through the silent rooms, touching familiar objects, gazing at old photographs in lacquered wood frames. She tipped back Jewel's old rocking chair and listened to it creak. When she had come to terms with the silence and emptiness, Rebecca carefully went through Jewel's possessions. The clothing, utensils, and furniture were consigned to charity. She packed the photograph albums and personal mementos and had them brought out to the *Windsong*.

When the house was empty Rebecca made an appointment with the minister of Health and Welfare. At the end of the two-hour meeting she had the agreement she wanted. Jewel's house, renovated and expanded, would become the foundation for an orphanage. She knew it was a project Jewel would have loved.

For the next several months the *Windsong* prowled the Caribbean. Tides general managers were kept on their toes, never knowing if the next morning they would see the sleek vessel riding anchor off their property.

The *Windsong* visited all Tides II resorts. Often Rebecca would spend a week or more in each location, scrutinizing the operations, making hands-on inspections, and holding roundtable discussions with her employees. The problems, as Rebecca soon learned, were few and fairly minor. Her policy of training her own staff was paying handsome dividends. Incidents of theft, "spillage," and absenteeism were rare.

432

In the fall the *Windsong* anchored off the Angelines-British Honduras border and Rebecca took a helicopter to the mining sites. Each one had been converted into a self-sustaining miniature town, with cottages for the workers, a bar and movie theater, library, infirmary, and, most important, a state-of-the-art kitchen. Her investment in brand-new mining equipment, made before the manufacturers jacked up their prices, was proving a boon. Site foremen explained how they were able to dig deeper, faster, and retrieve more ore than any other operation in the region. The bottom line showed Rebecca this wasn't an idle boast.

Afterward Rebecca flew to Pusilha. There she watched the progress of the excavations and was amazed by how much of the ancient city had been unearthed. Her previous best estimate for uncovering the entire site had been five years. Now that figure could be halved.

Rebecca spent her days in the jungle walking with guides along trails her father and Dallas Gibson had blazed. It was here, in the middle of untamed beauty, that she felt closest to them both. Her nights were shared with the University of Chicago archaeologists, young men and women who poured every ounce of their intelligence and enthusiasm into deciphering the Mayan codices. They were excited and intrigued by the five oval jade pieces Rebecca had brought with her, a legacy Jewel had kept for her. Only one of the stones yielded any clues to its origin and secret. The rest stymied the archaeologists. Rebecca, who had needed only that one clue, disappeared into the jungles and wasn't seen for several weeks. When she returned she did not say where she had been nor what, if anything, she had found. The Mayans who had accompanied her remained mute.

As November passed into December, Rebecca happened to hear that Miss Potter's school had fallen on hard times. Miss Potter, who had given almost forty-five years of her life to the institution, had seen her endowment dry up when Tyne & Wear's largess was terminated by its new chairman, Andrew Stoughton. Since it was a private school, no government assistance was forthcoming. Without a benefactor the new year would ring in the end of an Angelinian tradition.

Rebecca admitted that she, of all people, had no obligations to Miss Potter's. Yet if she stood by and did nothing, Angelinian children would be the ones to suffer. Calling her Zurich banker, Rebecca made arrangements for a large sum to be presented to the school. There were only two stipulations: the benefactor would remain anonymous and the school would triple the number of scholarship girls.

With Christmas only a few weeks away, the *Windsong* steamed back into Angeline City harbor. Although her office had been inundated with invitations from around the world to share the holidays, Rebecca drafted polite regrets to everyone except Bix and Lauren. She knew they expected her to be with them. It would take quite a turn of phrase to explain exactly why she couldn't commit herself, what—or more precisely, who—it was she was waiting for.

Tony . . . No matter how busy Rebecca had kept, her thoughts invariably returned to him. Sometimes late at night she would open the safe secreted in her bedroom and take out the Tyne & Wear founder's shares. As soon as she touched them she felt their power and reveled in it. Yet just as quickly that same power turned against her. The shares became enticing bait, tempting her to accept them. Time after time the same thought ran through her mind: *When will he finally demand his price? How will he let me know exactly why he gave them to me?* But Tony had not attempted to contact her. Through sporadic references to him in the papers, Rebecca watched him guide and expand the Polaris hotel chain. It seemed he had forgotten all about her.

As Christmas approached, Rebecca found herself thinking about Tony in a different way. In spite of the pace of her life, these last few months had been terribly lonely. Eric's treachery only sharpened the emptiness she felt, made the tears she cried for Dallas Gibson and the memory of his gentle love all the more bitter. Inevitably she would see Tony in another light, as a man who had boldly entered her life and prevented her from making a terrible mistake.

Instead of gratitude I rewarded him with suspicion, Rebecca thought. Instead of accepting his reassurances, I've waited for the ax to fall. Yet in my heart I know he cares about me. It was in his eyes, the way he touched me, the way he realized I couldn't help but hate him for having exposed Eric. . . .

Suddenly Rebecca wanted very much to see him again. Pushing away her suspicions, she telephoned Polaris headquarters in New York, only to have a personal secretary tell her that Anthony Fabrizzi was spending the holiday with friends and could not be reached.

That's exactly what I deserve! Rebecca thought angrily and resigned herself to a solitary Christmas.

*   *   *

The multicolored lights strung across the *Windsong*'s super-structure made the vessel appear a fairy-tale playground. Yet for all the gaiety the decorations implied, they served only to accent the silence around the magnificent ship.

Rebecca had given her crew liberty for Christmas week. Knowing that their mistress would be alone, some of the men had volunteered to remain on board. Rebecca would not hear of it. On Christmas Eve afternoon she inundated them with presents for themselves and their families and after some holiday cheer sent them off to loved ones in Angeline City.

Fixing herself a cold supper from the grand buffet the chef had left behind for her, Rebecca settled herself in her cabin and placed phone calls to friends around the world. Because of the different time zones she had celebrated Christmas twice before the security alarms went off.

Rebecca reached for the revolver tucked into a panel beneath her bed and cautiously made her way topside. Because of the lights, there were few places an intruder could hide. Rebecca spotted him at once, standing silently on the fantail.

"Identify yourself!" she called out.

"Ho, ho, ho!"

Rebecca's heart leapt as soon as she recognized the voice. She slipped the revolver beneath the tarpaulin that covered one of the Danzi speedboats and walked toward her visitor.

"I'm afraid, Mr. Fabrizzi, that you're not exactly my idea of Santa Claus," Rebecca said, critically examining Tony's dinner jacket.

She looked up into his black eyes and felt their caress.

"What on earth are you doing here? Your office said you were away—"

Just as had happened that night on Contodora, she felt herself sliding into his arms. His cheek grazed hers, and his fingers gently cupped her face, forcing her to look at him.

"Have you been a good little girl?" Tony whispered.

"Mmm . . ."

Then very slowly he kissed her, his lips pressing on hers, his tongue pushing through her teeth until Rebecca opened her mouth for him. She wrapped herself around his body, feeling a long, exquisite shudder work through hers.

When they finally drifted apart, Rebecca murmured, "But Santa, you didn't even bring your bag."

"I sleep naked. And I always stay for breakfast. . . ."

*   *   *

As Christmas passed, then New Year's Day, the *Windsong* became their haven, a refuge the world could not intrude upon.

Sometimes, after they had made love, Rebecca would slip out of bed and in the privacy of the bathroom stare at herself in the full-length mirror. The woman looking back at her was the same yet not the same.

Rebecca couldn't deny that she was attracted to Tony physically. She loved his broad chest and smooth, well-muscled limbs. When they made love he demanded things from her she had never before experienced. He roamed over her body at will, introducing her to pleasures and sensations she had never been aware of. He took her at any hour of the day or night, in any place or position he desired. The moments of shame, brought on by her eagerness to please him, were fleeting. Quickly they metamorphosed from submissiveness into aggression. It was Rebecca who would step into the shower when Tony was there, fondle and stroke him until he grew hard, take his head and guide his lips across her breasts, then down, clutching him as he tongued her.

But even as she gorged herself on him, sating every bit of loneliness and hunger that had welled within her, Rebecca realized there was more to their union than just lovemaking. They were like the last two people on earth, lost in a journey of endless discovery. Sometimes the fury and passion of their commitment frightened her, yet she couldn't deny that every time they kissed or touched or held each other they only strengthened the bond between them, realized what, in the end, had to be their common destiny.

During those peerless January days on board the *Windsong*, Rebecca's office was awash in blueprints and construction specifications. Looking over her shoulder, Tony noticed that the plans had been drafted almost a quarter century ago.

"They belonged to my father," Rebecca explained. "Skyscape, our home, was his vision. The contractors assure me they can duplicate everything right down to the last detail."

Rebecca pressed her cheek against his hand, resting on her shoulder.

"I want a home, Tony, a real home where I feel I belong and which no one can take away from me." She glanced up at him. "A home someone would want to share with me."

Tony understood exactly what Rebecca was asking for. In the evenings, after the crew had retired, he would lead her to the upper deck and there, under the brilliance of spinning constellations, open his life to her. He told her about his father, Michele Fabrizzi, who had arrived in America from Naples at the height of the Depression and had carved out an empire that extended from the northeast ports to the meat-packing houses in the Midwest to the gambling palaces of Nevada.

"The war put my father over the top," Tony said. "When it was over he used his army contacts to get huge construction contracts in Europe. Today, if you want something built in France, Germany, or Italy, you're going to have to deal with the Fabrizzis one way or another."

There were moments when Rebecca was tempted to ask about the dark side of Michele Fabrizzi's legacy and Tony's role in it. She had read enough accounts to understand that while Tony's father had never been convicted on any specific charges, his name and organization had been indisputably linked to the drug trade, prostitution, and loan sharking.

Do I really have to know about that? she asked herself. Tony has nothing to do with that world. It can't touch us or what we have. I won't let it.

Tony went on to explain how his three brothers now ran the empire their father had founded, each responsible for a different fiefdom.

"As the eldest, you got the plum," Rebecca said. "The hotel group."

But that wasn't the case at all. Tony explained how he had watched the explosive growth of Las Vegas in the fifties. He had predicted that the boom in nickel-and-dime junkets would follow the course of the economy. In hard times these mom-and-pop players would melt away. The trick was to cultivate gamblers whose fortunes and business acumen would make them impervious to the winds of economic change.

"I conceived Polaris to be the very best—in shows, accommodations, amenities," Tony said. "Some people use interior designers. I went to Hollywood and got the top set-design talent. I have people in every major casino in the world telling me what the competition is up to. Every time some rocker makes his first million he's plugged into my circuit. I read *The Wall Street Journal* like the Bible because it's the best way to keep track of my clients. Whenever some tinkerer in a garage shop patents a better mousetrap I know about it. If he hits the jackpot, he's at my tables the next day."

"Naturally you run all this on the strength of your warm personality," Rebecca teased.

She flinched when Tony grabbed her hand, squeezing her fingers hard. His black eyes were riveted on hers, then slowly he released his grip and brought her knuckles to his lips.

"I preserve and protect anything that's mine," he said. "And I don't give a damn about the costs."

Rebecca pried back her fingers one by one.

"I am not yours," she said coldly. "Don't ever make that mistake."

"I won't," Tony replied. "But I love you and no one will hurt you again."

"Is that why you helped me, because you pitied me?"

"No, because I loved you. That's the only reason. You do things for love because of its very nature. You don't expect anything in return. Ironically, that's the selfish part about love. Still, if something does come back to you, you're very, very lucky."

"But you were serious about the offer you made to me at Contodora to buy my properties, weren't you?" Rebecca said.

"Yes," Tony replied quietly. "The offer was legitimate. Please don't ask me why I had to make it. I just did. And I was very happy you said no."

Rebecca swung her arms around his neck and kissed him deeply. She had been praying Tony wouldn't lie to her. When he hadn't, her last doubts about him disappeared. He belonged to her now.

With Tides II running smoothly, Rebecca accepted Tony's invitation to tour Italy and the Mediterranean. She had never been back to Europe for any length of time since the Volkswagen excursion with Bix and Torrey and was excited by the prospect of seeing countries Tony knew intimately. She wasn't disappointed.

They began their exploration in Venice which, in winter, was cold, misty, and damp. Bundled up in sweaters and overcoats, lying back in Tony's arms, Rebecca glowed as the gondola rowers steered the swan-neck boats through the ancient canals. Everywhere she looked there was history, from the sublime grace of the Piazza San Marco to the mournful half-hidden synagogues in the world's first Jewish ghetto, only a stone's throw from the Grand Canal.

Rebecca luxuriated in the sense of speed as Tony drove the Ferrari hard along the seemingly limitless *autostradas*, staying in the left lane all the way from Bologna and Florence and into Rome. They toured the Eternal City like the lovers they were, oblivious to its cacophony and mayhem. Rebecca shopped along the Via Veneto, buying smart calfskin boots for herself and a supple leather jacket for Tony. When she returned to their hotel, the Hassler Villa Medici at the top of the Spanish Steps, she found a diamond necklace on her pillow, specially crafted by Bulgari.

As they swept along to Naples, Rebecca became apprehensive. Tony had arranged for them to meet the branch of the family that had remained in the old country and Rebecca was worried about the impression she would make. The people of the south, he had explained to her, were more devout than their northern cosmopolitan cousins. Tony's relatives, especially his paternal grandmother, wouldn't fail to notice that Rebecca and Tony were living together but were not married.

I'll bet the first thing she asks me is whether or not I'm a Catholic, Rebecca despaired.

In fact, she did. And when *nònna* Fabrizzi heard that she wasn't, she patted Rebecca's hand, saying that she knew exactly the right priest to lead her through conversion before she and Tony married.

In the house of Fabrizzi, Rebecca discovered the warmth and joy that radiates from a large, tightly knit family. There were Milanese cousins, nieces who held court in Rome, and somber, ageless men who looked as though they had just come from the hills where sheep grazed under the shadow of Vesuvius. Meals were taken in the garden, at a long communal table where everyone gossiped contentedly. Rebecca endeared herself to the *nònna* when she joined in with her halting Italian, founded on her excellent knowledge of Spanish.

"They're wonderful people!" Rebecca exclaimed, hugging Tony as they made their way to separate bedrooms. "I guess I didn't know what to expect."

"At least you know we're not all like Mario Puzo portrays us," Tony said dourly.

Rebecca laughed. "How long can we stay?"

"If we're here for one more day, I'm either going to go crazy or declare celibacy," Tony vowed. "I can't stand not being able to sleep with you."

"Ah, but abstinence makes the heart grow fonder," Rebecca said, giving him a chaste kiss on the cheek.

"Not just the heart," Tony muttered, stomping down the corridor.

The next day's farewells were a mixture of tears and embraces. Rebecca promised *nònna* Fabrizzi that she would visit again soon and was deeply touched by the hand-woven lace shawl the matriarch presented her. In return she extended an open invitation to the Fabrizzis to visit The Tides anytime they wished.

From Naples, Rebecca and Tony flew to Capri, where they stayed at the Polaris hotel then on to Iglesias on Sardinia, Tunis, Tangier, and, finally, Málaga. Each Polaris property impressed Rebecca, as much by its attentive service and glittering locale as by its clientele. The guest registers read like the current world edition of *Who's Who*.

As soon as they were seen together in Tony's domain, the inevitable rumors began circulating. Gossip columnists hinted at an impending marriage while financial correspondents speculated on a merger between The Tides and Polaris, the resulting entity to become one of the most powerful hotel groups in the world.

"I wouldn't be surprised if *nònna* planted these stories," Tony grumbled. "At least the ones about our impending marriage."

"How dare you say such a thing about that sweet woman!" Rebecca chastised him.

Later, as they sipped a rare Castillo Ygay Reserva, a white Spanish wine made once every twenty-five years, and watched the sun set the plains ablaze, Rebecca mentioned the notion that had been teasing her ever since Capri.

"You're not thinking of expanding Polaris into the Caribbean, are you?"

"There're more than enough gambling dens in the Bahamas," Tony replied. "And not enough money to make it worthwhile."

"That's good, because this is what I have in mind."

Rebecca explained that she believed the sixties generation would become the entrepreneurial group in the mid-seventies and eighties.

"We're already seeing a swing in the advertising of such companies as BMW and Perrier."

"Overrated cars and wimp water," Tony pronounced.

"Maybe. But the young European professionals are gobbling up the product. Pretty soon it will catch on in the States. In ten years we're going to have a stratum in society that has more money than it knows what to do with. People who belong will want the very best, the brand names in everything from watches to chocolates.''

"And?"

''I think the only place for them to vacation would be Tides III, the ultimate in luxury, service, and amenities.''

Caught up in her own excitement, Rebecca described how Tides III would offer total seclusion, complete privacy, and an environment where the rich and famous could cavort without a care in the world.

''Rock stars, artists, designers, the Hollywood crowd, stock market wizards, anyone who has made it on sheer talent, guts, and drive. Those people are becoming the new aristocracy, Tony. They'll need a place like Tides III.''

Rebecca paused. ''Of course, I'm going to have to come up with a new name eventually, something suitably exotic.''

She reached out and covered his hand.

''What do you think? Will it work?''

''It can,'' he said slowly.

Rebecca misinterpreted his hesitation.

''I won't be competing with Polaris,'' she assured him. ''I'm not the least bit interested in gambling. Besides,'' she added with a wicked grin, ''didn't T. S. Eliot say that only the mediocre borrow, the best steal?''

''I'm flattered.'' Tony laughed. ''But don't you think you're moving a little too quickly? Tides II has just started. You've got the mining operations to look out for. You may be taking on more than you can handle.''

Rebecca was about to make an offhand reply, when she stopped herself.

''It's something else, isn't it, Tony?'' she said soberly. ''Something about Tides III bothers you.''

Confronted by silence, Rebecca ventured a guess.

''Is it your father? Would he see it as competition for Polaris?''

Tony had never concealed the fact that he knew the dark secrets in the Fabrizzi clan. Every so often, when Rebecca overheard a business call, she sensed that streak of ruthlessness common to all Fabrizzis color his voice. But she knew better than to ask whether Tony ever employed strong-arm tactics in his own operations or turned to his family contacts when a problem required special consideration. Of course he did. He had not hesitated to draw Celeste Lambros into a drug conspiracy when it was useful.

Yet for all the power Tony could command, Rebecca was not frightened of him. She had long ago solved the riddle of why their relationship worked. They were kindred spirits, two people whose destiny it was to be unlike anyone else. Each had created an empire based on a unique vision. Each had suffered setbacks only to rebound to greater triumphs. Each understood one could never be greater than the other. It was an equality founded on immense individual strength—and an equally great need.

"It was your father who suggested that you buy The Tides, wasn't it?" Rebecca asked softly.

Tony nodded. "He admires the hell out of you. What he admires he generally wants."

"And you promised him you would ask if I wanted to sell?"

"I promised." Tony smiled. "But I didn't say how or when I would ask, or how insistent I would be."

"You have all the charm of Mephistopheles." Rebecca laughed.

Tony leaned across the table, his face a golden bronze in the twilight.

"My father was just curious about you. Hell, he's still curious. I'd like you to meet him. *Nònna* has probably sent him a glowing recommendation by now. I think it would be good for the two of you to get together."

"I do too," Rebecca agreed. "That way he can give me his opinion of Tides III firsthand."

Tony was quite ready to leave Málaga and fly back to New York via the Azores, when Rebecca insisted they visit the tiny hilltop village of Zamarramala, fifty-five miles from Seville.

"You'll love it," she kept telling him. "It's a world away from this dustbowl. Besides, there's something I want you to see."

Intrigued, Tony rented a car to drive them along the tortuous country roads beyond Seville.

"I've never seen so many women in my life!" Tony exclaimed as they walked hand in hand down Zamarramala's one main street. "They're all dressed the same." He turned to Rebecca and asked suspiciously, "What's going on?"

"You'll see," she said, giving him a brief kiss and dragging him into a clothes shop.

Rebecca had purchased the complete traditional festive attire—a long, full skirt; a tight, embroidered corset; and a lace veil topped by a sequined hat. Tony was mystified by the last object the saleswoman handed Rebecca, a long, wicked-looking cushion pin. He became a little apprehensive when he overheard the saleswoman call it a *matahombres*, a man-killer, and exchange winks with Rebecca.

"What the hell is that thing for?" he asked her.

"Oh, you'll see," Rebecca replied airily. "It's part of the costume."

Tony shrugged and forgot about it once they were strolling in the streets. The sheer number of women—of all ages, all shapes and sizes, all wearing the same outfit as Rebecca—fascinated him.

"I wonder who does the work around here?" he thought aloud.

Outside every taverna they passed he saw groups of women sitting around, chatting, throwing back glasses of local red wine and eating hot spiced sausages. He crimsoned when some of them cried out bawdy comments to him and was shocked to see three women arguing fiercely with the village priest. When they reached the square Rebecca joined in the dance, her black hair flying as she whirled from partner to partner—naturally all women.

Tony sidled up to a mournful young man who, like the rest, was standing against the wall of one of the houses bordering the square.

"What's going on?"

The young man scuffed at the dirt with his espadrilles.

"I tremble like custard when they have their fiesta," he mumbled.

I tremble like custard . . . ?

Totally puzzled, Tony's next words were drowned out by the tinny blare of a horn, followed immediately by a blood-curdling female war cry. The men reacted as though poked by a live wire.

"Run, amigo," the young man shouted.

Tony took one look at the charging women, their *matahombres* held in front like lances, and thought the young man made sense.

Pounding up the street to the jeers and cheers of women spectators, Tony heard howls of pain from the men around him. Glancing over his shoulder, he saw *matahombres* find their marks.

They're out to kill us!

"Ouch!"

Tony jumped forward as the needle pierced his white linen pants, nicking him squarely on the left buttock. He swerved and caught a glimpse of Rebecca, eyes glinting, making another stab at him.

"Faster!" she cried. "Is that the best you can do?"

Several more thrusts convinced Tony he could do better.

Pursued by their personal Furies, the men ran all the way to the end of the village, where, on a grassy plateau, they finally collapsed. One by one the women fell in with them, kissing and embracing them.

"Wasn't that fun?" Rebecca gasped, laughing until tears flowed. "We should do this more often!"

"What . . . exactly . . . did . . . we do?" Tony gasped, rolling over on his back, his chest heaving.

Rebecca propped herself up on one elbow and brushed the hair from his eyes.

"We celebrated the liberation of Segovia."

"Oh. Being hunted down with cushion pins—"

Rebecca pressed a finger over his lips.

"In 1227 the citadel of Segovia was held by the Moors. The women of Zamarramala led the assault to recapture it. Every year, as a gesture of gratitude, men of the village hand over the local authority for two days to the married women. The women elect two mayoresses, give orders to the priest and constable, and sit back and let the men wait on them."

"When they're not trying to skewer them!"

Rebecca helped Tony to his feet.

"Come on. You're not done yet."

Tony saw the long tables set up on the grassy knoll. The women were seated along the bench while men ran back and forth with pitchers of wine and platters heaped with delicious-looking roasted meats. He groaned as a cheer went up—along with a flaming straw effigy of a man dangling from a makeshift gallows.

"Even my ancestors weren't this bloodthirsty," he muttered.

"Console yourself with this thought, dear," Rebecca said seductively. "I'll be needing you later on, to carry out my wishes in a very different way."

As he watched her rejoin her sisters, Tony suddenly remembered something Rebecca had said.

"I thought only married women took part in this barbaric ritual," he yelled.

"You want to quibble about that?" she tossed over her shoulder, laughing.

No, I won't, Tony thought. *I'll never quibble, not as long as there is laughter in your eyes.*

*   *   *

It was their second day in Zamarramala and Tony was exhausted.

"I thought we were coming here to rest," he mumbled, burying his head in the pillow, trying to ignore Rebecca, lovingly stroking his penis.

"You'll get all the rest you need back in New York," she cooed. "Meanwhile—"

The sharp jangle of the telephone interrupted her ministrations. The hotel desk had an urgent telegram for her and was sending it up immediately.

"How the hell did they ever find us here?" Tony wondered.

"Bix can find me anywhere," Rebecca said, throwing on a cotton robe.

When the owner-manager-chef had come and gone, Rebecca returned to the bedroom.

"Well, well, well," she said, handing Tony the piece of yellow paper.

Tony scanned the brief message and asked, "Do you want me to come with you?"

Rebecca's eyes narrowed.

"No, my love," she said softly. "I have to see Andrew Stoughton myself. I only wonder what took him so long."

· 50 ·

In London, Andrew Stoughton was asking himself a variation of the same question: Why had Rebecca not yet hinted—to anyone—that she was in possession of the founder's shares?

Everything else stemmed from that one mystery. The soaring architecture of Westminster, visible from Andrew's floor-to-ceiling living room windows, failed to inspire a solution.

Andrew stepped back a few paces, his Italian-cut gray suit blending in perfectly with the stark white, black, and gray decor of the room, highlighted by cadaverous Giacometti statues, an anguished Munch, and an almost obscenely disturbing Dali.

Whatever the reason, I'll know soon enough. All she's done by waiting is dig a deeper grave for herself.

Over the last six months Andrew had managed to convince himself of this. The faint peal of doubt had been all but silenced.

Like Celeste, Andrew had not dwelt on the past. As shocked and outraged as he had been by what he considered to be Celeste's monumental stupidity, he quickly realized there was nothing he could do to change the result of it. In spite of Celeste's refusal to disclose the details, Andrew had learned the gist of Anthony Fabrizzi's involvement with his ex-wife. The cocaine arrests of old Tyne & Wear hands throughout the Caribbean certainly bore the Fabrizzi imprimatur.

Nor had the Fabrizzi connection ended there. Andrew was first surprised then worried when he read the accounts of Rebecca's involvement with Anthony Fabrizzi. Even though these tended to concentrate on the romantic possibilities and were often nothing more than servants' gossip, Andrew could not discount the possibility of a business alliance. He knew that if Rebecca pooled her resources with Fabrizzi, she might well prove an overwhelming force.

As soon as he had signed the documents guaranteeing Celeste's annual income, Andrew flew back to London. There was a great deal to be done and he had no idea how much time he had to work with. Only one course of action was open to him: He had to get rid of board members hostile to him and replace them with his own creatures. The faster he could stack the deck in his favor, the stronger his position would be when Rebecca finally broke her silence. Andrew had no worries about Celeste. He had written a clause into their agreement stating that Celeste would lose everything if she ever said a word about her forfeiture of the shares.

Month after month Andrew had lived under the gun. Each day his hatred grew for Rebecca, who, with a few words, could bring him to his knees. Her image rose from the veil of cigar smoke when, alone in his office at night, he schemed to remove the men who would gladly destroy him if they suspected his vulnerability. Andrew looked for any vice, weakness, or careless gesture he could capitalize on. He drove Alan Ballantyne as ruthlessly as he did himself, demanding almost impossibly intimate details on men he now saw as deadly rivals. Some he had been able to buy out, at almost ruinous consequences to his own finances. In others he exploited a moment of indiscretion that resulted in letters of "voluntary" resignation. The most obstinate of them all, the chairman of Continental Fidelity Insurance, had suffered a fatal accident while climbing the New Zealand Alps. . . .

For those six months Andrew had lived as though every day would be his last. Driven like one possessed, he had achieved his goal. But as important and necessary as those victories had been, they had a hollow ring to them. There was still Rebecca to deal with.

Andrew's choice of his apartment as the confrontation ground had been deliberate. He did not want Rebecca at the Tyne & Wear offices, where prying eyes and loose tongues would have word of their meeting all over the City within the hour. A public place such as a restaurant or his own club was out of the question.

Contemplating the grace of Westminster, Andrew found himself anxious, almost eager to see Rebecca. Part of the anticipation lay in the fact that he was as prepared as he would ever be to meet her. There was nothing he could do until he knew her intentions. But there were also the memories.

For all the lovers he had had, Andrew had never forgotten Rebecca. How could he? She was the only person he had been unable to vanquish completely. Each time he had thought Rebecca was finished, she rose from the ashes of disaster like the mythological phoenix.

Rebecca's invincibility intrigued him. He thought back to that shy, coltish girl of thirteen who had had a crush on him, and the almost-woman of eighteen whom he had seduced. Rebecca was one of that rare breed of women who had no idea how beautiful she was. Once, her innocence had made her vulnerable, so easy to manipulate. Yet over the years the qualities Andrew had overlooked had shown themselves. The hesitation had turned into determination, the naivete had become a finely honed ruthlessness. Justin Lambros's fate was proof of that.

Old Silas was right, Andrew thought. *I am obsessed by her. But not for the reasons he suspected.*

Andrew was fascinated by Rebecca precisely because she was a different woman now. He was like a man who, running into an old lover, suddenly sees new qualities and dimensions in the same body. He forgets what it was that first drew him to her and what, in the end, made him leave. He sees only what he perceives to be new.

"There's a Miss McHenry to see you, sir," the doorman announced over the intercom.

"Show her up."

Andrew felt a stirring in his loins. He wanted this new Rebecca, a woman unbowed, who dared to hold him hostage. One way or another he would have her, humiliate her, and break her. Unlike the attacks he had orchestrated in Jamaica and Windemere Key, there would be no escape for her this time.

· 51 ·

Rebecca breathed a sigh of relief when Andrew's telegram was passed on to her. She had been expecting it for months.

Rebecca was also cautiously optimistic about the timing. The weeks spent with Tony, especially the time with his family, had warmed and rejuvenated her. Tony's attentiveness and concern had assured her she was not alone. His lovemaking had filled her with a profound joy, renewing a sense of life, even hope, that had been almost extinguished by Eric's betrayal and Jewel's death. Rebecca thought she was as ready as she was ever going to be to confront Andrew Stoughton.

Rebecca planned her meeting with Andrew with the meticulousness of an army field general. From Zamarramala she and Tony flew to Paris, where they took a suite at the Lancaster. Not having brought suitable clothing for a London winter, Rebecca shopped along the Right Bank, carefully choosing her wardrobe for the meeting. Back at the hotel the material from New York and Zurich had arrived. When Tony returned from visiting friends, he found the desk in the sitting room piled high with memoranda and bound reports.

"What's going on?"

"This is all the information I've gathered on Tyne & Wear over the last six months," Rebecca told him. "Breakdowns of its holdings, recent acquisitions, profit margins, and so on."

Rebecca knitted her brows. "There seems to have been a marked change in the character of the board," she said. "Andrew has managed to get rid of a lot of the old guard."

Tony bent over and kissed the top of her head.

"Don't work too hard," he whispered. "Remember, we have reservations at Maxim's."

Rebecca squeezed his hand in silent thanks.

She spent the rest of the afternoon and the whole next day plowing through the research. It helped to look upon Tyne &

Wear as a faceless entity, a corporation without a soul. This way she could banish Andrew from her mind completely.

From the information she had to work with, Rebecca thought Tyne & Wear was not in the best shape it had ever been in. Its Caribbean operations—insurance, shipping brokerage, and land leases—were frayed around the edges, inefficiently managed, using outdated business practices. Its textile factories in the Philippines, Korea, and Taiwan were coming under increasing competition from homegrown entrepreneurs. But in Europe the company had several long-term shipping contracts that were turning a profit. Tyne & Wear had also commissioned three supertankers from Japanese shipyards to carry Arabian crude to an oil-hungry United States.

It was a changing world, Rebecca reflected. Driven by his greed to consolidate his power, refusing to delegate responsibilities, Andrew Stoughton was losing ground trying to keep up to it. Nevertheless, he now controlled the board, and his fourteen percent shareholding remained a potent factor. She could never, ever make the mistake of underestimating him. With that thought in mind Rebecca made several calls to London.

"I have some business in London," Tony said to her on their last evening in Paris. "Do you mind if we leave together?" He held up his palms in mock surrender. "I promise I won't interfere."

"I'd love for you to be there," Rebecca whispered, sliding a hand across his chest. "Bix told me about a wonderful little restaurant in Kensington."

But as she drifted off to sleep, it wasn't the London of pageantry and pomp Rebecca dreamed about. Her mind's eye was filled with dancing flames bringing down Skyscape. Somehow Justin was there, on the roof, and he was falling, falling and screaming but never hitting the ground. . . .

In spite of her promise to herself to maintain her composure, Rebecca felt her body stiffen and the hair on the back of her neck prickle as soon as the limousine brought them into the city. She did not even hear the welcome from the Connaught management. Twice Tony had to ask her if she wanted to go up to their suite or if she was keeping the car.

"I'll go over right away, darling," Rebecca told him, feigning a lightness to mask her fear. "I'll catch up with you later."

"At Bright's in Kensington?"

"Yes, of course, Bright's . . ."

As the Daimler slid into traffic on its way to the City, Rebecca slumped back, closing her eyes.

Get a grip on yourself! she ordered fiercely. *If he sees you like this, he'll walk all over you!*

Deliberately Rebecca pushed everything out of her mind. She opened the vanity in the center console and critically examined her reflection in the mirror. Her features were composed, almost frighteningly so. The touch of red not only highlighted her lips but set off the golden skin of her cheeks. Her eyes did not waver but they were huge, the only giveaway of the turmoil churning inside her. The severely styled midnight-blue jacket perfectly set off her white silk blouse, accented by an antique cameo Tony had given her. A full-length sable coat spilled over her shoulders.

What will he look like? What will he say to me? Will he touch me? What will I think when I see him? What will I remember . . . ?

Rebecca had the answer to only the last of her many questions. Staring straight ahead, she saw not the pale windswept grayness of a London winter afternoon but the fire on a humid Caribbean night.

"Oh, Max," she whispered. "Help me, please!"

"Hello, Rebecca. You're looking lovely—as ever."

She held his gaze, imprinting his image in her mind. Of course Andrew was older now. There were silver streaks in the impeccably coiffed hair. The once-taut skin was creased around his cheeks. Three horizontal furrows etched his forehead. But there was laughter in the eyes, something Rebecca hadn't expected, and an easy smile that revealed meticulously cared for teeth.

Rebecca tried to imagine that face as a mask of rage, the manicured fingers gripping the weapon he had used to murder Violet, his father's nurse. Those same fingers ripping away the intravenous feeds that sustained Max's life, then later, carefully placing the lighted candles through the house, sloshing gasoline all around them . . .

"Hello, Andrew," Rebecca said, and swept past him.

Rebecca hated the room on sight. It had the feel of a cave or a lair, not a home; the monstrous artwork reminded her of cannibalistic trophies. She did not take off her coat.

"Not planning to stay long?" Andrew said, holding his arm out to take the sable.

"Just long enough to hear what you want."

Andrew retrieved his cigar and walked over to the bar.

"A drink, perhaps."

"No, thank you."

"Then at least make yourself comfortable," he said, indicating the sofa.

Rebecca chose an overstuffed chair instead.

Andrew laughed. "My, my, aren't we defensive."

Rebecca kept silent. She wouldn't give him anything more than was absolutely necessary, not one extra word or gesture to use against her.

Andrew settled himself on the sofa opposite her and crossed his legs.

"You have Celeste's founder's shares," he said abruptly.

"They are my shares," Rebecca corrected him.

"Quite so," Andrew agreed. "How much do you want for them?"

"They're not for sale."

Andrew inclined his head. "Very well. Perhaps we can make a trade, something you want—or need—from Tyne & Wear."

"There's nothing you have that I need—or want."

"Then we seem to be at an impasse," Andrew said, spreading his hands.

"An impasse implies that two parties can't agree on a deal," Rebecca told him. "I didn't come here to negotiate. Only to listen."

Andrew leaned forward, elbows on knees, fingers intertwined.

"Rebecca, we're both a little too old and certainly too busy to be playing games. You've built The Tides into an extraordinary corporation. I salute your achievement. On the other hand, I can make the modest claim that Tyne & Wear hasn't done too badly under my leadership. So it seems to me that we've both come out rather well in our respective corners."

"What's your point, Andrew?" Rebecca asked quietly.

"That now we're on the verge of butting heads," Andrew replied. "You're in control of thirty-five percent of Tyne & Wear. I grant you that's a very strong position from which to influence company policy and direction. However, Tyne & Wear is my turf. I have never interfered in your operations. Now I'm asking you to show me the same courtesy."

Rebecca struggled to maintain her composure. She couldn't believe the arrogance of the man, the cold-blooded way in which he could dismiss the past.

What about Max and Skyscape? And in Jamaica, who was

*responsible for running my car off the road, murdering Mr.
Smith . . . and my unborn child? You bastard! Who had Dallas
killed?*

"There are a lot of things I could have done with those
shares," Rebecca forced herself to say. "But I didn't."

"That's because there's really nothing you can do," Andrew
told her. "You see, Rebecca, there's a difference between The
Tides and Tyne & Wear. The Tides is something you conceived
and executed. You had and still have complete control over its
direction and growth. Tyne & Wear is something else again. Its
operations are much more intricate, its scope worldwide.

"I think there is only one question you need to answer: Why
do I want to have anything to do with Tyne & Wear at all? I also
think you've been worrying about that question for the last six
months, without much result. In fact, this situation reminds me
very much of the fox in Aesop's fables. The poor creature
managed to reach into a hole in a tree and grab a juicy tidbit. But
when he tried to bring his paw out, he realized the prize wouldn't
fit through the hole.

"That's your dilemma, my dear. The prize is in your hand but
you don't really have it. Your options are equally limited. Either
you sit like that, clutching those shares, or else you release them
and go on your way."

Rebecca appeared to consider his words.

"What do you propose?"

Andrew got to his feet and began to pace.

"That's the real problem, isn't it?" he laughed. "I mean, if
you were an ordinary person, money would settle the issue. But
you don't need more brass than you already have. Still, that's the
only medium of exchange I can come up with." Andrew paused.
"Of course, the question is how much."

"A lot," Rebecca said softly. "There's not only the dollar
value of the shares but what they're worth to you, Andrew. If
you have them, you have Tyne & Wear as well."

Andrew moved closer to her. He reached out and touched her
cheek with his fingertips. Rebecca flinched, as though jolted by
a live wire.

"What did you have in mind?" he said hoarsely.

Rebecca felt waves of desire cascading off him. For an instant
she was flung back in time, to that moment when she and
Andrew had embraced beneath the sea and he had carried her
onto the beach and laid her down. . . .

Rebecca removed his hand and stood up.

"I don't think we have anything more to discuss—for the time being."

Andrew smiled lazily. "But we will very soon."

"Oh, I don't doubt that at all," Rebecca said.

At the door she turned and looked back at Andrew, all smiles and confidence.

"I'll expect to hear from you."

"I won't disappoint you," she promised.

As soon as she was in the limousine Rebecca telephoned the Connaught and asked the concierge to pass a message to Tony when he called. She then gave the driver an address. Checking her watch, Rebecca added, "Can we be there in twenty minutes?"

"Of course, ma'am."

As London flashed by, Rebecca gave silent thanks to her intuition, which had prompted her to make some calls from Paris. She had told Andrew she would let him know her intentions, and so she would. But not in the way he expected. Rebecca would have given anything to witness Andrew's expression had he been able to watch her pull up to the headquarters of the British Broadcasting Corporation, one of the largest and farthest reaching radio and television networks in the world.

The producer of *Business Forum*, the most widely watched financial program in Britain, also syndicated abroad, was waiting for Rebecca in the lobby.

"For a minute I thought you wouldn't make it," he said breathlessly. "We've only fifteen minutes to air time."

"Lead the way."

Rebecca made it onto the set with thirty seconds to spare. She shook hands with Sir Malcolm Beasley, the moderator, and settled back in her chair.

"I regret we didn't have time to go over the agenda," Sir Malcolm, once a financial adviser to the Crown, said. "But I am sure we can wing it, as you Yanks say. The gold-mining operation might be an interesting topic to discuss in some depth—"

"I have something much more exciting," Rebecca told him.

Sir Malcolm raised an aristocratic eyebrow, but before he could ask a question, they were on the air.

After a general review of the week's financial business, Sir Malcolm introduced Rebecca and shot the ball directly into her court.

"Miss McHenry, before our broadcast you mentioned that you

had something of a surprise for us. Perhaps you would care to elaborate?''

Rebecca smiled directly at the camera.

"Yes, Sir Malcolm, I do have an announcement. Quite recently I acquired the so-called founder's shares of Tyne & Wear, representing thirty-five percent of the controlling interest in that company. It is my intention to use those shares to acquire full and effective control of Tyne & Wear.''

For the first time anyone watching could remember, Sir Malcolm was speechless. Rebecca picked up the slack easily.

"The name of my new corporation, which will proceed with the takeover bid, is . . .''

She remembered Andrew's indulgent reference to Aesop's fable about the fox.

"The new corporation will be called Vixen.''

· 52 ·

The news of the challenge for control of Tyne & Wear not only electrified the financial world, it wreaked havoc with Tyne & Wear stock.

Since Rebecca's announcement came with only a few minutes of trading left on the Royal Exchange, the London price of Tyne & Wear remained unchanged. By contrast, the situation in New York was chaotic. At ten o'clock the market took Tyne & Wear's silence in the face of Rebecca's announcement to mean that the company was in grave financial difficulty. Traders were swamped with sell orders. By one in the afternoon, when Andrew Stoughton issued his declaration to fight the takeover bid and was supported by Tyne & Wear's consortium of banks, the trend was reversed. Market analysts had already figured out how much an unfriendly takeover would cost Rebecca's Suncorp. They had also concluded that a major source of revenue would be the producing gold fields. As long as the price of bullion remained high, there was a good chance that Suncorp could fuel the battle and ultimately emerge victorious. By the time San Francisco came into the picture, the net worth of The Tides had been factored in. Tyne & Wear stock, which had plummeted twenty points, rebounded, closing only five points down from where it had started the day.

Having dropped her bombshell, Rebecca slipped out the back of the BBC studios, leaving a dazed Sir Malcolm on the set and a pack of reporters chafing in the front lobby. She instructed her driver to take her to Bright's restaurant in Kensington.

Bright's was justly famous as one of London's premiere seafood restaurants. Its oval-shaped ceiling, with hand-painted sea nymphs frolicking with lecherous Neptunes, was so godawful it had become a city landmark. Rebecca arrived just as the last lunch patrons were departing. The maître d' greeted her like a long-lost relative and assured her the kitchen was at her beck and call.

Tony rose in the corner booth and crushed her cheeks with his lips.

"You are one surprise after another, lady," he said. "Why the hell didn't you tell me?"

"How the hell did you hear?" Rebecca shot back.

She grabbed Tony's vodka martini and gulped it down.

"It just so happens I stopped by my broker's place on the way over," Tony said. "The poor bastard was running around like a chicken with its head cut off."

The waiter appeared with a bottle of Montrachet from Bright's special reserves.

"You want to tell me what happened?" Tony asked.

Rebecca took a sip of her wine, and the alcohol gradually calmed her. She told Tony about Andrew's offer to buy up the founder's shares and the way in which she had led him to believe she would sell.

"*You sandbagged him?*" Tony said incredulously.

"He never knew what hit him," Rebecca said, exultant.

"Jesus, I hope you never get mad at me," Tony muttered, then, on a more sober note, added, "Why, Rebecca, why now? Have you really thought this through?"

Rebecca was silent until the waiter had served their lunch.

"Tyne & Wear has been in the Caribbean for hundreds of years," she said soberly. "They ran slave ships, lured vessels onto the reefs to plunder them, and over the years developed a choke hold on many of the islands. Silas Lambros was the last in a line of great pirates, Tony. What he left behind was an indentured people who were—are—servants in their own lands."

She paused. "And Andrew is as bad, if not worse, than Lambros ever was. He has no feeling at all for the people. To him, they're just a source of cheap labor. When he can find a better deal elsewhere, he'll close down Tyne & Wear operations in the Caribbean and move on—without a single thought to the ruined lives he's leaving behind.

"I've watched this go on far too long. I don't really care about Tyne & Wear's operations in the rest of the world. I want control to change what they do and how they do it in the Caribbean."

As he watched Rebecca wolf down her Dover sole, Tony said, "And now is the time to correct past injustices, when you have Tides III in mind?"

Rebecca put down her knife and fork.

"I have thirty-five percent of Tyne & Wear right now," she said quietly. "All I need is another fifteen point one to give me

458 PHILIP SHELBY

majority control. Think of it, Tony! Less than half of what I already hold! There won't be a better time for a takeover.''

Tony realized he couldn't argue with her logic. Nonetheless something did not seem right to him. A warning note was sounding deep in the back of his mind.

"Darling,'' Rebecca said, covering his hand. "Please don't worry. This doesn't change anything for us.''

Tony smiled back, masking his concern. He promised himself he would make sure that that was exactly the case.

For Rebecca, it was a case of déjà vu. The telephone was ringing off the hook the minute she and Tony returned to her home in New York. As had been the case when she announced the reopening of the McHenry gold fields, so now Ramsey Peet demanded to know whether or not she had lost her mind. Her anxiety-ridden accountant left messages all over town to the effect that he had dusted off his suicide pact and would make good on his threat if Rebecca didn't tell him immediately what was going on. When she met with him, Rebecca brought him a very loud cashmere sweater from London and a carton of Pepto-Bismol.

"There's no stopping you, is there?'' Ramsey said, shaking his head as he drummed his fingers on the globe. Rebecca thought that if Ramsey had indeed been God, there would be a huge crater in the middle of the Australian outback.

Rebecca relaxed in the familiar office, comfortable with the man and the surroundings. So much of what had molded and charted her life had started here.

"I suppose you want me to tell it from the beginning,'' she said.

"Even the Bible starts there,'' Ramsey said dryly.

Rebecca recounted how she had come by the founder's shares and detailed her meticulous examination of Tyne & Wear's assets and current financial status. She fished out the list of the company's shareholders who would most likely sell her the stock she needed—if the price were right.

"Two questions,'' Ramsey said, lighting his pipe. "First, why did you wait six months? We could have done a lot of groundwork during that time.''

"That's how long my research took,'' Rebecca told him. "Besides, if we had approached any of the names on the list, a leak would have been inevitable. Andrew would have heard and had time to marshal a defense.''

"That's my second point," Ramsey said. "Don't you think you've already given Andrew a headstart? He's had six months and he's used them effectively. Just look at the way he's changed the character of the board."

Rebecca shrugged. "The lesser of two evils. He's consolidated his hold on Tyne & Wear but that doesn't mean he has the full support of the shareholders."

Ramsey conceded the point but Rebecca could tell he was still troubled.

"What is it, Ramsey?" she asked. "Something is bothering you and I don't think it's how we're going to get the fifteen point one percent."

"I've read the papers, Rebecca," he said somberly. "So have a lot of people . . . about you and Anthony Fabrizzi."

Rebecca had known the moment would come. But knowing still didn't prevent her heart from lurching.

"What about Tony and me?" she asked tightly.

"You're aware of his background. You must know what people think of him—rightly or wrongly. There's no escaping the fact that his father is a major underworld figure, and that leads to guilt by association."

"Ramsey, that's not fair!"

"I never said it was," the attorney replied. "But it doesn't change the fact that what I've said is true."

"What are you really telling me?" Rebecca demanded.

"Bottom line?"

"Bottom line."

"If you do not disassociate yourself from Fabrizzi, we're going to have a very tough time snagging those shares. He's a completely unnecessary complication—and one which I assure you Andrew will exploit to the hilt."

"If he utters a single word about me and Tony, I'll hit him with the biggest slander suit in history!" Rebecca said, eyes blazing.

"Perhaps. But I don't think Andrew will fall into that trap. Your relationship with Tony has been plastered all over newspapers around the world. All Andrew has to do is make sure Tyne & Wear shareholders are aware of it. He can let them draw their own conclusions."

"But what about my reputation?" Rebecca cried. "Doesn't that and what I've achieved count for anything? Wouldn't the stockholders realize that I could make even more money for them?"

Ramsey reached out and gently took both her hands.

"Even though Andrew won't tell them how you got the founder's shares—because it would make him look like a fool, unable to control his ex-wife—the shareholders will ask the same question I have: How much does Anthony Fabrizzi really control of Suncorp, of The Tides . . . of you?"

Rebecca's head was spinning. She couldn't believe the insinuations her longtime adviser was hinting at.

"Tony doesn't have one penny in The Tides," she said coldly. "I'll be happy to open up the company records if that will satisfy anyone—including you! For God's sake, Ramsey, without Tony I wouldn't have the founder's shares."

"That's exactly why everyone is going to suspect an under-the-table deal," the attorney said. "Why should Tony have given away so much for nothing in return?"

"He got my love," Rebecca whispered. "Not that he had to give me the founder's shares for it. But I suppose that doesn't count for very much in this case, does it?"

"I'm sorry," Ramsey said.

Rebecca paced the room, trying to burn off her anger. A part of her understood that Ramsey was right. Her association with Tony would be sensationalized. Given her public profile and the magnitude of the takeover bid, the media could scarcely ignore it. Yet another part of her raged that it was nobody's business and, at the same time, cried out for a little understanding if not compassion.

Rebecca folded her arms across her breasts.

"I'm not going to send Tony away," she said flatly. "Even if I hadn't lost so much to Andrew I wouldn't do it. But he murdered Max and Dallas. If I break with Tony, Andrew will have won again. And I'm not going to let that happen."

Rebecca hesitated.

"But I have to know one thing, Ramsey. Regardless of what you think of Tony, do you really believe that he has any control over me?"

Ramsey Peet looked at Rebecca, whom he loved as if she were his own daughter.

"Of course not."

"Then you'll stand by me on this?"

"All the way down the line."

Rebecca ran to him, flinging her arms around his neck and kissing him loudly on both cheeks.

"Now that that's out of the way, let me tell you about my new project, Tides III."

Ramsey blinked at her, then shook his head and retreated to his globe, giving it a furious spin.

By the end of the week Rebecca realized that while she might have had the advantage of surprise and the first shot, Andrew was fighting back hard. On Friday, through what was obviously a well-timed and orchestrated move, full-page ads appeared in the business sections of the world's leading newspapers. Using a strong, direct approach, Andrew characterized Rebecca's attempt to gain controlling interest of Tyne & Wear as a gross example of corporate raiding. He pointed out that Tyne & Wear shareholders had already seen the value of their investments drop and predicted further decline. He warned that the money needed to fight the takeover would not only erode earnings but prevent the company from expanding and postpone or cancel altogether future acquisitions.

Andrew concluded his brief by asking all shareholders, even those who had only one share, to support him and current management by rebuffing Vixen Corporation's attempts to buy outstanding stock. But it was the last three sentences that infuriated Rebecca.

"The shareholders should be made aware that Suncorp's president, Miss Rebecca McHenry, has absolutely no experience in any of the enterprises Tyne & Wear is involved in. Unless, of course, she is going to rely on the expertise of her current associate, Mr. Anthony Fabrizzi, son of indicted underworld figure, Michele Fabrizzi. As chairman of Tyne & Wear, I have grave doubts about the efficacy of such an arrangement."

"The bastard!" Rebecca shouted, hurling the paper across Ramsey's office. "He's slandering me! Ramsey, isn't this grounds for a suit?"

"Andrew hasn't said anything that isn't already in the public domain," the attorney replied quietly. "Your relationship to Tony is no secret."

Rebecca bridled and took a different tack.

"What about the reference to Tony's father? That indictment was handed down ten years ago! And quashed!"

"Then Mr. Fabrizzi may decide to sue," Ramsey Peet said. "But that's up to him, not you. And in my opinion, he won't. Dredging up the past is not in his best interest."

"So you're telling me there's nothing you can do," Rebecca said, still livid.

"In this case, no. But I hope you have a rebuttal prepared. This is only the opening round."

"I'm ready," Rebecca told him grimly.

During the next two months the battle for control of Tyne & Wear became one of the most vicious and costly in the history of corporate takeovers. The dueling fields were the front pages of *The New York Times, Wall Street Journal,* London's *Financial Times* and a dozen other prestigious publications. Rebecca's public relations specialists booked her on every influential television interview show in the English-speaking world. In Europe they arranged for her to appear with translators. Rebecca crossed and recrossed the European continent, where most of Tyne & Wear's shareholders were found. In private meetings she addressed money managers who controlled vast insurance and retirement pools, urging them to cast their vote for her. She lunched with the heads of Europe's stock exchanges, explaining Vixen Corporation's intentions for Tyne & Wear should the takeover succeed. She even met with groups of ordinary individuals—housewives, tradesmen, clerical workers—who had formed investment clubs and whose portfolios included Tyne & Wear stock.

All the while Suncorp's security division kept her up-to-date on Andrew's movements and speaking engagements. He was, Rebecca concluded, matching her stride for stride. For the moment, at least, it seemed they had fought their way to a draw.

On the first day of May, Rebecca broke the stalemate. Tyne & Wear stock had been languishing at a few dollars below its pre-takeover announcement figure of $160. Rebecca huddled with her financial advisers, and between them they came up with what was thought to be an irresistible offer: $180 per share plus a fraction of Vixen stock.

Rebecca made her announcement on Monday, timing it so that it hit the early morning news in all financial centers. That day brokers' phones were ringing off the hook. Orders to accept the offer poured in from the smaller investors, in spite of warnings that Tyne & Wear would probably match the offer. It did, but too late. In forty-eight hours Rebecca had scooped up nine of the fifteen point one percent of the Tyne & Wear stock she needed for control. But the big investors hadn't come to the party. They were gambling that Rebecca would have to sweeten the offer, driving the value of the shares even higher. Whatever would happen hinged on a single question: Which giant, Tyne & Wear or Suncorp, would be the first to inflict the mortal wound?

The rolling hills along the Hudson River's northern reaches form some of the prettiest landscape to be found in New York State. For generations, old money had retreated there, to summer in rambling country mansions well away from the stifling heat of the city. A stone's throw—as several hundred acres were measured here—from where President Franklin Roosevelt had his favorite fishing hole, a new generation of wealth had quietly settled. The restored clapboard farmhouse, with its huge wraparound veranda that bordered the river, was home to Michele Fabrizzi, a man who had arrived in America with two pairs of pants, thirty dollars, and a savage desire to succeed.

"Antonio, it is very good to see you."

Tony Fabrizzi embraced his father, feeling the air rush out of his lungs as two very strong arms were clamped around him. Gripping each other by the shoulders, the two generations took stock.

He never seems to change, Tony thought. For as long as he could remember his father had been as strong and commanding as he appeared today. Michele Fabrizzi had the short, stocky build common to Neapolitan peasants. The shock of white hair was as thick as ever and the restless black eyes were unclouded by time. Even now, when he surrounded himself with the best of what he wished to have, Michele Fabrizzi still had traces of earth in the callused skin of his fingertips. It was more than just a sign that he enjoyed growing herbs and vegetables for his kitchen. It was his heritage.

The two men sat at a round table covered with snowy linen and set with heavy gleaming silverware and old crockery. Although Tony knew his father had a retinue of a dozen people on his estate, not including his bodyguards, there was no one else on the veranda. The paterfamilias hoisted a bottle of Ceratti's Greco di Bianco, uncorked it, and poured.

"You know how they make this?" he asked after a quiet salute.

Tony rolled the sweet aperitif wine over his palate.

"By immersing freshly picked grapes in boiling water before crushing them."

"*Bene!*" his father commended him. "You might be a bigshot hotel owner now but you know what is important."

To Fabrizzi, family, honor, America, and things Italian were important, in that order.

Father and son sipped their wine, silently contemplating the razorlike trim of the lawn that ran to the stone wall by the river and the sparkling carpet that was the Hudson. Michele Fabrizzi refilled their silver goblets, then rang a tiny crystal bell. Tony rose immediately. A thin pale woman, dressed completely in black, hurried toward them, carrying a platter of antipasto. Tony bent down and kissed his spinster aunt who had cared for his father since his wife had died twenty years ago.

"It's been too long since you were here, Tony," Michele Fabrizzi said, plucking a queen olive and wrapping a wafer-thin slice of *braciòla* around it.

"I know, Papa. But there was work to be done."

The old man regarded him roguishly.

"Work? Your *nònna* tells me she thinks you weren't working too hard."

Tony laughed. "I was in Europe. I stopped to pay my respects."

"You are a good boy," his father said solemnly. "Family is important." He popped the *braciòla* into his mouth and chewed. "Family is everything," he amended his thought.

"I know, Papa," Tony replied quietly.

"So tell me about her."

As the soup was served, in a gleaming, ornate tureen, Tony explained how and when he had met Rebecca and what she had come to mean to him.

"You love this lady?"

"I love her, Papa."

"You gonna marry her?"

"I don't know. Maybe one day."

Michele Fabrizzi set down his spoon.

"You're never gonna marry her, Tony, she isn't family and never will be. She's not even Catholic!"

"That doesn't change what I feel for her," Tony said, his voice hardening.

Michele Fabrizzi waited until his sister had brought in the fish course, razor clams, *cappe lunge*, with risotto.

"You did what you did for her because you love her," he said.

Tony understood that his father's statement was really a question and that he already knew most of what had transpired between Tony and Celeste. In his oblique way he was asking Tony for his version.

"So you end up giving this girl the shares, thirty-five percent of a big corporation," Michele Fabrizzi said. "All for love?"

"The man who runs that corporation murdered her father," Tony said. "He also tried to kill her."

"It's not your fight, Tony. If you didn't want to profit from it you should have stayed out."

"It was my decision."

The old man nodded. "And you think you can live with it. But now this girl is threatening you."

"Threatening, Papa?"

"Tides III. Deluxe resorts. She's gonna steal the people who come to your tables, Tony."

Tony waited until his father had uncorked an early Barbaresco and the veal with wild mushrooms had been served.

"Tides III will be no competition, Papa."

"I think maybe you should make her another offer for The Tides, *molto dolce*, very sweet. Now, when she's fighting with Tyne & Wear . . ." He spread his hands, leaving the obvious unspoken.

"Rebecca will never sell The Tides," Tony said. "She would die first. Besides, I don't see the new project as any threat. Rebecca doesn't like gambling and even if she did, she'd soon realize there's too much competition in the Caribbean already."

Michele Fabrizzi accepted this. He concentrated on his meal, slicing up the veal into tiny pieces before popping it into his mouth. For the next twenty minutes neither man spoke. The elder Fabrizzi used silence like a weapon, making his enemies so uncomfortable that they would inadvertently give themselves or their intentions away. But Tony had learned the technique at his father's feet and had become a master of it himself.

"Tony," the old man said suddenly, "I am disappointed in you. You had in your hands what other men would willingly kill for: control of Tyne & Wear. It was your obligation to bring this to the family. Instead, you chose a stranger over blood."

"To you Rebecca is a stranger," Tony replied quietly. "And you want to keep her one by not ever saying her name. But you can't change the fact that she is the woman I love—and who loves me."

Tony paused. "You're right. I did place Rebecca ahead of family. But she is not so different from us, Papa. No one gave her what she has. She went out and built it, sweated and schemed for it. She is a proud, strong woman. Even you expressed respect for her achievements."

Michele Fabrizzi shrugged off his son's parry. True, he had mentioned something about the woman's accomplishments. But that had been done in the abstract, before she became involved with his son.

Michele Fabrizzi grimaced at the camomile tea his sister placed before him and glanced covetously at Tony's cappuccino.

"The doctor says no more caffeine," he grumbled, then reached for the bottle of Fernet-Branca, a deep purple liqueur whose bitter herbs settled the stomach. "All right," he said, pouring them shots. "What is done is done. But you know, Tony, I have always believed that you would be the one to succeed me. You have the best brain. This thing you did will count against you on the family council."

Tony sipped his coffee, giving himself time to formulate an answer. He had to be very, very careful.

"Papa," he said, "you will outlive us all."

The old man snorted.

"But if God feels he needs your advice so badly, then I promise you I will do my part to preserve and protect what you've built—no matter who takes your place."

Michele Fabrizzi gripped his son's hand.

"I know you will," he whispered. "I know, too, I am a stubborn old man, fixed in his ways. But there is hope for change. One day—not now—but one day, you bring your lady. Maybe she can seduce me the way she has cast a spell over you." He laughed.

Tony left shortly after lunch. As he watched his son descend the flagstone steps to his car, Michele Fabrizzi found himself intrigued by Rebecca McHenry. Tony was a strong man, the strongest of all his sons. Either this woman was even stronger or she was a *strega*, a witch.

Michele Fabrizzi banished his doctor's admonitions about sweets and asked his sister to bring him a rum baba, a favorite of his she made so well. As grudging compensation, he had another quart of San Pellegrino mineral water.

The elder Fabrizzi spent the rest of the afternoon on the veranda, oblivious to his sister, who silently cleared the table, then withdrew. He was not disturbed when the phone rang and visitors who were expected were pointedly told to wait.

Michele Fabrizzi turned the problem over and over in his mind until he was certain he had seen every facet of it. Had it concerned anyone but Tony, he would have dealt with it swiftly and decisively, as he had always where family was the issue. But that was the thorn. Where Tony was concerned he could not go to the family, not unless he wanted to diminish Tony, the heir apparent, in their eyes. The alternative was perhaps the lesser of two evils, although Fabrizzi could scarcely convince himself of this. To protect Tony from this *strega* meant going to the one man who knew her better than anyone else. But someone who was also outside the family. Being put in such a distasteful, even humiliating position rankled Fabrizzi. It was a sentiment he had the *strega* to thank for.

The sun had turned the river into molten mercury by the time Michele Fabrizzi stirred. He reached for a telephone and dialed the number in New York. When he spoke, his clipped, dry words betrayed none of his loathing.

"So what do you think?" he demanded, having outlined the details.

"I think," Andrew Stoughton said softly, "that we have a real problem."

"Come and tell me the remedy!"

· 53 ·

When Andrew Stoughton had eagerly grasped Silas Lambros's outstretched hand to help him avoid prison, he hadn't known that he had also come to the attention of other parties. Nor that one particular person had kept an eye on him even after he had disappeared into the bowels of Tyne & Wear.

Andrew had started out as a minor paper-pusher in Tyne & Wear's financial division, which kept track of the company's investments. Another man would have thanked his lucky stars and stuck to his ledgers and tables. Not Andrew. Before his first year was out, he knew more about the day-to-day mechanics of the division than its vice-president. By spending long nights going over dusty memoranda Andrew also discovered how the vice-president was feathering his own nest by accepting bribes from Ceylonese officials responsible for tea export.

Andrew could have reported the matter to the head office and left it at that. Instead, he carefully gathered enough dirt on the Ceylonese culprits to have their government throw them in jail, and quietly renegotiated the terms of Tyne & Wear's agreement. Only then, with executed documents in hand, did he go to Silas Lambros.

To Andrew's surprise Lambros accepted the findings with equanimity. He had known that the vice-president was rotten and had deliberately waited to see whether Andrew would carve out a piece of the graft for himself. Having finessed the matter to Tyne & Wear's benefit without scandal, Andrew had proven his loyalty to his benefactor.

Andrew's singular talent for finding corruption was based on his own larcenous nature, something Silas Lambros capitalized on. What better way to rid one's house of sly moccasins than by planting a king snake? Lambros rewarded Andrew's efforts by having him fired very quietly.

As soon as all evidence of Andrew's ever having been at Tyne

& Wear had been erased, Silas Lambros took him aside and explained what he had in mind. An astonished Andrew found himself working for an obscure company called the Severn Group, whose holdings included mining concerns across the world. But this, as Lambros explained, was only a carefully arranged front. The Severn Group was wholly controlled by Tyne & Wear although the connections had been buried far out of sight. Its purpose was to monitor Tyne & Wear's operations and employees worldwide. As acquisitions manager, Andrew could, on the pretext of being an interested buyer, examine the operations of any Tyne & Wear office in the world, scrutinize its records, and investigate its employees. He was to report any malfeasance directly to Silas Lambros.

As financial gunslinger, Andrew circled the globe many times. He dredged up information on foreign leaders, ministers, and bankers that became invaluable to Silas Lambros in plotting Tyne & Wear policy. He discovered stock scams in New York and duplicate factories in Hong Kong. He pried open Swiss bank accounts and tracked down embezzlers in Rio. Once, he had even been instrumental in fomenting a civil war in a Central African nation.

Yet for all his success and the glowing support he received from Silas Lambros, Andrew realized he was—and would remain forever—an employee. The irony was that he truly enjoyed his work, matching wits with men who betrayed their masters and then one another all the while pretending to be pillars of society. Still, he hungered for more, for the power to control not only his destiny but that of a great corporation with its thousands of individual lives. Andrew had no illusions: As long as he served at Lambros's pleasure, his dream would be stillborn. Convinced that there had to be a way to realize his vision, Andrew began to search for a new, more powerful patron.

The circumstances seemed accidental at the time. A young man from an influential Greek family, who was also an assistant manager in Tyne & Wear's Athens office, had run up massive gambling debts in the private casinos that dot the Aegean. To cover his losses he agreed to make slight alterations in cargo manifests so that certain clients were double-billed while those whom he owed would have their consignments shipped gratis. It was an old variation of an even older scam that Andrew was very familiar with.

Andrew had slotted thirty seconds to fire the man and a full day to clear up the paperwork. He had deliberately chosen to do this on a Friday in order to have the weekend to savor the Greek capital's many delights, historic and otherwise. But instead of finding the assistant manager behind his desk, Andrew was confronted by a stranger whose name most certainly did not appear on the Tyne & Wear payroll: Michele Fabrizzi.

Their privacy guaranteed by a phalanx of Fabrizzi *soldati*, the two men spent a quiet afternoon contemplating the glory of the Acropolis. During their stroll, one of the most powerful crime figures in the world paid Andrew the ultimate compliment. He had been following Andrew's career at Tyne & Wear and was impressed by the results Andrew produced. He was also privy to how Andrew had come to work for Silas Lambros and the hold the wrecker had over him.

"He has you by the balls, my young friend," Fabrizzi said. "If you make the slightest move to get away, or even to try to earn what should be yours by your talent, he will squeeze your jewels until you kneel. That is no way for a man like yourself to live."

They walked on without speaking. Andrew, too, had learned how to use silence although he had no idea how greatly Fabrizzi admired this quality.

"I propose we strike a bargain," Fabrizzi said at last. "I have substantial interests in the Caribbean. Your Tyne & Wear is the most important and established company in the region. Become my eyes and ears. Tell me what is going to happen, whether it is because of Tyne & Wear or somebody else. Let me glimpse the future."

Andrew waited for the other shoe to drop.

"In return, my young colleague, I will lift the veil as it pertains to *your* future. I think many people will be amazed by what they believe is your foresight, daring, and cleverness." Fabrizzi laughed.

"That doesn't solve the problem of Lambros's hold on me," Andrew told him.

"Not immediately," Fabrizzi agreed. "You have the gift of silence. You must cultivate the virtue of patience. There will come a time when I may help you even with that. . . ."

"I think that time has come, Mr. Fabrizzi," Andrew said, taking a seat at the table that the spinster had cleared and recovered with a fresh cloth.

Even after all these years of association, Andrew never addressed the *capo di tutti capi* with any familiarity.

"May I smoke?"

Fabrizzi waved his hand. "Please. You have excellent taste in cigars. Even if I can't indulge, the smoke brings back good memories."

Fabrizzi watched as Andrew carefully lighted the Romeo y Julietta.

"First you say we have a problem. Then you say the time has come. Which do you mean?"

"In this case my two comments are related," Andrew said, breaking the wooden match in half. "With all due respect, your son's handing over the founder's shares to Rebecca McHenry was a problem that is now compounded by his obvious infatuation with her. The fact that Rebecca has the shares, and is using them to try to gain control of Tyne & Wear, has made it necessary for me to remind you of our agreement. Again, with respect, I feel that the time has come for you to assist me in gaining undisputed control of Tyne & Wear."

"And what do you suggest?" Fabrizzi asked.

Andrew shrugged. "I have learned a great deal from you, Mr. Fabrizzi. For example, when you placed the information about Alan Ballantyne's involvement in heroin traffic at my disposal, you literally put his life in the palm of my hand. That life has proven to be of considerable value to both of us. With Rebecca McHenry, exactly the opposite is true. She is a threat to both of us: To your enterprises through Tides III, to myself . . . well, that's clear. In my mind there's only one solution. She must be killed."

"You tried that, Andrew," Fabrizzi said softly, permitting himself a Cheshire grin.

"That is why I am bowing to the expertise to be found in the ranks of your associates," Andrew said, parrying gracefully. "After all, neither of us would have a problem if Tony hadn't been so stupid."

The chill around the table was almost palpable. Andrew felt it immediately and knew he had said the wrong, possibly fatal words.

"Please, Andrew," the old man invited, his voice almost a whisper. "Tell me how stupid Antonio has been. I'm very interested to hear."

"All I meant, Mr. Fabrizzi, was that Tony should have brought the shares to you," Andrew said, backtracking very carefully. "After all, he must have known about our association—"

"It's not like you to make assumptions," Fabrizzi said.

For a second Andrew wasn't sure he had heard him correctly. Was it possible for Tony *not* to have known how close his father was to the head of Tyne & Wear?

"Not only possible," the paterfamilias said, reading Andrew's mind. "It was—and is—a fact."

Andrew was stunned. Over the years he had come to appreciate and respect how tightly knit the Fabrizzis were. It was part of their strength. Not only did they present a united front to the world, but one never knew when a member of the clan was looking over one's shoulder, ready to report the slightest indiscretion or disloyalty.

"Mr. Fabrizzi, I'm truly sorry," Andrew said humbly. "I know how fond you are of Tony. I naturally assumed . . ." Andrew corrected himself. "I made a mistake."

"Fond, yes," the old man said. "Because Tony has always been different, will always be different—"

Michele Fabrizzi caught himself. He had never voiced his doubts and fears about Tony to anyone in the family. He would have cut out his tongue before uttering a single word to a stranger.

In Tony, Fabrizzi saw a new generation of the family. He and his other sons were of the old school. Their actions were governed by the ancient code of *omerta*, silence, which gave the family its great strength. Tony had gone beyond the family. He had stepped out into the world, mastered its best schools, and had made a shrewd marriage of his innate cunning with modern business techniques. His success with the Polaris hotel chain had demonstrated that the family could thrive and prosper in purely legitimate enterprises.

Yet precisely because Tony had been so successful, Fabrizzi harbored a dark fear that he was distancing himself from the rest of the family. There was resentment of Tony's achievements among his brothers and other relatives who clung to the old ways. The resentment turned to bitterness when they remembered that Tony was his father's favorite, destined to succeed him.

To Fabrizzi, Tony represented the future. He had solved such riddles as electronic banking and offshore mutual funds, probed the weaknesses of the American banking system and made it work for him. Somehow he had even managed to get the Republicans to hold their major conferences at his hotels. But because he had also distanced himself from other family enterprises, he had brought suspicion on himself. Suspicion that had grown deeper since his involvement with Rebecca McHenry.

Michele Fabrizzi could make the family forgive Tony many things, but he could not force them to accept this woman. He himself could not fathom the attraction. Rebecca McHenry could cripple Tony, deny him the leadership that was his by right. And this, Fabrizzi vowed, the *strega* would never do. . . . No matter how much the father had to hurt the son.

"I'm gonna help you against Rebecca McHenry," Fabrizzi said at last.

Andrew, who had been carefully searching for any clue as to what was going on behind Fabrizzi's silence, was relieved.

"I offer you my sincere thanks," Andrew said solemnly.

"However, this help will come when I say it comes."

The warning bells went off in Andrew's mind.

"Mr. Fabrizzi, surely you're aware of Tyne & Wear's current position," he protested. "We've spent millions fighting the takeover. Rebecca McHenry needs only six percent of the outstanding stock to control the company. I don't see how we can wait any longer."

The old man sat back and surveyed the tranquil Hudson.

"Sometimes you worry too much, Andrew," he said gently. "You're forgetting how close Tony is to this woman. Let him get closer still. Very soon he will bring us something we can use to deal with her once and for all."

Andrew did exactly what was expected of him. He pretended to weigh Fabrizzi's words then, after a suitable interval, concurred. Fabrizzi would have been suspicious had Andrew agreed at once. He would have never allowed Andrew to leave had he been able to read his mind.

· 54 ·

There comes a moment in corporate dueling when, by unspoken mutual consent, the two equally matched parties withdraw to their respective corners. Each licks its wounds, takes stock of how costly the battle has been, determines what reserves are left, and searches for new resources or allies with which to continue the battle.

By the middle of May, Tyne & Wear and Vixen backed away from each other. Rebecca was only three percent short of gaining controlling interest of the huge conglomerate. Every instinct in her screamed not to retreat at this point. She could almost taste how close Andrew was to defeat.

Cooler heads prevailed. Ramsey Peet was quick to point out that if more millions were spent immediately in trying to push Andrew over the edge, Rebecca would have to go outside for financing. Even though Tides II was already showing a profit, the price of bullion had stabilized. The revenue from the gold fields would barely cover the costs Rebecca had incurred thus far.

"I'm not saying that gold won't continue to move up," Ramsey told her. "But we'll have to wait for the market to give it that push."

"Three percent!" Rebecca gritted her teeth. "I can't believe I'm so close. It's got to be out there somewhere!"

"It is," Ramsey said soothingly. "And we'll get it. Believe me, we're in much better shape than Tyne & Wear. Their profits are down almost fifteen points this quarter."

The attorney looked at her closely. Over the past few months Rebecca had looked hollow-cheeked and pale. Ramsey had heard from Bix that she was seeing her doctor on a weekly basis. He had broached the subject of her health but had received only evasions.

"I want you to take a holiday," he said firmly. "You've been running yourself so hard that there won't be anything left of you when you do win!"

"A holiday! At this point? Ramsey, you're nuts!"

"If you don't take some time off, I'm going to speak to your doctor," he replied. "And that's not an idle threat!"

"But we're so close!" she wailed.

"I'm not saying we have to stop completely. Look, we're three percent short. Instead of going head-to-head with Stoughton, let's chisel that amount out of him."

"What do you mean?" Rebecca asked suspiciously.

"Let me work on the individuals and small corporations who hold what we need," Ramsey explained. "Maybe I can make some kind of deal. Maybe there's something we have that they want. It will take time and patience, but what do we have to lose?"

Rebecca thought the proposal over carefully.

"So we wouldn't be giving up altogether," she said slowly. "Just concentrating our resources."

Ramsey beamed. "Exactly."

"And you'd keep me informed every step of the way."

"You have my word."

"I suppose you're right," Rebecca admitted. "This thing has left me a little tired. Maybe a rest isn't such a bad idea."

"I'm glad you agree," Ramsey said quickly, moving to seal the agreement before Rebecca could change her mind. "Now go home and start packing."

Tony was waiting in Ramsey's outer office.

"Everything all right?" he asked.

"I don't want to see this young lady's face for at least a month," Ramsey told him sternly. "Take her to the ends of the earth if you have to."

"As long as there's a telephone," Rebecca said, laughing.

"I don't know what's going on," Tony said. "But I'm not about to look a gift horse in the mouth."

As they hurried down the corridor, Rebecca whispered excitedly, "Do you think he fell for it?"

"Are you kidding? You were carrying on like an Arab at a funeral! Even I bought it." Tony shook his head. "You should've auditioned for Broadway."

"As long as Ramsey thinks my going away is his idea, no one will suspect a thing," Rebecca said.

As they waited at the elevators Rebecca slipped her arms around his neck.

"Tony, are you sure about this? Absolutely, one hundred percent sure?"

"I've never been surer of anything in my life," he said softly. "I have never loved anyone as I love you."

The first month sped by so quickly it might never have existed had it not been for the scent of sandalwood that lingered, refusing to dissipate, even after they had left the magic isles.

From New York, Rebecca and Tony flew to Honolulu. After a two-day respite to recover from jet lag they boarded an aircraft for a direct flight to Bangkok. In spite of the steambath humidity, Rebecca was enthralled by the city, which was overlaid by a fine golden dust that seemed indistinguishable from sunlight. Amid a constant cacophony of cymbals, bells, and whistles, she shopped in the bazaars for bolts of silk for Bix and antique Burmese puppets for herself. She haggled over the price of a suit for Tony at the Jim Thompson Thai Silk Company and was thrilled when Tony presented her with a ring dominated by an enormous sapphire, her favorite stone, set in a cluster of tiny diamonds.

After a week at the Royal Garden Resort on the Gulf of Siam, where they were guests of the Thai royal family, Rebecca and Tony flew to the Seychelles, which had been proclaimed by General Gordon in 1881 to be the original Garden of Eden. Rebecca was quick to see why. The Seychelles were home to one of nature's most curious trees, the coco-de-mer palm. The female tree bears a large nut whose shape is identical to the female pelvis. The male trees produce a large phalluslike catkin.

"Did you know," Rebecca whispered to Tony as they listened to the pounding surf from their balcony, "that the sound of the coco-de-mer crashing against each other is their love song?"

"And anyone who spies on them won't live to tell the tale," he replied, finishing the legend.

"There's no one spying on us. . . ."

Their next stop took them even farther into the vast Indian Ocean, to the Maldives, where they traveled four hours by speedboat to the archipelago of Nika and the exclusive sixteen-bungalow resort. Since Nika was on the fringe of Ari Atoll, some of the world's best scuba diving was literally at their doorstep. Even at night they had the water around them. The resort's Venus nightclub was built on an artificial reef with spectacular underwater lighting.

"Too bad I didn't think of it," Rebecca said wistfully. "The idea would be perfect for Tides III."

This leg of their journey lasted twice as long as Rebecca and Tony had anticipated. By the time they arrived in Hong Kong it was almost the end of July. The Peninsula Hotel became their temporary business headquarters. During the day both fielded messages from the United States and drafted replies that kept the hotel's telex machine humming. But by mutual consent all work ceased at five o'clock, when they retired to the bar to watch Hong Kong's fabled taipans conduct the really important deals of the day. Afterward there was a table at Gaddi's, perhaps the finest restaurant in all of the Far East, waiting for them.

By the time July was over Rebecca felt more and more uncomfortable traveling.

"Then we're going home," Tony said firmly as they rested in their sunken bath in a losman at the Oberoi in Bali. He reached for her tenderly.

"I can't tell you how happy I've been these past few months. They've been everything I imagined . . . and so much more."

Rebecca traced a fingernail across his lips, then brought them to her own, her mouth hungry for him.

"No one can take this away from us," she whispered fiercely. "We're beyond the pain now."

As they clung to each other in the garden that surely must have been God's favorite, each believed that no other truth could possibly exist.

On the one hand Ramsey, Bix, and Torrey were surprised that Rebecca and Tony didn't return directly to New York from the Far East but elected to go to Cayos de la Fortuna instead. Nonetheless they agreed among themselves that Rebecca could just as easily keep tabs on what was happening with Tyne & Wear through the elaborate communications system on board the *Windsong*, berthed off the island. No one even came close to guessing the real reason.

Standing on the terrace, Tony reached out and drew Rebecca to him, gently running his hand over her breasts and belly.

"You never fail to amaze me," he whispered. "A miracle. That's what you are, a miracle."

They cradled together like that, listening to the ocean ripple and hiss along the beach below.

"Andrew still bothers me," Rebecca murmured into his chest. "I don't know how Ramsey's done it, but he's managed to chip away another two percent of Tyne & Wear stock. Obviously it's just a matter of time before we get the last point we need to put us over the top. We're so close to taking over—and yet Andrew hasn't gone on the offensive.''

Tony shushed her, stroking her hair. Still, he silently admitted that he shared Rebecca's concern. On his brief trip to Europe and the States that August he had made a point not only to meet with Ramsey and go over his information but also to touch his own sources. Everything pointed to the fact that Andrew, while maintaining his own public relations campaign against Rebecca, had not come up with any bold, decisive moves.

''He's got nowhere to run,'' Tony said with quiet finality. ''It's just a matter of time before Ramsey pries that one percent out from under him. Then he's finished.''

''I wish I could believe that,'' Rebecca said. ''I want to believe it. But to do nothing isn't Andrew's style. Something's going on. Something we don't know about.''

''Maybe somewhere else,'' Tony said. ''But not on Cayos de la Fortuna. There's nothing Andrew can do to us here.''

Tony was right that Cayos de la Fortuna was a secure haven. But it was not impregnable.

The killer had studied the island with all the care of a scientist recording the movement of tiny life forms beneath his powerful microscope. He knew that the few hundred people who lived in the mainland village of La Ceiba, the jumping-off point for Cayos de la Fortuna, all spoke favorably of the gringo who had come here five years before and who lived quietly among them. Anthony Fabrizzi was different, they would say. He paid the workers generously who looked after his home. Unlike the other two residents of the island, he never tried to bribe local girls to come out and act as ''hostesses'' when he entertained. He had been the first to help when, several years before, a hurricane had torn through Honduras, devastating La Ceiba. Anthony Fabrizzi had worked tirelessly, unloading the helicopters that ferried in food and medicines. Only later had the people learned he had helped organize and pay for the relief.

It was ironic, Andrew thought as he sat in the fighting chair of the small cruiser, pretending to troll for marlin. It was precisely because of Tony's Samaritan instincts that he had learned so much about him. The people of La Ceiba spoke openly and generously about him. They had told Andrew everything he needed to know, including the fact that he had chartered a plane to fly him from La Ceiba to Houston in two days' time. Andrew had been counting on that. August 29 was Michele Fabrizzi's birthday. It was an occasion Tony wouldn't miss, one to which he most certainly couldn't take Rebecca, and the one time Cayos de la Fortuna would be vulnerable.

On the morning of August 29 Andrew Stoughton took the cruiser out by himself. He had spent every day out on the sea and taken the controls often enough to satisfy its owner of his seamanship. A hefty deposit erased whatever lingering doubts the Honduran may have had.

It was still dark when Andrew entered the channel, running at low revs. He had to position himself directly in front of the sun so that he could see Tony as he swept by him toward the mainland but in turn could not be seen.

As he waited Andrew felt a deep calm descend upon him, as though he were walking through a dream. A month ago Rebecca had managed to add another two percent of Tyne & Wear shares to her portfolio. That had left Andrew no option. It no longer mattered what Fabrizzi thought or counseled. It didn't matter what the risks were. Andrew knew he was on the verge of losing everything. Rebecca's death was the only way to prevent that.

Andrew smiled in the darkness, remembering how clear his mind had been when he had committed himself to this course. From that moment on it seemed as though he could do no wrong. Everyone around him sympathized when he had told them he needed to take time off. There were murmurs of concern for his health and his personal secretary had been visibly relieved when she made the arrangements for him at an exclusive spa in Palm Springs.

Andrew had gone to California. In fact he was still registered at the Nirvana Estates. That he hadn't been seen by its staff for over a week was unimportant. The spa's clientele flew in and out all the time. It wasn't unusual for guests to organize trips to the coast or mountains. Andrew had made sure the spa director knew he would be spending a few days fishing in the Sea of Cortez in the company of a junior senator from the Midwest. The politician would swear, if he ever needed to, that Andrew had never left his cruiser.

Nor was there anything to fear from the Hondurans. The man who had arrived in La Ceiba had a three-day growth of beard and was dressed in ragged cutoffs and a stained T-shirt. He said little and paid in cash, which dampened curiosity. He went under the name of Thompson and carried a Canadian passport to vouch for it.

Andrew had used such ploys many times when he had been Tyne & Wear's most effective and merciless troubleshooter.

The sun was a blinding streak of light across the horizon. Then slowly, majestically, the corona appeared, banishing the darkness. Andrew focused his binoculars on the dock at the foot of the steep ramp that led from the house to the water. Rebecca was standing with her back to him. There could be no mistaking her long dark mane. He saw her arms circle Tony's neck, bringing his lips to hers.

Andrew watched their embrace impassively and slowly brought the binoculars away from his eyes, letting them hang around his neck. It wasn't that he felt self-conscious or ashamed at having invaded such a private moment. He was a master at using people's intimacies against them. But there was something in the way Rebecca had reached out for Tony that stirred a deep, almost forgotten memory within him. At that instant he remembered exactly how Rebecca had tasted and felt beneath his touch, the anticipation and eagerness he had felt in his own body when she lay beside him.

Maybe, Andrew thought, she can bring back that moment one more time.

Andrew squatted on the boat's Astroturf carpeting and opened the compartment hatches. There were two full five-gallon plastic containers of gasoline, the kind any prudent sailor would carry. Wrapped in plastic was something of little use on a vessel, a bundle of twenty-odd candles. Beside the candles was a wicked gaffing hook, its curled point gleaming with machine oil.

Andrew rose when he heard the rumble of engines break the dawn peace. He watched the cruiser pull away from the dock, its course set for the mainland. A man was standing on the flying bridge, both hands on the wheel. Andrew bade Anthony Fabrizzi godspeed and hoped he would have a pleasant time at his father's birthday party. It would be his last happy moment in a long time.

Andrew waited a full half hour before steering his vessel toward the dock at Cayos de la Fortuna. He wanted to make absolutely certain Tony wasn't returning.

From the gossip in La Ceiba, Andrew had learned that the maids and cook wouldn't be arriving until nine o'clock or so. He still thought it curious that Rebecca wouldn't have any live-in help and that the servants never even caught a glimpse of her. He had also heard the rumors about a doctor visiting regularly. Idly he wondered if Rebecca was ill.

In another hour it wouldn't matter.

By the time he reached the dock Andrew had completely divorced himself from the horror he was weaving. He made his vessel fast and stepped onto the pier, the two plastic jerry cans seemingly weightless in his arms. The gaffing hook was snug underneath one arm and the candles were tucked securely in his jacket. Andrew took the steps of the steep incline without losing a single breath.

The house was completely open, just as he had expected it to be. He stood on the wide circular patio, the stone parapet on his right, able to see into the timbered living room on his left, and listened keenly. It would have been so much easier to find Rebecca had she been singing to herself. . . .

Andrew lowered the jerry cans, placed the candles on top of them, and gripped the gaffing hook by its leather-bound handle. It was swinging lightly as he entered the house, the sunlight making the tip sparkle.

In calm, measured steps, Andrew explored the living room, his sneakers falling silently on the gleaming mahogany floorboards. He moved through the dining room, with its magnificent view of the reef, and into the kitchen, still wrapped in the delicious smell of coffee. Then he heard a chair scrape.

To the left of the kitchen was a self-contained area he assumed to be the master suite. Andrew's footsteps fell on the gaily colored Mexican tile, past the huge bed with a fan turning lazily above it. He saw the shadow first.

There was a terrace beyond the open sliding doors of the master bedroom. Andrew saw a white patio table with a cup of coffee and a newspaper on it. He also saw the shadow of the person sitting in the chair beside the table. He tightened his grip on the gaffing hook, raising the weapon until it was shoulder-high.

It could have been so different for you. For us.

An instant later the illusion was shattered. The chair scraped again. The figure moved as though to rise. For a split second Andrew was paralyzed. Then he screamed like one of the damned and the gaffing hook blurred through the air, the tip burying itself in the object of his terror.

A red haze filmed Andrew's eyes as he brought down the hook again and again. After several blows he gripped the leather handle with both hands, bringing his full weight behind every strike. He never knew, even when he collapsed to his knees, lungs burning, that the haze was real, created by the sprayed arterial blood that streaked and dripped down the sliding glass doors. Only when he saw his own blood-spattered reflection did he realize the truth.

· 55 ·

Rebecca had tried to convince Tony to attend his father's birthday party but he wouldn't budge.

"I'm not leaving you and that's final."

"But he'll be so disappointed!"

"When he learns why, all will be forgiven," Tony had assured her.

"Well, I'm going into La Ceiba to buy him something anyway," Rebecca had said.

She could have had Ramon bring the *Windsong* around from the leeward side of the island and ferry her to La Ceiba by tender. But she had gotten to know and trust the boatman who had been serving Tony. Like Tony, she preferred to give the work to the locals when possible.

"It'll be the first time in months since they've seen you in La Ceiba," Tony had said, chuckling, as they prepared for bed. "You're going to cause quite a stir."

Rebecca had asked that the boatman pick her up before first light. Although she could hardly say she had become claustrophobic, she eagerly looked forward to this brief trip. She loved the village and its people and daydreamed about enjoying her coffee on the docks, watching the fishing boats go out.

In spite of the hour and the sleep in his eyes Tony saw her off at the wharf. For an instant, when she held him so close and smelled the tangy odor of his skin, she almost changed her mind. But she stepped onto the cruiser, and the boatman, having made sure she was comfortable, scrambled up to the flying bridge. As they pulled away she saw the silhouette of a vessel lying a mile or more offshore.

La Ceiba was tranquil in the cool, early hours. Rebecca strolled through the dusty streets, empty save for the fishermen on their way to their boats. She joined them, accepting a cup of coffee but passing on the homegrown rum, which Rebecca was convinced must be distilled from white lightning.

In spite of the easy conversation with the fishermen Rebecca couldn't shake the feeling that something was wrong. She couldn't put her finger on it but her thoughts kept returning to the vessel she had glimpsed lying off La Ceiba. She was sure it wasn't a fishing boat and it didn't belong to either of the other two property owners on Cayos de la Fortuna.

Rebecca asked the fishermen if they knew anything about it but received only shrugs, until one of the men told her it was probably the gringo who had chartered Manolo's vessel to try his luck at marlin. The rest of the men laughed. How lucky that Manolo was! To find himself a gringo who believed marlin ran in August when the season began only in October. . . .

The premonition that something was dreadfully wrong finally galvanized Rebecca. She hurried toward the harbormaster's office, one of the few places with a telephone. Her throat was dry as she dialed and waited for Tony to answer.

The phone rang and rang, then abruptly the connection died.

Rebecca saw the vessel again as her cruiser approached Cayos de la Fortuna. She was sitting in the belowdecks cabin and through the porthole watched the unknown pilot execute a perfect turn against the swells before aiming the boat for the mainland. The figure on the flying bridge glanced once in her direction, but the distance between them, a hundred yards at least, and the salt-coated glass made identification impossible.

Who are you? What were you doing here?

As the boatman made the cruiser fast, Rebecca was tempted to have him call the police in La Ceiba to intercept the stranger.

And for what reason? Intuition? You don't know who he is much less if he's committed any crime.

Even if there had been foul play, a determined criminal could easily elude the two-man constabulary. Alternatively he could keep running out to sea. The Hondurans had no coast guard to speak of.

Dammit, you're seeing ghosts! Tony's probably on his way down right now, worried out of his mind that something's happened to you.

The boatman helped her onto the dock and Rebecca made for the staircase. Careful to hold on to the steep pipe railing, she took the first step, then suddenly cried out as her leg flew out from under her. She fell heavily on her hip, and a searing pain knifed through her abdomen.

Oh God, please, not like this!

The boatman was scrambling toward her as Rebecca rolled over on her back, gasping. She drew herself up on one arm and tried to grasp the railing. When she looked down, she screamed. The steps, and now her right hand, were spotted with blood.

"Go to the *Windsong*. . . . Tell Ramon to come quickly!"

Rebecca clutched the boatman.

"Please," she whispered. "Nothing on the radio. Just get Ramon!"

The boatman hesitated. Summoning the last of her strength, Rebecca shouted, "Go! Now! I'll wait here!"

She held back until the cruiser was well away from the dock. That minute gave her a chance to get her breath back, fight off the terror welling within her. Rebecca gritted her teeth and staggered to her feet. Clinging to the railing, using an arm-over-arm motion, she began her climb up the precipice.

The pain was never-ending, as though fed by some bottomless spring. It raced through her legs with every step she took, hitting her abdomen like a molten shaft. Whenever Rebecca felt her knees buckle she tightened her grip on the railings; the rust and flakes of paint mixed with the blood on her palms, searing her already tender flesh. But she refused to stop. Something evil had descended upon Cayos de la Fortuna. Something that had come to destroy her and Tony.

She was panting when she reached the summit. The wind, normally cool and brisk, now seemed like a tempest.

It's just the dizziness. . . . That's all it is. Rest for a moment. Clear your head. Take deep, deep breaths. . . .

Rebecca leaned against the railing with both arms. The blood was roaring in her head, which seemed impossibly heavy.

Now!

Summoning the energy from the pit of her stomach, Rebecca threw her head back. Using the technique her doctor had taught her, she took two long, deep breaths, inhaling and exhaling like a weight lifter preparing to tackle a seemingly immovable barbell. Little by little the world stopped spinning and she dared to open her eyes.

There was blood on the terrace as well, just a few drops, but enough for a trail. Slowly Rebecca moved into the living room, her ears straining to catch the tiniest sound. There was only the

wind moaning through a partially open door or window somewhere in the house. Then another one, the tinkle of brass against
brass as Rebecca lifted the poker from the rack next to the
fireplace.

She gripped the poker with both hands, holding it high over
her head. The fear was gone now, replaced by a cold, furious
hatred. Someone had been here, might still be here.

Rebecca slipped through the kitchen. The wind changed direction suddenly and she almost gagged on the stench.

Gasoline!

The poker clattered to her feet when she saw the candles laid
out in a neat row, running from the door of the bedroom to the
foot of the huge bed. The sun almost blotted out the whispering
flames, but Rebecca caught their evil winks, like the blink of an
old yellow-eyed cat. Suddenly her feet were wet and cold. At the
same time, they began to burn. The gasoline was pooling around
her, trickling through her toes. . . .

Rebecca didn't see him until she followed the trail of candles
and looked up. She couldn't stifle her involuntary cry. With
every step she took she saw more and more blood until she
realized Tony would never hear her screams. . . .

Put out the candles! If they burn down far enough . . .

"No!" Rebecca shrieked.

The thin bedspread felt like a bloated sponge beneath her
hands and knees. Rebecca crawled across the bed on all fours,
squeezing her eyes shut against the blood. She opened them only
when her fingertips found Tony's face.

"Oh, dear God, what have they done to you?" she whispered
through cracked lips.

Tony was lying on his back, his entire torso drenched in
blood. One side of his skull was oddly misshapen. There was a
gaping hole near the back of his neck through which blood still
seeped.

"We'll make it, darling," Rebecca gasped. "I'll take you out
to the balcony first. Then the candles . . . Yes, I have to
extinguish them. We don't want our beautiful home to burn
down, do we . . .?"

Rebecca climbed over his body and gripped Tony under the
arms. She cried out as she jerked him forward. Rebecca got a
better hold and slowly backed away toward the patio.

"Tony . . . please, help me, Tony!"

But it wasn't in her pleas that Rebecca found courage. It
wasn't Tony she was dragging to safety. It wasn't their home.

The fiery memories of Skyscape and what must have happened there that terrible night fed her fury.

Choking on the fumes, sobbing because she did not believe she could endure another second of this pain, Rebecca dragged Tony onto the terrace. She lowered him as gently as she could but still heard a sickening crack when his head touched the concrete. Unable to hold back any longer, Rebecca whipped her head around and threw up.

Her chest heaving, her lungs on fire, she staggered back into the bedroom. The taste of bile was so overwhelming that it kept her from losing consciousness. Yet for some reason the flames of the candles had become blurred, swimming from side to side as though teasing her.

Damn you to hell!

Rebecca felt the dead cold of the gasoline soak her shift as she lowered herself on her side. The candles were burned down until they were only inches above the fuel. There was no way she could stand and stoop over to extinguish them. Pushing herself along with her feet and arms, careful not to let her fingers touch the gasoline, Rebecca slithered toward them. When she reached the first candle she wet her fingertips with her tongue and pinched the wick.

It was like crawling through hell, the iciness of the gasoline set against the whispering flames that beckoned her forward. After the third candle Rebecca stopped wetting her fingertips. She had to feel the pain to fight the intoxicating smell of gasoline.

Only six more . . . just six, then we're safe. . . .

Her shoulder muscles screamed in protest as time and again she reached for the flame, willing her arm not to shake. Three . . . four . . . five . . .

You monster! You cheating, murdering monster!

At the end of the row stood a seventh candle, shorter than the rest, the flame almost as high as the wax column. As mesmerized as she was by the fire, Rebecca knew she would never reach the candle in time.

She began to back away, her eyes riveted to the flame, praying that the wax would hold for just a few more seconds. Rebecca felt her legs touch the bedposts and she maneuvered her way around them. She was so close to the balcony she could feel the breeze on the soles of her feet.

Suddenly she heard a clatter and a deep-throated roar. Twisting around, she saw the *Windsong*'s helicopter bank in a sharp turn, hover for an instant, then swoop toward the house.

"No!"

Rebecca's frantic warning was drowned out by the whine of turbines. The helicopter swooped in, its blades creating a whirlwind that slammed into the terrace doors, rattling them. The jet of air that escaped through the opening was enough to carry the flame of the last candle toward the gasoline before it was snuffed out. Rebecca staggered through the doors, yanking them together a second before the bedroom exploded in crimson.

Her home was burning, the gasoline-soaked bed erupting in a fiery column. Rebecca craned her neck to see Ramon crouching by the open rear door of the craft. Because the *Windsong*'s helicopter often flew over water, the manufacturer had installed an electric winch with remote control as well as a horse collar rescue device to pluck capsized victims from the sea. Rebecca watched as Ramon strapped a harness to his waist, fitted the collar over his chest, and cinched himself to the winch wire. The electric motor keened as he began to lower himself.

At that instant one of the glass balcony doors exploded. Rebecca screamed as a hundred razorlike splinters buried themselves in her skin. The force of the blast ripped the air from her lungs, throwing her against the railing.

This is the way it's going to end.

Teetering on the edge of the railing, she saw the jagged face of the cliff with twisted trees and brush growing out of it. A hundred feet below that was the beach. . . .

No, not this way!

Rebecca thrust herself away from the railing and turned to face the inferno. She felt something graze her hair and looked up to see Ramon reaching for her, shouting words Rebecca could not hear.

Rebecca shook her head. She kneeled and raised Tony's body, leaning it against her own. She brought her forearm under his jaw as though rescuing him from the water. The other she raised to the sky and felt Ramon's fingertips graze hers.

The second door exploded.

Tony's body took the brunt of the blast. Rebecca swore she could feel it jerk as though he were still alive and in terrible pain. As the shards cut into her forearm she cried out, instinctively trying to shield herself. That was when she lost her grip on him.

Twisting in the horse collar, Ramon saw his chance. Straining his reach to the limit, he seized Rebecca's wrists. Suddenly the helicopter jolted. Rebecca stared into Ramon's wild eyes, his face streaming with sweat, the forearms bulging as he struggled to maintain his grip. Even through the banshee wail of the rotors she heard his desperate cry.

". . . caught in a downdraft. We're going over."

The pilot had no choice. If he waited a split second longer, another gust would throw the craft against the house, plunging it into the fire.

Rebecca screamed as her arms were almost yanked out of her shoulder sockets. She craned toward Ramon, staring in horrified fascination as he pulled back. Then Rebecca felt her feet leave the ground. Desperately she tried to swing around, but Ramon's hold was too strong.

"I can't leave him!" Rebecca screamed.

It was too late. The helicopter drew away from the house, dipping at an angle that would bring it over the water as quickly as possible. If he lost his grip, Ramon wanted Rebecca to fall into the water, not on land. That way she would at least have a chance of surviving.

Every few seconds Rebecca felt another jerk as Ramon worked the remote control. The winch shrieked under the double weight. Using the helicopter's momentum, Ramon swung himself toward the open hatch and curled his fingers around a metal grip. Rebecca screamed as she was slammed sideways against the edge of the hatch. Then suddenly she was inside, Ramon hauling her in by both arms. Rebecca rolled over on her back, the pain exploding in her skull.

I can't lose consciousness now! she kept repeating to herself. *I have to tell them what happened . . . what we have to do.*

As Rebecca struggled to focus her vision, the faces hovering over her were receding farther and farther away. The words being said to her seemed to be traveling very slowly down a long, dark chamber. By the time they reached her they were barely whispers. It was the image of Tony's blood-streaked face that galvanized her.

"No hospital," she whispered hoarsely. "Only the *Windsong* . . . No one must know what happened . . . not yet."

· 56 ·

That news of the tragedy on Cayos de la Fortuna reached North
America as quickly as it did was due to a combination of fate
and one journalist's dogged persistence.

As soon as La Ceiba's chief of police heard the cries about a
fire on the island, he telephoned his superior in the Honduran
capital of Tegucigalpa, one hundred twenty miles to the south.
Not that the chief expected any help. There was only one pumper
in La Ceiba itself and no firefighting equipment besides what the
residents themselves had on Cayos de la Fortuna. When he saw
the plume of black smoke hanging over the island the chief
crossed himself. The fate of Señor Fabrizzi and the incomparably
lovely Señorita McHenry was in God's hands. He didn't have to
wait for the return of his constable, who had gone out to see if
the owner and his mistress had survived the blaze, to be certain
of this.

What the chief did need was advice from his superior on
exactly what to tell the press once it arrived. In fact, considering
the identity of the fire's victims, he would have preferred that the
National Police handle the matter themselves.

Jimmy Webber was an overeager, restless, twenty-two-year-
old stringer for CBS. For the last three years he had headquartered
himself in Tegucigalpa and considered himself an old hand, even
though none of his reports had ever made it to Walter Cronkite's
desk. During his tenure Jimmy had ingratiated himself with the
commissioner of the National Police at the cost of having to date
his overly plump daughter. There were days when Jimmy Webber
considered the amorous overtures of the buxom Juanita too large
a price to pay for virtually unchallenged access to police headquarters. That thought went out the window when Jimmy overheard the excited chatter at the switchboard about a terrible fire
raging out of control on Cayos de la Fortuna and the presumed
deaths of Rebecca McHenry and Anthony Fabrizzi.

490

Jimmy Webber forgot his lunch date with the fair Juanita, grabbed his camera bag, and raced to the airport. Two hundred American dollars bought him a pilot with a Cessna and more than enough fuel for a round trip between the capital and Cayos de la Fortuna. Fifty-five minutes later Jimmy Webber was screaming at the pilot to fly lower, *lower*! With every click of the shutter he felt one step closer to a network headquarters posting.

Another hundred dollars convinced the pilot that he had enough fuel to make Kingston, Jamaica. Looking like a washed-on-the-beach refugee, Jimmy raced for the Air Jamaica counter. His Amex card got him the last seat on the noon flight to JFK.

Ninety minutes after touchdown Jimmy Webber emerged from a darkroom at CBS headquarters and threaded his way down the corridor, clutching two dozen eight by ten glossies over his head. He barged past the startled receptionist in the executive wing, blew the transfixed personal secretary a kiss, and swept into an office littered with nautical memorabilia.

"Walter, old buddy, have I got a story for you!" Jimmy Webber crowed.

Bix was in her office at The Tides headquarters on lower Fifth Avenue, dictating a vituperative letter to a supplier who had failed to deliver on time, when the news broke. Bix had a habit of tuning in the news and listening to it with half an ear as she worked. As soon as she heard Walter Cronkite's solemn reference to Cayos de la Fortuna, she dropped the microphone and twisted the volume control.

The telephone was ringing even before Cronkite had completed the story.

"Have you heard?" Torrey asked without preamble.

"I was watching," Bix replied. "But what the hell was he saying? There was a fire, Tony's place was apparently destroyed. But there was no reference to either Tony or Rebecca. . . ."

"I'm certain they're all right," Torrey said quickly, catching the note of hysteria in Bix's words. "You know how the media loves body counts."

"Torrey, if Rebecca was all right, I would have heard from her by now!"

Torrey did not know what to say. He had been thinking exactly the same thing.

"I'm going to try to get through to the police at La Ceiba," Bix said. "Torrey, in case I don't, I want you to call your friend at the Marine Air Terminal. Ask him if he can have a jet standing by.''

"And call Ramsey," she added as an afterthought. "He may have missed the newscast."

"Are you kidding?" Torrey replied. "He's on the other line—and he's already got a plane waiting."

At Wildwood-on-the-Hudson, Michele Fabrizzi had been enjoying his second shave of the day, a ritual before dinner, when an assistant whispered the news. The barber, horrified, drew back.

For a moment Fabrizzi remained very still, saying nothing. Then he beckoned to the barber.

"Finish!"

While his associates filed into the room and the barber quickly completed his work, Fabrizzi made his own peace. When he got out of the chair he faced his men.

"The *strega*," he said softly. "I always knew she would bring grief to my house."

"We have no reason to think this woman wanted to harm Tony," a venerable *consigliere* replied. "We all know how they felt about each other."

"And Tony might still be alive, *padrone*," another added in hushed tones. "No bodies have been found—"

Fabrizzi's right hand moved over his heart.

"Tony is dead," he said as though speaking only to himself. "I can feel it here. He is dead and she is responsible."

He looked at the *consigliere*.

"If she is so innocent, why did I not hear this from her lips?"

The *padrone* turned to the whole group.

"Call our people in Miami. Tell them that by the time I arrive I want to know what happened."

He paused. "And tell them to find the *strega*!"

The *Windsong* was well out to sea, steaming southeast toward a predetermined position ninety miles off the coast of Jamaica.

The vessel had stopped only twice, once when the helicopter had taken off, then again when it had returned. Ramon Fuentes was pushing the craft hard to make up for the lost time. He had to put as much distance between himself and the Honduran coast as possible. He had also instructed the radio officer not to acknowledge any incoming transmissions. His mistress had made him promise the *Windsong* would run swift and silent.

Belowdecks, in the master suite, Rebecca was being ministered to by the doctor the helicopter had brought from Angeline City. The young black Angelinian, named Picot, who had been looking after her these past few months, shook his head.

"You really should be in a hospital," he said.

"No hospital . . ." Rebecca murmured.

"There may be complications," Picot warned. "You've had a terrible ordeal. The shock has weakened you—"

"I'll be fine," Rebecca whispered, opening her mouth to suck on the cool water-soaked washcloth Picot held out.

The lie was so obvious, Rebecca knew no one believed it. Her entire body ached and burned. Picot had washed her, emptying and refilling the bathtub three times before he was satisfied there was no residue of gasoline. The imbedded shards of glass had been carefully extracted, the cuts treated with disinfectant and bandaged. When Picot had refused to let her see herself in the mirror, Rebecca ran her fingers over her face. The skin was puffed and she detected angry welts where the glass had caught her. That had been the first time she cried. Not out of fear of disfigurement but because she was seeing Tony, and his face, a bloodied, lifeless mask.

Before Dr. Picot had arrived, Rebecca had kept drifting in and out of consciousness. The pain in her abdomen was unbearable, and by the time the physician had examined her, the sheets were soaked through with sweat. In spite of the agony, Rebecca stubbornly refused any medication. When the pain started to come at regular intervals she felt as though there was no strength left to carry on.

Suddenly Rebecca arched her back and screamed. She felt as though she was being torn apart.

"We can't wait anymore!" she heard Picot shout. "She's hemorrhaging!"

The tragedy on Cayos de la Fortuna continued to make headlines the rest of the week. Public fascination was fueled by the arrival in La Ceiba of crime overlord Michele Fabrizzi, who had come to take his son's body home. Although reporters tried to elicit a comment from the *padrone*, his bodyguards kept them well back. Only once, when he emerged from the undertaker's office, walking beside the casket, did one newsman overhear Fabrizzi utter a single word: *Strega!*

*   *   *

In New York, Ramsey Peet pulled out all stops in an effort to locate Rebecca. He flew to Washington and prevailed upon Senator Lewis Gibson to use his influence to request that the U.S. Coast Guard become involved in the search. The senator from California assured him that within forty-eight hours Coast Guard vessels out of Miami and New Orleans would begin extending their patrol ranges, with orders to relay any information on the *Windsong* to his office immediately.

Worried out of her mind and unable to sit still, Bix made a pilgrimage to Newport and begged her father for help. Admiral Ryan wasted no time. An Annapolis classmate was currently leading a squadron on maneuvers off Grand Cayman. He saw no problem in directing his Search and Rescue flyers as well as the pilots on the aircraft carrier *Kitty Hawk* to overfly certain sectors of the Caribbean Sea where the *Windsong* might have headed.

"All this high-tech stuff is well and good," Torrey told Bix, tapping the front page of the *Times*. "But if anyone finds her, it'll be these guys."

The aerial photograph showed a flotilla of small boats leaving Angeline City harbor. In every Caribbean port a similar scene was being enacted. Fishermen, lobstermen, charter captains, pleasure yachtsmen, were all putting out to sea in an attempt to find Rebecca McHenry. The word that her body hadn't been found on Cayos de la Fortuna had swept across the islands. Now the woman who had done so much for the people she loved was the object of their determination to find her. Every skipper who left port made the same vow: to go out today, the next day, and the next—as long as it took—to find the *Windsong*.

"I don't understand," Torrey said, pacing in Ramsey's office. Five days into the search and nothing, not even a sighting, had been recorded.

"We've had no communication from the *Windsong*. No one's spotted her. What the hell is going on? Why doesn't she talk to us?"

"Maybe she can't," Ramsey said quietly. "Maybe something happened on Cayos de la Fortuna that we don't know about. Or at sea."

Torrey's patience exploded. "The police have searched every inch of that island! The Hondurans have had helicopters and rescue vessels off its waters. Nothing! I can't believe Rebecca's dead. I won't believe it!"

"She's not," Bix told them both. "I would know if something happened to Becky. I'd feel it."

"Then what's going on?"

"I wish I could tell you, dear heart. But think about this: Ramon Fuentes is probably the best captain in the Caribbean. Those waters are his home. If he doesn't want the *Windsong* found, we don't stand a chance."

"You mean Rebecca's hiding from us?" Ramsey asked incredulously.

"No," Bix replied. "I think she's mourning."

Andrew Stoughton would never have dreamed of attending the memorial mass for Anthony Fabrizzi, held in the tranquility of the rolling hills on Wildwood-on-the-Hudson. He knew, too, that Michele Fabrizzi would not have expected him to be there. Theirs was a relationship of shadows. Nonetheless Andrew did send, anonymously, a large wreath for the service.

The fact that he was still alive told Andrew the *padrone* hadn't the slightest suspicion that he had had anything to do with Tony's death. Which meant that Honduran law enforcement, such as it was, was also looking elsewhere for clues and motives.

Why should they suspect me? Andrew thought. I'm not linked to the Fabrizzis in any way. As far as the old man is concerned, he would have to think I'm crazy to have murdered his son.

The thought of a grief-stricken Fabrizzi raging against forces he could neither see, touch, nor understand raised an idea in Andrew's mind. That Rebecca had disappeared also factored into the equation with an exquisite symmetry.

Audacious, Andrew thought, surveying a bikini-clad girl poised on the diving board of the Palm Springs spa. *Dangerous as well . . .* Only when she was certain every eye was on her did the girl take three steps, jump, and execute a clumsy entry into the ice-blue water. *But as long as Rebecca remains lost it can work*.

The rage of having been cheated at Cayos de la Fortuna, the fury that had compelled him to bludgeon Tony Fabrizzi to death, the insanity that had made him replicate the murder of Max McHenry, had all receded now. Andrew had fled Cayos de la Fortuna with what had seemed a paltry victory: the destruction of someone Rebecca loved. He had carved out a tiny piece of her heart and he fed his hatred upon it. Now he realized there was more, much more, that he could have.

Andrew didn't know where or why Rebecca had fled. He followed the newspaper accounts of the search very carefully, but they yielded no clues.

"Stay lost a little while longer," Andrew murmured. "Just a little while . . ."

"Did you say something?"

The girl in the bikini was standing beside his chair, her wet hair combed back, sleek as an otter's pelt. Andrew graced her with a dazzling smile.

"Yes, I did," he said. "I greatly admire your form, both in and out of the water."

Just as he expected, the idiot simpered.

"Permit me to offer my sincere condolences, Mr. Fabrizzi."

It had been two days since Andrew had left Palm Springs, twelve since the inferno at Cayos de la Fortuna. Andrew and the *padrone* were sitting on the veranda, at the same table they had shared before. Fabrizzi's sister, veiled in black, drifted in and out like a fallen angel, serving food and drink. Andrew thought she appeared even more cadaverous than before, if that was possible.

Tony's death had also taken its toll of the *padrone*. Andrew detected a rheuminess in the once-cold sparkling eyes and a hesitation in the speech that made Fabrizzi sound distracted. This, Andrew reckoned, was all to his advantage.

"I thank you for your kindness," Fabrizzi said after Andrew had offered his condolences.

"I only regret that I wasn't able to attend the funeral," Andrew replied.

"A great many people would have been surprised if you had."

Andrew nodded and ate a little of his antipasto, noticing that Fabrizzi left his plate untouched.

"Mr. Fabrizzi," he said, "I realize this is a difficult time for you. Unfortunately what I have to say can't wait."

"Of course," Fabrizzi replied. "One of your better qualities is that you do not waste time, yours or anyone else's."

"I must also tell you that this concerns Tony," Andrew said.

He was watching closely for a reaction but received none. It was as though the very mention of his son's name anesthetized Fabrizzi.

The *padrone* motioned for Andrew to continue.

"I believe," Andrew said slowly, "that Rebecca murdered Tony."

Michele Fabrizzi flinched. Andrew saw him grip the armrests of his chair, his knuckles white.

"Why do you say such a thing?" he asked softly. "Tony told me she loved him. He was very sure of that. He was willing to give up a great deal for her—family, honor, his achievements. . . ."

"And maybe he ended up giving his life to her," Andrew suggested. "Consider, Mr. Fabrizzi: Rebecca McHenry's body hasn't been found. The world believes, as do I, that she is alive. But if that's the case, why doesn't she come forward? We know from the Honduran investigation that she was in La Ceiba the morning of the fire. I'm sure your own sources have confirmed that she left the village quite unexpectedly. No one can guess why. She returns to Cayos de la Fortuna and suddenly the fire breaks out. Neither the boatman nor she is seen again.

"There was no one else on Cayos de la Fortuna that morning, Mr. Fabrizzi. Newspaper accounts have confirmed the where-abouts of the other residents. So unless you believe that Tony had enemies and that they somehow infiltrated Cayos de la Fortuna to murder him—but not her, a potential witness—that leaves only one person: Rebecca McHenry."

Michele Fabrizzi considered what had been said to him.

"You know by now that I never approved of my son's associ-ation with this woman," he said, careful not to mention Rebecca by name. "But you also understand that vengeance is not to be treated lightly. It is a matter of honor that I be certain she is responsible for what happened to Tony. Because whatever action I take then . . ."

The *padrone* spread his hands in a gesture of finality.

"My opinion is also tainted," Andrew said. "But I ask myself: Why did she run? Why doesn't she show herself?" He paused. "What does she have to hide?"

Andrew wet his lips with his wine and continued.

"You will never know if Rebecca McHenry murdered Tony unless you confront her, ask the question, look into her eyes, and read the answer."

"She cannot hide forever," Fabrizzi said. "I will find her no matter how long it takes."

"With all due respect, if the resources searching for her now haven't had any luck, you could end up waiting a very long time."

"You have an alternative," the *padrone* stated.

"I propose we force her to come to you," Andrew said.

"And how would you do that?"

Andrew realized this was the dangerous crossroads of his proposal. He had to make Fabrizzi accept both sides of the idea.

If either was rejected, he would lose this golden chance to be rid of Rebecca once and for all.

"If I may, Mr. Fabrizzi, I'd like to outline the benefits, to both of us, of what I have in mind."

"I expected no less," the *padrone* replied.

"If you should decide that my plan has merit, then not only will you succeed in flushing Rebecca McHenry, but you—and I—will hold her fate in our hands. Together we can break The Tides. As soon as Rebecca McHenry sees her creation threatened, she will have to come out of hiding. But by then it will be too late. The damage to The Tides will be irreversible and we will be in a position to take over the entire resort empire.

"Once that happens I would be willing to help you, if necessary, acquire all her properties and use whatever influence I have to obtain gambling licenses for them."

"And what do you get out of all this, Andrew?"

"Tyne & Wear," Andrew said. "Without The Tides, Rebecca is no longer a threat to me."

"That is one thing," Michele Fabrizzi agreed. "There is something else."

"My debt to you, Mr. Fabrizzi. I have much to thank you for. Without your assistance I would never have achieved as much as I have. But there comes a time when the balance must be restored. I wish to be master in my own house, Tyne & Wear, with obligations to no one. I ask that, if you agree with my proposition, you consider my debt to you paid in full."

The autumn wind brought a chill with it. Michele Fabrizzi cocked his head slightly as though he were listening to the rustle of leaves, watching their torrent of color as they fled the trees. Time, he thought. Too little time. Too many questions. Too old is the man.

The *padrone* rose and said, "Speak your mind to me. If I agree, I swear to you there will be no more debts between us."

· 57 ·

As September waned, even the stoutest hearts began to lose hope of ever finding the *Windsong*. The intense searches conducted by the government marine agencies of various countries were, one by one, curtailed. Individual efforts also stopped as islanders throughout the Caribbean accepted the inevitability of what the sea had done. The false sightings, which had sent men dashing across hundreds of miles of open ocean, served only to frustrate would-be rescuers.

In New York, Bix, Torrey, and Ramsey Peet struggled like Trojans to maintain The Tides empire on a steady course. The disappearance of Rebecca McHenry had cast a pall over the entire staff. It was as though without her vitality The Tides was just another holiday destination, with nothing to distinguish it from any other. Bix tried to pick up the slack, roving from one resort to another, giving pep talks and offering encouragement. Everywhere she went she ended her appeal on a common note.

"Rebecca is missing. She's not dead but *missing*. I don't want any of you to doubt that she'll be back."

Looking at the sad faces, Bix realized how futile her words sounded. Late at night, when she was lying in Torrey's arms, her hopes seemed hollow even to her. But she clung to them as she clung to her husband, knowing that if she ever abandoned them, she would lose something irreplaceable.

In the third week of September, two days after Bix had returned to New York from Mexico, Ramsey Peet called a meeting with her and Torrey.

"We have to make a decision," the patrician lawyer said gravely.

They were in Rebecca's office, and all three were conscious of the empty chair behind the elegant Valenti-designed desk.

"According to the articles of incorporation, the three of us not only have the power to run The Tides on a day-to-day basis, we may also determine its future," Ramsey continued. "That means we have to decide whether or not to continue to fight for that one percent Vixen Corporation needs for control of Tyne & Wear."

Bix looked at Torrey, who shrugged.

"What's the latest from Stoughton?" he asked.

"All quiet," Ramsey said. "In fact, he's tapered off his attacks."

"Smart boy," Torrey murmured. "If he went after Rebecca now, all he would do is increase sympathy for her."

"There's another side to that," Ramsey added. "Without Rebecca we're rudderless. Sure, we can control The Tides, but she *is* The Tides. Investor confidence has a tendency to wane when the chief executive mysteriously drops out of sight. We might—no, we will—have a tough time getting that last one percent."

Torrey and Ramsey debated the issue for a few minutes before they realized Bix hadn't said a word. When she was sure she had their attention, Bix said, "I don't even know why we're talking about this. As far as I'm concerned, nothing's changed. We have to finish what Rebecca began. Unless the two of you can give me a damn good reason why not!"

"Easy, honey, lighten up," Torrey said. "We're not shutting anything down—"

"It sounds to me as if you've given her up for dead!" Bix retorted, furiously brushing away tears.

Before either Ramsey or Torrey could convince her otherwise, Rebecca's personal secretary stepped into the office unannounced.

"I'm terribly sorry," he said breathlessly. "But this just came in over the telex from Bonaire. I thought you should see it immediately."

Bix read the message through, sucking in her breath.

"There's been a fire at the resort in the Netherlands Antilles."

Six hours later Bix and Torrey were carefully making their way through the charred, skeletal remains of what was left of the east guest wing at Tides II in Bonaire. Sixty of the resort's one hundred eighty rooms had been destroyed in the explosion and subsequent fire. It was a miracle that no one had been killed.

"Your people tell me that that wing was only half full," the fire marshal said to Torrey. "Since most of the guests were divers, they were out on the flattops on the reef or still at breakfast. The boats went out at eight o'clock in the morning, so the cleaning staff serviced these rooms first. If they had waited to do them . . .''

The air was still laden with smoke and ash. Torrey put a handkerchief to his nose and mouth and told Bix to do the same.

"Any idea what caused it?" he asked.

The fire marshal passed him a loop of charred wire.

"Could be faulty electrical wiring," he said.

"But you said there was an explosion," Bix countered, coughing as she removed her handkerchief.

"You use a lot of propane in your kitchens," the marshal replied. "The spare tanks are kept in a shed near one end of this wing."

"Faulty wiring there too, Inspector?" Torrey murmured through the cloth.

"We don't know yet, Mr. Stewart," the fire marshal said coldly. "But that's where this business started. The shed caught on fire, the propane exploded, and the rest, well . . .'' He waved his arm. "You can see for yourself."

Because daylight was fading quickly, further investigation was put off until the next day. Bix and Torrey retreated to the administration building, where they checked the arrangements for the guests who had suddenly found themselves homeless. Fortunately other hotels on Bonaire had enough space to take them in. Bix dashed off a letter to each guest expressing profound regrets over what had happened. She assured them The Tides would look after all expenses and asked that each guest draw up a list of personal effects that had been destroyed in the blaze. Insurance adjustors for The Tides were on the way to settle all claims.

It was one o'clock in the morning before Bix and Torrey finally turned in. They had talked with the kitchen and grounds staff about the propane explosion, but it was clear no one had any idea what had caused it. Neither of them had reason to doubt the staff's word.

"A fluke accident," Bix said miserably as she got ready for bed. "That's all it can be." She glanced at Torrey, looking for confirmation. "What's that?"

Torrey was sitting on the edge of the bed, toying with the loop of burned wire.

"No, it wasn't," he said quietly.

Bix froze. "What do you mean?"

"I've seen this kind of wire before," Torrey said, looking up at her. "At construction sites. It's used by demolition special-ists. . . ."

Torrey paused. "Whoever rigged the explosion knew what he was doing. Sabotage, Bix, that's what it is."

The next morning, after a sleepless night, Torrey was prepar-ing to take his case to the fire marshal. He and Bix were on their way to the administration building, when a young counselor intercepted them.

"New York's on the line!" the sailboard instructor said breath-lessly. "Mr. Peet wants to talk to you right away!"

A few minutes later Torrey was slumped forward in a chair, holding his head up by one hand.

"Are you absolutely certain, Ramsey?" he repeated. Torrey listened to the reply, then said, "I'll send Bix up in the Lear right away."

"What's going on?" Bix whispered.

"The Tides in Jamaica . . . There was an accident on one of the dive expeditions. Sixteen people went out this morning. According to what Ramsey was told they weren't underwater for more than five minutes when they started choking. Most of them were at sixty feet or better. They panicked, came up too quickly."

Bix, who had become an expert diver over the years, was shocked. She knew of the bends, the agonizing and crippling affliction that could kill a diver who surfaced too rapidly.

"What was the cause?" she demanded. "Faulty equipment?"

"Only one tank has been tested," Torrey replied. "Appar-ently the air was bad, with enough carbon monoxide to incapaci-tate the diver."

"But how—" Bix said, then stopped.

"It's the same thing, don't you see?" Torrey shouted, flinging the charred wire loop across the room. "Here they used demoli-tion. In Jamaica someone tampered with the compressor used to fill the scuba tanks. Andrew Stoughton hasn't backed off. The bastard's coming after us!"

In the next three days several more "accidents" befell The Tides.

On the Pacific coast of Mexico, a Tides bus carrying vacation-ers to the Ixtapa resort was ambushed by armed gunmen. The guests were robbed of their cash and valuables. Those who tried to resist were beaten.

The next disaster struck much closer to home. The resort at

Palm Cove had to close its doors when its drinking water was found to be contaminated.

Bix and Torrey raced from one location to the next, doing what they could to restore order. They quickly realized it was a losing battle. The police in all jurisdictions were conducting thorough investigations. The staff became demoralized when it was clear they were the prime suspects. In the growing climate of fear and resentment, guests were leaving in droves, angry, disappointed, and afraid.

"We're going to hell in a handbasket," Ramsey told Bix and Torrey from New York. "We've got a dozen lawsuits filed against us already, and I expect more each day. So far two people have died and another of the divers isn't expected to live. The press is having a field day with this."

One call to The Tides' central booking office confirmed Bix's worst fears. Cancellations were flooding in. New bookings were nonexistent. The Tides, whose name had been synonymous with safety and comfort, had suddenly become a pariah.

"If we don't turn the situation around," Ramsey warned Bix, "we won't have a fall season, or a winter or spring either! Our insurance people are screaming blue murder, arguing negligence and insufficient security on our part. Until that's settled, we're going to be paying compensation out of our own pockets. I don't have to tell you there's only so long we can do that."

In an attempt to prevent total collapse, Torrey contracted an agreement with local private security agencies in each Tides location. The cost was staggering and the sight of armed patrols did little to reassure staff or guests. Ironically the people they were protecting saw them as a constant reminder of the danger they were in. The exodus continued but the attacks stopped.

"We need a little breathing space to figure out how Andrew's orchestrating this," Torrey said, calling Ramsey from Ixtapa. "Either he's given it his best shot or else the security has scared him off."

"I hope you're right," Ramsey replied. "But Stoughton isn't admitting a thing. In fact, he's taking the opposite tack. He's issued a statement to the effect that he's had nothing to do with the attacks. His press people have given the newspapers his itinerary for the last few weeks, showing exactly where he's been and with whom. There's also been a not-too-subtle threat about lawsuits if anyone publicly connects Stoughton with the attacks."

"What about Tyne & Wear?" Torrey demanded. "Isn't anyone on the board the least bit suspicious of how nicely timed all this is?''

''Stoughton overhauled the board during the last year,'' Ramsey told him. ''They're as tame as circus bears. The bottom line is that without hard evidence of Stoughton's involvement, we can't go after him. So I hope you're right: that whoever set us up has given it his best shot. We can't afford to take much more of a beating.''

Their hopes went unanswered. After a three-day hiatus, night-time marauders destroyed ten *palapas* on Windemere Key, striking at the heart of The Tides.

· 58 ·

Newspapers and magazines were scattered across the vast expanse of the bed. On television a commentator was unctuously recounting the latest disaster to befall The Tides. Rebecca depressed a button on the remote control and the image and voice faded. She didn't need to hear or see anything more.

Rebecca propped herself up. In spite of the rest she had been getting and the mild sedatives Dr. Picot had insisted she take to relax her, she was far from well. The pain in her abdomen had receded and most of the cuts inflicted by the flying glass had healed. Her face and arms, which had taken the brunt of the explosion, were still swollen. Rebecca could trace the angry welts across her cheeks and forehead.

But the physical pain was only a fraction of her torment. In spite of the medication, her sleep was racked by nightmares in which Tony died over and over again. Rebecca kept waking up, drenched in sweat, curled up in a ball, clutching a pillow. She must have been screaming because Dr. Picot was always by her side when her eyes flew open.

The images of Tony never faded, never lost their razor sharpness. Sometimes, when she was nibbling at a particular dish or someone spoke to her in a certain way, Rebecca remembered Tony as he had been in life. For a while she was surprised not to see him when she looked around. Then she would remember and the agony of knowing she would never see or hear or touch him again washed over her.

As the weeks of her self-imposed exile continued, Rebecca allowed the horror to wash over her, sweeping away all considerations but one. She felt no guilt at not letting anyone, even those who loved her, know she was alive. The determined efforts to locate her, with their cost and risk, left her indifferent. Rebecca knew that because the attempt to kill her had failed, Andrew Stoughton would try again. The next time she would be ready.

Slowly Rebecca got out of bed and made her way across the master suite. She had insisted on walking a little each day, traversing the length of the *Windsong*, learning to ignore the pain. In time the dizzy spells grew less and less frequent. Her muscles began to respond to the steady exercise until she could even go into the water and swim around the vessel.

But I can't wait any longer, Rebecca thought. I have to go with what strength I have.

The ferocity of the attacks on The Tides had stunned her. Yet in following the newscasts she realized there was nothing beyond the measures Bix and Torrey were already taking that she could do. After his failure at Cayos de la Fortuna, Andrew had changed tactics: Instead of targeting her directly, he was using her disappearance and silence to mount a final offensive.

With whose help?

As vicious as she knew Andrew was, he could not have masterminded an attack with such clockwork precision. There had to be someone behind him, with resources and experience, someone to whom violence was a way of life . . . or had been once.

The only connection Rebecca could make seemed not only unlikely but insane. Yet the more she examined it the more its pieces appeared to fit perfectly. Rebecca was still trying to convince herself when news of the attack on Windemere came over the radio. Time had run out. If she waited any longer, there wouldn't be anything left to save. She had to play the only card she was holding—and pray that it was the right one.

Rebecca slipped into a rainbow-colored caftan and went into the radio room. Her conversation with Bones Ainsley lasted only as long as it took her to give him the *Windsong*'s coordinates.

In his mind Bones Ainsley had already accepted that Rebecca was dead. Day after day, as the rescue boats returned to port unsuccessful, the policeman found himself spending more and more time on the piers of Angeline City. He stared out to sea, praying that it would give him back the woman who was like his own flesh and blood. Yet because he knew the sea so well, Bones Ainsley had no choice but to accept its verdict. So when a startled radio operator had run into his office, breathless with the news that he had received a message bearing the *Windsong*'s call sign, Ainsley first thought it a cruel joke.

"Can you ever forgive me, Bones?" Rebecca asked softly. "I knew how badly I was hurting you, hurting everyone who cared about me. But I couldn't come back. Not then. Can you understand?''

Bones Ainsley nodded sadly. One look at Rebecca when he had come on board was all he had needed to appreciate the hell she'd been through.

"It's not over yet," Rebecca continued. "I have to stop Andrew or else he'll destroy The Tides.''

"You're not in any condition to stop anyone," Bones said gruffly. "You should have let me take care of that.''

Rebecca shook her head. "It can't work that way.''

"I won't let him get near you again," he said stonily.

"You won't be far away, Bones, I promise. I'm going to send Andrew a message to meet me at a certain time, at a certain place. I want you to be there and bring him to me.''

"I don't know if I can keep my hands off him," Bones growled.

"There's something else," Rebecca told him. "I need you to go and see a man. He has to be convinced to come here, to the *Windsong*, before Andrew arrives.''

Bones frowned. "Ramsey?''

"No," Rebecca said gently. When she told him the name, Bones Ainsley shuddered.

"Have you lost your senses, girl?" he said under his breath.

Rebecca touched his arm and calmly explained what she had to do.

"It's the only way to stop all this, Bones," she said. "Innocent people are being killed. More will die unless I do something. I don't have any choice.''

"It's a terrible gamble," Bones said.

"It's the last and only chance I'll have.''

The message arrived over his private telex. Andrew Stoughton read the words avidly and smiled. His ruse had worked. He had forced Rebecca to show herself.

The message was succinct: CALL OFF YOUR DOGS. THE SHARES ARE WAITING. COME TO THE ANGELINES ALONE. FOLLOW THESE INSTRUCTIONS TO THE LETTER.

The details confused him. He was to fly into Stann Creek Town, where Bones Ainsley would meet him. He would be driven to the docks, and a boat would take him up the coast.

Up the coast to where?

Andrew turned the instructions over in his mind, trying to fathom Rebecca's intentions. Finally he sent a telex to the

Windsong requesting clarification. All he received was a duplicate of the original message.

Andrew telexed back an affirmative reply. He had nothing to fear from Rebecca. For all he knew, she could be crippled, even dying. Besides, he still had his dogs whom he could unleash the minute he suspected any treachery.

Andrew called Michele Fabrizzi with the good news and left for the Angelines the following afternoon.

Rebecca followed Andrew's progress very carefully. Bones called her from the Stann Creek Town airport after a customs and immigration officer had quietly told him Andrew was in the process of being checked through. The next call came from the docks: Andrew was on his way.

Rebecca joined Ramon Fuentes on the pilotdeck.

"It's time," she said. "Notify any vessels you pick up on radar to stay well away from us."

Ramon Fuentes, who, in the past weeks, had hidden the *Windsong* in innumerable coves and inlets across a dozen islands, set his course and brought his vessel out of the bay. Majestically the *Windsong* sailed off toward the sunset, her owner uncaring who might see her now.

Rebecca was standing on the bow, the wind streaking across her face as she stared out to sea. The sun was sliding softly in the west as the *Windsong* hurried toward her rendezvous.

After all this time it will finally be over, she thought to herself. *One way or another*.

The *Windsong* reached her predetermined coordinates and the engines were cut. The only sound around Rebecca came from the radio room, where the communications officer answered the excited chatter of skippers who wanted to know if they had seen a ghost or the real vessel. Warnings went out to all not to approach the *Windsong*.

Rebecca didn't have long to wait. She heard the engines before she saw the boat. Taking out her binoculars, she focused on a red and white speck riding high in the waters. Without realizing it, she tightened her grip on the binoculars, pressing the rubber pads hard against her eyes.

Just a little closer . . .

The pilot of the other cruiser was following her instructions precisely. Rebecca watched as the vessel made a slight course alteration, then sped for the mainland.

"He's come, Max," Rebecca whispered. "He's mine now."

As Andrew's boat passed over the spot where she had consigned her father's body to the deep, Rebecca let her arm drop. The *Windsong*'s diesels thundered to life and the vessel made for the mainland. Rebecca was confident she would arrive there in time.

At first Andrew thought it was an apparition. As the cruiser approached the shore and the looming stone face that reared up from the beach, Andrew glimpsed a structure set on top of the cliff. Then the boat veered and all he saw was thick jungle.

He shook his head as though to erase the image. Obviously he was suffering from fatigue. The flight from London had been bad enough, the aircraft buffeted by strong headwinds, and his reception at Stann Creek Town had further unnerved him. Bones Ainsley hadn't said a word during the short drive to the docks. Andrew had found himself glancing frequently at the huge man, finding his silence ominous.

The skipper edged his vessel against what seemed to be a newly built dock and gestured for Andrew to disembark. Like Ainsley, he had said nothing.

"Where the hell am I supposed to go now?" Andrew demanded angrily.

Silently the boatman pointed to the top of the cliff, then reversed throttles, leaving his passenger alone on the dock. Andrew craned his neck, and there was a mocking smile on his lips. Now he knew exactly where he was—and why. It hadn't been an illusion after all.

"So the bitch wants poetic justice, does she?" he rasped, feeling the last fury of the sun beat down on him. "Then that's what she'll get!"

With his jacket over his shoulder Andrew started across the beach where he and Max had sat and plotted the future of McHenry Enterprises. He paused when he reached the familiar stone trail that zigzagged across and up the incline, and poured the sand from his shoes. As he began his climb Andrew imagined the sight waiting for him: the blackened ruins of Skyscape, overrun by jungle, the last of the structure rotting away and collapsing under decay. What was Rebecca trying to do, frighten him? Raise the ghost of Max McHenry?

It's too late for that, Andrew thought grimly, breathing hard but determined to maintain his pace. Max isn't going to come back from the dead. If she thinks some sort of hocus-pocus is going to save her now . . .

Andrew clambered up the last few steps and stopped short in amazement. He ran a hand over his forehead to wipe away the sweat and blinked rapidly. But the mirage did not dissolve. It was perfect in every way. Suddenly Andrew began shivering uncontrollably. The sun had disappeared and shadows were falling quickly.

From a second-floor window Rebecca watched his approach. For a full minute Andrew did not move. He remained at the foot of the terraced staircase, staring wildly around himself as though searching for a way to escape. But Rebecca knew he could not flee. She had resurrected a perfect past for him and led him into it. Now he was caught as surely as the butterfly in a funnel-web spider's deadly embrace.

Rebecca didn't take her eyes off him. She saw Andrew move cautiously across the verdant lawn, freshly mowed, exactly as Max had always kept it. He looked at the flower beds and shook his head. Rebecca laughed softly. The same flowers, in the exact arrangement, had grown there when her father had been alive.

Come, Andrew, come . . .

And he did. Across the crushed-stone circular drive, toward the great black door, with its lion's-head brass knocker, left partially open. Rebecca knew his fury, and his fear, when the door was slammed shut.

Andrew moved slowly through the house, like a sleepwalker who can neither dispel nor awake from a nightmare. As though drawn by an invisible force, he drifted toward the kitchen. The sliding glass doors were open to the deep maroon sky; the wind whistled through the crack. On the counter were two metal cans of gasoline and a handful of candles. . . .

"Is this what you used to kill Violet?"

Andrew whirled around at the soft voice. He barely caught sight of Rebecca before he threw up his arms. The iron bar she had tossed at him struck him on the elbow and clattered to the floor. Andrew sucked in his pain and staggered after her.

"Rebecca!"

The scream reverberated throughout the empty house. Andrew turned the corner and found himself in the main corridor, dark except for a row of lighted candles that reached all the way to the foot of the staircase. . . .

"Come, Andrew, quickly! I'm up here."

Her voice, coming from the second floor, taunted him. Andrew swore viciously and took the staircase two steps at a time, hurtling toward what had once been Max McHenry's bedroom. The door slammed against the wall as Andrew threw his weight against it.

Again, everything was the same, the furniture, the ornately carved four-poster, the hospital machines that had been there ten years ago, keeping Max McHenry alive. . . . Except this time it was Rebecca who was in the room, standing at the foot of the bed.

"It all looks very familiar, doesn't it, Andrew?" Rebecca said softly.

Andrew felt a tremor ripple through him.

"What do you want?" he demanded hoarsely.

"Many things, Andrew," Rebecca replied. "We'll get to them, one by one."

"Don't toy with me!" he hissed. "One telephone call and your precious Tides will be hit again, over and over, for as long as it takes to finish you!"

Rebecca shook her head. "No, Andrew, that's all over now." She paused.

"There's a terrible irony here, Andrew, one which I'll have to live with for the rest of my life. When I decided to take over Tyne & Wear, I had no idea that you had already made your deal with Michele Fabrizzi. Neither, as it turned out, had Tony. By continuing to challenge you for control, I drove you to retaliate . . . except it was Tony you murdered instead of me. My ambition to strip you of everything you ever had resulted in your killing the son of your silent patron. . . ."

Rebecca moved across the room to the windows, turned and faced him.

"It was your boat I saw that morning I left for La Ceiba, wasn't it? Somehow you had learned that Tony was supposed to fly out that day to attend his father's birthday party. What you didn't know was that the evening before, Tony's aunt had telephoned to say that I wasn't welcome to come with him. Tony refused to go under the circumstances. The man you saw get into the cruiser was the boatman—after I had gone belowdecks.

"That's when you made your move, and you lost control when you discovered that I wasn't there. That's why you ended up mutilating Tony. . . .

"And the gasoline and candles . . . just the way you murdered Max, wasn't it? Was it the symmetry that appealed to you, Andrew, or were the candles meant to give you enough time to escape . . . ? Just as you escaped from Skyscrape that night, in time to get back to the office before the fire started . . . In time for me to find you, become your alibi . . . That's something else I'll never be able to forgive myself for.

"That was the way you killed Max, wasn't it?" Rebecca said, her voice rising.

"That's *exactly* the way Max died," Andrew said savagely, pinpricks of madness dancing in his eyes.

"And you used the same method to murder Tony, didn't you? Then you ran to Fabrizzi and convinced him I had done it, knowing that in his grief Tony's father would give you whatever you needed to destroy The Tides."

Andrew chuckled to himself.

"Talk all you want, Rebecca," he said. "Max is dead. Tony is dead. No one could prove a thing against me, even if I *were* to let you live to testify in a court of law. But I'm going to spare you that, Rebecca. I'm going to kill you now. Since everyone believes you're dead, I'll walk away from this too."

"Why don't you ask yourself, my young friend, *how* Rebecca learned of our relationship? If you didn't tell her, then who did?"

Andrew, who had taken two steps toward Rebecca, froze then. He could not believe he had heard that voice. But there was no mistaking Michele Fabrizzi as he stepped through the door of the adjoining room, a revolver rock-steady in his hand, its barrel pointed at Andrew.

"*Padrone* . . . surely you don't believe—"

"Do not address me by my title." Michele Fabrizzi, his eyes glittering, spat out the words. "You are not of my family!"

"But she's lying," Andrew screamed. "Can't you see that? Do you really believe I would have dared to murder Tony?"

"You are insane," the *padrone* whispered. "Like a mad dog which bites and tears anything it is close to, you destroy innocent lives. And like the dog, you will be destroyed."

"You must believe me!" Andrew pleaded. "I didn't murder Tony. There's no proof. . . ."

"I have seen the proof!"

Andrew recoiled as though Fabrizzi had struck him. At that moment Rebecca, who had disappeared into the next room, returned, carrying a bundle in her arms. Andrew heard a soft gurgling sound, then a weak cry.

"Look!" Fabrizzi ordered.

Andrew got to his feet and watched as Rebecca withdrew the edge of the blanket. Nestled in her arms was a baby, with his mother's huge eyes and his father's strong chin.

"That is my proof—my grandson," Michele Fabrizzi said, unable to keep his voice from cracking. "You want me to believe that a pregnant woman who was carrying my son's child turned on him and murdered him? She tried to save Tony's life when she found him. . . ."

Andrew stared at the infant in disbelief.

"I didn't know," he stammered. "*No one* knew! No one had seen her for months!"

The final realization dawned on him, and he said to Rebecca, "That's why you hid away on Cayos de la Fortuna—"

"I didn't hide, Andrew. I went there because I wasn't going to take any chances. Not this time."

"This time? What do you mean?"

"Do you remember Jamaica, Andrew?" Rebecca asked softly. "The day you forced me off the road, almost killed me? I was pregnant then too. With your child."

Andrew's expression of amazement crumbled. He closed his eyes and slowly shook his head.

"You almost killed me on Cayos de la Fortuna," Rebecca said. "But I swore to myself you wouldn't take this baby, Tony's son, from me. I was over eight months pregnant, Andrew. I gave birth prematurely, on the *Windsong*. But my son survived. And so did I."

Rebecca adjusted the blanket around her baby. She ignored Andrew's arm, outstretched to her, as though in supplication.

"Get him out of my home!" she told Fabrizzi.

EPILOGUE

It was the kind of December day Rebecca remembered from her own childhood, a blue sky stretching forever over an aquamarine ocean. She looked inside the makeshift tent beside her blanket and smiled when she saw her son sleeping peacefully in his crib. As so often happened when she was alone with him, the tears came unbidden. Every day it seemed that Anthony McHenry looked more and more like his father, a man he would know only through pictures and the stories Rebecca was waiting to tell him.

Rebecca leaned across and nuzzled her son. Her hair tickled his nose and he rubbed two tiny fists across it. Rebecca brushed away her tears lest Anthony wake up and see her crying. The crying, she told herself again, had to end, just as so many things had at last resolved themselves.

Three days after she had watched Michele Fabrizzi lead Andrew out of Skyscape, Rebecca had read about his body washing up off Stann Creek Town's golden ghetto, where Silas Lambros had once ruled. The predators of the sea had done their work but there was enough left for a positive identification. Since no witnesses came forward, Bones Ainsley closed the case. Andrew Stoughton had been the unfortunate victim of pirates who had first robbed then murdered him.

Shortly afterward, Rebecca received Michele Fabrizzi at Skyscape.

"You don't have to worry," the old *padrone* assured her, conscious of Rebecca's suspicion and the fiercely protective way she kept him away from her son. "I have not come here to lay claim to Anthony. He is flesh of my flesh but you are his mother. He belongs with you."

Fabrizzi took her hand in both of his.

"You are a formidable woman. Even if there was no bond between us, I would not wish you for an enemy. To think that I came so close to destroying you—and with you, my grandson—is something I will have to live with the rest of my days. To make those days easier to bear I beg you to forgive me and allow me to visit Anthony from time to time."

Rebecca weighed the *padrone*'s words carefully, searching for deceit. But all she saw was a tired old man whose power could not return to him the life of the son he loved.

"I want you to swear to me that you won't interfere in Anthony's life—or mine," Rebecca told him.

"You have my word," Fabrizzi said softly.

"I also need your promise not to interfere with Tyne & Wear."

Michele Fabrizzi smiled faintly and nodded. The news that Rebecca's Vixen Corporation had at last gained control of the venerable Tyne & Wear had made headlines across the financial world. For his part, the *padrone* wanted no part of the entity whose head had murdered his son. He had his revenge and would have to make do with its cold comfort.

In spite of the hundreds of questions Bix, Torrey, and Ramsey had besieged her with, Rebecca did not say a great deal about the time between her rescue from Cayos de la Fortuna and her confrontation with Andrew. Anthony's birth had been difficult, she explained, the problems compounded by the horrible circumstances of Tony's death.

Her friends accepted the little Rebecca told them and left the rest alone. For them, it was enough that she was alive and on the mend. They were confident that there would come a time when she would want to fill in the missing pieces. They would be there for her then.

With a final, loving gaze at Anthony, Rebecca rose and looked up at Skyscape. The wind was blowing off the land and she heard the staff laughing as they prepared the great house for its first Christmas party, just as Max had dressed it for the two of them and their guests so long ago.

Rebecca smiled when she remembered Bix's words.

"You had this planned all along, didn't you?" Bix had said, eyes gleaming. "You started rebuilding Skyscape because you knew that's where you and Andrew would meet for the last time!"

Rebecca had neither confirmed nor denied it. But Bix was wrong. Skyscape had been built for an entirely different reason.

Rebecca undid the string of the chamois bag tied to her bikini. As she lifted it the five jade stones which Max had found, whose mystery Dallas had not lived to solve, poured into her palm. Rebecca knew now what they meant. She had found the single missing clue to their inscription at Pusilha. Later, when she had retreated to the Angelines after Eric's treachery, she had followed the message on the stones deep into the jungle. It led her to Apho Hel, to her mother's grave.

From that moment on, Rebecca had dreamed about bringing her mother home, completing the task Max had been unable to finish. Contemplating the stones, she realized she would never do this. Apho Hel had been buried in a secret place reserved for Mayan priestesses. It was hallowed ground that not even love could intrude upon. Instead, she would hold on to her secret, and when Anthony was old enough, she would take him there and show him his heritage.

Without realizing it, Rebecca found herself ankle-deep in the onrushing tides. The waters swirled around her, receded then pounded back. Constant motion, constant churning, a reflection of the tumultuous ebb and flow of her own life.

Past life, she corrected herself.

Rebecca's fingers curled around the sea horse pendant and with one jerk the thin chain was broken. Rebecca stared at the figurine intently. All it did was reflect the past. It told her nothing about the future. That was hers to decide.

So be it!

Rebecca drew back her arm and suddenly the sea horse was flying across the waters, the sun catching the gold and diamonds and rubies. For a few seconds it seemed that the pendant would fly forever. Then a giant wave crashed off the reef, snatching it out of the air. The sea horse and the past blended together and, in the blink of an eye, disappeared. The fury of the tide died, too, until Rebecca heard nothing but the steady rhythm of a newborn heartbeat.

DON'T MISS
THESE CURRENT
Bantam Bestsellers

Special Offer
Buy a Bantam Book
for only 50¢.

Now you can have Bantam's catalog filled with hundreds of titles plus take advantage of our unique and exciting bonus book offer. A special offer which gives you the opportunity to purchase a Bantam book for only 50¢. Here's how!

By ordering any five books at the regular price per order, you can also choose any other single book listed (up to a $5.95 value) for just 50¢. Some restrictions do apply, but for further details why not send for Bantam's catalog of titles today!

Just send us your name and address and we will send you a catalog!

BANTAM BOOKS, INC.
P.O. Box 1006, South Holland, Ill. 60473

Mr./Mrs./Ms. _____
(please print)

Address _____

City _____ State _____ Zip _____
FC(A)—10/87

Please allow four to six weeks for delivery.